ALSO BY JULIA GLASS

Three Junes

The Whole World Over

The Whole World Over

JULIA GLASS

PANTHEON BOOKS · NEW YORK

All rights reserved. Published in the United States by Pantheon Books,
a division of Random House, Inc., New York,
and in Canada by Random House of Canada Limited, Toronto.

Pantheon Books and colophon are registered trademarks of
Random House, Inc.

Due to limitations of space, permissions to print previously published
material can be found following the acknowledgments.

Library of Congress Cataloging-in-Publication Data

Glass, Julia, [date].
The Whole World Over / Julia Glass.
p.   cm.
ISBN 0-375-42274-9
1. Women cooks—Fiction. 2. September 11 Terrorist Attacks, 2001—
Fiction. 3. Marital conflict—Fiction. 4. New York (N.Y.)—Fiction.
5. Pastry industry—Fiction. 6. New Mexico—Fiction.
7. Governors—Fiction. 8. Maine—Fiction. I. Title.

PS3607.L37P54 2006   813'.6—dc22   2005054043

www.pantheonbooks.com

Printed in the United States of America
First Edition
2   4   6   8   9   7   5   3   1

For Dennis

"Black as the Devil, heavy as sin, sweet as young love," is the way an Englishman has described the ceremonial cakes of his country; solid, romantic, and frequently good, but with quite a different kind of goodness from our own more casual sort.

—Louis P. De Gouy
The Gold Cook Book

Do you know where I found him?
You know where he was?
He was eating a cake in the tub!
Yes he was!
The hot water was on
And the cold water, too.
And I said to the cat,
"What a bad thing to do!"

"But I like to eat cake
In a tub," laughed the cat.
"You should try it some time,"
Laughed the cat as he sat.

—Dr. Seuss
The Cat in the Hat Comes Back

I

A
Piece
of Cake

ONE

THE CALL CAME ON THE TWENTY-NINTH OF FEBRUARY: the one day in four years when, according to antiquated custom, women may openly choose their partners without shame. As Greenie checked her e-mail at work that morning, a small pink box popped up on the screen: *Carpe diem, ladies!* Scotland, according to her cheery, avuncular service provider, passed a law in 1288 that if a man refused a woman's proposal on this day, he must pay a fine: anything from a kiss to money that would buy her a silk dress or a fancy pair of gloves.

If I weren't hitched already, thought Greenie, I would gladly take rejection in exchange for a lovely silk dress. Oh for the quiet, sumptuous ease of a silk dress; oh for the weather in which to wear it!

Yet again it was sleeting. Greenie felt as if it had been sleeting for a week. The sidewalks of Bank Street, tricky enough in their skewed antiquity, were now glazed with ice, so that walking George to school had become a chore of matronly scolding and pleading: "Walk, honey. Please walk. What did I say, did I say WALK?" Like most four-year-old boys, George left his house like a pebble from a slingshot, careening off parked cars, brownstone gates, fences placed to protect young trees (apparently not just from urinating dogs), and pedestrians prickly from too little coffee or too much workaday dread.

Greenie was just shaking off the ill effects of what she called VD whiplash: VD as in Valentine's Day, an occasion that filled her with necessary inspiration as January waned, yet left her in its wake—if business was good—vowing she would never, ever again bake anything shaped like a heart or a cherub or put so much as a drop of carmine dye in a bowl of buttercream icing.

As if to confirm her fleeting disenchantment with all that stood for romantic love, she and Alan had had another of the fruitless, bitter face-offs Greenie could never seem to avoid—and which, in their small apartment, she feared would awaken and worry George. This one had kept her up till two in the morning. She hadn't bothered to go to bed, since Tuesday was one of the days on which she rose before dawn to bake brioche, scones, cinnamon rolls, and—Tuesdays only—a coffee cake rich with cardamom, orange zest, and grated gingerroot: a cunningly savory sweet that left her work kitchen smelling like a fine Indian restaurant, a brief invigorating change from the happily married scents of butter, vanilla, and sugar (the fragrance, to Greenie, of ordinary life).

Dead on her feet by ten in the morning, she had forgotten the telephone message she'd played back the evening before: "Greenie dear, I believe you'll be getting a call from a VIP tomorrow; I won't say who and I won't say why, but I want it on the record that it was *I* who told him what a genius you are. Though I've just now realized that he may spirit you away! Idiot me, what was I thinking! So call me, you have to promise you'll *call me* the minute you hear from the guy. Bya!" Pure Walter: irritating, affectionate, magnanimous, coy. "Vee Aye Pee," he intoned breathlessly, as if she were about to get a call from the Pope. More likely some upstate apple grower who'd tasted her pie and was trolling for recipes to include in one of those springbound charity cookbooks that made their way quickly to yard sales and thrift shops. Or maybe this: the Director of Cheesecake from Junior's had tasted hers—a thousandfold superior to theirs—and wanted to give her a better-paid but deadly monotonous job in some big seedy kitchen down in Brooklyn. What, in Walter's cozy world, constituted a VIP?

Walter was the owner and gadabout host (not the chef; he couldn't have washed a head of lettuce to save his life) of a retro-American tavern that served high-cholesterol, high-on-the-food-chain meals with patriarchal hubris. Aptly if immodestly named, Walter's Place felt like a living room turned pub. On the ground floor of a brownstone down the street from Greenie's apartment, it featured two fireplaces, blue-checked tablecloths, a fashionably weary velvet sofa, and (Board of Health be damned) a roving bulldog named The Bruce. (As in Robert the Bruce? Greenie had wondered but never asked; more likely the dog was named after some fetching young porn star, object of Walter's cheerfully futile longing. He'd never been too explicit about such longings, but he made allusions.) Greenie wasn't wild about the Eisenhower-era foods with which Walter indulged his customers—indulgence, she felt, was the province of dessert—but she had been pleased when she won the account. Over the past few years, she had come to think of Walter as an ally rather than a client.

Except for the coconut cake (filled with Meyer lemon curd and glazed with brown sugar), most of the desserts she made for Walter were not her best or most original, but they were exemplars of their kind: portly, solid-citizen desserts, puddings of rice, bread, and noodles—sweets that the Pilgrims and other humble immigrants who had scraped together their prototypes would have bartered in a *Mayflower* minute for Greenie's blood-orange mousse, pear ice cream, or tiny white-chocolate éclairs. Walter had also commissioned a deep-dish apple pie, a strawberry marble cheesecake, and a layer cake he asked her to create exclusively for him. "Everybody expects one of those, you know, death-by-chocolate things on a menu like mine, but what I want is massacre by chocolate, execution by chocolate—*firing squad* by chocolate!" he told her.

So that very night, after tucking George in bed, Greenie had returned to the kitchen where she made her living, in a basement two blocks from her home, and stayed up till morning to birth a four-layer cake so dense and muscular that even Walter, who could have benched a Shetland pony, dared not lift it with a single hand. It was the sort of dessert that appalled Greenie on principle, but it also embodied a kind of überprosperity, a transgressive joy, flaunting the potential heft of butter, that Protean substance as wondrous and essential to a pastry chef as fire had been to early man.

Walter christened the cake Apocalypse Now; Greenie held her tongue. By itself, this creation doubled the amount of cocoa she ordered from her supplier every month. After it was on his menu for a week, Walter bet her a lobster dinner that before the year was out, *Gourmet* would request the recipe, putting both of them on a wider culinary map. If that came to pass, Greenie would surrender to the vagaries of fleeting fame, but right now the business ran as smoothly as she could have hoped. She had a diligent assistant and an intern who shopped, cleaned, made deliveries, and showed up on time. The amount of work they all shared felt just right to Greenie; she could not have taken an order for one more tiny éclair without enlarging the enterprise to a degree where she feared she would begin to lose control. Alan said that what she really feared was honestly growing up, taking her lifelong ambition and molding it into a Business with a capital B. Greenie resented his condescension; if Business with a capital B was the goal of growing up, what was he doing as a private psychotherapist working out of a back-door bedroom that should have belonged to George, who slept in an alcove off their living room meant for a dining room table? Which brought up the subject of George: was Alan unhappy that Greenie's work, on its present scale, allowed her to spend more time with their son than a Business with a capital B would have done?

"Delegation," said Alan. "It's called delegation."

This was the sort of bickering that passed too often now between them, and if Greenie blamed Alan for starting these quarrels, she blamed herself for plunging into the fray. Stubbornly, she refused to back down for the sake of greater domestic harmony or to address the underlying dilemma. The overlying dilemma, that much was clear. Through the past year, as Greenie began to turn away clients, Alan was losing them. His schedule had dwindled to half time, and the extra hours it gave him with George did not seem to console him.

Alan, two years away from forty, had reached what Greenie privately conceived of as the Peggy Lee stage in life: Is That All There Is? Greenie did not know what to do about this. She would have attacked the problem head on if the sufferer had been one of her girlfriends, but Alan was a man, chronically resentful of direction. When he was with friends, his argumentative nature was his strength, a way of challenging the world and its complacencies, but in private—alone with Greenie—he fell prey to defensiveness and nocturnal nihilism. She had known this before they married, but she had assumed this aspect of his psyche would burn off, under the solar exposure of day-to-day affection, like cognac set aflame in a skillet. Next year they would be married ten years, and it had not.

In their first years together, she had loved the wakefulness they shared late at night. After sex, Alan did not tumble into a callow sleep, the way most men claimed they could not resist doing. Like Greenie, he would be alert for another half hour or more. They would talk about their days, their dreams (both sleeping and waking), their notions on the fate of mankind. When it came to worldly matters, the voice of doubt would be Alan's—mourning or raging that genocide would never end, that presidents would never be moral, that children would always be abducted by men who would never be caught—but he was invariably passionate, and back then, Greenie saw hope in that passion. He loved Greenie expressively, eloquently, in a way she felt she had never been loved.

When they had been sleeping together—or not-sleeping together—nearly every night for a month, she asked, "Why do you suppose we're like this? Why can't we just go to sleep, like the rest of the exhausted people around us?" They were lying in Alan's bed, in the never-quite-dark of a city night.

He said, "Me, I think too much. Not a good thing."

"Why? Why is that not good?"

"It wears down your soul. It's like grinding your spiritual teeth," he said. "Dreaming is the healthy alternative. Even nightmares once in a while. Sometimes a nightmare is like a strong wind sweeping through a house."

Greenie had noticed early on that first thing every morning, often before getting out of bed, Alan wrote his dreams in a leather book the size of a wallet. "What about me?" she said. "Do I think too much?"

"Not you." He pulled her closer against his side. "With you, I can only imagine that some part of your waking soul just can't bear to see another magnificent day in the life of Greenie Duquette come to an end."

"That's very poetic," said Greenie, "but it's malarkey."

"When I'm with you," he said, "I love not getting to sleep." He kissed her and kissed her, and then they did fall asleep. The next day, on the phone with her mother, she said she'd met an incredible man, that she had fallen in love. Her mother teased her that it wasn't the first time, and Greenie said yes, this was true, but she had a hunch it would be the last.

Consistent with all the evolutions and revolutions of married life, their wakeful late-night musings came to an end when they had George. In those early months, starved of sleep, their thinking selves would plummet toward oblivion once they lay down. But Alan still slept so lightly that he was nearly always the first to rise and comfort George when he cried. By the time Greenie stumbled to consciousness, there was her baby, in his father's arms, being soothed until she was ready to nurse. Alan's only complaint was that waking up so often and so urgently made it hard for him to remember his dreams. Along with so many other habits once taken for granted, the little book went by the wayside. Now Greenie wondered if Alan had needed it more than she understood.

Greenie could not point to a specific moment when Alan's sober but passionate view of the world might have tipped into a hardened pessimism, and she reminded herself that he was still a loving, patient father—but what if that pessimism was genetic? Could it lie dormant in George?

When the loaves and cakes she had baked sat cooling on racks, Greenie filled the larger sink with all the loaf pans and whisks, cups and spoons and mixing bowls. Sherwin would show up later to wash them, but Greenie wiped down the counters herself, several times a day. She had made this place—an old boiler room in the basement of a nondescript tenement building—into her private kingdom. Around the perimeter, the walls and cupboards were white, the countertops made of smooth, anonymous steel, but the linoleum tiles that Alan had helped her lay on the floor were gladiola red. The only windows ran along the ceiling at sidewalk level: wide yet narrow, like gunports in a bunker. Sometimes, organizing bills or tinkering with recipes, Greenie sat on a stool at the butcher-block island and watched the ankles passing by these windows. Now and then a dog pressed its face between the bars against the glass, spotted her and wagged its tail. Greenie would smile and wave before the dog was yanked along on its way. She came to recognize the neighborhood regulars: the aging black Lab with the heavily salted muzzle, the twin pugs with their Tammy Faye mascara, the Irish setter who marked the windows with his wayward tongue. Sometimes dog faces were the only ones she saw for hours. Even toddlers were visible only up to the hems of their shorts or jackets. Walter was the one person who would lean down, knock on a pane, and give her an upside-down grin, The Bruce right there beside him.

She would know that spring had arrived when green crept into her rabbit's-eye view, as the small plots of earth around the trees in front of the building filled with hardy weeds or the floral attempts of residents longing in vain for gardens of their own. (The dogs were no help there.)

Just below the windows, Greenie had hung her copper and stainless-steel bowls, in pairs. It was a minor joke she still enjoyed: displayed this way, they looked like pairs of great armored breasts, the warrior bosoms of Amazons, of Athena, Brunhilde, and Joan of Arc. *Count me in!* Greenie told herself while inspecting her private battalion. *Carpe diem, ladies!*

She addressed them as she sang, which she liked to do when she worked alone. A cassette player, beside the wooden spoons, gave her reliable backup from Dinah Washington, Nina Simone, Billie, and Aretha, though lately she had taken to buying old-fashioned sound-tracks, musicals, so that she might belt out toward her feminine army songs like "My Boy Bill," "Gee, Officer Krupke!" and "I'm Gonna Wash That Man Right Outa My Hair."

When the phone rang, she was tying up the last box of hot cross buns for Sherwin to deliver to an East Village coffeehouse. Along with Julie Andrews' mother superior, she sang "Climb Ev'ry Mountain," heedless of the notes she couldn't reach, and had looked up just long enough to watch a pair of man-size schoolboy galoshes, complete with ladder clips, pass from west to east. "Happy Leap Year Day," she answered.

Greenie was thrown off by the way in which the caller addressed her—for Charlotte Greenaway Duquette had an assortment of names, each of which identified the user as belonging to a particular period of her past. To relatives and friends of her parents, she would always be Charlotte, unabridged. To schoolmates and other people who had known her in the town where she grew up, she was Shar; to a certain clique with whom she'd hung about in high school, Charlie. In college, her first roommate had taken to calling her Duke. Liking the tough, feminist ring to this name—it made her feel as if she'd pierced her navel without going to such physical extremes—she had let it follow her on to cooking school and then to New York City.

Within a few months of moving to the city, she met Alan, who dis-liked this nickname and told her so on their second date. "It's too butch, and you are anything but butch," he had said, boldly touching her long, unruly hair as they walked down the street. "I can tell you're strong, but you are much too agreeable to have the kind of name a boxer or a pimp would choose."

For a time, he insisted on calling her Charlotte. One night when he spoke her name in a searing whisper, she told him that she was sorry, but she felt as if a member of her family were making love to her. "It's sort of like if you wore my father's aftershave," she said, "even though he doesn't wear one."

Later, as they lay awake together, he murmured her whole name aloud several times, as if to search out every pocket of air in its vowels. "Well, Miss Charlotte Greenaway Duquette," he concluded, "I'll have to make up a name of my own." That was when, with a secret thrill, she'd become Greenie; when, looking back, she had become his bride.

When it came time to name her business (her business with a little b), she was tempted to use this new name, but it still felt private then, like a love charm she should be careful not to bandy about. With more calculation than sentiment, she decided on Pastries by Miss Duquette. She opened during the craze for all things Creole, zydeco, Margaret Mitchell: to steely New Yorkers, just about anything with a southern flair had the wistful allure of cotillion chiffon, and Greenie liked to think of her surname as calling to mind the pink oleander, mannerly verandahs, and ubiquitous angels of New Orleans (though she had no such personal claim to make, having grown up west of Boston). On the pale green boxes in which she packed her sweets, the name swooped from corner to corner, a flounce of curlicued purple letters trailing wisteria blossoms.

People who called her for business nearly always asked for Miss Duquette or "the manager" or, if word of mouth had sent them her way, Greenie. On this occasion, she picked up the phone to hear "Would this be Charlotte Duquette?"—her name pronounced "Shallot Dee-oo-kett" by a young woman who sounded as southern as Greenie was not.

"That's me," said Greenie, and she waited to hear how this woman was connected to her parents. Not even the four banks that issued her credit cards knew her as Charlotte.

"Shallot Dee-oo-kett," the woman repeated, "will you please hold, then, for the guvna of Nee-oo Maixico?"

A ratcheting of telephone connections followed, clearing the way for a hearty male voice: "Girl, excuse my informality here, but you make one hell-and-back of a coconut cake."

Helplessly, Greenie burst out laughing.

"Oh, and I see you are prone to easy amusement. I like that in a person, I do." He laughed briefly, easily amused himself. "Well, this is Ray McCrae, and you are excused if you can't quite place the name, being as you are from these distant, more sophisticated parts, but as your friend Walter will have told you, I have a proposition, Miss Duquette, based solely on that knockout punch of a cake I sampled yesterday. No, did not sample, Miss Duquette, that would be inaccurate. A fib. Ate—no, ravished—one gigantic slice and scraped the plate clean with my fork. Then ordered a second to go and gobbled the whole thing down in the car. Ate the crumbs right off the seat."

"Thank you. I'm flattered." This had to be a prank, friends from cooking school colluding with Walter, but why not play along?

"So now, right now as a matter of fact, I'm just about to pull up to your city hall for face time with your powers that be. I'm hoping you won't mind if Mary Bliss, my assistant here, takes over and does the explaining—but," said the charming impersonator, "I do hope we'll meet in person, Miss Duquette. I do."

"Well, I do too," said Greenie, after which she covered the mouthpiece.

"Miss Deeookett?" The southern belle was back on the line.

"Yes, that's me, but could you please explain what's going on?"

"That Walter fella didn't ring you up like he promised, now did he?" the southern belle said pleasantly. She explained to Greenie that there was a job opening in the Santa Fe Governor's Mansion. House chef. "Now I know this sounds fah-fayetched," said Mary Bliss, and Greenie could tell that she thought it was more than that, "but it so hayapens that the guvna has a sweet tooth the sahz of Mount Rushmoah, and the sweet spot in that sweet tooth hayapens to be coconut cake. So he has this impulsive notion, see, that you just might like to . . . audition for the job while he's here on your turf."

Greenie contemplated her bulbous reflection in a steel mixing bowl. She remembered the time one of her more ambitious classmates, now sous-chef at a Park Avenue bistro, had been invited to make a six-course meal for Princess Diana and an unnamed companion. All on the QT, the classmate was told, so she mustn't discuss the meal with anyone. She had delivered it to the Carlyle only to be met in the lobby by a group of her girlfriends, all wearing rhinestone tiaras and hooting with laughter.

Greenie would throttle Walter.

"Miss Duquette? Would you do me a favor and humor us here? I know it may sound outrageous . . ."

"Humor you? Oh, in any way I can, just you name it!"

"Well you know, make him a nice meal while he's here in town, tell him you'll consider the offer? We'll pay you a bundle, whatever you'll lose in work that day and more. Does this sound a little insane? Probably does."

A long pause. The woman was serious. If there was a punch line, it was much too long in coming. Greenie said carefully, "But wait. I'd be moving to Santa Fe. If I got the job." Except for a week's vacation with Alan in San Francisco, to visit his sister, she had never been west of Saint Louis. She pictured cartoonish saguaro cactuses, Spanish missions with ruffled terra-cotta roofs, honest-to-goodness cowboys herding honest-to-goodness cows. Wouldn't George love that.

"Yes," said Mary Bliss. "That's what I mean by insane."

"For what it's worth, you ought to know I'm a Democrat," said Greenie. Now she recalled why Ray McCrae was in New York. Sherwin had complained about traffic during the previous day's delivery; apparently—though he didn't find this out till he was mired at an intersection, standing still through three green lights—a convention of Republican governors had cut off most of the Upper East Side, causing bipartisan gridlock all the way over to Chelsea.

"Oh Miss Duquette, we know plenty more about you than *that,* we wouldn't waste the time on this call without at least a thumbnail daw-see-ay." Mary Bliss's tone told Greenie just how much she enjoyed opening people's government files and spying on the haphazard details of their lives. Greenie was on the verge of telling her where she could stow that thumbnail daw-see-ay when Mary Bliss added lightly, "Besides which we're equal opportunity employers and love nothin' so much as a house full of friendly debate."

As opposed, thought Greenie, to a house full of unfriendly debate. She could just see Alan's face if she were to tell him later tonight that she'd turned down this blue moon of an offer. ("You did what? You refused the chance to impress a head of state? Who knows what connections you could've made?")

"I'll make the guy a meal. Sure," Greenie said. "Why not?" How often did she get a break in her routine, a professional lark? She named a price that was three times her usual income for a day's production—which Tina could, with a little overtime, cover in Greenie's absence—and asked about the governor's favorite foods. All right, so she would spare Walter's life.

LIKE OTHER BOYS HIS AGE, George loved dinosaurs, poop talk, and reminding his parents about The Rules (no shoes on the furniture, no talking with your mouth full, no saying "Jesus!" not even under your breath and never mind why). He had outgrown his fascination with men working under the city streets and his early, oblivious tolerance of broccoli and peas. When George grew up, he would be an astronaut palaeontologist, digging for fossils on other planets. Pluto, he told his mother this evening, was not a planet anymore.

"Oh? What is it?" Greenie asked, genuinely curious.

"It's make-believe. Like aliens. There is no such things as aliens."

"Not that we know of," said Greenie. Poor Pluto, she thought, now to be accorded the same disdain a teenager held for Santa Claus.

George frowned at her, as if she'd spoken out of turn. "There's not! We *know* there's not!"

His vehemence cowed her a little. "Right!" she reassured him. Alan, resolutely truthful, would not have colluded in such simplification, but she had learned that splitting hairs with a four-year-old was counterproductive. And Alan was working late. He had a new couple; such referrals were generally for a limited time, six or ten weeks to steer (if not determine) the fate of a courtship or marriage. The high stakes of this particular work—the work of just a dozen hours—astonished Greenie, though Alan had told her that quite often all he did was guide these couples toward recognizing and voicing decisions they had already made in their hearts. "I don't have as much power as you might suspect. At least I hope I don't."

Begrudgingly, George was working his way through the three baby carrots Greenie had exacted as the price of a heart-shaped Linzer cookie (thawed from a freezer stash of VD overrun).

When she handed him a small plate holding the cookie, he beamed. "A story, a story!"

She went to his bookcase and ran a finger across the bright narrow spines. "*The Sneetches*? We haven't read *The Sneetches* in a long time."

"I am taking a break of Dr. Seuss," George declared imperiously. George was an articulate child, already a language person, just like his father, but he spoke like a not-quite-fluent foreigner, tenses and prepositions often skewed.

"How about just a little Dr. Seuss and then something else?"

"No. I want the dinosaur book with the flaps and the one of the wide-mouth frog and *Me and My Amazing Body*," he answered. Alan claimed that George's confidence in his choices was a trait that came from Greenie, but she believed it was simply a fact of four-year-old life. "I want *Me and My Amazing Body* after I've putted on my pajamas."

"*Put* on my pajamas," Greenie said.

George laughed at her. "Not *your* pajamas."

"You're right. Mine would be way too big, wouldn't they?"

Greenie searched for the books he'd named, reluctantly passing her favorites by. The more she read Dr. Seuss, the more brilliant she thought he was. She had become even mildly smitten, the way one customarily felt about a movie star: Andy Garcia or Kevin Costner or, if you were younger, Leonardo DiCaprio. That's how Greenie felt about the late Ted Geisel. (Twitterpated, her mother would have said.) *Horton Hears a Who!* was a tale that brought altruistic tears to Greenie's eyes every time she read it; others, by simple recitation, could dispel almost any anxiety or minor attack of the blues. Tonight, she craved the curative absurdity of "Too Many Daves," a brief story about a certain Mrs. McCave who had twenty-three sons and foolishly named them all Dave—twenty-four lines of shamelessly silly verse that, Greenie once remarked to Alan, triggered in her brain the release of more serotonin or some other feel-good neurochemical than any dose of Zoloft ever could.

Nevertheless, she read the dinosaur book (not a story but a patchwork of scientific facts and speculations) while George ate his cookie, retrieving every precious crumb from the table around the plate. Then he stretched his arms out toward her, a wordless request for her lap. She folded her son's slim, bony form—the nimble body of a mountain goat—into her lap and read him the fable about a frog whose bragging leads to fatal consequences.

George chose his flying saucer pajamas over the ones with the fire-breathing dragons. Greenie brought him the book he wanted and sat beside him against his pillows. "*I* will read it," he told her, and he dove right in, as if the book were a pool, lending great emotion to human anatomy, bones and muscles, organs and veins.

" 'My blood can't move through my body all by itself,' " he read with decorum. " 'It needs my heart—a group of strong muscles in my chest—to move it. My heart is like my own little . . . engaah . . .' Mommy, what is e-n-g-i-n-e?"

"Engine. A machine that makes something run, like in a car."

" 'Engine! It pumps blood through my body all the time, even when I'm sleeping! If I put my hand on my chest, I can feel my heart beating.' " Here they stopped, as always, to place George's hand under his pajama top and slide it around till he felt his heartbeat. Then Greenie let him feel hers.

"God made a weird thing about lungs," he said after turning the page, breathing dramatically to make his point.

"You think lungs are weird?" said Greenie.

"They blow up like balloons, but they don't go up to the ceiling. They're inside you."

"Yes. And they're a lot tougher than balloons." Even though George had never shown signs of being especially fearful, Greenie worried sometimes that he would develop unnecessary fears by thinking too much—in this case, that his lungs might explode or wither down to nothing.

Having taught himself to read, George now preferred books to videos. Perhaps because books were involved, he rarely resisted going to bed. In these ways, he was not so typical of boys his age. Greenie also wondered if other little boys marveled so often at the quirky motivations of God when their parents never spoke to them of any god whatsoever. Greenie had long ago discarded her parents' anemic Protestant rites, the stuff of white clapboard churches plain as any tract house or government office; Alan's parents, one Jewish and one Christian, had shown no enthusiasm for their inherited faiths, defining the various holidays so loosely that they had become almost secular by attrition.

"Why did God make liquid?" George asked once, with exasperation, when he spilled his juice. Scolded for the umpteenth time about his boyishly unsanitary manners, he complained, "But if you're not allowed to lick your hands, why did God invent the words *lick your hands*?" Why did God invent noises that hurt your ears, shoes that had to be tied, animals that liked to eat other animals? Arguments—why did God invent *those*?

Greenie answered his questions without raising doubts about God—though she asked him who had mentioned God and learned that one schoolmate seemed to be the chief missionary. "Ford says God is everything," George told her one day when she was washing dishes. She shut off the water and turned to face him. "God is *in* everything?" she asked, to clarify what he'd said. George rolled his eyes and said, "No, Mom, God IS everything. IS everything. Ford says so." And then he turned his attention to his Buzz Lightyear doll; there was nothing further to discuss. He had merely passed on his latest bit of knowledge, a fact no less certain, and perhaps no less remarkable, than the fact that T. rex had two claws on each foreleg while Allosaurus had three. A four-year-old brain was a cataloging device, an anthology in progress, collecting and retaining its own uniquely preferred scraps of enlightenment and misperception. Greenie would have loved to see an index of George's brain, exactly what assumptions and generalizations it had thus far made about the world.

Assumptions and generalizations, facts and rumors: all our lives, they mingle without segregation in most of our minds, thought Greenie. Look, for instance, at what she herself "knew" about Raymond Fleetwing McCrae. She'd skimmed past his name in the newspaper three or four times, in stories about concerns dire to western states, quaint at best to residents of Manhattan or even the rural Northeast (the severe ongoing drought; the civil feud over grazing lands; the summer forest fires that raged across states she'd thought of naively as nothing but sandy, uninflammable desert). She'd read somewhere that his Indian name was phony and so, too, the color of his hair (black as a polished stretch limo). She recalled that, without being a Catholic or a Baptist or even a husband and father, he was unabashedly pro-life. While standing in line at the A&P, she'd seen a headline about his relationship with a divorced Hollywood star renowned for doing nude scenes without a body double.

That was Ray McCrae, according to the politically indolent brain of Greenie Duquette. And now, thanks to Mary Bliss, she knew that, with the exception of sweet potatoes and snow peas, he liked his vegetables well disguised; that he liked beef and pork, but lamb best of all; that he had an aversion to game, though he was a sharpshooter when elk and antelope season lured him north to Wyoming; that he could not stand, in any context, flavors in the neighborhood of licorice (no aniseed, no fennel, probably no tarragon); that he loved to eat fluffy egg dishes while bragging about his low cholesterol count. No curries, no raw meat or fish, no leafy salads. His soft spots were ice cream, whipped cream, creamy French sauces, nuts, citrus flavors, and yes, yes indeed, coconut cake.

"And there you have it: the key to that man's heart—that *unmarried* man's heart, just *waiting* to be plucked," Greenie's mother would have said if she had been around to say it. Greenie's mother had been a fine old-fashioned everyday cook. When Greenie was no older than George, her mother taught her to sauté onions in butter and to melt chocolate in a double boiler. "Two great beginnings to so many magnificent things," she had said with an air of pride and mystery.

Alan came in just after George fell asleep; Greenie could hear her son's little lungs working quietly away behind the bookcase they had constructed to turn his space into a facsimile of a bedroom. The shelves facing out toward the living room were filled with books of Alan's: books on ego and self, on pleasure and love and libido and marriage. It amused Greenie to think of George, when he slept, with his head just behind this tower of scholarly effort to understand all these lofty yet intimate things.

From the darkened shoulders of Alan's coat, from his glittering hair, Greenie could see that the weather hadn't changed. Nor, from the expression on his face, had his mood.

Alan seemed perpetually unaware that his emotions were so transparent; Greenie could only guess that he must have another, more enigmatic face for the people who brought their own emotions to him for guidance. She said, "The session go all right? Is this a tough one, make or break?"

"Baby crossroads," Alan said succinctly as he hung his coat on the rack by the door to their apartment, bent to untie his hiking boots.

This was his shorthand for couples sparring over whether or not to become parents. Usually, by the time such a couple reached Alan, the woman had given an ultimatum to the man, his time had expired without a decision, and she was holding out one last chance: a third-party catalyst. Greenie figured this sort of crisis was to her husband what a busted transmission might be to an auto mechanic: either you fixed it, at no small expense but ending up with a car that drove like new (though who could say for how long), or you gave up the car altogether, sent it away for scrap. Alan and Greenie had been through a baby crossroads of their own, arguing and stonewalling through months of Alan's doubt and resistance. Just as Greenie was about to propose that they seek a third opinion, Alan had suddenly given in. She had been demonstratively grateful, though secretly her reaction had been, in a word, *Finally*.

Alan sat beside Greenie and set a hand briefly on her leg. "But here's a twist," he said. "It's two men."

"Oh my," said Greenie.

" 'Oh my' is right. I've never had to think out the conflict in quite these terms. And it does make a difference." He laid his head against the back of the couch. Greenie waited for him to say more, but he simply closed his eyes. She felt her modest hopes—for a lively conversation, for the company of a man with his vigor renewed, for a glimpse of her husband's warmly sardonic old smile—plummet in a familiar, tiresome way.

"George is reading just incredibly," she said at last, knowing it would be a mistake to push Alan further on any subject related to his work.

"That's great," he said quietly. "Though you have to wonder how much is memorization."

"Sometimes—sometimes yes. But this evening he read the directions on the box of spaghetti while I was making his dinner. That's not memorization."

"Great, that's great." Alan was always worn out after the sessions he had to hold at night to accommodate working couples, but Greenie was irritated all the same.

"Could you maybe have just a little knee-jerk pride in your son's talents? I'm not saying he's a genius; he's just a good reader—an amazing reader, as a matter of fact! Other boys his age aren't reading yet at all," she said.

Alan raised his head and looked at her as if he were peering through fog. "Comparisons are odious, Greenie. And did I say I wasn't proud?"

"No . . ." She might have told him that comparisons were the basis of science, the soul of metaphor.

"I'm sorry. The point is, I don't worry about George. Not a bit. George is terrific. Of course I'm proud of George. I'm worried about other things."

Greenie hesitated, then said quietly, "I know you're concerned about money—"

"Money? Oh, you name it!" Alan laughed. "Everything but my prostate gland! Hey, physically I'm in terrific shape!" He flexed his arms, braced his fists against his chest.

"Alan, I know I've said it before and it pisses you off, but you really should call Jerry . . ."

"Jerry does not, as you seem to believe, hold the key to the inner meanings of the cosmos or the source of all joy or even the divine secret to finding a *real* two-bedroom apartment in New York City without selling your nubile sisters into the white-slave trade," said Alan. Jerry was the analyst Alan had seen during and beyond the years he was training at the institute. Alan had stopped seeing him years ago, though sometimes they met for a friendly drink or exchanged referrals. Greenie wondered what Jerry would have made of Alan's remark about his prostate gland. It was true that the one place their life seemed as happy as ever was in their bed, but sometimes Greenie suspected that Alan used sex these days as the sole form of conciliation between them—which only served to create an insidious distance in her head whenever he made love to her in the wake of a disagreement.

Greenie started toward the kitchen. "Let me get you something to eat."

"That's okay; I'm not hungry."

She laughed. "I can't even do that—feed you!"

Alan stood up to join her. He held her from behind. "Greenie, Greenie, about Jerry, it's just . . . you know. Been there, done that. Done that exhaustively, inside out, to the sun and back again. That's not what I need right now."

"What *do* you need? I want to know, even if it isn't something I can give."

"Space," he said sharply. "Sorry if that sounds too California. Peace. A break from the interrogation." He squeezed her tight, her back against his long, slender ribcage, before he let her go and walked into the kitchen. Greenie saw him glance at the upper shelf that held the bottles of liquor. He sighed and turned to the sink, filled a glass with water and drank it down.

He crossed the room again and went behind the bookcase to look at his sleeping son. Greenie resisted the temptation to follow. Space he'd asked for, so space he would get. For now.

When he emerged, he told her he needed to sleep. His next session would be at eight the following morning: tedious timing, since after that he would be free for two hours. Later, however, he could pick up George from his nursery school and spend the rest of the afternoon and evening with him.

That would give Greenie extra time to cook for Guvna McCrae. She had agreed to serve him dinner the evening after next. As she cleaned the kitchen, she realized that she had yet to tell Alan about the phone call, but by the time she walked into their bedroom, he was already asleep. A sleep posture—could that be passed on through genes? Because George, when he slept, was a perfect miniature of Alan: on his back, mouth wide open, left arm (always the left) thrown up over his head, right arm along his side, legs spread in an attitude that looked in the man almost wanton but in the boy simply trusting, ignorant of threats to his dreams or to the eagerly growing cells of his wiry limbs.

After closing the bedroom door and pacing a small circle of frustration, Greenie sat on the couch, beside the table that held the photographs of their eleven years together so far: Greenie in Maine (wet hair, black swimsuit, too many freckles), squinting into the low, rosy sun, Alan the photographer's shadow draped on the rock beside her. The two of them at a dinner party all dressed up, exchanging a glance that said, *Oh here we are and aren't we lucky!* Greenie in white, hair wound with freesia, being kissed by Alan the groom. Greenie on this very couch six years ago, opening presents on her thirtieth birthday. Alan and his sister flanking their small, perplexed-looking mother. Then a copiously pregnant Greenie laughing, raising an arm in vain to ward off the camera. All these images soundly upstaged by George, George, and more George: tiny and rumpled by the pressure of birth, Greenie's lips on his cheek; casting up at Alan one of his very first smiles; cradled between his parents on the carousel in Central Park (a snapshot taken by a stranger); holding a toy backhoe in the playground sandbox; petting his grandmother's cat; up on his father's shoulders beneath a maple tree sunstruck with autumn.

Greenie wanted the history to continue, to go on and on, all of them together in recombinant images, in ones and twos and threes, stepping out sometimes with other people but always belonging together. And she wanted there to be a fourth, though any fool would know that now was not the time to talk or even think about that.

They lived on the parlor floor of a small apartment building that was wedged in a row of brick houses. It was a rear apartment, quiet but also cavelike. Greenie had brightened the place with pattern and color: calla lily curtains from the 1950s; a great pink armchair; two oil landscapes of southern France, hayfields under summer skies, which she had persuaded her mother to give her. "Premature inheritance," Greenie had joked—a joke that had come back to haunt her.

"You want to *live* with that color? Are you serious?" Alan had said when he first saw the armchair, which Greenie had paid two boys to lug in off the street. But he'd laughed and told her that maybe pink was just what his life had been lacking—though mainly, he said, all his life had ever lacked was *her*. It was a lap-sitting chair, a chair made for romance. "If I were a decorator," Alan had said, "I would name this color concupiscent rose." Greenie loved the remarkable words that came from her husband's mouth in the most unlikely moments. ("Smart is more important than rich," her mother once said. "Trust me on that.")

Rain clamored against the windows. Greenie picked up the phone. At eleven o'clock on a cold, rainy weeknight, Walter would be as close to relaxed as he ever came, relinquishing control to bartender, chef, and busboys.

"So, who put you up to this?" she said.

There was only the briefest beat before she heard his machine-gun laugh. "Sweetheart, this was among the most selfless gestures I have ever made."

"Oh, wait. You mean you meant to give me your winning lotto ticket?"

"Listen, you. Today, the Governor's Mansion in Santa Fe—I mean, who wouldn't kill to live there for a while?—tomorrow the White House. Or how about Air Force One? I've heard there's a chef just for Air Force One!"

"To tackle your assumptions in order: One, you mean, what queen of your acquaintance wouldn't kill to live in Santa Fe, which is only about nine thousand miles from the nearest ocean, and you know how much I need the ocean. Two, I am one of the people who would kill *never* to live anywhere *near* Washington, D.C. And three, you might not know this, Walter, but I am not fond of flying."

"Well, aren't *we* grateful for the leg up."

Over the sound of clattering dishes, they burst into collaborative laughter.

"The unbelievable thing," said Greenie, "is that I am actually going through with trying out for this hypothetical job. I've got to be out of my mind."

"Wait till you meet this guy. I mean the size of his personality. Though, come to think of it, maybe you'll be able to verify rumors as to the size of his something else."

"Walter!" Greenie pulled her knees up, gratefully scandalized. "Walter, I'm a married woman, and what would you stand to gain? From what I've seen in the tabloids, the guy is profoundly heterosexual. You don't get to be governor of a landlocked state if you've so much as air-kissed the cheeks of a Frenchman. Except for maybe Vermont."

"Lovey, you can buy off the tabloids," said Walter. "And you may be married, but in my opinion, that intellectual sleepwalker you call a husband could use a wake-up call. A wake-up *smack*."

"Alan loves me—"

"In his own way!" trilled Walter. When she failed to laugh, he apologized. "I know he's a great guy, it's just that I also know he thinks I'm a lightweight. Which I can't quite deny." Deftly, he changed the subject to pie. What did Greenie think of grasshopper pie? Or no, perhaps key lime; they'd drop the lemon meringue. "Could you do it with tequila so there'd be a little buzz?" he asked. "The doldrums approacheth. The Idolatries of March!"

"I don't make desserts that get people sloshed," she said.

"Oh you righteous Bostonian you."

On they talked, Greenie lying back on the couch—as if they were in bed together, she realized the second time she yawned. They talked for half an hour, Walter stopping now and then to speak with a waiter or cook.

She looked in on George, the last thing she did every night, after turning out the lights. His left leg hung over the guardrail. She lifted it carefully and placed it back on the bed. She slipped Truffle Man, his favorite bear, in the bend of a small elbow but stopped short of pulling the blanket over his back. Like his father, George shrugged off the covers in his sleep, summer and winter alike. He slept with a sheen of sweat on his smooth, pale hair, as if his brain were exerting itself in the manufacture of complex, beautiful dreams.

In her own room, in the dark, she took off her clothes and slipped into bed beside Alan. Though he did not seem to wake, he turned toward her and wrapped his arms around her from behind, just as he had in the living room an hour before. Then he exhaled noisily over her shoulder, half snoring, as if he'd been holding his breath till she arrived.

TWO

WALTER LOVED IT WHEN A FRIEND CALLED just as the final
guests were leaving. It helped him past the brief chill when the
restaurant fell silent for a sliver of an instant, for the first time in five or
six hours: the tide-turning moment when the clamor changed over from
chatter and laughter to clinkings, slammings, and mechanical growl-
ings, the sounds of the nightly overhaul. The restaurant was like a ship,
Walter mused (though he wouldn't know a ship from a Pogo stick). He
could imagine the sailors (delectable sailors) tightening screws and riggings, swabbing decks, polishing bollards (what in the world *was* a bol-
lard?), scraping barnacles loudly from the hull. Each night, Walter felt
this transition as the tiniest slump—but a slump nonetheless.

That night he carried the phone to and fro as he battened down the
culinary hatches, prolonging the conversation until Greenie exclaimed,
"Walter, look what time it is! I'll be a wreck tomorrow."

"A magnificent wreck," said Walter. "Like the wreck of the
Hesperus—was that a glorious wreck? The raft of the *Medusa*? No boring old *Titanic* you."

"Walter, good night."

"A wreck with a brilliant transcontinental future."

"Walter."

"Greenie." Walter sighed. "Well then, nighty noodles," he said, the
way Greenie said good night to her son. He'd never been to her apartment, and he'd met her little boy just a few times, when they'd come to
the restaurant for dinner; but one night, on the phone with Walter, she'd
interrupted the conversation as her husband was putting the boy to bed.
Walter had heard all the kisses, the endearments, the knocking-about of
the phone caused by hugging. Oh the daily embrace, the urge toward
sweet dreams: things one should not take for granted.

"Nighty noodles yourself," she answered now. After she hung up, he whispered, "Dreamy doodles," the reply he'd heard from the boy in the background that time.

Walter felt protective toward Greenie, and it wasn't just that he liked her company as well as her cakes. Perhaps a shade melodramatically, he thought of her as an orphan; two years ago, not long after they met, her parents had died in a ghastly accident, plummeting off a cliff while on vacation. When she told him the news, so unnecessarily stoic, so contrite about the missing cheesecakes and Boston cream pies, he'd confided that his parents, too, were in a fatal crash. Walter was thirteen, but even though he'd been so much younger than Greenie, in other ways the accident had been less tragic, for Walter's parents had driven themselves just about literally, willfully, to their deaths.

But really now, did this perfectly successful, obviously confident woman need anyone's protection? Of course not. The one thing that did surprise Walter about Greenie—and worry him a little—was the husband, whom he'd met the few times they came to the restaurant as ordinary customers. On the surface, Alan was more than suitable: fine-looking and shamelessly brainy in that Ivy-nerdy way, if a drab, very hetero dresser (oh, those cuffed *and* pleated khakis). Tall and dark, of course, made up for so many shortcomings. But as for suitability of sentiment, Walter had his doubts. The hint of discord was the affection that the man lavished on his son . . . and did *not* appear to lavish on his wife. Walter saw the small caresses, the gestures of love and reassurance Greenie gave to Alan—unreciprocated, all of it.

So Walter, no pussyfooting, asked outright. About a year before, alone with Greenie in her kitchen, he said, "Now that husband of yours, does he treat you like the queen you are?"

She'd laughed and said, "You mean, the kind with the crown and the corgis? Or the kind with size-thirteen high heels?"

"I'm asking you a serious question," he said brightly.

She blushed and all at once, to Walter's alarmed satisfaction, looked miserable. She said, "The simple serious answer is no. Not recently. But that's the nature of marriage, wouldn't you say?"

"Lovey, you tell me."

"Walter, there are hills and valleys, you know? Or maybe you're lucky not to."

So he had pried, and he had tried to be an ear, but in the end, what had he accomplished? Could he challenge the ingrate to a duel? Show up in the guy's office and have a man-to-queer talk? Imagine the oblivious khaki-wearer caught in *those* headlights.

After hearing Greenie's concerns about money, about how this husband of hers was losing patients (significant pun?), Walter had concluded that either the man was losing his knack or he hadn't had much of a knack to begin with. After all, this was New York City, playground of the rich and narcissistically needy, of the overly pampered whining id. (Whenever Walter saw that ubiquitous sign on the door of a club, VALID ID REQUIRED, he'd think, Oh yes *indeedy*.) Who could want for psychic fodder in a place like this?

"Want a look?" The bartender pushed a pile of credit card slips toward Walter.

Walter pushed them back. "Tomorrow. And tomorrow . . ."

Ben held up a single, admonishing finger. "Shakespeare got his last call an hour ago."

"Cloak?"

"Wearing the very item."

"I missed him?" said Walter. "Please tell me he's applying to law school by now. Sam Waterston's got nothing on that guy."

Organically, over time, Walter and Ben had developed a shorthand for their favorite and least favorite regulars, especially at the bar. Out-of-work actors were, for Walter, the worst. The poor devils made him shudder, since there but for the grace—the maliciously *arbitrary* grace—of God went his truly. Cloak and Dagger personified the two ends of that humiliating spectrum: one of them certain that his turn at Hamlet was just around the corner, the other one bitter and paranoid. (According to Dagger, Spielberg, the Weinsteins, and Tom Hanks ruled a second evil empire.) When the two showed up together—especially if Cloak wore his eponymous Zorro-esque cape—Walter had to avoid looking Ben in the eye. If he did, the two of them would laugh uncontrollably.

Not a guest remained, and it was barely eleven-fifteen. Beastly outside, it wasn't the sort of night on which people lingered. Recently, the climate had not been conducive to profit. Frigid temperatures kept customers coming, longing to toast their backsides at Walter's faux-Colonial fires in authentic Colonial hearths—but freezing rain kept even the upscale cruisers at home, marooned on cable. The Bruce had positioned his own backside close to the fire by the door. He was curled up so tight that he resembled a small beige ottoman. Oh to be a *dog*.

Walter fished in his pocket and pulled it out: Gordie's business card. He did not need to look at the numbers (work, home, cell—all those self-important area codes) to know them by heart, but he liked running a finger across the blue figures, raised like Braille. He had done the call-and-hang-up thing (the cell phone, not the home) just once. He would never do it again. He would not be a Glenn Close stalker. He put the card away and sighed, as if the extra air would clear out his heart. *Changez la subject!* he scolded himself.

"Ben, tell me what you think: do we need these newfangled vodkas, these Martha Stewarty concoctions with verbena, rosemary, hooey like that? Have you *seen* those giant billboards all over creation?"

Ben shook his head. "Hooey. Like you say." He was loading the dishwasher and did not look up. With those dark curls and that heavy gold hoop distending an earlobe, the man resembled a pirate. Give him an eyepatch, a parrot, a treasure map, and *le voilà!* Resolutely, Walter did not focus on the arms, the shoulders, that perfect parcel of a derriere (speaking of treasure). He had taken home many a prime derriere from this bar, Walter had, but here was one line he did not cross: hot for an employee.

But hot—hot was not the problem anymore. Not that hot had ever, really, been a *problem*. Oh for the days of such an uncomplicated itch. Walter remembered the very apex of those days, five and a half years back, when he had been thrilled and amused to realize what a cornucopia he'd made for himself. It was just after the restaurant had hit its stride, the first summer Sunday of sleeves rolled high, of crisp new shorts, the first stretches of smooth skin made brown by the sun, not by some phony, viperous purple lamp. (No inauthentic tans for Walter.) Solicitously cruising the dining room and the patio out front—cruising legitimized!—Walter had had a revelation: running a restaurant gave you a free look at the local wares. And here in particular—well, the men who relished eating this way were the men Walter relished himself. None of those chalky, bare-boned boys who ate at macrobiotic cafés, places that smelled of soy sauce, sawdust, and low-rent pot. Those places were for people who planned to live forever, paying the price of pinched exuberance in everything they ate, read, and probably even dreamed. Yoga, yogi, yogurt: all to be avoided like . . . like sock garters, beer from Milwaukee, and flat-bottomed ice cream cones made of packing foam.

How he wished that unrequited hot were the problem. No, the problem was love. Walter had fallen . . . no, had *somersaulted* into love— a tender yet lunatic devotion to *this* man, this man and no other, ad infinitum. It did not matter that this was what he'd always craved (who didn't?). He'd felt safer, however, when the craving was generic, when it was simple, bland loneliness late at night, a predictable given, and not this desperate, specific yearning. But he had not hunted it out! It had fallen quite rudely upon him, a piano let go by a busted pulley ten stories above the street where he happened to be standing. No one knew, no one *would* know—of that he'd been determined—for he had suspected he could wait it out, just let it fade, however slowly.

Well, he had suspected wrong. He had now turned the corner from suffering to scheming, and nothing good, he suspected, could come of it. But, once again, he could be suspecting wrong.

PLANNING FOR THE FUTURE: that was what got him in trouble. As he had watched the men around him—friends, customers, neighbors— dropping not like flies (what a trivializing expression) but like soldiers in World War I (the far too numerous deaths all senseless, gruesome, way too early, so painful to witness that even remembering the lives preceding these deaths became unbearable), he had seen up close the messy complications that arose when they'd made no formal will. Lovers disenfranchised, pets put to sleep, objects of sentiment smashed or sold in acts of contentious revenge. In short, pandemonium.

Walter hated pandemonium. Take, for example, his closet. Open it and you would see an array of modest garments (yes, the occasional silk this or that, the one pair of cashmere trousers bought in a wave of despondence and now mostly shunned by association), but it was an array so orderly you'd have guessed the wearer of these garments to be a Swiss sanitation engineer or a microbiologist with the CDC who dabbled in butterfly collecting. The walls of the closet were lined in cedar, sachets of dried rosebuds suspended above to obfuscate the scent. (The drawback to cedar was that it made you smell like a Colorado forest— unfortunate shades of John Denver.)

Walter cared not for costly rugs or antiques—his furniture was new, sharp and sleek—and he loved his dog too much to care about hairs on the sofa. Walter wasn't anal (make that *compulsive*), but when he left home each day, he walked out into the world looking as much like a model as he could. Not a fashion model—though he *was* tall and strong, he did have that—but a role model, a model of . . . well, of propriety and seemliness, his Lutheran grandmother would have said. She, not his slovenly, self-destructive parents, had been his example and personal muse, and he tried to live by her principles—most of them. Like her quite correct loathing of street vernacular: "the language of stevedores and ruffians." Not a *damn* or a *Christ* would escape Walter's lips, and certainly not what Granna had called the Carnal Words—though in certain exceptional contexts, he did not mind hearing such words from other men's lips.

In Walter's kitchen, the one bit of decor that clashed with his marble counters and leather-saddled stools was a trio of samplers Granna had stitched:

Pleasant hours fly fast.

Ask favors neither of the tides nor of the wind.

I will live in a house by the side of the road and be a friend to man.
This one was his favorite. It depicted a cross-stitched house with a red roof, a stream of blue *x*'s drifting like motherly kisses from the chimney, a pink-and-green rosebush like a polka-dotted golf ball, and, in the foreground, a large black angular Scottie. Did the sentiment come from the dog? You had to laugh freely at that.

One night the previous fall, after coming home late, Walter stood in his kitchen, drank too much bourbon, and dolefully contemplated the samplers—as objects, not as wisdoms. Naturally, they made him think of the past—which he had been doing already that night, grieving over what he hoped, yet again, would be the last early death of a good friend: Michael B, who'd waitered with him (on roller skates!) nearly twenty years ago at a big touristy restaurant across from Lincoln Center. Walter had gone directly from the memorial service to work that evening, thus having to endure not only seven extra hours of his funeral suit but thoughtless remarks from regulars such as "My but aren't *we* looking spiffy" and even—this from a rich young twerp straighter than a Mormon Eagle Scout—"Yo, did someone die?" Of all the friends who became sick, Michael B had been the one to hang on longest, so that finally no one took his hospital sojourns too seriously, not even Michael B himself. "He's in again," someone would say, making a brisk round of calls. And then everybody would visit, but they'd no longer visit with great bouquets of lilies to hide their fearful expressions. No, they'd make the visits a bit of a party now. They came in twos and threes, bringing phallus-shaped cakes, obscene magic tricks, balloons with foofy children's TV stars: Blue, Barney, that purple Teletubby who'd been outed by some clearly closeted televangelisto. Resilience incarnate, that was Michael B.

And then, a triumph, it turned out that he had hung on long enough to get the magic pills, the protease inhibitors. "Inhibitions, bring 'em on!" Michael B had cheered, raucous with relief, when the drugs began to do their thing and, for the first time in years, his body began to fill out, his skin regaining a modest glow. His appetite returned full force, and he loved to drop by Walter's Place for lunch, eat an oozing meaty Reuben and a butterscotch sundae.

But then something backfired. His liver didn't like the drugs or his T cells tanked; Walter hadn't really listened to the details that Michael B so urgently explained. Walter had gone to the hospital, as always, and this time, standing mortified beneath a genital piñata, unable to look at the table where someone had blithely placed an orange lava lamp, he had known that this was the last time in for Michael B. "Almighty fuck," he had said when he walked out of the room (H. E. double hockeysticks to Granna's silver rule). Within a week, Michael B was in a casket winging toward the heartland. Though he had told various friends to please take various items from his marvelous collections of party clothes and snuff bottles and Japanese fans, his parents had simply shown up like a band of deaf-mutes with a U-Haul and, faster than you could strike a set on Broadway, taken the whole production away to Ohio. Good-bye to all that in the blink of a Bible Belt eye. And his rent-stabilized apartment, the one he'd promised to pass on to Gwen? Gone with the wind (that is, after renovation, onto the open market at five times the price).

You could remember without artifacts; how pathetically superficial if you couldn't! But Walter realized that, blessed though he was to have escaped this plague, he might not escape a car crash or an embolism or, heaven forfend, an *actual* piano from above. He was not without assets and treasures, not without friends and other worthy potential heirs. He had, for instance, a nephew in California, and though he did not know

Scott well, the boy seemed a good enough egg. At seventeen, he played baseball and GameBoy, but he also wrote poetry, strummed a guitar, and treated Walter like a person, even a likable person, not the Strip-o-Gram Guy Who Came for Dinner.

Walter saw Scott only once or twice a year because his family lived just over the Golden Gate Bridge from San Francisco (like Paris, but with your own language and no Turkish toilets). Last visit, Scott had invited Walter to a "poetry jam" at a Berkeley bookstore rank with patchouli and bohemian dust. Walter had sneezing fits but enjoyed himself immensely among the young pierced peers of Scott (who had wisely, discreetly—on his uncle's advice—pierced nothing more than a single ear). Afterward, Walter took Scott to Chez Panisse, along with a willowy girlfriend who weighed about as much as a dish towel and whose "thing" was turning Emily Dickinson's poems into "soft rap." Walter had a hard time not laughing at her earnest countercultural spiel when surely her parents owned twin Volvo wagons and a hot tub the size of his living room. But she and Scott made Walter feel weightlessly young, even fleetingly, unprecedentedly *cool*. After telling the teenagers numerous tales about running a restaurant (and here they were at the sine qua non of modern eateries), Scott smiled at him in that adolescently catlike fashion and said, "Dude, your life so rules." Well, perhaps it *did*. Walter was charmed.

Unfortunately, you could have the rest of that family: Scott's sister, the snooty little cheerleader (though maybe she'd straighten out yet); Walter's supercilious brother, Werner, Prozac poster boy; and Tipi, the anorexic, mosquitoey much-younger wife (though at least his original wife).

No, Walter realized in his bourbon funk after Michael B's sorry send-off, no by golly NO; he would not want *them* to inherit so much as a shoelace. The samplers brought the worst of Walter's brother to mind when he recalled seeing Werner toss these and other mementos of Granna into a trash can (to be salvaged by Walter).

No: he would not give Werner a second chance to fling such treasures aside—or, worse, to spend Walter's greener assets on predictable follies like that ghastly "gaming hall" he'd added to his already monstrous house or the RV he planned to buy for his *very* early retirement.

So then, "Which one?" Walter had asked Ben the following night, freed from his funeral suit but held in the vise of a colossal hangover.

They were standing at the bar, spying on a table by the front fireplace. "The one in the sweater or the stuffy blue shirt?"

"Stuffy," Ben answered with his customary bluntness.

The couple in question were a pair who had been coming to Walter's Place several times a year since it opened. About Walter's age, they looked rich, fit, obscenely well educated and, most irritating of all, perfectly matched. They'd been together for who knew how long, and every time they ate here, they *talked*. When Walter passed their table, he'd eavesdrop; what could they possibly talk about together with such perpetual enthusiasm? Well, they talked about theater, opera, ballet, and they gossiped with connubial glee—about people Walter didn't know, of course, but sometimes about famous people involved in those sequined culture things. (So they were connected too.) Never had he overheard them discussing illness or death, topics far too common at so many other tables.

Walter could already look back on this horrific era with what he believed to be an uncanny clarity for someone so deep in its shroudlike folds. He could see these recent years as a timeline: how at first no one spoke about It (or not out loud), then how everyone spoke about It but not in terms of who had It, then how suddenly everyone knew, almost by osmosis, who had It and who didn't (and who might). Who was on the Quilt, who died fighting, who found God, who went back to Boise or Billings or hopped a final plane, first-class, to the finest hotel on Maui.

A particularly vile social phenomenon was the kind of couple who, when the topic came up, leaned just a little closer, forming a personal tepee, their unified expression this pious, phony guilt-trip look that said, *Please don't hate us because we happen to be monogamous!* Or celibate. Sometimes that was the dirty secret. Couples stuck in lustless unions, maybe because of real estate, because no one would budge from the deal-of-the-century rent-controlled apartment, and then, presto, their prison became a refuge. Sexless but safe. Oh now, SAFE. What a loaded, political, euphemistic, convoluted word that one had become.

Walter was one of the inexplicably blessed—footloose but healthy— so when he felt resentful toward these couples, it wasn't for their smug vitality. No, he envied them something else entirely: the no longer having to try so hard, no longer having to cruise with that creeping, escalating doubt, sliding down that laundry chute toward the puddled, sunless cellar of age. If he were entirely honest with himself, he'd admit that he longed, more than just about anything else, to be part of that club, the men who stood on the High Ground, snug and dry in the cozy, bread-scented kitchen.

Up There is precisely where he saw this couple at the table by the fireplace, but he could hardly despise them for their altitude, could he? He always greeted them warmly, and he knew their first names, but he had not known their professions. Now it turned out that Stuffy (Gordie) was a lawyer *and* a financial advisor—who, according to Ben, had become a fiscal priest of sorts, specializing in legal last rites for those who'd faced up to their imminent end. But even as a generalist, he was the best in the business, said Ben.

The next day had been one of those crisp September days that fill your lungs with virtue and resolve. Resisting superstition, Walter looked Stuffy up in the phone book and made an appointment.

THE WRETCHED SUN. Blame, to begin with, the wretched autumn sun, coming in that window and catching the maple highlights in the man's youthful hair, herofying his jawline and gilding the curvature of a hip just as Walter stepped into his office.

"Oh hello! Why *hello*," Gordie effused. "You're *that* Walter. I should have put two and two together! We love your place—and if I had my way, we'd come a lot more often, but Stephen's always trying some new kind of diet. We were there last week! I'm practically addicted to your beef bourguignon."

Walter thanked him. "The beef bourguignon is Hugo's, not mine. I started a restaurant because I'm a hopeless cook but love to be fed." He told Gordie it was the bartender who'd recommended him—and they joked about that to break the ice. Walter had expected to feel unnerved at this meeting, but not in this way; somehow, all at once, Stuffy seemed outlandishly charming (yes, his flattery helped), and that day he wore something nicer, softer, less prepossessing: mossy old corduroys and a loose copper-colored shirt (you could be sure the price had been more like platinum).

Gordie sat at his desk; Walter capsized in a fat green sofa.

"Where's your famous dog?" asked Gordie.

"At home," said Walter. "About pets and children, you should never presume acceptance."

"I love dogs!" Gordie protested. "We'd have one ourselves if our schedules weren't so insane. . . . You're lucky you can bring one to work."

"Actually, I'm lucky I haven't been closed. I'm waiting for the hygiene police to stop by and tell me I'm not exactly in Paris. Alas."

They looked at each other pleasantly, through a narrow shaft of silence. (Our first silence, Walter reflected later on. Most people noted first fights as a landmark; Walter thought first silences far more memorable.)

Gordie asked if he'd brought his financial information; Walter placed his folders on the desk. As Gordie began to page through tax returns and bank statements, Walter felt almost naked. This *was* a thorny business. He jumped slightly when Gordie pointed past him and said, "There's coffee, tea, and, speaking of Paris, some great French cookies. That's my vice—really expensive cookies."

"If you don't mind my saying so, that's a pathetic vice," said Walter.

Gordie's laugh was one of professional nicety (Walter knew that laugh quite well; a lesson in humility, this). "Perhaps I should amend that to say it's the only vice I'll confess to my clients."

"Ah. Say no more."

Second of all, blame that wretched Scotsman from the bookstore. (Now *there* was a bona fide Stuffy—though Ben had christened that one Bonny, short for Bonny Prince Charlie.) When the phone rang, Gordie answered. On the speaker thing, before Gordie picked up the receiver, Walter heard enough to recognize Fenno McLeod's distinctive voice.

"God it's been ages, how are you?" said Gordie. "I'm sorry we haven't been in to say hi, we've just—well, we were in Turin and Venice for all of July, the Berkshires in August, and now—maybe it's just me, but the fall is still like back-to-school: too much homework, playing catch-up at the gym, that feeling like you're about to start getting graded again. I'm with a client, but what's up? I'd love to call back and hear about your summer." He mimed to Walter that he would be off in a minute and swiveled his chair to face the one vast window, which looked out into the branches shading Union Square. Gusts of wind were beginning to strip away the turning leaves.

Gordie let out a cry of dismay. "Oh no. I'm so sorry. I am so sorry to hear that, Fenno." More silence. "I always thought he was like this . . . old soul in the corner there, such a reassuring presence. You must miss him so much."

Walter deduced that McLeod's dog had died. Walter wasn't much of a reader these days, though he still knew his plays, so he rarely entered McLeod's place, but the man's dog was as much "the bookshop dog" as Walter's was "the restaurant dog"—half a block apart. Like The Bruce, Rodgie was a local personality on Bank Street, the two dogs longtime acquaintances through frequent sidewalk encounters. Whatever Walter might think of his owner, Rodgie was one of the few male dogs with whom The Bruce did not feel compelled to stage that tiresome growling face-off. While the two dogs had made their olfactory small talk (small sniff, could you call it that?), Walter and Fenno had exchanged more or less the same pointless information, updated: current climate, volume of business, the relentless rise in real estate prices; yada yada *nada*. Dog people in New York loved to brag about how their pets made them important connections, but no one ever mentioned how much tedious obligatory chitchat came with the package.

After Gordie said good-bye, at first he did not turn around. Perhaps something down on the street had captured his attention. But when he faced Walter again, he was wiping his eyes with a sleeve. "I apologize," he said, with a small self-conscious laugh. "Excuse my emotions, I'm a bit of a sap, but a very nice dog I've known for ages died. . . . I should be glad it's you I have here, shouldn't I?" Gordie pulled a tissue from a box on his desk.

"It's not a bit sappy. Sometimes I'm sure I'd be lost without The Bruce," Walter said automatically. "He gets me up every morning. I know that."

With deliberate gravity, Gordie turned his attention back to Walter's papers. "So—I'm sorry—remind me about your objectives?"

"Well, it's not as if I'm dying or anything like that." Now it was Walter's turn to feel awkward. "Oh dear. I didn't mean to sound so glib."

"I'm aware of my reputation," said Gordie. "The fiscal undertaker, that's what I'm called, even to my face. Sad but true. One client joked that he's hung a sign by the checkout desk at his doctor's office: RESERVE YOUR PLOT AND CALL GORDIE UNSWORTH."

Walter rushed on: "So it's just—well, I suppose it does have a lot to do with everyone dying around me. Not everyone—you know what I mean. Good grief, I can't believe how rattled I am by all this. The point is, it's ridiculous, isn't it, to reach your forties and not have a will? Worse than not flossing your teeth."

"I know parents with children in college who've never gotten around to a will. It's a surprisingly hard thing to do." Gordie spoke earnestly, without condescension. His eyes still glittered. Walter had underestimated Stuffy's depth of feeling. Not the first time Walter got an F in character sleuthing.

So he relaxed. He explained to Gordie how the restaurant had done quite well these past few years, how he'd done nothing more creative with the surplus than dump it in a money market account with old-lady interest rates—and how, most important, he wanted to make sure that, should the accidental piano fall, his gas-guzzling Republican brother wouldn't walk off with the profits.

Gordie held up a folder. "This tells me everything about the business?"

"Yes."

"No partners, silent or talking?"

Walter hated this part. "Extremely silent now. I bought him out when he got sick. Four years ago."

Gordie's expression was one they had both seen too often: a look of dread, of pain, of a question you weren't sure you should ask yet had to. How many times could you have this same ghoulish, *plus ça change* conversation?

Walter rescued him. "Two years more, he made it that long. He took the money and went to Key West. Had a devoted lover. Not me." To hear himself speak of this tragedy so telegrammatically was depressing, but such shorthand had become a necessity in his world.

Gordie (who surely understood this shorthand better than anyone) said he was sorry, after which they observed the Respectful Moment of Silence.

"All right." Gordie paged back and forth, back and forth. "Debts?"

"None." In reply to Gordie's admiring glance, Walter said, "I can't pretend to be a wizard with money. But my grandmother was, and she left me just enough so I could cut up all that hateful plastic."

Gordie's smile was sly. "So I guess you'll be paying me in more than a lifetime supply of beef bourguignon."

Please let this be flirting, Walter thought.

Walter told Gordie about his nephew, his desire to leave a small gift to an animal charity, his fantasies for retirement. Walter had never been in therapy, but he imagined it must be quite a bit like this. At moments, he felt like a child talking about an imaginary friend. (Honestly now, who *was* this fellow daring to say that he dreamed of an old age on Cape Cod, a little house on the dunes? Dream on, buster!) But Gordie listened keenly, asked straightforward questions, never mocking. When Walter had finished reciting his fantasy life, Gordie began to explain about trusts and executors and mutual funds and things that Walter had always thought the province of movie stars, *Mayflower* descendants, and neighbors who monopolized four-story brownstones.

"To put it simply," said Gordie, "you can't just leave a three-star restaurant in New York City to a teenage boy who lives three thousand miles away. Or you can, but you might as well be leaving him an elephant or, for that matter, a circus. You see what I mean."

Walter laughed. " 'Hey dudes, guess what? My queer uncle in New York City just left me an elephant! Like, awesome!' " He pictured the look on Werner's face. He wished he *did* have an elephant he could leave to Scott.

"Not that you plan to go tomorrow—unless of course your piano phobia comes to fruition."

"Or the proverbial plane goes down."

"There's that too," said Gordie. "It happens."

"Oh, enough of the gallows; I begin to worry about my precious karma—just in case there's such a thing."

By now, Gordie had rearranged Walter's affairs into a tidy, prioritized stack. He stood and gave Walter a few pamphlets and a handwritten list of concerns to review before calling to make another appointment.

"Homework!" Walter exclaimed. He hadn't realized he'd get to return so easily. "I guess it *is* like back-to-school, isn't it?" Too late, he saw that this was a reference to the conversation with Fenno McLeod, not with him.

Gordie didn't seem to notice. He stood by the window. "Have you seen my view? I have to show it off or it's not worth the rent."

Walter joined him. It was Friday, so the farmers' market was in full autumnal swing, a sea of potted chrysanthemums and bushel after bushel of apples, pears, Fauvist gourds, and pumpkins with erotically fanciful stems. On one table stood galvinized buckets of the year's final roses; on another, skeins of yarn in muted, soulful purples and reds.

Walter loved this part of the season—and not just because it was the time of year his restaurant flourished, when people felt the first yearnings to sit by a fire, to eat stew and bread pudding and meatloaf, drink cider and toddies and cocoa. He loved the season's transient intensity, its gaudy colors and tempestuous skies. It felt, to Walter, a lot like loving Shakespeare (which he always would, even if he'd memorized his last soliloquy several years ago now).

"Do you shop there?" said Gordie. "I hear all the best neighborhood restaurants order from farmers."

"Hugo gets pheasants and squab from someone down there—corn and heirloom tomatoes in the summer. I leave all that to him, and just as well. Last spring he bought *fiddlehead ferns*. Well, I walked into the kitchen and shrieked. I thought I was looking at a bowl of dead caterpillars, that's how much I know!"

"Look—are those dervishes?" Gordie pointed down at a performance, three dancers in red skirts pirouetting on a stretch of open asphalt.

From the side, Walter stole a concentrated look at Gordie's face; it was so . . . kind. All its lines, still subtle, seemed to bookmark the places expressive of joy. *Greet the morning early and with joy:* Granna had embroidered that wisdom on a cushion. Walter leaned against it in bed when he watched the nightly news—never mind that, given the choice, he'd always rather sleep late.

He edged slowly closer to Gordie, till he sensed their sleeves just touching. Close enough to tell that Gordie did not wear cologne. Walter hated phony scents as much as he hated phony tans.

Gordie turned away from the window and reached out to shake Walter's hand. "I like this—having really met you. It makes the city feel nice and small," he said. "Stephen makes fun of me, but I'm someone who *misses* that part of living in the boonies."

"Well, you're in the minority there, dude—as my nephew would say—but you may be the wise one among us." If he'd been honest, Walter would have agreed with Gordie, but he decided it wasn't the note to end on, not this time. The calculations had begun.

When he left, he walked slowly, half dizzy, his brain buzzing like a hive, through the farmers' market. The dancers had vanished. He examined the flowers and the yarns and the pumpkins up close, as if to make sure they weren't all part of a heady dream. At one point, he looked up, just a furtive glance, to locate Gordie's window, to see if he was being watched. He was stunned to see eight or nine stories of windows just like Gordie's and could not remember which floor he'd been on. Up there, looking down, he'd felt as if the two of them were remote and alone, in a tower.

WHILE WALTER DYED HIS HAIR at the bathroom sink, The Bruce sat on the mat and watched. Funny how a dog could look puzzled (or angry or elated or grieving or guilty—all the same shades of emotion a person's face could reveal). This was only the third time Walter had done it, so he was still nervous about the results. His hair remained thick and basically blond, but a few months ago he'd noticed that the color was looking a little dusty alongside his ears. He'd just turned forty-four, so this seemed fair—but still.

He was surprised how much he liked this new task, how the tinted water swirling down the drain made him feel as if he were purging himself—washing something away, not covering something up. He only hoped that, sometime in the future, he would recognize the point when the lines on his face began to mock his hair, shriek at the vain deceit. You should age with dignity, not denial: Granna had not said or stitched this, but she might have. Before she died, her face had been nothing but folds and creases; to Walter, it looked like the topographical map of some mystical place, like a terraced mountain in Tibet.

He assessed his newly gilded hair in the mirror. So far, so good. Perhaps the dregs of winter, however dreary, wouldn't be so lonely after all.

"Now your turn," he said to The Bruce. The dog trotted briskly back to the bedroom, vaulting his stocky frame up onto the bed. Walter sat beside him and took the soft brush and the currycomb out of his nightstand. Like so many purebreds, The Bruce had a few chronic maladies; the worst was his eczema, for which Walter had creams and shampoos and special grooming utensils. Probably because he itched a good deal of the time, the poor dog loved all this close attention. "Does that feel good, lovey?" Walter crooned as he pushed the currycomb through T.B.'s short coat. The hair was a uniform grayish beige, but his skin resembled the hide of a pinto pony, pinkish white with patches of black. As Walter brushed him, the dog grunted vaguely—a canine purr—and drooled onto the towel Walter had placed beneath his head.

Walter had adopted T.B. as an older puppy. The shelter volunteer who helped him make his choice was a girl around Scott's age who wore lipstick the color of pot roast. (Was there nothing attractive left to be cool? Had fashion tripped into a black hole, or was Walter just too old?) "People hate dogs that drool, they think it's gross," she said as they looked into the cage, "but he's way cute. Looks a lot like Bruce Willis, if you ask me."

This had amused Walter greatly. "Well, if you ask me, Bruce Willis is anything but cute, and I doubt he'd be flattered. Man *or* dog."

Every Tuesday and every other Saturday, a misanthropic young woman named Sonya came by to borrow T.B., taking him to a nursing home in the Bronx, where he let the oldsters coddle him for hours. Sonya had that hackneyed Morticia Addams look, powdery skin and shoe-black hair, and smelled like stale cumin. When he attempted small talk, just about the only thing Walter got out of her was that she worked for some off-the-grid animal welfare group called—valiantly, he did not laugh—The True Protectors. Shades of Flash Gordon.

Walter went along for the first visit, just to make sure this theoretically Samaritan act was on the up-and-up. One of his regular customers had suggested this enterprise, pointing out that T.B. was perfectly suited because he was so well socialized. Walter, who'd been feeling guilty that he did not "give back," was happy to make T.B. his proxy.

Thus did Walter—after a silent ride with the unpleasantly perfumed Sonya, for whom gum snapping was evidently preferable to speech—find himself one balmy weekend on a narrow balcony in Riverdale, overlooking the Spuyten Duyvil Bridge, telling a pair of proud grandmas about his own Granna, playing gin rummy for pocket change, drinking sherry that tasted like stagnant Pepsi, and allowing himself to be quite absurdly flirted with. After that, he sent The Bruce back there alone. It pleased Walter to think of T.B. conducting his own private social life in a separate borough.

Tuesdays, Sonya arrived at seven, Saturdays at ten. She would pick up The Bruce and return him almost without a word to Walter, but if he looked out his front window after she took the dog downstairs, he'd see her nattering sweetly away as she settled him in the back of her van. That was one very odd girl.

Saturday was the only day Walter wasn't the first one in at work. He loved arriving to the smell of eggs and pancake batter and, this time of year, two newly laid fires. Today he surveyed the brunch reservations and snipped the dead flowers off the cyclamen plants inside the front window. At eleven he unlocked the door; the first customer to walk through it was Bonny.

"Greetings, neighbor," said Walter. "What brings you to Casa Cholesterol? Dating a gaucho?" The first time Fenno McLeod had come into the restaurant, along with an older woman, they'd looked at the menu and joked that some witty individual they'd known would have given this nickname to Walter's Place. Walter felt briefly offended—but it was accurate, was it not? Heart Attack Central, an otherwise benevolent reviewer had called it, but Walter liked Bonny's version better.

"Dates are for after dark," said McLeod. "Most days I eat fruit for breakfast, but I'm in the mood for eggs Benedict."

"Consistency is the hobgoblin of people who never get laid," said Walter.

McLeod gave him a stiff smile. Oh gosh, thought Walter, I *forgot* about that Conan Doyle walking stick stuck up your bottom. Not a bad bottom, though, if one were to steal a glimpse.

They did the requisite weather dance—Wasn't March always a letdown, a tease? Those poor little crocuses, hoodwinked again! Well yes, jolly so, but the *Ewe Kay;* well, there it would be bloody cold and *twice* as damp—and then McLeod laid a book on the table. How anyone could read while eating (even the newspaper) was a mystery to Walter. It was always an awkward mess: dabs of grease on the pages, a crick in your neck.

The two waiters were busy in back, so Walter brought out the wooden box of tea bags himself. Brits rarely drank coffee. None of that when-in-Rome stuff for imperial them. McLeod chose Lapsang souchong as Walter wondered if seeing this man would always, now, remind him of Gordie, of the way Walter had fallen for Gordie's sentimental reaction to the death of a dog. He wished Granna had stitched a sampler to warn him against such emotional triggers. *Lovers of animals doth not make the very best lovers of men.* Too wordy. *Beware ye the tears of easy sentiment.* Better. *Falleth not for married men.* Far more to the point. And blameth not the poor departed bookshop dog.

The first week of October—the week between his first and second meetings with Gordie—had been agony undistilled, bliss transcendent. Every night, in vain, Walter had hoped that Gordie and what's-his-name would return to the restaurant so that he could assess the surely obvious cracks in their conjugal veneer. Finally, having tucked his homework in a new manila folder, having changed his clothes twice, Walter walked to Union Square. The sky was a moody rush of lavender clouds, reflecting the state of his nerves. *Voolishness, voolishness, voolishness,* he heard Granna say in her small but confident voice with that shameless Wagnerian accent.

Nothing is going to happen, you idiot: that from Walter himself.

But all it took was the onset of the storm. They had been at their places on either side of the desk (and yes, he had brought T.B. along this time; the dog lay firmly ensconced in a sofa cushion) when the first crack of thunder sounded and the first flash of lightning lit the room like an opalescent strobe. A wind, out of nowhere, lashed at the sycamores in the park. The branches thrashed frantically, as if the trees were attempting to flee, and their leaves tore away in swarms. A spectacle of nature the two men had certainly seen before, but it drew them to the window like children. "Oh!" Walter cried out when a large limb cracked off and fell to the ground. Gordie turned toward him, and they stared at each other, neither laughing nor solemn, mutually strange in that strange green light. Puzzled, perhaps, but then they were in each other's arms—their mouths fervently joined—and then on that welcoming couch (rudely displacing The Bruce) and then on that parking lot of an oriental rug.

Gordie's skin was as smooth and hot as an oven door. With a distant surprise—irrelevant to the turmoil of their abrupt entanglement—Walter noticed, in glimpses, that Gordie's back and arms were manically freckled. If they had revealed their bodies more slowly to each other, this might have put Walter off, but his desire, returned so swiftly, could only gain momentum.

Gordie issued terse questions, but softly, about just what Walter needed: "Like that? Tell me . . . there, just there? Yes, baby, *there* . . ." Walter was quite beyond words yet touched by all this urgent thoughtfulness. The only words he could summon, and only in his mind, were those for body parts: knee, elbow, shoulder, thigh . . . and several others for which Granna would have to forgive him. He would later reflect on how *courtly* Gordie had been—if you could be courtly, hot, and aggressive all at once.

Walter fell asleep after he came—perhaps for just a fraction of a second; he knew this only by the instant of waking, of feeling his slippery skin against Gordie's. Walter lay on his back, with Gordie's face against his neck, a wide smooth palm across Walter's left nipple, as if to shield his heart.

I will not be the first to speak, thought Walter. If I open my big Teutonic mouth, I will say something completely doltish.

They lay there, breathing audibly, listening to the rain and the retreating thunder, for several peaceful minutes.

"I'm sorry," Gordie said at last, clearing his throat because he was hoarse, "but I'm afraid I have to know what time it is. I wish I didn't." He climbed carefully across Walter's body. "Yikes," he said. "We have to get dressed."

As Walter collected his clothes, he remembered The Bruce. Looking every well-fed inch the martyr, T.B. lay against the office door.

"I don't know—God, I don't—listen . . ." Hastily, Gordie tucked in his shirt, smoothed its front, ran his fingers through his hair, touched a folder on his desk. Finally, thank heaven, he smiled at Walter, who sat on the sofa, stunned, dressed except for his feet. The smile was warm, not guilty or evasive. "Can you come tomorrow afternoon? I mean, at least to finish up the terms of your bequest to Scott."

Walter said, "I like the 'at least.' "

"God," Gordie said, "I don't know. I just—"

"Oh sure you do," said Walter. "No 'just' about it." He stood and leaned across Gordie's desk. He grasped Gordie's arms and pulled him toward an embrace. The desk was wider than he'd thought, so their faces barely touched, but Walter could feel it: that Gordie still ached to kiss him, that it wasn't already a thing in the past, an impulse spent.

Gordie pulled away. He said with delight, "Whatever you do, don't come around this desk. You have to go now. I've got someone coming in five minutes. I have to . . ."

"Calm down?" said Walter, and they laughed. At the door, The Bruce looked tremendously annoyed, as if their joking were infantile.

"No Jiminy Cricket from you," Walter said in a low voice after Gordie had closed the door behind them. "I will not own a dog who thinks he's my conscience, got that?" He paused to scratch The Bruce on his neck and behind his ears. T.B. pushed back against his fingers. So kinetic with joy that he could not bear to wait for the elevator, Walter clipped on T.B.'s leash and made for the stairs. They trotted down all seven flights.

In the square—it was market day again—he led The Bruce down the lane between the vendors' tents. For the dog, he decided on a beef empanada from the pastry man (T.B. consumed it in two noisy gulps); for himself, roses.

"Those," he said. "I'll take those."

"How many?" said the girl.

"The whole caboodle. I'm feeling rich today."

Wielding twine and scissors, the girl hoisted the roses from the bucket and bundled them together. Before she hooded the blossoms with tissue paper, Walter leaned in quickly and touched his face to the petals. Plush and blousy, the roses smelled like a church prepared for a fancy wedding—potent, ecstatic, sacred—but they were a radiant orange, the color of torches, not of veils and modest lace gloves. Quite a different kind of vow.

The affair—that's what it had been, after all, though thinking in such terms made Walter wince—lasted two and a half months. It took the claustrophobic shape of passionate meetings in Gordie's office (without that prudish chaperone of a dog) and furtive weekday lunches in Chinatown, Hoboken, Yorkville, Long Island City—places where Gordie was convinced nobody would know them. Walter didn't care; he liked to think he'd be happy if they were "discovered." For most of that time, neither of them mentioned Stephen, and Walter began to let himself hope that Stephen had decamped (perhaps Walter was the grand consoler!) or been dismissed (Walter was the love of Gordie's life!).

Such wishful oblivion lasteth not forever; Walter knew that. He had been determined, however, that the breaker of the pact would be Gordie—and it was, though Walter was the one who blew his cool. It was the week before Thanksgiving week (the biggest week in the year for guilt trips). They were holding hands under the table at a romantic but oddly macho restaurant on the New Jersey side of the Hudson; out the window, from afar, they could see the rump of the *Intrepid*. The food was Low Italian, so dependent on bread and pasta and cheese that it made Walter's Place look like a Weight Watchers clinic. The clientele were mainly men, most of them wearing polyester shirts, wide shiny ties, and navy blue suits with garish buttons.

Gordie poked his lasagna as if it might contain a booby trap. Walter was contemplating his veal chop with ardor, though he did not want to remove his hand from Gordie's, which he'd have to do to cut the thing. He was wishing that he, too, had ordered pasta just as Gordie said, "Stephen wants to do pheasant this year—pretentious, if you ask me, but he's bored stiff with turkey. I know you mentioned Hugo does pheasant; do you think he'd share his recipe?"

So there it was: cuckold out of the bag.

"I'm sure he would." Walter was careful not to sound petulant.

Gordie didn't thank him or say, *How great!* Or, *What a relief!* He continued to perform a postmortem on his lunch. "Well, that was sensitive," he muttered.

"What?" said Walter, almost breezy.

"I don't know why I did that."

"I don't know what you mean."

"Mentioned Stephen. Mentioned Thanksgiving. For all I know, you have no family, no . . ."

"Friends?" Walter laughed. "Flatter me some more, darling."

"No, no," said Gordie. "No *plans*. You know, Thanksgiving's the big do for Stephen—he loves having friends with kids, letting them decorate the table with dried leaves and felt Pilgrims' hats, make place tags, all that. It's really very down-home, and I like that, I always have. But this year I'll be thinking about . . . about you, too. I guess I just assumed that because you have the restaurant—"

"Well, exactly so!" Walter interrupted. "After the crowd of lonely-hearts and can't-open-a-can-of-cranberry types go home, we're having our own family fling: Ben and his lover and Hugo and June and her husband and brother, maybe a few orphans yet to be determined—we're doing a late-night thing with paella and six kinds of wine and chocolate bread pudding. Don't you feel sorry for *me*."

Gordie smiled at him, the rapturous, admiring smile to which Walter had become addicted. "I don't. Forgive me for even implying I did."

"Nothing *to* forgive." Walter beamed. And perhaps there wasn't.

But Gordie had little to say as he drove them back to the city, and Walter decided that something had to give; they had to break the constraints of their ossifying routine. Gordie had to see more of Walter, had to have a taste of what it might be like not to watch the clock or the faces passing them on the street.

So Walter did the foolish thing, the fatal thing: He reserved a room at an inn on Cape May, for the weekend before Christmas. Once Stephen's name had been spoken, it came out again, every so often—and one day

Gordie happened to mention that lucky Stephen was off to Santa Fe for nearly a week, to hobnob at a benefit for the opera company, one of the artsy clients for which he apparently harvested money. Walter took the revelation as a hint.

How happily he had sealed the inn's brochure, with its pictures of tourmaline ocean and canopied beds, in a plain white envelope and placed it inside a necktie box from Barneys. He wrapped the box, tied it with a big red bow, and presented it to Gordie while they were sitting naked on the great fluffy couch in their aerie (office? this was an office?) above Union Square.

"Early Christmas!" Walter exclaimed.

"But I didn't—"

"Of course you didn't. I'm being impatient, that's how I can be," said Walter. "As you well know."

Gordie stared at the gift. He hesitated, but he was smiling like a child seated at the foot of the family tree. "I thought you hated the knee-jerk fashion thing," he said as he took the box from Walter.

The ribbon slipped across Gordie's thigh, down the velvet slope of the sofa cushion, and pooled on the floor. "Fooled again," said Gordie when he saw the envelope. He opened it slowly, not as eagerly as Walter would have liked.

Gordie unfolded the brochure and examined it, front and back. "I've heard of this place. I've always wanted . . . I've heard it's incredible." He looked up at Walter, and there were his easy tears again, but what did they mean?

Walter decided they meant that he was deeply moved. "Two weekends from now. I have a car lined up, first thing Saturday morning. I'll get Hugo to pack us breakfast for the road. Order whatever your heart desires."

Gordie folded the brochure back into the envelope. The gift box had fallen to the floor, its two halves face down across the spill of red satin ribbon.

"Oh Walter, I can't do that. I'd love to, but I can't."

"Don't tell me you have work—and I know you haven't got pets!"

Gordie leaned away from the couch to retrieve his pants. He pulled them on. "I've been a complete ass—to Stephen, but mostly to you—and I kept telling myself that by Thanksgiving . . . and then by Christmas . . . I'd . . ."

"You'd dump me." Walter said this so that Gordie would object. He wanted to be told he was wrong, so wrong; after all, he was not the intuitive type!

"Walter, I'm . . ." The tears were now mobile, making their way down Gordie's cheeks.

"You're crazy about me," whispered Walter. He couldn't touch Gordie, because Gordie was standing some distance across the room now. He was looking down at his shirt, which he held uncertainly in both hands, as if he'd forgotten what it was for.

"I am," sighed Gordie. "But that's not—that can't be something I turn my life upside down for."

"It can be that for me!" Walter stood; he was the taller man here, and he would not be looked down upon. Defiantly, he did not reach for his clothes.

"But your life . . ." Gordie shook out his shirt, almost angrily, and started to put it on. "I thought you always knew this had nothing to do with Stephen."

"How could it have nothing to do with him? Everywhere we go—all these hinterplaces where garment workers and Mafiosi hang out!—all that hiding was precisely about Stephen, wasn't it?"

"Yes!" said Gordie with unexpected fury. "Okay, you're right! Okay, I have a vice a little messier than delicious cookies!" He gestured toward the shelf holding tea bags, mugs, and plates. "I'm sorry."

"So, is it over?" said Walter. Surely *this* would elicit a denial.

Gordie came toward him, stopping just short of where they might touch. "It has to be, Walter. It just has to be. I'm such a spineless ass."

"Gordie, dear, the only bit of spine in an ass is the tailbone, that useless vestige of when we used to swing from the trees. Yes, that would describe you exactly, right at this moment." This insult made no sense, but never mind. Breathing through his mouth to keep from crying, Walter finally reached for his clothes. There seemed to be so many pieces to button and zip; oh for a jumpsuit and shoes that would package him up, neat and ready to go, with just a few tidy straps of Velcro. He was glad The Bruce was safely, ignorantly at home, no witness to this dreadful scene.

TWO MONTHS WENT BY BEFORE WALTER ran into Gordie on the street, just after Valentine's Day. Walter was hurrying because of the cold, looking down so as not to stumble on the buckled antique flagstones that paved his way to work (treacheries of the past, just waiting to trip you up). He was passing the bookstore when he heard the bell on the door as it opened and then a soft "Walter." He saw the feet before he saw the man. When he exhaled sharply in sweet, pained surprise, his breath exploded in a cloud.

"It's good to see you, Walter," said Gordie with a tenderness that sounded almost desperate.

"The fiscal undertaker himself. Hello there."

The Bruce sniffed at Gordie's expensive leather boots.

Gordie looked miserable. He leaned down to stroke the dog.

"Sorry," said Walter. "How are you?"

"Okay. Okay." Though it sounded like he was anything but.

"You're fabulous. Be honest, don't insult me."

"Say no if you want, but can I stop by for a drink at the bar sometime? I hate the way we left things."

"Oh you do?" Walter laughed harshly: another white explosion in front of his face. "Well, how about now?" It was five o'clock, on the cusp of dark. Gordie would make an excuse, and that would be that.

"Now's fine," said Gordie. "That would be great."

The path through the snow on the sidewalk was narrow, so Gordie walked behind Walter and The Bruce. They did not speak until Gordie had checked his coat, Walter had gone to the kitchen to speak with Hugo, and they were seated at a table in the back of the dining room.

Gordie ordered a Scotch; Walter ordered soda with lime, though his heart was clamoring for something far stronger. More than anything (well, except to look at Gordie, to have that face to himself), he wanted to keep Gordie on edge.

"How's business?" Gordie asked.

"Thriving. Hugo did a dinner last month at the James Beard House. Pennsylvania Dutch. He got a standing ovation."

"Which he deserves," said Gordie. "I'm so glad."

"I'm glad you're glad."

"Walter—"

"Yes, Gordie?"

"Walter, it would be cruel to say I miss you, because that would imply . . . and the problem is, you know, Stephen and I have this very complicated life. It's like a web."

"So then, I guess I didn't hear you say it?"

"What?"

"That you miss me."

"Oh Walter . . ."

Walter leaned suddenly across the table and touched Gordie's hand. It was so wonderfully warm. Physically, Gordie was always warm, out to the tips of his fingers and toes. Just a touch made Walter ache. He said gently, "This really isn't the place, you know. And please don't 'Oh Walter' me. We could've been together, and I could even, I bet, have fixed up Stephen with someone perfect for him . . . but that was then, as they say."

"I know. Maybe we—"

"Stop. I don't want to hear your maybes. Turn them into certainlys and then you can talk till the moon turns green." Walter wanted to hear every last one of those maybes, but oh how they would dither with his head. Now he laughed lightly, calling up his very best thespian skills. "But you know, I'm really fine about everything now. Once I thought about it, I realized that the last thing I'd want to have on my head is breaking up a monument like you guys."

Gordie took a deep breath: the relief of reaching the surface, not having drowned. "The irony is, Stephen and I are going through some pretty heavy stuff, and we may have to take a break. I just wanted to be the one to tell you, in case that's what happens."

"You're breaking up?" *Careful, you vool.*

"No. But there's this issue, something I never thought would come up between us in a million years—I'm sorry, I promised Stephen I wouldn't talk about it to other people." He finished his Scotch. "This is ridiculous, isn't it? I just saw you and wanted . . . your company, I guess. This is selfish."

Walter sat back and looked at Gordie as he imagined a loving parent might. "You don't have to tell me anything. I like your company, too— as you know." For emphasis, he laughed the artificially carefree laugh again. And then, as he watched Gordie looking awkward, bereft, clearly wanting to confide, he had a diabolical idea. "You know, it's none of my business, and please feel free to bite my head off, but I have a good friend whose husband is supposed to be a fantastic . . . counselor. You know, for couples. He's right in the neighborhood."

Gordie groaned. "That's exactly what Stephen wants. For us to 'see someone.' Work things out like that. I grew up in Montana, though. That's not how you solve problems in Montana."

"No," said Walter, "but I don't see you driving a truck with a gun rack. And"—Walter looked pointedly at Gordie's lovely corduroy shirt— "I'm not sure how many guys in Butte wear purple."

Gordie's smile was a scold to Walter's memory. "Bozeman. And I bet you could find at least three guys there who wear purple. Purple socks, at least."

"Under their cowboy boots and spurs."

"Yes." Gordie smiled at Walter, as if remembering something he'd forgotten. Forgotten and *missed*.

"I'll get you this guy's number. I'll leave it on your machine at the office."

Gordie's expression lightened, and he regarded Walter for a moment as if Walter had fixed things already, made things right in his life.

Walter took in the world beyond their table: three couples had been seated, older people who liked eating out when they could have a conversation without turning up their hearing aids. He stood. "Time to schmingle."

Gordie stood as well. He placed a twenty-dollar bill under his empty glass.

"Oh please." Walter picked it up and thrust it back at him.

Gordie took it. "Thank you. I'm glad we . . ."

"Buried the hatchet? *Didn't* kiss but made up nonetheless?"

Deliberately solemn, Gordie held Walter's gaze. "You don't have to be so witty all the time," he said. "I was just going to say I'm glad we saw each other, I'm glad we're in a better place, that we can talk without . . ."

Scenes. Walter smiled. "I agree. Now follow my advice, go be with *him* and try to make it work. Sitting on fences does not become you. Even if you did grow up on the range."

WHEN WALTER WAS THE FIRST ONE IN, he'd switch on the lights to find the place just as he'd left it the night before—three rows of tables like children waiting to be dressed, chairs above, floor below, long bar beckoning from deep in the shadows—and The Bruce would shove past him to bolt for the kitchen, where he knew his master would find him a treat. Following his dog, Walter would think, I'm here for *life:* always a moment of deep pleasure, always interrupted by barking. "Patience!" Walter would shout at The Bruce, though fondly.

Today, he found a note from Hugo on the butcher block saying that he was out at the meat market. *Veal Oscar?* Hugo had written. "Oh goody," said Walter as he went to the nearest Hobart to see what Hugo had set aside for T.B. Sometimes it was a bone, sometimes a handful of giblets.

Once The Bruce was contentedly, boorishly gobbling down leftover bacon, Walter went to the desk in his tiny back closet of an office and ripped the previous day off the calendar. And kaboom! Here was March, the sneaky month. "In like a lion, out like Richard Gere will never be," he muttered happily, and then something less entertaining occurred to him: Werner's birthday. *Obserf all your family's special occasions, even venn you'd rather not.*

He sat down and looked at his watch: just after six in California. Rising early was a Granna virtue that Werner did happen to honor, though it had to do with something like markets in Tokyo or Lagos, some sort of globalized money voodoo, not with emulating his wool-spinning, log-splitting forebears. Werner liked to brag about still seeing stars in the sky when he got up. He went running at dawn and ate some gargantuan but überhealthy breakfast, laced with brewer's yeast or seaweed, before the rest of his family had even begun to stir.

Werner picked up on the second ring.

"Happy birthday, brother dear."

"Well. Hey. Is this the annual reminder from the bureau of 'Don't forget you're aging'?"

"Hey yourself. This is someone thinking of you nearly halfway around the world. Not so long ago, that wasn't even possible."

"Thank you," Werner said (attempting warmth, to give him credit).

"So? News?"

"It's sixty-five degrees already today, and the jasmine's in full bloom. I can smell it right here through the open window. We've had a spectacular week—and out at Tahoe they're still skiing."

You couldn't avoid it: every conversation with his brother began with a prelude that Walter called The Weather According to Werner. You could practically time it: two full minutes, at least, just to remind you that northern California was Shangri-ladeeda. Walter held the receiver out to The Bruce and let him lick it as Werner gave a full report on wind-surfing conditions.

Walter reclaimed the phone in time to hear Werner say, "Eating your breakfast?"

"Eggs and ham," Walter lied.

"My omelets are whites-only now, and even turkey bacon's off limits. It's the sulfites that'll get you."

"Don't worry, you'll outlive me even if you don't give up the cocktails," Walter said. "How's Scott?" He added quickly, "And Candace?"

"Candy—God, she's dating, Walter. My baby is . . . Jesus, I don't even want to think about it. But the guy she's going out with owns a tie or two, I'll give him that. Has a good handshake and looks you square in the eye. Tipi says I've been muttering in my sleep again; little wonder there!"

"And Scott?"

Werner groaned. "Scott—get this. Scott now has this notion of not going to college next fall, of—he *says*—taking a year off. Which I'm horrified to say his mother's fallen for hook, line, and sinker. My buddy Rourke—remember Rourke? You met him on the tennis court last year? My buddy Rourke already put in some muscle for the kid at Stanford. And for what? So Scott can say no thanks and go start a rock band with the losers who won't get in anywhere? Please. He gave me this speech about how college is a waste of money if you don't know what you want to 'do' with your life."

"That makes sense, don't you think?" Walter massaged the folds of skin below T.B.'s jaw.

"Did I know what I wanted to 'do with my life' back then? Did you? Please. For Christ sake, all I had in mind when I was seventeen was finding the best weed, crankin' up the Stones, and screwing every blonde in sight! I did okay on my grades, took a little of everything—but a major? That was a babe with breasts the size of volleyballs. A master's? That was a golf tournament. And look at me. I did more than fine."

Your bank account's done more than fine, thought Walter. Your broker's done more than fine. As will your wife's plastic surgeon a few years from now.

"College is about structure," Werner continued, "about *not* doing other stuff you'd live—or wouldn't live—to regret."

"Oh, I don't think a little music would ever be regrettable. Or life-threatening."

Werner laughed. "Music? Man, are you ever not the parent of a teenage boy. I'm more sympathetic with our parents than I ever thought I'd be."

"As if they paid enough attention even to disapprove. We could've joined the Symbionese Liberation Army and they'd have thought it was Boy Scouts." Not to mention that they had been dead for most of Walter's teenage years.

He had to let The Bruce lick the receiver again while Werner gave the you-couldn't-possibly-imagine speech about being a father, but he wrestled it back when he heard, "The kid's even threatened to go east and work for *you*. Will that win me a little sympathy?"

Walter looked at the picture of Scott he kept on his desk: the poor boy had a large red zit on his chin, and his hair looked primeval in its lanky filth, but how happy he looked as he hugged his big shiny black guitar. Joy like the top of a Ferris wheel lit up that boy's face.

"I'd take him in with open arms, as a matter of fact."

This earned Walter a rather satisfactory silence.

"You would, huh?" Devilish chuckle.

"I would, and *huh* to you." Would he? But poor Scott; in Walter's mind, he was at the head of the class for domestic refugee status. If spiritual growth could be stunted, he had just the parents to do the job.

Now Werner laughed a long yuk-yuk sort of laugh. "Walter," he said to his wife, who had just come into the room and asked for caller ID. "He says he'll take Scott off our hands. What do you think?"

"Hi, Walter!" Tipi called out in her best wifely falsetto. "Watch out for that brother of yours, he's a sly one!"

Staring at Scott's picture, Walter thought, *Why the heck not?* Suddenly, he thought it made spectacular sense for everyone involved.

"I could use an apprentice," he said. "I could take him in July, after school ends. I promise I'd put him to work. And tell him I mean *work*."

"Walt, man, you have got to be pulling my leg."

"What—now the rock band looks good?"

"You don't know what you're proposing."

"So what if I don't? So what if it's a full-blown disaster? Like you wouldn't take him back? Like you think he'll return to you *co-rup-ted*?" Walter waited for more laughter. None. "I want you to propose it to

Scott and see what he thinks. Or I'll call him myself, tonight, while you and Tipi paint the town and she helps you blow out that battalion of candles."

Rarity of rarities, Werner was speechless. Which gave the man greater pause: facing his age or turning his grown son over to his homosexual brother? "Hello? Have we fallen into the San Andreas Fault?" said Walter. He wondered if Werner could hear his grin.

WALTER BUCKLED ON THE LITTLE PLAID COAT he had just purchased at the dog boutique on Bleecker. The Bruce looked suspicious and vaguely offended, and Walter understood completely, but the vet had suggested that T.B.'s sensitive skin be well protected from the cold whenever possible.

"I know, I know," soothed Walter as T.B. tried to wriggle free of the garment by rubbing against the doorjamb. "Believe me, sweetheart, this was the most masculine option." The jacket had a Sherlockian air— perhaps the skirting on the shoulders, suggesting fogbound London alleys. As compensation, Walter had bought T.B. a new, more intimidating collar: wide black leather with silver studs. Briefly, Walter wished he had a dog who didn't have to dress—a rugged dog, like that bookshop collie. He'd always laughed at the booties and raincoats on Upper East Side poodles. But truth be told, perhaps The Bruce was more like Walter himself: finicky about his surroundings, a sensitive kind of guy who loved his comforts just so and would rather be celibate than live in the woods.

Walter felt almost completely happy for the first time in ages, and when the two of them left the building to make their way through the gently meandering snowflakes—glinting overhead in the beams of the streetlamps, green in the traffic light, then vanishing like kisses on the well-traveled pavement—T.B. seemed to forget his troubles, too. What was it about snow: was it the silence, the perfect whiteness, the lovely paradox of icy and soft all at once? If the sight of falling snow didn't give you the itch to run out and play, there was a void where your soul ought to be.

They crossed Hudson Street and entered the small park beside the playground, where towering linden trees grew in straight rows, formal as a parading platoon. Both park and playground were deserted, and once they were under the trees, Walter let The Bruce off his leash so he could browse along unfettered, explore and reciprocate the scents left behind on numerous vertical objects. An inch of snow had managed to settle undisturbed on the bricks, so that Walter could feel and hear that pioneering crunch beneath his boots. The air was almost warm, pleasant though disappointing, since it meant that the snow would vanish by morning. But for now, here it was, just as plainly elegant as it would look in the country, as it had looked on Granna's lawn in Massachusetts every winter of Walter's youth.

This must be like finding out you're pregnant, he thought with secretive delight. Expecting—yes, he was now *expecting*. And just the night before, he hadn't had an inkling. He was pleased with his generosity and his spontaneity, as well as with the concrete thrill that he and T.B. would soon have a roommate; or, in Victorian terms, a "ward."

More responsibility, that's what I've been craving, thought Walter. And needing. He did not, after all, need a lover. Not now. (Let Gordie spin his amorous wheels in the muck of married life.) His calling Werner at just the right time had clearly been the hand of Granna. He looked up, though he thought heaven a pretty outlandish idea, and said, *"Danke Schoen!"*

Snow struck him full in the face, and he stopped to prolong the sensation. T.B. shook himself, blinking and sneezing, then grunted at Walter as if to ask why they were stalled in their habitual journey.

Walter looked back and saw their steps in the snow, crisscrossing, interlacing, like two strands of yarn woven close in a blanket. He looked over at the playground, locked and empty and yearningly white, from the slides to the seats of the faintly swaying swings. The sandbox was a drift of fluorescent blue.

With elaborate affection, he brushed the snow off T.B.'s face and head and his absurd diminutive trenchcoat. As they turned onto Bank Street, he clipped the leash back onto the collar. Midway down the block of dignified houses and trees, light from an open doorway stenciled the sidewalk ahead. A man was sweeping a path to the sidewalk; a cloud of fine dry snow rose before him like a sparkling explosion of glass.

"Evening," said McLeod as Walter passed.

"Picture postcard, isn't it?" Walter replied.

"Why, yes, long as you're staying put."

"Which I hope there'll be plenty of people doing in front of my fireplaces tonight!" Walter knew he should stop and make further conversation—over McLeod's shoulder, he saw no customers in the shop—but he continued toward the restaurant, savoring solitude for a change. He was glad to be a sentimentalist, unashamed of the homeliest pleasures. Walter would teach Scott to love all these things just the way he did, to take not a bit of beauty or tenderness for granted.

THREE

"SNOW ON A WOMAN'S SHOULDERS—now that's a sight I find just about fatally romantic, I do!" These were the first words out of Ray McCrae's large, lovely mouth when he opened the door to his hotel suite. Greenie was stunned. She had assumed that some third-tier assistant would greet her and take her straight to the kitchen.

"Miss Duquette," he said simply then, as if her name by itself were praise. He took the two shopping bags from her hands. He called out loudly, "Chop chop, Mary Bliss! Our hifalutin chef's arrived!"

He turned back to Greenie. "Miss Duquette—or, pardon me, *Ms.* Duquette—can I offer you a drink?"

"No, no, I'm here to work. And I'm Greenie," she said, trying to reclaim herself. It wasn't that he impressed her as a celebrity but, rather, that he was so shockingly handsome. He looked nothing like the few thirdhand images she must have skimmed over in the *New York Times.* They would not have shown the vibrant shine to his nutmeg-colored skin, nor that his eyes were the green of shaded ferns. Nor would they have shown the tall, dependable shape of the man, cutting a silhouette from the air immutable as a standing stone.

When she shrugged off her backpack, the governor took that as well, while deftly removing her heavy coat. Mary Bliss came in from the next room—and she, too, surprised Greenie: hardly the delicate blonde Greenie had imagined from her honeyed voice but a woman as physically impressive as her boss, with big, friendly features and a jubilant halo of dark brown hair. Both she and Ray McCrae wore cowboy boots, and Greenie wondered briefly if the tourist board of New Mexico required that its civil servants wear them—along with a string tie like the governor's, fastened at his throat with a corpulent turquoise bear.

"Hey," said Mary Bliss, holding out a hand. "Let me get you settled."

"Settle this woman in a chair for a minute," said the governor, and Greenie found herself steered toward an armchair by the window. She could hardly take her eyes off the view, a high vista of Central Park through falling snow.

Ray McCrae sat on a couch facing her, leaning forward, legs apart. "So, Queenie, you got a family, am I right?"

"Greenie," she said quietly. What was she doing here?

A phone rang in another room, but the governor paid no heed. "Well, I have to say I do like Queenie," he said. "But Greenie it is."

"I have a family, yes." She thought of the dossier. "My husband and my son."

The governor nodded. "Your son is four. Starting kindergarten soon."

"Next fall." She wished he would let her get to work.

"We have some fine schools in Santa Fe, I just want to assure you of that. And your husband's a shrink, right? Well, Greenie, we got ourselves plenty of kooks, if I may speak freely, rich kooks and not-so-rich kooks. Garden-variety neurotics, substance abusers, identity-crisis abusers, wife beaters, impotent lawyers, depressed unemployed craftspersons, you name it." He must have misread her discomfort because he said, "I'm not long on political correctness, Greenie. Forgive me."

"It's not that," she said. "It's just that I haven't even cooked for you, Mr. McCrae, and I do have a business here and I—"

"One thing at a time, absolutely. We'll see what you have up your sleeve and go from there. But I get hunches." He tapped the center of his forehead. "I got one female trait, and that's my intuition. It's how I know I never need fret about runnin' for the White House, so I can misbehave my butt off. Within reason. It's how I know I ain't met Miss Right so far, though I've been around the hacienda a few times and back. I have." He gave her a wide, charming smile and stood. "And here's the etiquette: you can call me Mr. Governor or, and I far prefer it, Ray. Call me Ray, would you, Greenie?

"Mary Bliss! Mary Bliss, where's George got to? Give him the cattle prod, would you?" Greenie started at the sound of her son's name. This George, it turned out, was Ray McCrae's driver.

"Excuse me for headin' out on you here, but I have a meeting, a dinner meeting at some swanky fish restaurant, where I will abstain from the eats as I expect even swankier food from you, Ms. Duquette—or maybe less swanky but superior. I am unimpressed by swanky." He took his coat from Mary Bliss. "Back in an hour and a half, that suit?"

"Does that suit you?" said Greenie.

"Suits me only if it suits you," he said, and then his cell phone rang and he pulled it out of his pocket. He walked out of the suite laughing and talking.

"Doesn't he have bodyguards?" Greenie asked Mary Bliss.

"The men in black are next door. A weird crew. Probably listening to your whole conversation on some big ear attached to the wall. . . . Sure you don't want a drink? Ray would hate my treating you like a maid. He hates my treating his *maids* like maids."

Greenie followed Mary Bliss into the compact kitchen. "He sounds a little too much like the perfect boss."

Mary Bliss laughed. "Oh honey. Cranky or arrogant, no, hardly ever, but demanding? He works us right down to the quick of our pinkie toenails."

Greenie worked that hard already. But wait. Was she considering the job? Hadn't she thought of this as little more than a lark?

On the kitchen counter, all the equipment she'd asked for stood in a row beside the handwritten list she'd sent to Mary Bliss. From the shopping bags, she took two dozen plastic containers, components of a meal showier than any she had cooked since she was in school. What did Ray McCrae define as "swanky"? she wondered with apprehension.

She felt a surge of panic, but it was followed by the same greedy calm she felt whenever she knew she was just about to perfect a new cupcake, cookie, or tart. How satisfying, all the colors and textures and tastes laid out before her, a palette of pigments before a painter. No one else confronting this array of ingredients (some common, others fancy; some raw, others mingled, blended, simmered, and spiced; some minced or sliced, still others puréed) would have done with them quite what she planned to do.

She opened the refrigerator and lifted the lids of the two green boxes delivered that afternoon by Tina. She needn't have checked on how their contents had made the trip—Tina never failed her—but Greenie wanted the reassurance of their solid perfection, a reminder of why she was here.

"Have to confess I had a peek myself." Mary Bliss stood in the doorway. "I've got a bad old sweet tooth too."

"There's plenty to go around," said Greenie.

"He does have a whale of an appetite. Just warnin' you, in case you decide to join us. Triple the recipe—that's sort of a motto I have when it comes to makin' Ray happy, and I'm not just talking foodwise. Though, mind you, triple's what you get in return if he likes the job you do."

Greenie put on her apron. "The two of you talk as if there's something I don't know, as if I'm about to be plucked off the ground by the hand of fate—I just haven't noticed the shadow over my head."

Mary Bliss laughed. "Something like that. But please excuse me." She let the door swing shut behind her, summoned by another ringing phone.

Greenie placed her own rack on the roasting pan Mary Bliss had found. She poured the soup into a heavy pot and spooned the chutneys into two tiny dishes—intended for butter, but they would do. She unwrapped the cakes of cheese: Vermont feta and Humboldt Fog, a goat cheese from California striped with ash. She laid paper oak leaves on a china plate and put the cheeses there to soften. She filled a steel tray with the pale, pulpy liquid she would stir into an ice to cleanse the gubernatorial palate. She placed it in the freezer.

"Do fancy food," Mary Bliss had said when Greenie asked what sort of a meal she should make. "Fancy but not pretentious, know what I mean?" So Greenie fantasized that she was cooking for dignitaries from abroad, showing off wholesome American plenty—and showing off to Ray McCrae that she could hold her own with more indigenous chefs. She felt pride along with a familiar unease. The opulence of the meal—counting ingredients, she stopped at sixty-three—was shameful in a way, but this was a fact of modern life at its most inequitable. When you made only desserts—when what you squandered, if anything, was chocolate, not corn (you wouldn't think about the flour)—you could fool yourself into believing that your professional dealings were in fantasy and art, removing you from the workaday morality of food, of excess here and hunger there.

Whether because of her personality or the lessons learned by her generation, Greenie's mother had been a thrifty woman. She had washed out plastic Baggies and polished her windows with yesterday's news. Beside her kitchen sink she'd kept a basin for all remotely edible waste, from tea bags and onion skins to leftover rice on the verge of fermenting and the fat trimmed from a roast. Every night before going to bed,

Greenie had carried the basin across their backyard and dumped it over a stone wall into a plot of forest owned by the town. And every morning, were you to have checked, you'd have found not a single trace of what had been discarded (what, in most households back then, was pulverized in a sink disposal and swept away, sight unseen, as sewage). "I can't feed the orphans of Southeast Asia, but I can feed the wildlife," Greenie's mother had boasted.

Living in the city, Greenie often wished for that basin, for its prudent circling of the food chain—but here, what would you feed if you tossed your leftovers into the night? Rats and roaches? Though, really, could you convince yourself they were much different from foxes, rabbits, and owls? Were their souls any smaller? Earnest little George would have argued their case.

Not long after George turned two, Greenie's parents took an anniversary trip to England and Scotland. As her father drove them along a coastal cliff in the Highlands, along a mere ribbon of road with a famously grand view, he missed a curve, sending their rental car to the rocks far below. This was what the chief inspector of the small Scottish town told Greenie in an awkwardly tinny phone conversation (the day after she had been notified, confusingly, by the chief of police in the town where she had grown up). "We warn the tourists how treacherous the roads are hereabouts," said the Scottish chief inspector mournfully, "but there's no other way to see these views without taking a little risk. I'm sorry as can be, miss, but I hope you don't find it disrespectful if I say, 'twasn't a bad way to go."

She clung to the odd false comfort in the chief inspector's lyrical *r*'s, in the quaint, pretty way he pronounced "tourist": *teeyoorist*. "Therabouts," perhaps the people were exceptionally courteous and charming, by American standards at least, their cobbled hamlets genteel and safe. But in America, the roads would have been safer, too. Along an American road of the kind this man described, there would have been heavy concrete barriers, like the ones placed around embassies to thwart car bombs, because an accident of this type would have set off a chain of lawsuits. The barriers would have marred the view, but never mind. If anyone was to blame, Greenie knew it was her father. Behind the wheel, Professor Duquette had been affably devil-may-care, casual with speed. Everyone made mistakes, thought Greenie, but why did his have to be fatal?

There would be an inquest, the policeman was quick to tell her, but that was a formality. Would she be coming over? She could hear through his well-mannered tone that he hoped she would not. Some bereaved children would have been impatient to catch the next plane, to see the exact spot where their parents' lives had ended, to ask futile questions, perhaps to see the bodies if time allowed; but Greenie found the prospect of such futile scenarios deeply depressing—especially as they would have to take place in a corner of the world renowned for its beauty. She chose, with guilty relief, to make the "arrangements" long-distance. She took a bus to Massachusetts and, along with the funeral director from her parents' town, went into Boston to claim the caskets and see that they were taken safely home—if the graveyard a mile from their house could be called "home."

Throughout the transactions and the filling out of forms, Greenie felt as if she were drugged, separated from her grief by a gauzy scrim, a tissue of incredulity. One of her Boston cousins had insisted on driving her and helping her accomplish the formalities. Greenie, in turn, had insisted that Alan stay in New York with George, at least until the day before the funeral.

After the caskets were unloaded at the funeral home and she had filled out yet more forms, Greenie asked the cousin to leave her—alone—at her parents' house. She had her own set of keys, and she knew where they kept the keys to their cars. It was a hot, sunny evening in early June, and when she let herself in, the rooms were unbearably close, the air thick as wool. She went about unlocking and opening windows, turning on the ceiling fans her mother had had installed the year before (no air-conditioning; what a wanton luxury!). She tried to glide blindly from room to room, focusing on none of the familiar things around her.

And then she went—as she had always done when she arrived home, ever since their move to this house when she was five—to the kitchen. Her mother's kitchen was a minor utopia, camellia white from ceiling to floor, smooth and clean and free of clutter. There was nothing on the counter by the window but the quavering cutwork of shadows cast by the leaves of the maple tree out back.

Without thinking, Greenie went to the refrigerator—for ice, she told herself, though she had not yet bothered to take a glass from the cupboard. It was a large refrigerator, its double doors neatly quilted with notices and lists, each held down with a magnet bearing a silly motto or advertising local commerce. IF I WERE ORGANIZED, I'D BE DANGER-OUS held down the schedule of seasonal events at the Museum of Fine Arts. Her mother had circled an upcoming lecture on the portraits of John Singer Sargent. A handwritten list of twelve friends (a planned dinner party? people to thank?) lay pinned beneath a flat red cow emblazoned in white ANGELO'S FINE CUTS — EUROPEAN VIANDS — GAME IN SEASON. And the schedule for her father's academic year, the year just ended, was clamped down by a magnetized business card from the family dentist. (The man who filled all of Greenie's cavities had seemed so ancient when she was small; how could he not have retired by now?)

Greenie found herself mesmerized—and briefly, falsely reassured—by the bric-a-brac of her parents' lives as of the moment they had left this house and, knowing her mother, as of the moment they were to have returned. It felt as if the entire house were poised for that moment, still unaware of the terrible news.

Reflexively, Greenie opened the right-hand door and found that, efficient as ever, her mother had nearly emptied this part of her refrigerator. There were a dozen well-preserved condiments in jars, but no eggs, milk, or juice to spoil, certainly no leftovers sprouting gray fuzz.

But then she opened the left side, the freezer, and this was when she found her true sorrow. Predictably, the freezer was full, stocked with carefully labeled foil packets (chicken breasts, turkey sausages, home-made raspberry muffins, chestnut purée), containers of chicken and shellfish stock. A dozen red velvet cupcakes, unfrosted: probably awaiting a visit from George. There was even a large plastic tub filled with blueberries picked in Maine the previous summer—destined for pies and preserves and a special pancake sauce that George had just learned to adore the way Greenie always had. Looking into the smoky hum of the freezer, Greenie saw in its generous cargo all the mothering that had belonged, every moment of her life till then, to her and her alone, along with the grandmothering that would henceforth become the sole domain of Alan's well-meaning but mostly hapless mother.

She stood there a long time, clinging to the freezer door and sobbing, letting the cloudy chill bleed out into the room, flow heedlessly around her body. She heard the inner workings of the refrigerator grind in protest, but still she felt incapable of closing the door, as if that act would be too unbearably final.

The indignant call of a crow startled her; she turned to the window and released the freezer door. She went to another door, the one that led to the backyard, unlocked it, and walked out. The swing her father had hung from the elm tree was still there—a swing that George, at two, was still too cautious to trust, even in a grown-up's lap—and as Greenie stood there, listlessly gazing, she realized that she would have to give it all up, literally dismantle her past. This house, where she had grown up, belonged not to her parents but to the university where her father taught (oh, *had* taught). Where would all her parents' belongings go? Still crying, she left the house, called Alan from a pay phone in the village, and told him to come at once. She had finally understood the monstrosity of her loss, which, each succeeding time she looked at it, compounded itself, sprouting head after head, cruel as a hydra.

Ultimately, from among her mother's things, she took a few pieces of jewelry and a white cashmere sweater wonderfully preserved from the fifties (which, though she loved it, Greenie would never bring herself to wear—perhaps, she came to suspect, because the label bragged that it had been made in Scotland). Most of the rest of her parents' incidental belongings she set aside for the church thrift shop; she was grateful when Alan insisted on packing and taking them over himself. The furnishings that she thought they might want in the future, if they ever moved to a larger apartment, she arranged to store at a warehouse in the middle of nowhere in western Massachusetts.

When all was said and done and paid for, she inherited just enough money to cover her business loan and George's nursery school tuition, along with a real but unquantifiable—and regrettably undisposable—share of a family cabin on an island in Maine. There were also her father's boats, a Whaler and a small, much-loved sailboat, but they had already been put in the water that year. Greenie called the Boston cousin and told him he could keep both on indefinite loan. Perhaps they were worth a lot of money; Greenie had no idea. She knew only that she could not imagine going to the island without her father picking her up at the marina and her mother, swanlike and stylish, serving her perfect meals. Gently, Alan told Greenie that she would probably change her mind, but this time she was the one with the dark, doubtful perspective. No, she said; no, never.

MORE SERENELY THAN SHE HAD EXPECTED, Greenie went to work on the governor's dinner; the suite's kitchen, though small by her mother's suburban standards, was royal compared with the cubbyhole in Greenie's apartment downtown. She measured the cornmeal. She held the roast above the marinade, allowing it to drain. She trussed it, painted it, laid it on the rack. She oiled two ramekins. She cracked eggs into a bowl. She grated nutmeg. She measured cream and salt and the garlic she had minced that afternoon. Half an hour before the governor was due back—the roast crackling in the oven, cakes and cheeses all plated and waiting to be devoured—she set the table and propped a handwritten menu against the hotel's vase of synthetic-smelling roses. Ordinarily, whenever she had to write something to show, she'd ask Alan to check her spelling, but this time she did not ask, not after the ghastly argument they had had when she told him about this adventure. Instead, she'd spent half an hour cross-checking her words in various cookbooks. She paused to read the menu one more time:

SWEET POTATO BISQUE WITH CRABMEAT
·
GRAPEFRUIT ICE IN A SWEET TORTILLA CRISP
·
LAMB SEARED IN ANCHO CHILI PASTE ON POLENTA
TWO CHUTNEYS: PEAR & MINT
ASPARAGUS FLAN
·
AMERICAN GOAT CHEESE, EAST & WEST, WITH RED-WINE BISCUITS
·
AVOCADO KEY LIME PIE
PIÑON TORTA DE CIELO & CHOCOLATE MOCHA SHERBET

She'd invented the cake just for tonight; the sherbet came from Julia Child, a remarkably simple confection made with sour cream. Torta de cielo was a traditional wedding cake from the Yucatán, slim and sublime, light but chewy, where pulverized almonds stood in for flour. This time, instead of almonds, Greenie used the fat, velvety pignoli she ordered from an importer on Grand Street, mincing them by hand to keep them from turning to paste. She did not know whether you could tell the best

Italian pine nuts from those grown in New Mexico, but, she caught herself thinking, and not without a touch of spite, she might soon find out.

PERHAPS WHAT UPSET HER MOST about the current state of her marriage was how often she guessed wrong, dead wrong, when it came to predicting Alan's reactions to just about anything she might say. Commenting on the *weather* now made her nervous. Last week, she'd complained, as she wiped up tracks on the floor from George's boots, that she was tired of sleet and snow. Alan snapped, "Ever notice the headlines all fall about drought? Ever stop to think of the farmers? The food we eat, the showers we take?"

Yesterday, Greenie had gone home for her typical midmorning break, after putting Tina to work on Walter's white rolls and sending Sherwin out with the day's deliveries. Knowing that Alan was free as well, on his own break between appointments, she took along a box of apricot scones. And there he was, at the table, reading the op-ed pages of the *Times*. She kissed his right ear and placed the box beside him. "Your favorites."

He pulled the box toward him and opened it. "Ooh, still warm." He looked up with widened eyes, just as George would have responded to a treat. "Can I have both?"

"Help yourself. I've been nibbling on pie all morning." She poured herself the last of the coffee, turned off the machine, and sat down.

"Ecstasy—the legal kind," he said as he took the first bite.

"Honeylamb, we aim to please," drawled Greenie, channeling Mary Bliss.

"Authentic pleasure, that's something you do sell to your clients," said Alan. "That much I don't deny."

Before she could stop herself, she said, "But . . . ?"

He shrugged. "But nothing." His attention returned to the paper: an article about diplomatic relations with China, hardly anything urgent.

"I heard the implied 'but.' Like there's something you do deny," she said.

"I was going to say, but the pleasure is ephemeral. I was thinking how it's too bad the joy of sugar can't last." Perhaps his smile was apologetic; Greenie saw it as condescending.

"You, on the other hand, you sell your clients lasting pleasure, pleasure that makes it past the tongue. Pleasure of the soul."

"Pleasure that doesn't make you fat, that much at least. Or guilty. Well, the last I can't guarantee." When she did not laugh, he said, "I'm only joking. You take me too literally, Greenie."

"I suppose." She sighed. "I came back because I had a tale to tell you."

"A tale? I never tire of tales."

She closed her eyes briefly, to suppress her irritation. "This should amuse you." Alan smiled when she mentioned Walter. He laughed when she mimicked Mary Bliss again, the bit about the daw-see-ay. Greenie relaxed.

"You are pulling my leg," said Alan.

"No, wait!" said Greenie. She told him how Ray McCrae had come on the phone, calling her "girl."

"The environmental fascist in that *High Noon* getup?"

When she told him what the governor had in mind, he said, "Man, what a nerve the guy's got. Like the life you have here must be some flimsy rag you'd toss aside to run away and join his frontier circus!"

Greenie had been pleased at Alan's amusement, but now she paused. "Well," she said quickly, "so I said I'd make the guy dinner. Tomorrow night."

Alan had just polished off the first scone. He wiped the crumbs from his lips with a napkin. "Now you *are* joking."

"I am not."

He stared at her for an instant before he said, "You really are. You are cooking for him. You're what, maybe planning to poison the guy? You know, you'd be the heroine of Greenpeace, the Nature Conservancy, and the purist holdouts of the Sierra Club they haven't managed to bribe into silence out there."

Greenie said, "I thought you'd see this, at the very least, as an opportunity for me to make connections."

He stared at her again, this time as if she were crazy (the way he would surely never look at any of his patients, even if he thought the same of them). "Connections to . . . what . . . the Republican restaurateurs of the Southwest? If you're planning an expansion, that's great, but Long Island or New Jersey might be a more realistic place to start."

"Let's see. Is there someone around here who tells me I don't network enough?"

"Networking refers to *useful* connections, Greenie. Like, do you see me handing my card out to couples fighting on the subway?"

"Well maybe you should. Maybe that would open things up a little."

"What do you mean by that?"

"Sorry. That was insulting. But look—I mean, who knows? Maybe we should consider something like this. Maybe a move wouldn't be the worst thing. We're always talking about how we can never make enough money here to give George the life he should have, give ourselves that life!"

"I know I've said that. You're right. But we have a good life. And this—come on, Greenie, this is not an option." He sighed. "I'm sorry. I don't mean to sound so critical."

Yes you do, she thought. She hadn't meant to tell him she was considering this job in any serious way—she wasn't (was she?)—but now she'd dug in her heels. "Tell me why we couldn't do it. Just hypothetically."

"Forget the clients I do have, and forget that we have a decent place to live and good friends and your successful business—"

"Which you've told me isn't successful enough."

"Greenie, that's not what I've said. I've said it could be *more* successful. Your business is your business. I don't mean to—"

Greenie felt her heart accelerate with indignation. "What is the matter with you! What makes you so completely, predictably negative!"

Alan was clearly stunned by her sudden rage—though that's how her rage, which was rare, would emerge, surprising even Greenie. He veered back in his chair, as if she'd struck him. Greenie leaned forward, her forearms pinning down an overturned section of the paper. Paralyzed briefly by frustration and fury, sorrow at both, she could not help reading the upside-down but all-too-familiar slogan between her elbows. It was one of those self-congratulatory ads the *Times* ran in space that must not have sold to purveyors of yet another bloated car or party-colored laptop.

She stood up and pointed at the words. "Expect the World!" she shouted. She laughed briefly but loudly. "Expect the *world*. That was me when we got married. Okay, so I was an idiot, a typically blind romantic idiot, right? So I learned my lessons like any new bride, and I didn't marry the wrong guy, did I, Dr. Glazier? But now, now it's like, expect a world of doom and gloom, expect a world of no praise, no support—no emotional support—a world of *but this* or *no not that.*

Expect to have everything I feel hopeful about just pushed right into the mud. Expect a hole in the ground. That's what it feels like, that's me now. Am I deluded? Am I wrong? Tell me! Please!"

The sharp sound of barking drew Greenie's attention beyond the window by the table, into the garden behind a brownstone that belonged to a neighbor they had seen for years but never met. The neighbor's small dog clamored at the sliding glass door. Unable to meet Alan's gaze of wounded surprise, Greenie focused on the dog, a terrier of some sort, watched him jump at the glass, each of his yips a briefly visible outburst of air.

"You are very angry." Alan's voice was quiet and solemn.

Duh, she thought, the rude little expletive that George had recently picked up and Greenie was trying to expunge from his proud, precious repertoire of slang. *Can we talk about that?* also crossed her mind, the next thing she'd have heard from Alan if he had been her therapist, not her husband. She wished the dog would shut up.

"Oh Greenie, why are we always fighting?" He sounded sad, even penitent.

"You're the shrink. You tell me." She turned back to look at him. He was bent over his lap, looking between his legs at the floor. Instead of his face, she saw the cowlick of dark brown, barely graying hair that George, riding aloft on his father's shoulders one day last week, had pressed with a finger. "Look!" he'd said, giggling. "Daddy's hair is the color for dirt!" Alan had muttered absentmindedly, "That's me. Mr. Dirt."

Outside, the glass door slid open for the terrier, slid shut behind him. It looked like a magic act, as if the door had opened by itself, for the owner was obscured behind a reflection of brick walls and barren trees. In the exaggerated silence, Greenie felt forced to speak. "Is this really news to you?"

Alan looked up. "Yes and no. I didn't know you were *this* angry."

"Well, now you do," said Greenie. *And now I do.*

Alan looked at his watch and gave her a pleading look. "I'm so sorry, this is very bad timing, but I'm afraid I have a phone session now."

"Maybe that's what we need—a prearranged session."

"Greenie, don't be sarcastic. That's not like you."

"I'm not. Being sarcastic. I mean, by the time we're together, without George, without conflicting schedules, we're . . . dead on our feet." Or you are, she thought. "Look, I'm doing this thing because I agreed to. I'll be over at the kitchen this evening, and I'll try to be back by nine, and we can talk then, okay?"

"Okay," said Alan. "Okay then."

"Kiss George for me," she said. "Tell him I'll walk him to school in the morning and pick him up in the afternoon. I have to be at Governor McCrae's—at the environmental fascist's hotel—at seven tomorrow evening."

"Okay," said Alan. He stood, looking as if he might like to touch Greenie, but she turned away and carried her mug to the sink. She was ashamed of her outburst, but it had been necessary, hadn't it? Alan retreated to his office, and Greenie left to shop. That night, when she came back at a quarter to ten, she found Alan asleep next to George in the bedroom. They were turned toward each other, both snoring, the boy's head against the man's chest. *Oh Say Can You Say?* was splayed open beneath her husband's hip, several pages bent double. So much for the break of Dr. Seuss.

HAVING JUST FINISHED THE MAIN COURSE, his plate stark naked, Ray McCrae appeared to be talking loudly to himself, though in fact he was having an impassioned conversation on one of those telephonic earpieces. As Greenie cleared the dishes, he was facing his high-priced view and waving both arms about, as if he might persuade the trees spread out below him to burst into passionate song. "It's a frigging weed! A weed, Archie! What gives? You know, look, I got no quarrels with the redwood huggers and the give-it-all-back-to-the-wolves city folk buttin' their coastal noses into our business, that's par for the democratic course, but Archie, there's wildlife and then there's . . . weeds! Even my cows won't touch 'em!" As Greenie arranged the biscuits in a crescent flanking the cheese, there was a long silence, and then the governor let out a theatrically exasperated sigh. "Bundled up with welfare-to-work? Oh now that was demonic, pure sly-dog tactics. How'd we let that one slip past, Archie? Who snoozed through that one, huh? Just tell me who. You do."

Greenie realized the conversation was over only when he turned around, looked straight at her, and said, "Do you have any idea what kind of devilish mayhem can break loose in a state full of cattle when a plain old weed—I mean the thing doesn't even *flower* or *smell nice*— gets promoted from 'threatened' to 'endangered' in the EPA's fancy-ass lexicon?"

"I can imagine," she said as she set the cheese plate on the table and refilled his beer glass. (When she'd told him she knew next to nothing about wine, he'd made a dismissive gesture and said, "Wine's for the likes of Ralph Nader, people who like stuff designed to get picky about.")

"With all due respect, young woman, you cannot," said the governor. "This is the stuff of my worst nightmares, stuff that can whup you upside the head when you're happily trimming your toenails. Stuff you think of as footnotes, but don't be fooled! You easterners picture New Mexico as a land of Pueblo Indians and fancy turquoise trinkets, like I run one big exotic Disney World pawnshop, a few exits off Route Sixty-six. But let me tell you: when the going gets tough, it's the men with the cattle who open up their big fat rawhide wallets. If the Archduke Ferdinand's assassination could set off World War One, well, the canonization of a scruffy plant that some kind of owl needs to scour its gullet could boot me clear out of a job and a mansion. I kid you not. Troublemakers come through the backyard, that's what my dad used to say.

"But speaking of gullets!" This one-sided conversation was his first acknowledgment of her presence since he'd sat down to the soup. Now, giving her his full, robust attention, he said, "Greenie, you are a sorceress. Those oysters Rockefeller and tuna ballyhoo I turned down at the fish place? Canned stew compared to this meal."

"Thank you. I'm flattered." You had to wonder if there was anything of substance behind this man's relentless bluster, yet Greenie found that she was beginning to like both the man and the bluster. Despite her exhaustion, she was sorry that she would have to leave soon, probably never to see him again.

"Pull up a chair," he said. "You have any dinner yourself?"

"I had a sandwich late this afternoon. I'm fine."

"Sit, girl!" he said. "That's an order from a card-carrying chauvinist who just may be your future boss." He stood, pulled up another chair, held it out till she sat down, and went to the kitchen. He came back with a plate bearing two slices of lamb and a sliver of polenta, the only food remaining from the previous courses. "Is it me or is it your dainty eastern portions?" he said when he set the plate down before her.

"A little of both."

"I do like leftovers. Have to dock you half a star for that." Abruptly, he called out, "Mary Bliss! Hold off the calls a half hour, would you? And bring us another glass from the bar.

"If you work for me, especially in my kitchen, you got to like me at least a little. Vice-a versa I'm already sure of," he said as he filled the second glass with beer. She accepted it, even though she was one of those Ralph Nader folk, a lover of wine. "Not that we'll sit down for meals together, not much. But you'll see what I mean. And of course, I need to say, you won't be playing waitress. There's plenty of staff for the fetch-and-carry. Nice people, too."

Before she could ask if he was offering her the job outright, he asked about George, her George; and if the bachelor was bored by the subject of four-year-old ways and means, then the politician trumped that boredom with what appeared to be genuine curiosity.

After hearing about George's talent for reading, he said, "When I was little, my favorite books were just about anything to do with the sea. Pirate books, to be sure, and that Jules Verne book *Fifty Thousand Leagues Under the Sea*—Captain Nemo and the giant squid. But even books on seashells, sea birds, sailors' knots, books about sea battles— Spanish Armada, you name it. I was just *dyin'* to get a glimpse of the sea."

"I grew up taking the sea for granted," said Greenie. "I can't imagine living too far from the ocean."

When he gave her a scolding look, she realized what she'd implied.

"We may not have the sea out west, but we have ourselves a glorious ocean of sky, Ms. Duquette." He drank the last of his beer. "So, as you may have guessed, I joined the navy. Just before Vietnam, as both my fans and foes like to point out. You can look at it any way you want— bravery, cowardice, dumb luck—but I joined up without a whit of politics in mind. Needed to get away from home, like any normal guy, and wanted to see the sea. What's that Gene Kelly song?"

" 'We Saw the Sea.' I think the singer's Fred Astaire," said Greenie, though she knew for certain he was. She sang the chorus, her voice quavering only a little.

"The woman cooks . . . and knows her old movies, too. She does!"

"Her sappy old movies," said Greenie. "Or the music. But you were saying . . . about the navy."

"Yes. I landed in the Mediterranean. A little later, a lot less luck, I'd have drawn the China Sea instead." He licked a bit of cheese off a thumbnail. "But now—but now, dessert! What I've been hankering for all day. Bring it on, Ms. Duquette."

Greenie carried in the cakes, both at once, on a tray with a foxhunting scene she had found in the bar. The sherbet was in a paper carton nestled in a bowl of ice.

"My God in heaven, girl," he said when she put the tray down on the table before him. Addictive or simply relentless, the man's enthusiasm never seemed to quit. She was reminded, fondly, of George.

The governor did not converse much this time as he ate; he might have been contemplating the flavors she'd assembled or brooding about the accursed weed. Greenie excused herself to sort things out in the kitchen. Mary Bliss had insisted she leave the dishes for the hotel staff, so Greenie rinsed out only the items she had brought with her.

When she returned to the living room, Ray McCrae was standing at the window, looking at the citified forest below. The branches of the trees were gloved in glistening ice, so deceptively beautiful. From her childhood, Greenie could remember the sound of limbs cracking off in the middle of a winter night, the ice too much for the trees to bear; in the frigid, hollow darkness, the echoes carried like gunshots.

Something fell from the sky yet again; up here, at this privileged altitude, the something was snow, but farther down, at street level, it was probably sleet. Oh what would it be like, she yearned, to escape this city, this dreary precipitation, these slippery sidewalks—escape the anxieties of how to get along with an angry husband, how to afford a home where her son would have a real room, how to get this son into a school that wasn't motley, crowded, and overrun with irate, pushy parents? Such anxieties—the kind that linger—had only recently begun to afflict her. For most of her life until now—even for her first year or two as a mother, at least until her parents were killed—Greenie had been someone whom other people admired for the ease with which she made decisions, the way she faced the world straight on, with little confusion or doubt.

She was startled when the governor spoke. She could see his face only as mirrored in the window. "Out where I live, the elements don't spare us, Ms. Duquette, but they're not so underhanded. Snow is snow. Rain's rain. And boy oh howdy, is heat ever heat. I'd call it a man's meteorology—off the record, because that would be sexist, right?" Turning around, he smiled at her in a different way. It was a prolonged, complicitous look, as if they had a secret to share. He held out his right hand. "Greenie, you've made me a happy man tonight. Mary Bliss will call tomorrow. I have a feeling you might be hard to pry loose from this place, but we have our ways. We do."

He walked her to the door and took her coat from the closet. "George is out front with the car; he'll drive you home."

Greenie thanked him, and she thanked Mary Bliss, and then she was alone in the hallway, and then in the elevator with its lion-footed bench and gilt-framed mirror (in which she avoided her own eyes), and then in the lobby, where a solitary bellboy snoozed on his feet by a luggage trolley. Across a prairie of carpet printed with red acanthus leaves, she could see the polished revolving door that led to Fifth Avenue and, beyond it, a black town car. Perversely, or just because she felt too tired to make small talk with a stranger (she hadn't been raised with hired help and did not know how to ignore anyone politely), she turned left, toward the side door that led to the cross street.

The dreary precipitation had ceased, and the air was milder than she had expected. She fastened her coat beneath her chin, pulled up the hood, and started downtown on foot. Though it was late—nearly one, she was stunned to learn when she looked at her watch—there were several people out on the avenue, many alone, many talking on cell phones. Greenie disliked these phones, which she saw as security objects for people who were afraid to be alone with their thoughts, afraid of real independence. You'd walk along the street and hear isolated snatches of gratuitous chat: "I'm heading down Perry now, and I'll be in the subway in five minutes, though I have to buy tokens. . . ." At the grocery store, in the produce aisle: "Yeah, the broccoli looks kinda yellow today, so I don't know . . . asparagus? Only wait, it's pretty overpriced, so how about artichokes? Yeah, not too bad, they're sort of in season, aren't they?" As if such decisions could no longer be made in private, at a visceral layer of the brain, while you dreamed, deeper down, about far more complex, significant matters. When she'd told Alan her theory, he agreed: "Internal conversations are the hardest ones; they include the voices we wish we could drown out rather than discipline."

The thoughts she was left alone with now were thoughts of Alan.

When they met, Alan and Greenie were starting out in their respective fields, both happily exhausted by all there was to learn and both—as they figured out while lying ecstatically awake in bed one night a month or so after they'd fallen in love—setting out to ease the world's pain, on a modest scale and in very different ways.

Flirtatiously, they teased each other about it.

"Ordinary unhappiness," said Greenie, remembering something she had once read in a magazine about the goals of psychotherapy. "I think German chocolate cake aims higher than that. And it costs a whole lot less."

"It does," he answered, "but it promises no progressive improvement, no way to internalize the remedy it offers."

"Digestion doesn't count, I guess."

"Doesn't digestion result in externalization?"

Through the silliness, they had felt the forging of an altruistic collusion, a shared conviction that what they did when they got up every morning made the world a brighter place to live, one hour of talking, one piece of cake at a time. And then, though Greenie had to expend every ounce of her patience to persuade Alan past his customary agonizing, along came George. For a time, he deepened their collusion.

But then, gradually, over the past two years, Alan seemed to undergo a kind of souring—not on fatherhood but on something indefinable that Greenie could think of only as his way or his direction. It was as if he'd been strolling a wide thoroughfare that had subtly begun to narrow, until one day he realized it was little more than a dirt track threatening to fade into the brush, into brambles and swamp. In such a predicament, Greenie would have bushwhacked it wide again, swung her machete this way and that, and if it slowed her passage, well that's the way it would be for a while. Alan, in tough times, turned inward—not in defeat but rather, as a tortoise might, securing himself in a safe, dark place until the storm had passed. Greenie's prodding at his shell was ineffectual and foolish, but she couldn't seem to help it.

Last month, three of Alan's patients had quit. All three gave financial excuses. Greenie made the mistake of telling him that he need not panic; her revenues had risen. A few days later, one night early in February, he stayed up late and drank far too much Scotch, a poison he resorted to only when he was feeling low (and which, after briefly raising his spirits, made him feel even lower). After Greenie told him that she thought she might land a new account, a good one, he launched into an angry speech about the disillusionment of the millennium. "It's like, last year or the year before, they all took up therapy—took it up like tennis or bowling—or devoted themselves to yoga and Buddha, or went vegan, because they thought this arbitrary flip of the digits would initiate some kind of presto change-o!" He spoke bitterly, pacing the living room, glass in hand. "Like they were vestal virgins awaiting their sexual-spiritual epiphany, as if those three fat, indolent zeroes entitled them to be enlightened—hey, there's the title of a best-seller waiting to be written. *Entitlement to Enlightenment!* . . . And now, now that nothing happened overnight, when they didn't wake up in the new millennium anything other than just plain hungover as usual, now they dump all those disappointing, no-money-back yearnings, go whining back to their old shopaholic ways. Now they eat lemon meringue pie instead of sitting down to ponder their dreams. You get the clients I lose. At least *somebody* here's in the black!"

Greenie had listened, speechless, appalled. She knew he was unlikely to remember much of what he was saying. The next morning he would apologize, but that night, lying beside him as he snored with abandon, she wondered if their collusion had changed—for Alan and without her noticing—into a competition.

By the time she reached the public library at Forty-second Street, her feet were cold. She paused to look up at the building (a palace, really) and noticed, on the steps, the dark hummocks of people huddled under blankets. She had a brief image of Alan as one of these drifting, frigid souls. *You have a tendency to exaggerate,* she could hear him say. His voice was one of the voices in her own head that, lately, she found herself having to discipline. *And so what?* she retorted in silence.

She walked to the curb and waved toward an empty cab, entered its dark, stale warmth with grateful surrender. Alan would be long asleep, she knew that, but she had hoped to find a note, just a few words hinting at reconciliation. When she found no words at all, she went into George's alcove and stood beside his bed. He slept in his habitually trusting sprawl, pajamas rumpled, his belly exposed in the golden glow of his nightlight. She laid a hand lightly on one side of his rib cage as it rose and fell. His flesh was silky and warm. He did not stir. The mobile of the planets that hung above him, however, bobbed and turned eerily in the air displaced by her presence. She noticed that the planets were dusty. It occurred to her that George had long ago outgrown mobiles, at least as infantile entertainment; perhaps she should take this little cosmos down.

She went over to the shelves that held his books and toys; her eyes fell on his wooden United States of America puzzle. She pulled it out quietly and placed it on George's small table.

New Mexico was a luscious maraschino red, with two details: a white star marking Santa Fe and a green lizard with a long curlicue of a tail (the cowboy on the map belonged to a purple Wyoming). Greenie held the piece of painted plywood to her lips as if it might have a magical taste, offer a fairy-tale moment of truth. But no, she was not one of Alan's millennial brats, expecting epiphany; she was no vestal virgin, no virgin of any sort. When she put the piece back in the puzzle, next to those other western states—all so much more clear-cut, more decisively shaped than their eastern companions—it made a small, solid click.

FOUR

A DEFIANT OBSTACLE—HARD, SMOOTH, AND CHILLY—
confronted Alan Glazier's left middle toe when, for the first time in
months, he stepped into his running shoes. When he turned the shoe
over, a chrome marble fell out, rolled across the rug, and stopped when
it struck the leg of a chair. Alan picked it up. When he smiled, he saw his
smile reflected, tiny as an eyelash, in the silver surface of the marble.
"Oh George," he said, and if anyone had been there to hear him, they
would have heard love and sorrow, futility and frustration all jumbled
up together in his voice.

He walked into George's room. On the bureau, in his spherical bowl,
Sunny appeared to glance directly at Alan and put a little extra verve
into his circular swimming. "You already got your breakfast," Alan said
to the fish, his sole roommate now for two weeks. He tapped the glass
with a knuckle, and the fish flipped about, startled.

His son's small bed was more perfectly made than it had ever been
when he slept there, and the shelves against the wall were nearly empty.
The books that remained were the dog-eared cardboard books, the ones
George had chewed on before he could comprehend their function and
purpose. The stuffed animals and the games, too, were those that George
had outgrown—except for Mousetrap, which he had left behind, reluctantly, because it was missing one of its two essential marbles (and you
had to have precisely these marbles, weighted just right, or the bucket
wouldn't spill down the rickety stairs, nor the backward diver land in
his tub). "We have to buy a new one, we have to!" George had wailed
the week before he left.

Alan, already bereft and in shock at his family's impending departure,
would gladly have run to the nearest toy store and bought a dozen
games for his son, but Greenie said calmly, "George, we are taking

plenty of things, and I promise you, there are lots of toys in New Mexico. We're not going to the ends of the earth."

Oh no? thought Alan as George asked, "Ends? The earth has ends? Where are the ends?"

Greenie had laughed—laughed!—and said, "Georgie, it's just an expression. It means somewhere completely different from the places we know, without all the things we know and love."

Well then I, thought Alan, I am the one consigned to the ends of the earth! But all that talk, all the talk that Greenie would accept, had already taken place. This, the packing and leaving, was a strange kind of aftermath that Alan had to suffer meekly through. Too little too late, she had told him—for the time being. It was not, she'd said, as if he didn't have options: he could pack up and join them! "You can take your time, that's perfectly fine," she had said, as if he were George's age, just another child. She wasn't leaving him or running away, she pointed out. She was gaining distance. She was opening a window. She was breaking them up to keep them together. One cliché after another, as shiny yet leaden as this marble he held, tumbled blithely from the mouth of the smart, charming, still youthful woman he had married. At one moment, he was appalled to find that he actually wanted to hit her, if just to bring her to her senses. But that was a cliché, too, was it not? And by then he felt too tired to fight any further.

Forget the run, thought Alan. He pulled off his shorts and threw them onto George's bed, went back to his own room and found a pair of jeans in the tangle of clothes on the chair beside the dresser. This locus of turmoil disturbed him because it reminded him that Greenie's anger and even her decision to leave him alone with himself were not unjustified. How could he have told her what goblin, aside from his petty financial woes—his wounded breadwinner ego (our most primeval, panther-killing pride, he liked to tell his male patients)—was truly holding him hostage? Worst of all, she was right: he ought to be talking to Jerry. If ever there was a time to talk to Jerry, it was now—though Greenie did not know why. If she had known, she would most certainly have left him for good, behind in the dust, without a leg to stand on. Here, clichés would have been all too apt.

It was the first tantalizingly warm day of the year, the first day that promised summer before its true arrival, when you could not help feeling, *Ah, the worst is over.* In some years this day came in February; now *that* was heartbreak. This year, however, summer had postponed such flirtation, for it was now the beginning of May. Throughout the neighborhood, slender pear trees had put forth a cloud bank of blossoms; daffodils and tulips were already fading.

Waiting in line at the postal truck on Tenth Street, he stood in the sun and felt as free of despair as he had in days, at least viscerally, content just to feel the wash of heat as he waited to send his son a surprise that would bring him joy. Along with the now-complete game of Mousetrap, Alan had enclosed a few brand-new superhero comics. George had discovered this old-fashioned pleasure in just the past few months; for reasons that Alan found illogical, Greenie did not like to buy them. Did spite play a role in his sending along these treasured objects? Perhaps a little. Perhaps more than a little.

As he stood at the end of the line, he heard a faint mewling, the sound of new kittens or puppies. Looking around, he located the source of the sound in the arms of a young woman standing nearby, holding a cardboard box. Face bent toward the box, she was speaking in soothing high-pitched tones, motherly nonsense. She swayed from side to side, the habit of a parent accustomed to holding an infant. Every so often she'd look up, toward the oncoming traffic on the avenue. Alan watched her for a moment; when he turned back, he found himself at the head of the line.

He mailed the box and asked to see the most picturesque stamps, choosing a series that showed endangered mammals. He bought a sheet for himself and another sheet to send George in his next letter. He tried to write at least a few lines every other day.

When he had folded the stamps and slipped them in a pocket, he turned around to see that the woman with the box stood a bit farther away, in the middle of the block, but she was clearly waiting. Feeling magnanimous, Alan approached her. "Can I help you get a cab?"

"No, no. Thanks anyway," she said cheerfully.

Simultaneously, he saw that the box held six squirming spotted puppies and that the woman's face was asymmetrical, one of her eyes sharply narrowed, the two corners of her mouth in discord. One of her cheeks was smudged, and her long brown hair, though combed back into a ponytail, was oily and dull. The lapels of the wool jacket she wore—all wrong for the weather—were frayed. At a glance, she looked like someone leading a vagrant or hapless existence, yet she did not have the slouch or the glassy-eyed expression of the chronically homeless. Alan guessed her to be about thirty. It was something of a curse, his clinical eye, because it refused to take time off.

"Cute," he said, nodding at the puppies, before he turned to walk home. He felt relieved yet also unsettled and embarrassed. But then the woman called out, "Wait! Could I ask a different favor?"

He turned around.

"Do you have . . . one of those personal phones?" she asked. "I always carry quarters, but the pay phones around here are busted. None of them work nowadays, since rich people don't need public phones anymore, do they?"

Alan had just bought a cell phone, which he carried everywhere, placing it beside his wallet on his dresser at night so that he would never forget it. With George so far away, he felt more alert to the possible emergency, the possible change of heart from Greenie, the possible moment when George might miss his father so much that he needed to hear Alan's voice right then, exactly then. Only Greenie had the number, and she had yet to use it. When she was the one to call, she called their home number, sometimes at an hour when she ought to know he wouldn't be there.

So it took him a moment to remember that he did have a phone, and when he took it out, he fumbled at getting it open. He supposed this could be an elaborate scam (of course it was!), but he decided to let himself think the best of this woman. To hell with his clinical eye. Here was another change since George and Greenie had left: though he wasn't the slightest bit religious or superstitiously inclined, Alan acted as if he were trying to accumulate what he could only think of as positive karma, just in case it might tip the Fates in his favor (why not keep all your mythological bases covered?).

"I don't use it much," he said.

The woman set the puppies on the sidewalk between them and took his phone. "Here now," she said. "You guard the little guys, would you? But no petting! They haven't had their shots."

He listened as she spoke to someone's answering machine. "Stan, I'm on Sixth and Tenth, like we arranged. Where are you? I've been here half an hour. Pick up, Stan." She waited, squinting at the sun. She sighed. "Okay. Okay, Stan. I'll try you later, but I guess I'll just take them over myself, since you gave me the address. I guess what I can do

is—Oh I hate that. He's got one of those guillotine message machines."
She pronounced the word "gillateen." She closed the phone and handed
it back to Alan.

She put her hands on her hips. She scanned the avenue. She made a
motherly noise of disapproval. As she leaned down to pick up her box,
Alan said, "Is there anything I can do?" Like most New Yorkers, his
instinct was to remain sealed inside the safety of his individual shell, but
by profession he was supposed to be a helper, and there was nothing
worse in his book than a hypocrite, especially a hypocritical helper.

"Well now that is an offer I cannot afford to ignore," said the
woman. "I'll tell you my situation. This friend of mine, or not really a
friend but a guy I work with, he was supposed to pick these guys up to
get their shots and help find them homes. He's a busy guy, so maybe he
got hung up. So." She craned her neck to look down the avenue again,
as far as she could; as she did, a cloud passed over the sun and the air
became abruptly chilly. She glanced at the sky and frowned briefly.
"Okay, here's the plan."

She put the box of puppies in Alan's arms and took a large card out of
her pocket. She looked at it, mouthed something, looked up at the nearest street sign and back at the card. She started uptown. For one ghastly
moment, Alan thought she might simply abandon him with the puppies,
but a few steps away from him, she turned back and said, "Follow me,
okay? I hope you don't mind, but my arms are tired."

"No," said Alan, suddenly charmed by her sense of purpose. He had
planned to catch up on reading professional journals, but he did not
have patients for another four hours, and in truth, he would probably
have gone home to brood, since this was the time when he ought to have
been picking up George at his preschool and taking him out for a snack
or to the library or, if it was warm enough—as it was now—to the playground. His life felt so thin without George.

Catching up to the woman, he said, "I'm Alan. Alan Glazier."

"I'm Saga," she said. Despite a minor limp, she walked along quickly,
slowing only to look at the street signs and back at the card she still
carried. "It's just a block or two from here. You okay with that?"

"Yes, fine—did you say Saga?"

"Like the blue cheese," she said.

Or like a story, a grand story, he thought. Finding out stories, decod-
ing them, that was his job—what was *her* story?

She did not seem interested in making conversation, so he followed without asking questions. They turned one corner, then another, until she stopped in front of a tenement building with dirty windows. She stood by an iron staircase leading down to a basement door that announced itself as the entrance to a veterinary office. Alan probably passed this building five times a week, but he had never noticed the sign.

"You with me?" she said.

"Lead on," he said, and down the stairs they went.

The waiting room was small, windowless, empty of people, and lit with a long fluorescent fixture that hovered too close from the low ceiling and buzzed intermittently. The smell of disinfectant was strong, but not strong enough to hide the stench of kennel. No receptionist sat at the white Formica counter where a small sign read RECEPTION. Saga leaned across this counter and called out, "Yooooohoooo!"

From somewhere close but out of sight, two dogs began to bark.

"Coming!" A few footsteps, and then a man in a white smock emerged from the door behind the desk. "Hello again—you're Stan's friend, am I right?" he said pleasantly. He glanced at Alan. "Are you with Stan's group, too?"

"No, he's with me," Saga said before Alan could answer. "Stan couldn't make it. Some kind of appointment. I thought I could just bring them by on my own. Is that okay?"

"Today's my day without an assistant, but if you help out, I can take care of them now." He was young, this doctor, the kind of young that made Alan realize how old he was becoming—for though the vet was probably nearing thirty, to Alan he looked like he was barely out of high school. Skinny and pale, he might never have left the unpleasant cave of his subterranean office.

"You're a gem," said Saga. "A true gem." She took her precious cargo from Alan. Without speaking, she and the vet went into the room behind the desk; the vet closed the door.

Alan stood in the empty, buzzing room for a moment. Should he leave? He could knock on the door and say good-bye. But then he heard the first puppy yelp. "It's okay, it's okay, it's okay, you're a brave little guy!" he heard Saga saying, her voice raised but gentle. "All done, there you go. Skedaddle." Right away, the next puppy yelped.

Alan sat down on an orange plastic chair. He looked around and laughed. He could have described this episode to Jerry and passed it off as a dream; he felt that off-balance, that disembodied. This was just the sort of room you encountered in dreams—in dreams about to morph into Alice in Wonderland nightmares. An urban rabbit hole, this place. "All right, so I'm dreaming," he said aloud, to hear his own voice, something familiar. From behind the closed door, he continued to hear the pups getting their shots, each one comforted loudly by Saga. Was that her real name? Perhaps she'd been the child of early hippie parents, the people who so thoughtlessly gave their offspring naïve or grandiose names like Storm, Sequoia, Moonbeam, Cosmos. Right before Greenie, Alan had dated a younger woman named Truce, whose parents loved to brag about how many times they had been arrested for demonstrating against the Vietnam War. They claimed to have conceived her while in jail. They *told* her this.

When the door opened, Saga and the vet were discussing the next round of shots. This visit was free, he said; next time, he would do it for the cost of the vaccine. Could she or Stan come up with that?

She was about to answer when she saw Alan. "Oh! Are you still here? I'm sorry, I was so involved, I didn't think to say thank you. Thank you!" She smiled broadly—on one side, at least—and Alan noted (another guilty diagnostic appraisal) that her teeth were all there and in decent shape.

She turned to the vet. "Stan has to give you that answer. He's the only one who knows about the money."

"I'll pay for the shots," said Alan. "I could pay you up front, now." Had he really said this? But Saga's look of asymmetrical astonishment pleased him. The vet, who hadn't acknowledged his presence till now, named a price higher than Alan had expected, but he took out his wallet.

"No, wait," said Saga. "Stan wouldn't . . ."

"I don't mean to insult you."

"Oh *insult,* no!" she said. "I just can't predict the future. Stan might have the money, it depends on donations, and I wouldn't want you to spend your money before the fact, you know?"

"All right. I'll give you my number and you can call me. I mean it. I'd like to help. I would."

Now it was Saga who seemed to be assessing Alan, staring at him in a friendly but penetrating fashion. "Walk me out," she said. Once again, she handed him the box. She took a few small packets from the vet—

worming pills—and stuffed them in the pockets of her jacket. She shook hands with the vet and thanked him again.

Outside, the midday sky had darkened luminously. The passing clouds of half an hour before had pulled in a thunderhead; its mountainous form glowed yellow at the edges. The rumblings were still far off, somewhere over New Jersey. Alan hesitated in the doorway, but Saga said, "Let's hurry!" and without asking where, he followed her down the street. A block later, the rain did not fall so much as collapse from the sky, as if a great tank of water were being dumped on a forest fire. Gusts of wind carried it sideways.

Saga took off her jacket and draped it over the box. "There!" She pointed across the street to the awning of a bookshop. Already three people stood against the window, waiting it out. "We'll fit, come on!" She dashed across.

Under the awning, their fellow refugees moved aside grudgingly. Standing shoulder to shoulder with Saga, Alan thought he could detect the smell of mildew. A few minutes later, the rain had not let up; two of their companions had left, resigned to a drenching. The puppies began to whine. Saga shivered.

"They must be terrified, poor things," said the one remaining stranger, a woman in a green silk suit. "You shouldn't have them out here."

Alan was about to tell her to mind her own business when Saga said, "You're right, you know? But we were caught unawares, the same as you in your pretty outfit." Her voice shook with her shivering, but she smiled.

The woman in green silk said nothing.

When the storm showed no intention of abating, Alan leaned toward Saga and said, "Now it's your turn. Follow me."

Saga held on to his arm. "No. I can't go out in that."

Looking at her, he saw that her shivering might be dread, not a chill. She scanned the sky, as if a squadron of bombers might appear. "Trust me," he said.

At a clap of thunder, she tightened her hold on his arm. She shook her head vehemently.

Was she unstable after all? Schizophrenic, hearing voices in the thunder? For God's sake, he admonished himself, a fear of thunderstorms was perfectly normal. Alan would have put an arm around her shoulders if he had not been holding the box. "Two blocks, that's all," he said. "Otherwise these guys will get soaked."

That convinced her. "Okay," she said. "Ready when you are."

He waited until the traffic light at the intersection turned, then dashed across the street and around the corner. He ran carefully, eyes clenched against the downpour, and looked back only once to make sure she was right behind him. He was thinking, I'll make us tea. I'll let her take a shower. I'll find something in Greenie's closet, something clean and warm and dry.

"GORDIE HAD THIS PHENOMENAL DREAM," said Stephen. He was sitting on one end of the long, soft couch; deliberately, Gordie had seated himself at the opposite end. The cushions rose up like a small black hill between them. But this did not stop Stephen from leaning across to squeeze his partner's knee. "Tell him!"

"I didn't think it was that remarkable," said Gordie.

"Tell it anyway. Let Alan be the judge," said Stephen. He looked at Alan. "You know, we have this huge double shower in our bathroom. It's like being at a spa. Cost a fortune, but it was worth every penny. In the morning, every morning, we talk about our dreams while sudsing up." Stephen's expression, so often deferential or even fawning toward Alan, turned briefly hard. Was he looking for Alan's reaction to the image of this shower, of the two naked men "sudsing up"; checking for homophobic disapproval, envy or admiration? And why had he mentioned the cost? Did he suspect—well, in this office meant to be a bedroom, who wouldn't?—that Alan could never afford such a thing?

"Do you want to tell the dream, Gordie, or is something else on your mind?" asked Alan.

"Fine, fine, I'll tell it," said Gordie. He crossed his arms. "There's this store below our apartment, it's like a fancy newsstand–tobacco shop. In real life. But in this dream, I go downstairs one day and it's turned into a clothing shop that sells pants, I mean only pants. I go inside and it's mostly jeans—like, every kind you can imagine, in every color. And I'm really happy about this—which is surprising because, actually, I never wear jeans, I can't stand how stiff they are. But in this dream I'm . . ." He shrugs, with a baffled, self-conscious smile. "I'm glad the store is there."

Alan waited for him to continue.

"That's it. That's the whole dream. Or what I remember."

Stephen said, "But the point is, jeans make him happy when they didn't before. I mean, look at the pun; aren't dreams famous for puns, Alan?"

Alan nodded, but before he could say anything, Stephen said, "G-e-n-e-s, that kind of genes! And in a space that's holding up our building, holding up *our home*! Good God, how symbolic can you get? The strength of men and their continuity through their children—"

"There were women in that shop, too," Gordie said to Stephen. "And there were jeans with sequins and flowers, pink jeans . . . And whose genes are we talking about here anyway? I thought you wanted to adopt."

Stephen leaned forward and raised his hands in exasperation. "God but you're literal when it suits your purposes. And pink jeans—well obviously those are girls! Who says we couldn't raise a girl?"

"Guys, let's not race too far ahead," said Alan. "Last week we'd just started talking about what it might be like if—*if*," he emphasized to Gordie, "you were to go with Stephen's wishes. What you imagine it would be like."

Stephen stared pointedly at Gordie. This was the predictable dynamic in this type of counseling; apparently, gender made no difference. In the first session or two, Alan tried to get to know the individual members of the couple, then draw out their history as a couple, then listen to their respective sides of the "story." But once that was taken care of, once the battle lines were drawn, the one who wanted something cataclysmically new—children, marriage, a move, more sex—nearly always assumed that Alan was his or her automatic ally (the agent for change was generally female).

"Gordie," said Alan, "you said that you do like spending time with children. You love your brother's kids, you enjoyed the visit from your friend Jill's daughter—"

"Which I now wish I'd never agreed to."

"It's painful to find out what you've been missing!" Stephen blurted out.

"One week. She stayed with us *one week*. And she's twelve, practically an adult! That is so *not* what parenthood is all about, Stephen. And based on that—on that, I admit, perfectly fabulous game of house we got to play, and all because Jill's mom was dying an awful death—because of that you decide we must have a baby!"

"Gordie, I am not a cretin," said Stephen. "It's just that . . . as you know, I always wanted this, but I put it aside, I gave it up for you—I don't mean to sound the martyr here, because maybe in those days I just didn't think it was possible. I was a coward, but now . . . and then, when I saw you with Skye—that night you were doing her math homework with her—I mean, you were a natural. And it just . . . it reawakened things. Because times have changed! Look at Eric and Roberto!"

"Eric is a social worker."

"So? Like that makes him more nurturing than we are? Or because my job is raising money, I can't raise kids as well?"

"No!" said Gordie. "Of course not! But that child practically fell in their laps! They were already a part of the system."

"Well, I want to be a part of the 'system,' too, Gordie. The system of life."

There were tears in Stephen's eyes, and anyone could see that Gordie was deeply affected by this. Alan leaned forward. "Stephen, I know how passionate you feel, but I want Gordie to talk now, and I want you to listen. Remember Fran Lebowitz? I don't know what's become of her lately, but my favorite thing she ever said is that the opposite of talking isn't listening, it's waiting your turn."

Stephen smiled weakly. "Guilty as charged, I fear."

"So, Gordie, what are you afraid of—or, no, what do you object to most about having a child? Is it how drastically your life would change—because it would," Alan said, looking briefly at Stephen. "Or is it the responsibility? Or something else entirely?"

Gordie sighed. "Can it be just everything?"

"Okay, but give me the details of everything."

"Like parties—we give these great parties. Which are crucial to Stephen's work! I mean, look, Stephen, can you imagine us giving that black-tie thing with Beverly Sills and that guest tenor and . . . and with a baby crying in the bedroom you've proposed we turn your study into? Like, 'Oh, excuse me, Bev, please help yourself to the gravlax while I go change Junior's diaper and warm a bottle.' "

"We're rich, Gordie! We can afford live-in help if we want, we can—" He stopped when he saw the chiding look on Alan's face. "Sorry."

"You so don't get it! It's not playing house; it's *being* house," said Gordie. "You can't return a baby like that table you decided was all wrong after we'd had it for two months."

"You make me sound so superficial and shallow—oh, I *am* sorry, Alan."

"I want you to talk to me, Gordie, okay? Not to Stephen," said Alan. "Just for now."

"Look. It's true I like kids, and sure, I've had pangs, or probably we wouldn't have been together so long, would we? It's not just great sex and compatible furniture or shared fear of plague. We're envied by just about everyone we know, and I would hate to see that change."

"I assume you don't mean the envy," said Alan, then realized that teasing was all wrong. His instincts had been thrown off since Greenie's departure; at his worst moments now, he felt like an imposter when it came to the work of reconciliation.

"No! What we're envied *for*," said Gordie, looking offended. "For sticking together because we want to, never mind the rough times, for thirteen years! You know, I hate being a know-it-all, or sounding like a broken record here, but Stephen is an only child, whereas I was the oldest of seven, and so I know what babies and kids are like, the stress they make, how they can turn even something like going shopping into a major expedition, how you're never on time again anywhere, ever, how tired the parents always are. And we don't have jobs where we can be exhausted all the time!" He glanced at Stephen, who looked as if he might cry again. "I don't mean to sound cold, but these are the facts."

"Well, in part, they're the facts of your childhood," Alan said carefully, "as you felt them. Or they seem like facts, but they're really impressions, colored a great deal by how your parents ran things. Remember that one kid is a long way from seven, Gordie, that your parents did get divorced, and that they didn't have money. Stephen's right about one thing: money can make a big difference when you have children. But, Stephen, you should hear what Gordie's saying about how wonderful your life is now, as it is. I can tell you guys have a rich history, incredible commitment—or you wouldn't be here—but to have a child, no matter how much you love each other or how long you've been together, is to trade up for an even more profound commitment. Don't take for granted that being good at one will make the other a piece of cake."

Alan looked at the two men on the couch before him, both well kept, well dressed, and in their late thirties. They lived in the neighborhood, and before meeting them, Alan had noticed them more than once: in the expensive wine store, in the video store, just walking down the street. In public, they were talkative and affectionate. Now, getting to know them, he marveled that they had been together longer than most straight couples Alan and Greenie knew, longer even than Alan and Greenie. And both men wore rings. When Greenie and Alan had been planning their wedding, she had been disappointed when Alan told her he was sorry but he just didn't feel comfortable wearing jewelry of any kind. Why had he been so stubborn, so prissy about it?

Alan took a deep breath. "Gordie, like it or not, Skye stayed with you, and she brought up something for Stephen that was probably going to come out soon no matter what. The two of you are here because of what we call a logjam. Ordinarily, I hate jargon, but I like this term. This is as hard and real and turbulent as a river choked with logs, and right now it seems impassable. What we have to do is break it up. I can't predict which way the current will flow when we do it, but do it we will." Or do it he hoped they would. This referral, which baffled him, had come from a restaurant owner down the street who knew Alan only as Greenie's husband. When Stephen had said, "Walter says you are the *best*," Alan had to guess that the referral came out of pity, that Greenie had told her client about Alan's financial woes.

"I'm going to be honest here," he said. "I've never tackled this problem with two men—I mentioned that before—but perhaps the only obvious difference is that neither of you has a biological clock to tick." He saw Stephen open his mouth to protest. "But—but there's such a thing as a stage-of-life clock, too, and if you want to be considered as candidates to adopt—and despite the change in the times, Stephen, it isn't going to be easy—I think you'd do best to start investigating your options. Let me tell you, these days it's not even easy for straight couples." He let them absorb this for a moment, and then he told them that he wanted them to sit down together for at least an hour, unplug the phone, and make those old-fashioned lists of pros and cons. They could talk about the lists if they both wanted to—but only if they could do so without fighting. If they began to argue, they had to promise to put the lists away and change the subject. Either way, they were to bring them to their next session with Alan.

AFTER SEEING GORDIE AND STEPHEN ON THEIR WAY, Alan called New Mexico to speak with George, something he had done so far nearly every night. A sad silver lining of the literal distance between them was the two-hour time difference; if George had been at home in New York, Alan would have missed saying good night because of the late therapy session.

"I have a new friend," George said right away when he came on the phone.

Alan asked the new friend's name.

"He's Diego. Do you know what he has?"

"What does he have?" asked Alan, expecting to hear about toy armies and guns, things that western Republican parents would have no qualms about giving their little boys in ample quantity.

"A squirrel."

"A real squirrel?"

"*Yes*, Dad," said George, in a tone that prophesied his adolescence.

"Wow, a real squirrel. That's amazing. Is it a gray squirrel or a red one—or do they have flying squirrels out there?"

"Dad, squirrels don't fly. It's brown. It comes on his roof and it eats things Diego puts out the window. Diego can touch it and put the food in his hand so it eats from his hand. It likes peanuts and string cheese. Mom let me take some cookies she said got scale."

"Does it live in the house?"

"No, Daddy. It's a squirrel. It lives in a tree. There's lots of trees. The house is into the woods. There's a barn with horses and three dogs. The dogs live in the house. Daddy, can we get a dog when you come here? Our house is in the city part here, so I know we can't get a pony, and we don't have a tree like Diego's tree, or a roof like that, we don't really have a roof because we're not in a house with a upstairs, so we can't get a squirrel, but could we get a dog? Please?"

"Well, that's an idea. It's certainly an idea for us all to talk about."

"Is it a *good* idea?" asked George, sometimes too careful a listener.

"We'll see," said Alan. He smiled at his son's understanding of this distinction, but he was furious at Greenie (how little it took, at such a distance, with such provocation!). He wondered just how sharp a picture she had painted of his moving out west. Still, he had to be happy that George had offered conversation of any kind.

Unlike a lot of children his age, George had no attraction to the phone. One time, while Alan waited to speak with his son, he had heard Greenie whispering fiercely, coercively, "It's *Daddy*. Daddy wants to talk to you.

Daddy misses you!" Another time, George came on the phone and said, at lightning speed, "HiDaddyhiDaddyhiDaddy, Irodeinastretchtoday, That'sallIhavetosay, goodbyehere'sMommy!" Alan hadn't spoken a single word to his son, and George had refused to return to the phone after handing it back to his mother. She'd explained that the governor's chauffeur took George for a ride in a limousine and let him push all the buttons in back. Greenie said, "He told me there are stars in the roof you can turn on and off, and terrible me, I didn't believe him. But George—I mean George the chauffeur, that's his name, too—said that George, our George, was right. Can you imagine that? Stars on demand?"

Alan had despised what he took in her voice to be an air of superiority, for being there to experience George's simple joy in person. ("Our" George? Oh thanks for sharing!) But Alan was too smart to let on. And perhaps his son's callow haste meant only that he felt secure, that he wasn't worried, that he was having a good time where he was—and wasn't that what Alan should wish for? The lesser of two anxieties?

Tonight Consuelo, the babysitter, was the one to begin and end Alan's call. ("Mr. Alan," she called him when she answered the phone, or "George's Daddy," as if he were some lord-of-the-manor and not this discarded, remote appendage to the family, like a far-flung cousin.) Consuelo told him that Greenie wasn't there, which meant she was at the Governor's Mansion, in that other man's kitchen, cooking up a feast. If she had been in New York, she might be off at her own kitchen, cooking for others as well, so Alan's jealousy was misplaced. But he would have liked to ask exactly what George (not the damned chauffeur) thought this separation meant, how he envisioned the future.

OH, THE IRONIES OF "TREATING" COUPLES with threatened unions when your own was fractured. What sort of list would *he* make, Alan wondered as he ate his plate of prawns in garlic sauce later that night. (Now that he was living by himself, Alan made a point of never eating takeout right from the disposable cartons; this would be akin to drinking alone . . . though *that*, alas, was something he did do now, more often than in the past.)

So then:

Pros and cons of living without Greenie (about living without George, there were only cons, or that's how it looked right now):

Pros:
- Leave toilet seat up (the bed was another story; that he made, thus far at least).
- Be silent whenever you like, for as long as you like.
- Watch sports without the burden of covert disapproval or irritation (though baseball, his favorite sport by far, had yet to gear up and give him the kind of solace that nothing else could).
- Take showers the length of TV sitcoms.
- Leave bath mat on floor and shower curtain pushed back.
- Order take-out sushi (his alternate dinner) without a warning on tapeworm as regular and redundant as those recordings in taxis that told you to "bat-buckle up."
- Read sections of the Sunday *Times* in whatever order he liked and throw out those he hated before he even brought the paper in the door.
- Snore without being poked, awakened, and told to turn on his side as if he were a piece of rotisserie chicken.

Cons:
- No apricot scones or devil's food cake on demand; no loaves of French bread in the freezer.
- No one to do most of the shopping, all the laundry, and some of the cleaning up.
- No one to sit close against while watching a movie.
- No one to enfold in bed or, of course, make love to (even when it felt like a task—vacuuming, say, or pairing socks—giving satisfaction but leaving you unmoved).

Alan stopped here, mainly because he had finished his food and it was time for the news. Normally, he wouldn't watch the news because Greenie hated the intrusive angst at a time when you were supposed to be winding down toward sleep. "If something's happened in the world that matters so much you can't wait till the morning paper, it's probably something you can't do anything about," she reasoned, though he thought her reasoning faulty.

In truth, there was only one con to living without Greenie: the absence of Greenie. He did not miss having someone to talk with every day; he missed having *Greenie* to talk with every day. She had claimed, before leaving, that he did not talk to her anymore. Was this true? Or had he so internalized Greenie that he did all the talking in his head?

And look at his pathetic list of pros. He did not agree with Greenie that the separation wasn't a true break, but even so, he felt no urge toward courtship or even frenzied coupling with strangers—oh, of *that* he was cured! After all, shouldn't the pros include the freedom to investigate, once and for all, the truth about Marion's son? Or was he too cowardly to find out, and what would that mean about everything else he believed himself to be?

The anchorwoman, who wore a red suit that would have made anybody look fat, started off with a rapid-fire list of later news items whose promise was intended to hold you through the meatier though ultimately less tantalizing stories. Something about Tom Cruise's love life, something about a deadly bacteria carried by squirrels (Please, not in New Mexico, Alan prayed), something about a breakthrough in curing prostate cancer (which would be based on a retrospective study with maybe seven subjects, but the newscasters wouldn't tell you this).

Alan had just switched off the TV when the phone rang.

"Okay, how many?" she said without a greeting.

"How many what?"

"Drinks. I am monitoring you. The tough-love thing."

"I had one beer with my Chinese food and one before. You can't eat Chinese without beer. God, you're obnoxious."

"That has *always* been part of what makes me so good at everything I do," his sister said gaily.

Back in his normal life, Joya had phoned Alan once every two weeks or so (she didn't seem to mind that he was rarely the one to call), but since Greenie's departure she "checked in" every three or four nights, and while this hovering annoyed Alan, it also touched him. He knew he should find a way to tell her so, but he couldn't. Almost always, because of the time difference, Joya called too late for him to think in any clear, energetic way—and energy was necessary to keep pace with Joya.

Tonight, without much prelude, she told him that he was making a mistake by not coming clean with Greenie. Too tired for debate, Alan told her she was probably right.

"So will you call her? Write her a letter?" persisted Joya. "Of course, you should have done it before she left. Maybe you should just fly out over the weekend. Tell her in person. That's what you should do."

"Joy, I don't know if there's anything *to* tell, do I? And it's not like I have a Learjet at my disposal."

Joya made a noise of contempt. "God, even my brother's a typical caveguy asshole. Aren't you being a little dense for a shrink? What do you mean, nothing to tell? Hello?"

"Your sympathy is much appreciated," he said. "You're not even married, may I point out. You don't know what the stakes really are. Honesty can do more harm than good."

"Oh, 'may you point out' indeed. Thanks, yeah, that's right, caveguy. Don't think you can hide behind that Jeremy Irons diction. Though clearly, what right-thinking woman needs marriage if all she really wants is kids? Which, as time goes on and I get to know the ways of testosterone on a more intimate basis—and boy, do I *ever*—seems to be the most sane approach."

"Should we hang up? I think we're both tired."

"Speak for yourself. I am about to go out on a *date,* speaking of my pathetic spinsterhood. A fourth date."

"That's great," said Alan. "Did you mention him before? Someone you met at work?"

"No. I was fixed up. That's why I didn't say anything. Generally these things are doomed, but I am nothing if not desperate."

"So you like him." Joya was hard to take when she was lonely, and it pained Alan, who had no remedy to offer. She was, in many ways, too smart for her own good—or for the good of finding a man who wouldn't flee. Out in San Francisco, she was a mediator in union disputes, and though the art of compromise was supposedly her vocation, she hated being wrong more than just about anything else in the world.

"Yeah, I like him. A lot. . . . A nice surprise," she added. "And he's cute—I mean, I don't even have to *convince* myself—except for this grotty little mustache, which I'm sure I can get rid of, no problem. And he likes to dance, and his wife left him five years ago, and he's had it with being skittish."

"A seasoned Prince Charming."

"And he's Jewish."

Alan paused. "Which would mean . . . ?"

"Oh, don't be so damned ecumenical, Alan. Jewish men like brainy women. It's one of those true clichés. And anyway, I got all the Jewish genes in our family. You got all the white-churchy baggage from Mom."

"Thanks. Like you ever went to a seder."

"As a matter of fact, more than a few." Joya sighed. "We are off the subject."

"Right. Your incredible catch."

"But that's the thing. There *is* a catch," she said, with a small, bitter laugh.

"Let me guess. He's . . . a cross-dresser? A drummer? . . . Oh no. He's a union leader."

"He has *two teenage daughters.*"

"You've met them already?"

"No, but I can tell he's worried about that. I know my vibes. Reading vibes is my forte. He thinks they'll eat me alive. And if he thinks they can, they will. They'll sense it, like blood in the water."

"Be a little open-minded, maybe? And Joya: teenage girls have got to think you're cool because you're sexy but you've got this macho job. The guy can't see that angle. Besides, their mom's the one who left."

"Oh Alan. Who better than you to know how many different versions there are of *Rashomon.* And I may not be married, but *you* are not the father of teenage daughters."

Alan loved her boomerang wit, but he worried about its effect on men who hadn't had Joya as their protector when they were thirteen, awkward and gangly, red-faced with alternating bouts of shame, acne, and hopelessly immature longings. She had been so much more powerful than any pumped-up big brother, respected for the way she could throw around words, not threats or physical blows. You could borrow that aura, just enough of it, even when she wasn't present.

"Go easy," he said. "Be a little dumb. What I mean is, let it unfold without all your brilliant second-guessing. That gets you in trouble."

She sighed. "I know. I will try to keep a tiny pipsqueak version of you perched on my shoulder for the rest of the evening—and maybe beyond. You know, like Rick Moranis in *Honey, I Blew Up the Kid.* Though shut your eyes later, would you, 'cause this could be the big night." She sighed again. "Oh God, remember when it wasn't so cautious, when you got this part over with practically first thing of all? Got to see where the other person was hairy and bald and scarred and tattooed?"

"Yeah. Do I ever," said Alan. "Thanks for reminding me."

"I'm sorry. I didn't mean it that way."

"I know. But on that note, I've got to get to sleep. I have a seven-thirty tomorrow. Weird how all my remaining patients are at the beginning and end of the day."

"Means they're productive citizens. Maybe you can even take credit."

"Joya, what don't you have an explanation for?"

"The fuck-up you got yourself in, my dear little brother." She told him she loved him, loved him anyway, and then they did say good night.

FIVE YEARS BEFORE, Alan had gone to his fifteenth high school reunion. He had never been to a reunion of any kind, never intended to do such a thing, but he'd needed whatever kind of jarring he could get, because he and Greenie had arrived at precisely that crisis on which he had so smugly advised perhaps two dozen couples by that time. They were at Baby Crossroads: Greenie so all-consumingly certain; Alan, if anything, more doubtful than ever. In a way, Greenie's unclouded enthusiasm for parenthood made the prospect that much more worrisome. She seemed, suddenly, more naïve than confident.

But something had to give, and the giving (or giving in) probably had to be his. So anything he could do that was to any degree out of the ordinary gave him hope. Small changes tend to precipitate the large, he told his clients. Of course, what he meant was *relevant* changes. He did not mean that changing the color of your eyeshadow might change your attitude toward joint finances (though, really, who knew?).

It was Joya who suggested that he stop acting so superior and go to the reunion; since she was five years older, she would also be at hers. Would that give him enough courage? They could stay with their mother and get extra credit. "You'd never guess, but these things are a hoot," said Joya. "And you've got Greenie—she'll be like Debbie Reynolds, the perfect socializing spouse. You probably won't have to say a word, just look at everybody's name tag and go, 'Oh wow! Do you look fantastic!' and Greenie'll do all the schmoozing. The food at *my* fifteenth was surprisingly good, and I won a weekend in the Poconos by remembering more teachers' names than anyone else. Of course, I also remembered which ones had been sleeping around and with *whom*. Too bad I wasn't so great at memorizing presidents or capitals."

In the end, Greenie did not come, because they'd had their worst fight yet two nights beforehand. She was barely speaking to him the Friday morning of the reunion, and he was still too raw to apologize. Screw *her,* he thought as he threw his clothes into a bag and called New Jersey Transit. This rage and his longing for Joya—who would give him a rough time but drink him under the table and make him laugh—carried him in full righteous dudgeon all the way to the rail station parking lot in Hazlet, where his mother picked him up. In the car, he discovered that a threatened strike having something to do with the BART had kept Joya back in San Francisco. "Darling, you'll have a lovely time," said his mother. And she proceeded to name various neighbors happily greeting their grown children for the very same occasion. She did not ask why Greenie wasn't with him. This was the one advantage to having a mother who lived in constant fear of the unexpected.

In his old bedroom—now a guest room with twin four-poster beds and a large pastel portrait of his mother as a teenage girl with cocker spaniel hair—he threw his bag down on one mattress and collapsed on the other. "Darling?" his mother called up the stairs after an hour had passed. "Darling, your party starts in half an hour, I think. You can keep the car as long as you like." Her querulous voice irritated him, if only because his mother, poor woman, now carried all his projected fury at both his wife and his sister. Well, screw the lot of 'em, he just *would* have a good time. Without bothering to shower or change into the white shirt and festive red tie he'd packed at Joya's urging, he went downstairs, kissed his mother and, as if he were seventeen all over again, took the keys to her car.

Gyms. Jesus. Why did they hold these affairs in gyms? The associations—teams you didn't make, games you lost, coaches who bullied you . . . girls who refused to dance when you finally got up the nerve to ask—were all horrendous. And the smells; you didn't even have to conjure those up from the past, since a fresh crop of youthful armpits had seasoned the space that very afternoon.

Alan made his way to a long table with jugs of budget booze. Because he had driven so fast, he was one of the first to arrive. He'd glanced at the waiting array of name tags and spotted several familiar last names, but often the first names attached were those of siblings to the people he'd known. The one high school friend with whom he stayed in occasional touch wouldn't be here; he lived in Texas, and his wife (though Alan had not told Greenie) was eight months pregnant.

As the men arrived, Alan saw with grim satisfaction that every one of them wore not just a tie but a jacket. Those jackets would be shed, but still, here was Alan in a denim shirt that seemed to shout, "Look how cool and rebellious I am!" A statement Alan the therapist would have deemed vaguely hostile in a context like this.

Alan's high school was the sort of place that sent just about everyone safely off to college—to colleges from which they would emerge, also safely, into lifelong servitude (sometimes happily) as lawyers, dentists, accountants, and sales reps. To wind up as a shrink; well, Alan might as well have become a dedicated surfer, traveling the world in search of the perfect monster wave. I should have worn a *Hawaiian* shirt, he reflected as he cruised the room with his second gin and tonic.

He roamed from one end of the basketball court to the other, scanning chests more often than faces since he could not remember too well what some of these faces might have looked like fifteen years before—forget how they might have evolved. As he did this, looking up now and then to exchange a quick rodent grin with yet another stranger, his roving glance was stalled when he ran into someone wearing what appeared to be the very same denim shirt that he wore. Before he could read the name tag on the shirt, he recognized the voice.

"Little *brother*," said the voice, and a long-forgotten chill shot through Alan, pleasure and sorrow all at once, from one end of his spine to the other.

Alan, as Greenie had so accurately assessed him soon after they met, was a man of cool temper. ("Whatever's the opposite of Latino—that's you.") But before Greenie knew him, Alan had been a boy, a teenage boy, with a body as tortured as any other boy's, and it was his body that remembered the voice.

"So, where is she? Did she wimp out? I bet she did."

"Marion," said Alan, and suddenly he felt the cheap gin quite viscerally: in his bloodstream, in his brain cells, in his fingertips and pupils. "Marion!"

She took hold of his right upper arm, just a shade too tightly, the way she had done when they were kids, a gesture of teasing domination. "How are you, Alan?"

"I'm fine," he said.

"Not to ignore you—because, God, here you are all grown up and looking like a wild one, like one who escaped!—but where's Joy? I meant to call her, but since I saw her at the last one, I just assumed I'd see her here."

"She's in San Francisco."

Marion laughed. "She lives there? How funny. I'm moving there in a couple of months. To Berkeley."

It was the same shirt, the exact same shirt—oddly, covering a chest far less enticing than the one he remembered from the upstairs hallway, the breasts he could just make out through her nightgown whenever she'd spent the night in Joya's room. And now Alan was the taller of the two—though he still felt small beside her, small yet happy. (God, he had forgotten all about gin.)

Her hair. In high school, Marion had forced her bushy, obstinate hair into a braid that fell below her waist. Now, it struck Alan, her hair looked almost identical to his: short, curly, and dark, brindled with gray, standing up fiercely away from her head. She looked . . . militant, Alan decided. Was she gay? How odd that would seem. Alan might not remember the faces of classmates he'd passed in the halls for four years, but how minutely he could remember trying to listen, often successfully, to the conversations between his sister and Marion on the other side of his bedroom wall. He could remember trying to use a terra-cotta flowerpot as an amplifier, placing its wide mouth against the wall, pressing his ear to the drainage hole. How many boys had he heard the two girls dissecting like frogs in science class? How many nights had he gone to bed just a hand's width from Marion's body, only inches of wall between them, bringing his agony and fascination to a hard, thrilling crescendo just before sleep?

"So, little brother—*not*-so-little brother—are you married?" She glanced around and behind him suggestively.

"I am. But my wife couldn't make it. And please stop calling me that."

"Children? Pull out the pictures."

"No. Not yet anyway."

"Watch out there. We are not as perpetually youthful as so many of us seem to be assuming."

Marion did not appear to be drinking anything, but she did seem charged up with mischievous elation. Someone had made the studious decision to put not just people's names and classes on their paper badges but their professions as well—or, apparently, whatever they had filled in on that line of the reunion questionnaire. Marion's name tag identified her, in some cheerleader's round, girlish script, as LIFE STUDENT, AD INFINITUM. (Alan felt doltishly envious; his read PSYCHOTHERA-PIST/COUPLES COUNSELOR, the last word squashed below the other two, as if cowed into the corner of a room.)

"I like your chosen career," he said.

"I didn't really choose mine, but I do like *yours*," she said. "What's your score on the couples?"

Alan rattled the ice in his plastic cup. He laughed nervously. "Score?"

"How many've stayed, how many split?"

"I don't keep track," he said. "Maybe I should."

"People don't ask when they come to see you? Like, who'd hire a broker without asking how many good investments he'd made?"

"No," he said. "Kind of funny, I guess, now that you make that analogy. But in theory, I'm not a fixer. I'm a . . . sounding board, a safe zone, a giver of permission to say whatever you need to say without . . ." He faltered as he tried to read her expression. Was it mocking?

"Without being tossed in the wood chipper? That's hard work. I'm serious." She looked at his hands, at the rattling ice. "Let's fix you up there."

They walked to the bar, where Alan poured himself another metallic-tasting cocktail and Marion poured herself cranberry juice. Had she quit her hellion ways? Because *she* had always been the wild one, so if she was now on the wagon, he had to admire her bravery in coming to one of these sloshfests.

At the drinks table, Alan was accosted by a classmate he barely remembered, a guy who claimed they'd been in Boy Scouts and swimming lessons together. Jim and his wife, Stephanie, ran a small company that sold prostheses. Alan fought the childish urge to guffaw at their earnest description of how they'd fallen into this line of work (she'd been a physical therapist, he an M.B.A. with entrepreneurial yearnings). Alan examined their limbs as surreptitiously as he could, but all eight appeared to be quite real. Over their shoulders, he kept an eye on Marion, who had wandered across the gym and seated herself on the bleachers. She was reading something.

"Know what?" said Alan after he'd listened for ten minutes or so.

"I'm going to check out the old locker room. Nice to meet you, Stephanie."

"Do you have a card?" said Stephanie. "We're collecting everyone's card. We're in the city, too, and we might do a post-reunion reunion sometime. What do you think?"

Alan told her it was a great idea and fished his card from his wallet. Without heading for the locker room even as a pretense, he crossed the gym, straight toward the bleachers.

He sat beside her. "Maybe it's my turn to look after you," he said.

Marion looked skeptical. "When was it mine to look after you?"

"Well, you and Joy, the two of you . . ." Alan blushed.

Marion saved him. "I do remember the time we got you into that R movie when you were so obviously a baby. When you were about to be humiliated in front of that long line of older kids. What was it, *Taxi Driver*? *Mean Streets*? Something with Robert De Niro. We had the hugest crush on him, Joya and me." She squeezed his arm again. "I'm not sure that constitutes 'looking after.' Maybe the opposite."

He glanced at the flyer she was holding. It was a "newsletter" from her class. "Are you in that?" he said.

"Oh no. Coming to this thing is geeky enough. Sending in my snapshot or listing my dubious achievements, no way."

"Why are you here?"

"Let's see . . . I'm a glutton for punishment?" She folded the newsletter twice and set it beside her. "It so happens my parents are packing up the house before they move south. They're joining the flamingo set. Dad's wearing white shoes. Unbelievable. I think he thinks he's an elderly Bing Crosby. So this is my last chance to go through the old Barbie dolls and those gimp bracelets from Camp Watusi. Salvage my mementos. Or not, as it's turning out. I won't lie: from where I sit now, my childhood looks almost beautiful—or innocent, just the way it's supposed to. But the remains look pretty grotesque. A mouse made a nest in the shoebox where I kept all of Barbie's stewardess outfits and cocktail dresses."

"And what about your . . . your dubious achievements?" Alan knew that Joya and Marion had stayed in touch through college or longer, that some Christmas a few years back he'd heard his mother ask about Marion. Joya had said she was in Tanzania or Thailand, doing something valiant and hopeful, like vaccinating babies or building thatched schools or teaching first aid.

Marion did not answer right away. "Well, they're not a lot different from yours, Alan. I mean, I help people. Fundamentally. Or try to." She stopped there, as if she'd said too much already.

"Are you trying to avoid telling me you're a lawyer?"

"God no," she said. "Thanks a lot, little brother."

"Teacher."

"No. I don't have that kind of masochistic patience, I'm afraid."

"Wait. I didn't ask *you*. Are you married?"

"Oh no," she said. "I'm a member of the female generation that somehow missed that bus. Pretty stupid, to tell you the truth. But I'm fine about it now."

"What, you think it's too late?" Like his sister, who was still fervently aiming herself toward marriage, Marion would soon be thirty-eight.

"For me at least. But like I said, I'm fine about it. At this point, I'd make a horrific wife. I'm not too good at give-and-take."

Neither was Greenie, thought Alan, recalling how cool she'd been that afternoon when he left for the train station. "Have a good time," she'd said, with the same tone and rhythm you'd use to utter, "Makes no difference to me."

Marion looked around at the growing crowd—including, noticed Alan, too many lone souls meandering about as if the gym were an art gallery and the climbing bars and basketball hoops and scoreboards were objects of aesthetic fascination. Joya had been wrong: this was depressing.

"Listen," she said. "You want to go have dinner somewhere? That road joint you guys used to take us to when you wanted to get laid? It's still there, can you believe it? I passed it on the way over. I'd love to see if they make the burgers as greasy as they used to. One last time."

Alan knew the place she meant, though he'd been there only two or three times in the past and never (alas) for the purpose she'd stated. He suspected that the only reason the place survived was its fame as one of the bars where Bruce Springsteen had played before he was anyone special.

They took Marion's car, and they didn't say much on the way. Marion would point out landmarks: places where the relics of their youth had survived, places where they had not. No one at the reunion had noticed their desertion or tried to stop them, as Alan half-wished someone would—and not because he wanted to stay.

When they got out in the dusty parking lot, they could hear the thumping pulse of whatever godawful band was booked at the bar that night. They looked at each other across the roof of the car, and Alan's guilty hesitation was vaporized, gone in a flash too quick to overrule. This was his past; he had the right—even the responsibility—to explore it, to seize this strange, unexpected chance at looking backward so far and so clearly.

"Shall we, little . . . Alan?" Marion held out her hand in a way that suggested he should make a hoop of his arm and escort her formally in. When her arm was tucked inside his (their identical fake-western shirts from the Gap linked together, as if they were partners in a square dance), Alan stole his first close look at her face in so many years and saw there a kind of admirable clarity: no makeup, few creases, a plain old-fashioned pallor. The earring he could see was a small cascade of silver beads, like a sip of icy spring water.

A pink fringe of sky persisted still, the rim of a wide rosy ocean beneath the ever-descending night. An evaporating ocean. A last chance, a last glimpse of innocence, thought Alan as the present enclosed the past like a long soft glove and the two of them stepped into the clamorous dark. Marion pulled him toward the only empty booth, though the table was strewn with someone else's dishes.

ALAN CARRIED THE LAST OF HIS rice and prawns to the kitchen; he would eat it for lunch the next day. When he switched on the light, the plate and mug in the sink reminded him instantly of Saga's visit that afternoon. In a peculiar way, this cheered him up. Her story (which he had not managed to get, at least not through subtle methods) was surely not a happy one, yet once she had come inside, out of the storm, she'd exuded an air of confidence, almost contentment. He had said, as she left, that he hoped he would see her again, and he'd made sure she had his phone number, written clearly on a heavy piece of paper in permanent ink. (His card, he thought, would scare her off for good.)

She told him she'd be in touch; she had to return the clothes he'd lent her. She said she could not keep them, not without the explicit permission of the woman to whom they belonged. But would she, a day later, care about or possibly even remember Alan? Her appearance had implied she might be homeless—and often people living at such extremes, no matter how "normal" they seemed, were in such a psychic muddle that each day wiped clean the day before. The inability to keep time continuous, one day distinct from another, might be the very reason such people had to live like feral cats.

But Saga had not seemed the least bit feral; a little simple, a little careless about her appearance, but not wild, uncivilized, crazy. She had wiped her feet vigorously on the mat inside Alan's door, and she had asked for an old newspaper to set the box on, so as not to stain the floor. (Later, she asked for a new box, and he found one—the one that had been too small to hold George's Mousetrap game that morning.)

"Where are you going to take those puppies?" Alan had asked as he led her to the bathroom.

"My place."

"Where do you live?"

"Oh"—she laughed, the laughter of private jokes—"downtown a bit. Sometimes."

"If you need a place to live—"

"I just said I have one, didn't I?" She sounded testy, but then she smiled. Her right eye, the narrow one, did not give in to the smile; nor did that side of her mouth, as if the muscles there were contentious or unwilling. The good eye, only by comparison with the other, looked as if it were open extra wide, as if half of Saga were in a state of perpetual astonishment.

She said, more gently, "This is very generous of you, taking us in. It's not often strangers do things like that. But I do take care of myself." She glanced at the puppies, sleeping off the trauma of their shots and the storm. "And of my little friends. Till *they* get homes, and they will. One way or another, I'll make sure of that." Alan's irrepressible judgment must have shown on his face, because she added, "Do you think I'm a little eccentric? Hey! Don't answer that."

He began to protest, but she interrupted. "Know what? I'm freezing."

So she had showered, while Alan made her tea and put out a plate of crackers and cheese. When she came to the kitchen table, she was wearing the sweatpants and T-shirt he'd taken from Greenie's bureau. The T-shirt was red, stamped with the white silhouette of a lobster and the name of the restaurant in Maine where he and Greenie had celebrated their anniversary four years in a row. The restaurant had been a favorite of Greenie's, on the coast looking out toward the island where she'd spent a part of every childhood summer, in a tiny house on the rocks with kerosene lamps and an outhouse. After her parents' death, Maine had become too sad for her. That was two years ago; she and Alan had not returned since. Nor had she worn this T-shirt, Alan suspected.

Saga stayed for only forty-five minutes (twenty of which she spent in the shower). While they were seated at the table, she asked Alan about George, whose face hung in every room.

"He's four. On a trip with his mother right now," said Alan. He asked if Saga had children.

"Oh no." Her mouth was full, and she covered it with a napkin, as if to hold back something else she might have said.

"Parents?"

He tried to sound casual, but she eyed him sharply, warning him she wasn't so simple. "Long gone," she said.

Saga ate the entire plate of crackers and cheese, using a thumb to pick up the last of the crumbs—just as George would have done. Alan wished he had put out more food, but to put out more now might insult her. She looked out the window often, and as soon as the rain seemed to have let up for good, she said, "I should go now, but would you mind if I made another phone call? It's local, I promise."

"Oh please," said Alan, and he took her back into the bedroom and pointed to the phone. He closed the door to give her privacy. He carried their plates from the table to the kitchen. He found a sponge and worked at the gray crud around the faucets and the drain.

"Success!" Saga stood just outside the kitchen. "Thank you! You've been the soul of kindness, Mr. Alan Glazier."

Alan was startled, not just by her sudden closeness. She smelled like Greenie—like the shampoo Greenie had left behind. "I've done hardly anything," he said.

"Perhaps you'll do more," Saga said brightly. Within a few minutes she had collected her soggy, soiled clothing in a plastic bag, her box of puppies, and Alan's number, which she stuffed in a pocket of Greenie's sweatpants. After she put on her damp sneakers (Greenie's feet were much smaller, Alan's too large), he saw her out the door. She refused his offer to pay for a cab and set off toward Seventh Avenue. Alan watched her cross every intersection—carefully—until she turned a corner.

When he wandered, idly, into the bedroom, he found her wet towel folded neatly on the bedspread and the bar of soap from the shower on his dresser, placed in the ceramic dish where he put his keys and coins each night before he went to bed (it was in fact a soap dish, one he had pilfered from a fancy hotel in Paris before he knew Greenie). On the nightstand, beside the phone, Saga had left two quarters.

He checked the bathroom when he took the towel in to hang it up, but he found nothing out of order there. Sheepishly, he opened the medicine chest, and at first his heart foundered at the sight of all the empty spaces where vials and miniature boxes had stood—but then he realized that these were just the spaces so recently occupied by Greenie's benign little remedies: Motrin, Q-tips, Chapstick, hand lotion, a tiny beaker of colored barrettes, and a cylinder of powder (a scent called Rain, as if you could begin to capture such an elemental smell). Against his will, he felt the longing for her things, her presence, spread across his chest like a burning rash. "Oh Greenie, what a mess," he said. He closed the cabinet, which left him facing only himself. How well a mirror could say, *I told you so.*

FIVE

"THREE DAYS IS MUCH TOO LONG," said Uncle Marsden. "You are going to worry me literally to death if you keep on disappearing like this. And then you'll be in a pickle, won't you, my girl?"

Arriving on foot from the train station, Saga had found her uncle on his knees in the garden, weeding the peony bed. His white hair, blown loony by the wind, made him look like that god—Who was that god? What was his name?—about to hurl a thunderclap.

"I'm sorry," she said. "I didn't disappear. I left you a note. And yesterday I left you a message. You were out." Or did she leave the message? She remembered planning to leave the message.

"Oh thank you very much!" he scoffed. "A note and a message! As if they assure me you're safe. I wish you would let me find a room for you down there. I'm sure I know folks who'd put you up, maybe even let you have a key. At least I'd know where you're sleeping, that you're safe." He tossed his dirty gloves into the wheelbarrow and grasped her shoulders, as if he might shake her, widened his eyes and uttered a long growl. "Rrrraghhh!" Then he kissed her on the cheek.

As she followed him into the mudroom, it came to her. Zeus. The god was Zeus. Uncle Marsden was nothing like Zeus, he was more like . . . Hephaestus? Was that the blacksmith god? Saga had loved the Greek myths when she was little, known all the gods and muses and famously doomed mortals by heart. She'd like to know them again. She would have to find that book. It had a yellow cover; that much she remembered, but not where she had last seen it. Had it even survived the move from her mother's house? It might be in one of the boxes on the third floor. She would have to look—if she could remember to look. She took out her notebook to write a reminder.

"Did you do what you needed to do with those creatures? Poor things," said Uncle Marsden as he took off his rubber boots.

"Yes. But I have to go back in at the end of the week. They're with my friend Stan, but I want to keep an eye on them. Until he finds them homes."

"Is that where you stay? With this Stan fellow? Who in Constantinople *is* this Stan fellow?"

"I stay there sometimes," she lied. "But he's not a boyfriend, so please, no lectures."

Oh, *Stan* might have liked that, no doubt about it. Stan wasn't really even a "friend"—in terms of personality, he was a jerk—but there was no reason to worry Uncle Marsden with the details of her history with Stan. Stan was a big drinker, and basically, Saga had decided, he didn't much care for people. Drunk or sober, however, he was devoted to the animals he rescued.

Uncle Marsden growled again, but quietly. Gradually, he was giving up the struggle of trying to reason with her or find out where she stayed when she went into the city. She knew he suspected that he wouldn't like the answer, and it was true: he wouldn't. Last year, when he'd told her that her secrecy was dangerous, she'd told him it wasn't secrecy. It was just that she needed some of her life to remain private, all her own. "If I don't make a boundary or two," she had explained, "I'll have to keep reminding you I'm thirty-three years old, I'm not a child." Poor Uncle Marsden had to agree.

She hadn't had a seizure in two years, so he couldn't very well use this caution, either, as an argument to keep her close to home. They had a complicated alliance but one they both loved. At times—late nights, on the front porch when it was warm, by the front fireplace when it was not—she fancied that this must be a little bit like marriage.

She caught him eyeing the borrowed shirt she wore, but all he said was "I'm going to assume you were *not* in Maine these past few days. Though God knows that might be safer." He looked again and, this time, pointed at the shirt. "Lobster, lobster . . . nice idea there. How about lobster on Friday? Just for a change of pace."

"I'd love that," she said. Briefly, she wondered why she was clutching her notebook. She put it back in her knapsack and hung the knapsack on a hook. She dropped the plastic bag containing her wet clothes beside the washing machine. For a moment, on the train, Saga had completely forgotten what the bag contained. She had been surprised, when she opened it, to see her yellow dress and her tweed jacket, the remains of a suit she'd bought for job interviews in her previous life.

Inside the house, heat rose contentiously through the antique vents like the mumblings of a hungry stomach. Saga walked carefully through the kitchen and the rooms beyond, turning on lamps. Just to see where you were going, you had to turn on half a dozen. Because of the outdated wiring, Uncle Marsden insisted on weak bulbs, and most of the shades had turned cloudy and yellow with age. "Can I make you a drink?" she called out.

"You may, my dear!"

She went to the bar in the parlor and stood on the library stool to reach the shelf with the bourbon and the cherries. "Shirley Temple for me," she said when Uncle Marsden passed her on his way upstairs. Even when he hadn't been in the garden, he changed his clothes for dinner.

He leaned across the banister. "And forty lashes. As if they'd do a bit of good."

Saga looked out the front windows at the house across the street. Standing at the door was the giant schnauzer who lived there. He never barked or scratched, just showed up and waited. Saga didn't need to look at a clock; this meant it was probably five to six. Every night, precisely at six, the porch lights flanking the door winked on, and Commodore Perry was admitted to his house. That was the kind of life Saga kept thinking she longed for. Really, though, it was the kind of life she could have right here, for the time being, if she chose—a life of perfect safety, ample comfort, and easy kindness amid all these deep, lumpy sofas and thick-limbed tables in rooms as grand as circus tents.

Uncle Marsden's house was so nice, so intensely, so magically *nice*— not magazine nice but fairy-tale nice. Saga had loved it forever, all the way back to when she was a little girl and came for summer visits with her parents. Even then she had wished she could live here, and not just because it would be wonderful to live near the beach. Uncle Marsden's house had lots of funny forgotten stairways and cupboards and chutes, just the way a person had blood vessels and organs (some of them essential, some nearly obsolete) hidden beneath all that skin. It had a dumbwaiter that still worked, though no one used it—or not since Saga and her cousins had been children, pretending, when the adults weren't around, that it was an elevator, a spaceship, a diving bell. In the old smoking den, Uncle Marsden had installed blue lamps and a purring humidifier. This was where he kept his personal plant collection; he called this room the Salon of Mosses. It smelled exactly like a forest.

There were chandeliers that might have come from Cinderella (though Cinderella would have kept them free of cobwebs), and halfway up the front stairs, which changed direction twice, there was a deep windowseat, as if you just might need to rest on your way to bed—which, for a while, Saga did.

Everything was big and old: the tall imposing beds, the crooked raftered ceilings, the Arabian rugs—worn from plush reds to dusty pinks—and the front porch, which felt like the sheltered deck of a ship, cluttered end to end with sagging wicker chairs and flocks of pillows with sun-faded faces, their undersides peppered with mildew. It was the kind of house people called stately, with rooms on the highest floor that Uncle Marsden referred to as "maids' rooms" even though he'd never had any maids, or any that Saga knew about. Three of these rooms were filled with boxes and unused furniture, and when you opened their doors, the smell of mothballs hit you hard and made you sneeze, but the fourth room had a bed, a dresser, a cracked-leather armchair, and a painting of a tulip field in Holland (complete with rickety windmill). In one corner stood a tiny green sink, and out the one protruding window— this was the best part—there was a view of the ocean and some tree-tufted islands in the distance. This was the only room in the house where you could really see, not just hear, the ocean, and Uncle Marsden had given it to Saga.

That long-ago wish of Saga's—getting to live here—hadn't come true in the best of ways, but she sometimes got a kick out of the fact that it *had* come true when so many others had not. She didn't like to think about how long it would *stay* true, though unless Uncle Marsden lived practically forever, she would almost certainly have to think about that. Saga had moved in just over a year ago, when her mother died. Uncle Marsden had sold his sister's house and furniture and put the money in a bank account for Saga. "No question, my dear, you'll move in with me," he had said right up front, before the funeral. Saga, too proud to say that she could not live alone, had never felt such relief. Uncle Marsden was, if not a god, a saint for sure.

On a good day, the only serious drawback to Saga's altered life was Uncle Marsden's allergy to cats and dogs—which meant she couldn't have so much as a single kitten in the house. Two years ago, for several months, she had fed a group of feral cats behind the garage, cats abandoned by the fickle kinds of people who came to stay in the summer cabins a few miles down the beach and somehow thought that pets, like bathing suits, were a seasonal thing. But Uncle Marsden's snooty neighbors had put an end to that. It broke Saga's heart to have to catch them—which wasn't hard, since most of them had come to trust her—and drive them over to the shelter, a few at a time. She would rather have driven them back to the overturned boat where they had gathered and managed to survive before she became their caretaker (and then their betrayer), but she knew that nothing would have stopped them from returning to the garage, and she did not want to make trouble for her uncle.

Uncle Marsden told people that Saga had wanted to be a vet and that it was such a tragedy her accident had made this impossible. This wasn't really true, or not completely. Saga had loved animals from the time she was little, and when she was eight or ten, she told all the grown-ups that's what she wanted to be, a vet, maybe a zoo vet. But by the time she finished high school, she knew full well that she didn't have the kind of brains it took to ace all those science courses. Because vet school, she'd found out, was harder to get into than med school, and once you got there, you had to learn how to be a doctor not just for one species, like human doctors did, but for a whole bunch of species—pigs and horses and cows, even if you knew from the start you just wanted to care for dogs and cats (never mind zebras and camels and snakes!). As part of your schooling, Saga had heard, you had to slice open ponies, just to explore their insides, and cut the beaks off chickens the way they did on factory farms. Well, that would have done Saga in. Learning science was peanuts compared to *that.*

When she was in college—nowhere like Yale, where Uncle Marsden taught—she'd gone to a career workshop and decided that travel agent would be a great job, so that's what she'd set her mind on, taking classes in French and business and even a little modern history. So *that* was the profession which now, because of the accident, she could no longer pursue. There were just too many details you had to keep straight. In fact, it was exactly the sort of job for which she was now *least* qualified. Sometimes that seemed funny, too. Almost funny.

But Saga held back from correcting Uncle Marsden. She understood that for him, a tenured professor at a fancy university, to say that his beloved niece had been thwarted from a career as a *travel agent* by a serious head injury would have been . . . well, it wasn't tragic enough. And anyway, a lot of the time when she heard him tell his version, she wasn't even in the same room. The very network of passageways and hollow compartments that made the house seem so alive also made it a place where conversations traveled unlikely distances—like straight up the dumbwaiter shaft to the heating vent on the floor in Saga's room. So if she was up there and people were talking just a little loud in the kitchen, she'd hear most of it without trying, or wanting, to.

This was how she'd sometimes hear her cousins Pansy and Michael and Frida discussing *her*. To her face, they all treated her as if they loved and cared about her as much as their father did, but actually, when Saga was absent, Frida was the only one who ever came to her defense. They all worried, and you had to admit this was logical, about what would happen when Uncle Marsden died. Would *they* have to look after Saga? Absurd—especially since surely there was some kind of work she could do to support herself; Uncle Marsden hadn't tried hard enough to help her find it.

But Michael, she'd found out, made merciless fun of her.

One morning last summer, before she had gone down for breakfast, she'd heard Michael's voice, like the voice of a pompous ghost, reverberate through the floor: "Rubber bands, twisties—*twisties!*—tinfoil, wax paper, and *stuff* . . . can openers, corkscrews, *et cetera*. . . . Oh, I like this one: large utensils except wooden spoons, *wooden spoons go in jar beside laundry door!*" Laughter—mostly his.

Michael was reading out loud, to his sisters, from the labels Saga had placed around the kitchen to help her remember where to put things away, and where to find them again. (The antique cupboards had glass panes, so there she had only to look right through to see the dishes and food inside.) She cooked and cleaned for Uncle Marsden, though at first he told her she shouldn't feel obliged to do anything special; all he needed was her charming company. But Saga liked organizing tasks in ways that made her feel like anyone else and that might, despite what some doctors said, sharpen her mind again. Uncle Marsden had also nailed a big blackboard on the one blank wall, taking down a rooster weather vane that had been there as long as Saga could remember. (She'd been told that most of the long memories were just fine in her head—but how could anybody know for sure? How could she, much less anyone else, know what she'd once remembered and no longer did?) On that board, Saga and Uncle Marsden wrote down telephone messages, events for the week, and things to shop for, anything that might slip their minds.

Tactful Uncle Marsden claimed that in fact he'd been lost in this room before they added the labels and the board. And it was true that his wife, Liz, had been entirely in charge of the kitchen until she died. Uncle Marsden was as old-fashioned as those wavy-windowed cupboards, cooking out of cans when he had to cook, which was only when no one else was there to do it for him. (Chili overdose, Saga called it, when she came back from being away and saw all those cans in the recycling box.) Left on his own, he'd pile dishes in the sink till none remained in the cupboard. Pansy had scolded him for assuming that "some female" would come along and wash them, but Saga defended him. He was seventy-five years old. If men his age could cook and clean, they were gay or they were chefs.

When Aunt Liz had ruled over the kitchen, she kept a radio on, a neverending backdrop of NPR, even when others were there to keep her company. If you stayed for long in the house, it began to feel like a stream that flowed beyond some unseen window, a stream of news delivered with accuracy and taste (Cory Flintoff's pious voice had never deserted Saga); of book reviews, bluegrass, Bach, and curious jokes about Scandinavian people; of "all things considered"—or at least all appropriate and dignified things. When Saga moved in, she found this patchwork of information, especially the news in the morning, its words words *words,* an assault on her tender senses, but she did not feel she had the right to complain. One morning, when Uncle Marsden saw her turn the volume down, he walked across the room and pulled out the plug. "You know what?" he said. "I loved my wife dearly, but this, I never liked this. Who wants to start the day with shootings, lootings, and stock market plunges?" To Saga's quiet delight, that was the end of radio in the house; soon after, they decided to do away with the TV as well. They agreed that nothing was lovelier, more soothing and peaceful, than to hear the ocean in the distance, to gauge the state of their own modest world by the changing rhythms of wind and water rather than by the voices of reporters, even if they did sound like heroes from leather-bound novels.

The morning of Michael's ridicule, Saga heard Uncle Marsden argue that her presence kept him from turning too far inward, possibly losing his marbles—and he had always liked her. He would never, he said, take in a "student boarder," as Michael had suggested. What a preposterous idea. "And aren't you afraid that said individual would hang around till I became senile and then dupe me into leaving everything I owned to him or her, not you? Some small-time Basia Johnson? Say, why don't I let a room to a comely buxom blonde from my department who can tend my garden *and* my doddering but still intact libido, then marry me on the sly and sell this place to a developer when I croak? White elephants like this make fabulous upscale condos, you know. Just have a look at what those sharks from Hartford are threatening to do down the beach!"

Saga loved it when Uncle Marsden stood up to his children like that. It always silenced them. She hoped he would live to be a hundred. She fed him lots of salads and green vegetables and slipped tofu into his soups; gratefully, he ate what was put before him. For her absences, she stocked up on cans of organic chili and bacon made of free-range turkey. All he asked was to have a big rare steak and a banana split every Friday night, the night he "went to town." Literally speaking, he almost never went to town, except to give an occasional lecture. Mostly he stayed right there: reading, gardening, poking about in his collection of mosses, fixing all the things in the house that, as if in a relay, were constantly busting, one right after another.

She typed for him, too. Though he didn't have to—at least, not to keep his title at Yale—he still published articles in scholarly horticulture journals. He knew a lot about intimate relationships between plants and dirt and snails. People in the neighborhood referred to him as the Famous Snail Guy or sometimes the Famous Salad Guy, because a long time ago he had made some discovery that revolutionized the productivity of lettuce growers, repelling snails and other pests without the use of dangerous chemicals.

Saga had no trouble reading her uncle's prehistoric cursive; it looked so much like her mother's had looked, the siblings having been taught by the same lone teacher in the one-room schoolhouse back in rural Wisconsin. So she'd take his handwritten yellow pages and type them up. This took longer for her than it once would have, since she was still relearning the layout of the keyboard and sometimes had to hunt for letters one by one. But Uncle Marsden had never known how to type, and now that he was semi-retired, he shared his New Haven secretary with, as he put it, the "faculty sproutlings."

It was Uncle Marsden's idea that she make labels, just like the ones she'd made in the kitchen, to put on all the drawers and pigeonholes of the captain's desk he used like a miniature warehouse. It would help them both, he said.

Well, last weekend Michael had shown up with his wife, Denise, and you didn't need the dumbwaiter or the servants' stairway to hear his bellowing through the entire house. "Jesus H. Christ, this piece is Federal, Dad! You let her put these labels on the wood? They'll rip off the original varnish. Jesus!"

"And whose desk is it, Michael? Is it mine, or is it already yours?" she'd heard Uncle Marsden calmly reply.

"Don't you give a damn about anything? This desk isn't 'yours.' It's been passed down through the family and happens merely to be *in your care* at this moment in time!"

"Yes, and it's your hard luck, young man, if my 'care' happens not to be museum-quality. I am not a curator at the Frick. If the furnishings in this house make you lose sleep at night, then it's hardly worth—"

Michael groaned. "Oh Dad, please don't start with the yard sale threats. That may have worked on Mom, but it won't work on me. Stop covering up for her! We have to find a *real life* for her—I'm talking about what's good for Saga. You think you're protecting her, but you're not. You're only postponing the hard facts of reality here. I never agreed with you when—"

Uncle Marsden cleared his throat loudly. "So! So let me see, what's good for Saga is to respect the varnish on the furniture?"

Michael uttered a noise of strangled frustration, and Denise said, "Calm down, sweetie. You had a very stressful day."

Michael had an all-around very stressful *life*, as far as Saga could tell, and only by choice. He was some kind of money trader in the city, and when he wasn't arguing with his father, he was on the phone reciting numbers. His wife wanted babies—everyone could see that from the way she looked at the visiting grandchildren who ran in and out of Commodore Perry's house across the street all summer long—and Saga suspected there was some kind of tension for Michael there, too. She could feel it in the air around that couple when they were together, just the way you could feel fear or shame or rage in the air around a dog. None of Saga's cousins had children; Frida and Pansy weren't even married, though they were both past thirty. Saga knew they weren't happy about this, either. Uncle Marsden, on the other hand, seemed oblivious; he loved and tended his plants. At his age, that was nurture enough. He'd had his children late, he told Saga, and never assumed that grandchildren were part of his life package. Nor would he pry into what he considered his children's private lives. Saga wouldn't have contradicted him there, but sometimes she got the feeling that Pansy and Frida felt neglected by their father, that they *wished* he would pry. She'd seen them trade pointed looks at the dinner table when Uncle Marsden did not pursue certain topics they brought up on their own.

While Michael had been in the study that previous weekend, having his outburst, Saga had been in the kitchen, peeling onions for dinner. Quietly, she'd gone to the mudroom, put on her jacket, and walked down the road toward the beach. Michael's temper was quick; if she came back in an hour, he'd behave nicely toward her, or he'd be on the phone spouting his numbers, and Denise would compliment her on the soup, and things would be . . . civil. After dinner, Frida and Pansy would get out the Scrabble board. It was a custom that went back to their teenage summers, when the three girls hung about on the porch in their wet, sandy bathing suits. Now they'd insist that Saga take a thirty-point handicap. She still liked playing, but words could be devilish: when she searched hard for one, sometimes the effort unleashed a whipcrack of too many other, unnecessary words. Say she had a V on her rack; her mind could spew forth, too raucously, top speed, *vivid, vivacious, verve, valve, vulva, Vesuvius, valorous, voracity,* words by the dozen. It was like a crowded escalator when someone who reached the bottom got off but stood still.

Or a single word would pop out in relief, on display, like a peacock fanning its tail. The word would fill her mind for a few minutes with a single color: not an unpleasant sensation but still an intrusion. V a s c u l a r . . . v i v i s e c t i o n . . . v a l e d i c t o r y . . .

On the way to the beach, she had stopped by the culvert, and that was when she had found the puppies. This wasn't the first litter she'd found there, and sometimes Saga imagined that a rumor had spread: if you had puppies or kittens you had to get rid of, this critter lady down by the beach would pick them up. Saga didn't know if she liked this idea or not, if she should be angry or relieved.

Because the fact was, if you took them to the nearest animal shelter, the one where she'd made the mistake of taking those poor wild cats she'd betrayed, they would probably be dead inside the week. It was the only shelter for miles around, so it was way overcrowded—and out here, off season, there wasn't much demand for pets, even for the most adorable puppies. That was how, talking to the one nice guy who worked at the shelter, Saga had heard about Stan and the place in Brooklyn where they kept the animals for however long it took to find them a home, where they never put an animal to sleep unless it was terribly sick or too badly injured. ("They," as it turned out, was basically Stan.)

The pups had writhed about in their cardboard box, with nothing but a dish towel for warmth. According to the calendar, it was spring, but the wind off the water in the evenings was bitter. Saga tried hard not to think about the puppies' mother, how desperate she must be to know where they'd gone.

She'd sat on the edge of the damp, cold cement and picked them up, one by one, pressing them against her belly, under her jacket, for a dose of warmth.

"Time for a little commute," she said as she slowly lifted the box. "No cause for alarm." Before heading back up the road, she had turned for a moment toward the sea. In the late afternoon light, the water was gray wrinkled with orange. Tiger water, she called it when it looked like that. Rhino water was smooth and leaden, dull as smoke. But her favorite was polar bear water, when the moon hung low and large, as if too heavy to rise very high, and scattered great radiant patches, like ice floes, across a dark blue ocean.

She'd looked all around for the moon, its sly early ghost. Not yet.

"The moon is my friend," she murmured to the puppies, something she would never have spoken aloud to another person, hadn't even told the doctors and therapists who swarmed about her for nearly a year. Or at least she didn't think she had. There was so much she would never remember and so much she would forget again and again.

She had shown the puppies to Uncle Marsden, then taken them out to the garage. There, she had lined a larger box with newspapers and raggedy bath towels, plugged in a heat lamp, and transferred the puppies into their nest of clean, pink warmth. Not a mother, not even close, but better by far than a damp cement cave. She'd fed them warm milk, from the baby bottle she kept in the pantry, then finished making her soup.

At dinner, there'd been discussion of a feud over valuable land not far up the shoreline. A condominium developer had offered a large sum of money to the widow who wanted to sell the land and move to Sarasota. Uncle Marsden's neighbors, the owners of the biggest houses, were trying to persuade the Nature Conservancy to buy the land, to keep it for the nesting birds—though really what they wanted to keep was their open view.

"Maybe you should just marry her, Dad," joked Pansy.

"Hoo *hoo*! My dear, she's a good fifteen years older than I!"

"Oh, and that's right. You have Saga after all." She smiled at Saga. "He doesn't take advantage, does he?"

Saga blushed. She decided Pansy didn't mean to embarrass her. "He takes advantage of my housekeeping abilities—such as they are."

Uncle Marsden frowned at his daughter. "Hanging about with teenagers is making you crude." Pansy counseled kids in a poor high school, one thing Saga held in her favor no matter what she said—but Uncle Marsden had hoped his children might become academics. None of them had.

"Have a sense of humor, Dad. Studies show it helps keep your arteries open."

Michael had been mostly absent from the table, making and answering phone calls. Uncle Marsden had learned to ignore his son's attachment to the phone. Saga imagined that Michael's attitude toward his clients was like that of a brain surgeon toward his patients: nothing personal, everything dire.

After loading the dishwasher, Saga had played Monopoly with Uncle Marsden, Denise, and Pansy. (Frida lived up in Boston and came down only every couple of months; Pansy lived in New Haven, an hour away, and dropped by most weekends.) She'd let them buy up all the little houses and red hotels so she could go bankrupt first and slip away to bed. Her plan had been to wake up early on Saturday morning, even before her uncle, and she had. She'd eaten a quick breakfast, called Stan, left her note, fed the puppies and cleaned them up, then smuggled them onto the train in her big plumber's bag. She'd had to stay in the city for a few days—Stan had been elusive—but the corner she had carved out for herself had made it feel almost perfectly safe.

SHE OFTEN WENT OVER THE AWAKENING, the first memories she had that came after the accident itself. It began with sounds, few and faint, like the sounds of a fish tank. She'd never had an aquarium, but her dentist did; looking at it was supposed to calm you down while you had your teeth cleaned and drilled, your cavities filled. So there in the dark, automatically, she'd thought of her dentist's office, of the brilliant fish, some blue, some striped black and yellow like waterborne bees. The burblings, watery whispers, and sighs of the machinery and tubing. But she'd known she was not at the dentist.

As her eyes adjusted to the dark, the air about her settled to a tabby gray, lit only by a glow outlining a sharp-edged form that quickly volunteered it was a door.

She was in bed, and her throat hurt, and her head hurt even more. She tried to lift it but couldn't. From her hips up, she lay on an incline (oh: a hospital bed; a *hospital*), so she was glad, at least, to be able to make out all of her body in her limited view. Something—a deeply physical reluctance . . . a drug?—kept her from testing her body, from checking its responses to her brain.

Her brain. Was it her brain that hurt, or was it her skull? Could you tell the difference? Could your skull even hurt?

"Hello?" she tried to call out, but her throat felt swollen, inflamed, and all that emerged was a rasp, like a wooden chair creaking under the weight of a very large man. The effort paved a searing pathway across the back of her head, pain like the rolling out of a brightly colored carpet. Fear rose through her, vertically, sap through a tree.

A tree . . . something about a tree. Something awful. Very bad news.

Now she saw another source of light: a window, to one side. If she tipped her head just a little to the left—this she could do if she did it slowly—she could look almost straight out the window.

And there was the moon. A warm and visible greeting, a beacon of relief. Full, unshrouded, its edges crisp. It looked like an airy wafer—what were those crackers that came in the big green tin? She stared at the moon and thought about the fact that she was breathing. Fact of breathing, fact of life. This she could control: slow down and speed up her breathing, despite the pain in her throat. She'd never really looked at the moon, never really seen how intricate the etchings on its yellowy silver surface. Bowl of a spoon in candlelight. When she'd looked a long time—*I see the moon, and the moon sees me*—a glimmering ring like a rainbow materialized at the rim. In the memory she still retained, as clear as a framed snapshot, a portrait worn in a locket, Saga stared at the moon that way for hours, and it kept her company, it kept her sane, it kept her in one piece, it kept her alive. It was proof, fact, patience, faith.

But no, she was told by a doctor sometime later, that wouldn't have been possible, because nurses checked her room frequently, at least every twenty minutes because her condition had been so severe; surely not much time had passed before the nurse found her conscious and fretful, gave her water and more of the medications designed to lighten her mind, not just her pain.

Over the week that followed the accident, even while she had been in the ICU, she had been conscious several times. This is what her mother told her the next day. But she did not remember those earlier wakings.

What she did remember, as her days in the hospital stretched into weeks, as she discovered that she would have to learn how to use her right arm and leg all over again, was the accident itself. It had been raining hard—*a whopper of a storm,* her mother's words—and Saga had been walking alone to her apartment. She carried her black umbrella, she remembered that, the big one with the wooden handle that had belonged to her dad. She watched the ground for puddles because she wasn't wearing proper boots. The rain was so noisy, the thunder frequent, and one of the cracks she heard must have been not the thunder but the bough that fell, that she could swear she remembered seeing as she dipped the umbrella aside and looked up. She was transfixed, the way you always are by something that looms unexpectedly, that seems to be aiming right for you. More sharply than the sight of that bough, she remembered the *sound* of it inside her skull, as if her consciousness were the occupant of a very small house and the bough had crashed down on its roof: a universally resounding hollow crack, a muffled gunshot. And she remembered one instant thought: *If I die, Mom will be crushed.* Because her father had died of cancer the month before.

They told her this was probably a dream she had much later, and for a while she argued with them. Then she pretended to agree. Now she no longer mentioned it to anyone, but it remained a marvel: this crystal-clear memory, like a church bell rising over the din of an entire city, over all the confusion and pain and humiliating inability to recover parts of herself that she could almost recall, that she felt sometimes she was carrying around in her pockets like lovely stones, things you can fondle but never really *own*.

"Think of your memory as very badly bruised," one of her therapists had told her early on. "Some of it will recover fully, but some of it could remain permanently numb."

That wasn't how Saga saw it. She now thought of her entire memory as a distinct and separate being, with moods and feelings, as if she'd been born into the perfect marriage and then, bingo, the marriage had crumbled into an unpredictably bumpy relationship, but one that could not be severed or traded in for another, no matter how discouraged she became.

She looked at the material world around her and sometimes thought she was making small discoveries. Riding on the train, she'd notice how highway signs were precisely the same green and white as those woven plastic lawn chairs (was that on purpose?), how she felt like a drop of water sliding fast through a long glass tube, how railroad ties were no longer made of dark motley wood but plain old concrete. But perhaps she had known and felt all these things before. At such times, she saw her brain as one of those pocket puzzles composed of numbered square tiles in a grid; the tiles had merely been mixed up like crazy, and now her work was to move them side to side, up and down, till she got them back in order.

Oh but numbers: numbers were one thing that she seemed to have lost almost completely. She knew what they were, she could count and tell time, all that; but when she looked at actual numbers—at those figures, whether on paper or on a street door or on one of those traveling headlines on the stock market channel that Michael kept on the TV during his visits—they were mostly meaningless. She knew them as words—*seven* or *two and a half* or *three thousand six hundred and seventy-four*—but as symbols on bank statements and grocery receipts, they were, except in rare eureka glimpses, little more than rows of tiny ballet dancers. Uncle Marsden had bought her a wristwatch, large and sleek, where all the numbers were represented by their names, and he made her a card—of which he had dozens printed—bearing a chart that read:

o zero   1 one   2 two   and so on. When people gave
her phone numbers, she could rewrite them as words. Laborious, but it
worked.

Words, they were more unpredictable, more fickle. At times, she
could actually sense the voids, nearly palpable, where reservoirs of
words had deserted her mind. The three years of French she had taken,
though what she had learned was no doubt elementary, had mostly fled
as well. But then, like windows into the past, there would be periods
when all of Saga's non-numerical knowledge felt harmonious, when
words, at least in her own language, came easily without falling into
torrents, when events for days on end seemed as clear and orderly as pictures in an album, when she could open the refrigerator without encoun-
tering a box of cherry tomatoes or a jar of mustard she had bought the
day before and regarding its presence there as a baffling surprise.

SHE WAITED NEARLY TWO WEEKS before she went into the city again.
She would meet Stan, she reminded herself as the train pulled into Grand
Central, and then she would stop by to see that Alan fellow, the one
who'd offered so kindly to pay for the vaccinations. (Stan, of course,
had seen the offer as suspicious.) She couldn't remember his face, but
she remembered his help and that he had given her a cup of tea. If it got
too late, she would spend the night in her secret place. It was warm
today, really warm for a change, and she had remembered to bring
her sleeping roll. She liked the open sky when it was nice out. That
night, the moon would be nearly full. She had checked the calendar.

Before leaving home, she always wrote her day's plans, step by step,
in the notebook she carried. There were things she'd forget anyway,
things she'd skip over, but later she'd know about it.

This time, as promised, Stan was where they'd agreed to meet, by the
arch in Washington Square.

"Here they are," he said, without any kind of hello. She didn't blame
him that he wasn't friendly. She no longer took it personally, since she'd
seen him with other people and this was simply how he was.

She looked at the flyers Stan had printed. "You did a nice job," she
said. "Color copies are expensive."

"Yeah, well, let's just say my butt is crapola if my division manager checks the counter on that machine. So you know where to put them up?"

"East from here over to Avenue B, come back through SoHo, then up west. Okay?" She would take most of the flyers to the veterinary clinics and the pet supply shops in those neighborhoods. Others she'd put up in cafés and college buildings that let outsiders put things up on their bulletin boards. She kept a map with every one of these places marked—though she'd never have shown it to Stan. Saga knew that Stan wasn't well liked, not personally, but people liked what he did. He didn't care one way or the other—"Life ain't no popularity contest," he'd say—but he knew it was best if other people did the footwork. He didn't have the time, and he was prone to picking arguments with people who, as he put it, deluded themselves into *thinking* they were animal lovers when an animal, to them, was little more than a fashion statement, a bed warmer, or a creature to boot around in this miserable world.

He handed her the list of vets, the places she had to go. "Think your scrambled brains can handle this?"

She didn't answer that; she knew why he had to insult her. "Can I come down and see them tonight?" she said instead.

Stan smirked. "Call around six. If I'm there, I'm there. No promises."

"I'll try you then," said Saga.

No better at good-byes than he was at hellos, Stan strode off across the park, back to the subway, to his job at the phone company.

Saga stayed on the bench for a moment to feel the sun on her head and shoulders. Sometimes she liked to imagine that if she could just sit still long enough, the sun could heal her brain the way it made leaves and flowers sprout, multiply, glow. She let herself reach up, just briefly, to feel the long furrow that remained along the top of her head, entirely hidden by her hair, which had quite indifferently grown out (speaking of growth) to cover this anatomical crisis.

She pulled her hand down and made herself look at the picture Stan had taken for the flyer. It was true; he had done a nice job. The puppies were cozied up together on the big plaid cushion in Stan's kitchen, all of them facing the camera. They looked playful and bright and would find their new homes quickly.

The flyer gave Stan's number over and over on little rip-off tabs at the bottom. When people wanted to adopt an animal, Stan took it to them, so he could see where it would live. He never let them come to his place. Saga supposed he knew how his way of living would appear to the outside world, so sometimes she still wondered, a little shamefully, about the way he'd so easily let her come over that very first time, about how naïve she had been.

Stan lived in a skinny, sinister-looking house out in Brooklyn. Though it had clearly come first, it looked as if it had been squeezed into a crevice between the two large brick buildings on either side. Because of this, it was almost constantly in shadow. But hey, as Stan had pointed out when Saga remarked on the darkness, it was a *house*. A house in New York Fucking *City*. He'd bought it at a foreclosure sale. Deal of the fucking *century*.

When she had first phoned him, last year, after getting his number from that shelter worker in Connecticut, he had given her directions to get to his place. Without worrying about her safety, or about who this man really was, she had eagerly followed those directions, carrying a small stray, a Norwich terrier, in her plumber's bag on the subway. She had already put up a notice in the post office and the grocery store and on telephone poles around Uncle Marsden's town and other towns nearby—IS THIS YOUR DOG? HE MISSES YOU!—but no one had called. When Stan agreed to take the dog, she'd told Uncle Marsden she was going to a museum in the city.

Stan worked, so she'd had to wait until the evening to see him. To kill time, she had taken the dog to Central Park, walking him past the back of the Metropolitan Museum, so that what she had told Uncle Marsden became almost the truth.

Setting foot inside Stan's house had been a shock. Saga was almost obtusely brave (that was how Uncle Marsden put it once when he lost his temper), but for a moment even she had second thoughts about her safety. At a glance, the place was a nest of bedlam and grime, cats and dogs everywhere, in frayed, chewed-up baskets, on tattered armchairs, in open metal dog crates lined up against a wall where you'd expect to find a sofa. And this guy Stan, in his buttoned-to-the-neck white shirt (gray at the cuffs) and shiny black pants, had a kind of leering undertaker quality. He had this long, thin, pale face (somewhat like the façade of his house), spiky brown hair, and huge, intense blue eyes that looked a little creepy when he smiled, because his smile was faintly mean. Or maybe, to be fair, this effect was just because of his jumbled, slightly pointy teeth. When he closed the door behind Saga, the look he gave her was the look you might imagine on the face of the old woman in the forest who takes in Hansel and Gretel: Now *here's* a tasty meal!

Stan was obnoxious, you couldn't get around that, yet Saga decided that maybe he was just one of those people cursed with a face that put you off no matter what he was thinking. The first thing he said that night was "Where is he? Let's see him." Rude, but this was business.

He'd taken the dog from Saga's bag and simply held him close for a few minutes, until the dog stopped shivering. Then he'd examined him, all over but gently—looking for fleas and rashes, Saga figured. Stroking the dog's belly, Stan muttered, "Wormy as hell, poor guy."

While he made his inspection, Saga forced herself to look around. The furniture was coated with gray fur, the windows so filthy the panes had no shine. No bookcases, no rugs, few pictures on the walls. But she also noticed that the fifteen animals she could count looked clean and healthy. Two larger dogs had come over to Stan and tried to jump up to check out the terrier; Stan lifted a knee, ordered them down, and they obeyed. He used a calm voice. She liked that.

Finally, still carrying the dog, Stan led Saga upstairs. He did not invite her to follow him, but he didn't tell her not to. They went into a small room, and he shut the door behind them. Newspapers covered the floor, and except for a food bowl, a water bowl, and a cushion, the room was empty. (The "room," Saga noted, was smaller than the pantry at Uncle Marsden's.)

The terrier ran straight to the water.

"He has to stay in here alone?" said Saga.

"He has to be quarantined—obviously—till I can get him to the vet."

Well, of course, thought Saga. She sat on the floor by the cushion and waited for the dog to stop drinking.

"So what kind of a name is Saga?" Stan said.

"It's one of those childhood names that just sticks. I'm Emily, really. But nobody calls me that." Nobody other than her doctors.

"Like you told big lies—or what?"

"Something like that." She was glad she'd found Stan, because of what he did, but she didn't feel much like talking to him. She wondered if she should say good-bye now and leave, if despite his own rough manners he'd find *her* rude.

He crossed his bony arms and, for a moment, watched Saga petting the dog. He gave her another unnerving smile. "Want a beer, Saga? Seeing as you came all this way." He opened the door. "He'll get along fine. I watch over everybody here. No-brainer, it ain't about money or fame."

So she followed him down to the kitchen. Stan washed his hands at the sink and made sure Saga did the same. "Sit," he said in a neutral voice as he went to the refrigerator. The counters were covered with stacks of papers and magazines. The only place to sit was at a table taken up almost entirely by a cage in which a white rabbit—fat, immaculate, sleepy-looking—chewed mechanically on a turnip, devouring it end to end. While Stan's back was turned, Saga sneaked a finger between the bars and stroked the rabbit's shoulder. The rabbit turned its rosy eyes toward her and pushed its nose against her finger. "Hi," she whispered, putting her face close to the cage.

"Kindergarten bunny," said Stan, startling Saga. "Did his time with several rounds of the poky little monsters and then, all because one of 'em one year had an allergy, was about to be shipped off to the torture labs of Monte Fucking Fiore." As he talked, a dog slipped through a flap in a door that must have led to a backyard. (Saga imagined a narrow patch of dirt, a space no less dreary than the space indoors.) "So, Budweiser do? That's it around this watering hole."

Since the accident, Saga hardly ever drank alcohol, but she accepted the beer because she thought it might make her less nervous. She asked Stan how he'd started taking in animals.

"When I learned, not a minute too soon, that taking in people— wives, girlfriends, moochers, assholes, whoever—is a miserable waste of time."

Stan must have been about fifty. Was he implying he'd had a wife, even more than one? Saga wondered who would have married the guy. She wondered if he had children; she hoped not. But then he told her about the group of people he'd organized to look out for strays, rescue abused animals, take calls in the middle of the night if someone found an animal hit by a car. They posted leaflets all over the city to broadcast their services. "That so-called Animal Welfare Society up in Manhattan? 'Society'? More like charnel house," said Stan. "Penitentiary. We're like the Guardian Angels of the animal world. And it ain't a world of charm and style, let me tell you. Some people get us, some don't. They don't? Well, to put it politely, tough excrement." He told her about cockfighting, dogfighting, satanic sacrifice. Someone in the group had a big back-yard on Staten Island; he took in the roosters and goats. Snakes, lizards, and ferrets went to a vet who lived on Long Island, birds to a flutist from the Metropolitan Opera who had a soundproofed loft on Liberty Street. "Like they say, it takes all kinds."

Stan opened a kitchen drawer and pulled out a sheaf of lime-green papers. "Here. Take some to fancy-ass Connecticut. Can't hurt. Maybe get us some bleeding-heart patrons from the retriever set." Saga took the leaflets. They read:

We are the **TRUE PROTECTORS** of the urban animal kingdom.

We look after, heal, and give shelter to: **DOGS, CATS, PARROTS, BIRDS, PIGEONS, LIZARDS, TURTLES, IGUANAS, SNAKES, MONKEYS, RABBITS, GUINEA PIGS, GERBILS** . . . everything except rats from the subways and mice from your stove.

We have **ADOPTION SERVICES** for pets of all kinds. We know **THE BEST VETS** all around the city and beyond.

WE REFER FOR LOW-COST SPAY AND NEUTER—DO IT NOW!! HELP US HELP THE ANIMALS. CALL US ANYTIME. WE NEED VOLUNTEERS. WE ARE THE ONLY TRUE PROTECTORS!

There were no pictures, no decorative borders. It looked serious, political. Like a . . . Saga groped for the word. It was a red word. If she'd told Stan what she was thinking, he would probably have said, "No-brainer, honey."

All at once she felt envious of Stan, never mind his grubby little house. She was sorry that she didn't live in the city (where people could be odd without explanation), that she couldn't be a part of his group, that she wasn't quite independent enough to make these choices. Stan said the group met every Tuesday night at a falafel joint around the cor-ner. (What was falafel? Had she ever known?) "Come if you like," he said, without encouragement.

Manifesto—that was the word, the red word she'd been searching for, she realized as she watched the bunny lick its paws.

She had another beer. (Why hadn't she left?) She noticed that Stan had already drunk four or five. She said she had to go, but could they check on the terrier first? Up in the quarantine room, they found the little dog fast asleep on the cushion in the corner. "Happy?" asked Stan as he closed the door.

"Who's that?" said Saga as they stood in the hallway. From the floor above, she heard voices. As she listened, the voices turned to music.

"Radio. Jazz and blues tonight," said Stan.

Saga must have looked as if she expected more, because he laughed and shook his head. "All right, Nosy Parker. I have a cat of my own who likes the radio. She gets my bedroom to herself, because she doesn't get along with the guests. She's this Siamese vixen that nobody else would take because she clawed nearly everyone who met her. Well, I discovered it's true after all, that thing about music and the savage beast. Wanna meet the little terror?"

Saga looked at her watch. With a pang of anxiety, she noticed that it was already too late to catch the last train to Connecticut. "Can I use your phone?"

"Sure. But come meet Sing Sing. I promise not to let her maul you."

The beer had softened Stan, or maybe it had softened Saga toward him. She followed him up a staircase that tilted badly toward the wall. The banister was chipped in places, exposing paint in four or five different colors. You had to hold on or you'd fall to the side.

Stan got to the top first and turned to see her moving cautiously, slowly. "Great sobriety test, my stairs. And honey, looks like you might just *flunk*."

"I don't have my full equilibrium," she said defensively—though she had to admit that two beers had affected her far more than she would have guessed.

"Hey, who does?" said Stan as he opened one of two doors at the top of the stairs. Inside was a room that Saga had imagined (or hoped) would be a crisp, clean oasis of domesticity, another likable surprise about this sandpaper man. But no. The first thing she saw was a movie poster—*The Maltese Falcon*—tacked to the wall. Below it, a gooseneck lamp cast a cone of light onto a hastily made bed, navy blue sheets without a blanket or quilt. At the foot of the bed cowered a Siamese cat with shredded ears and a stump for a tail.

The cat began to whine at that eerie pitch unique to feline distress. On the radio, a lady singer with a big voice happened to be yowling as well.

Stan turned the radio down and then swept the cat up in his arms, as if receiving a low pass in a football game. "Now now, none of that, you she-devil!" he said between clenched teeth. To Saga's alarm, he tossed the cat up toward the ceiling, so that she flipped over in midair, then caught her with ease. He thumped her rhythmically on her backside several times and imitated her earlier moans. "Yeeeaaah-oooo, eeeaaah-ooooooooo!" he moaned. When he stopped, the cat was purring, kneading her paws on the sleeve of his shirt.

"See?" said Stan. "I've just got a way with the dames." He pointed to a phone on a table and motioned for Saga to sit on the edge of the bed. Picking up the receiver, Saga had to be careful not to topple a tower of books (science-fiction novels), three bottles holding various amounts of beer, and a glass of cloudy liquid with a dusty film on top.

"Yuck," she said quietly. The receiver was sticky.

"Oh chill," said Stan. "Everyone else you know has a maid. I don't squander my money like that. Other ways, but not that way."

Uncle Marsden was out at a lecture that night, she remembered with relief when she got the answering machine. "I missed the last train, so I'm staying with a friend," she said. "I'll see you tomorrow afternoon."

"Ho *ho*," said Stan. "Would I be that lucky friend?"

"Of course not," said Saga, though she was no longer in touch with anyone in the city and did not know yet what she would do—probably sleep on a bench in Grand Central Station. (Could you even do that anymore, since the fancy renovations? What if you couldn't?)

And right then, just like that, Stan pulled her to him and kissed her—not in a forceful or threatening way, but surely and calmly, as if there wasn't a chance in the world she'd refuse his advances.

At first she did, not shouting but pushing at his chest. She was angry and shocked, not afraid. How could someone who took care of helpless creatures be a menace? "Stop," she managed to say, though he wasn't letting go of her body.

"Oh really?" He was smiling his unpleasant smile, but then he was running his lips around her ear—the ear on her good side, the sensitive one.

"Really," she said. "I do not know you!"

"Oh please let's dispense with knowing, Story Girl," he said in a whispery voice against her neck. "Knowing is so . . . cumbersome."

Cumbersome. She saw something like a large puffy white-blue bank of clouds. And in the opportunity of silence that opened as she contemplated her picture of this word, Stan slid a hand under her shirt and beneath the elastic band of her bra, slipping it up past her breasts.

He'd pushed her back—without resistance, really—against the pillows, which smelled musty and earthen. The ceiling that Saga could see beyond his head was textured, patterned in curlicued squares. It was light blue, just like her vision of *cumbersome.* Odd coincidence, she couldn't help thinking.

So almost by accident she paused, letting him caress one breast and kiss her mouth, and then she found herself wondering merely if she could get pregnant this time of the month. She had a sudden elusive memory of the last time she had wondered such a thing . . . and here was David's unwelcome face.

It was so very long ago, or it seemed so long ago, that she had last been held like this. (*Is it all right?* whispered David's face.) Because she was curious, even eager, to remember how it felt, or perhaps because she wanted so badly to banish David, she let Stan continue. She could feel his hard penis like an exclamation point right up against her thigh. He wasn't rushing it. Reaching for common sense, she pushed at his chest again. "No, really. Stop."

Now he was on top of her, and a part of her knew she should fight, but she didn't. Stan pulled himself up from the waist to look her in the eye. He was panting slightly as he said, "You take a while to make up your mind, Story Girl. I don't think that's really fair in a situation like this, do you?" And he resumed kissing her.

His mouth tasted like beer—as hers did, too, no doubt—but it wasn't a bad taste. It was one of those tastes that called to her from her past, her not-too-distant yet light-years-away prehistory, when she had assumed so many things (for instance, that it was stupid to go to a strange man's house without anyone even knowing where you'd gone). But how senseless and silly so many of those assumptions had become in hindsight. Why not this one, too? That he was essentially raping her, or at least taking advantage of her.

The word *rape*—a very dark purple, strangely royal—sent a tangible chill through her body, like a halting of her blood. But this did not feel like what she imagined rape to feel like. She liked the warmth of his body, and she liked the softness of his mouth.

When she put her arms around his narrow shoulders and began to kiss him back, he murmured his approval. The radio still played, though more quietly than when they'd come upstairs, and Saga was vaguely aware that the cat was still on the bed, near their feet, no longer objecting to her presence. *Tain't nobody's business if I do,* sang a woman in a sassy, girlish voice.

"You're a sexy lady, know that?" Stan whispered as he unzipped her pants.

She had no answer; she kept her eyes closed and sank into the music. His naked penis, when she felt it against her bare skin, was a shock, mostly for the desire it beckoned from Saga's marrow.

"So touch me, Story Girl," he said.

Still she said nothing and kept her eyes closed. She felt Stan's pubic hair, like a prickly sea creature, move in circles on her thigh. Then, another shock, she felt his fingers. She tried to pull away, but she knew her resistance was only halfhearted. Away to the side, on the floor, she caught sight of her pants.

"Oh no," he said gently. "Oh no. You're liking it, you are. I can tell."

And he was right, she *was,* in a strange way that denied her surroundings, the man's disturbing smile, the smells of this bed. It was as if only the music and her body existed. His body—that was less real.

When he raised himself slightly away from her again, she opened her eyes only long enough to see that he was taking a condom out of a drawer in the table that held the books and the phone. She closed her eyes again and let herself sink further down, or come more fully to the surface, she wasn't sure which. Because he was so thin, his body wasn't heavy, and when he entered her, the harshness was only brief. Right away he moved slowly, smoothly, and she knew without looking that he was *paying attention* to her, to what her body wanted, all on its own, without any heed to her mind, and she felt herself yield.

And then before her inner eye, a tide of words leaped high and free, a chaotic joy like frothing rapids: *truncate, adjudicate, fornicate, frivolous, rivulet, violet, oriole, orifice, conifer, aquifer, allegiance, alacrity . . .* all the words this time not a crowding but a heavenly chain, an ostrich fan, a vision as much as an orgasm, a release of something deep in the core of her altered brain, words she thought she'd lost for good. It nearly deafened her (but not quite) to the other, more alarming wave— the groaning and happy cursing that came from Stan.

"Oh *shit,* Story Girl," he said as he pulled away and collapsed face-down beside her, one arm across her waist. Before falling asleep (quick as you'd fall from a ledge), he reached over and turned off the radio.

The lamp, however, still cast its oval of tawdry light, straight down on Stan's head, on his thinning dust-colored hair. And from a corner of the room, the cat's eyes glowed accusingly at Saga. Together, the silence and the illuminated squalor filled Saga with shame and terror—terror at herself and at what she had allowed (not even passively) to happen.

As she crept down the two flights of stairs, clutching the banister to keep from falling, hoping the dogs wouldn't bark and wake Stan, Saga couldn't help thinking of Uncle Marsden, of how much he worried when she went off on her own, of how truthfully she'd always told him there was nothing to worry about; after all, she was not a *child.* In that year after the accident, during all those therapy sessions and walking lessons and silly games with balls, she'd often thought of how people think they might wish for a second childhood. Well, she was here to tell them that no, that was nothing to wish for!

She'd been glad, once she found her way back to Uncle Marsden's (this time reassuring him falsely), that Stan did not know how to reach her. She had hoped never to see him again. But then other animals came her way, and within two months she had to call him. "Well well well, if it isn't Story Girl," he said, but he did not mention what had gone on between them. Almost as soon as she entered his house, however, he'd begun to put his hands all over her body. She made the mistake of thinking that if she told him what had happened to her—explaining how, because of the accident, she made mistakes in judgment sometimes—he might sympathize a little.

He laughed. He said, "Right, so you're a sicko *and* a slut. Next sob story? Hey, just kidding." He winked meanly. But he had never touched her again, never even tried.

"I AM EMILY ALMA TALAMINI. On my birth certificate."

"I am twenty-eight."

"I live in West Hartford. I live with David Hayward. David, the guy you just sent out to wait in the hall."

"This is . . . is this 1996?"

These were some of the answers she gave, whispered because her throat still hurt, the day after her "real" waking up, the one she could remember. A young male doctor nodded and took notes, but it was the nurse who said, "This is wonderful. This is such good news, Emily. Now don't try to move too much, okay?"

When she asked why, the nurse said softly, "Because some of you isn't quite moving yet. But it will, with some help. We just don't want you to panic."

Saga realized then that the right side of her face felt swollen or numb, as if it had fallen asleep. She felt alarm when the nurse reached out to dab at that side of her mouth; was she drooling?

Oh God, I'm a vegetable, Saga thought. David is going to leave me.

And he did—but not before staying long enough that she'd come to believe he wouldn't. Through the first month of therapy, after many long weeks in the hospital, he came for lunch every day and sometimes took an afternoon off to sit on the sidelines while she walked laps or worked her fingers around a tennis ball or practiced holding pencils and forks. She stayed at her mother's house so she wouldn't have to struggle up the two flights of stairs to the apartment she shared with David; often he drove her back after therapy and stayed for dinner. Sometimes Saga's mother went out, to give them time alone. It was hard for Saga to go to restaurants; she hated being stared at. She had been back to their place only once, to point out what clothes and other items David should pack. He had carried her up the stairs, like a bride, and back down again.

The David of her memory was mostly kind—she could remember arguments, though nothing ferocious or mean—but the new David was emphatically gentle and patient. Before long, this invalid treatment felt claustrophobic and creepy. Everybody around her hovered, and sometimes she had the strange feeling that there was something else they kept waiting for her to remember. The person she thought of as her reading therapist said more than once, "If new memories crop up, even suspicions you might have, let's be sure we talk about them. Okay?" Saga thought of it as the knee-jerk okay: the tendency of her caretakers, along with the rest of the world, to finish nearly all their statements to her with a little "okay?" as if she were two years old and might have a tantrum at the slightest change of plan.

One day when they were eating lunch and David leaped to retrieve the fork she'd dropped, Saga joked, "Stop being so nice all the time, would you? I want a boyfriend, not a Moonie or a guide dog."

David looked hurt. "But nice is what you need, honey. You need—you deserve a lot of nice."

"I don't mean to be ungrateful, but normal is what I need. *Truckloads* of normal. If that's possible."

He smiled nervously, silent at first, as if to imply that it wasn't possible.

"When you're ready, we'll get a new place," he said. "I want a place with miles of books around all the walls. Maybe we could rent a little house out near the beach. I wouldn't mind the commute. How about that for a dose of normal?" A tiny version of Uncle Marsden's house: that had always been Saga's fantasy. Though the part about the books made her sad. David was a librarian, so naturally he'd want that, but he didn't seem to think about Saga, for whom books had become a chore—surmountable, getting easier, but a challenge rather than a refuge, a reminder of how the most ordinary things were no longer that, how in a way nothing was.

It was a book that gave him away. Having missed a few recent lunches, he brought Saga a box of lavish takeout from a French bistro—roast chicken, green beans, and tiny red potatoes. A Styrofoam cup of chocolate mousse for dessert. He'd gone to the bathroom after setting the food on a table. Ravenous, Saga started in on the chicken. It needed salt. Thinking that there might be packets of salt in the paper bag David had stuffed in his satchel, she fished it out.

Under the crumpled bag, which contained no salt, she saw two books: a biography of Truman Capote and a slim volume called *How, Voyager? A Practical Primer for Moving Abroad.*

Abroad: a bold orange word, like a fat painted line down the center of a street, stretching out of sight.

"Who's moving abroad?" Saga asked when David came back.

He looked at her blankly, and then he started to giggle.

"Someone who's a fool?" she said.

Not even a smile remained on his face. "Maybe," he said quietly. "I'm sorry I didn't mention it before. I didn't want to upset you. Though I was thinking you could come if . . ."

"Where? Come where?"

"Zimbabwe. . . . They need someone to train librarians. I saw the ad in a journal, and just to see if I could ever get . . . I didn't think I'd really . . ." He added desperately, "I haven't decided."

"Yes you have," she said quickly, trying hard to keep spite from her voice. "It's the decision you have to make, isn't it? How in the world would I come to Zimbabwe when I can't even get up the stairs to our apartment!"

He had looked stunned, as if she were the one with the bad news, and she said, "I understand," because she was just too tired to say much else. And it was true. Who *wouldn't* understand?

"You let him off the hook!" cried Saga's mother when she heard the story. She was enraged at David and refused to speak with him at all the two or three times he called before he left. "What a coward. What a traitor. What a *cad*," she would mutter. Saga thought that, objectively, her mother was overreacting; these days, people lived together all the time and then split up, over much less than this. But her mother was from a generation that hadn't done it that way; and perhaps she was secretly most upset because David's departure left her alone with her daughter's plight. Perhaps, Saga sometimes reflected, her mother had already sensed that she would not be around much longer to care for her daughter. In any case, how could she have been foolish enough to think that David would stick around with a woman who just might become a permanent cripple and certainly wouldn't ever again be completely "right" in the head, completely the woman he had known and lived with? Maybe it was true that people never changed, not voluntarily— but they could, Saga knew now, become altered. Changed from without if not from within.

David told Saga he would write, and he did send three letters—his brief persistence almost valiant, considering that she sent not a word in reply. Over was over, that was one thing she'd always been blessed with knowing.

Still, when Saga heard about (and, in rehab, witnessed) the ordeals of all the other patients who had taken a blow to the brain yet managed to survive, she wished that she could be one of those who'd lost a solid chunk of time from the past rather than bits and pieces of her ongoing life; her memory had come to resemble Swiss cheese. How much better, and more convenient, if she had just lost a definable wedge from that wheel of cheese, just the two and a half years in which she had come to know and love, and then live with, David.

~⁀∽

LUCKY THING HE'D WRITTEN DOWN his name and address. On this street, so many buildings looked alike—dark red brick, with steep stairs and big shaggy trees out front, rug-size gardens tucked behind black iron railings—and she couldn't quite remember which one it had been. But here was the buzzer: *Glazier, 1R.* She rang a third and last time. Well, it was silly not to have called ahead.

She sat on the top step and set her knapsack and the flowerpot beside her. It was late afternoon, the sun still fairly high in the sky now that the clocks had skipped ahead. She had two hours to wait till she could call Stan. Through an open window across the street, a trumpet played a jazz song that sounded familiar. That was her life: so much felt familiar yet fuzzy, just out of reach. Could Saga have learned to play an instrument now? There was a neglected grand piano in Uncle Marsden's study; Aunt Liz had been the musical one. The children would crowd on the bench beside her and sing along while her hands romped through folk songs out of a green book used so often that many of its pages were held in with layers of jaundiced tape.

A piano player. Imagine being a piano player. All those zillions of notes, like daisy chains, garlands and garlands all wound through your head. Even in Saga's former life, her brain could not have managed that, no way.

She unzipped a pocket on her knapsack, took out her notebook and a plastic bag of oatmeal cookies. She ate two while she looked at her list. She could go by the veterinary clinic where she'd taken the puppies; she should thank the vet, too, though she hadn't brought him a present. If she did something like that, Stan would probably yell at her. He liked things done his way. But she could say thank you. He couldn't object to that.

She took one of the notices about the puppies and wrote a note to Alan Glazier on the back, telling him she would come by the next morning. She taped it to the bottom of the intercom box. Then she took out her notebook and, under THURSDAY MORNING, wrote, "Visit Alan Glazier, Thirty Five Bank St." As she walked down the steps, the sun dipped below the roofline of the buildings across the street. The quick, surprising chill of evening rippled through the air.

Saga was slightly relieved to find the veterinary clinic closed. She started back east, in the direction of the subway she would take, and found herself, after turning a corner, once again on Alan Glazier's block. She'd come the opposite way this time, and she saw something new: a tiny shop at the bottom of a very skinny house. A bookshop.

A string of bells jangled on the back of the door and, like a cuckoo springing from a clock on the hour, a man's head protruded from behind a bookcase. "Hello," he said quietly. "Lovely day, isn't it?"

"Hello, yes it is," said Saga.

"Please let me know if I can help you." The man had a pleasant accent of some British variety (like the jazz tune, familiar yet fuzzy). He crossed the shop with an armload of books and went about his work as if he were all by himself. Except for Saga, he was.

Whenever she entered a shop, Saga was almost always happy to be ignored. Relaxing now, she looked around. On a wall toward the front of the shop hung several large, stylish pictures of birds (Audubon; this one she knew without effort, as he was a favorite of Uncle Marsden's, two of his birds in the dining room). The most colorful one showed green and yellow parakeets. She looked them over closely. They were gorgeous.

All of a sudden, she heard a loud squawk. "Oh!" she exclaimed.

At the back of the shop, a door stood open to a garden. Through it Saga saw an armchair, on the back of the armchair a big red parrot.

"Oh my. Is that your bird?"

"She's called Felicity, and no, I am hers." The man with the accent walked through the door ahead of Saga and held out his arm. "Had your spot of sun?" he said to the parrot. She jumped right on and sidestepped rapidly up his sleeve, coming to rest on his shoulder. She leaned forward, like a bird dog, pointing toward Saga with her beak, and squawked again. The tone (if birds could have a tone!) was imperious, as if she were saying "You there!," about to give a command.

"I'd call her Marie Antoinette. Or Sheba. She seems like a queen," said Saga. "Can I touch her?"

"Scratch her just here." He scratched Felicity behind one of her downy, unbelievably scarlet cheeks. To Saga's delight, the bird allowed her to do the same.

"Who could look at books with you here?" Saga said to Felicity.

Felicity accepted her affection without comment.

"It's a trade-off," said the man. "She's an attraction but also a distraction. Some people come by just to see her—after a while they feel guilty enough to buy a book or two. She's not the most efficient marketing tool, but she gives us a certain reputation. People walk in and say, 'Oh so *this* is the place with the parrot.' " He stood still for a few minutes while Saga stroked the bird on his shoulder.

"You're lucky."

"I am indeed," the man said. He did not realize that Saga had been talking to the bird. What a life she must have, this beautiful creature. Pampered, unthreatened, nothing to do but entertain and be entertained.

"Maybe you could teach her to say, 'Spend a little money!' " said Saga.

The man laughed. "A clever student—that's one thing she's not."

"Can she fly?"

"Yes."

"She doesn't fly away?" Saga looked at the sky.

"She never has. I'm not sure why."

"Maybe this is all she knows?"

"Oh, but she strikes me as the kind of lass who leaps before she looks." The man put a hand up to his shoulder; the bird stepped on.

Lass. Saga turned away to hide her smile. How like a fairy tale, that word. Rapunzel. A tall tower by a deep emerald lake. A dark green word, *lass.*

As she turned, she saw the bookcase beside the armchair—right out there in the garden! It was filled with paperback books that looked as if they'd been read about a hundred times each. She saw *Pride and Prejudice,* she saw *Middlemarch* and *The Quiet American.* Titles she had seen forever on the shelves in Uncle Marsden's house.

"What if it rains when you're not looking?"

"These are the books everyone likes to read again and again, books you can lose because they'll reappear the minute you turn your back. They replace themselves," he said. Saga pictured this man with the dashing accent as the rescuer of Rapunzel. It wasn't outrageous in the least. He was handsome enough, though neither tall nor dark. His skin and hair were faintly golden, or they had been once upon a time, and his hands were long and slim like the hands of a prince. Piano hands, Aunt Liz would have said. He looked to be several years older than Saga, maybe not too much older than Michael.

"Can I sit here?" she asked.

"Last I knew," said the bird prince, "that's what chairs were for."

"I don't know any bookstores with chairs in gardens," she said. "Or any gardens with bookcases." She would have to tell Uncle Marsden about this place.

"So now you do. Make yourself at home." He left her alone then, carrying his glorious bird back into the shop. He needs a crown, thought Saga as she watched him go. He wouldn't look the least bit silly. Even his posture was regal. She leaned back in the chair and looked straight up. Branches waved calmly; a few thin clouds flowed along like blossoms fallen in a stream. She would have to ask the bird prince for a card, to make sure she could find her way back. She reached toward the bookcase and took out a pink book with a water-stained jacket, poems by E. E. Cummings. She opened the book and let her eyes alight on random lines: *I'd rather learn from one bird how to sing / than teach ten thousand stars how not to dance.* She read the entire poem, but then that sad leaden feeling descended, the reminder that reading was a labor, not a reflex, something she had to do with a conscious will, as if she were eight all over again. She remembered enough to be certain she'd never read anything terribly difficult, but she had been a fast reader. She would be again, Uncle Marsden assured her. Uncle Marsden knew a great deal, but the rest he bluffed. He'd never say he didn't know. That was his biggest flaw.

She closed the book. She did not want to leave, but just the thought of reading disturbed her right now. She looked around and saw, at the edge of the garden, a row of stone planters—old ones coated with moss. Beside them stood several plastic pots containing geraniums and orange pansies, waiting to be planted. Red with orange: odd but nice.

Saga went to the door of the shop. "Excuse me?" The interior now seemed murky and obscure, her eyes were so accustomed to the sun.

"Yes?" The bird prince appeared from behind a row of shelves, just as he had when she'd come into the shop.

She pointed back at the flowers. "Do you need these planted? I could do that for you . . ." The bird prince approached her, smiling, but he looked puzzled. "I have this time to kill," she said. "I'd like to."

He came out into the sun. "That's jolly kind of you. All right then." He went back into the shop and emerged with a pair of gritty work gloves, a trowel, and a plastic container. "Bonemeal."

"I know about bonemeal from my uncle," she said. "He says it's not good outside because it attracts rodents." Suddenly, she worried that she would sound like a lunatic to this stranger, though his kind expression did not change. "My uncle's a professor of horticulture at Yale." The truth was, people always relaxed when she mentioned Yale.

"Fortunate fellow, to have a knack with plants," said the bird prince. "I have to choose the easy ones, the ones nobody can kill. So thank you." He took back the bonemeal. "I tell you what. Why don't you choose a book when you leave? Any book." He was about to go in but turned again. "What's your name?"

"Emily." Somehow, with this man, she felt self-conscious about the name she used everywhere else. She knew he would have asked about it—he was that kind of attentive—and she wanted to be alone with the plants and the parrot and the waving trees. He would leave her alone, she figured, only if he thought she was perfectly normal.

He shook her hand. "I'm Fenno," he said, and then, of course, hearing his odd name, she wished that she had told him hers. He was the sort of person who (unlike Stan) you wanted to find a connection with, something to keep his interest or earn his respect. Not because it looked like a hard thing to do; in fact, because it looked so easy.

STAN LET HER GO TO BROOKLYN and visit the puppies. In just a week, they'd grown so much bigger. It was becoming obvious they were part wirehaired something, part something with short legs and maybe something with tall pointed ears. They were white, with brindled spots, their coats (thanks to Stan's care) clean and shiny as party gowns. Stan fussed with papers at the kitchen table, sighing loudly, while Saga sat and played with the puppies on the floor. "I'm only letting you do this because they need the socialization," he said when she lay on her back so the puppies could climb across her breasts and lick her face.

"Thank you," she said. "I appreciate it."

"Well, what else do you have to do with your stunted life?" he said in a voice that was, for Stan, good-natured.

When the doorbell rang, he went to the front door. He returned to the kitchen with a girl holding a carrier that contained a yowling cat. "Third and Thirteenth," she said, handing it to Stan. "I'm double-parked, so I can't stay long." She saw Saga on the floor with the puppies. "Hi. I'm

Sonya," she said, the introduction of someone who needed nothing in return.

Sonya's hair was dyed black to make her skin look shockingly white. Piano keys, thought Saga.

She was about to stand up and introduce herself, but Stan was already talking. "I'll have to keep him out back. I've still got this litter in the small room. Can you come back tomorrow, leaflet the block where you found him?" He put the carrier on the kitchen counter and bent to see the cat through the small, prisonlike window. "Hi there," he said softly. "You are freaked out, I know that, yes I do. Sorry, fella."

"Yeah," said Sonya. "Yeah, sure."

"I'll do the Polaroid and copies," said Stan. "Go before you get a ticket. Thanks." He touched her on the back, a friendly touch.

Sonya gave Saga a circular wave, still no smile. "Next time," she said.

In just those few minutes, Saga noticed how much more humanely Stan spoke to Sonya than he did to her—how he expressed real *gratitude* to Sonya. Sometimes Saga felt, even after all these months since they'd had sex, that she deserved his contempt. Sometimes she looked at him when she thought he wouldn't notice and asked herself if she could ever be this man's girlfriend. What would that be like? What would it be like, now, to be anyone's girlfriend?

"Okay, I'm closing up," he said after Sonya left. "So back to the burbs, Story Girl. Want me to call you a car?" Where Stan lived, you couldn't hail a taxi on the street.

"I'm fine on the subway," she said. She helped him carry the puppies upstairs. As soon as she left, Saga knew Stan would attend to the panicky cat on the kitchen counter, make the guy a soft place to sleep and give him some food, maybe cook him something warm and meaty.

She went back to Manhattan. She had plenty of time to catch the last train home, but the night was mild, and she liked the idea of staying, of sleeping outside in her special place. She got off the L train at the end of the line. She wandered south through the part of the city where meat was sold, where the streets were still cobblestoned. She walked carefully when crossing these streets; not long ago, forgetting herself, she had fallen and skinned both her knees. She followed Hudson Street several blocks south, till she got to the café with the umbrellas, turned west and then south again, down Washington. She liked this part of town best, because only a few of the streets were named for numbers. Most of them had real *names,* like Charles and Leroy and Jane.

That first night alone in the city the year before—ashamed and stranded, having fled Stan's bed and house—Saga had taken the subway to its last stop and wandered, aimless, along this very route. On a corner, in a neighborhood of dark, sleepy buildings, here was a tall iron gate, left open a sliver, that led into a shallow patio in front of a restaurant. At first, Saga went into the patio just to sit and think, to calm down. She found herself secluded from the street by a pair of enormous flowerpots—tree pots, really—that held two tall, thick evergreens. She'd sat there a long time, uncertain what else she could do, till she fell into a doze against the wall. She awoke at dawn when a street sweeper came hissing by a few feet away, scattering dust and broken bits of dead leaves through the patio gate. Alarmed, she stood quickly, but she was alone. She saw her reflection in the plate glass window of the restaurant; through her reflection, a menu. *Tagliatelle, pappardelle, perciatelli . . .* If she cupped her face against the glass, she could see a sleek, fancy interior: red velvet benches, coppery modern lamps on the walls, light wood tables.

She had to pee badly. She let herself out of the gate, closing it behind her, and walked quickly east, where she found a coffee shop open on a corner two blocks away. After tea and a muffin, she called Uncle Marsden collect from a pay phone. She told him she had stayed with that friend, just as she'd said in her message. Oh, a friend from college, someone she'd bumped into on the street. It was the first lie she had told him since she'd moved into his house, perhaps the first real lie she'd ever told her uncle. It surprised her, but she never took it back.

Some weeks later, she'd decided to go into the city again, this time for no urgent reason. She found herself telling Uncle Marsden that she might stay over, might visit that old friend again. She saw him consciously holding his tongue, respecting her "boundaries." It was that easy; her age won her freedoms that, after all, she deserved. Didn't she? She took a sleeping roll she'd found in the top of a closet when she was airing the upstairs rooms. Late that night, after a lot of trial-and-error wandering, she found the spot again.

That time, the gate had been locked with a heavy chain. But the street was deserted and Saga, driven by a mysteriously stubborn urgency, would not be turned away. She tore the inside of a trouser leg on the top of the iron fence, but she got herself over. Once inside, she felt a moment of animal panic; with the gate locked, she was caged. But after she'd settled in against the planters, this time with her bedding, she felt both secure and free, the dark sky far above the pointed tips of the potted trees. Occasionally, a couple would walk past deep in a conversation they thought private on this quiet street, removed from the commerce and brilliant glow at the heart of the city. Once, a dog sniffed avidly on the other side of the fence; Saga heard an impatient owner yank and scold, yank and scold. That was the closest she came to discovery—or the closest she knew of. She slept in a surprisingly deep state of restfulness. Sometimes when she slept there—not always, but often enough—the moon's path would intersect with her avenue of sky, and then she would be happy, strangely and unsentimentally happy. It was a kind of happiness so much more felt than reasoned. Had she known this particular feeling before her life had been—as others put it—derailed?

So she would return to this corner every so often as if it were her home away from home. Each time, very late, she would climb the fence. And then, very early, after watching to make sure the street was empty, she would climb back over. One morning, Saga nearly fell onto a jogger coming around the corner, but he merely swerved into the street, too preoccupied with his exertions to care about where she had come from.

When it was warm, she might allow herself to stay here two nights in a row. If she chose a Sunday, she could even sleep just a little bit late, because the restaurant was closed on Mondays. Now and then, when she was in the neighborhood putting up flyers for Stan, she'd spy on the restaurant's life by day. Three café tables filled the little patio where she slept, all occupied on pleasant days by stylish-looking diners. It made her laugh out loud. The thought had crossed her mind, They are eating in my bed! Goldilocks. She was a real-life Goldilocks, but older and far more sly. Sly: that's what she was on those daring nights.

In her life with David—a life that, mercifully, she thought less and less about—she had loved to dance. David had belonged to a Morris dancing troop, and she had enjoyed watching him leap about with bells on his knees (though the first few times, she had laughed so hard she cried). But together, they had dressed up and gone to modest charity balls (often for literacy causes, through David's library job) just so they could dance. They'd even learned how to waltz. She remembered taking the lessons but did not remember how to waltz.

They had played tennis. Neither played especially well, but they'd had long, graceful rallies every so often. She remembered that, too, the sweet give and take, the crisp hollow smack of the ball. When it was warm, that was what they'd done with their Saturday mornings.

Now she lived what she thought of as the Life After. This life had its own pleasures, not all of them different, but it was a life as meek as milk, and in the midst of it this was her one defiant thing, sleeping outside in a quite unlikely place where no one would have guessed to find her. Sometimes she even thought of animals asleep in a zoo, in their make-believe jungles and savannahs, meticulously cared for by day but, sleeping at night, wild as could be in their dreams, watched by the silent, all-seeing, all-forgiving moon.

SIX

ON MOST DAYS, GREENIE ARRIVED AT WORK between six and seven. George rose early by nature, just like his mother, so he would go with her, taking along his favorite books or toys. They drove down a sluice of narrow curving lanes, between walls draped in blossoming vines, through the center of town and out again, up to the Governor's Mansion. Greenie thought of it as a *ranchion*. Built on one level only, a trainlike clustering of vast boxy rooms, it sprawled across a hill overlooking the Rio Grande Valley.

George loved switching on the battery of lights in the kitchen and later, if there was baking or roasting to be done, helping Greenie set the oven dials. "I'm learning my hundreds!" he liked to proclaim to anyone new he might meet.

They would play tapes and sing along together—Woody Guthrie and Pete Seeger had joined Greenie's repertoire now—but sometimes George would veto the music. Sometimes he had important things to tell his mother while she kneaded dough, chopped vegetables, or mixed a marinade. She had a sous chef and, when she needed them, other assistants, but she still preferred to start her day working alone—or alone with her son, even when it was trying.

"Diego's mom says Mr. McCrae made a really big mistake," he said to Greenie that morning. "They put those fires on purpose, she said. Isn't that pretty stupid to do?" He sat on a tall stool, spinning around, braking himself with the counter, reversing direction. The stool creaked; Greenie reminded herself to ask Mary Bliss for household oil.

"Don't pinch your fingers," she said. "You know, George, this doesn't sound like it makes sense, but sometimes you have to light small fires to stop bigger fires from starting. Or spreading."

George stopped spinning and looked at her as if she were nuts.

"It's like this," said Greenie as she pulled three bowls from a cupboard. "You've seen how there are not just woods here but also fields, big spaces with lots of smaller bushes, right?"

"No."

"Well, there are, and when the bushes and the dry grasses in the fields and the canyons catch on fire, they can spread the fire to the forest, to the bigger trees, much faster. So if you can get rid of the bushes by burning them up first, with the firefighters watching, then you can . . . you can stop them from spreading fire when no one's watching." She was glad this explanation had no adult witnesses. It did not sound logical and probably wasn't entirely accurate.

"So why don't they just chop the bushes *down*?"

"Good question. I guess it takes too long to do that. Burning's faster."

"But it didn't work because it made the fire bigger. So it was a big mistake. Like Diego's mom said."

Greenie smiled at George. "Yes, I suppose she's right. But don't tell that to Ray. A lot of people have already told him so—and it wasn't his decision."

"But he's the boss of Mexico."

"New Mexico. He's the governor, which is kind of like the boss, but he has a lot of helpers who decide things, too."

"Well, the helpers are big mistakers too."

She thought about trying to explain that the fires were the work of the National Park Service, but she said, "Yes, George, you're right. And they're sorry, and they're trying to fix it." Conversations with George were often circular, and Greenie found them exhausting, but she envied him his pure, uncluttered logic.

At seven-thirty, Consuelo arrived to pick up George. Consuelo Chu was a large, grandmotherly woman who was married to Mike Chu, Ray's head gardener. Consuelo's three children were in their early twenties, and she liked to say that George was her "practice grandchild." On weekday mornings, she took him to a playgroup in Tesuque, where the children did more than occupy themselves with blocks and books. They made collages from leaves and colored sand they collected themselves, played soccer, and paddled about in a tall round pool. George's skin had taken on a pale brown hue that made him look healthier and older than he had in their city life. A dozen boys, all around George's age, were also driven out from the city, but he had attached himself with fierce monogamous loyalty to Diego, an older boy who hung around because his mother and aunts ran the group. Diego's father worked at a ranch next door, where sometimes the children were allowed to ride a pony.

In the afternoons, Consuelo would retrieve George and take him with her on errands, buy him a sweet, and bring him back to the governor's kitchen for lemonade or milk. On the nights when Greenie had to stay late, to oversee a formal dinner, Consuelo would put George to bed and wait for Greenie to return.

"Her name is like a sneeze," George had said the day he met Consuelo, almost as soon as she was out the door. "Oh say oh *choo*!"

Greenie had not laughed so hard in months. "Consuelo, honey. It means 'comfort' in Spanish. Lots of people have Spanish names here."

"Do I have a Spanish name?"

"George in Spanish is Jorge," said Greenie.

"Hor-hay! Hor-hay! Hor-hay!" chanted George. "Like horses eat hay. That is so weird. Horse-hay. I like 'George' better."

Sometimes spending an evening or a Saturday with George felt like hanging around with a talk show host while he tried out new jokes— most of which were doomed to be tossed. After hours of his ingenuous quips, Greenie would long for Alan's company, for the leavening of adult intelligence. But rarely did she give in and call him. She wanted Alan to stew, to miss her, to understand what he had given up—and to see his way to joining them. Most therapists took off the whole month of August; why didn't he come for August? All right, he'd said, he would come for three weeks—but for part of that time he would take George to see the Grand Canyon. Just George.

Greenie had not thought about how much she would miss being close to her New York friends, even those with whom she had communed almost exclusively by phone. Speaking on the phone across two time zones and several ecosystems was not the same as speaking on the phone when you could walk out the door into the same stale humid air, with the same ruddy starless sky above your heads, the same sticky frost-warped streets beneath your feet. And the time difference made it tricky. She spoke more now to her single friends—to her surprise, Walter most of all—than she did to her married friends with children.

Walter was in a state of proud anxiety, readying his apartment for the arrival of a grown nephew from California. "An apprentice!" he told Greenie. "I'm going to be like some Old World mentor, like those guys who ran guilds in the Renaissance. Ergo, I am shelving pleasures of the flesh—of which I must confess there have not been many—and I am fluffing up my father-hen feathers. Nesting!" He told her that Alan had been to the restaurant a few times since she'd left. "Lugubrious personified," he said. "And he always orders dessert. If he can't have you, at least he can have your creations."

"But he *can* have me, Walter."

"No, my dear, I don't believe he can."

"What do you mean by that?"

"I mean that you refuse to see exactly what you've done. And it's a good thing you've done, in my opinion. You've cut the line, you've chosen freedom. I may live to regret saying this, but he is not worthy of you. He is a perfectly okay guy, but he is a moper and an emotional tortoise. Well, I have said *way* too much."

"Oh Walter, I know he looks that way now—"

"Honey, he will look that way till the cows come home unless something pretty heavy falls on his head and rearranges his brain."

"Your proverbial piano, Walter?"

"The very one, my dear!"

In a strange way, Walter and Ray began to seem increasingly similar: both loud and unabashed, both taking on the role of a second father that Greenie was sure she had never implied she wanted. Alan, meanwhile, seemed to have stepped back into the shadows. She wanted to believe that his distance was a sign of respect and contemplation, but unless he could tell her so, she had no way of knowing.

So Greenie's primary dose of face-to-face adult intelligence came at about the time when Consuelo picked up George from the kitchen. That was when Ray showed up.

The governor rose—without an alarm clock, he boasted—at dawn. According to Mary Bliss, he began each day with a call to his ranch manager, to check on his herd. Then he attended to e-mail, ate a hard-boiled egg, and went for a run. He came home, took a shower, and met with his press secretary. He drank coffee and scanned the news as represented in the *New York Times,* the *Christian Science Monitor,* the *New Mexican,* and the *Albuquerque Tribune.* Then he had breakfast in the kitchen with Greenie.

He came in that morning just after Consuelo and George had left.

"Damn but that kid of yours is smart. And damn if he isn't an insolent puppy." Ray went straight to the household refrigerator, the one where Greenie kept what she thought of as food-in-progress. "I say, 'Hi pardner, how ya doin'?' and the little guy looks me straight in the eye and goes, 'Mr. McCrae, fire does not beat fire. Water beats fire. Mom says you're sorry, but sorry's not always enough.' " Ray laughed loudly. "I take that on a might-as-well-be-empty stomach, I do."

"I'm sorry," said Greenie. "He's asked about the fires. I'm not very good at explaining."

"Hell, nobody's any too good at explaining any of it now. And listen to the man: Sorry's not always enough. As the voters may feel bound to tell me come election time. Try saying the words *prescribed burn* to a wall of TV cameras. Pretty damn lame as justification for burning down two hundred houses. 'Got a light?' I heard one reporter say to another, and you should've heard the yukkin' it up that spread through the room." He looked at the clock over the sink. "So what did we have for dinner last night? Seems about a week ago."

This was his morning ritual: he opened the fridge and rummaged through the remnants of whatever Greenie had made for dinner the night before, laid various items on the counter, and helped himself. He loved cold soufflé, cold rice, cold potatoes, cold stew, cold soup, even cold meat in a cream sauce that had congealed. Along with two slices of whole wheat toast, he often ate these foods straight from their storage containers, washing them down with a glass of milk. Unless he had an early meeting, this was his breakfast of choice.

"Lamb chops! Ratatouille! Ooh, and . . . can I have whatever's in this thingamawhosit, or is it something you're saving for later? Smells dandy." He held up a plastic tub filled with something brown.

"That's leftover consommé. I used it in the sauce for the lamb. Help yourself." Greenie winced as he spread the cold meat jelly on his toast.

Once he had composed his peculiar breakfast, Ray would take it to a corner counter, away from Greenie's workspace. While he ate, he talked: weather, movies, Greenie's history or even his own. Greenie went about her work, letting him steer the conversation.

That morning, he said, "So before that little guy was born—Mr. Hose Is Mightier Than the Torch—did you have a lot of sonograms, that amnio-whadyacallit?"

"I did have a lot of sonograms, yes," said Greenie. "As a matter of fact."

"And why was that?"

"If you want the gruesome details, they thought for a few months that part of my placenta might be detached. It was amazing—I mean, seeing him so much before he was born. It's like we got to know George a little, spy on what he was going to be like before he was even born. So amazing."

"Must be. And you saw his little heart beat?"

Greenie turned around to look at Ray. She never knew what he would bring up. Ray's press secretary was pregnant; wouldn't it be just like Ray to coax her through fears of early tests, as patronizing as he was loving. "They had just improved the technology so we could see it—or maybe hear it, I can't remember which—at six weeks. I'd known I was pregnant for less than two. It was amazing. Terrifying."

When he said nothing in reply, Greenie turned around again. She had finished dicing leeks and scooped them into a colander. She carried it to the sink on Ray's side of the kitchen.

Ray set down the remnant of a lamb chop. "Greenie, you're pro-choice. I'd bet fifty head of my cattle, including Wally, my best bull. I would."

She laughed and turned on the tap. "You're not getting me into this argument, Ray."

"Oh honey, yes I am."

"Burnt lunch would not impress your Water Boys."

"Oh let 'em eat silage. They're the least of my worries these days. It's the Fire Crew got my chaps all rucked up."

Greenie sprayed the leeks with cold water. She set the colander on the drainboard. A thin layer of sand remained in the sink; spraying again, she rinsed it down the drain.

"Okay, Miss Coolhead Duquette. Here's what." He held out a folded copy of that day's *New York Times*. On the front page, she saw headlines about Israeli politics, national unemployment figures, and accusations aimed at her old city's child welfare agency. Nothing about the fires in New Mexico or anything else of local interest. To the rest of the country, the fires were old and distant news.

"What's what?" she said.

"You tell me how we are all so hot and bothered, so outraged, as well we should be, when a child suffers torture at the hands of its parents, but we defend the right to say to a kid in your belly who's already got a thumping heart—who's got, according to *you*, a personality brewing— 'Sorry, bub, you're not wanted out here, so we're as good as turning you out with the compost. You'll make a fine shrub, you will.' You're smart, Greenie. You defend that logic. Convert me."

"Ray, I am not getting into that trick debate of when life begins. That's not what it's about. It's about women choosing their fate. I hold the line there."

"Well, what if these evil parents right here in this story said, 'We are not getting into that trick debate of who's in charge of how these kids get brought up.' There's no more an iron divide at the cervix than there is at the door of these folks who ought to be gutted and shot." He slapped the paper. "And *choose your fate*? Who do you think you're kidding? So what about the poor sucker who gets AIDS from one slip of the libido? Can you abort *that* consequence?"

"Oh Ray, that is so much not the same thing, and you know it."

"All I'm saying is sex has risks. I'm not preaching abstinence, boy oh howdy no. I've been eighteen, alone with a girl in a pickup out in the desert under those carpe diem stars. Talk about a freight train! But far more unstoppable forces have consequences we can't turn back. They do—and hey, that don't kill us neither. I don't even have to go religious on you here."

Greenie looked out the window. The world it showed her could not have looked more different from the one she'd seen while working back in New York. Instead of ankles, weeds, and the tires of parked cars, she saw mountains, treetops, and sky. But the sky, for nearly a month, had been yellow, the mountains sheathed in smoke; after dark, flashes of flame might appear. When at last the fires were contained, the horizon came into focus again, but it was gray, a landscape painted with tar and ash.

How odd it felt to share a kitchen most mornings with a man whose face she had seen in the news, without caring, for years. She was no longer intimidated, but sometimes she saw him across the room and thought that he must be a hologram, a figment, that she was far lonelier than she could admit.

"Look, Ray," she said, "I was lucky enough that I never got pregnant when I didn't want to be pregnant. So I never made the choice I'm in favor of preserving. But I do think it's private."

"And child rearing's not. Apples and kumquats, that what you say?

Welfare, reverence for safety and well-being, for plain old *being*, begins when the cord gets cut. That's what you say?"

Greenie put down her knife and turned fully around, leaning back against the counter. Ray was looking at her as a father might regard a child who had disappointed him, just the way Alan had looked at her the night she told him that yes, this was her decision; she knew it was right and not just for her.

"That's not what I say," she said quietly. "Not at all. But there are some places where what we know in our hearts just can't be the same as what we stand up for in the world."

"Sheep manure."

"I'm, what, not just your cook now but your ideological guinea pig, too?"

Ray did not smile, but he winked. "Bet your eastern liberal ass."

"Then I demand a raise," she said.

"No, but here's your bonus: How'd you like to come out to the ranch weekend after this one, you and that back-talking boy? Only condition: you got to bake. McNally does barbecue fine, but I would love a pie or two. We're entertaining a buyer. George can watch my boys get the cows fit and parade 'em around like peacocks. He'll see guys who wear Stetsons and spurs when it's not Halloween."

"He'd love that," said Greenie. All at once she thought of her father, the pride he'd taken in his boats not unlike the pride Ray took in his cows: the way he'd spent nearly as many hours polishing, scrubbing, and refitting as he had spent out on the water.

Greenie knew that the fires were eating at Ray's conscience. At night, if she turned on the news (something she'd never done in New York), there he would be—his televised self always shocking to her for an instant, as if her own life had leaped to the screen. Without fail, he looked stubborn and sure, defending the early decisions made by the National Parks Service. But his cook knew something that others might not: Ray's appetite had dwindled. After he left the kitchen that morning, she saw that he had eaten only two chops and hadn't touched the ratatouille.

Greenie had come to understand that there was something sacred and separate to Ray about his morning ritual. Whether or not it had anything to do with her, she felt both flattered and uneasy. He might arrive looking haggard or angry, but he never took it out on Greenie. Let the chaos and recrimination flutter frantically about, like papers thrown to a reckless wind; not even Mary Bliss was permitted to interrupt this sliver of his routine.

There were days when the smoke drifted everywhere, disparate yet durable as rumor. It would defy the closed windows and doors, leaving a fine dark grit on all the polished steel and tile surfaces of the kitchen. Except for the way it smelled, the smoke reminded Greenie of the fog in Maine: of its curious solidity, the way it could sit right up against a window screen, soft yet firm like a pillow, and its equally curious ubiquity, the way you could open a latched closet and find that it had invaded, leaving your clothes droopy and damp. But Maine was farther away than it had ever been before. When she took her clothes from the closet, they smelled of cinders, not of the sea.

SHE HAD DOUBTS, but she was not homesick. The mournfulness had come at the beginning.

Greenie and George had left very early one morning, and Alan had decided not to see them off at the airport. "Greenie, how weird would that be? I'm sorry, it's too sad," he'd said to her the night before, after they had made love. To George, over a sleepy breakfast, he said, "I have way too much work today, guy. There are people counting on me to be here later this morning." He carried George on his hip out the front door. Together, they each raised an arm to flag down a cab. After lifting suitcases into the trunk, Alan reached into both of his pockets and held out four plastic dinosaurs, two in each hand. "Two herbivores," he said, passing them from his left hand to George's right. "And two *carnivores,*" he snarled, passing them to George's left.

"Wow, Dad, velociraptor and parasaurolophus!" George exclaimed in grateful awe. "But I'm going to keep them away from these guys." He waved the fist that held the stegosaurus and the dimetrodon, their sharp plastic limbs and tails protruding between his fingers. Alan kissed his son on the top of his head, his wife on one cheek (pointedly far from her lips). He picked up George and hugged him tight.

"We'll call when we get there," said Greenie, and in the cab, as they pulled away, she struggled not to cry. Already, George was staging a showdown between the two meat-eating creatures. Alan, wise in these matters as ever, had provided just the right face-saving decoy. By the time they were deep in the Holland Tunnel, Greenie felt fine, her emotions under control.

Within an hour of takeoff, George fell asleep. And then, so hard and fast it stung, the anticipation of regret and loneliness overcame her. She turned to the window and let herself cry, as quietly as she could. In four hours, she never took out her book. Suburbs with affectedly curvaceous roads and pools gave way to country highways and farms, their geometry laid out in confident trajectories so absurdly unlike life: perfect circles, perfect squares, fields rolled out like bolts of rugged cloth. For a time, the plane passed over a seemingly endless prairie of clouds, their unbroken surface like gently foaming milk. But this they also left behind, to glide above a glorious calligraphy of rivers and then, as they approached Denver, the rising mountains. The sun was so bright that Greenie could watch the plane's raptor shadow undulate over and down the peaks, always a little ahead, leading the way like a phantom guide. *Oh what have I done?* thought Greenie as they hit the bumpy air before they landed.

But when she woke George, he was cheerful and refreshed, and by the time she had bought the two of them chocolate milk shakes and they had boarded a second plane, Greenie felt the certainty she had expressed to Alan the evening she told him that this was their chance, this was *his* chance, not just hers—if he was brave enough to take it.

"This is so rash, Greenie," he had said, shaking his head. "I can't believe you are doing this to our family."

"I am doing this *for* our family," she said. "It's time for something new. This didn't fall into my lap for nothing. It was a message, loud and clear."

She had expected him to make a sarcastic remark about hearing voices, but he had simply continued to shake his head, looking deeply sad; and then, to her surprise, he had held her very close.

"Are you crying?" she had said, for an instant willing to take it all back, to call Mary Bliss and say she was sorry, very sorry, but she had made a mistake.

He pulled away from her. "I wish I were, Greenie. I wish I could."

Over the next two weeks, as she packed, prepared Tina to take over in her absence, and answered all of George's questions, Alan had been weirdly calm, even helpful. She half-expected to see him packing his things as well. "Surprise!" he would say the morning of the flight, and the three of them would fly west together, and as they did, Alan would shed his recent angst, like an astronaut leaving gravity far in his wake. But this was nothing more than a dream.

MARY BLISS HAD FOUND THEM a furnished guesthouse to rent, under a copiously weeping willow on Acequia Madre, an old, quietly elegant street where the houses and walls seemed to rise organically from the burnt red earth, where an old irrigation ditch would brim and flow whenever there was rain. The two small bedrooms opened onto a brick *portale* and a garden planted with herbs. When the doors and windows were open, the rooms smelled like lavender and thyme. In the living room, the fireplace nested in a corner like a beehive, and the beams supporting the roof were so massive that at first Greenie felt the instinct to duck whenever she entered the room. Two hanging Indian rugs, pale red zigzagged with brown and white, faced each other from opposite sides of the room.

"Look. Lightning's on the walls," said George when they arrived. "I know what that's for: that's our protection. So we won't get stuck."

"Stuck?" asked Greenie.

George frowned at her confusion. "Stuck by lightning, Mom. Ford says it's called voodoo, from another religion, not the one about God." He looked at the ceiling. "Are those *whole trees*? Is this a house made from trees? That's crazy."

"You've seen plenty of houses made from trees, George. Like Nana's house in New Jersey. The trees have just been sawed into boards. And log cabins—those are made of whole trees."

"Yes, but log cabins are into the woods, *with* the trees," said George, patient with her misconceptions.

She gave George the larger bedroom, where Mary Bliss had put an extravagant gift from Ray: a hobbyhorse, the old-fashioned kind that bounced up and down (the kind now banned because fingers might catch in the springs). The bed was large, with a puffy mattress and a four-poster frame stained blue. On the bureau sat a lamp made from a worn cowboy boot filled with plaster, another gift from Ray. Greenie asked Mary Bliss what made Ray so generous. Mary Bliss said, as if it were obvious, that Ray had no children of his own.

"Do you think he wants them?" asked Greenie.

"I believe so," said Mary Bliss, standing in Greenie's kitchen. "I hope so." She smiled at Greenie, who wasn't sure how to comment. Sometimes Mary Bliss said things that were almost shockingly forward. Greenie admired this trait, and it made her feel more comfortable when surrounded by politicians who were anything but blunt.

Greenie's bed, like George's, was massive yet soft. In her bedroom, the beams (*vigas,* Mary Bliss had corrected her gently) were plastered over, so that the ceiling resembled a great white ruffle. Lying awake her first night there, Greenie found herself amused at the notion that the interior of the little house looked as if it had been frosted, as if the hidden walls were made of sponge cake. She thought instantly of Alan, how she'd love to report this curiosity to him (how she would have, so naturally, had he been lying beside her), but she would not call him a second time. As soon as she and George had been left alone by Mary Bliss, she'd called him right away, to say that they had arrived safely.

"I'm glad to hear it," he'd said, "though *safely* is a relative term."

FIRE MIGHT HAVE CAPTURED THE HEADLINES—government probes, impending lawsuits, calls for emergency supplies—but Ray McCrae knew that a far thornier problem, a problem that would only grow worse as time went on, was water. He tried to talk about it in public as little as possible; talk of water, he told Greenie, was something he delegated whenever he could. But this was a year of exceptional drought, so talk about it he must.

The Water Boys, as he called them, were a loose and shifting posse of commissioners, lobbyists, and freelance know-it-alls on everything from Navajo water-rights litigation to the sorry future of the aquifer feeding the middle Rio Grande basin. They met every other Thursday for lunch in the dining room of the mansion. The group included the state engineer, members of a drought task force and a water conservation committee, lawyers, ecologists, developers, miners, ranchers, tribal elders, and what Ray called the BLM grunts. ("Big-ass Louts and Morons, but that's between us, Ms. Duquette.")

Greenie did not serve the meals she cooked, but through the swinging doors she heard talk of irrigation, reclamation, river diversion, groundwater mining, snowmelt, shelterbelts, dead pool, Godwater, ditch bosses, cow urine, fishing seasons, growing zones, acid rain, and tribal claims to water that wealthy ranchers took for granted and eastern transplants like Greenie used with abandon to wash their cars, nurture their gardens—and, thought Greenie, blithely rinse sand from leeks down their kitchen sinks. Sometimes the talking turned to shouting. The Water Boys were destined, by virtue of their fanatical and quixotic aims, rarely if ever to find a consensus on anything.

That day a small pack of Water Boys entered the dining room already in the midst of an argument. "So *here's* an idea," Greenie heard one man say. "We hold a statewide lottery, and the losing third of the population gets to move to northern Wisconsin. Where they can plant roses to their hearts' content *and* join the great northern fossil fuel grab. Let's kiss a few *more* Saudi asses. At least the water's ours. We don't take that project on the Gila, Arizona will."

As Greenie's sous chef, Maria, placed bowls of soup on a silver tray, she rolled her eyes. She picked up a shaker of chili pepper flakes and made a threatening gesture over the soup bowls. "These gentlemen, would they call for water *then*!"

Greenie laughed. "No women today?"

"Oh no. That's why they so loud so soon. The ladies keep the manners."

Maria and Greenie looked up to see Ray leaning into the kitchen. Maria blushed and picked up her tray. Ray held the door for her as she passed through, then let it swing closed. "Greenie," he said, "I never do this to you last-minute, but any chance of that orange soufflé after lunch? I got fifteen cranky men out there I need to impress. Or placate. Or drug with sugar. Any or all of the above. There's this redneck dam broker from Albuquerque, stupid enough to turn me into a socialist, and I got me a new fish hugger from out east, courtesy of my favorite senator. I have to drive to Los Alamos in an hour and won't be back for dinner."

"You don't need reasons," said Greenie.

"I do not," he said, "but I like to be reasonable all the same. And while I'm on my wish list, next weekend—angel food cake?"

"I thought you wanted pies," she said, but he was already through the door, changing places again with Maria.

Greenie laid out plates in two rows and put the steak sandwiches on them. Maria dished out the jicama coleslaw and shoestring yams. This was a staple menu for lunches where pads of paper and small computers would occupy most of the dining room table. On the center island, Greenie began separating eggs. The shell of the thirteenth crumbled, and a shard fell into the bowl of whites. As she reached for a discarded shell and began to fish for the shard, she heard the door to the dining room open. It would be Maria, with the Grand Marnier.

"Pardon me."

When Greenie turned, she saw an unfamiliar man. Except that, as she stared at him, suddenly he wasn't unfamiliar.

He held one side of his jacket away from his shirt, as if about to bare his heart. "I was told you might—" He stepped closer. "Charlie?"

"What are you doing here?" said Greenie.

"Good God, it *is* you, Charlie. Way out here!"

"No, Charlie, it's Good God *you* way out here."

They should have embraced, but he still held his jacket in that awkward way, while she held her hands in midair, her fingers slippery with egg. She wiped them on her apron as he let go of his jacket.

"Oh Charlie," she said after they had hugged, "what *are* you doing here? Don't tell me you're a Water Boy."

"A water boy?"

The fish hugger. The fish hugger from out east. She laughed. "You *are*. You're here to save those fish." How long had it been since she had seen someone from high school, never mind someone from that briefly tight clique that had formed in their final, smug year, when they'd pretended to be daring (driving too fast, drinking too much, talking too loudly outside their parents' bedrooms), when she had gone from Shar to Charlie? *Other Charlie*, her girlfriends had called this boy. Everything about him—but from so long ago—came flooding back to Greenie.

"I'm afraid that's almost accurate," he said. "But you. Mom told me you were in New York."

"I was in New York; you knew that. I was there before I was married." That's when she'd seen him last: at her wedding. Afterward, Greenie heard about him from her mother: how he went to law school and joined a corporate practice in Boston. But for the past two years she'd been cut off from hometown news.

"Well," she said, "here's where I am now. Since April."

He told her he'd arrived only three weeks before. And then he remembered about her parents. He told her how sorry he was. As they talked, she looked at him carefully, feature by feature. His pale hair was shorter, blanched by age or the sun, and his jaw seemed larger, as if the bone had continued to grow, to jut forward with greater determination. Other Charlie had always been determined. And he must have met with resistance, for his face bore so many new angles and lines. He was thinner. Resolution, she thought. He looked like a man of resolution.

He wore jeans and laced leather boots, but also this pale linen jacket, an awkwardly urban touch. There was a long brown stain on one lapel.

"You came in here looking for club soda."

"I did," he said. "But, wow. Look at what I found instead."

After she gave him a bottle of soda and a dish towel, she went back to breaking eggs. "How is it fish get defended by lawyers these days?"

"I was a lawyer. Okay, I still *am* a lawyer. I just went back to school. I tell people I wanted to do some good. I just wanted to be outside more often. Desks make me antsy. I thought that would change when I grew up, but no. Or else I just haven't grown up. More likely that."

Greenie remembered a tipsy midnight exploit: an illicitly borrowed canoe with too many passengers, a bottle of Mateus rosé, a paddle fumbled overboard. She remembered Other Charlie diving deep down in the middle of the lake, staying underwater so long that everybody got nervous. When he surfaced, he seemed a football field away. She'd thought of the seals in Maine. Was that when she had begun to notice him apart from the other boys in their group?

She said, "I've been ordered to make a soufflé so you'll be nicer to one another." She pointed toward the dining room. "The notion being that civilized food inspires civilized manners. I'm skeptical. You can keep me company, but who'll be in there defending your helpless clients? What kind of fish are your clients anyway? Are they likely to be on one of my menus?"

"Silvery minnows. I don't think so." He'd made a futile attempt at cleaning the soup off his lapel. The stain was now surrounded by a broad wet patch. He sighed and took off the jacket. "I have another meeting in Albuquerque," he said, as if to explain why he'd overdressed. He handed her a card. "I go back and forth, but mostly I'm here. Would you call me? I don't know much of anyone other than lobbyist types. Them I'd rather steer clear of."

"I don't know anyone either," said Greenie. "Outside this house."

"But your husband's here."

"No. He's back in New York. For now he is." She said nothing about

George; other Charlie would know about George from his mother. "I have a job to do," she said. "Grating orange zest. Go back out there or you'll know all my secrets."

"I wouldn't mind that," he said.

"I would." Greenie waved at him, to let him go—to make him go. She needed to concentrate, not on the past but on the present, on whisking and folding and baking and, above all, on serving this dessert. The only tricky thing about a soufflé was its timing.

SEVEN

THURSDAY WAS THE ONE MORNING Alan had no appointments, so the phone call at seven-thirty hauled him up from deep in a dream about George, about waking to find George in the apartment, in his own bed, never having left.

"Oh God, did I wake you? I'm sorry."

Alan cleared his throat. "It's all right. I ought to be up by now."

"Oh God."

Alan heard weeping. "I'm so sorry," he said, "but who is this?"

"It's Stephen, Stephen Campbell. Oh God. I'm going to hang up."

"No you're not," said Alan. "If you do, I'll call you right back. Stephen, talk to me." He waited.

"He moved out! He—just like that, he actually moved out!"

"What do you mean? Last time I saw you—"

"He *moved out*! He left me this . . . left me this goddamn note I am staring at here, and he actually just sneaked out in the middle of the night, like some burglar in reverse, took his biggest suitcase and all his meds and he . . ." Stephen broke down again. "I can't believe this!"

Alan sat on the side of his bed. His head was still thick with the dreamed presence of his son. How he ached for George.

"Stephen, do you want to come over and talk in person? I think it's a good idea. I have an opening in half an hour." Opening? More like a chasm.

"Do I want to come over and talk? No, I want my life back! That's what I want, for God's sake!"

Well join the club, thought Alan. "Can you go into your office a little late today, or call in sick?"

"I can do whatever I please, I'm the boss!" This came out as a wail of sorrow, not anger or pride; could Alan have held Greenie fast if he had been capable of wailing at her with such passion?

"Then come," he said, making it sound as much like an order as he could.

Half an hour later, a deeply distraught but beautifully dressed Stephen sat on the couch in Alan's office. He had to pull himself together by one o'clock, he told Alan, because he had an important lunch with two board members of the San Francisco Ballet. "One thing you've got to do," he said, "is help me stop crying. I cannot show up at Lespinasse with the sodden blubbery face of a walrus. You wouldn't have any cucumbers, would you?"

"Well, over in my kitchen I think I might have a shriveled tomato. Sorry." Alan handed him the box of Kleenex, smiling sadly.

"You're a shrink, not a salad bar, right?" Stephen attempted a laugh, then blew his nose.

Alan wondered if it had been wise to let Stephen come over on such short notice, but perhaps the crisis was partly Alan's fault. It had been a stupid idea to assign those lists, as if the two men were teenage girls thinking about what colleges they should attend. He might have misread Gordie, but he had taken him for a guy who thought in balance sheets.

When Alan asked what had happened, Stephen explained that they had indeed sat down, the night before, to list the pros and cons of becoming parents. They had done this in silence after a nice dinner. Stephen had made pork loin stuffed with prunes, one of Gordie's favorite meals. Stephen was optimistic, because Gordie had been relaxed and said he'd had a good day at the office.

He had brought along both lists, which he now handed to Alan. Alan was dismayed but took them; he shouldn't be looking at Gordie's list, or discussing it, in Gordie's absence, but of course the next thing Stephen said was "Okay, so look at his list, would you?" His eyes were teary and desperate.

Alan was struck right off by two things. First, by the similarity of the two men's handwriting. Both of them wrote in a broad cursive with generous masculine loopings. Superficially, the only difference was the left-handed slant of Gordie's script. Second, Gordie's list (the two columns studiously scored off with a cross) comprised nearly as many pros as it did cons. Alan was contemplating the pros when Stephen broke in.

"Look at the last item in the right column, the nays."

Alan looked across the divide. Gordie had written there a dozen items, marked off with bullets, each one tersely expressed in just a few words. Last on the list of reasons to forgo children came *Issues of fidelity.*

Oh no, thought Alan. What an idiot I've been.

"I was flabbergasted," said Stephen. "I said, 'Just what does fidelity have to do with this?' And maybe it wasn't a great idea to make a joke, I know, but I said, 'Well, we'll probably be too exhausted, in the beginning at least, to be anything other than faithful!' He didn't think this was funny at all. He glared at me and said that if anyone should take this whole thing seriously, it was me. So I asked him if he was making a threat, and it just went downhill from there."

Stephen bent forward, elbows on his knees, face in his hands. Was he crying again? Alan said, "Fidelity. Wow. Well, you can't say he hasn't been thinking hard about this. But that's something we didn't really talk about before. The whole monogamy thing. Are you guys on the same page there?"

"Oh God." Stephen's expression, when he uncovered his face, was weary and remorseful. "Oh, well, to be truthful, it was . . . well it's gotten more complicated lately. I think."

"Complicated how?"

Stephen told Alan how being monogamous, for him, was essential to their living together, their being a couple from the time they moved in together. Gordie was less insistent, but when they had decided to make their union official, have a ceremony, he had agreed that not "straying" was important to him as well.

Stephen looked at Alan and sighed. "The truth is, this was always a bigger sacrifice for Gordie, even though we never put it that way, because I'm . . . well, I like sex fine, don't get me wrong, but when I'm working like a maniac, which I practically always am, it's just . . . not that big a deal. I mean I'm sexual, it's just . . ." He sighed, this time very loudly. "Oh, what's the point? This is over, isn't it?"

"Stephen, thirteen years are not erased in twelve hours. Believe me."

"Gordie is the most incredibly decisive person I know."

"What, he never changes his mind? He never does anything rash?"

"His note was so cold."

Alan softened his voice. "Did you bring the note?"

"I couldn't. I'm sorry."

"Did he say your relationship is over? That he's breaking up with you? That he plans to move out?"

"Not in those words. But it doesn't matter."

On first meeting them, Alan had liked Gordie more than Stephen. When you worked with couples, that's how it was: at a gut level, you'd almost always prefer one to the other. And your preference rarely changed, which made the work more challenging—but now Alan wondered if there wasn't a plain-Jane logic to Stephen that would make him an excellent spouse, maybe the *better* spouse. He was the proverbial Swiss watch: dependable, easy to read, well made through and through, from his psyche to his large, strong hands.

"I think I should go now," Stephen said. "I'm wrung out."

"Will you call me this evening? Please."

"If that's what you think I should do."

"Stephen . . . what will you do with your day, other than go to that lunch?"

"I won't call him, I promise you that. And I will resist the catty urge to pack his belongings in Hefty bags and leave them on the curb."

"Good." Alan stood up. "I don't think he's really left. I can't be sure, but I doubt it."

"I hope you're right. At least, I think I do," said Stephen. "Though it makes me mad to think he might come back in a week and then think that this . . . scare will warn me off the whole child issue. Because it won't."

Alan nodded. "I'll walk you out." He led Stephen down the dim hall; through the frosted glass on the front door of the building, he could see that someone was seated at the top of the steps. A woman, he could see from the curly sunlit hair, and for a moment he felt an irrational leap of hope, a thrill. How naïve his emotional reflexes, how wishful his battered heart.

He opened the door and was about to say good-bye to Stephen when the woman on the stoop turned around and smiled at him.

"Saga?" He stepped out beside Stephen. The men stood side by side as Saga rose and turned. She held a stack of papers. "I'm glad to see you again."

Saga reached out to shake Stephen's hand and introduced herself.

Stephen reciprocated, but he was blushing. Alan realized that Stephen must think she was another patient. "Saga rescues animals," Alan said. "We met when she was walking around with a box of puppies."

"And here they are." Saga held out one of her papers; it was a notice with a photograph, the puppies on the floor in someone's kitchen. The notice declared boldly, NEEDED: GOOD HOMES WITH GOOD, DEPENDABLE PEOPLE.

"Well, perhaps that's what I need. A puppy," said Stephen. "Am I dependable? I used to think so."

"Here, take a few," said Saga. "Put them up somewhere. Like your office?"

Stephen took several sheets and said, "Keep up the good work. Who knows, I just might give you a call. Seems I have an unexpected vacancy."

After Stephen was gone, Alan and Saga stood facing each other on the stoop. "I brought something for you. To thank you." She bent over and picked up a potted plant with dry-cleaning plastic wrapped in a quirky turban around its top. "I hope you can grow these somewhere."

Alan couldn't help examining Saga. Her jacket was wrinkled, but her hair looked clean, her jeans and sneakers almost new. He should probably invite her into his apartment—though now, so early in the morning, being with her felt more awkward than it had the first time, when there was an urgent purpose.

He accepted the plant and held the door. "Would you like some coffee?"

"Tea would be nice," she said, "if that's not too much trouble."

"None at all," he said. "Why didn't you ring the bell?"

"When I got here, I thought it was maybe too early," she said.

"My work starts early and ends late," said Alan, "often with too much free time in the middle." He carried the flowerpot into his living room and set it down on the table in front of the sofa. In the kitchen, he filled a kettle. When he returned to the living room, Saga had unwrapped the flowerpot. From the dirt protruded a dozen tall green spears. They resembled asparagus stalks.

"Peonies," said Saga. "My favorite. I brought them from my uncle's garden; he doesn't mind, he has lots." She looked around the room. "Though I realize now, maybe you don't have a garden. I didn't remember that. Sorry. Where I live, everyone's got a yard."

Alan smiled at her. "I thought you told me you live downtown."

Saga blushed. "Just sometimes," she said.

Alan waited a moment, hoping she would explain. When she didn't, he said, "Well, I do have a fire escape that gets a couple hours of sun." He carried the plant through George's little room and opened the window. Saga followed.

"You have a fish!"

"My son's fish," said Alan. Sunny was doing his jackknife laps, hopeful. Alan hadn't fed him yet. He reached for the food shaker.

"How old is he? Is he in school?"

"Excuse me?" said Alan.

"Your son."

"No. Away on a trip with his mother. He's four." Alan remembered that he had told her all about George before.

"Maybe he'd like a puppy," said Saga. "You'd be the one who'd have to take care of it. But you could surprise him. If you wanted. Stan thinks these are part corgi. Corgis are nice, like little dogs with big-dog personalities."

Alan laughed. "Oh, he'd like that all right. But it's the old dog-in-the-city dilemma. When you grow up with dogs in the great outdoors—even the suburbs—the city seems too cruel." The kettle began to whistle.

Saga was clearly startled. She frowned. "Oh no," she said.

"What?" asked Alan.

"The clothes, the ones I borrowed. I forgot them. Till just this minute. I'm sorry."

"It doesn't matter. There's no need to return them."

She looked at him fiercely, as if he'd insulted her. "Oh, but I will," she said. "I absolutely will."

So Saga would visit again, thought Alan. However much she might keep him off balance, he didn't mind the prospect of seeing her again. "So," he said as he poured the tea, "tell me more about those puppies."

FOR SO LONG, ALAN LIKED TO SAY that he knew Greenie was the one he should marry long before she knew the same of him. Among friends, Alan's scripted tale was one that had always flattered them both, in each other's eyes as well as in the eyes of those around them. A decade into their marriage it was set in stone, and Alan would typically tell it like this:

"There I was, doing my white-glove psychoanalytic training at this mausoleum on the Upper East Side, and there's Greenie, working behind the counter at this equally uppity French patisserie just down the street, where all my teachers buy their café au lait and pain au chocolat every morning before they sit down to become these quasi-Freudian deities from nine to five. Well, thank heaven I'm a good student and follow their every example, down to that pain au chocolat, because who gets up while it's still dark and makes these sinful confections?" A laugh, a look across the room, because the story was told this way only if Greenie was present.

"Cut to the chase, to our very first date—a drink at a local bar, because I wasn't a guy with much in the way of guts or imagination. Or money.

"We're going over the usual ground, and of course I ask her about what she does for a living—this pastry business, how you fall into something like that—and she looks me straight in the eye and says, 'I'm one of the lucky ones. I knew what I wanted to do with my life from the time I was five years old. I've had it easy.' And me, I'm a little speechless, because here I am leading this double life of full-time psychic excavation—in therapy *and* analysis myself, while seeing my first patients. Their doubts and regrets and agonies, along with mine, would make quite a fruitcake, I tell my date, and she says, 'Just because I've had it easy doesn't mean I don't wish sometimes that I got to this place by a road that winds a little more.' And I am smitten. I am down for the count. Certainty. Clarity. Packaged up with modesty. Oh dear God, I thought. Don't tell me this is it. I practically fled right then and there."

After a few sessions of silent listening, then a few of devil's advocate quibbling, Alan's therapist, Jerry, had to agree: from any angle—but certainly from the angle Alan had, lying on a couch—this girl was a catch. For as long as Alan could remember, his mother had been chronically if never dramatically depressed, and his father had apparently chosen to coddle her yet also to ignore her despair—a paradox obvious to Alan and Joya surprisingly early on. It was not a colorful despair, of tempers and sobbing and accusations, but a blue resignation, a despair of drawn shades, slippers worn at dinner, laundry left out on the line for days.

By the time he was off at college, safely removed from the prevailing winds of hometown rumor, Alan found himself wishing that his mother would do Something Big—not suicidal but crazy, like burn furniture on the lawn or have a weeping fit in the grocery store—something that would force his father not just to see the depth of her sadness but to act on it properly. But nothing like that ever happened, and then Alan's father died of a heart attack after mowing the lawn in the August sun, leaving Alan's mother well provided for. And even this did not change her weary but tolerant demeanor, her habit of always saying she was perfectly fine when she knew you knew she wasn't. She did not partake in arguments of any kind.

But Greenie, oh Greenie knew how to argue. And after an argument, she did not sulk. If she was anxious or sad or angry, she said so. If *he* was anxious or sad or angry, she called him on it—not always with the greatest of tact; but clarity, he could remember thinking, is not obliged to be tactful.

After they came to the place in their new life where they began to spend idle evenings together after dinners at each other's apartments—Alan almost always reading, Greenie paging through cookbooks and taking notes or watching something funny on TV—she said, out of a long silence, "Do you know how much you sigh?" Alan looked up from his book; she was smiling.

"I sigh?"

"Oh, quite a lot sometimes."

"Huh." And then he heard himself sigh, and they laughed.

"I'm sorry," he said.

"Don't be," she said. "I just wondered if you knew."

"It's something I'd better attend to, considering what I do," said Alan. "I can't believe no one's mentioned it before."

"Maybe it's just because you're in this very intense time of your life," she offered. "Or maybe it's just me who's noticed. My mother's like that; she notices things that other people don't. Sometimes that's good, and sometimes it isn't."

Alan set down his book. He realized something. "You've never talked about your mother." He, meanwhile, had told Greenie plenty about his.

"Oh," said Greenie, "my mother is wonderful. I'm very lucky. You'll meet her, and you'll see for yourself."

Two months later, when they had been seeing each other for almost exactly half a year, Greenie invited him up to Maine, to the "camp" where she had spent part of every summer since she was born. She laughed when Alan asked, trying not to hide his dread, if they would be staying in tents. The last camping Alan had done was in Boy Scouts, in a state park somewhere off the New Jersey Turnpike (he could remember the all-night whoosh of the not-so-distant traffic, along with the whine of the mosquitoes). Greenie explained that there would be no electricity, no plumbing—yes, you did have to use an outhouse—but there were walls and a roof and screens, batteries for lamps, bug spray, an oven and a stove on a generator, and real, quite comfortable beds with sheets and pillows. Here, she leaned into his ear and whispered, "Though the walls are thin, I should warn you."

They drove a rented car to a boatyard, where they were met by Greenie's father, the George after whom they would one day name their son. Greenie had said he would pick them up in a "whaler"; Alan imagined some sort of schoonerlike craft, a scaled-down version of the *Pequot*. So the noisy, gleaming white boat that turned out to be their conveyance unnerved him a little—as did the tenacious handshake and gaze of the original George. "Alan Glazier!" he exclaimed when he turned from his daughter's embrace. "My girl is crazy about you—that because you're a shrink? Ha ha!"

Before Alan could grope for a clever reply, Greenie's father had grabbed up their duffel bags and thrown them into the boat. Alan had barely seated himself before the man called out, "Time and tide!" and revved up the motor.

Swiftly, without seeming to notice the rise and smack of the boat as it bounced from wave to wave, he guided them through a cluster of tiny rock-rimmed islands—many of them occupied, even monopolized, by toylike houses that appeared far too trusting of the elements. All the while, shouting over the roar of the engine, he delivered a tour guide's monologue, pointing broadly to left and right. Alan tried not to look nervous, clinging as discreetly as possible to the bench on which he was sitting. Greenie stood next to her father, leaning over the windshield, her face lifted gratefully into the wind and the stinging spray of cold ocean water.

"String of Pearls!" shouted George Duquette as they passed an island with an ornately trimmed cottage and an oriental bridge leading to a second, even tinier island with a guesthouse not much larger than a tool-shed. "Island bought by a sea captain back in the days of the China trade! Present for his wife! Rumor was, she told her friends she'd rather've gotten a string of pearls, ha ha! . . . That one over yonder—

Tetcheval, shaped like the head of a horse! Off to port, Little Oslo! Now there's a pile of new money—the first with juice wired straight from the mainland! Tacked on a third story and put in a pair of those compost toilets! Ask me, more trouble than they're worth! Don't know what you're doing, they stink to high heaven!" Every few minutes, Greenie looked back at Alan and smiled.

The island they were fast approaching was a good deal larger than these little knobs of land, and it was covered nearly end to end with thick pine forest, the trees so uniform in height that the island looked as if it were sporting a mammoth crewcut. "Circe's dead ahead!" George called out, pointing at a trio of weathered cabins, a long gray pier reaching toward them like a beckoning arm. "Charlotte, stand by!"

Greenie's true name startled Alan as much as the oddly Odyssean reference—but not nearly so much as the sudden swerve of the boat when George cut the motor and steered them sharply to the side just before they would have struck the pier and literally lost their heads. (Or so it looked to Alan.) Just as quickly, Greenie vaulted from the side of the boat to the pier, a long rope in one hand. Now she bent over the edge, performing some sort of cat's cradle with her father, lashing the boat in place. Alan's ears still buzzed from the din of the motor. His legs felt gelatinous. "Here," said Greenie, who must have read his expression. "Grab my hand." She pulled him to the dock. Already, George had seized their bags and strode ahead, sure-legged, up a wooden gangway laid across a sloping apron of smooth gray rock.

"My God, does he drive like that on land?" Alan said as he accepted her help, without which he was sure he would have keeled over into the water.

"He likes speed, all right," said Greenie. "It's sort of funny, because everybody sees him as the absentminded professor. I think behind the wheel is where he tries to prove them all wrong. My dad, the Italian roadster in disguise." After Scotland, this remark would come back to Alan, but he never mentioned it to Greenie.

There on the dock, regaining his balance, Alan remembered that these cabins were the shared property of Greenie's mother, two uncles, a great-aunt, and several cousins. "Oh, we are so far from rich," Greenie had said when Alan reacted to her mention of a house in Maine. "They sort of used to be, I think—Mom's great-grandparents—and she has the manners to go with money. But now if any of us are, rich I mean, it's a matter of who they married. Mom married a professor. An *English* professor. In the age of easy tenure, thank God." Greenie explained that their part of Smith's Rock (the name of the island itself) was a "compound," though hardly Kennebunkport or the Kennedys' Hyannis. It had been named by Greenie's classics-loving great-great-grandfather, who had tried but failed to rename the island Ithaka. The arrangements of who stayed where and when had grown complicated now that there were so many cousins, but Greenie's parents still took the same cabin for the same three weeks every July.

From way ahead, George called back, "Get your fellow a bunk, get him a drink—or, hey now, reverse that sequence!—then help him get his bearings. Your mom's on her constitutional, hoping to find a few berries as well. Never a single bird, that woman, never a single bird!"

"I feel like such an oaf," said Alan, trying not to cling to Greenie as he searched for his equilibrium. He glared back across the water, which looked perplexingly calm.

Greenie put her arms around him and kissed him on the neck. "Between sailors and oafs, I choose oafs. We're on land now, and no one'll force you back on the water until we have to go. Did that drink sound like a good idea or not?"

So there was a martini—something he hadn't tasted since college— and there was wine, and there was a dinner most remarkable for a meal produced at a "camp": smoked mussels (gathered and smoked right there on the island, he learned), ratatouille, a salad with pears and blue cheese, and a three-layer chocolate cake with whipped cream and cherries, all of it made by Greenie's mother, who would not accept a bit of help. But all that came later. First and foremost, there was Greenie's mother and the entrance she made.

As instructed, Greenie assigned him a bunk, of the genuine boyhood variety, in a spartan creaky-floored room with pine plank walls that looked like they were crawling with eyes. Not that the room was creepy; far from it. The largest of two windows looked toward the mainland, a view many tourists would have shelled out hundreds of bucks to enjoy. Glad to be alone for a time, Alan set his martini on the small plain dresser and circled the room, touching everything, opening everything, from the three paperback books on the side table to the closet and the drawers. *Atlas Shrugged, Kon-Tiki,* and *Is Paris Burning?* were speckled and swollen from years of damp. The closet, too shallow for hangers, was simply a cupboard with hooks. And most of the dresser drawers, which squeaked loudly, were empty. The top drawer held a bar of Dove soap, a flashlight, a bottle of aspirin, and a pair of ruffled tiebacks to phantom curtains (both bedroom windows were naked, perhaps to make the most of their views).

He heard children's voices nearby; leaning out the side window, he saw another house through a row of pines. He could make out a screened porch, where a family was already sitting down to dinner. A bed of coals smoked in the small yard, and Alan smelled steak. He was ravenous.

Following orders, he put on his swimming trunks and went downstairs. Here was Greenie, by a window, looking through binoculars at the smaller islands and the harbor from which they had come. Her father sat at the table, a picnic table with fixed benches, polishing a number of small brass objects that looked to Alan like parts of an antique harness. Greenie's room was down here—right next to her parents' room, which Alan realized was directly below his. He couldn't help wondering if this was on purpose.

There was still no sign of the mother.

"Out! Let's go before the bugs arrive," said Greenie. She handed Alan a towel. In the cooler air of the late afternoon, he felt pleasantly chilly as he followed her along a dirt path through a prickly green thicket blooming with pink and white flowers. The path wound away from the houses, around several curves of rocky shore, to a patch of dark pebbled sand.

Greenie threw her towel on a rock and sprinted into the water. "Oo-hoo!" she exclaimed, and "Yowza!" But she did not pause until she was treading water, up to her neck, looking back at Alan.

Alan clutched his towel. "Here comes the dare to the city-slicker oaf."

"It's worth it, believe me!" she called out.

"I don't like the arctic quaver in your voice."

"Just make a run for it," said Greenie. "That's my motto in life."

"Well, mine is 'Always test the waters.' " Which he did, with his toes, and was instantly sorry. "No," he said. "Definitely no."

"Suit yourself, city boy." She dove under, the soles of her feet the last of her to vanish. He watched her surface a remarkable distance away, then swim, gracefully and languidly, around another bend of the shore. He began to clamber along the rocks, to follow her, when he was stopped short by a voice.

"Hello, young man—though you're not exactly young by the standards of my day."

The most striking thing about the woman standing behind him, at the foot of the path, was the bathing suit she wore. It looked as if it was made of white satin, reflecting sharply the last bright sun of the day. An oddly mixed fashion statement, it was cut low on top but draped down into a modest skirt, reaching nearly to the middle of the woman's thighs. The woman herself was tall and athletically slim, and though she was clearly on the far side of fifty (only the looseness of the skin on her limbs showed her age), her hair was a convincing shade of auburn. It was the hair that made him certain.

"Mrs. Duquette. You surprised me."

"Well, thank you. I like surprising people," she said. She did not move to shake his hand but bent to place her folded towel carefully on a rock, away from the damp sand. She looked him up and down with ambiguous pleasure. "You haven't been in."

"I think I'm not," he said. "Going in."

"Oh, but the cold is worth the shock. The air feels splendid when you come out."

He was going to tell her that she sounded just like her daughter when, just like her daughter, she ran and plunged. She, too, turned to face him, treading water at almost precisely the place where Greenie had. She said, "How was your trip? Was the traffic horrendous? I hope not."

Greenie resurfaced, right beside her mother. "Boo," she said. "Hi, Mom."

"Hello, my darling." The woman who liked to surprise people did not appear surprised in the least. She kissed Greenie on the cheek, and Greenie kissed her back. How absurdly decorous, this floating kiss between these disembodied heads.

"Children," said Mrs. Duquette, "the hors d'oeuvres are out, as I know you must be famished. So go on up and I'll join you after my swim. I'll do the Reader's Digest version. And Charlotte, don't let your father begin another project. Make him be a host, however much it pains him." Whereupon she turned around and swam straight out. She did not hug the shore, as Greenie had, but seemed bent on challenging the boats that crisscrossed the thoroughfare between her island and the next.

Dinner was by candlelight, with French wine procured from a picnic cooler of ice, the table spread with a cloth. George Duquette still wore his polo shirt with the logo of a boatyard, half tucked into baggy madras shorts, the fabric worn so thin in places that the pattern looked smudged. His wife, however, after returning from her Reader's Digest swim, changed into a close-fitting shirtdress, white again. It looked like a well-preserved dress of the fifties, the kind of thing Alan's mother wore in his earliest memories, with so many careful details—pearl buttons, thin belt, pleated skirt—that it gave off a military air, except for its attention to the wearer's curves. ("I have to warn you of one thing: Mom overdresses just about all the time," Greenie whispered to Alan before her mother emerged from her bedroom. "Though she doesn't expect the same of anyone else." Later, when Alan asked if her mother always wore white, Greenie said, "Except to funerals and weddings.")

As soon as they were seated, Alan said, "Thank you so much for inviting me, Mrs. Duquette."

"Olivia, please," she scolded. "Do not make me feel like the grande dame I'm fighting every second from becoming."

Throughout the meal, Olivia quizzed Alan about his work. She told him that she'd always preferred Jung to Freud, as if they'd been opponents in a crucial election. Alan told her that his interest was in human emotions and personal histories, why people make the individual choices they do and how they can be helped to understand their motivations.

"That's bold," said Olivia, looking intently at him. "But also risky, wouldn't you say? To actually *understand* such things about oneself? Just the wondering could leave you quite neurotic." She smiled.

"Beats me what motivates *my* self," George joked.

Olivia did all the serving, all the taking away, stacked the dishes in the cabin's small sink. Dessert, however, she invited her daughter to serve. "You're the one with the professional knife skills," she said. "Not that that should make you nervous, Alan."

He laughed, as expected, while Greenie cut tall, fine slices from the tower of a cake that her mother had concocted. "Oh, the baking I did off island," she said when Alan expressed his amazement. "Every fine meal should end with a cake."

As they all began to eat this indispensable cake, the only sound, besides the urgent ruckus of crickets and the occasional snap of a moth against a screen, was the nicking of forks on plates. "Greenie's right," said Alan. "You're an extraordinary cook."

"Who?" said Olivia. "*Who* speaks so highly of me?"

Greenie said, "That's me, Mom. Alan calls me Greenie."

George said, "I'll be!" He laughed loudly. "You know, I like that. 'Greenie.' Yes. Sounds sweet. Innocent. Yearning."

"Charlotte was her grandmother's name," said Olivia. What she meant, of course, was that Alan had messed with tradition."

"Mom, outside the family nobody calls me Charlotte anymore."

"Perhaps you're tired of the name?"

"Of course not! It's just . . . well, Alan met me as Duke."

"Oh that. That was your college phase, wasn't it? In my sorority, I was called O.J. Lucky thing *that* name went the way of the saddle shoe!" Olivia pushed her plate aside, having eaten only two or three bites of her cake.

"Livvy," said George, "am I permitted seconds? To paraphrase my students, this stuff is to perish upon." What *he* meant, of course, was that his wife should permit the subject to be changed.

So this is high WASP, thought Alan, whose father was a lapsed Jew, his mother a deflated Methodist. He'd never quite realized, because she did not dress or speak or socialize the part, just where Greenie came from.

When dinner was over, George lit a battery-powered lamp and went back to polishing his brass. "Got everything you need there, Alan?" He murmured his approval when Alan held up his book.

"Not enough readers in this world, that's a problem nigh on to rival global warming; what would we call that, literary cooling? Ha," said George, and then he gave his full attention to his project.

"The girls," as he called them, went through a complex ritual to wash the dishes, draining water from an outdoor barrel (rainwater gathered from the roof, explained Greenie) and boiling it on the stove. Alan, once again, was told to behave like a guest. Since George had the one good lamp on the table, Alan had to sit across from him to read, but it was impossible to concentrate on Winnicott when his girlfriend's father, close enough to kiss, was humming the *1812 Overture*. After pretending to read for a few minutes, he got up and wandered out the front door onto the porch. The night was more beautiful than he could have imagined, and he felt the thrill of good fortune: the company of a girl he adored, a fine meal, a clear night, and a setting unlike any he had ever known.

From the next cabin, music drifted sporadically through the pines. Listening hard, Alan caught the harsh sorrow of an Irish ballad. The children he'd heard before were probably asleep. The crickets had also gone silent—puzzling, though perhaps they, too, had a curfew—and a slight breeze had risen, ruffling leaves and swelling the beach towels that hung on the laundry line. From the direction of the water came an occasional, arhythmic sound, like a spoon striking an empty tin can.

Wrapping his arms around his chest for warmth, Alan started down the dirt path, choosing the way toward the dock. As he passed through the waist-high thicket, he found himself surrounded by the green Morse code of fireflies, sparking the colors of the roselike blossoms about them. Did they drink the nectar, like bees? He bent toward one of the flowers; it smelled of nothing to his urban nose. How little he knew of the natural world; it was shameful. As he stood there, looking toward the dock for the source of the metallic tattoo, he was startled for the second time that day by Greenie's mother.

Just behind him, quite close, she said, "You appreciate our little bit of heaven." It sounded like an order, rather than an observation.

"Yes, I do," he said.

"This is your first time in Maine." Another statement; Alan felt slightly resentful, though why shouldn't Greenie have given her mother such details?

"Yes. And now I have to wonder why."

Her laugh was rich and relaxed. "You do indeed."

"You grew up coming here?"

"Oh yes, sometimes for entire summers. I was quite spoiled. I still am!"

Having just met her, he couldn't disagree without sounding absurd, so he tried to laugh lightly, and she made no effort to rescue him from his own wooden reaction. Alan looked out at the water. Even at this hour, boats threaded the channels between the islands, and in the still air he heard the stealthy muttering of motors.

"Charlotte's rather spoiled, too, of course." Greenie's mother spoke abruptly, as if there'd been no pause in the conversation. "She's very talented, I'm sure you know that. She's also very forceful."

"Yes," he agreed. "She knows where she's going. I like that."

"You may like it now, but be careful," said Olivia. "My daughter is a very strongheaded young woman. I say that only because I've known her so long and I love her virtues dearly enough to recognize her flaws—relatively few though they may be."

You say that, Alan thought reflexively, only because she's young and you're not and she's taking your talents to a height you never did. But he said, "We all have flaws. Like me—I don't know a thing about these flowers, all these trees, about anything more natural than a well-watered lawn in the suburbs."

"Oh, that. That's not a flaw, because it can be corrected. Give my husband the time and he will gladly do the job. But be forewarned! The expression 'ad nauseam' comes to mind." She laughed. Alan could not tell if she was speaking fondly or critically. "These flowers? Prunus maritima. More commonly, beach plum. Come fall, I make a pretty mean jam from the fruit. I'll send some to you, shall I?"

"Thank you," said Alan. "I'd be honored." And then, like a baffled sailor spotting at last the beacon of a lighthouse, Alan saw the pennant of Greenie's yellow T-shirt approaching through the beach plum.

"Darling!" called Olivia. "We were just speaking of your talents!"

"Mom thinks she has to sell me," said Greenie as she joined them.

Alan hugged her to his side. "What's that noise?" he said, eager to change the subject. "That clanging."

"Halyards against the mast of a sailboat," said Greenie. He loved the feel of her hand on his waist. "Daddy's pride and joy. He'll take us out tomorrow—or you and I could go out on our own."

Alan wanted to say no, no thank you, but he just smiled. If she wanted to sail, he would go along. If she wanted to climb a tree or scale a cliff (well, a small cliff), he would follow. Next day, he would brave the cold of the water.

She led him toward the boats. "I'm taking him down to show him the phosphorescence," she said to her mother. Alan hoped this was code for "See you tomorrow, Mom." To his relief, Olivia kissed them both good night.

Later on, as he lay alone in his bunk, he heard Olivia's voice, in the

room below his yet alarmingly close, as if she lay on the floor under-
neath his bed.

"I think he's too handsome for her." She spoke softly, but every word
was clear.

"Oh, what's handsome got to do with the price of tea in China?"
Greenie's father answered.

"You're a man, George. You couldn't possibly know the perils of
handsome. To a woman."

"Well, you were sure friendly enough to Boy Handsome."

"I like him. I didn't say he wasn't pleasant. Or smart. He's just a
little . . . a little too prominent for Charlotte."

"Prominent? Like the fellow's in *Who's Who?*"

"No. Like he knows he can do better. Like he's biding time. Would
you want to see her hurt?"

"Livvy, you underestimate our girl," said George.

"No, George, I protect her. That's a mother's job."

"Huh," said George. "The dad's job, I guess, is to bring home the
bacon, right? So let the dad get a good night's sleep."

The floor was so permissive that Alan heard even their good-night
kiss and, shortly after, George's grumbling snore.

In the years that followed, before she went over that Scottish cliff
with her husband, Olivia was nothing but gracious to Alan, yet the
longer he knew her, the less he liked her—and the more he marveled at
the cheerful admiration with which her only child seemed to regard her.
There were times when he wanted to tell Greenie, outright, that her
mother was not the generous, loving woman Greenie presumed her to
be, but he knew better. Maybe some fortunate children were born with
platinum emotional shields, protecting them from harm and keeping
them, also harmlessly, oblivious.

When he helped Greenie go through her parents' house after their
death, empty its drawers and closets, he kept expecting, almost hoping,
to find some deviance that Greenie's mother had kept from the world.
They never found anything of the sort, not so much as a diary or an
accessory to unconventional sex. The closest thing they found to a secret
was a list Olivia had compiled in a journal of menus she kept: a list, person by person, of her all friends' food allergies and metabolic quirks.
In the midst of perpetual tears, Greenie sat down at the kitchen table

and read it with interest. "I had no idea Mrs. Austin was diabetic," she murmured.

By then, however, Alan wasn't one to point a finger at secrets.

FOR CLOSE TO A YEAR after sleeping with Marion—until Greenie gave birth to George and started to nurse—Alan's guilt was the most extreme when he touched Greenie's breasts. Every time he did, he thought of the thick, sinuous caterpillar scars, ridged and warm, he had felt on Marion's chest in the dark. He had felt them before she had let him see, but because she had told him, they were a surprise only to his fingers and his mouth. Because she had told him so calmly, whispering in the dark as they undressed, the scars were a marvel, not an obstacle. The third and last time they made love, very early in the morning, before she drove him back to the high school where he had left his mother's car, he came all over her chest as he looked at the scars, long and straight, magnolia purple against the pale tight skin and blue veining around them.

Over dinner at the roadhouse—the same greasy cheeseburgers of days gone by, two patties served naked in a pool of pink juice on an oval platter, large white biscuits on the side—Marion had told him about the cancer, the wide rough detour it had made in her life. She'd been in Kenya when she felt the lump. By the time she came back to the States six months later and got a proper diagnosis, she felt she had to do the most aggressive thing.

When she saw the look of horror on Alan's face, she laughed. "Hey, my prospects are good. I took the meanest motherfucker drugs they had to offer, and I decided I'd think about reconstruction—love that term, like hard hats are involved—I'd think about that part later. And when later finally came, I didn't really care. I liked feeling so light, like gravity didn't own me there. And I didn't want any more surgery either."

She'd still had nothing strong to drink, and Alan wondered how she could tell him these details with so little inhibition, especially since they practically had to shout to hear each other over the band. Hardly conducive to intimate confessions. Yet her story made him feel safer than he had in the parking lot when they arrived; after all, how could you talk about things like tumors and chemotherapy and then fall illicitly into bed?

"Marion . . . I don't know what to say," he said. "I am so sorry. And all your beautiful hair . . ."

"Oh, little brother, losing my hair was the least of it, let me tell you. Even losing my breasts. I found out, you know, that I have a pretty gorgeous skull. Except that I have to work with people it might scare, I might've kept that Amazon look. I might've commissioned a great tattoo right across the back of my cranium. 'You lookin' at ME?' 'Keep on truckin'.' Anything, really. I could've grown my hair back over it, but I'd know it was still there, my own subliminal message." She laughed softly, as if she were reminiscing about a sports event or a party. "No, the worst came later, when the doctor broke the news to me that I'd almost certainly be infertile because of the chemo. It was like he just up and punched me in the gut. And when I asked him why he hadn't told me this before, he said—and I quote—'It's my job to buy you as much life as possible. I couldn't risk that you'd say no to the drugs.' Move over, Nancy Reagan."

By then Alan had seen two patients with cancer, but they were men, both reassuringly older than he was. "You can't have kids?"

"I can adopt, and you know, with the work I've done, that's very plausible to me—but it doesn't make me great wife material, if you know what I mean. So the irony is, the asshole might as well have told me the chemo would make me an old maid. Not that I was counting on being a wife, but it was down there on my list, somewhere between 'fulfilling work' and 'organic garden.' "

Alan, of all people, ought to have known what to say—that plenty of men could take or leave kids, that Marion was still incredibly sexy, that sensible people knew cancer wasn't a stigma—but the more she told him, the less he felt he could safely tell her.

Marion reached across the table. She put her hands over his and held them firmly. "That was three years ago, and I'm absolutely fine with it now." She sat back. She turned to look at the band and the gangly teenagers dancing in the confetti of light from the strobe.

"Joya will kick herself she wasn't here," said Alan.

"Oh, never mind Joya now. I like this, having you all to myself. When I call you little brother, I'm only half joking. It's like you were my brother, too."

Marion insisted they share an ice cream sundae, and then she asked him to dance. It was a rare slow tune, and he held her reverently close, feeling through their twin shirts her flat, nearly concave chest. He was clumsy, stepping on her feet more than once. "Good thing I'm driving," she said when the song was over.

Once they were both in the car, the doors closed, Marion sat still for a long moment. She was looking down at the keys in her lap with a secretive smile, then she looked at Alan. "I'm not at my parents' house. My old room is full of boxes. I'm at the Red Coach Inn."

"That sounds nice," he said quietly, and that was all he said for the next few hours.

At three in the morning, he told her (for God knew what ridiculous, self-serving reason) about Greenie wanting a baby, about how he was far less than sure, about wondering whether they'd split up, about trying to work it out in his head as if he could be his own therapist. Marion listened for a while and then said quietly, "Just about every couple I know have been through this; it's normal." Because they were in the dark, with the curtains drawn against the bright light of the highway out front, he couldn't tell if she meant to express sympathy or scold him for treating her like a big sister while behaving in a most unbrotherly manner. So he shut up, and he went back to what they had set out to do.

They got dressed when the clock told them it was five. Marion pulled open the curtain. It was almost but not quite dawn. The air looked sweet and palpable and white, like milk. He came up behind her and kissed her neck. He was terrified, but he didn't know if it was because he wanted to see her again as soon as possible or never lay eyes on her from that day on, forget her very existence.

In the high school parking lot, his mother's red car stood entirely alone, absurdly bright in the mist—as obscene, thought Alan, as the lies he would have to concoct. He looked helplessly at Marion. Before he could speak, she said, "Listen," in a strong, startling voice. "I have one thing to say to you, little brother. Go back and have that baby." She reached across him and opened the door. She kissed him and nudged him with a fist.

"Thank you," he had said. (Thank you!)

George's birth washed clean so many things, as Alan had heard (and read) that the arrival of a child, especially a first child, will do. In all the high-wire busyness, his guilt over Marion seemed to shrivel and then disintegrate; or so he thought. Greenie proved to be five times more energetic than Alan had ever imagined a person could be—and poor

Greenie, he remembered thinking sometime that first month; perhaps *proved* was the telling word. Because when he'd agreed at last, out of numb desperation and self-loathing as much as anything else, she'd exclaimed a hundred joyful promises of all that she would be, take care of, provide for, no matter what. When her determination broke down after George's first cold—an ailment whose symptoms were normal yet, in his tiny person, ferocious—Alan had watched her fight back the despair and tears born of dirt-dark exhaustion.

"Please go ahead and fall apart. I know I'm going to," he had said, and both of them had cried together along with George, a collective frustration so loud that in no time it silenced the baby, who stared at his parents with an expression in which curiosity overruled alarm.

If George did not wholly redefine their routines, he gave a new substance to the mortar of their lives. He changed the nature of his parents' simplest social exchanges: with the grocer and the token seller in the subway, with teenage boys on skateboards in the street ("Cute baby, man!"), with all the other parents they already knew. *Welcome,* all those parents seemed to say. *Step across the threshold. Sorry the place is so messy, but you'll be glad you came.*

Alan's practice grew along with his infant son, and sometimes he felt that the latter must be responsible for the former, that fatherhood must make him radiate a greater knowingness, if not an outright wisdom. This was just a hunch, but it gave him a sense of relief that he had, if only by groping in the dark, done the right thing.

Life rolled smoothly along until the accident, not long after George turned two, in which Greenie's parents died. For several months, Greenie vacillated between a testy depression and righteous anger. But her work did not suffer, and gradually, she found her optimistic center once again. We can weather anything, Alan thought smugly. Perhaps they would even have a second child—unlike so many of their city friends, who felt that life with one was both splendid and complicated enough. To his astonishment, the very thought of another baby—a baby, not just a child—filled him with nostalgic yearning.

Alan had just shared these thoughts with Joya, during one of their catch-up calls, when she said, "Oh, speaking of babies! You'll never guess who's out here, too, whose name I saw on this list of lectures at Berkeley. I'm constantly thinking I'm going to sign up for stuff and get myself some enlightenment, learn about something completely new—

such a ridiculous idea, but hope springs eternal! So I see this online post-
ing for a lecture on volunteering in the cancer community and guess
who's giving it?"

Alan was crossing the room, only half listening, because he was in
charge of George while Greenie was out working. George had just disappeared into their bedroom carrying a crayon. "No, George! Only on
the paper!" he hissed as he confiscated the crayon, sparing the closet
door. George began to cry.

"Marion! Remember Marion?" he heard Joya say as he carried his
struggling son toward the kitchen, whispering, "How about a pretzel?"

He dumped several pretzels into a dish and placed it on the seat of a
chair.

"You've got to remember Marion. I mean, you were like smitten with
her when you were twelve. It was hilarious watching you try to conceal it."

"Of course," said Alan. "I remember her."

"So I looked up her phone, and it wasn't listed, but I actually went to
the lecture and saw her after. It was so incredible—I think she's too busy
to hang out with, but we had coffee, and it was great to see her. Anyway,
she's done this totally modern thing, having a baby on her own—he's
like three now, she said—and moving out here and getting another
degree, and she's teaching, and she's really involved in some food co-op
and a church and—"

"She adopted a baby?" said Alan. He was watching George crush
pretzels intentionally into the fabric of the chair seat.

"No, no—had it on her own! I saw a picture, and he looks like her
dad, it's sort of hysterical. That huge, serious forehead. She said she
never got married or lived with anyone after the Peace Corps, and then
she had cancer—and you can guess how many guys are mature enough
to commit to a woman after that."

"But who's the father?"

"For God's sake, Alan, you sound like one of our parents," said Joya.
"Who cares? I'm not sure she does."

"How is she?" he said quickly.

"She looks great," said Joya.

George began chanting for more pretzels, and Alan used it as an
excuse to get off the phone. Two nights later, when Greenie went out to
work after George had fallen asleep, he called Joya back and told her

about the reunion. At first, after telling Alan what a schmuck he was, she laughed at his vanity, at the ridiculous thought that the child could possibly be his.

When she finally understood what he was suggesting, she said, "Jesus, Alan, Marion would never use anybody like that. You are acting like an asshole."

"You don't really know Marion. Not anymore. She's been through a lot more than she'll let on to anyone, I think. I wouldn't blame her for putting her own interests ahead of anyone else's." Strange that he was defending her. He thought of the scars on her chest, of her stubborn desire to preserve them rather than hide or replace them.

Joya was silent for a while. He waited. She sighed twice, first with exasperation, then with what sounded like pity.

"Alan, I doubt I'll see her again, unless we run into each other."

So she had sensed what he wanted to ask. Still, Alan waited; Joya was generous, but you had to let her offer the favor herself.

She said, "No, Alan. This is your problem. I can't help you with this one. I can't." She sighed, this time with pure impatience. "Oh *Alan*. I'm so—I can't talk to you right now, I'm sorry. I can't even think about poor Greenie. I'll call you in a few days, but . . . I'm sorry," she said, and she hung up. Two days later, she left him a message during the day. Just an address, nothing more. It took him three months to write, and all he could say to Marion was that he'd heard she was out there, he wondered how she was—her health, her life, her "dubious achievements." He did not tell her about George or say that he had heard about her child. It was a cowardly, dishonest letter that did not deserve a reply. It did not get one.

BEFORE ALAN WENT OUT THAT EVENING, he checked on Saga's peony plant, as if it might have been stolen or taken flight. He opened the window and reached out to feel the soil in the pot. It was damp. He closed the window and just stood there awhile, staring at the plant, as if there were something else he could do for its welfare. He noticed that the tip of each stalk had opened into a feathering of tiny leaves, olive stained with crimson.

He had told Saga, before she left, that he'd like to have another look at the puppies; he couldn't think of any other way to make sure he'd see her again. She had given him the phone number of the guy named Stan who hadn't shown up that first day. Couldn't Saga take Alan to see the puppies? No, she'd said, but if he adopted one of them, she would be sure to check in. She should call or drop by anytime, he told her awkwardly. She thanked him but laughed, as if their continuing to know each other was patently absurd. In a way, it was, but Alan couldn't help worrying about her. He still knew nothing about where she lived or how she made her way in the world. She could be a wealthy eccentric, for all he knew; it really wasn't his business.

The air was soft and beguiling, and outside Walter's Place, four couples waited on the sidewalk for the few outdoor tables, all occupied. Alan had hoped to eat outside, but he did not want to wait alone. He was not in the mood to converse with strangers, and he had brought nothing to read. When he stepped inside, Walter was right there.

"Husband of my runaway confectioner, hello!" He shook Alan's hand with vigor.

Where did all this ready wit come from? Alan thought bitterly. "Greenie says hi," he said, just to say anything.

"I spoke with the traitress herself just a few days ago. I told her that Tina is a princess, but nevertheless I am suffering, I am wasting away." Walter clasped a menu against his heart. He led Alan by the arm toward a hearthside table, a prime spot in winter. "The special tonight—and this one's really special—is Hugo's brandade Cape Cod," Walter confided. "There's just one left; shall I nab it for you?"

"Fine," said Alan. "Sounds great." He had no idea what he had just ordered, but he did not want an extended conversation with Walter. He wanted a meal that he didn't have to cook and that was meant to be eaten with a knife and fork. He wanted to ignore his jealousy, stop wondering what Greenie would talk about to Walter now that she was so far away.

Gazing aimlessly about, he was stunned to see Gordie seated at the back end of the bar, eating alone—or waiting for someone to return. Alan tried to look away, but Gordie had spotted him, too. The other man waved, smiling, as if everything were normal, as if he'd be seeing Alan, side by side with Stephen as planned, just a few days hence. Or would he? Alan gave in and waved back. Gordie returned to reading a magazine and eating his meal.

Alan saw the diners around him now as he often saw any gathering of people: a collection of invisibly layered lives, like a display of minerals he remembered from the Museum of Natural History, the one he'd known during his childhood rather than George's. You'd go into a dim booth where a glass case held a homely assemblage of plain old rocks. But when you punched a button, a light would click on, transforming the rocks into primitive jewels, pocked and striated in glowing shades of green, purple, red, and blue. Halfway through his training at the institute, Alan had been struck by the memory of this transformation. That's it, he'd thought, that's what my work will be like: revealing all this hidden color and light.

Across the room, the waves of laughter, the general gaiety of spring, he stared for a moment at Gordie, who was still reading his magazine. Right then, to Alan, Gordie appeared as dark and dense and gritty as any other person there. Alan thought of George, for whom the world was still mostly aglow, so eminently knowable, even waiting and eager to *be known,* and except that Walter was now approaching—grinning, flourishing a large white plate—Alan might have wept.

II

The
Realm
of
You

EIGHT

WHEN ALAN CALLED, IT WAS OFTEN BEFORE Greenie came home from work. He would talk to George, and she would call him back when she returned, if it wasn't too late in New York. Rarely was Alan the one to call back.

That night, she came in early enough to read to George but late enough that she had missed his father's call. The ceiling fan spun on its wobbly axis above their heads as Greenie read a book she had brought from the library called *Mordant's Wish*, about a mole who wishes for a friend and the whimsical way his wish comes true. It involved a bug that lived in a bowl of antique buttons, a pool of melted ice cream shaped like a hat, and a girl who read a secret message in a shopping list she picked up off the street. It was a book about how a chain of seemingly trivial actions and free associations could change somebody's life. (Or was it about how wishes came true in the oddest of ways?)

"I loved that story," she said when she closed the book. "Did you?"

"It was okay," said George. "I like stories with dragons better. I like when scary things happen. Actually." He enjoyed this new word and tried to use it whenever he could.

"I'll look for that kind next time," said Greenie. She turned off the lamp and lay down next to George. She would rest for a minute under the cool stroking of air from the fan. The occasional breezes from the open window smelled lovely for the first time in weeks. They smelled of pine trees—but of green boughs and needles, not of burning sap. The fires had been contained.

The phone in the living room woke her, and she stumbled out into the light. As she picked up, she saw Other Charlie's business card on the table beside her address book. It had been sitting there now for a week. They'd promised to call each other, but so far they hadn't.

"Greenie?"

"Oh Alan. Hi." She sat down. "I fell asleep beside George." She looked at the clock; it was nine-thirty.

"I'm sorry. I know you get up early."

"No, I . . ." She was going to say that she needed to take a cool bath and make some lists, but details like this now felt awkward to relate to a husband so far away for so long. "I'm looking forward to your visit," she said.

"Yes," he answered simply.

"I am. I want you to like it here."

Alan sighed. "I'm sure I will."

"I wasn't trying to make you say that. I know it's complicated."

"To state the obvious." But then he said, "I miss you both."

"We miss you all the time," she answered, but strangely, the affection in his voice—the sentiment she was always longing to hear—made her nervous. She glanced down and saw Other Charlie's card again. "Did I tell you that I've run into a childhood friend here? At work, at the mansion."

"Oh?" said Alan. "No."

He did not sound curious to hear more, but Greenie went on. "Charlie Oenslager. Do you remember him from when we got married, that party my mother gave the week before?"

He told her that he didn't. She was about to describe Other Charlie when Alan said, "Listen. I called because I have something important to tell you."

Greenie felt her mind come to attention, as if pulling away from her will. Did he sound solemn? Joyful? Spiteful? "Yes?"

"I'm getting a dog."

Briefly, Greenie laughed.

"I thought I should tell you. Before I tell George."

"A dog? You're getting a dog? Just like that? I mean, without . . ."

"Without consulting you?" Now Alan laughed. "For starters, maybe I'm lonely. Maybe I'm not used to coming home to an empty house. Unless you count Sunny. Poor Sunny. Sometimes I wish he weren't such a survivor."

"Alan, how did you suddenly decide to get a dog?"

"I'm getting her from a woman I met."

Very deliberately, Greenie could tell, he let the silence persist. He was trained, she'd always thought, to use silence the way the Old Masters used white. The surface of a pearl, the shaft of light from a window, the glint on a chalice or a dagger.

She gave in. "A woman you met."

"On the street. She was carrying a box of puppies. It's a long story. I suppose it was an act of charity—the puppy, I mean."

"To the woman or the dog?" said Greenie, unable to hide her irritation.

"Good question."

"It's late, Alan. I think we're both tired. I think we should talk tomorrow."

"Don't you want to know anything about the dog?"

"Okay. What kind of a dog is your dog?"

"Don't be sarcastic, Greenie. She's a funny, mixed-up kind of dog. Just the way she looks, I mean. Part corgi, I'm told, but smaller. You know, the kind of dog the Queen Mother has. But not that color. White with brown spots, almost tiger spots. Brindle, that's what it's called."

Greenie marveled at his tone. It was so . . . lively.

"Is she house-trained?" This was the wrong question.

"No, Greenie, I'll be instructing her to pee all over everything here that belongs to you. For God's sake, you act like I'm letting another woman move in."

"What's her name? Does she have a name?"

"I want George to name her. She's called Molly, but she's still very small, so we can change it."

"Are you bringing the dog with you? Out here?"

"I am," said Alan. "The airline lets one pet travel in the main cabin of the plane. I made a reservation for her, too."

Greenie wondered how much it cost to fly a dog cross-country, then hated herself for wondering. "So you'll . . . take her along with you and George?"

"I already found a couple hotels that take pets."

"A dog," she said. "We own a dog." She waited for him to correct the "we," but he didn't.

"Have you hidden from me that secretly you hate dogs?" he asked.

"Of course not. We had a dog when I was in grade school. Hero. You've seen him in pictures."

"So is it that you're now in charge of all the big decisions? Because something about this is pissing you off."

"I'm not pissed off. I'm . . . I don't know, 'thrown for a loop' is what my dad used to say. You know, I've already told George we can't have a dog here. It's too much responsibility, I told him. Because, of course, the responsibility would be mine. Or Consuelo's."

"Well, there's the beauty of it," said Alan. "I bought the dog a round-trip ticket, just like me, Greenie. The dog will be my responsibility."

"So now George can miss you *and* a dog back in New York."

"Jesus, Greenie, this isn't some calculated move to screw up your . . . big promotion, or whatever it is you consider that job."

"This job is good," said Greenie. "This job is actually great, as a matter of fact. This job could pay for all of us to live here for a while. Which it could never do back there. Which, it seems to me now, very *few* jobs could do back there."

The silence that followed was not an artful silence. Greenie knew she had succeeded, cleverly and stupidly all at once, in making her husband even angrier at her than he had already been.

"You want me to drop all my patients just like that and move out there next week? It's doable," said Alan. "That way, George could get the dog he's been wishing for, and you—you could have a dog of your own, a human lapdog! How's that for an idea?"

"I'm sorry," she said. "I'm sorry, Alan."

"You'd save the money you're spending on that . . . nanny you've gone and hired, and it sounds like we could be filthy rich. Maybe get to sit on the other side of the door you work behind. Drink expensive California wines and discuss the evils of unionized labor and state parks too darn big for the public good."

"Fuck you," Greenie whispered viciously, mindful of George.

"You will not get me to hang up," said Alan.

Greenie began to cry. "You'll say I'm not acting like it, I know, but I love you. Why are we like this? Why can't we talk anymore?"

"Because there's this pretty big decision we didn't make together. That's my best educated guess."

She heard him breathing; she imagined he could hear her breathing, too. She would not speak until she felt calmer. At last she said, "We're nothing if not educated. We're smart enough to work this out. We simply will. So tell George about the dog tomorrow. Whether or not I'm here. And send a picture; he'll want that as soon as he can have it."

"You're right," said Alan.

"About something. Thank heaven." What was she *doing*? She softened her voice and said, "I'm right about this, too: we do belong together."

"I hope so."

"I know so," she said, and after they hung up, she knew how it would be. As if they were together in bed, they would each lie awake a long time, imagining conversations with the other, ones they'd had in the past, ones they might have in the future. Greenie saw this as clearly as she could see the Milky Way above the trees once she had turned out the light. She still did not understand how you could be a part of something that looked so unbelievably far away.

TO VISIT THE RANCH was to see Ray turned inside out, his childhood worn on his sleeve. Greenie and George had made the drive following Ray's entourage, pulling up in time to watch Ray greet his three dogs, all big hairy herding dogs who would have been miserable in town, all mottled brown and dusty, just like most of the landscape around them. He lay down full length on the gravel drive so they could trample him with their bearlike paws and lick his face.

"I can't wait to meet Treehorn," said George when he saw this display.

"You will, honey, very soon," said Greenie. When Alan had given George the news, George had named the puppy in an instant. No, he did not need time to think about it, Greenie heard him say to his father. He chose the name of the character in a book Consuelo had checked out of the library for him that week. Never mind that the character was a boy, the dog a girl.

Ray's ranch occupied a plain of scant grass and scrub juniper that stretched north toward a wide mesa and, beyond it, the Sangre de Cristo Mountains. Up close, the cows were massive creatures, with an almost industrial rather than animal weight.

The silvery glinting Greenie had seen from a distance revealed itself now as the corrugated metal roofing of three adobe barns; away to one side stood a great square house built of stone. Three black-and-white goats sauntered in the shade of a dozen cottonwoods, which surrounded the hacienda like a council of dignified elders. The trees were in full leaf but so dusty that they resembled trees in a sepia photograph from long in the past. Greenie thought she noticed birdhouses high on some of the trunks; once she was out of the car, peering up into the branches, she realized that they were cameras.

"I want to see the horses," George said.

"Let's go inside first," said Greenie.

The house was just as she had imagined it would be: a place of *almost* genuine rustic charm. The furniture was dark, blunt, and stolid. The native rugs and blankets that gave the rooms their only color were beautiful, an ancient geometry of reds and browns, but they were also worn and tired, scuffed paper thin by generations of steel-toed boots. Except for one large, murky landscape over the fireplace, most of the pictures were documentary: photographs of Ray with family, of Ray with other powerful men, but, more frequently, of livestock. One wall of the living room was covered entirely with prizewinning Angus and Hereford cows. Each one stood in perfect profile, hooves primly together, like a cookie-cutter cow. In every picture, the cow's handler stood squashed against the margin, holding aloft the lead rope attached to the halter. A ribbon draped the animal's neck, or the handler (always a man) held a trophy in his free hand. Along an adjacent wall stood a long glass case lit from within. Greenie was reminded of her high school gymnasium—except that the prizes on display here had been won not by teenage athletes but by cows.

Yet everywhere amid the tarnished trophy urns and the heavy furniture gleamed the sleekest of stereo systems, laptop computers, and telephones. A tangled sheaf of electrical cords passed under a table supporting a lamp made from a stuffed porcupine.

"Mommy, is he real?" gasped George.

"Well, honey, he was."

"Do you think he was shooted? Diego says people shoot animals because they don't like them. Or actually for fun." George looked up at her with concern and disapproval.

The porcupine, posed on its hind legs, was a creature of enormous girth, the size of a well-fed raccoon. "It's a shame when people do that," she said. "I don't know about this guy, but he looks like he was pretty old when he died, so maybe he just died fat and happy."

"How old do porcupines get?"

"I'm afraid I don't know that either, sweetie."

A maid waved timidly from the doorway. She took their suitcase and, without a word, led them upstairs to the room they would share.

George knelt on one of the beds so he could look out the window. "Hey, a weather vane!" he cried out, pointing.

Oh my New York City child, thought Greenie, touched by how exotic he found such ordinary things. As for the ordinary things he found disturbing—well, many of them *ought* to seem disturbing.

"Do the horses get their own barn?"

"We'll ask," said Greenie, tired of telling him how much she didn't know.

"Mom, what does it mean when you break a horse?"

"It means taming a horse. Teaching a horse to wear a saddle and let people ride it."

"Why do you have to tame a horse?" said George. "You don't tame a cow or a sheep or a chicken. They're not like lions."

"No, they're not. Maybe it's just teaching them to wear a saddle and be ridden. The way you learned to ride a tricycle or walk in snow boots."

"Actually, it's not like that," said George. "No one's riding *me*."

Greenie was struggling to find a better analogy when she heard Ray calling her from below. She led George down a staircase to the kitchen, the only room that did not smell aggressively of sawdust, leather, and mothballs. The ranch cook, McNally, had a body as dense as a stump and nearly as short. He looked as if he'd been sustained for his sixty-some years on a diet of jerky and buckshot. He was clean-shaven, his gray hair combed neatly back, but his cheeks blazed with broken veins and acne scars. Two of his fingernails were black right down to the cuticle. Greenie had spoken with McNally on the phone, but this was the first time they'd met.

"Cake Lady!" he exclaimed. "Come to sweeten our lives."

"That's me. Sweetener of lives," she said.

"Ray says you're going to teach me a thing or two about pies."

"I can do that," said Greenie. "Pies are just know-how and practice. The only secret's a light touch."

McNally squinted. "I look like a light touch to you?"

George, still standing beside her, said, "I want to see the horses now. Can I please?"

McNally yelled toward the living room, "George! Tall George!"

Small George shrank against Greenie's leg at the force of McNally's voice. Clearly, this was not a sedate household of intercoms, like the mansion in Santa Fe. It was a house of men shouting from room to room.

Ray's driver appeared in the doorway. "Yo there, Small, my wish is your command. Nowhere else I got to drive today. Hey, we forgot!" He held his hands up and the boy slapped them hard, laughing.

"Five up, five down, five twist around!" the two Georges chanted in unison, performing the ritual greeting they had devised.

"I want to see the horses, Tall," said Small, and out the door they went, hand in hand, without a backward glance at Ray's two cooks.

"When does the buyer get here?" Greenie asked McNally.

"Tomorrow lunch. I got that squared away. For tonight, I got ribs, I got potatoes in foil, I got three-bean salad. You just conjure those pies and I'll look on. About the fanciest dessert I make in this kitchen is whiskey poured over coffee ice cream."

"Sounds good to me," said Greenie. She asked McNally if he stocked lard.

"More flavors than Baskin-Robbins." He pointed to a freezer the size of a toolshed.

Greenie made enough pastry for five pies. She showed McNally how to divide it into flattened cakes, wrap them, and put them away to chill. Using fruit she had brought from the city, they filled two shells with apricots, two with cherries, and one—for Small—with butterscotch custard.

At dinner that night, Greenie was the only woman. It was an easy, inclusive meal. Everyone ate at the wooden table in the kitchen, a table about as long as a stretch limousine—still only half the length of the dining table at the mansion. The maid had left, but five cowhands remained, along with Small George, Tall George, McNally, two security men, and Ray. The cowhands said grace in Spanish and then talked mostly among themselves; one security guard (jacket discarded, holster and gun fully exposed) punched away at a GameBoy; Ray talked intermittently on a cordless phone; and the Georges colluded like playmates, their bantering inaudible from where Greenie sat. McNally grilled Greenie about New York City. When he told her that he subscribed to *Gourmet,* she had such a hard time not laughing that a green bean nearly lodged itself in the back of her nose. He told her that he read the restaurant reviews and kept a list of the places in other cities where he'd like to eat if he were to travel.

After three and a half pies had been demolished, Tall took Small to see the horses again. "We'll watch 'em do bed check," said Tall. When McNally insisted on washing the dishes, Greenie caught up with them.

The center aisle of the horse barn was floodlit, its glazed brick floor shinier than the floor in Ray's Santa Fe kitchen. The order and cleanliness of the place—the martialed hay bales, the detailed feeding schedule chalked on a blackboard, the racks of harnessings and silver-pommeled saddles—took her by surprise. At the far end, she saw Tall lifting Small so he could stroke the nose of a speckled gray horse.

"Mom!" he called when he saw her, "Ray's favorite horse! Mica. It's a she. She's the mayor of the barn, like the mayor of New York City."

Tall George smiled at Greenie. "Hey, Small, a mare is what you call a lady horse. But you're right. She probably is the boss of this place. She be the queen."

The barn contained twelve stalls, all occupied. The horses looked up as Greenie passed, yet they were clearly used to strangers. It *was* odd that people could control these enormous animals, "break" them. She thought of the circus, of elephants made just as docile. Greenie had ridden horseback one summer, at a camp, but never since. She knew much more about controlling a sailboat. Perhaps the sea could be said to have a mind of its own, but never the boat.

"Pet her!" Small George commanded.

"She's very soft." Greenie smiled at her son, held in the arms of a man who was not his father, who looked nothing like his father yet with whom he seemed completely happy.

She looked into a room beside Mica's stall. She saw a locked glass-front medicine chest holding pharmaceutical vials and boxes; a rack supporting two long guns; and, stopping her for a moment, a crucifix—small and dark but gruesomely detailed—hanging alone on a white wall. One of Ray's men, passing by with a bale of hay, must have seen her staring. He paused and, assuming she'd focused on the guns, said, "Do not be alarmed if you hear shots in the night. Coyotes."

"Coyotes would kill a cow?"

"Cows, no. But when we have calves . . . and dogs, goats. Cats—ah, cats are very tasty." He grinned like a hungry predator.

"Oh," said Greenie, aware how dumb she must have seemed to these men. The night, she realized when they left the barn, was noisy and filled with unseen activity of so many kinds.

On the way out, she heard Small George whisper loudly to Tall, "Look at that bit. That is a horrible kind of bit." She looked back and saw them standing before a pegboard hung with bridles.

"Hey, Small, I bet that's an antique, up for show," said Tall.

Small shook his head. "Look how it's pointed. That goes on the tongue of the horse."

Tall swung the boy's arm. "You are some kind of sharp-eyed guy, but don't let that imagination go nuts." He led Small away from the bridles.

As Greenie tucked George into bed that night, he said, "Actually, I saw a horse in a blindfold."

"Here?" said Greenie.

"No. At Diego's dad's farm. I think he was being punished."

Greenie did not know how to answer. She kissed George on the forehead. "Ray's horse is beautiful, don't you think?"

George smiled. "She's like silver."

Greenie climbed into her own bed. When George fell asleep, she turned out the light. She listened. No coyotes (and no gunshots), but she heard relentless crickets, the mild complaint of a cow, the jingling of a dog's tags as it was called into the house long after she'd thought the rest of the household asleep.

Next morning, McNally took care of breakfast. Ray liked to go for a long ride at dawn; before setting out, he would eat a platter of steak and eggs. It was Ray's voice, after his return, that woke Greenie and George. He stood by the nearest barn, calling orders to his men. Cattle were being paraded in and out, soaped up, scrubbed, hosed down, brushed. Some of them protested loudly.

"That doesn't sound like mooing," said George. "That's like *yelling*. Is Ray being mean to the cows?"

"Once upon a time you hated baths, too," said Greenie. "You should've heard how loud *you* yelled."

An hour later, she and George were standing under the cottonwoods—the only cool place out of doors—feeding handfuls of grain to the goats, when a pickup cruised down the drive, a truck larger and more macho than those she'd seen coming and going, driven by the hired hands. It pulled up at the house.

As a tall woman got out of the cab, Ray came running from the barns.

"Claudia, Claudia!" He pronounced her name *Cloudia* and bent to kiss her hand.

Claudia pulled her hand from his, but she looked pleased. "None of your chauvinistic nonsense. And none of your Wal-Mart Italian." When Ray straightened up, Greenie saw that this woman stood an inch or two taller than he did. They hugged in a slapping, comradely way, a hug between men.

"Long time, Claudia Rose."

"Ray, only my dad calls me that nowadays. And yes, thank you, I'd love something cool to drink. Shall we go inside?"

"You are one step ahead of me all the way," Ray said as he followed her into his own house. "You are."

Once Ray took Claudia out to the barns, Greenie, McNally, and the two Georges had the house to themselves all afternoon. Outside, it was over ninety degrees, so Greenie had insisted that George stay in. He whined in protest, but Tall said he'd teach him a new game. They sat in the living room, drinking lemonade under a fan, shouting "Spit!" and slapping cards on a table. Small George squealed with abandon.

The maid had closed all the windows and drawn the upstairs curtains; the thick walls of the hacienda would hold the cool night air for a few hours still. Greenie worked in front of the kitchen windows that faced the barns, where cattle and people had stirred up a pall of sunstruck dust. Through it, she could make out Claudia and Ray sitting on a bale of hay in a narrow strip of shade against a wall, eating the sandwiches McNally had made before Greenie even came downstairs that morning. The most audible voice was Ray's, typically clamorous, whether it sounded ornery or joyful.

McNally had no copper bowls, so Greenie rubbed vinegar and salt on the surface of a deep ceramic basin. Angel food cake required perfect egg whites, stiff and lofty. After she had finished the beating, she paused to watch McNally coil two layers of bacon around several filets of beef and thought of Walter, with whom she now spoke at least twice a month. She imagined him working here in her place. Walter would like McNally; vice versa might be a different story. Not that the two would ever, in a million years, come face-to-face.

McNally looked up when he heard Ray shouting his name. He opened the window. "Set an extra place!" yelled Ray.

"Roger and out!" McNally yelled back. He slammed the window. Greenie started laughing.

"What?" said McNally, smiling at her over his shoulder.

"It's just so . . . hilariously male around here. Even this buyer—this *Cloudia*—what's her story?"

"Hoo boy," said McNally. "He don't know it, but that man's met his high noon. Ray went to school with her big brother. She goes off to get some fancy-ass eastern degree, works in Washington as a lawyer, marries another shiny-butt lawyer, gets divorced, finally comes to her senses and hightails it back out here. She called Ray a couple months back and said she's got herself a ranch up across by Telluride. And is that woman a pair-a legs or what!"

"That woman can literally look down on Ray," said Greenie. "He'd never go for that."

"Who knows what that man would go for! His time's come, that is all I can say. Nearly all of us, our time comes. Pairing up, same as death. Difference is, you need to be smart enough to see it." McNally tapped the spot between his crinkled eyes. He placed the filets in two iron skillets. Over them he poured most of a bottle of brandy.

"What about your time, McNally? When was your time?"

He turned to her with a look of amusement. "Oh my time? Well, I ain't so smart. I figure it came and went in a big bright whoosh, like a wildfire gunnin' through, but likely I was passed out cold and missed it. Can't even tell you her name, that's how dense I am. But that's why I'm a ranch cook, not a governor. The dense part." He put the brandy bottle to his lips to drink the few swallows left in the bottom. He winked at Greenie. "Hey, Small!" he bellowed, and George came running through the door, faster than he would have come for Greenie.

As McNally ignited the filets and rolled the skillet to spread the flame, the front-door knocker sounded. Greenie could hear the vacuum cleaner on the second floor and knew the maid wouldn't answer, so she wiped her hands and went to the door herself. Back in the kitchen, she heard Small George exclaim in amazement.

She opened the door to Other Charlie. They both laughed.

"I'm stalking you," he said, kissing her cheek. He walked past her and stood in the living room, gazing around. "I've been granted a private audience to plead my case. Will I get another great meal in the bargain?"

"You will," said Greenie. "You'd be the extra place we've been ordered to set."

He followed her to the kitchen and drank a glass of water. She pointed him toward the barns. Through the window, Greenie watched him shake hands with Ray. They walked around one of the buildings, out of sight.

The angel food cake that Ray had requested was to be a birthday cake. The birthday was Claudia's, Ray told Greenie that afternoon, clearly pretending that this had just occurred to him. "How 'bout with some kind of berry sauce?"

"That's her favorite cake?" said Greenie.

"I have no idea what the woman's favorite cake is. Everybody likes angel food, right?"

"Maybe," said Greenie suggestively.

Ray gave her a testy look. "I got cows to sell here."

"How many candles?" goaded Greenie.

Ray considered this. "Don't know as we have birthday candles on hand," he said. "But you get McNally to fork over some sparklers from his personal munitions. And how about pink frosting? The feminine touch." He walked out the door before she could tell him that Claudia did not look like a woman who needed or even wanted the feminine touch.

Dinner was late, so Greenie gave George a hot dog and put him to bed while McNally quartered heads of iceberg lettuce and smothered them with blue cheese dressing. A basket of Greenie's whitest bread sat smack in the center of the table; no flowers here. Nor were there candles, which would have guttered in the cross breeze created by numerous fans, the only relief from the heat that had finally breached the stone walls. By the time Greenie sat down, the conversation was nothing but cattle: the best way to ship sperm (UPS, over dry ice, the general favorite); whether calving was safer when induced (higher vet bills but fewer stillbirths and less time wasted waiting, Claudia argued); whether the Brits and their idiotic denial of mad cow disease had blown their beef industry permanently to hell (the farmers over there were downtrodden wimps and losers, said Ray).

Ray's and Claudia's voices were so strident—with Ray's men joining in—that Greenie and Other Charlie sat mostly in silence. They'd wound up on opposite sides and opposite ends of the long table, so all they could do in their shared exile was exchange their covert amusement from a distance, especially when Ray and Claudia began to debate the ideal way to bed a barn with straw once calving season came.

"High, deep, and fresh is best for babies and mamas," said Claudia.

"I see *you* don't clean the barns and haul the manure," said Ray.

"You do?" she shot back.

"We aim to conserve on this ranch. Waste not and all that."

Claudia laughed. She took the last piece of bread from the basket and wiped the last gravy from her plate. "Oh Ray, cows are never about conservation. Switch to soybeans and we'll talk conservation." She took a bite of the bread and stared kindly at Ray as she chewed. "Here's how I see it. The cow's udder is just like a dinner plate." She gestured at her own plate, cleaned nearly to a polish. "If it's dirty, the baby's exposed to more germs. Not good, right? Know what? More straw, less dependence on antibiotics. Now never mind the public hysteria; which costs more, straw or drugs?"

Ray listened, sipping his beer.

"And the hauling and spreading, smart guy? More straw makes for better fertilizer out on the fields and gardens. I rest my case." She finished her bread with relish. Greenie could see that she was the kind of woman who ate to her heart's content without a second thought, without gaining an ounce. She had the body (and the voice) of a warrior goddess. She seemed impervious even to the warmth of the kitchen, the only one at the table whose face did not shine.

Greenie caught Other Charlie's eye. They laughed openly, helplessly.

"You eastern slugs just help yourselves to more mashed potatoes," said Ray. "Let the cowfolk reign supreme." He waved his fork in the air, lasso style.

"Don't pretend you know a thing about roping," said Claudia. "I've seen you out there."

But when the sparklers were lit, the warrior cowgirl had tears in her eyes, tears of pleasure and surprise. Ray looked happy, with himself and with her. Other Charlie smiled down the table at Greenie.

"Okay, McNally, douse those things," Ray said after the applause. "Burn my house down and the vengeance of my ancestral spirits shall track you like a pack of rabid wolves. The nonendangered kind we're still allowed to shoot."

After dinner—after Other Charlie made a laughingstock of himself by asking for herbal tea instead of coffee—Greenie told McNally it was her turn to wash up. Other Charlie lingered while Greenie loaded the dishwasher and filled the cake pans with hot soapy water. "Fish and the law," she said. "Does that make you an ichthyological lawyer?"

Other Charlie groaned. "Oh, fish are the least of it. Right now, I am having a demolition-derby education in the measurement of dissolved-solids concentrations and the effects of selenium on migratory water-fowl. I am up to my neck in eco-legalese."

As Greenie listened to him speak, she recognized his precise enuncia-tion, something their schoolmates had mimicked, not always meanly, behind his back. He'd been one of those kids you wanted to mock but couldn't help admiring. She felt as if her brain were undergoing a pal-pable change, a realignment of the present with her distant past, an unforgetting.

He told her about the dam he was fighting. He told her about the ways in which the irrigation systems of the Southwest had filled the rivers with salt, pesticides, and other invisible pollutants; how down-stream, across the border, entire regions of Mexico that were once fertile now lay fallow and useless.

"You can't borrow water from a river like money from a bank," he said. "Money that's soiled and crumpled doesn't lose its value. But water—well, there's no interest you can pay that will restore water to its original purity."

"So the fish die," said Greenie.

"Yes, but listen, the fish are . . . it's a longer story."

Greenie had turned to oiling McNally's iron skillets. The first won-derfully chilly night air began to drift through the windows. When Greenie stopped to close the one right beside her, she saw Other Charlie, his passionate gestures, reflected in the glass. Except for the roiling of the dishwasher, the house around them was silent. Greenie realized, briefly, that she did not know if Claudia had left or stayed. "Tell me the longer story," she said.

So Other Charlie told her about dams, how they had irrigated but would ultimately ruin the West. In the desert, he told her, dams sent water to places where there would have been none—and took water *away* from places where there had been, perhaps, just enough. He told her how, every summer now, stretches of the Rio Grande went dry for miles on end, stranding the fish.

"The truth is," he said after a long pause, "I don't really care about the fish—or I do, I do, but not like the biologists who want to preserve them. To me, the fish are a wedge. Defending wildlife is a way to defend the land, foil development, try to make people see the idiocy of what they're doing to the aquifers, to the rivers, to the whole system of life in this part of the world. It just wasn't meant to include so many people! It wasn't meant to grow cotton or grapes, forget about Kentucky bluegrass and heirloom roses!"

Greenie confessed that she hadn't known what an aquifer was before she came west. "If you'd asked me to guess, I'd have said a piece of scuba diving equipment, like the mouthpiece you breathe through."

Other Charlie did not laugh. "Nobody knows these things! Everybody knows what a Jacuzzi is, what a pulsing-massage showerhead is, but what do they know about water itself and where it comes from? Nada. That's what."

"I'm glad you're so passionate," she said.

"Yes! And I shouldn't feel so alone!"

"My mother always said you were a boy prematurely sure of yourself." Greenie saw his frown deepen. "She meant it as a compliment, Charlie. She said you were someone to keep an eye on."

"Your mother had a lot of opinions."

"I miss her opinions," said Greenie.

He was quiet for a moment before he said, "They were still pretty young, weren't they?"

"Yes. And they were just beginning to really enjoy George. My George."

"Was that your George, running around the house before dinner?"

"Yes." She asked him if he had children.

"I wish I did. I've never been married. Almost, but no. Too much school, too much moving around."

Loudly, the dishwasher shifted cycles, startling both of them. Other Charlie looked at his watch and exclaimed at the time. The roads would be empty, she reminded him. It wasn't her place to offer him a bed, and Ray had long since disappeared.

Greenie closed the front door behind Other Charlie and waved him off, glad to have seen him, but again—as she had felt in the kitchen at the mansion, breaking eggs for the Water Boys' orange soufflé—also glad to see him go.

WHEN GREENIE AND OTHER CHARLIE were in high school, Greenie's mother hired him to cut grass, trim hedges, rake leaves, shovel snow—all the chores generally done back then by the fathers in Greenie's neighborhood. George Duquette exempted himself from lawn work to tinker obsessively with his sailboat. The vessel, its mast removed, its deck protected by canvas, wintered not in a boatyard but high on a cradle that dominated the Duquettes' back lawn. It was a fine old wooden boat, a folkboat sloop, and as Greenie grew older, watching her father stroke, sand, smooth, varnish, sometimes merely stand back to contemplate the cetacean curve of its hull, she came to see exactly why boats were and would always be unquestionably female.

Greenie and Other Charlie weren't friends, not exactly, but they had friends in common. So in addition to seeing him at school and at parties, some afternoons she would come home to find him at her kitchen counter, sweaty and rumpled, eating her mother's homemade cheese sticks and drinking iced tea. Olivia would prepare dinner while quizzing Other Charlie about algebra or baseball or what he might know about changing the washer on her sputtering faucet.

Sometimes it felt to Greenie not as if she had a classmate who worked around her home to make pocket money—the way Greenie did by babysitting and passing trays of deviled eggs at cocktail parties—but as if she went to school with the family handyman. Sometimes she would blush when she saw him in school, as if he didn't belong there.

The summer before they went away to college, Olivia hired Other Charlie to paint the house. Greenie was around that summer, working as a waitress at a steak house. In the mornings, before she went to work, she would loaf around the house and read, or sunbathe on the patio. More than once, she would look out a window and see, right there, Other Charlie's studious, slightly scowling face. They'd wave at each other and smile, but the windows were closed against the heat, so they rarely spoke.

One day, waking late, she went into her bathroom and was stunned to see the small window occupied entirely by a very close view of a man's naked chest, speckled with white paint. The man's head (and she knew it must be Other Charlie's, not that of the assistant he'd hired) was well above the window, and she could tell from the movement of the muscles that his left arm was reaching, over and over, to paint the triangular space under the peak of the roof above her. Before she closed the inner shutters for privacy—she wasn't quite sure whose—she put her face close to the glass, mesmerized by the long band of hair that ran down the center of his torso, widening slightly at the navel. It was the translucent blond of honey. So was the patch of springy hair in the pale hollow beneath his outstretched arm.

Because she was dating someone else, Greenie became confused when Other Charlie invaded her dreams with his lean, furry chest and striving arms. In one dream, he was speckled white not with paint but with sugar. She was relieved when the house was finished and she no longer had to confront this alluring yet distant boy in her kitchen, in her waking views of the world, even walking on the roof above her bed, his casual steps resonating quietly through her being, commanding her from a height. Her relief was undermined when Olivia announced that dear Charlie Oenslager had done such a superb job that he deserved a vacation. She had invited him to bring a friend and be their guest up in Maine. "I think he's a darling, don't you?" said Greenie's mother. Greenie had no choice but to agree.

NINE

"THIS IS YOUR ROOM, AND THIS, more significantly, is your door. Any bedlam in which you care to live ends there, and you close it so that I do not have to share the scenery." Walter swung the door to and fro, as if demonstrating a revolutionary product. "You may strew clothing every which way in here, as long as I can't smell it, but no food. Food attracts roaches. You may not know about roaches in swanky Corte Madera, but they are repulsive, dirty, and look like creatures out of Japanese sci-fi movies, a genre I do not care for."

He led Scott to the kitchen. "The fridge. Basically empty because I let other people feed me. That's why I do what I do! If you prefer to feed yourself, that's fine. Only please keep an eye on the science projects. Ditto my caution about those Japanese films. Sponges, by the way, are in that drawer to the left of the sink. We encourage the use of sponges." He crossed the room and opened the pantry door. "Because this is New York, where closets are about as common as Tasmanian devils, you will find clean sheets and towels up there"—he pointed to a high shelf, above the jarred spices he never used—"and laundry, by the way, gets done on the other side of the playground. I'll give you a neighborhood tour on the way to the restaurant.

"Speaking of the neighborhood—I will say this only once because your mother would have my hide—but the closest and most varied source of inexpensive condoms is the chain pharmacy at the end of the block: go out the front door and turn right. As for nightly visitors, all I ask is that you remember about the door, about noise, and by the way, no drugs. Period. Nancy Reagan was right about that.

"And speaking of thin Republican women, your mom asked that I try to ensure you pierce no further body parts while under my roof nor deface them with permanent illustrations. I don't see how I could practically prevent such actions, were you to suspend what I have a hunch is your generally decent judgment, but if you consider my generosity in other areas, I'm hoping that may count for something. Sort of like Mafia protection. Think of me as your personal Don Corleone, without the hit men."

"Like don't you mean Tony Soprano?" This was the first evidence that Scott was actually listening. For most of Walter's speech (which he had rehearsed silently on the bus to Newark Airport), the expression on Scott's face was disturbingly akin to blank. It did not help that he arrived wearing a T-shirt which read, in a font you'd expect to see on a law firm's letterhead, GRABBER, BOODIE & DEWITT. (Honestly now, if you wanted vulgar, you could execute it with far more verve than *that*.)

"So you're with me?" said Walter.

Scott smiled. "All sounds cool to me, Uncle Walt. You're the man."

"You may call me Walter. I think that will go over better at work, don't you?"

"Hey, it's copa. Whatever suits. Am I supposed to like not be your nephew?"

"Of course you're my nephew. I can be as nepotistic as I darn well please. I'm the boss," said Walter. "As you say, I am *the man*."

Scott sat down on the leather couch—could sitting and sprawling be a single action?—right next to The Bruce. T.B. had been feigning relaxation; throughout Walter's tour, his eyes had never left Scott. Scott started petting him now, and T.B. accepted the affection with wary pleasure.

"You know," said Walter, "if you don't mind, I was thinking you could also walk this guy a couple of mornings, which would permit me to get to the gym before work. It much improves my mood." He also liked the idea of Scott doing the hand-off to surly, gum-snapping Sonya. The two of them might just have something in common. Now that Scott was actually in Walter's home—complete with grotty duffel bag, guitar case covered with holographic stickers, and a gaudy medallion that looked like something Prince Charles had worn at his Duke of Earl coronation—Walter did see him as a prototypical teenager. But after all, this was part of the adventure! Like hosting an ambassador from one of those brand-new African countries that kept cartographers on their toes.

"Unpack, have a beer, whatever," said Walter. "And why don't you call your mom; I put a phone in your room. I'll take you over to the restaurant in an hour. Hugo's got his hands on the first truly fabulous corn of the season."

BACK IN EARLY JUNE, WALTER HAD HAD a moment's hesitation, wishing he could take back his offer to Scott, when he discovered that Gordie had moved into a place of his own. Walter found this out from his trainer at the gym, who was the trainer of every important homosexual man between Fourteenth and Canal and the only person Walter knew who seemed to get the dish before Ben overheard it at the bar. The first few days after hearing this news, he was constantly alert for the phone, sure that Gordie would call. Walter imagined their reunion in various locations: perhaps Gordie would summon Walter to his office—now inconceivable to Walter as a place in which to do business—or perhaps they would meet somewhere public, at the restaurant or in the park by the playground, all their mutual longing inflamed by their inability to act it out there and then. The public scenario was sexier, but either would be fine, so Walter dressed each morning prepared for Gordie's summons, choosing clothes that were silky or crisp, fine to the touch and easy to remove.

After the third or fourth day without a call, Walter told himself Gordie needed to settle in first. He imagined Gordie unpacking possessions—not many, because the one who is left is the one who gets to keep the goodies—and carefully lining up books in a new bookcase, plates in a new cupboard, shirts in a new closet. Walter tried to dream up the perfect house gift: maybe an antique Pendleton blanket, to acknowledge Gordie's nostalgia for his western roots? No, those were passé. A bowl? Too formulaic, too *passive*.

One day Walter went into an ethnic-goods shop run by a fellow whose eye for beauty made up for his infuriating ennui toward customers. (With lessons from Walter, or maybe just a good dose of Paxil, the man could have had a chain of successful shops, a far more sophisticated version of Pier 1.) There, he found a shirt from India, ivory linen embroidered, almost invisibly, with elephants and monkeys. It had the same collarless neckline that Gordie seemed to favor when he didn't have to wear a tie. Walter wrapped it himself, in orange rice paper tied with chartreuse ribbon.

This cheerful present sat on Walter's neglected dining table for two weeks before he realized that Gordie was never going to call. The indifferent shopkeeper took the shirt back in exchange for a huge black basket that Walter placed in a corner of his spare room. Scott could use it for dirty laundry.

One of Walter's waitresses fixed him up with a flutist. Except for mild middle-age spread, the guy was handsome—and quite enduring in the sack—but during their third week he confessed to a slight anxiety that Walter's astrological sign was generally not a good match for his. Would Walter go to the flutist's astrologer and let her take a look at their moons and other mitigating factors? "It's on me, of course," said the flutist.

"I would not," said Walter, though he smiled as he said it. "I do not think in purple, I'm sorry." They lasted another week, and then the flutist went on tour. At least the ending was easy. No fuss, no muss.

And then, of course, it happened. In the pharmacy, in the toothpaste section. Walter was searching for the mint-flavored dental tape he liked best when the hand touched his shoulder. He jumped, as New Yorkers will at any unexpected touch in public.

"Oh—I never meant to scare you, I'm sorry! How *are* you?"

Walter knew desperate phony cheer a mile away.

"Gordie," he said smoothly. "I thought you must've moved to Argentina."

"I'm just so busy now, and I've been spending my weekends out in Sag Harbor. But I've been wanting to call."

Walter smiled at Gordie and held his gaze but said nothing. He wanted Gordie to falter.

"You heard I moved to Chelsea. I imagine everyone has."

"Yes, I heard that."

"I've been wanting—needing time alone. For a while."

"Poor Stephen," said Walter.

Gordie frowned. "That sounds odd, coming from you. Don't you think?"

Walter sighed. "I guess I have to empathize with him at some point, wouldn't you say?"

Now Gordie looked angry. "Well, I do too, in fact. You don't even know what went on between us. And actually, we still see each other and talk. It's not like I don't know what a schmuck I've been, but I still hope we're going to be friends. It's hard, harder than you can guess."

Walter put a hand on Gordie's shoulder. "You're right. I'm not in your life anymore, so I'm in no place to judge. We're also in no place to talk about this. I mean, at the dental floss display?" As he gestured at the legions of little white boxes suspended in midair, he saw it, the one he wanted. He took it down.

Gordie said, "Walter, someday I'm going to call you, you know. It's not like I think it's over between us. But this is not my finest hour, and I . . ."

"I know," said Walter. "You have to go it alone."

Gordie stared at him, perhaps searching for any hint of sarcasm. In truth, there was none. Walter did not want to understand—he did not want Gordie to seem anything other than ignoble, yellow-bellied, glib— yet understand he did. He wanted to tell Gordie that his heart was still broken, though that would never be wise, least of all in the CVS, within reach of a placard on gum disease, complete with graphic photos.

"You know exactly where to find me," he said, and did something unexpected to both of them. He kissed Gordie on one of his lovely clean-shaven cheeks. Just one.

Vell and graciously done, said the spirit of Granna when Walter left the store by himself and welcomed, for just an instant, the onslaught of midsummer air. Two days later, Scott arrived.

AT LEAST TO BEGIN WITH, Scott was elaborately thoughtful. He seemed to pad through rooms like a cat walking through broken glass; he closed doors with extreme tact; he left not a single dirty mug or sweat-shirt lying around the apartment. He also took The Bruce on walks far longer than Walter did. Scott would come back with reports of the places he'd discovered: Tompkins Square Park, the concrete Picassos off LaGuardia Place, the building painted with parachuting pigs, the block where the Hell's Angels parked. T.B. began to seem both more rested and more alert. His eczema faded.

At the restaurant, Scott was responsible for collecting and tallying receipts from Ben and for running Hugo's errands. Though Ben and Hugo already liked their jobs, they liked them better than ever now. Walter was indeed The Man.

Late at night, Walter would sometimes wake to a muffled wailing. The first time, it alarmed him so deeply that he crept out into the dark living room carrying a glass paperweight he kept on his bedside table. The next few times, he lay awake fighting the urge to get prissy. But then he became accustomed to the sound of teenage angst in musical form, accompanied by instruments that sounded like colliding trains. He would go back to sleep thinking how proud Granna would be. Tolerance, she'd told him once, was *also* next to godliness. It was like a cleanliness of temper, she explained. The young Walter wanted to ask her just how tolerant she thought *God* was, but he kept that to himself, along with the void where his piety ought to have been.

He could not help seeking parallels between himself as Scott's generous uncle and Granna as his own kindhearted warrior angel. There was a pretty significant difference, however. Werner and Tipi might be many deplorable things, but unlike Walter and Werner's parents, they were not a pair of drunken, selfish losers deluded by a lethal mix of narcissism and cultural indignation (okay, perhaps a little war trauma, too). Thanks to Granna, Werner and Walter had grown up to be highly functioning, productive citizens—but if you were to ask Walter, Werner had a far easier time of it and lived his life with the sanctified nonchalance of those who will do anything to avoid dissecting their souls.

Walter and Werner's father, August—ha! as if there'd been a grain of nobility or summery splendor in the man!—had the bad fortune to fight in Vietnam (though he did so by choice). This was followed by the more ambiguous fortune of being shot—clean through the center of his right palm, so that he did not come close to dying but did require prolonged therapy to regain the use of his dominant hand. Despite a nearly complete recovery (the hand ached in cold weather, and the palm did not flex), he returned home to his wife and children a political cynic and grade-A drinker. He was predictably unpredictable and around home too much for everyone's comfort.

Werner, who was five years older than Walter, retained earlier, kinder memories of their father—he could even recall the bowling alley where August had kept the long runways polished, the sodapop stocked, the rental shoes lined up on their shelves like soldiers awaiting deployment—

but Walter had been too young to remember those days. All he could remember now was the impossibility of knowing whether the dad he would see at the end of a schoolday would help him with his homework or complain, in an escalating rant, about the injustice of the world.

When the bowling alley closed, August Kinderman had enlisted, and his wife and two sons had moved from Boston to the small town in western Massachusetts where August's mother lived. Granna was still vigorous, recently widowed, and happy to help with her grandsons. Walter noticed that she was a little bossy with his mother—he could remember Granna resetting the table when Rose didn't do it quite her way and wondering aloud if the younger woman's skirts were just a little too short—but she treated her grandsons with pure adoration. She would sing Bing Crosby songs as she washed and pressed their little shirts for school, as she baked them strudel and kugel ("Oh vould you like to sving on a star, carry moonbeemps home in a char . . ."). She papered her kitchen walls with their paintings and crookedly penciled compositions and let them run freely about until dark to play with other children down her nice little street of matchbox houses and beds of striped petunias.

Best of all, moving into Granna's house meant that Walter got a separate room from Werner, even if his was the smallest. It was the only room on the third floor, with a view over chimneys and roofs toward hills that blushed brilliant red in the fall. "Greylock, tallest mountain in the state," Granna had told him, pointing out the wide, lofty hill. It looked too tame to be a real mountain, but its superior status compelled respect. Looming to the west, it hastened sunset, lengthening the longest of winter nights. Walter would look out his window sometimes and whisper that name, the name of a magician or mythological trickster. Or a horse ridden by a knight in King Arthur's court.

After nearly two years away, August returned. He moved Rose, Walter, and Werner to an apartment over a Woolworth just a few blocks from Granna's house, but he had trouble finding work. Walter supposed that there simply weren't many bowling alleys out in the country. Granna suggested that what August needed to do was finish college. In retrospect, it didn't take brains to figure out that August's inability to find employment had little to do with the supply of jobs and that choosing to stay in the country made it easy for him to use that fiction as an excuse.

Commitment to booze, all its rituals and the changes it wreaks on grown-ups (first the hour-to-hour changes and then, more subtly, the long-term changes), is a confounding thing for a child to observe, let alone understand. After their dad came home, Werner and Walter were often split between their parents. Many evenings, Werner went out with their mother, because he was the older one and could entertain himself during evenings of sorority-sister bridge, reading a Hardy Boys book or rearranging his stamp collection, while Walter stayed home with their dad. Father and son would sit side by side on the couch watching *Hogan's Heroes* or *Get Smart* or *Saturday Night at the Movies*.

This was not an unpleasant way to pass the time, but along with those hours in front of the TV, one of Walter's earliest serial memories was of being hustled into the car by his dad after dark and cruising from town to town in search of a bottle. It was such an important bottle, no doubt about that, and you couldn't get it at just any store. Sometimes the right store would be closed—there would have been a mad, cursing dash in the car, way too fast—and this would lead to bouts of cursing and yet further speeding dashes from town to town. Walter did not need to be told that he wasn't to tell his mother about these trips. Once in a while, however, she would come home while they were out on their mission—that's what August called it—and she would be waiting and angry. Walter and Werner would go straight to their room and lie awake listening to the uproar. The two brothers never spoke about it, perhaps because it always happened in the dark before they fell asleep, and when they woke up, the tumult felt unreal or diminished by intervening dreams, dreams that for Walter were often more dramatic, more highly colored, than any of the accusations his parents made in the dark.

And then one day, very early, Granna dropped by with a cake for Werner's birthday. It was a Saturday, and Walter was the only one up, watching cartoons. Granna walked into the living room in her shiny, snub-nosed high heels and stood between him and the TV, white gloves on hips, her head turning this way and that, like the head of an owl.

"There vuz a party?" she asked him.

Walter told her no, there'd been no party, as he saw her gaze travel from the coffee table to the floor beside the armchair to the top of a glass-front bookcase that had belonged to her hardworking, book-loving husband (a publisher of hymnals and prayer books in Germany and then, in the immigrant's trade-off, a typesetter at a newspaper plant in Pittsfield). All these surfaces were occupied haphazardly by bottles, glasses, ashtrays, matchbooks, and pretzel shards.

"No party," she repeated with soft-spoken furor. Walter had been eleven years old. He knew the subtle emotions by then as well as the obvious ones.

Within weeks, he and Werner and their mother went to live at Granna's again while their father went away. "It's a special kind of vacation," their mother said brightly, but you could see she was angry: not at her husband but at Granna. At dinnertime, she and Granna worked around each other, never touching and almost never speaking. They reminded Walter of those black and white Scottie dog magnets that repelled each other when held in contradiction to their polarity.

"Where did he go?" Walter asked his brother, wondering if their father could have sneaked off to Disneyland without them. Like any normal eleven-year-old in 1967, Walter dreamed of going to Disneyland. Sixteen-year-old Werner had said, "He went to dry out. Any dope could figure that one out."

"He went to what?" said Walter.

"Granna wants him off the booze. She says it's why he can't get a job or be a good father," said Werner. "Jeez, are you a knucklehead." Werner had reached the age when he couldn't tell his little brother much of anything without throwing in a pinch of contempt.

When their dad returned from his "vacation," about which he had no stories and of which he had no snapshots, they did not move back to their own house but stayed at Granna's. August drank a lot of Coca-Cola and coffee, smoked more cigarettes, and often went to bed by ten o'clock. Another difference was that it began to seem as if the parents were in cahoots. They went out after dinner sometimes to take walks together; when August turned in early, so would Rose. Walter longed to band together with Werner, but by then Werner had thrown himself into school sports and girls. He had also worked his tail off as a lifeguard at an indoor pool to buy himself a rattletrap Impala. He would come home after one kind of practice or another to drop off half his books, shower and change clothes, contemplate his important self in the mirror, eat something right out of the fridge, and declare that he was off to the public library. (No one other than Walter seemed to wonder whether that's where Werner really went.)

Granna—who'd be at the stove, preparing a stew or pot roast—would scold Werner: Dinner was time for family. Eating while standing was the habit of beasts. Werner would get intestinal cramps and risk driving off the road.

Werner, who stood a foot taller than Granna by then, would bend down and kiss her on the forehead. He'd say something like "Beasts don't have algebra and a buttload of Norman Melville to read." Walter, setting the table, would watch his brother saunter out the door, listen to the Impala roar away toward freedom.

August would be in the living room, supposedly checking the paper for new job listings. But when he came to the table, what he'd talk about was the news, reciting story after story with derision. He'd rant about the stupidity of the war, the stupidity of the president, the stupidity of the first lady and her stupid obsession with flowers, the stupidity of the gooks and how, ironically, it just might help them win. "Hey, what's another fricasseed village or two when the Mouseketeers are beating down your door? Man but the world is full of jerks."

Granna's sacred tolerance began to crack. One night she told her son to show some respect and native pride: for a president who would not give up on a difficult fight, for a first lady who knew that to love the beauty of nature was to love God, and—more pointedly—for a country that would continue to send good money to a man so determined never to make a living.

"Like you've ever had to support a family," August said.

Granna stared hard at him and seemed to consider whether she ought to reply at all, but she did. "I am doing ziss now, ziss very past year and more."

There was a pause, like a quick inhaling, and then August laughed, loud and short, a gunshot laugh. "Touché, Mother!" he said, raising his glass of Coke. "The only catch being that whatever money you're using here comes from Dad's fat pension."

Granna stood up, almost demurely, and carried her plate to the sink. She came back to her place, sat down, and stared once again at her son. "Perhaps you and Rose might go down the street for ice cream. Walter vill help me clean dishes. Perhaps you vill bring him a chocolate sundae."

Walter (who always helped with the dishes anyway) watched his father turn to his mother and say, "Hear that, Rose? We are being shown the door."

As he waited, without much real optimism, for his chocolate sundae to arrive, Walter finished his homework and went to bed. He was awakened by a car screeching into the driveway, radio blaring. Boy, is Werner going to get it now, he thought—until he heard his parents' voices. They were singing "Blue Moon," warbling the chorus like third-string opera singers.

Next morning, they were not at the breakfast table. Granna said very little as she made oatmeal for Walter and Werner. She looked as if she had been crying, but one thing you did not ask Granna about was her emotional state. If you did, she would say something like (if she seemed sad) "I am bearing up, as we all must do" or (if she seemed light on her feet) "Joys, they are butterflies; never should you try to hold them, not even so much as touch the vings."

Seventh grade was a year of retreat for Walter: retreat to his attic room, retreat into reading, retreat from the realization that spin-the-bottle and gym dances left him feeling as if everyone around him had shared a special drug when he wasn't looking. He became aware that the reason he loved to watch *Lost in Space* had nothing to do with sci-fi, which he generally hated, and everything to do with the actor who played Major West.

Then came the summer that would stand out forever as a uniquely vivid, turbulent summer in Walter's life. It was the summer he met beautiful, nervous Joel, his first requited crush; the summer he read *In Cold Blood* (and every night for weeks locked all the doors and windows); the summer of Manson's rampage; the summer his father, having sold his own car, crashed Granna's Buick into a phone pole the next town over, killing his wife then and there, himself after nearly a month in a coma. Along with Granna, Walter and Werner visited their father and his machines every day he lay there in limbo, and not once did Walter wish for the man's recovery—though, at his grandmother's side, he went through the motions of stoic prayer. She was the one he felt bad for. He knew she was convinced she had failed in the gravest way a person can fail: as a parent.

August died, fittingly, at the end of August. In September, a week late, Werner went off to start college at U. Mass. The idea was that he'd be near enough to come back on weekends, though he might as well have gone to UCLA. He came back at Thanksgiving, but Christmas he spent with a girlfriend in New York City. The following year he did go to California, transferring to UC–Santa Cruz. "Haight-Ashbury, here I come," he said to Walter. How he'd evolved from a would-be flower-child to a Republican moneyman would always be a bit of a mystery to Walter. But people, no matter how well you knew them, never ceased to surprise.

AFTER SCOTT HAD BEEN THERE just over a week, it occurred to Walter that he had not shared a home with another person since living with Granna. Even in college he'd never had roommates; he'd rented the teensiest, grungiest studios and fixed them up to a fare-thee-well. The highly peopled occupations he'd chosen—theater first, then restaurateering—meant that once he went home, privacy signified far more than space.

So now he experienced all sorts of odd, unexpected emotional symptoms, exacerbated by the ambiguous nature of his affection for Scott. Even after he learned to sleep through Scott's faintly caterwauling music, he would sometimes awake for no discernible reason. Hearing nothing more than the murmur and groan of the city outside, he'd wonder if the boy was in the apartment or out at large. He would resist the urge to go into the living room and put an ear to Scott's door. Even then, he might not know. What he felt in these wakings was a mixture of tenderness and agitation. Was he worried for Scott's safety? Not really. Was he envious—or, worse, jealous!—at the notion of his nephew out with a prospective lover, dancing and kissing, sitting with legs intertwined on a pair of barstools? Or was he simply feeling the misplaced wishful yearning of someone who'd been single for too long?

The Bruce, meanwhile, took Scott's presence completely for granted. When Walter opened the bedroom door first thing in the morning, T.B. shot across the living room and sniffed greedily at the gap beneath Scott's door. Scott would emerge, squatting down to tussle with the dog, greeting Walter as a sleepy afterthought.

"Hey, Walt, how they hangin'?" Scott would growl in his sexy teenage morning voice.

Walter tried not to stare at his nephew's lovely naked chest or the scandalously low point at which the blond hair on his abdomen disappeared behind the drawstring of his flimsy shorts. Early on, Walter had given up on reinstating the second syllable of his own name.

The first two weeks, Werner called nearly every night—at the restaurant, to Walter's annoyance. Cocktail hour at Kinderman West coincided with dinner rush at Kinderman East. Walter would call Scott away from setting tables, sweeping the sidewalk, or answering the front phone. The boy would have a short conversation with his parents, his end a series of cheerfully sarcastic quips like "No, Mom, I stay out all night at leather bars" and "Like anybody has time to read when we're right up the block from the triple-X video store."

Every so often, Walter would be summoned to the phone after Scott said good-bye. He'd reassure Tipi that Scott was being fantastically helpful (code for kept out of trouble) and that he was a perfect roommate (code for spending the night where he was supposed to spend the night). "Rest assured that I'm exploiting your son's talents to the max," he might say. "I've worn him out so completely that his fancy guitar is gathering dust."

As summer wore on, calls from the Coast dwindled in frequency, and rarely did Walter and Werner trade more than a brief greeting before the phone was passed to Scott. Scott was the one who had to suffer through The Weather According to Werner. Walter would overhear remarks like "Yeah, humidity's been awesome" and "You mean the waves at Stinson?"

It was a summer of work more intense than Walter had ever known; Scott's extra hands were a blessing. Was everyone suddenly richer? That's not what the papers said, but that was how it felt. Certainly, the boys in the 'hood seemed all at once healthier, the sickest among them passed on, the ones who'd managed to hang on this long filled with the hope and energy purveyed in a new set of potions and pills. The number of black-bordered cards in Walter's mail diminished—as if he were living life backward.

And then there were the new "dieters," people who'd given up bread and pasta for steak and butter. "Fight fat with fat, it's so intuitively homeopathic!" said a sleek guy from Walter's gym who suddenly showed up all the time, renouncing his vegan ways. Honestly, thought Walter, people were so absurd about food. But if the fads had turned in his favor, who was he to rock the boat?

Walter did worry a little about Scott's social life—surely the boy needed creatures his own age to hang with—but he heard no complaints. Contrary to what Walter had told Tipi, Scott spent a lot of his free time playing guitar in his room or combing the music listings and going out to places like CBGB and The Bottom Line. It was all very post-counterculturally wholesome. Perhaps Scott genuinely liked his own company, a rare talent in someone his age. So far, the most vulgar, juvenile thing about Scott was his never-ending collection of wisecrack T-shirts. One day his chest would proclaim, JESUS HATES YOUR SUV; the next, SUCK ON THIS. ("You know," Walter said cheerfully when the latter message emerged, "there are people in this town who might act on that imperative." Scott grinned and said, "Let 'em try." But the shirt did not make a return appearance.)

The apartment grew vaguely collegiate around the edges. Old halves of deli sandwiches dried out, forgotten, in the fridge. Scott's sneakers seemed to migrate about the living room, spreading their subtle pungence. Here and there, magazines lay crinkled and slumped like dead birds. Walter had expected this. He spoke calmly to Scott, whose sloppiness went into periodic remission, but with business as good as it was, Walter also hired a housekeeper, a daffy actress friend of Ben's who sometimes left rags in the tub but could be trusted not to steal Granna's silver or Walter's collection of cuff links.

"Are you still writing poetry?" Walter asked Scott one afternoon as the two of them took a late lunch break.

"Well, yeah, sure, but I'm merging it with my music."

"Lyrics. Of course," said Walter.

Scott looked at the ceiling, audibly chewing his pastrami, playing with that Duke of Earl medallion. His T-shirt du jour, innocuous for once, proclaimed I'D RATHER BE IN MANITOBA; the menacing face of a polar bear filled the O. "Not lyrics, not conventional like that," he said. "It's more like I'm turning the poetry into the music. Like the music's eating the words, digesting the emotions. Know what I mean?" He redirected his gaze at Walter. Walter noticed for the first time that his nephew had sprouted one of those fungus beardlets known as soul patches. Bad decision for anyone. And when had he traded the tasteful star in his earlobe for a miniature demon's mask with, however tiny, a protruding tongue?

"Like John Cage? Or maybe Enya," said Walter.

"Who's John Cage?" said Scott.

To act shocked would have been dishonest. Walter himself had heard only snatches of John Cage, always on basement FM; every time, he'd changed stations. "Oh, well. Pots and pans, vacuum cleaners and subway brakes. That sort of thing," he said. "Cacophony before anyone else was doing it."

Scott looked perplexed but did not ask for elaboration.

"Personally, I do like my songs with a melody and lyrics," said Walter. "But I am musically bourgeois."

Scott nodded gravely. "I've seen your CD collection. But never judge a man by his music. You're cool enough to be, like, nowhere near your age. That's what I told Sonya."

It took Walter a moment to make the connection. "Sonya? Sonya who takes T.B. to entertain the oldsters?" Whatever the opposite of cool was, that was surely what Sonya thought of Walter.

"Hey, did you know Sonya plays flute? Like even classical stuff sometimes. She introduced me to Rampal, the Bach cantatas."

"Will wonders never cease," said Walter.

"She took me to the Kitchen, where we heard *seven dudes* play flute together. The high notes were, like . . . like noise from outer space. It was so fine. It's like you become a bat or a dog."

"A bat or a dog?" said Walter. Good Lord.

"You know. Like you can hear on some higher frequency. Like your ears hurt at first, but then they're supernatural. You're inside this awesome tunnel. It's genius. You *are* the noise. Know what I mean?"

Walter leaned forward, smiling, and put a hand on his nephew's arm. "No, Scott, I haven't the remotest notion what you mean. But have fun with it." Ben was waving him over to the phone.

"Walter's Place. The man himself," he answered. As he watched Scott from across the room, he saw the boy swaying from side to side in his chair, touching his medallion to his nose, his upper lip, his chin, as if in some weird benediction.

The caller was Bonny Prince Charlie (*the book dude,* mused Walter in his nephew's lingo). He wanted to know if they were still serving lunch. "For you, my dear, whenever. Come right on over," said Walter, though anyone could have had lunch all afternoon. If you ran an eating establishment in New York, you had to be a total rube to stop serving food anytime between noon and midnight—unless you ran a restaurant in Midtown, which, in Walter's terms, was the same as being a rube.

He returned to Scott and picked up their plates. "Back to work, Bat Boy. Hugo is going to show you the proper way to trim asparagus."

"Yo. Cool. Is there like an improper way?"

"Like yes," said Walter. "Believe it or not."

THROUGH HIGH SCHOOL, Walter lived with Granna. Because of her weakening hips, she no longer slept on the second floor but made a bedroom in the small den off the living room. She still drove, shopped, cooked, and went to church. In addition to her needlework, she took up making wreaths for charity: bay leaf in the spring, dried flowers in the summer, juniper in the fall, fir and red ribbons for Christmas.

Walter kept his room at the top of the house, so the second story became a ghost floor—not gathering dust, because Granna cleaned it once a week, but holding unaltered the beds on which Walter's parents and brother had slept, the pictures on the patterned walls, and the books, all leather-bound, all in German, left behind by the grandfather Walter could not remember. Sometimes it seemed as if even Werner were dead too—until he phoned, as he did about once a month. But it wasn't the possible company of ghosts that kept Walter from moving downstairs; it was the very real company of boys, beginning with Joel, whom he sneaked upstairs for sex—at first awkward and quick, with the pretense of shared homework or a new record; then purposeful and more prolonged, even half a night sometimes.

This was the only thing Walter felt guilty about. He did not smoke dope or drop acid or even, after his father's example, drink more than the occasional beer. Almost as compensation, as purification, he took an after-school job at the public library. Reshelving books, he began to notice plays. Toward the end of Dewey Decimal 822, Walter became acquainted with a two-foot stretch of small blue clothbound books with gilt titles on the spines. The plays of Shakespeare. They fit so nicely in the pocket of a jacket that he checked them out one by one and carried them about, whispering the speeches aloud when he was alone. For their passion to entertain, Walt Disney and William Shakespeare were Walter's twin idols. (You could have *Barbarella* and *Easy Rider*; *Fantasia* put them to shame.) He had yet to discover Billy Wilder, Peter Sellers, or Matthew Broderick in *Ferris Bueller's Day Off*.

Walter's first role on a real stage, his third year in high school, was Petruchio. He suspected that he won the part not because he had any real acting skills but because he knew the lilt and strut of Shakespeare's words far better than any of his classmates. Bluff: that's what got him into acting. When he practiced his lines at home, he would pace the short length of his attic room (which, as he grew taller, provided less and less pacing room, since two of its walls slanted down to the floor), sometimes addressing Mount Greylock, out the window. The night before dress rehearsal, he paced up and down buck naked, reciting the "I am he am born to tame you" speech to Stuart, another naked boy, who lay in Walter's bed giggling.

Granna was downstairs, forming hoops of dried statice and watching *Celebrity Squares*. Walter had grown complacent about what Granna could and could not hear from far below. The next morning she was unusually quiet at breakfast. As he gathered his books to leave and catch the bus, she stopped him and turned him to face her, both hands raised to his shoulders. Like Werner, he was now far taller than Granna, but when she was stern, his pulse still quickened. She looked up into his face and said, "Let a fire burn too hot in your heart, and smoke, it vill fill up your head." She gave him the same brief, hard gaze once reserved for his father, and then she released him, wished him a fine day, and opened the door. He was touched and astonished by her evenhandedness, her lack of revulsion. (Only years later did he realize that, perceptive as Granna had been, she must have believed his midnight guest a girl.)

After the applause of the next three nights, he began to dream of moving to New York City, becoming an actor, and changing his name to Walter Greylock. Strangely, he never climbed the mountain he had gazed at for so many hours from his tower room and on which he'd projected so many hopes.

He was glad that Granna got to see him graduate from college, that she also got to see him in an Off-Broadway production of *Ah, Wilderness!*, a play she could appreciate and understand. That was the best role he ever had in New York. She also lived to see him start the restaurant. She told him how pleased she was to see him serve stuffed pork with cabbage, inspired by her own.

One autumn day she pulled into the parking lot of her beauty parlor and had a stroke. The woman who parked next to her saw Granna slumped over the steering wheel. On the seat beside her lay one of her bulky purses, a pair of her stubby shiny pumps in need of new heels, a bag of daffodil bulbs, and a Whitman's Sampler, which she always bought when she knew that Walter would be coming to visit. Awkwardly, a police officer gave Walter a plastic bag containing these things when he arrived to claim Granna's body.

"Way to go, Granna," he whispered tearfully when he saw her at the funeral home. He knew that the only thing she'd have done differently would have been to go to the hairdresser *first,* to look her best for Karl, the local undertaker. Walter planted the daffodil bulbs on her grave and, before he turned the house over to a real-estate agent, stood in his room on the third floor and had the satisfaction of seeing his old mountain for the last time in all its October glory.

WALTER'S FAVORITE PHOTOGRAPH OF GRANNA sat on his front hall table with a number of other family pictures. Granna stood in her garden, in front of a hedge of white peonies. She looked uncomfortable, standing stiffly, arms at her side, but she had a big proud smile for Walter, who had insisted she pose for the picture the day he graduated from high school. He told her that if she could insist on pictures of him in his silly cap and gown, she must submit as well. She was wearing a tweedy ivory dress, a shade too warm for June, with the gloves she wore to church. On her head sat a pie-shaped blue straw hat; she'd set her purse in the grass because she couldn't figure out how to hold it while posing.

One morning Walter saw Scott examining the pictures as he devoured a bagel. As usual, the boy could not sit still while eating. Walter thought of Granna telling Scott's father that only beasts ate while standing, but he kept this to himself.

"I like this one of you and Dad," said Scott, smiling.

The picture in question showed the brothers, before their parents had died, sitting together in a bumper car at an amusement park. They had matching crew cuts and matching plaid camp shirts. Werner was making horns behind Walter's head with a victory sign.

"Ah, we were young, were we not?" Walter said. Then he saw Scott pick up Granna. "Does your dad tell you stories about her?" he asked.

Scott put the picture down and wiped cream cheese from his upper lip. He sucked briefly on his finger. "Not much."

"Really!" said Walter. "Well, she practically raised us. Me, she raised entirely. I consider her my true mother."

Scott looked at Walter with an odd, almost embarrassed expression.

"What?" said Walter.

Scott shrugged. "Dad says she was like totally mean to your parents, especially your father."

"Mean?" Walter gasped. "She gave him about twenty thousand leagues of rope." He thought for a moment. "Scott, your father did tell you our dad was a drunk, that he killed our mother along with himself in that car wreck? I don't see how either of us could ever forgive him for that."

Scott, for all his effortless youth, seemed to understand that he was walking along the edge of an invisible ravine. He sat down on the couch. "Well . . . he told me how your dad had like post-traumatic war stress and stuff. Like how 'Nam wrecked his life and there wasn't much help in those days. And like how your grandmother didn't get it. How she was so cold and drove him so hard. Dad says he wouldn't have drunk so much if she . . ." Seeing Walter's expression, he giggled nervously. "Yow. Pretty heavy stuff, I guess."

"Heavy stuff indeed," said Walter with disgust. "Sorry. I'm not angry at you, but your father has it all wrong. Or part wrong. All Granna did—besides put a roof over our heads—was try to help your grandfather get back on his feet. Which if he had managed to *do* might have meant that he could have known you. Never mind *us.*"

"You and Dad are like pretty different guys," Scott said. "So I guess you'd see things different ways. Like me and Candace. She is just totally Valleyed out."

"Scott, your father and I lead very different lives, but this . . . this bit of history, I believe, is not up for dispute."

"You guys've never talked about this stuff?" said Scott.

"Your father isn't one for serious talks." Walter tried not to sound bitter.

"Yo. Five on that." He put down his hand after he realized Walter did not plan to reciprocate the gesture. "It's like golf, tennis, the Dow Jones, and how I'm fucking up my future are his favorite topics when I'm around. In that order."

"Don't you worry about your future, you are doing fine," said Walter, deciding to ignore the expletive. "And I am running late. After the paddywagon comes for T.B., why don't you take the morning off. I'll see you at noon."

From weight lifting to menu check, the morning went smoothly for Walter, but in the back of his mind he was seething at his brother. Was his take on the way they'd grown up really so different? They'd never spoken much about what went on in the years after August returned from the war—the majority of Walter's childhood—and now the little chat with Scott had put a different, malevolent spin on Werner's attitude toward everything in Granna's house, his urge to heave it all out when she died. It had little to do, after all, with Werner's glib taste or generic lack of sentimentality.

Just before noon, Walter went out front to nip the dead buds off the geraniums and petunias in the window box. It was hotter than Hades, with the terrace in its brief midday bath of full sun, and he did the job as quickly as he could. He used nail scissors; you did not greet guests with a molecule of dirt on your hands. He did have time, however, to notice the familiar van parked across the street and to see that in the front seat two people were making out with a teenage vengeance. The two people were Sonya and Scott.

WALTER NOW UNDERSTOOD WHY SCOTT was so cheerful and worked so hard. He was having sex. Everyone in the world was having sex except for Walter. It was August, and lust was in the air—at least for those who had not fled the city. Maybe his problem was that he had too much dignity, that he rode too high a horse. So on a night when the heat had broken and the air felt crisp as a water cracker, after asking Scott to take the dog home, Walter left the restaurant and walked along beneath the lovely swishy murmur of the leaves until he reached the building where Gordie now lived. His name was right there, inside the foyer on the buzzer beside number seventeen.

"Oh for crying out loud, just get it over with," Walter muttered to himself, and then he rang, the briefest touch. In all likelihood, Gordie would be out of the city, like any self-respecting power queen. But still Walter stood there until, stunningly, Gordie's voice crackled through the intercom: "Who is it?"

"Oh my stars," said Walter, a hand to his blushing face.

"Walter, is that you?" said the intercom.

"Oh who else," he said, his lips nearly touching the steel box.

"Well, come up then," said Gordie. "I'm on five."

And I'm on *fire*, thought Walter when the buzzer released the lock on the door.

TEN

RAY HAD MADE TIME TO INVITE THEM to the mansion for dinner. Maria cooked the meal, her chicken with mole sauce and a vegetable rice casserole.

To eat in the dining room where Greenie's meals were served every day yet where she herself never ate, this was odd enough; but now Alan was present, as well as George, who sat high on a plump cushion borrowed from a couch, his short legs swinging and clumping against the chair legs. This was the first time Greenie had seen a child at this vast formal table. That it was George made her want to laugh every time she looked across at him. Mary Bliss sat next to George. She'd made him a paper cootie-catcher; quietly, they took turns telling each other's fortunes. "You will fall in love with a hairy goblin," Greenie heard George whisper loudly. "Ooh, I hope he loves me back!" Mary Bliss replied.

"The food here is amazing," said Alan, after complimenting Maria's sauce. "In this city, I mean. When you come from New York, you forget that you don't have the market cornered on good restaurants."

Ray said, "You do not. Although"—he looked at Greenie—"seems I had to go there to import my chef. My *irreplaceable* chef."

Mary Bliss looked up from choosing yet another fate. "I thought he'd gone off the deep end when he fixed on that notion. But sometimes he gets these devilish brilliant hunches." She winked at her boss. Greenie knew what was going on here. Alan was about to be outflanked.

"So now the question is," said Ray, "how do we get you out here, Dr. Glazier?"

"Alan," said Alan. There was a nervous sheen on his forehead.

"Same question, Alan," said Ray.

In the candlelight against the stylishly stippled salmon walls, Alan's face looked as smooth and pink as a cameo. The shadow of a mounted cowboy, a bronze Remington on the sideboard, wavered gently behind him, as if the pony were loping home after a long, hard day on the range.

"Right now," said Alan, "I have a few patients I couldn't abandon."

"Well, maybe they can be weaned onto someone else, so to speak," said Ray. "Calves have a hard time of it, beller for their moms a night or two, but they manage—and they got to do it cold turkey. No phones, no e-mail, no nothing."

Alan forced a laugh. "Psychotherapy patients aren't calves. Or turkeys."

"No indeed," said Ray. "All the same, thought I'd give you these, and you can run with it." He passed a small packet of business cards across the table. "Mental hospital directors and the like. People whose funding depends on me, if I may put it bluntly. Most of the time I do." He grinned at Greenie. This was the side of Ray she liked least: the charm that was so conspicuously oiled.

"I've given them all the heads-up," said Mary Bliss.

Alan flipped quickly through the cards. "I appreciate it. Thank you. I'll . . . make a couple of calls." Watching him closely, Greenie knew that he did not appreciate it much at all, that he found it demeaning. She tried to smile at him. To be sharing meals with her husband again was both wonderful and worrisome. This was their sixth day together here and still it seemed surreal. Their entire shared life had been framed by New York, its tensions and tall buildings, its crowded geometry, the shade and scents of its leafy, well-watered trees. Here, as they walked down the streets, the air tinted by red dust, the astonishing ocean of sky overhead (just as Ray had promised), she felt as if they were explorers on a voyage together, with no familiar landmarks to navigate by. As if Alan also felt the need for an anchor, he held her hand nearly everywhere they went, something he had not done much after they married.

George said, "Ex-ca-yooz me, but I am full. Can I wear that mask on the wall there?"

Greenie was about to tell him no—the mask was a Hopi artifact on loan from a museum—when Ray said, "It's kind of big and heavy for you, Small, but let's have a closer look." He crossed the room and took the mask off the wall. He held it up with both hands so that he and the mask were face-to-face. "What the heck," he said, turning it around and holding it against his face. Leaning toward George, he began dancing in place, as if he were standing on hot coals. The feathers affixed to the brow of the mask fluttered lightly; one of them drifted to the floor. George squealed.

"Oops," said Ray. "I could be in biiig trouble."

"You *are* in big trouble, mister," said Mary Bliss.

"Well, Mary Bliss, one of your jobs is to keep my secrets, am I right?" Ray hung the mask back on the wall, handling it now with exaggerated care.

"That's raaahhht."

Ray picked up the stray feather and tucked it into a bowl of glass fruit below the mask. Looking at George, he placed a finger to his lips.

"Mr. McCrae, you are a goofus," said George.

"Back atcha," said Ray.

Alan looked beyond uncomfortable now. He looked disapproving. "George," he said gently, "you should address him as Governor McCrae."

"Oh sheep manure. Too much of the world calls me that, and not with a whole lot of respect these days, I might add."

"Diego's house has masks," said George.

"Like this one?" Greenie asked.

"Sort of. But not yellow. And not feathers. They're black, with big googly eyes. Actually, I used to suppose they were pretty scary."

"They sound like old masks. I hope you don't handle them without permission."

"Diego's allowed," George said defensively. "So it's okay for me, too."

"Just as long as his mom knows," said Greenie.

"Diego says they can make us invisible if we want."

"Maria, that mole was stupendous," said Ray as she brought in a dessert of Greenie's, a ginger cake with tangerine icing. "After this, how about you take that boy home to bed, Greenie, and I give your man a little tour. Mary Bliss, you work too many nights. Head out and have some fun, for God's sake."

Both Alan and Mary Bliss looked, for an instant, disconsolate. It was Mary Bliss who wanted to be alone with her boss, Alan who would have preferred to flee. Greenie had begun to understand, though Mary Bliss had never fully confided in her, that she was smitten with Ray, that her dedication was the deepest of pleasures. More than a workaholic, she was a bossaholic.

As for Alan, Greenie had no intention of rescuing him. She wanted there to be a chance, any chance, for Alan to understand why she liked this place, why she lived happily with the governor's flamboyant, even pompous manner because it came with the largesse of his heart, why she felt safe here.

"Is there time for a video?" George said. "Actually, I want *Black Stallion*."

"We'll see," said Greenie. George had seen the movie at Diego's house. He had made Greenie check it out so often at the video store that she had finally bought it. There were sinister, even terrifying scenes, especially when the ship carrying the boy and the horse caught fire and sank (a scene that had crept into one of Greenie's recent dreams, something she wouldn't tell Alan).

Ray took only two bites of dessert, but Greenie knew the cake was not to blame. Not since the Cerro Grande fires had she seen his appetite diminish the way it had in recent weeks. Nor had she seen him look at his reflection so often and with such obvious anxiety. It had become clear to her that Ray was falling in love (and not with Mary Bliss). But for McNally's "high noon" speech, Greenie might not have noticed. Ray went to the ranch nearly every weekend now; much more often than before, he mentioned matters of animal husbandry in casual conversation. To Greenie, over breakfast one morning, he'd rhapsodized about the natural beauties of Colorado.

GREENIE HAD GONE TO BED by the time Alan returned from the Governor's Mansion. He came into the bedroom followed by Treehorn, who had waited for him beside the front door. When George had been disappointed that the dog wouldn't sleep in his room, Greenie explained about dogs and their loyalty, how Treehorn would grow to love George as much as she loved Alan, maybe more.

As Alan undressed, Treehorn sniffed loudly at his body. Greenie wondered why the dog seemed so intrigued by Alan; she laughed when he climbed into bed beside her. "You do not smoke cigars!"

"That's right. But I do not say no to that man," said Alan. "I do not!" he bellowed in Ray's cocksure tone. He stroked Treehorn until she lay down on the floor beside the bed. "The weird thing is, I found it completely impossible to hate him, even while having a tour of his stuffed elk busts and his Indian arrowheads dating back to the rape of the West. There was a whole wall of cavalry sabers in his dressing room. He admitted they weren't too PC, but he didn't want to offend the historical society, so he just moved them out of the living room." Alan's left hand rested, beneath Greenie's nightgown, in the crook of her waist.

"You didn't bring up the fires, did you? Or tell him he's an eco-fascist?"

Alan looked into her eyes for a long moment, smiling. "You've been hovering over George too long. We did not talk politics, Greenie. We talked you. Your talents and virtues. Your assets, as the governor called them."

"Did you volunteer any, or did they all come from my boss?"

"I named plenty, believe me, Greenie. The first two I named were your breasts." His hand moved up from her waist.

"Be serious."

"I can't be, not right this minute! I've been shacked up with a goldfish the past four months."

"Did you like him, even a little?"

"Sunny?"

"No, Alan. *Ray.* Just a minute here." Greenie laughed. She held his wrists away from her chest.

"Greenie, he's a politician. Read: an emotional mannequin. I can see that he's charming, and he sure as hell thinks you are the Bengal tiger's pajamas. He told me how he starts off his day in your kitchen. 'Like a guaranteed sunrise,' he said, or something to that effect. If he gets voted out of office next term, he's a shoo-in at Hallmark. So how can I hate the guy when he loves the woman *I* love? But have *you* caught a glimpse of this man as a person?"

"Several glimpses," she said. But had she? She knew details of his story, interesting details, and they had debated this or that political issue . . . but all of it could be a front. "What exactly do you mean by 'a person'?"

He answered without hesitation. "Someone acting or speaking with-out motive."

She thought this over. "But we always have motives, don't we?"

"No, I don't believe that," said Alan. "Falling in love, for instance—that's not a sensible thing to do at all. Whatever the outcome, there's always pain involved, always separation." He kissed Greenie's mouth. "We don't need to have this conversation. Not now at least."

She let go of his wrists. She said quietly, "Sometimes, you know, I wonder if what we do need is another child."

Alan's body, against hers, responded with a jolt of surprise. "Wow. Talk about something we shouldn't be discussing *now*."

"Why *not* now? How old are we, Alan? Is there much more time, if any? Maybe this would make all the difference in the world."

"That's what you said about moving out here."

Greenie sat up. "And I was wrong? You sound sure of that."

"Well, we're not living together, and I'm not living with George, and those facts hardly amount to what I would call a *positive* difference in the world. My world, at least. If my world counts."

"This afternoon, in that church, you told me you thought this place was amazing!"

"There's amazing and there's practical," said Alan. "And there's also not feeling coerced."

"Tell me you never coerce anyone in your work."

"I never do. I persuade, and I elicit, and I guide."

"Well saintly, superior you." She meant this half in jest, but in the dark it did not come across that way.

Alan, who was also sitting up by now, turned to her and sighed. "Oh Greenie . . . do you need to hear that I love you? I do, I've never stopped." He pressed his hands against his eyes. He lay down. "Let's go to sleep. Let's have a civilized breakfast. George and I have to get an early start." He pulled her close, her back to his chest. He kissed her neck.

"I like that," she said.

"I do too," he said. "I've missed it."

They made up in their usual physical ways, and in others. Quite unlike himself, Alan fell asleep right away.

When Greenie woke up, George was still asleep, but she could smell breakfast. From the kitchen doorway, she watched Alan remove bread from the oven and tenderly fold it into a napkin. When he saw her, he said, "I'm sorry about last night, that I got so belligerent," but this was all the intimate conversation they were allowed until he returned three days later—and by then everything had changed. The everything was private, invisible to everyone but Greenie. She could only have described the sensation as that of a large glass vessel cracking deep inside her, releasing a flood of something dark yet delicious, viscous and warm, through all her arteries and veins.

For their "guy weekend," Alan drove George and Treehorn south and then west, out Route 66 to see Acoma and Chaco Canyon. They would stay in a corny old-style hotel in Gallup where the rooms were named after movie stars who'd camped there when westerns were filmed in the real West. Mary Bliss had arranged for them to stay there with Treehorn. "I think we're in the Gene Autry suite," Alan told Greenie. "Dale Evans was taken."

The night after she saw them off, Greenie's doorbell rang at eight o'clock. She was home, reading Marcella Hazan. Ray was in Taos for dinner.

She had not seen much of Other Charlie since the weekend on the ranch. For the second time, she answered the door to be startled by his face, this time behind a handful of daisies. "Is this too rude? I saw your lights on."

"And you happened to be in the neighborhood. With flowers."

"I always carry flowers. Just in case."

She took the flowers and told him to come in.

"I should have called, shouldn't I?"

"Don't be silly." Greenie held the flowers with their heads toward the floor, as her mother had taught her when she was small. She looked at Other Charlie's face and recognized a nervous habit from long ago: he set and worked his lower jaw so that the muscles beneath his ears stood out like small marbles. She had always seen this look of consternation as the look of a boy playing at being a man. Endearingly, it seemed no different now that he had become a man.

She said, "You worry too much, Charlie." He followed her to the kitchen. She pulled a glass pitcher off a shelf and filled it with water, consciously—because here was the ultimate Water Boy—not turning on the tap until it was right above the mouth of the pitcher.

Other Charlie sat quietly at the table while Greenie trimmed the flowers. He said abruptly, "Charlie, I still can't believe it's you, here."

"It's me," she said, "I'm here, and you can call me Greenie."

"No. No, I don't believe I can. It's not . . . you. The you I know. Or remember."

"I'm probably not the me you remember." Greenie felt the insincerity of the teasing, the way it was meant to cover their genuine astonishment, their mutual excitement at stumbling onto someone so familiar—almost familial—in a place where they were both happily occupied but out of place. *Fish out of water,* she might have joked. But wanting to lighten rather than deepen the moment, she laughed and said, "My mother always put two aspirin in the water. Viagra for flowers!" She set the pitcher on the table.

"Charlie," said Other Charlie, his tone almost urgent, "please stop talking about your mother. I've hated your mother for so long. I'm sorry. No, no I'm not, as a matter of fact. I'm not sorry."

Greenie turned away. She laid the cutting board and the knife in the sink. Speechless with anger, it took her a moment to turn around and sit at the table. "Is that what you dropped by to tell me?"

"I make it a policy never to dwell on the past, but seeing you? I keep on remembering that weekend, the time she invited me up to your place in Maine. No, *her* place; that was clear."

Greenie sat still, hands in her lap. "Yes. That was ages ago. Eons."

"Do you know what happened that weekend?"

Greenie had no idea why he was torturing her. In return, she was blunt. "We slept together, and you went off to college and didn't call me. That was pretty cruel, wouldn't you say? But youth is—what's that word?"

"Callow. Which I never was. Many stupid, thoughtless things, but never that."

"So. Do you need me to forgive you?"

"It's not me you'd have to forgive." His jawbone worked incessantly, a piece of machinery fixed inside his scowling face. "Do you know how much I wanted you the whole summer I was painting your goddamn house?"

"I guess not." She thought of his naked chest framed in her bathroom window. She laughed.

"What's so funny?"

"Now that you mention it, none of this is funny. I don't know what my mother has to do with it, Charlie. Especially now. My poor mother is dead."

"I don't care if your poor mother is back among us in the body of the

Dalai Lama," said Other Charlie. "Do you know how much she was out to undermine you when she was alive? She was so smart, Charlie, so clever with her little comments that it took me years to figure it out, how she chipped away at you, made you seem so, I don't know . . . impossible." His voice turned mincing and learned. " 'My daughter, you know, is quite particular about people.' 'Charlotte has her eye on about five boys this year.' 'She's going to make a fine challenge of a wife one day, that girl of mine.' "

"Oh, I heard her say those things. That was just her way of . . ." *Her way of what?* thought Greenie. She remembered when her mother had said to Alan, "Creativity and brains compensate for quite a lot. Just ask *my* husband."

"Her way of making sure you didn't get the things you deserved."

"But I *have,*" said Greenie. "I have more than I deserve. If there's such a thing in life as deserving. Which there isn't."

"Like a husband who's nowhere in sight?" said Other Charlie.

Greenie might have told him that Alan was just around the corner, that things between them looked fine, that they were working out logistics . . . but she was mute. She realized that she had never mentioned Alan's visit to Other Charlie. She might have asked him to join them for dinner one night.

She realized that he would stare at her now until she answered him. "What happened back then can't matter that much now, can it?" she said.

"Yes it can." His hands were pressed flat on the table, as if he might leap to his feet. "Or it can now that I see you again. I don't mean I've thought about it much all these years, but when I have, I've felt such fury, such—"

"Let me get you a drink," said Greenie.

"I don't need one."

"I do." Greenie took a bottle of red wine off the windowsill. Alan had bought it: fancy, Ralph Nader stuff, bottled the year of their wedding. She took her time opening it. Night had fallen, swift as a curtain on a stage, and Greenie saw herself in the window, her face dim beside the bright explosion of daisies. She could not help remembering how much she had cried after Other Charlie's abrupt disappearance that summer. Her mother had come upon her once and had magically seemed to *know.* "Boys will be boys, even big boys," she'd said. "My dear Charlotte, a city boy—a city man—will be much better for you. Just wait till you get to New York." So it had seemed, later on, as if her mother were a prophet.

She set two glasses of wine on the table. When she did not sit, Charlie stood.

Greenie folded her arms. "So what did my mother tell you that weekend?"

"A lot of crap. That you had a boyfriend. That I wasn't the first guy you'd flirted with too much. That I was too good for you. You didn't have a boyfriend, though, did you? Later I figured it out."

"That you were too good for me!" Greenie recalled her longing. Then she recalled her mother's insistence, years later, that Charlie be included among the guests at her wedding. The thought of his presence even then had pained her, but his parents had been invited because they were long-time neighbors; how petty and rude to leave *him* out, her mother had said. "Jesus," said Greenie.

"It's not like I've wanted you all these years, not like you're the reason I . . ." He looked down into his wine.

Haven't married? thought Greenie. She couldn't stand what she was hearing, but she needed to hear it. All of whatever it was he wanted to say.

He laughed. "Man oh man. I did not come here tonight to say these things! Hey—where's your son? Already asleep? I thought I might get to see him, really meet him this time. That was part of why I dropped by."

"You mean the flowers were for him?" Greenie smiled. She finished off her wine, felt it rush through and brighten her body. "He's away for a few days. He'll be back on Sunday." If he asks where or with whom, I will tell him, she thought.

He said, "I'm sorry. How did we have this conversation anyway?"

"Charlie," said Greenie, "you are just as intense as ever. Some things never change."

He drained his glass and set it down. Empty-handed, speechless, he stood right next to her.

"I really am married, Charlie," she said. "I really am."

"I'll have to take your word for it," he said. "At the last minute, I skipped your wedding. Did you notice? Bet you didn't even notice."

"I wondered where you were." This was a lie; after wishing she didn't have to invite him, she *hadn't* noticed his absence—not till weeks later, when she had gone through the proofs of the wedding pictures. He had been to her mother's engagement party but not to the wedding.

"Since you're alone, let's go into town," he said. "Let's walk and look at the stars. We didn't have stars like this in Massachusetts, did we?"

"Sometimes we did," said Greenie. "Let me grab a sweater."

Other Charlie smiled. "You always had to argue; I remember that about you. Even about the little things. But everyone liked you too much to care."

"I thought you were the argumentative one," she said as they left the house, "the one who always had to be right."

As they made their way toward town, Greenie resolved not to think about (or mention) her mother. Other Charlie seemed less tense. Perhaps he was relieved to have said his piece.

Greenie pointed them toward the bar of a sophisticated restaurant on Palace Avenue, one where she was likely to see state officials she knew, if only to greet in a quick impersonal fashion.

They stood and talked till they could sit and talk. They talked about the years between her wedding day and the day that ended with the two of them sitting right there, wanting the bar never to empty and close, wanting not to be alone together yet not to part until they had filled in all the missing space between them. When Greenie told him the story about the implausible way in which she had landed her job wih Ray, she had to tell Other Charlie about Alan's resistance. He was quick to defend the other man's caution as necessary, probably even wise. At first, Greenie was annoyed, but then she realized how generous Other Charlie's reaction was. He might be, like Greenie, a creature of impulse and passion, but he was the more empathic one. That was when she ought to have told him about Alan's visit, but how would this look when she had neglected to mention the visit hours ago?

Other Charlie walked her home, along the sinuous route of the acequia, under the willows and cottonwoods and aspens fortunate to grow along its banks, under leaves that rustled more crisply than eastern leaves. As they walked through the gap in the wall that led into Greenie's tiny garden, he said, "Wait. I have something for you."

Other Charlie owned a car but bicycled everywhere he could, even to meetings at the mansion. In the governor's parking lot, his bike looked especially comic alongside the town cars and Hummers. Now, in the dark, he fumbled with bungee cords that fastened a package to his bike rack.

The package was so heavy that Greenie nearly dropped it. When she took off the newspaper, she burst out laughing.

"A brick?"

"It's to put in your toilet tank." He blushed. "Okay, I know how geeky it is. It's nothing personal; I always have three or four in the trunk of my car, and tonight I just thought . . . I get obsessed about these things. I've learned to go with it. I sleep better."

"So you just happened to cruise by my house on your bicycle with daisies and a brick." Greenie clasped the brick to her chest. "Well, that's nothing if not charming. Sort of."

"Sort of charming," he said. "That's a whole lot better than obnoxious, which is something else I can be."

They said good night while they were laughing. Once she was inside, Greenie raised the brick to her face. It smelled like any other brick, like a flowerpot, like soil. She went to the bathroom and opened the back of her toilet. Careful not to jar the flushing widgets, she maneuvered the brick down into the tank. She waited till the ripples settled to close it again.

ALAN DROVE UP TO THE HOUSE two nights later, after midnight. Greenie had begun to worry, even to wonder, in her wildly distracted state of mind, whether Alan would do something as rash as kidnap their son and head for Mexico. She felt acutely ashamed when she saw the car. Treehorn jumped out first, avidly patrolling the borders of the yard.

Alan carried George, fast asleep, straight to his room. Without a word, Greenie pulled back George's bedspread and removed his sandals. On his little feet, the pattern of the straps was outlined precisely in red dust. She turned on the fan, then bent to kiss his grubby cheeks.

Alan told Greenie that George had been fairly quiet for much of the trip. The heat and all the driving had made him sleepy, though he had enjoyed running freely around the ruins of Chaco Canyon. "He does love this dog," Alan said.

"Did you have a good time?"

"Oh yes. But I promised him he could tell you about the dance on the mesa and the bison heads in the hotel."

A band of rosy skin lay across Alan's nose, from one cheek to the other. Greenie was glad to see him look so alive, so out in the world.

"I brought you something," he said.

She lifted the lid of a white box. It contained a turquoise necklace: a string of rough beads, pitted like moons, in various shades of green. She held the coiled necklace in her palm. "It's gorgeous," she said. "Is it old?" She fastened it behind her neck before she realized that he had hoped to perform this intimate task.

"Yes, but it's not pawn," said Alan. "I couldn't get over all those pawnshops filled with all that exquisite jewelry. It gave me the creeps."

"I've heard about that. Even saddles turned in to get money for booze. That's what they say. It's all for booze. Even those beautiful patterned blankets."

He touched the beads where they lay against her throat. "I didn't like the idea of some forsaken heirloom around your neck."

But isn't that what all antiques are? thought Greenie as she looked at her reflection in the bedroom mirror. Isn't it all discarded, abandoned, whether by choice or compulsion? She had recently noticed that her red hair was fading in the sun. She wasn't outdoors a great deal, but she had lived here now for two seasons and the climate was making its mark.

The next day, Consuelo took George to Diego's house for the day. Greenie and Alan went to the fine arts museum. Everywhere they walked, Alan kept an arm across Greenie's shoulders. They did not separate, as couples often do, to look about at their individual paces. They saw Georgia O'Keeffe paintings and squash-blossom necklaces so heavy and battered they reminded Greenie of armor. They saw real armor, the armor of Spanish conquistadores. They saw blankets, baskets, and rugs that filled rooms with a geometric frenzy. They saw Madonnas appealing to heaven from beneath so many layers of aging varnish that they looked as if they were literally drowning in sorrow.

So many beautiful, solemn things to hold the eye and anchor the mind, yet Greenie could think of nothing but Other Charlie—or, more exactly, speak to no one else inside her head. She told him about the weeping Virgin surrounded by butterflies, about the seven-course dinner she would be making for the attorney general of California at the end of the week, about George's new passion for masks. She told him every detail she remembered of lying down with him in the soft yet prickly needles carpeting the woods behind Circe (how the needles had stuck to their bodies like iron filings to a magnet, how she had pulled those needles from her clothing and hair, her bedsheets, for days after he had left the island). She told him what it was like to start her business, what it was like to fire up her oven long before dawn on a frigid New York morning, what it was like to give birth, what it was like to get married in front of all those people she'd known forever, what it was like to have slowly forgotten him since then, let him slip into the sea behind her sailing ship, sink out of sight so that she believed him blessedly lost till here he was, having washed up on shore right before her eyes. All these things she chattered about to Other Charlie inside her head, sometimes even while Alan, the real man beside her, was talking.

After Alan left, three long weeks passed during which she heard nothing from Charlie. By now he was just Charlie; there was no Otherness to him, none whatsoever. There was not even, to Greenie, a time she could imagine when he had been absent from her soul. There were merely all the years when he might have been a part of her physical, geographically rooted life but, inexplicably now, had not. She saw no shades of infidelity here; wasn't it fair to say that as you grew older you understood that marriage was not the exclusive domain of emotional attachment, that deep connections formed elsewhere too, with men as well as other women? She told herself that even if Alan had already pulled his act together to move here (which he had assured her now he was doing, though his characteristic caution, so charming once, had become an aggravation), she would still have been glad to see Charlie. She would still have wanted to feel this connection to her youth. The intensity, she reasoned, was also tied to the loss of her parents.

Even the start of school for George did little to distract Greenie; in fact, there was no longer time for him to spend mornings with her at the mansion. Now consistently alone in the kitchen before Ray arrived, Greenie found herself singing along, once again, with Billie Holiday and Sarah Vaughan. No more Julie Andrews or Mary Martin.

Finally, one Saturday morning, he called.

"Hey there," he said, as if she should have expected this call. "It's me. I have something to show you. Can I pick you up in fifteen minutes?"

Greenie paused. "I have George, you know."

"Bring George! I was hoping you would."

As usual, Ray was at the ranch, McNally in charge of his sustenance. Greenie had spent the early part of the morning playing Go Fish with

George. Then Alan had called. He told her he had two new referrals: couples, short-term. Their sessions should end by the new year. Greenie told herself to be patient. They talked about Christmas in New York, what fun it would be for George.

While she spoke with Alan, George had wandered back to his room. She found him there now, reading one of the comic books Alan had sent him.

"We're going on an adventure," she said.

George looked up but did not shut the book. "What kind of adventure?"

"It wouldn't be a true adventure if you knew just what to expect or precisely where you were going."

"No adventure. I want to stay here."

"We'll get ice cream—or some kind of treat," she said, realizing that she had no idea where they were going, either. "You'll meet my friend Charlie. I've known him almost since we were your age. Since we were Diego's age, I think."

George brightened. "Can Diego come?"

"No, sweetie. Not today."

"Then no."

Greenie sat down on George's bed beside him. "Honey, I already said we would go. Please."

George exhaled the long kind of *aaaalll riiighhht* that every parent knows will exact a price (later outcries of "You promised!" "You said!").

"Pick out some toys to bring in the car," she said.

She packed juice, pretzels, and Oreos. She cajoled him into the bathroom, smoothed sunblock onto his arms and face. By then, Charlie was at the door.

He looked first at George. "I am so glad to meet you."

George stared at Charlie but said nothing.

The awkward silence did not last. George handed his mother two plastic horses. "Will you carry them?" he said. "*Please* will you carry them?"

Sometimes she wondered if she ought to be worried about George; he had grown more solemn, less silly, in recent weeks. But he had also grown taller and slimmer, and perhaps these changes were logically aligned. She held the horses in one arm and laid her opposite hand on top of his head as they walked to the car. Perhaps, like his father, he needed a little distance from Greenie. She felt a twinge of loneliness.

"I can't promise anything," said Charlie as he pulled away from the curb, "but I have a hunch."

"Stop with the teasing," said Greenie. "How're your clients doing, your little fish?"

"Not well. An upstream battle. Ha ha." He told her about a panel of federal judges known as the God Squad, who could be asked to override the Endangered Species Act if the consequences of enforcing it meant that people would be adversely affected. "The whole point of the act was to trump this kind of selfishness! No one wants to talk about 'adversely affecting' an ecosystem!"

To leave Santa Fe by car was nothing at all like driving out of New York. New York was a city whose reach seemed never-ending, even greedy; for miles and miles, the only perceptible changes as you tried to leave it behind were a diminishing of scale and encroaching grime, as if you were leaving a literal heartland, heading out to the extremities of an old, weary body with poor circulation. But as you drove away from the heart of this town, you might turn your attention from your surroundings for just five minutes and look up to find yourself somewhere altogether different, driving between rustic tin-roofed shacks where goats or chickens loitered in the shadows; crossing empty arroyos, stretches of sagebrush and cowering pine (much of it still visibly singed by the fires). You'd enter and leave villages that, but for their satellite dishes and cars, looked nearly ancient, lost in time. Civilization remained ever-present in the grand houses perched on hills and ridges—haciendas of Old World ranches; glinting glass mansions built by the newly wealthy—yet how far you would feel from the city's galleries, restaurants, and street shows. In the time it took to get from the Empire State Building to the middle of Queens, you'd find yourself rising toward the arid austerity of pine groves and mountains.

Charlie paid frequent attention to the sky before them, dipping his head and squinting his eyes every minute or so. It looked as if a storm might break—or that was how an easterner would have read this sky; by now, Greenie was accustomed to the false anticipation, the fleeting showers that never became true rain.

She could hear George, in the backseat, muttering some sort of dialogue between his horses. She heard the words *buckskin, pinto,* and *hackamore.*

When they passed a horse alone in a field, she said, "Look, George."

She heard a break in his wordplay, but he did not comment.

She turned around. "Did you see that horse?"

"He's lonely," said George. "He needs friends. Actually, you should give animals friends."

"Yes," said Charlie before Greenie could equivocate. "That's true, George. Animals should be kept in twos, at the very least. Maybe except for cats. Cats like their privacy."

"Yes," said George. "Cats are hunterers, and hunterers do the best hunting alone."

"Treehorn's happy with you and Daddy as friends," said Greenie.

"Actually, Treehorn gets to meet other dogs on the street, Daddy says. So she can talk to other dogs sometimes. Dog-talk, not real talk."

"Right. That's one good thing about the city," said Greenie.

George did not reply, and Greenie heard the critical echo of her remark, as if there weren't much to recommend the city at all. For months, Greenie had braced herself for George to be homesick, to say how much he missed not just his father and now Treehorn but his old haunts and friends and other touchstones—yet he hadn't. And although he'd been told that his father would be moving out soon, he did not ask when this would happen.

Charlie turned off the road, onto a dirt track. "There," he said. "There we go." He drove for several yards and stopped at a gate. He got out, and Greenie followed his lead. She expected him to open the gate, but he leaned against it, then beckoned to George.

They were looking at a stretch of rough, meager pasture enclosed in barbed-wire fencing. The vista was still and bleak.

"Where are we?" asked George when Greenie opened his door.

She looked at Charlie, but he was staring at the sky.

"I'm staying here where it's warm," George declared.

"Fair enough," said Charlie, and then, to Greenie, "Look at that." He was pointing to the horizon—above the horizon. "See those clouds?"

"Hard to miss," said Greenie. In contrast to the wind-flattened landscape below them, a gathering of elephant-colored clouds stretched upward in towering formations, ominous in their verticality. Their rising force seemed infinite, yet the bottom of the cloud mass was so perfectly planed that it might have been resting on a thousand-acre sheet of glass.

"Cumulonimbus. But what do you see below them?"

"The land. Nothing much."

"No. Right below them."

Greenie shaded her eyes, for though the sun was hidden, the very expanse of the sky exerted a milky brilliance all around them. "Haze."

"Rain," said Charlie. "That's rain." He invoked this ordinary noun like the name of a lover.

"That's great," said Greenie. "That's good news. Isn't it?"

"Look again. It's rain, and it's not rain. It will never reach the ground."

Greenie could see, then, that the veil stretching from the bottom of the cloud mass dwindled to invisibility. "Why? Why won't it?"

"Because the air is so impossibly dry. The rain evaporates before it reaches the ground." He looked at her again. "The other day, you asked me why there's so little rain. It's not that there's so little rain; it's that we don't receive that rain. It's taken back before we can get it. That's half the story of why this part of the world is the way it is. People wish otherwise—they think they're wishing for rain when what they ought to pray for is humidity. But that's not in the *nature* of this place. If farmers could run acequia straight from the clouds, it might be a different story."

Greenie shivered. "It's cold out here."

"Well, that's it," he said sharply. "You asked about the rainfall, why there's so little. I like to *show* that to people. It means a lot to see how the rain disappears, how the air just drinks it up."

"Mommy, I'm hungry," said George. "You said we'd get a treat."

"First, how about lunch?" said Charlie as he looked over his shoulder, backing toward the road.

He took them to his apartment. When they arrived, Greenie could tell he had planned their visit beforehand. "I'm very good at grilled cheese," Charlie told George. "Do you like grilled cheese, maybe with tomato?"

"Not tomato," said George.

"But the cheese? Is that okay?"

"Yes, I like cheese. Is it cheddar cheese?"

"It is," said Charlie. "All the way from New York. Nice and sharp. And George, come in here a minute."

While Greenie looked around the one room that served as everything but kitchen and bathroom, George joined Charlie in the tiny kitchen. "Oh wow!" she heard her son cry out. "Wow, T. rex!"

She wondered what had rekindled his interest in dinosaurs; he ran to her from the kitchen and said, "Mom, he can cutten the cheese into a T. rex!"

Charlie leaned out the kitchen door. "You want a grilled T. rex, too? I have T. rex and stego." He held up a pair of oversize cookie cutters.

"Mom, choose stego," urged George.

"That's fine. I'm a pacifist, so I prefer stego," she said.

"What's a pacifist?" asked George.

"Someone who likes things peaceful, who doesn't like violence."

"Stegos can fight, Mom. They can crush things with their tail."

"I'm sure they can. Or could. But . . . well, I like their shape, too. I like their . . . fins. Are they called fins, George?"

"Plates. They are called plates," George said emphatically.

Charlie's place was spartan yet also, in a quiet way, filled with treasures. His bed—a mattress in a simple frame—took up one corner, covered with a faded patchwork quilt. In the center of the floor lay a single rug, a gray-patterned rug made by local Indians. Stretched across the wall above the bed was a map larger than any she'd ever seen, nearly the size of a garage door: the Grand Canyon, intricately surveyed in pinks, purples, blues, and tropical greens, swarming with infinitesimal numbers and jigsaw lines. At the opposite side of the room stood a couch, a coffee table, and two antique folding chairs with wooden pockets on their backs—chairs from a church, designed to hold hymnals or prayer books. Three small paintings, all desert landscapes, hung on the wall above the couch.

But Charlie's most interesting possessions were the smallest, laid out evenly on a table against a third wall. The table—a peeling turquoise door laid across a pair of filing cabinets—doubled as a desk and a natural history display. Around a modest clearing that held a laptop computer lay bones, pot shards, fossils, dried seed pods, mysterious tarnished implements—and dozens of stones, each distinctive and striking. There wasn't a mote of dust on anything.

"Come and get it," Charlie called from the kitchen. George emerged with his own plate, on it two sandwiches shaped, as promised, like

Tyrannosaurus rexes. George looked up at his mother, grinned, and made a loud snarling noise. This was the silliness she had missed.

"*Rrraaar* yourself!" she said. "Just wait till I get my stegos. They know how to fight; you told me so."

"But not as good as T. rex. You cannot vanish T. rex." Carefully, George transferred his plate to the dining table just outside the kitchen.

From Charlie, Greenie took a tray holding their sandwiches (Charlie had chosen T. rex, too), a bowl of sliced pickles, and a dish of baby carrots. Greenie's stegosauruses looked as if they were bleeding; beneath the cheese, Charlie had tucked slices of tomato. She told him the sandwiches smelled delicious.

"No disingenuous compliments from *you*."

"I love grilled cheese," said Greenie. "My mother taught me how to make it with horseradish and coleslaw."

"This is what they call one-upsmanship," Charlie said to George. "Does she always show off like that?"

George was already eating. He looked up at Charlie and giggled.

Charlie asked George about his new school. Greenie learned more in those fifteen minutes than she had managed to get from quizzing her son for days on end. She learned that his teacher, Mrs. Rodrigo, was teaching them a little Spanish; that she owned twenty-three finches, which she kept in a cage that filled most of her living room; that her husband operated a crane. (She had shown the class photos of the finches and of her husband in his crane.) She learned that Mrs. Rodrigo had read them a book called *Owl at Home*, which was really, according to George, "a bunch of stories squished into one."

"I must say," said Greenie, "Mrs. Rodrigo seems to like birds. I mean, finches . . . a story about an owl . . . and even that her husband drives a *crane*."

"Mom, not *that* kind of crane," George said impatiently.

Greenie glanced at Charlie, who listened with pleasure and amusement to her son's assertions. She stacked their dishes on the tray and carried it into the kitchen, a stunningly bright little alley of a room, almost completely enclosed in glass. When Charlie joined her, she was taking in the long terra-cotta planter filled with cactuses, the barometer (identical to the one her father had kept in Maine), and the great wooden barrel on the floor by the sink.

"No washing dishes. I do that."

"Oh please," said Greenie.

"No, really." He smiled apologetically. "I have my own eccentric system."

She noticed that there was no dishwasher. The dish rack beside the sink was rigged to drain through a slot in the lid of the barrel, along with a hose that snaked down from a hole drilled in a window frame. Charlie said, "It comes from the gutter. I get some of my rinse water that way. Not much these days, but some."

She laughed. "That's how we got water in Maine."

He nodded. "And there you have more water than anyone here could ever dream of. That is, if people here were realistic."

"What is *this*?" George called from the other room. Charlie left the kitchen to join him, but Greenie lingered. Beyond the barrel and its Rube Goldberg riggings, she saw nothing out of the ordinary. Three yellowed cookbooks were stacked on the only shelf, next to a framed photograph of Charlie's parents in front of their house in Massachusetts. On the counter stood an old-fashioned rotary telephone and a wooden pepper mill. Greenie placed an index finger in the aperture framing the zero on the phone. She pulled it around to feel that long-outmoded sensation, of making a phone call back in high school.

"Hey!" Charlie shouted from the other room. "Stop snooping in there!"

George stood at the large table, asking Charlie about his stones, lifting them one by one. On the bottom of each stone, Charlie had inked in white the place it had come from. *Champlain–Vt.* on a gray egglike stone bisected by a protruding white vein. *Wading River,* long and smooth and mauve, like a tongue. A lump of black pumice as light as down, *Etna;* sage green with bits of glitter, *Trapalou–Ikaria;* a jagged cube of granite, *Central Park.*

"When were you in Central Park without looking me up?" said Greenie.

"I didn't know you'd care to have me look you up."

"I like this one," said George. He was holding the biggest, in both hands: a hunk of sparkling rose quartz. "Little Compton," he read aloud from the underside. "Where is that?"

"Rhode Island," said Charlie. "Would you like to have it?"

"Yes!"

Greenie did not try to discourage this gift or even get George to say please. She was through, for the day, with being the disciplinarian mother. Idly, she picked up a sliver of blackish rock, thin as a piece of cardboard. The perfect skipping stone, she thought, remembering contests with cousins when the tide was low and the swimming cove was placid. She turned the rock over: *Circe, Smith's Rock.* She put it back quickly, but not before Charlie noticed.

"That one I'm not giving up. I'm not sure I could replace it."

Greenie laughed nervously. She lifted another rock. "Tierra del Fuego," she read. "Where haven't you been?"

"Lots of places," said Charlie. "I'm one of those people who can't stop searching my way around the world." Abruptly, he returned to the kitchen.

George played with several of the rocks, lining them up, stacking them, talking to himself about their qualities, while Greenie stood in the kitchen with Charlie. He took a dipper and, with water from the barrel, filled a plastic basin in the sink. He put their plates and cups in to soak.

"You wash dishes in that?" she said. "Water from your roof?"

"And from my salad spinner. I try to scrub them off without soap. Then I rinse them with hot water from the tap. That's enough. I'm not running a restaurant."

"And you take two-minute showers."

He smiled. "Three minutes. Every three days unless I go running."

Greenie laughed. "Charlie, you may be this big world traveler, but you've grown into such an old lady!"

George, who was suddenly beside her, clutching his large pink rock, said, "He is not an old lady, Mom. He is a guy. He is a man."

"That's right." Charlie did not take his eyes off Greenie. "I am a man."

Greenie tried to meet his level, superficially pleasant gaze, but she couldn't. George, who had not been so talkative in months, said, "Charlie, can I change my mind? Can I keepen the one from the volcano instead? The one with the little holes all over?"

"Absolutely," said Charlie, though Greenie was sure the pumice from Sicily, like the skipping stone from Maine, was irreplaceable.

"Thank you. Thank you a whole, whole lot!" exclaimed her glowing boy as he traded up, something large and shiny for something small and cunningly dark.

⟿

CHARLIE BROUGHT ANOTHER ODD PRESENT to Greenie a few nights later, though this time he called before dropping by. George was fast asleep.

Once again, she was fooled by the appearance of the gift, a small rectangular box that suggested a bracelet or earrings.

"Don't get excited," said Charlie. "You know me by now."

The bar of soap Greenie took from the box was brown, oval, and speckled like an egg. It smelled of almonds. "Nice," she said, embarrassed by her disappointment. "Though I hope you don't mean to imply that I'm not clean enough."

Charlie stood by her kitchen sink. He picked up the bottle of liquid soap she kept there for washing hands. "No," he said, shaking his head for emphasis.

Greenie laughed. "No what?"

"No antibacterial soaps." He went on to explain to Greenie how these soaps, just like an improper dose of antibiotics in the human body, flowed out into the streams and oceans, creating new and stronger bacteria, supergerms.

"But then why does George's doctor have that very soap in his office?"

"Two words: *free, samples*." He smiled forlornly. "Charlie, the world is full of shortsighted people."

By now, Greenie understood that to Charlie, an idealist almost by instinct (could you be a knee-jerk idealist?), this human failing was a monstrosity, a tragedy that made him chronically anxious. But she also understood that he was telling her, whether he meant to or not, that she could trust him with anything, because he was someone who, unlike Greenie, thought things entirely through, saw the consequences of actions and inactions both, their long trajectories through time. The gifts he had given her were signs of his very self: that he was as solid and square as the brick, as wholesome as the soap, as unassuming as those wide-eyed daisies. But now all she said was "And that's why you do what you do."

"I suppose so, yes, in a nutshell."

Greenie put the bar of soap where the quietly evil bottle had sat.

"What's that?" she heard Charlie say. He was pointing at a cake stand.

"German chocolate," she said.

"I'll have a very big piece," he said. "Please."

As she watched him dig into her cake, she saw the earnest boy in the man, and she understood something else, or two things at once: that she wanted Charlie to make a pass at her and that he never would. If that was how he wanted her—and did he?—he would leave it up to her, because she was the one with so much at stake.

As soon as he was gone, Greenie called Walter. "Oh Walter, something terrible is happening," she said when he answered. "I'm falling in love."

"Good for you, baby," Walter said softly, instantly. "Falling in love is never terrible, never."

Greenie said, "Walter, that's the stupidest thing I've ever heard you say."

"No," he said firmly. "It just depends on what you do with the love into which you have fallen."

"That's too complicated for me," said Greenie. "I'm desperately in need of simple. Simple, simple, simple." She heard summer thunder, all the way from New York City. She thought of Alan: *We do it without any sensible motive. It always involves pain.*

"Darling, *simple* is the childish prayer on everyone's lips," said Walter. "But here's what's crucial: does he love you back, this mystery man?"

"I'm afraid he might. Back to the time we were barely old enough to drive."

"Oh my heavenly stars." Walter let out a laughing, wrenching sigh, which was followed immediately by another, louder crack of thunder. Then Greenie could actually hear the rain fall outside Walter's apartment, pelting hard on the roof over Walter's head, the roof over Alan's head, roof after roof in the city where Greenie finally knew that, whatever else might happen, she would never make her home again.

ELEVEN

"WELL, EVERYBODY, we have some big news. I'm pregnant."

They were eating the main course of Thanksgiving dinner—
Saga's turkey stuffed with corn bread, Pansy's mashed potatoes with
too much garlic, Frida's Asian yam salad and brussels sprouts in cider.
Pansy's new boyfriend had just asked if someone would pass the cranberry relish (the one thing that wasn't homemade). That's when Denise
made her announcement.

Michael sat next to her, fully attentive; he hadn't been on the phone
once since arriving. He took his wife's right hand with his left, between
their plates. His thick wedding ring sparked in the light from the candles.

Pansy's face seemed to whiten. For an instant, she looked more anxious than glad and stole a glance at her boyfriend, who smiled blandly,
the way one does at the good news of strangers. She laid *her* hand on the
tablecloth, perhaps hoping the boyfriend would take it. He didn't.

Frida was the first to speak. "Oh Denise, that is so wonderful.
Michael! Congratulations to you both." She raised her glass. "Here's to
you, new mom."

"She's going to be the best," said Michael.

Uncle Marsden's smile wasn't much more personal than that of
Pansy's newcomer boyfriend. His eyes were dry as he murmured, "You
bet she will."

"How far along?" said Pansy. She put her unclaimed hand back in
her lap.

"Oh, about a minute," said Denise. "We just found out yesterday. I
know it's soon to tell anyone, but since we're all together . . ." She
looked at Michael, who beamed at her.

To Pansy, he said, "No reason to think we'll have problems. First
checkup was totally normal."

"Oh no!" said Pansy. "I never meant to imply you would!"

In her head, Saga counted carefully, twice before she was nearly certain. "August?" she said quietly. "Wow. A baby in August?"

The entire family looked at Saga: an unfamiliar sensation. Had she said the wrong thing? But Denise was smiling wholeheartedly at her, even gratefully. "August first, as a matter of fact. I can't imagine what I'll look like in a bathing suit by then." Again, she and Michael exchanged their starry look.

"August," said Uncle Marsden, "is when they're threatening to break ground for those blasted condominia. Unless the bird people pull themselves together. So don't get too smug about beach plans just yet."

Frida frowned at her father. "Dad, did you hear Denise? She just said she's going to make you a grandfather."

There was a hint of annoyance in the smile Uncle Marsden directed at Frida. His eyes were closed slightly—a little like a snake, thought Saga, surprised by the treachery in this image. He said calmly, "I heard the splendid news, my dear. I'm not a bit deaf." He turned to Michael and Denise. "That *is* splendid news, in case I didn't shout it from the rooftops. I shall have to dig up the cradle my father made. I think your mother kept you girls in it; Michael, I seem to remember you did not like the motion. You wanted your little bed on solid ground. That's you all over, isn't it? Well, may your little one find his bit of solid ground as well." He chuckled and raised his glass.

"Or *hers*," said Frida as she joined the toast.

"And now I need more of Saga's fine stuffing. Pass it on over," said Uncle Marsden. He set down his glass and made a summoning gesture toward the dish, which sat at the far end of the table, near Pansy's boyfriend.

Remarkable, thought Saga, how no one said another word about it for the rest of the meal—well, herself included. But if your own sisters and dad didn't want to talk about the first of a new generation—wonder about names, things like that—wasn't something wrong? Or was it that Denise wasn't their sister and daughter? Pansy was clearly envious. Look at Michael, though: he did seem softer, happier. He seemed, for a change, in the moment, not preoccupied by speculations, investments, trades. Maybe a lot of his crankiness over the recent years had been about this: worrying that they wouldn't have kids. Saga could understand that. And she could understand the wash of joy when that worry was behind you, like a wash of bright sunny blue watercolor brushed across a pencil drawing. Or she could imagine it.

Dessert was pumpkin pie made from a can by Saga and pear-ginger crumble made from scratch by Frida, served with Uncle Marsden's favorite food in the world: hard sauce with brandy. They talked about *The Perfect Storm*; everyone had seen the movie except Uncle Marsden and Saga. Pansy was upset that someone had exploited the tragedies of real underprivileged people who would never see a penny of what those actors and producers were getting. Denise said she thought the author had set up some kind of scholarship fund.

"Well, *I* read that he opened a hipster bar in New York City with his take of the loot," said Pansy.

"Maybe he did both," said Frida.

"The scholarship fund should be for the families of those rescue divers from the Coast Guard," said Michael, "who sacrifice their lives for spoiled, ignorant people on yachts. Did you read that part of the book? It wasn't in the movie. About that rich imbecile who sued the Coast Guard for forcing him off his boat? They should have left him to drown."

"Aren't those spoiled, ignorant people with yachts some of your biggest clients?" asked Pansy.

Michael gave her a brief hard glance, an "Oh *please*" sort of expression.

"Frankly," said Uncle Marsden, "I am not interested in watching a movie where you know from the start that you will see the main characters drown. Unless they're murderers or former Gestapo, perhaps. And big waves—we've seen plenty of those right here, no special effects needed. What's the hoopla?" That brought the conversation to a halt.

Saga took orders for coffee; over her objections, Pansy's boyfriend insisted on helping.

"You have a nice family. Mine can't get through a meal without a big fight," he said as he measured coffee grounds and water. While they waited through the coffeemaker's burblings, he gave her the dinner plates one by one so she could rinse them. They had eaten off Uncle Marsden's Yale plates because those could go in the dishwasher.

"That's too bad," said Saga as she rinsed off Harkness Tower, then Woolsey Hall and the arch that led to the athletic fields. Funny how, from washing their images on dishes, she knew these places by heart when so many others, places she'd really been to, were hard to retain. "We do okay here; we're pretty high on the scale of family niceness. Most of the time." Had she just said "we"? Saga wondered if maybe, tonight at last, she was feeling accepted by her cousins. And she wondered what Pansy had told the boyfriend about her.

He said, as if reading her mind, "Pansy says you're looking for a job in animal welfare."

Saga ran a sponge across the counter. "I do volunteer work. For now."

"I run a career counseling service in New Haven," he said. "Pansy said maybe I could help you out. Nonprofit might be a good place for you." He held out a business card. She put it in the pocket of her apron, Aunt Liz's apron.

"Thanks."

He said, "I know you have . . ."

She looked straight at him. "Disabilities."

"That shouldn't discourage you. Obviously you—"

"Let's go have more of that yummy crumble," said Saga. "I'll call you." She stared into the cupboards, hoping he would take the hint. For a minute, she wasn't sure she would recognize the coffee cups, know them from soup bowls or ramekins. I know all these words, she reassured herself as she reached for the saucers. *Ramekin:* a sturdy cube of a word, spinning in the air like a juggler's ball. Maroon.

She knew she was stacking the cups too loudly on the tray. Slow, she told herself. Calm.

The boyfriend said, "Please, let me—"

"Oh yes," said Saga. She put the cream and sugar on the tray and handed it to him. "Put this on the sideboard. We'll serve ourselves."

When he had left the kitchen, she walked through the mudroom onto the side porch to feel the shock of cold air. She took a deep serrated breath, almost a sob. The boyfriend was nice; it was Pansy who'd put him up to that nasty little mission. Or was it thoughtful? Maybe Pansy did care for Saga, about Saga's life.

The unseen waves were loud, almost as loud as thunder, slamming the beach. A fine snow was falling, flakes as tiny as dust motes but sharp and distinct when they hit your face. She leaned out from the overhang and looked up. How thick were the clouds tonight? She walked down the steps and away from the house. No, *there* was the moon, murky yellow, half lit, a thick potato wedge. Hello. Hello, dear friend.

There was the falling snow, visible only in the light from the dining room windows. There were Michael and Denise, perhaps the only ones in the room now, kissing. There was the house. *House:* a word as big and gray as a summer storm cloud, but flat, solid, quiet. *House. Ramekin. Boyfriend* (china blue, Yale blue). *Baby* (white as the innards of a milkweed pod). Four delicious words.

SHE HAD GROWN TO LOVE THE BOOKSTORE, and it had become as vivid a place in her mind, and in her memory, as her room at the top of Uncle Marsden's house. The bird prince let Saga come and go as she pleased, and he welcomed her modest help. She'd started with the garden and moved her way in. After planting the window boxes, she'd put pachysandra along the fence and a rugged moss between the flagstones. She consulted Uncle Marsden's books, choosing things that were easy to grow. She copied down their names, and Fenno bought them. In the early fall, she planted daffodil and tulip bulbs in a patch of sun, hostas among the pachysandra. She loosened the hard soil around the magnolia tree and weeded, weeded, weeded. Sometimes the parrot kept Saga company, watching with those strange black eyes, tilting her head every which way as if she could never get a clear impression of Saga. Just who *are* you? she seemed to wonder. Will I know if I look at you this way? This way? How about *this*?

In October, Fenno had asked Saga if she'd like to help him do a reshelving project. He warned her that there would be a lot of carrying, upstairs and down. Could she do that? He also told her that he would not allow her to continue doing anything if she would not accept payment. "Oneeka gets paid, you should get paid." Oneeka was his real assistant, though she wasn't there all the time.

Saga now tried to go to the city a few times a week. Stan's frosty behavior bothered her less and less. She brought him a litter of kittens she found in a box when she went for a walk along the Hudson River, putting up flyers asking for donations and volunteers. Fenno let her put Stan's flyers right on the sales counter in the bookstore.

Sometimes, as she walked around the Village doing Stan's footwork, she would pass the Italian restaurant, "her" little courtyard, and feel a jolt of longing. On one of the last warm afternoons in October, she'd taken a table there and ordered a piece of cake. These days, she spent all her nights in her own bed, even if it meant taking a rush-hour train, standing up for several stops, clinging to a pole as she struggled to keep her hard-won balance. She did not want to show up for Fenno looking anything but clean and neat.

She'd had a glimpse of Fenno's private life the first time she went down into the basement of the bookstore. Half of the low space was taken up by shelves—mysteries, science fiction, and horror stories—the rest by stacks of boxes, a desk, a rocking chair, a dog kennel, a folded baby stroller, and a bike. The bathroom was down here, too. It wasn't much more than a cubbyhole with a toilet and tiny sink, but its walls swarmed with information.

Next to the mirror over the sink hung a bulletin board. Tacked to it were notices of readings around the neighborhood, a pamphlet claiming to list the hundred best books of the twentieth century, a water-stained handwritten sign that read PLEASE: NO REFUSE IN TOILET, and a photograph. Here was Fenno, sandy hair blowing, eyes crinkled up in a smile, standing in a field that stretched away like a green and stormy sea. A moor, she thought. *Moor:* a long word, a purple word, a dark satin ribbon of a word.

In the photo, Fenno knelt on the ground enfolding a child in each arm: a boy and a girl, though you could tell this only from the way they were dressed. Both had short, fine blond hair and wide pink cheeks. He was a father! Saga felt unexpectedly strange at this discovery, excited yet also unhappy.

Covering most of the opposite wall was a bird-watcher's map of the world. It made the birds look like conquerors, their colorful shapes crowding every continent like game pieces or markers on a battle plan. Birds had such wonderful names, Saga thought as she let her eyes roam the map. Way down in Australia, Rainbow Lorikeet, Satin Bowerbird, Tawny Frogmouth; in Africa, the Green Wood-Hoopoe, the Sacred Ibis, the Fulvous Whistling Duck. (Fulvous?! Was that an ordinary word with an ordinary meaning? A word swollen, tender, and pink, like a nursing breast . . .) In Europe, her favorites were the Chiffchaff, the Fieldfare, the Stonechat, the Capercaillie; to the far north, Oldsquaw and Parasitic Jaeger.

The birds' migration routes crisscrossed the map like a craze of telephone wires, swooping gracefully from one coast to another. They seemed almost to *secure* the world, all these well-traveled paths in the sky, the way ribbon or twine secures a precious gift. And yet, it occurred to Saga, all the creatures pictured here, though they might venture the whole world over, returned in the end to their separate colonies. Could you be a roving homebody?

Is that what I might be? she wondered: someone who roams and roams yet always goes home to roost?

After leaving the bathroom, she stopped to look at the desk against the back wall. There, pinned to another board, was another picture of those same two children, younger perhaps. They sat in the lap of a pretty woman with milky skin and red hair threaded with silver. Saga had been in the store many times by now and was sure she would remember if she'd seen this woman before. Or maybe she wouldn't. Or maybe Fenno was divorced. There was also a picture of a Border collie lying against a bookcase. That must be the dog he'd lost, the one he missed. Saga touched the dog's nose—graying, just like the hair of the pretty woman. A dog who'd lived to a ripe old age; that pleased her. Fenno took good care of those he loved—but where were his children?

For most of the time since the accident, certainly since David had left, Saga had assumed that she would probably never find someone to marry, certainly never have babies. Her doctors did not bring it up, and neither did she. She had her periods—the part of her that could nurture a baby was healthy—but until two years ago there had been the seizures, and even now she had spells of vertigo, numbnesses that came and went, the headaches. Whenever she felt a longing—as she did when she heard Michael's news—she couldn't help feeling that to ask for too much was to tempt fate. She was lucky to be walking, conversing, leading an almost regular life.

And she had her shared life with Uncle Marsden. Alone together, they joked about what it must look like to people who didn't know them. "Look at that bozo. He thinks you're my child bride—my trophy wife—and I don't mind one bit!" Uncle Marsden had said one evening last summer. It was a gorgeous evening, the air about them soothing and pink. They'd been playing Parcheesi on the front porch as neighbors and their weekend guests walked along the road and waved. Uncle Marsden and Saga waved back. Sometimes they took a picnic to the beach just as the sun began its slide toward the west. Uncle Marsden might take a book of poems and read to her. It was awfully close to romantic.

But ever since the strange, frightening day when Saga had met Stan and they'd had sex, the impression of that physical encounter had trailed her like a ghost, one that grew less malevolent with time. Saga could not forget the orgasm, nor could she stop herself from re-creating it—and when she did, she thought not of Stan (certainly not!) but of men she'd seen yet did not know, men from the train, the beach, the supermarket. Across the street, in Commodore Perry's house, there was a grown son who came to visit on weekends: he had long dark hair, wide shoulders, and a smooth golden chest. In the summer, he walked about in nothing more than a skimpy black bathing suit and sneakers.

It was as if she'd rediscovered a flavor of life that the accident had erased from her mental palate—a flavor she now craved, as maybe she had in the time before. Had David fulfilled that craving? She supposed he must have, though she did not recall sex with David very clearly. The memories had faded naturally, or they had been blurred.

And then she had stumbled into that bookstore, and she had met Fenno: the bird prince, the man who made her think of Rapunzel, the princess trapped in the tower, the tower in the garden. Not that Saga was Rapunzel, certainly not. And not that Uncle Marsden's wonderful, wonderful house could ever be seen as a prison. No, it was a palace, the place a princess would want to end up, would want to live happily ever after. If, of course, it was rightfully hers.

WHEN SAGA ARRIVED AT HOME THAT NIGHT, she found Uncle Marsden sitting on the living room floor. Beside him, on a patch of newspapers in the middle of the Persian rug, stood an antique cradle, dark wood with long graceful rockers and spindles carved to look like slender pine cones. There was also a pile of rags and a bucket of gray water. The air smelled heavy, like varnish.

"Hello, my dear! Will you come have a peek at this grand little treasure I've rescued from oblivion and rot? My father made it. I could hardly manage so much as a balsa toy plane! I missed out on *these* genes." Uncle Marsden ran four fingers along the rail he had been polishing.

He stood and went over to the sofa. He lifted a lumpy rectangular object. "Horsehair," he said. "I can hardly believe I let our daughters sleep on this. Ouch! Like a pincushion now. Feel how heavy." Saga took the mattress from her uncle. It was prickly and leaden and smelled like mildew.

"You'll need to get a new mattress," she said as she leaned it against a wall. She began opening windows. The air that poured in was fresh and cold, a relief from the stifling chemical smell.

"Yes, some newfangled fireproof organic-wool moth-resistant never-wrinkle sort of thing that will cost an arm and a leg—which bringing this thing down two flights of stairs nearly cost me as well."

Saga ran her own hand along the cradle. Cleverly, it had been made to rock not side to side but head to foot, the way a mother would rock her baby in her arms. The pine cones must have taken forever. Words were carved into one of the plain pale slats in the bottom; she knelt to look. PRO FILIO MEO 1925. A small thrill ran through Saga; this cradle had been made by her own grandfather. Had her mother slept in it, too? "*Filio*—isn't that 'son'? Uncle Marsden, this was made for *you*."

He looked over her shoulder. "Young lady, you will not carbon-date *me*. Now stop snooping into chronological matters and make me a drink. Please."

As she stood at the bar, Saga watched her uncle reach into a cardboard box. He shook out a parcel of tissue paper and held up a tiny lacy dress, impossibly long and lapsed from its original white to the yellow of untended teeth.

"Oh my." Uncle Marsden peered at the dress. "Michael's christening gown." He smoothed it out against the back of the sofa. "Oh my."

Saga gave him his drink. The gown looked like an object from a museum; hard to believe that Aunt Liz would have dressed a baby in this garment. Had this, too, been Uncle Marsden's before it was Michael's?

The box was labeled BABY MICHAEL. Her uncle reached into it and pulled out a grubby stuffed elephant in a clear plastic bag; a wooden fire engine, its red paint cracked and peeling; a tiny three-legged stool painted with a fleeing dish and spoon; a pair of brown leather shoes that had curled and petrified; and three picture books: *Roar and More*, *Wee Gillis*, and *The Cat in the Hat Comes Back*.

"Oh my goodness, my goodness me," said Uncle Marsden. "I do remember reading *this*." He opened *Roar and More*, a yellow book with a crouching lion on the front. The spine snapped. "If a lion comes to visit, don't open your door. Just firmly ask 'What is it?' and listen to him . . . ROOOOOAAAARRR."

Saga and Uncle Marsden laughed loudly. She sat beside him on the couch as he flipped through the book, murmuring with pleasure. "Oh, this verse I always loved. 'Fishes are finny, fishes are funny. They don't go dancing. They don't make money. They live under water. They don't have troubles. And when they talk, it looks like bubbles.' " Uncle Marsden attempted a bubbling noise.

Saga looked closely at the illustration of pastel green fish. She felt a gust of cold air from an open window. She was sure she could remember Uncle Marsden reading this book to her, this very verse, along with her cousins. He paged slowly to the end—past a cat, a pack of yellow dogs, bees, a mouse, a giraffe—and closed the book. He let it sit on his lap, both hands flat on the cover. Saga noticed all the brown spots on his hands, the sliver of fragile white skin under the edge of his wedding ring.

"Let me see that one." Saga reached across her uncle and picked up *Wee Gillis*, a book with a plaid jacket and a drawing of a boy in a jaunty Scottish cap.

Uncle Marsden winced and set his book aside. He clasped his left shin with both hands.

"What is it?" said Saga.

"Oh, I bollixed myself up good when I was trying to get the cradle around that turn on the landing."

"Let me look." Saga sat on the floor at Uncle Marsden's feet. He did not protest when she lifted his trouser leg. Sure enough, there was a nasty red and purple scrape below his knee. "You don't want this to get infected."

"I think I'd look dashing with a peg leg, don't you?"

She went to the bathroom and brought back alcohol, cotton, a large Band-Aid, and a tube of ointment.

"Let's go hunting for lichens this weekend, shall we?" said Uncle Marsden as she tended to his leg. "We're supposed to have a last little warm spell, and I need to add to my slide show for that lecture I'm giving in March. Freshen my material. Though, alas, morphology is now passé. It's all about DNA."

Saga agreed to the expedition. Unless Stan summoned her, she rarely went to the city on weekends; the bookstore had so many customers then, and Fenno did not work on Sundays. Perhaps he spent Sunday with his children.

The house still stank of turpentine, so Uncle Marsden decided they would go out to dinner. At the Oyster Shack, a place with dusty fishing nets and lobster traps suspended from the ceiling, they ate fried clams while Uncle Marsden reminisced about what it was like to take on fatherhood in his late thirties, how his best friend's children had been applying to college when Marsden was helping Liz, for the second and not the last time, warm bottles at four in the morning. "I was the laughingstock of the department. And now," he said, "only now does it occur to me that Michael's doing the same thing—though nowadays it seems to be the norm, does it not? *Now* I wouldn't be snickered at, would I? I'd be doing the *mature thing*. Parenthood as a *rational choice*."

"People want to pack a lot in now," said Saga. "Before they have kids."

"I saw people pack in plenty back then, even with kids in tow," said Uncle Marsden. "We weren't so finicky. Everything wasn't so scheduled. Everything wasn't so absurdly safe. People drove across the country in station wagons with half a dozen children bouncing around like billiard balls."

"I don't think wanting to be safe is bad," said Saga. Her remark came out accidentally as scolding, and Uncle Marsden looked at her intently. She knew the look: it meant he was thinking about her in some critically tender way. This always made her nervous. She didn't want him to comment on her "progress" or ask when her next checkup would be or, worse, how her friend Stan was doing.

She said, "A year from now, we'll have a baby around." She smiled.

"Yes," Uncle Marsden said quietly. "Won't that be something." He was still giving her that look, but when he next spoke, he was back on the condominiums again, how they must be stopped.

Only later, as she climbed into bed with this curious book, *Wee Gillis*, did it occur to Saga that Uncle Marsden had asked her nothing about her day.

SAGA HAD LOVED BEING AN ONLY CHILD. She'd had the best of both worlds: all her parents' attention when they had time to play, all her grandparents' attention when the cousins were not around—and then, whenever they went to the big house (her grandparents' summer place before it was Uncle Marsden's all year round), the easy company of her cousins.

How different it had been when they were small. Michael was always a little bossy, but you had to excuse that behavior in an oldest child— and in an only boy, which back then counted for a lot. Frida and Pansy, only two years apart, were close in those days. By junior high, they'd formed a plan to grow up and be stewardesses for TWA. Sometimes together and sometimes apart, they would fly to every continent; by the time they grew up, there would be regular service to both poles as well. Fatefully, they would meet foreign princes in first class. Having read an article about the world's young royals in *Life* magazine, they kept a list of the candidates, along with other titled heirs.

The sisters would marry their princes—preferably in countries not too far apart, like Monaco and Greece—and each would have her own private jet, which she would already know how to fly. Frida said that if you were a stewardess, you had to learn to fly a plane, in case your pilot had a heart attack while he was in the air. So they would visit back and forth whenever they pleased, borrow each other's ball gowns and learn each other's second languages. Their royal husbands would be best friends, soul mates, each godfather to the other one's children. Frida wanted seven children, Pansy just three.

Saga admired their plan and their complete confidence that they would carry it out. It was decided that Saga, with her love of animals and her fantasies of seeing the world, would create and run a wildlife park in each of their countries. Saga would meet and marry someone like James Herriott or one of the Leakeys—a "prince of science," as Frida put it.

Michael, meanwhile, planned to become either a magician or the doctor who would cure cancer. He would not need the use of their silly, frivolous jets. Sometimes the girls gave in and played Michael's games: they submitted to being sawed in half, or they were the nurses in his clinic.

When the four children were not constructing the future, they would dig great holes on the beach, down to where the sand became a glistening black, or hunt in the tide pools among the rocks or, back at the house, play board games or sardines. Charades was a favorite after dinner, though the grown-ups would insist on joining if they had nothing better to do. They drank their golden cocktails and clowned around like the apes Saga would one day have collected for her twin royal wild-life parks if Frida and Pansy hadn't let life—real, nonroyal boyfriends and down-to-earth college professors and summer jobs—distract them from their plans.

Now Pansy was a school psychologist in New Haven, and Frida ran a hunger project in Boston. They had not married princes, not yet any-way. They had not married anyone. Pansy was thirty-five, Frida thirty-seven. They wanted to be more than aunts. They had never discussed this in depth with Saga, but you'd have to be an idiot not to know it.

SHE WAS DOWN IN THE BASEMENT. Oneeka was off for the day, so Saga had volunteered to flatten the week's cardboard boxes and stack them up for recycling. She worked carefully with the box cutter, a tool she would not have trusted herself to use two years before.

The first time she heard a customer talking to Fenno upstairs, she laid down the box and the cutter and went to the desk. She sat in the chair, facing the bulletin board with the photographs of the children. Slowly, she opened the center drawer. In its trays she found the usual things: pencils, pens, paper clips, rubber bands, a box of staples, a roll of Wint O Green Life Savers, a nest of crumpled receipts. Under a pack of book-plates with the store's trademark owl, she found a Polaroid picture of Fenno with Felicity. He looked a little younger—maybe just because he was laughing. Felicity's wings were a blur; she might have been about to take flight from his shoulder. They were indoors somewhere, but it didn't look like the store.

She closed the drawer quietly when she heard Fenno say good-bye to the latest customer, heard the string of bells on the door jostle and jingle. "Faring well down there?" Fenno called out.

"Oh yes!" she answered. She went back to slitting seams on the boxes until she heard Fenno talking on the phone.

The drawers on the left contained business: invoices, order forms, let-ters from publishers, best-seller lists. In the top-right drawer she found Scotch tape, scissors, a stapler, three rubber stamps, a stamp pad, a bag of sunflower seeds.

On her final round of snooping, in the right-hand bottom drawer, she found a soft plaid scarf (struggling, in vain, to find the word for that very expensive, very fine wool; was it from goats?), a compact umbrella, and a framed picture where Fenno—definitely younger, with blonder hair and rosy cheeks—stood in front of a blooming lilac bush with two other men. Had he mentioned brothers?

She was jolted, and nearly slammed the drawer, when Fenno called down, "Leave the rest, why don't you, and come up for tea."

It was no longer warm enough to sit in the garden, so Saga joined Fenno at his upstairs desk (she supposed there was no way she could explore *those* drawers). Fenno made a series of phone calls to customers waiting for books. Saga sipped her tea. She was happy listening to his voice, which could carry you off to some green hilly place in Scotland. Saga had never been to Scotland, but she had a clear image of the land. The landscape in *Wee Gillis*, that book from Michael's box, looked a lot like the landscape in the photo of Fenno with those children.

Cashmere. There: that was the soft, expensive wool. A deep lavender word, an early twilight word, expansive as the folded hills of the Highlands but pillowy, gentle.

When Fenno finished his calls, he thanked Saga for her help, the way he always did. "I'm not awfully good at hiring new people when I need them," he said. "So it's a blessing of sorts that *you* found *me.*"

Saga blushed. "You have Oneeka."

Fenno laughed as if she'd made a joke. "Yes I do, and she's smashing. But in a way she found me, too."

It wasn't Oneeka that Saga wanted to know about. She had a sudden idea. She asked, "Do you have children? Someone to take over the shop? So you could be, like, 'Fenno and Son'?"

He gave her a cockeyed smile, and at first she was terrified that he had seen her snooping in the desk. He poured milk into her tea, remembering the way she liked it. After a pause, he said, "I'm not even married, Emily. I am quite far from being a father. Quite."

He still called her Emily, and though she'd felt for a little while as if the name were a lie, now she liked the old-newness of it. And she liked that Fenno was the only person in her nonmedical life who called her by her very first, her original name.

Hoping it would sound innocent, Saga said, "So the children on the wall in the bathroom, whose are they?"

"My brother's twins," said Fenno. "Camilla and Paul. Altogether, I have five nieces and one nephew."

The bells on the door jingled then, saving her from having to make conversation out of her nosy misunderstanding. She said good-bye to Fenno before he had finished helping his customer find a book on secret codes. Fenno looked confused at her sudden departure but called out, "Cheerio!"

On her way to the subway, Saga walked down Tenth Street instead of Eleventh. She was pleased to find that she had remembered correctly: yes, here was the baby store with the tiny rocking chairs in the window. She did not go in, but she paused to look at the silk booties displayed at the foot of the chairs and at the tiny kimonos, red and orange and blue, suspended on fishing line above them. They looked like little Japanese ghosts—happy ghosts, dwarf ghosts—hovering, looking out at the real people on the sidewalk, not longing for lives of their own but curious: about what it might be like to have tasks and homes and people to take care of. The ghosts seemed to wish Saga well.

THE FRIDAY AFTER THANKSGIVING WEEKEND, Michael and Denise came to visit again. Except in summer, it was unusual for them to show up two weekends in a row, but Saga could well imagine they wanted to bask in their good family news.

At least they'd given warning so that Saga could plan for bigger meals on Saturday and Sunday. Friday night, they drove out from the city straight to Uncle Marsden's favorite steak house.

"Dad, I gotta say, you have simple standards for dining out," said Michael when his prime rib arrived. "This broccoli nearly matches my suit."

"Are you complaining?"

"Come on, Dad, this place is great—I mean, I loved it when I was ten, it brings back great memories—but it's amazing how they've survived without changing a thing. Like, a menu on a cutting board? Cottage cheese with pickles and breadsticks? There's retro, and then there's antediluvian."

"Saga and I are happy with old-fashioned things, aren't we?" He took Saga's hand and started to sing. " 'We're old-fashioned, and we don't mind it.' "

"Dad," groaned Michael, "your voice is as overcooked as the broccoli."

"Ah well." Uncle Marsden kissed Saga's hand and dropped it.

For a moment, Michael and Denise were both smiling fondly at Saga. Had pregnancy really made them this nice? Denise started to speak to Saga, but Uncle Marsden interrupted.

"Speaking of old-fashioned, I have quite the surprise for you two when we get back to the house." He'd had a foam mattress cut to fit the cradle; Saga had picked out sheets. "Even you might shed a little tear, my sophisticated son."

"Oh that'll be the day," said Denise, but she was clasping Michael's hand on the table. They touched so often now that you could almost imagine the teeny-tiny baby taking its earliest food from Michael as well, carried right through its mother's skin.

Michael's phone rang in his pocket. "Excuse me a minute," he said, and carried his conversation out the door of the restaurant.

"Are you hoping for a boy or a girl?" Saga said to Denise.

Denise pursed her lips as if she were about to laugh, as if Saga had asked a silly question. She looked out toward the parking lot, where Michael could be seen pacing and gesturing, making some kind of deal. "Actually . . ." She looked at Uncle Marsden. "Well, we have a surprise for you too."

Uncle Marsden had finished his steak and was cutting his baked potato into cubes. Onto this grid he would slather sour cream, then cottage cheese, and then he would savor one small bite at a time. The broccoli he had discarded onto his butter plate.

"Well, my girl, will you spit it out, this secret of yours, or shall we talk about the *Farmer's Almanac* predictions for winter? I hear it's to be a mild one."

Denise ventured one more glance toward the parking lot. Her sigh was like an exclamation of pure amazement. "Well." She blushed at her plate, then looked up at Uncle Marsden. "We found out yesterday we're having twins. They thought so last week, but now it's certain. We heard two separate heartbeats."

Saga thought of the twins at the bookstore, the picture in the bathroom. Uncle Marsden gasped. "Good Lord. Will that age me double-quick?"

There was an awkward pause, and then Uncle Marsden stood, startling Saga. He leaned across the table, grasped both of Denise's hands, pulled her toward him, and kissed her on the mouth. "My dear," he said, "you must both be very happy." When he sat down, there were curds of cheese on his necktie and tears in his eyes. Using his napkin, he wiped the tears away. As unobtrusively as she could, Saga reached over and used her own to wipe off his tie.

"Oh yes," said Denise. "Yes, we are."

Uncle Marsden stood abruptly again. "I am going to get that negligent son of mine. I do not care if he is trading Long Island Sound for the Caribbean."

Alone with Denise, Saga said, "Wow. I mean, *wow*."

Denise looked flustered. "You'll have to be an honorary aunt," she said.

"Thank you," said Saga. "I would love that."

Denise seemed on the verge of saying something else, but then she just kissed Saga on the cheek. Why was Denise suddenly so attentive to her? Did getting what she had wanted make her sorrier for Saga?

When father and son returned to the table, Uncle Marsden had possession of Michael's cell phone. He grinned as he put it in his own pocket.

"I'll pay for that," said Michael, but cheerfully.

"Oh nonsense," said Uncle Marsden. "The world will turn quite happily without your help." He called the waiter and ordered cold duck, the closest thing they had to champagne.

Michael kissed Denise and said, "I want you to know, babies work as an excuse in my line of work for about fifteen minutes. And let's not forget that now I'll have *two* new mouths to feed."

Denise kissed him back. "And a bigger apartment to find."

Michael raised his hands in surrender. "House of cards. What can you do?"

Back at the house, Saga found that she was too exhausted to clean up the day's dishes, a ritual she often shared with Uncle Marsden, though mostly he liked to sit nearby on a stool, drink tea, and talk.

"My dear, I will do it with the help of Mr. High Finance here. You two girls get on up to bed. Tomorrow we have our lichen expedition."

"Oh," said Denise, "can I go along?"

Uncle Marsden looked pleased; even Michael looked pleased. He was putting on his mother's apron as Saga led the way upstairs, turning on lights.

In her room, she took her notebook from her knapsack. Out of it fell the picture of Fenno and Felicity. She held it, hands trembling. She remembered finding it, but she did not remember stealing it. Saga stared at it for a moment and then propped it against the lamp on her bureau. Well, she reasoned, it *had* been buried in a drawer beneath things that were probably never used, hadn't it?

As she put on her nightgown, she heard the reverberations from the kitchen, carried upward along with the heat. She heard plates clattering too loudly against one another, the way they always did in the hands of men. She heard, though at first they were muffled by running water, the voices of the men manhandling the plates. And then the water stopped.

"It's just an idea," said Michael. "I've been thinking I could start my own little firm in New Haven, maybe by next year sometime. I could commute for a while before then, if I had to."

"You'd better not expect me to babysit," said Uncle Marsden.

Michael laughed. "One day, we might just have to babysit for you. I can see it now, the Snail Guy wandering up and down the beach in his mad-professor daze, hurling insults at the residents of the new condos."

Uncle Marsden made a growling noise. "What 'mad-professor daze' are you referring to, young man?"

Water ran briefly again. "Listen, Dad, I called that broker we grew up with, the one who used to lifeguard at the club, and she told me there's a small house coming up for sale in a few months, closer to the village. An old one, a gem. A captain's house. It would be perfect for you. If I put our apartment on the market right away, I'm sure I could—" Water again.

Saga stood directly over the vent. Warm air filled her nightgown, soft and feathery up across her belly and breasts. The gown swelled like a tulip in bloom, like a pregnancy. She moved to the side and bent over. Now the warm air blew, less pleasantly, straight in her face.

When the water stopped again, she heard Uncle Marsden say, "—Saga. That would have to be a condition."

"Sure," said Michael, but Saga could hear his reluctance, along with his agreement, ricochet all the way from two stories below. "Dad, we have to talk about Saga, not just about where she's going to live. With Denise pregnant, I've been—" The dishwasher changed from a hiss to a roar.

AFTER A FINE WEEKEND OF WEATHER that yearned back toward summer, a sea of flat, monotonous clouds moved in. It rained for days.

Saga spent Monday and Tuesday typing up her uncle's notes on the lichens and mosses he had collected on their family hike. She helped him label slides and put them in the carousel. (His hands shook just enough now that this simple task was nearly impossible for him.) She felt glad to be useful, but she did not know what it meant that Uncle Marsden, through all this time they were spending together, said nothing about the proposal Michael had made that night in the kitchen. By Wednesday, she felt anxious and hurt, but what could she say? She decided to take an early train into the city, to hell with the tempest.

Fenno was opening the register. Oneeka was straightening books on the shelves, dusting the glass case that held all those odd bird-watching gizmos. "Hey, girl," Oneeka said as Saga came in, "would you pay four hundred bucks for a picnic basket? Like get real. What's in this thing anyway?"

"Fancy binoculars, three Sibley pocket guides, stainless flatware, and linen napkins printed with songbirds. That's what," said Fenno. "Hello there, Emily."

Beside the door to the garden stood a playpen. Saga had heard about Oneeka's baby girl but had never seen her. She was standing, clinging to the plastic rail, not quite able to get her chin that high.

"My mom couldn't watch her today," Oneeka explained, as if Saga had any authority at the store. "I just hope she ain't planning like one of her cranky days. She has one-a those, boy, you are in for some wicked shit."

Fenno gave her a parental look.

"In for some serious trouble," amended Oneeka.

"She'll have plenty of people eager to entertain her," said Fenno. "Rain brings in the hordes, who love nothing better than to drip on the books. Which reminds me. Where's the barrel for the brollies, Oneeka?"

"Oh man, will you quit with that Queen Elizabeth talk? You live here how long now?"

Fenno smiled at Oneeka. "Umbrellas," he enunciated slowly.

"Can I help out?" asked Saga.

Fenno told her that if she stuck around a bit, he could use her help in the basement, packing up returns. Oneeka could stay upstairs.

Seeing Oneeka with the baby made her look younger than ever, thought Saga. When they'd met, she had told Saga she was living with her mother, finishing high school at night.

Saga went over to the playpen and leaned down. "Hi, baby."

The baby looked at her with fierce attention; out of the small mouth flowed a buoyant fleet of syllables. Why were babies so intimidating to Saga? Were they so different from puppies? Just then, the baby let go of the rail with one hand and grabbed onto Saga's hair, her grip as firm as her gaze. Oneeka rushed over and pried her daughter's hand free. "Grab the whole world, that's her. Get that bad old world by the butt before it gets her! Sorry."

"Smart girl," said Fenno. "Tiger by the tail."

Saga looked around. "Where's Felicity?"

"I left her home today. Miss Felicity is not keen on babies," said Fenno. "They siphon off all the amazement and adoration."

Siphon. A forgotten word. A circular word, caterpillar green.

Oneeka went behind the sales desk and pointed a finger at him. "Put me in charge, you are one crazy dude."

"I aspire to be a crazy dude. The day I am an authentically crazy dude is the day I can die a happy man," said Fenno. "Shall we?" he said to Saga.

In the basement, he lined up several open boxes. He handed Saga small stacks of books to arrange inside them, showing her which books must be packed together. She examined his graceful hands for evidence that he'd ever worn a ring. *So far from being married:* was that what he'd said?

"I've brought a funny book to show you," said Saga.

"Have you indeed?"

"It's a child's book," she said. "From my house. It's about Scotland. I'll show it to you when we take a break."

"Show it to me now," said Fenno.

Saga's knapsack hung from the chair at the desk. She pulled out the book.

Fenno smiled warmly at the plaid dust jacket. He took his time looking at the title and copyright pages. "Nineteen thirty-eight! Oh what a bloody lot's gone on in the world since then. I'm betting this book's no longer in print." He looked at Saga. "This was yours when you were a wee one?"

"No, or not really," she said. Who knew how many books she'd once known and forgotten?

Fenno sat on the edge of the desk. He began to read the story. On the second page, he laughed loudly. He read, and it sounded delicious in his genuine Scottish voice, " 'His real name was Alastair Roderic Craigellachie Dalhousie Gowan Donnybristle MacMac, but that took too long to say, so everybody just called him Wee Gillis.' "

"You read it so perfectly," she said. "Read it all."

He gave her a wry look. "What's a rainy day meant for?"

He read on, fluidly, musically: about the dilemma of Wee Gillis, whether to choose a life in the Highlands, hunting stag with his father's relations, or in the Lowlands, herding cows with his mother's kin. Fenno looked up and said, "A book about finding out where you belong. Now that's a theme to warm my heart. Yours too?" He did not take his eyes off her.

"Yes," she said. She'd read the book a few times, because it made her laugh and she loved the old-fashioned black-and-white drawings. She hadn't thought about themes.

"Let me give you a book, since you've shared one with me," said Fenno. He went to a bookcase by the bathroom and came back with a new pink paperback. "My favorite poet shares your name," he said as he handed it to Saga.

Upstairs, the front door closed and someone exclaimed about the nasty weather, the adorable baby. Did they have any books on dream interpretation?

"Ah. The day begins in earnest," said Fenno. "But keep this, read the poems as you like." He bowed slightly before heading up to help his customer.

Emily Dickinson's name was entirely familiar to Saga, but it was unlikely she had read one of these poems since high school. She opened the book to the middle.

I have no Life but this —
To lead it here —
Nor any Death — but lest
Dispelled from there —

Nor tie to Earths to come —
Nor Action new —
Except through this extent —
The Realm of you —

"Oh," said Saga, as if someone had sneaked up and startled her. She should have begun sealing more boxes, but instead she sat down at the desk to read.

FOR LUNCH, THE THREE OF THEM shared Chinese food. Oneeka, though she was gracefully slim, ate twice as much as anyone else, emptying all the packets of sauce on her chicken and using the plastic fork instead of the chopsticks. Saga had to use a fork as well, but she could remember the days of chopsticks. David had loved his Chinese food spicy. Oneeka talked the most, too, telling Fenno just how ridiculous she thought most of her classes were. "Like geometry. Whoa. Talk about weird. All this proving how circles are really circles and stuff! What's the point of this proof business anyway? I'll show you a proof or two. Proof my baby's daddy is like the king of losers. Proof this Al Gore dude needs like a sex-appeal transplant. Proof we live in a twisted world."

Saga was grateful for Oneeka's easy banter, which allowed her to look almost unguardedly at Fenno's face lit up by amusement. You could tell from his eyes that much in his life had not amused him.

As soon as Oneeka took Topaz downstairs to nurse, Treehorn came through the door, eagerly preceding Alan by the length of her leash. What luck that Saga had chosen today to come into town.

"Oh hello, hello there, you!" she said, greeting the dog first of all.

Treehorn rolled over, inviting Saga to scratch her belly. Her tongue unfurled from the side of her mouth as she smiled.

Fenno shook Alan's hand. "Safe travels. I have your cell number, and the San Francisco number, so hasten away. Have a lovely visit with your sister."

"I'm so grateful. Are you sure she won't be too much trouble?"

Fenno shrugged. "And if she were? What then?"

"Then I'd take her." Saga wished that Alan had asked her to dog-sit—she felt almost as if she'd been passed over for the care of her own child—but then, Fenno would look more dependable to anyone than she did. And he did live right down the street from Alan.

Once she'd committed Alan's face and name to her fickle memory, Saga had decided he was a man who looked worried too much of the time. For a psychologist, maybe that was normal. He must listen to worrying all day long; he must absorb it. Now, however, he did look relieved. "Thank you both," he said.

"We will spoil her," said Saga. Perhaps she'd offer to take Treehorn for Sunday, Fenno's day off; perhaps Fenno would invite her to spend the day with him. Or she could take Treehorn to Stan's, to play with the other dogs, the ones that had been wormed and had their shots. They could run in Prospect Park.

Alan thanked them again and said good-bye, shaking Saga's hand, shaking Fenno's again, and waving awkwardly at Oneeka as she emerged from the basement, sleeping baby in her arms. She sang softly as she carried Topaz back to the playpen and wrapped her in a tiny blanket.

"I got to run out for diapers," Oneeka said in a low voice. She took an umbrella from the barrel and opened the door with exaggerated stealth, but still the bells jingled when it swung shut behind her.

Fenno knelt on the floor to scratch Treehorn under her chin. "Now we have two wee'uns to care for," he whispered. "We've nearly a nursery here."

Saga had never been so close to Fenno. She could see the silver hairs above his right ear, the cornsilk lines on his eyelid, a glint of gold in his mouth. He smelled wonderfully of nothing much: ordinary soap, the cotton of a nice clean shirt. For the moment there was no one else in the store.

The Realm of you.

Fenno sat cross-legged, stroking Treehorn with both hands, massaging the base of her tall pointed ears. Saga stood. "You are such a prince." She hadn't planned to say this out loud, but to hear it made her glad that she had. She stood still, hands clasped in front of her waist so she wouldn't reach out to touch his head. When Fenno looked up at her, she made herself hold his gaze. She would have told him that she had fallen in love, she had lost her heart, but she knew it would be too much.

And then came his reaction, his terrible reaction.

"Me, a prince? Not I." He started to laugh, but he stopped. He must have read her emotions too late. Now he looked almost fearful. "Oh lass," he said, "I am not the man you envision me. Oh Emily."

How was it, thought Saga as she stood there, making every effort not to cry, which meant not blinking or uttering a sound or even moving the tiniest bit, that life could give you so much experience, so much pain, yet leave you just as able as you'd ever been to make a fool of yourself?

It seemed to take him forever to get to his feet. He put a hand on her shoulder, just the way he'd have put a hand on Oneeka's shoulder, but somehow it wasn't the same. Saga knew apology even by touch. "Emily," he said, "come over here and sit down."

She wanted to run out the door, but instead she sat in the armchair. He sat not behind his desk but on it, close to Saga. He leaned forward, looking serious, like a doctor about to deliver a bad diagnosis. Saga knew the posture well. "I hope it's not selfish to say that I'm flattered."

"Of course not," said Saga. She couldn't help sounding angry.

"Listen. Could you stay and have supper? Tonight?" he asked. "Up in my not very princely digs? I will tell you my story if you agree to tell me yours. Yours, I'd wager, is the interesting one. Though mine may be a bit longer."

Still she wanted to run, or simply to let go and cry, but she did neither. She spoke as calmly as she could. "I can do that."

"Good," he said. "I have some frozen prawns. Do you like seafood? I can make a plain curry with yogurt."

To keep her voice steady, she took a deep breath. "I haven't had curry in a long time."

"Then it's fate," he said. And that was that.

"Thank you for the poems—the book," she said. She wanted to ask why he had given her a book of love poems—that's what they seemed to be—if he did not share a bit of her feeling for him. For a moment, she was afraid to meet his eyes, for fear she'd see the poisonous beginnings of pity. But when he said, "I want you to tell me what you think of them," she could hear that nothing, for him, had changed.

It took some effort to remember the task she had left off doing before lunch, before the poems, before this mortification, but she did. She started toward the basement just as Oneeka walked in the door. Treehorn, startled, let out one sharp bark. Topaz, awakened too soon from her nap, began to cry.

"Damn, girl, can you ever give a person a break, like maybe your mom?" said Oneeka as she wiped her feet on the doormat.

"I'll take her," said Fenno. He bent down and swung the baby up to his chest as if he'd been a father for years. Topaz continued to cry, but he rocked and shushed and paced, undaunted.

"Crazy dude," Oneeka said to Saga. "Crazy fairy godfather dude."

Fairy godfather, thought Saga as she made her way to the basement.

That's what he was, to her as well as to Oneeka. *Godfather:* Red as a ruby, a bottomless vibrant purplish red, a big word, impressive but airy, the silk dragon in a Chinese parade. Just as Saga reached the bottom of the stairs, Oneeka's baby stopped crying.

What, she wondered, would she remember of this day, and what would she forget? What, in a few hours' time, would she tell the first man she had fallen in love with, really in love with, since a tree limb, a plain old piece of wood, had spun her topsy-turvy? And why, she wondered—when she knew the man couldn't or wouldn't love her back—didn't she feel unhappy, miserably sad?

TWELVE

THE STREET RAN UPHILL, curving and tilting at once, as if to
ensure that every house would have a magnificent view of the bay.
Every house had been built on a slope, those to the left condescending
from aloft, those to the right set far lower, giving the appearance of faces
peeking over a windowsill. But if you looked between the low houses,
you would see that they were the larger ones, four and five stories high
at the back. There would be tier upon tier of rooms facing the cloud-
swept horizon, the bridges and ships, the city's distant pinnacles.

Marion's was on the left and, like all the others, old and asymmetri-
cally gracious. How could she afford this neighborhood? thought Alan.
Wrong question, he scolded himself.

A long flight of steps led the way to her front door, which was sheltered by an arch of twining wisteria vine. The topography of this address
made it both a frustration and a relief. A frustration because there
would be no spying—no peering into the house, since it stood aloof
from the street, its windows but a series of reflections, panels of sky. A
relief for the very same reason. Alan had not come to spy (or had he?).
A little research couldn't hurt, he'd told himself on the way out of the
city, riding the BART.

His plane had arrived the night before. Joya treated him to dinner at a
fancy vegetarian restaurant with a view of the Golden Gate Bridge. She
knew the menu well, and he let her order everything. At the moment, he
wished that all decisions could be taken out of his hands; never mind
that he had resisted Joya's most strident advice in recent months.

While they ate, he had been happy to discuss Joya's woes instead of
his. She had broken up with the guy she'd been seeing since spring. He
really did not want to have more children. Two—his teenage daughters—
were plenty. Ironically, the teenage girls had never been a problem for

Joya. As Alan had predicted, they adored her. She had liked them, too, and their adoration had made her feel young. She'd stayed with the father longer than she should have, knowing in her gut that nothing would change his mind. Or hers.

There was no right thing to say to a woman in this situation, nothing that would not make her angry or sad, especially if the person doing the saying was a man. Thank heaven Joya did not ask for his opinion, delivering her story as she might have reported to him yet another tale of disgruntled city workers, then promptly changing the subject to their mother, who had grown painfully slow in recent months. Alone with her at Thanksgiving, Alan had convinced her to have the hip replacement her doctor advised—only to realize that this would certainly delay his move out west. As if to compensate, he'd resolved to end, finally, what he had come to think of as the Mystery of Marion.

He had decided to make this trip quickly and in secret—three days, four nights—to find out once and for all whether the news he had heard from his sister was true. Even Joya, who was about as gullible as an aircraft carrier, had to be capable of mistaking rumor for fact. At the same time, Alan knew that he could never lie convincingly to Greenie about such an extravagant trip.

It was eleven in the morning; the only sign of human life on this Berkeley street was a man planting a row of trees on the slope that rose to the house next door to Marion's: clearly a gardener, undisturbed by Alan's loitering.

This was idiotic. Enough indecision.

Climbing all those stairs was torture, not physical but sentient; what if she was in the house, watching his approach? Alan thought of a medieval castle: soldiers in chain mail hiding behind the ramparts, watching from on high, waiting for the enemy to get just close enough before . . . He stopped and looked up at the house. Would Marion hate him enough to fire a catapult, dump scalding oil, let loose a rain of barbed arrows? (Whatever made Alan think she could hate him at all? One lousy, cowardly letter?)

He stood up straight and struck the knocker three times against the door. No dog barked. No voice called out that he should wait or identify himself.

When he turned to leave, he noticed that the stairs continued, after a jog beneath a trellis of thorny white roses. He started up these stairs. They led to a higher back entrance, a circle of garden enclosing a table and chairs, a red tricycle, a scattering of beach toys: a plastic shovel and rake, a Thomas the Tank Engine bucket, tiny shark-patterned flip-flops. He did not venture farther.

"JESUS CHRIST!" SAID JOYA. "Have you become a Peeping Tom or what?"

"You think I should have left a note?"

"What I think you should have done, you should have done ages ago." Alan could picture her face exactly, her lips tight, the furrows between her eyebrows deep. "What I think you should do now, if you even care, is call like a civilized person, on the phone, tell her you're here and need to see her."

"What if she says no?"

Joya sighed. "Alan, I don't know. You've let so damn much time go by. You're like . . . Gerard Depardieu in that movie about the guy who . . . no, no, maybe he gets the girl."

"Joya!"

"Sorry."

Alan stood in front of a hip grocery store on a shady street a few blocks from Marion's house. He'd eaten a sandwich in a café and drunk too much strong coffee. "I'm going to stay till she gets home. Don't wait up."

"And if she doesn't show up, you're going to sleep in a bush? Oh. Brilliant."

"I'll call you later, Joy."

"I'm sorry, Alan. I'm just—I'm . . . stymied by this. And not much stymies me. In fact, I don't think I've ever used that word before! Look. It's nearly four. Come back now and I'll make you an early dinner. We will really talk about this. I have a big meeting tomorrow, so you won't see much of me then. *Tomorrow* you can camp out there and sleep in a bush." She waited. "Please, Alan?"

He agreed to her plan, but after he put his phone away, he walked back toward Marion's street. When he stopped on the opposite side-walk, he saw that a light was on. A woman, not Marion, passed behind the front window. A roommate? A maid? What kind of a life did Marion have in this handsome aerie of a house? Not the simple life of an earthy idealist.

Now he noticed the plantings that formed a rolling carpet down the slope before the house: tiny dark green leaves with yellow stripes; a frothy vine that might be honeysuckle; artistically spaced eruptions of purple flowers that looked like exclamation points. The air was distinctly, expensively floral.

Strangely, he had found the nerve to come here because of Stephen—because he realized that he did not want to become Stephen. They had reached the point where Stephen, still as remorseful as he was angry, had begun to rehash the twists and turns of his relationship with Gordie that he believed had led them first to their impasse and then to their senseless breakup. He blamed himself as often as he blamed Gordie. For Alan, it was like listening to the survivor of a car wreck go over every turn and stoplight on a journey that, taken just a shade more slowly or by a slightly different route, would have evaded catastrophe. If the phone hadn't rung; if he'd found the keys faster; if that boy on the bike hadn't crossed so slowly; if he'd only gone *through* the yellow light three blocks before. . . .

Alan had sat very still and listened to every detail. He knew that all the fury and regret simply had to come out, like fluid from an infected wound, whether it happened in the sheltered space of Alan's office or out in a less controlled, less benevolent world. In therapy, there were revelations, there were explorations, there were breakdowns and breakthroughs, and there were rituals. This was a ritual, not unlike a dance. And then, a few weeks ago, Alan had a sudden flash-forward of himself in Stephen's place, only he was on Jerry's couch, and the anguish flowing out of him was all about Greenie: Greenie having left him because she'd found out about Marion. With or without that mystery child, there was still Marion, the fact of her, a fact that any wife had a right to regard as betrayal. Alan knew that he had not acted out of careless lust, that what he had succumbed to was a mixture of longing for the past and disdain for the future, of affection and anger, of permission and pity—each pairing perilous in its chemistry—but Greenie would have told him that once again he was mincing words. In far simpler words, he had fucked another woman.

So as he stood on this alien sidewalk, aimless yet urgent with purpose, trying to feel neither envy nor contempt (wasn't sheer misery enough?), growing colder as the sun sank away, a car pulled up and parked right below the stairs. Marion stepped out. He had time to notice that the car was modest compared with the house, that she wore a plain gray raincoat and plain flat shoes, that her hair had grown long again—all this in the instant it took her to see and recognize him.

She came straight across the empty street and faced him, up close, with an intense but indefinite expression on her face. She hugged him, and he held her tight, not wanting to see her face until he could know what she felt.

She stepped away just as abruptly as she had embraced him. "Alan, what in the world are you doing here?"

"I'm visiting Joya. She said you were living here now. I thought . . ."

She was watching him closely. She looked worried, or skeptical. She also looked so . . . tame compared with the Marion he had last seen.

"I'm here because of what I heard—that you have a little boy."

She seemed to smile and frown at once. "Alan, what are you talking about?"

Oh good, he thought. There *is* no little boy. He laughed. "Sorry. You know Joya. Full of stories . . ."

"Alan."

"You don't have a little boy."

"Yes, Alan, I have a little boy. His name is Jacob." Now she was, unmistakably, frowning.

Alan felt like a fool. A man walking a dog passed them, pulling on the leash as it sniffed at Marion's ankles. The sky was turning a rich pale purple.

"I know we never spoke after that reunion, and I think we should have."

Marion shook her head. "Because you felt guilty? I didn't. I hope you didn't tell your wife. . . . Is she all right? Did you go and have that baby like I told you to, little brother?" Her smile was tense.

"Don't call me that," he said. "Marion, is your son—was he my baby?"

Marion gasped. She looked up at her house. "Wow."

"Is he?"

"Alan, I don't know what's gotten into you. Are you all right?"

"Of course I'm all right!" He thought briefly of a tasteless joke he could make about what had gotten into *her*. He said, "I hear you have a baby just about nine months after we . . . after we're together, and after you tell me you can't have babies—"

"I told you that my doctors said I *probably* couldn't have babies."

"Oh. So you do remember telling me that. Interesting."

She opened her mouth. She closed it. She twisted her keys in her right hand; was she contemplating a getaway?

Ah, he thought, I've caught her. "Just tell me the truth, Marion."

"Alan, did you have this crazy suspicion when you wrote me that weird, cold letter—how long ago now?"

He softened his voice. "Just answer my question, Marion. Please? Can you understand how I felt when I heard about the baby? Never mind how I felt after we'd had that . . . that time together and you just vanished."

"Did you look for me?"

Before he could think of what to say, she said, "Well, not that you should have." Marion sighed and looked around, as if waiting for someone else to arrive, someone to get her off the hook or simply haul Alan away. Another man with a dog steered wide of them, across a grassy lawn. Had they been shouting? Perhaps the whole neighborhood was listening. Well, let them. That's when Alan noticed her ring. "You're married," he said.

"Yes, I am." She sounded defiant.

"Congratulations."

"Alan! What kind of a conversation is this? Why couldn't you have called me, for God's sake? This is no way—"

"This is a conversation I should have tried to have with you years ago. That's my fault," said Alan. "I screwed it up, and I'm sorry. All I want now is an answer. Wouldn't you?"

"Alan, my son is mine, and he is my husband's. He is not yours. I'm sorry if this has been a concern of yours all this time. You're right: you should have asked me your question long ago. If at all. Alan, we had a one-night stand. We were friends from a long time ago. It's *okay*."

"It is most certainly not okay if you got pregnant and had a kid!"

"Wow," she said again. "This is not a conversation we should be having like this."

"Then how *should* we have it?"

Marion looked at the ground. She turned and started across the street. "Come here." She got to her car and opened the door before he followed.

"In your car?"

"Well, I am not inviting you up to my house, not right now at least!"

Marion sat behind the wheel, Alan on the passenger side. Unavoidably, he thought of the last conversation they'd had, also in a car she was driving.

"Sorry—just move those," she said as he tried to work his feet around a jumble of notebooks and manila folders on the floor. She reached down and grabbed a handful, tossing them onto the backseat. "I'm afraid my office is basically my car."

Should he ask her what sort of work she did, make small talk? He took three of the notebooks and twisted toward her to put them in the back. They were labeled with the names of hospitals. What had Joya told him Marion did—cancer outreach? No, he thought, do not ask. Do not allow her to seem saintly by virtue of what she does for a living.

"Oh Alan," said Marion, and now her voice was mournful, "I've always been so fond of you. I don't want to have some . . . awful episode here."

"Episode! Is that what this is? Like an all-new installment of a TV show?"

With both hands, Marion clutched the top of the steering wheel.

"I'm sorry," she said. "That wasn't the word I meant."

"What word is there for an agenda like the one you clearly had—to go to your high school reunion and find a sperm donor?" All at once, Alan remembered how Joya hadn't shown up at the reunion, how supposedly there had been a strike to break. Had Joya colluded in this?

Marion stared at him. She looked sad but also determined. "Some women in my shoes would kick you out of this car, out of their lives right now."

Alan stared back. "Just answer my question, Marion. Then go ahead and call the cops if you want."

"My son is five years old," said Marion. "That's a mighty long time in a little boy's life. Alan, he has nothing to do with you. You don't know him, he doesn't know you. You have to let this be about him, not you."

"I want to meet him. Can I meet him?" He hadn't expected to ask this.

"So you can see if he looks like you?"

"Then he is mine."

"He is not yours!" Marion shouted.

"Are his genes—are half of his genes mine? Okay, *from me?*"

Marion laid her forehead on the wheel. "You are obsessed by this, aren't you?"

"What sort of a heart would I have if I weren't?"

Marion sat up. "I believed my doctors, Alan. They told me exactly what I told you—whatever it was I told you about not having babies. And Alan, I was honestly smitten when I saw you after all those years. I honestly was. Smitten and charmed off my feet. I did not get a hotel room to lure you or anybody else into a paternity trap. You have to believe me, Alan. You have to."

She should have been crying, thought Alan, but she wasn't. Or had all the turbulent experience of Marion's life—which made his look so damn soft—hardened her enough that emotions like this were chaff?

"Listen," she said. "I had other . . . there was another guy not long after, an old boyfriend. I had to—"

"Oh please. Don't insult my intelligence."

Marion startled him then by leaning across the emergency brake and kissing him on the cheek. "Alan, whatever mistakes I may have made, it's me who has to ask you please. *Please.* My life is complicated enough."

"Well, so is mine," said Alan, but his tone was more resigned than angry. Now they were holding hands. He could see, from a small clock attached to the dashboard, that it was six-thirty. "Tell me about your husband."

"He's older. He has two kids in college," she said slowly. She sighed. "He's an oncologist. I met him as a patient; he'd been divorced for years."

Alan's phone, in his breast pocket, trilled its irritating birdsong. Automatically, he took it from his pocket.

Marion laughed. "You are going to *answer* it?"

Alan stared at the phone. Still, after all these months, only Greenie had the number. No, that was no longer true; because he was looking after Treehorn, Fenno McLeod had the number. Alan let it ring out and stop.

"It could be George," he explained. "Or Greenie."

"George?"

"My son."

"Your son?" Marion squeezed his hand. Now, yes, finally, there was a hint of tears. "Oh Alan. It's wonderful, isn't it?"

"Yes, Marion, but that's not the point. Or it is the point, the point being that I have . . . that I fathered, that I—what, sired?—*another* child besides the one I love like the world I walk on. I would love both of them that way, wouldn't I? I'm not saying he's 'mine' in the way you mean, Marion. Of course I'm not! I'm not saying I have rights, I'm not saying you have to . . ." Alan was gesturing wildly now, sitting forward in his seat, but he stopped.

"Not saying I have to what, Alan? That part is important."

Alan looked up at Marion's house, where motion had caught his eye. He saw a face in the front window, dark and distant. A child, his palms flat against the window above his head. The silhouette of his hands looked like an elaborate crest, as if the boy were pretending to be a cockatoo or rooster. It had grown dark while Alan sat in the car with Marion. Their faces were lit now only by streetlights.

"He's expecting me," Marion said, following Alan's glance. "He knows my car. In a minute, he may just come running down."

"So I should go."

Marion took Alan's hand again. "At least for now."

"And for later? I'm only here a couple more days."

"I don't know. I'll call you at Joya's tomorrow."

"You need to consult with the big doctor, I suppose."

"I need to *think*." She dropped his hand. "You like to be contentious, don't you, Alan? I don't need to tell you that's not a good thing. Do I?"

Alan's eyes burned. "You might have told me. Even if it's true there was only a . . . possibility."

"And then what? Break up your marriage over a maybe?"

"That would have been my problem."

"And hers."

"Oh, the feminist alliance."

"Alan! Alan, stop it." Marion clamped a hand on his shoulder hard and tight, the way a mother would, then let go. "I am sorry. What's a word for sorry to the hundredth power? But I could not have lived with fucking up your life. I can't now, either! And forgive me, but I thought, stupidly, that this would stay a secret. From you. Why do you think I've been avoiding Joy? When I found out I was pregnant, I thought of you right away. I hoped this baby was yours. Okay? But I wasn't going to interrupt the plans I already had. I figured I had room for a child, but I didn't have room for a big domestic, emotional grown-up mess."

Which is exactly what I am in, thought Alan. He hadn't even considered whether he had "room" for such a thing. "I see what you're saying," he said. "But I—"

"Go to Joy's," said Marion. "I will call you tomorrow morning. I have her number. I promise." She got out of the car and walked around the front. She waited on the sidewalk until he got out, too. She started up the stairs to her house. She waved, but not at Alan. The boy peeled himself off the window and vanished from sight. Jacob.

Jacob. As Alan walked away, his momentum hastened by the slope of the street, he heard a familiar sound: a small boy greeting his mother as she came home from a day at work. *George,* he thought. *Greenie,* he thought. Same yearnings, new urgency. He pulled his phone out of his pocket, flipped it open, and watched its face light up in the dark like a greeting. George was the one who answered, a small cosmic mercy.

Since Treehorn, George often asked if he could speak with her first. Alan would hold the cordless phone to the dog's ear; if George was lucky, she might whine a bit or give a cursory bark. Tonight, Alan explained (a true lie) that he was out, so Treehorn wasn't with him.

"I miss my dog," George said. "When are you coming again?"

"I'll see you at Christmas," Alan reminded him. "That's not so far away. I can't wait!"

"Me either."

"How's school?"

"I miss Diego," said George. "I miss Diego *and* Treehorn."

"But you're making new friends, right?"

Alan heard George make a complaining noise, a small groan. "Yeah, but they're not the same."

"No friends are the same," said Alan. "Not the same as each other. That's what makes having friends so much fun—they're all different. But maybe you can see Diego outside school sometimes. Maybe on the weekends."

Alan had met the beloved Diego just before leaving Santa Fe. To his astonishment, Greenie had never thought of inviting the boy into the city before then.

Together with George and Treehorn, Alan had picked up Diego on a Saturday afternoon so that the boy could have dinner with them and stay overnight. Because he was older than George by a few years, this was no big deal for him, but it was George's first sleepover, and by the time they picked up his friend, he had nearly worn himself out with anticipation, counting hours, counting minutes, selecting the toys they would play with, wondering if his books would seem too babyish for a bigger boy.

Alan did not know many eight-year-olds, so he had no real expectations, yet something struck him about this boy as disproportionately young and old at once. As they ate dinner together on Greenie's small verandah, George chattered blithely on at his playmate.

"You know, we got hummingbirds here—see the feeder? It's water in sugar—I mean sugar in water." He giggled. "Mom makes it. They fly forever, I think. I don't think they ever stand on their feet. Actually, maybe they don't *have* feet."

"They have to stand," said Greenie. "They have to sleep."

"Maybe they sleep flying. Horses sleep standing up."

"I'll bet their feet are tucked up neatly into their feathers," said Greenie. "Do you have hummingbirds out at your place?" she asked Diego.

Diego shook his head. "We don't have bird feeders," he said. He ate well, taking seconds on corn and Greenie's tomato salad. He said please and thank you, put his napkin in his lap. He chewed his food slowly, almost solemnly, and gazed around the room while others talked, as if he were memorizing details. After dinner, he asked to be excused. The boys went into George's room and closed the door. Alan heard George's voice, not speaking but whinnying.

"What a gentle boy," Greenie had said as she watched Alan wash the dishes.

Alan looked at her in the window over the sink. "There's something a little haunted or overly serious about him, don't you think?"

"He only seems that way compared with George's manic enthusiasm. I didn't realize George was so infatuated." She'd laughed. "I'm glad Diego likes him back. I don't suppose it will last after George starts kindergarten next month."

Alan had nearly forgotten that George would be entering kindergarten. This was a rite of passage—the beginning of "real" school—about which Alan had once fantasized and worried: how he and Greenie, like other New York parents, would tour the different public schools downtown, perch on elfin chairs and listen raptly to teachers who would evangelize about new ways of spelling and learning to add. Alan had looked forward to inspecting the collages and crooked compositions in the halls of these schools, going home and debating with Greenie the merits of one playground or principal over another.

But in the end, Ray—Ray, the eco-fascist!—had chosen George's school. He had let George sit on the back of a "real" horse for the first time. He had enabled George to have a "real" bedroom all his own for the first time, too. Alan had listened to George's admiration of this surrogate godfather and managed to hold on to a smile—but now just hearing Ray McCrae's name could quicken Alan's heartbeat. This spite, however, he had learned to swallow.

Now, four months later, he knew that he would also have to pick up the phone and call the contacts Ray had given him back then. He told himself he would do this after he had finished with Marion.

AS HE MADE HIS WAY FROM THE BART to Joya's loft, Alan thought about the patients he'd left behind in New York, some of whose sessions that week he had canceled or changed. At the moment, he was seeing just seven people. There was the cellist who couldn't get a job, the woman who couldn't get pregnant, the man who couldn't get over his wife's having left him for a younger man, the couple who fought constantly because they couldn't get out of debt. And there was Stephen, who couldn't get past his broken heart. Recently, Alan had also started seeing a woman who claimed that her life was in fine shape (nice apartment, nice husband, nice grown children); she just wanted to know the meaning of her tangled colorful dreams. His practice bore out the theory of a cynical classmate in grad school: that psychotherapy patients were ninety percent "can't-gets" and ten percent idle rich.

Alan had it fairly easy: no one had a terminal disease, no one was suicidal, no one had lost a child. He should be able to—as Ray put it so rudely—wean them all in the next few months.

Alan was deeply enmeshed in these thoughts as he used the key Joya had given him to open her door. Before he had even climbed the stairs, he could smell something wonderful cooking.

"Well, well, fucking well," said Joya as he walked in.

"What?"

"It's nearly nine o'clock." She gestured at the table, set with linen napkins, candlesticks, flowers. She was wearing a pretty dress, and her bushy dark hair, now in disarray, looked as if it had been stylishly primped.

Alan closed the door quietly. "Is this a date?" He made the mistake of laughing.

"I thought you'd been mugged!" she yelled. "We agreed you would come right back, that I'd make you—" With the hand that wasn't holding her wineglass, she made an angry sweep toward the kitchen. "Well, how about some incredibly dessicated leg of lamb?"

"Joy, I'm sorry. I lost track of time. I was walking—thinking."

"For four hours?" She smiled meanly. "You saw her after all. Didn't you?"

Alan felt as if he were pinned against the door. "As a matter of fact, I did see her. Briefly."

"Who needs big sister's advice when you're a psychiatric prodigy, right?"

"I should have called you. I'm sorry."

"Why didn't you just stay in a hotel? Why even tell me you were coming? Oh, that's right, you're not exactly rolling in dough these days, are you?" Her consonants were fuzzy, and she leaned dependently on the island countertop between the kitchen and the dining table, the open loft.

When Alan put his arms around her, she pushed her face into his shoulder and started to cry. A rhinestone hairclip shaped like a butterfly tumbled across Alan's arm and onto the floor.

"Let's eat something," he murmured. "We should both eat something." On the stove, he saw a covered casserole and a pan of broiled cherry tomatoes, deflated and singed, in a pool of oil. When he began to steer Joya around the island, she punched him in the chest. "Ass," she said. "Men. Jesus."

"You mean pig. I am a thoughtless male pig," he said. Still holding her against his side, he opened a cupboard and took down two plates. The casserole held mashed potatoes. "Oh Joy, what a fantastic meal." He guided her gently toward a stool. He opened the oven, took the mitts from a nearby hook, and pulled out the roasting pan. He needn't have bothered with the mitts; the oven had clearly been off for a while. The lamb, posed on its rack, looked like a giant shriveled mushroom. Below the rack were limp snakelike forms. The scent hit him: fennel. "Oh Joya." She had remembered how much he loved fennel, a food that Greenie never cooked.

He turned a burner on under the tomatoes. He began carving the lamb. "Look, Joy," he said, pointing with the knife. "Still a little pink."

"Well, well. I'll be a monkey's uncle. I'll be the man from uncle."

"Come on," said Alan. He went to the table and held out a chair; she sat. He lit the candles with the starter for the gas burners. He shook out her napkin and laid it tenderly in her lap.

As soon as he had put down their plates, she said, "The thing is, little brother, Marion was always my friend, not yours! Who are you to barge in and ravish her like that? Get her pregnant—if that's what you did—and go on about your life? Then run to *me* for help when you figure out you've fucked up so royally. You know, Alan—you know, I don't really care what you do to your relationships, but this one was mine."

"I know," said Alan. "Eat, Joy. Eat first, then talk."

Joya ate, but she would not meet Alan's eyes. Suddenly she looked up and said, "You know, *speaking* of talking, Greenie calls."

"What do you mean?"

"Calls to talk to me. Every couple of weeks. Or so."

Alan focused on Joya's tone. It was either neutral or very, very angry.

"She really thinks I should adopt." Joya had reached over to the nearby counter and picked up the wand for lighting the stove. She flicked it on and pointed the small flame at Alan. "What do you think?"

"Is that what you want? Have you thought about it?"

"Have I *thought* about it? What, you think I live in medieval Estonia?"

Alan felt incredibly drained. In New York, it was past one A.M. "Foreign adoptions are tricky. You have to be careful about a lot of things," he said slowly. "George has a classmate who was adopted from Russia, and she's sweet, but she's in several kinds of therapy, and the parents are worried that—"

Joya's laugh was clearly intended to cut him off. For pure drama, she tossed her unkempt hair. "Careful! 'Be careful'! Look who's telling *me* to be careful!"

No more apologies. "Joya, I am so tired. Can we talk about this tomorrow? It's a very, very serious thing you're considering. If it's what you want, I would so love to help you out. I would—"

"You," said Joy, her voice stern. "You need all the help you can get, never mind me."

"Let's go to bed." Alan picked up their plates.

"So I might have told her." Joya was staring at him, and only now was it obvious, the quiet depth of her rage.

"Told who what?" he said, but only to buy time. He put the plates on the counter beside the sink.

"Greenie. About Marion. She called tonight. Asked what I was up to."

Alan decided that to say nothing was the only, the least foolish, alternative. Joya looked at him steadily. She wants me to break down, he thought. This is *her* way of breaking down. Say nothing, he told himself. He sat once again at the table, across from his sister. He took a sip of water.

"She was talking, like she sometimes does, about what a sourpuss you've been the past couple of years. How she thinks you're in this huge depression and she doesn't know what to do. She goes out of her mind trying to figure out what *she* did."

Like she's done nothing! Alan wanted to say.

"Are you with me here, little brother?"

"Right across the table, just like when we were kids." His voice shook.

She poured them both more water from a pitcher. As she filled Alan's glass, her hand wobbled. A thin pool spread smoothly across the table. She did not move to wipe it up.

"She was pretty upset tonight. She—"

"Did you tell her or didn't you? Joya, she doesn't even know I'm *here*."

"I'm always thinking of telling her. The words pass through my brain every time she calls, you know? Tonight I was so pissed at you, I just might've actually said something. Or not." She shrugged.

Alan saw what he thought was a flicker of pleasure in Joya's drunken expression. "Good night," he said quietly. "I can't talk to you right now. I'm too upset. I will talk to you tomorrow."

"I'll be gone early and back late."

"I will talk to you whenever." Without waiting for a reply, he walked to the extra bedroom—thank God she did well enough to have two bedrooms—and closed the door after himself. Immediately, he turned on the small clock radio and adjusted it to a jazz station, keeping the volume low. If Joya was going to rant or cry, he did not want to hear her. He sat on the edge of the bed. He pulled his phone from his shirt pocket and punched in Greenie's number.

There was George, on the answering machine. "Greenie," he said to the beep, "I love you. I love you, I love you, I love you. I want us in the same state, the same home, the same bed. I love you. I don't know what else to say. I'll keep on calling. Whatever else you might think, it doesn't matter. I love you."

He heard the toilet in the other bathroom flush. He turned out the light and curled up on his side, on top of the bedspread. He sat up only to take off his shoes, then lay down again. He meant to wait a while, then try Greenie again, but he fell asleep quickly. He dreamed he went back to New York to find out that he was married to Saga. He'd been married to her all along! It was comforting, and it was disturbing. She was warm and loving, and they had Treehorn, every bit as wonderful as a child, but whenever Alan tried to have sex with Saga—and he wanted to, he couldn't wait, it felt like the first time even though it wasn't— something would interrupt them. A phone call, a visitor, the need to eat a meal . . . She doesn't want to have babies, he found himself thinking. She doesn't want to be a mother because she has the dog. The dog is enough for her. And this made him terribly sad.

JOYA WAS NEVER THE STAR STUDENT. That was Alan. In the public school they attended, there were prizes: a prize from fourth grade on for every subject; awards for every major sport; awards for citizenship (the social kiss of death). Alan hated the prizes because at one point or another he won them all, and every single year he suffered the consequences. In eighth grade, he hit the jackpot. He won the art prize, the English prize, a volleyball prize, a tiny silver-plated bowl for the best short story (the teachers were the ones who submitted their students' stories), and a citizenship award. According to a rumor tauntingly pressed on him in the locker room after gym the next day, he would have won the French prize, too, if the teachers hadn't felt they had to draw the line somewhere. "Parlez-vous suck-up?" said one of the all-around jocks, making a lewd kissing noise.

Alan became very good at the impassive, hear-no-evil response to such taunting, and sometimes now he wondered if all that practice at refusing provocation had helped him in his work as a therapist. Had he even been steered toward that work by learning to establish a wall of a certain kind?

Alan's mother was never happier than when he raked in the prizes, an occasion that became one of yearly anticipation, so that by junior high Alan noticed his mother's mood begin to ascend in the middle of May, culminating in his favorite dessert—a big chocolate Duncan Hines cake—on the night after the awards assembly. At some point during the annual Alanfest, Mrs. Glazier would turn to her daughter and say something like "We are so proud of you, too, dear. After seeing those sculptured heads you made last fall, I was sure you'd have the art award sewn right up, but the judges are probably the sort who don't *understand* modern sculpture."

"Why would they?" Alan's father might have joked. "They're teachers of algebra and typing. Lord, the janitor's probably in on it, too. Equal opportunity and all that."

"What I mean to say is, Joya has talents aplenty that have very little to do with grades and prizes," their mother would say.

When the parents weren't looking, Alan could count on Joya to make a hideous face at him, a face that said, "Retard!" or "Pathetic loser nerd!" or to stick out her tongue when her mouth was filled with masticated devil's food cake. Again, Alan was impassive. Without comment, he allowed his sister to ignore him, or lock him out of the bathroom for ages, or "accidentally" leave her wet towel on his bed. ("I was just in there looking for my brush. Did you steal it?") The cold front never lasted more than a day or two.

Joya got into trouble now and then, generally with Marion, but it wasn't the sort of trouble to involve the police. The two girls made crank calls ("Mr. Woo, is that your rickshaw double-parked outside the IHOP?"), reset clocks, and tucked smelly cheese in more than one mailbox. At their best, Alan and Joya gossiped about teachers and traded the rumors they'd heard about each other's friends, but their academic disparity—they never spoke about that.

Alan had always assumed that Joya simply didn't care, but when he awoke early the next morning in her spare room, he lay in bed wondering if he had underestimated her resentment of all the things that had come so much more easily to him. How clearly he could now imagine her saying, in her deep, gutsy voice, "Why is it you get everything: the prizes, the good spouse, the child, the clients looking up to you like a surrogate dad, not the surrogate principal or cop!" Though she would never dream of saying such a thing.

He heard her showering, making coffee, then leaving almost right away. He was too exhausted to go out and confront her, and it would have been selfish. She did not have time for this kind of turmoil.

Ten minutes after Alan heard the apartment door close, he got up and checked his cell phone. There had been no calls. When he ventured out toward the kitchen, he found that Joya had left the after-dinner mess perfectly intact. The smell of charred meat was oppressive. The plates sat next to each other on the counter, littered with lamb fat and gristle; on Joya's, the mound of potatoes, crusted and yellow, had never been touched. Across one end of the wooden dining table, a pale maplike stain marked the place where no one had wiped up the water she had spilled. Their napkins lay on the floor, next to the butterfly clip that had fallen from her hair. As he picked up the glittering ornament, Alan felt shame at the effort she'd made. Even her brother, it seemed, could not reciprocate her love.

He opened the three large front windows. The sky was an assertive blue, the sunlight strong. It illuminated, too brightly, the ambitious grin of a sitcom actress on a billboard across the street. Alan groaned and sat on the couch. He glanced at the wall phone. If it were to ring, whose voice on the other end would he dread least? This was a sad state of affairs. If my patients could see me now, he thought, would they flee in disgusted pity? Or would his example give them courage, the comforting sense that if he—Dr. Alan Glazier, Ph.D., Phi Beta Kappa, summa cum laude, family man—could screw up so completely, well surely they were not after all so pathetic themselves.

The patient with the traitorous wife: now he would definitely have fired Alan. The cellist, facing so much disappointment in the world and its commercial, art-spurning nature, would probably have forgiven him. Recently, Alan had read about a debate in the real-estate world over something called owner disclosure. Must home owners disclose the results of any and all tests they performed on things like termite infestation and radon levels? Wouldn't it be fair if such a law governed psychotherapists, forced them to confess histories of divorce, infidelity, substance abuse, even chronic impatience with children or addiction to boring, formulaic cop shows on TV?

He called Joya's office number and spoke to her voice mail. "I don't know what happened last night," he said, "I mean how it got so out of control, but I'm sorry I made you angry. I shouldn't have been so thoughtless about the time. But I'm totally confused about what you told me, the part about Greenie, and I need to talk to you, Joy. Would you find a minute to call me? Are you speaking to me? You'd better be."

He called Greenie's number. Consuelo answered. "Hello Mister Alan, a good day to you!" she said gaily. "She has taken Mister George to the kitchen this morning, then school! She will teach his class to make biscuits! I will tell her you call! It is important?"

"Yes," said Alan. "Tell her to call my cell phone. I am not at home today."

"Yes!" echoed Consuelo with warm conviction. *Someone* did not regard him as the world's biggest jerk.

Alan had a number for Greenie at the governor's kitchen, but she had given it to him mainly for emergencies. Was this an emergency? Good question, thought Alan sardonically—but if Joya had told her about Marion, to call her there now would be calamitous, no matter how urgent his feelings.

When had Marion said she would call?

He would wash the dishes and clean the kitchen. If Marion had not called by then, he would clean the oven. If she had not called by then, he would take a bath. In a bath, unlike a shower, he could hear Joya's phone ring. If she did not call by the time he got out of the bath, he would check his own machine for messages back in New York.

He threw away the leftover, spoiled food. He filled the sink with soapy water and put the dishes in to soak. Under the sink, he found a sticky old bottle of furniture oil. He would try to restore the surface of the table.

Alan opened the dishwasher; it was full of clean dishes.

"Oh God." He sighed.

The proper places for plates, bowls, mugs, and glasses were easy to find. The silverware drawer was the first one he tried, the one he would have chosen for this purpose. Logical Joya. (Why had no one married logical, clever, admirably independent Joya, Joya with the killer legs? If she were not his sister, would *he* have married Joya?)

The incidental pieces—the spatula, whisk, and long knives—were harder to place. The third drawer he opened was stuffed with take-out menus and other papers; immediately, right on top, he saw a pamphlet about a "resource and support group" for single women who wanted to adopt a child. He lifted it daintily, as if it might mask an explosive device, and saw an envelope with the return address of a missionary service in India. Jumbled in alongside it were the business cards of two adoption lawyers and a social worker.

Why, before the previous night's disastrous conversation, hadn't he suspected that Joya would pursue this way of becoming a mother? Stephen was beginning to talk about adoption, too—though it would be much harder for him. No doubt there were support groups for single men who wanted to adopt—and whip-smart adoption lawyers who worked with tenacious idealism to help their gay clients—but Alan's job came before all that. So how could he have been spending the past two months probing the ins and outs of this monumental choice with a man who had been a total stranger just one year ago yet never have had a clue that his own sister was going through the very same struggle?

"Somebody shoot me," he muttered into the drawer before closing it.

The next one, of course, held all the wooden spoons, potato peelers, ladles, and knives in two spotless plastic bins. He put away the utensils he still held in his left hand and returned to the dishwasher. By ten-thirty he had it loaded. Only the roasting pan still lurked in the sink, filled with soapy water. He would wait to start the dishwasher because that noise, too, might drown out Marion's call. The oven, as it turned out, was self-cleaning; there would be no penance involving arms caked with the brown crud of baking and broiling, of splattering fat.

NOW IT WAS ONE IN THE AFTERNOON. Alan had dressed. Joya's kitchen phone had taken on a decidedly contemptuous air.

He called Fenno McLeod back in New York. It was while walking Treehorn one evening that Alan had resolved to make this trip; on their way home, as if to cement that resolve, he had stopped in at his favorite bookshop to buy a travel guide. Providing for the dog during his absence was a detail that hadn't occurred to him yet. In a rare stroke of luck—dumb luck, the only kind Alan deserved these days—Fenno had offered advice on which guide to buy and then, quite offhandedly, had offered to look after Treehorn. Now, Alan could hardly believe he'd imposed this task on a virtual stranger—even if McLeod *was* known about the neighborhood as someone who clearly loved dogs.

"Your lassie's asleep in the garden," the Scotsman told Alan over the phone. "Tuckered out from a long gallivanting run along the piers with Emily. Doesn't seem too mournful about your absence, I must tell you."

"I'm so grateful," said Alan. Though who was Emily? Another assistant?

"Not to worry," said McLeod. "You'll just have to buy more books now, won't you?"

"I will," Alan said. "Absolutely I will." Everyone he knew and loved, he thought as he hung up the phone, would get books for Christmas that year.

He called his machine. There were three messages: his mother checking in about Christmas ideas for George's gifts; Jerry wanting to catch up, wondering if he and Greenie were free for dinner some night; and Gordon Unsworth.

Gordon. Gordie. Gordie of Stephen and Gordie. Alan smiled grimly as he listened to the message a second time. ". . . I know you're seeing Stephen now, alone, but I was hoping I could just talk with you about . . . things." He left three phone numbers.

"Things!" Alan exclaimed to his sister's cool, indifferent loft, to the actress on the billboard, her manufactured smile no longer in the sun. Now her teeth looked gray, even predatory. "Things!"

He hunted below the sink for a scouring pad. He found one. As he scrubbed mercilessly at the roasting pan, he spoke to it. "Hello there, Gordie. You'd like to talk about things? What things would those be? Broken things? Unfinished things? Things you own? Things you regret? Please, I'm a thing specialist here! Talk to your heart's content about *things*. Oh, the shame and the glory of THINGS!"

At 1:32, according to the digital clock on the microwave oven, Alan laid the pan—probably cleaner than it had been since it was purchased—facedown on a towel. He dried his sore hands and punched Gordie's office number into the phone. To his surprise, Gordie answered.

"Alan Glazier returning your call."

He heard a long, grateful sigh. "Oh thank you. I thought you might not call back. I'd have completely understood."

"I always return calls," Alan said, trying not to sound cold. "Tell me what's up with you."

"What's up with me is I'm—I was going to say I'm miserable, but that's not it. I'm . . . baffled. I sort of can't believe I took the drastic step I did."

Alan let the silence stretch for two or three seconds. "You mean, leaving Stephen the way you did."

"Yeah. Like an ass. A royal ass."

Like a pig, thought Alan. Like a selfish, frightened, faithless pig. Wouldn't it be funny if Joya had a device that tape-recorded all her calls? It was entirely plausible, since she was in a profession that might attract threats.

"Do you want to see someone and talk, Gordie? Because I have a commitment to Stephen now. I could ask how he feels if I see you once or twice—or I could just refer you to someone else."

"I understand," said Gordie. "Could you do that? Ask him if I could just tell you what's going on with me?" Alan heard the disruptive click of call-waiting. "Because he doesn't return my calls anymore. I mean not that I've called him more than a—"

"Gordie? Gordie, I'm sorry, but I have to put you on hold. Can you hang on a minute?"

"Of course," said the repentant Gordie, and Alan switched to the alternate line. He heard a woman speak his name, but the din in the background nearly engulfed her voice. Was it Marion or Joya? "Hello? Hello?" he said, as if he wasn't sure they had any connection at all.

"Alan, it's me. It's a bad day, but I have a breathing space right now. I've left you three messages on your cell phone. . . . Maria, no, he said to use that tureen with the antler on top. It was a gift from one of these guys." Greenie laughed. "I know, it's revolting and tacky. Warm it slowly so it doesn't crack when we pour in the soup. . . . Alan? I'm completely stressed out. We're feeding governors from two other states, and this morning I made biscuits with George's class. They came out of the oven looking like a field of little meteorites."

"Greenie?" Alan pressed his free hand against his chest. "Did you get my message last night?"

"Well, yeah," she said. "And I happened to talk to Joya last night, too; she told me you were there! Alan, what's going on? Why would you go all the way out there? Is everything okay with Joya? I'm kind of worried about her."

There was a loud clattering noise on Greenie's end. He heard her groan. "Oh no, oh—can we glue it back on? Can somebody go find Bill and get a hold of some Krazy Glue? We can heat the thing up, put in the soup, then glue the antler back on. Wait a sec. Oh don't—Alan, I have to go, but we have to talk. I don't know what's going on—there or here. I won't be back till late tonight. Call George at least."

She said good-bye, and Alan realized he had said almost nothing. No lies, no excuses, no confessions, no explanations. No further declarations of love. But he was fairly certain that Joya had told her nothing incriminating about his visit. Still, Greenie had been speaking so loudly, with so many people around her, that he could read nothing into her voice. He hung up the phone. Immediately, it rang. Stunned, Alan grabbed it up. "There appears to be a receiver off the hook," declared a prissy robotic voice. "Please hang up and try your call again."

Gordie. Alan had left Gordie hanging until, quite reasonably, he had hung up. Alan struck the wall twice with the receiver. A shallow dent in the Sheetrock mocked his petty rage. The dent was shaped like a smile.

More than anything, he wanted to go out, to pace the city from end to end—perhaps to show up in person at Joya's office. He realized he had no idea where her office was, but if he ransacked another drawer or two, he'd find out. Where else in his sister's life did he need to meddle?

Hadn't Marion said she would call in the morning? It was well past morning. Why shouldn't he call her? Alan got his address book and called the number he had never used before. A man answered.

"Can I please speak to Marion?" he said without greeting.

"Marion's not here just now," the man said. "Who's calling?"

"Alan Glazier." He felt naked, stripped to his pale and quivering flesh.

"Hello, Alan. I'm Lewis." The man's voice was warm. It was, without doubt, the voice of a doctor. Did they teach you this voice in medical school, or if you happened to grow up with a voice like this, did someone steer you toward becoming a doctor?

Alan said nothing.

"I'm Marion's husband. I have to tell you that Marion's taken our son to visit friends for a long weekend. She needs to think a lot more about your request to meet Jacob."

"You mean, she's protecting you."

"No," said the calm, kind, enveloping voice of Lewis. "We talked about you last night, and I told her this is entirely up to her. As it should be."

"But if it were up to you, you'd tell her never to speak to me again."

Lewis sighed. "No, not at all. I have two children who are more or less estranged from me because of their mother. When it comes to family matters, I don't make judgments, and I certainly don't give advice. I could never do what you do."

"You couldn't begin to know what I do," said Alan. Alan wondered why he was even talking to this man. He wondered why he was acting so juvenile. No, that part he couldn't honestly wonder about. His belligerent pride was part of what had landed him here in the first place. Don't fool yourself, he thought, you've earned every bit of this trouble and humiliation, fair and square.

Briefly, Alan thought again of all those prizes he'd won as a child. Never once had they, or his fine high grades, made him feel secure. He had always suspected that once he reached the end of his glowing school career, some sort of comeuppance would be awaiting him, patiently, like a robber hiding behind a bush at the end of a finely gardened promenade.

"Alan?" Lewis said. "Alan, are you still there?"

"Yes," said Alan. "Yes. I don't know what to say."

"I'm sorry. I know you must be pretty angry," said Lewis. "She isn't doing this to be cruel. It's just so—well, obviously it's complicated. You haven't done anything wrong. She wanted me to tell you that. She felt terrible not calling you, but she was afraid that if she spoke to you, you'd change her mind. And she needs to think things through with as little pressure as possible."

"Oh." Trumped yet again by the wisdom and kindness of Marcus Welby, M.D.

"You know, this will sound presumptuous, but I have a feeling that one day we'll meet. Marion says we have a lot in common."

What was Alan to do now, thank the man for his generosity? Ask what he was doing home on a Friday—whether he, too, was low on patients?

"She promises she'll be in touch," said Lewis. His tone was more apologetic than reassuring, the tone he would use to tell a patient that while, yes, they'd caught the cancer early, there would still be evil medicine to take.

She promised she would CALL! Alan wanted to shout. She promised . . . But had she promised anything else? Oh, promises. As durable and easy to define as jellyfish bobbing up and down in the waves.

"Thank you, Lewis," he said, forcing himself to say the name. "Would it be inane to ask you to tell her I called?"

Lewis, bless him, did not laugh. "I knew you'd call—I mean, I would have called, too. So of course, of course I'll tell her."

Alan sighed, his chronic trademark sigh. "So that's it then," he said. He thanked Marion's husband again. In unison, the two men said good-bye.

"That's it then," Alan repeated, breezily, to the voracious sitcom actress, to Joya's view of industrial San Francisco. And hey now, as it turned out, there was plenty of time to see a few sights in this handsome city! Where had Alan put that guidebook he'd bought from Fenno McLeod? Had he even remembered to bring it with him?

THIRTEEN

REMARKABLY, ALAN WAS WAITING FOR THEM at the mouth of the tunnel leading from the plane. "I pleaded," he said, "and they took pity on me." He put down a large shopping bag and held each of them tightly a long time, first George and then Greenie.

"Am I ever glad to see you!" he said to George. He tapped his watch. "We have to catch up on this Christmas business. I got us a tree, and Santa came, even though he knew you weren't here yet. And how about some of Nana's fruitcake?"

"Yuck, Dad," said George. "You know I hate that. We all hate that!"

"All right then, no cake but your mom's." Alan glanced fondly at Greenie.

"Where's Treehorn?"

"She had to wait at home," said Alan. George made a face but did not complain.

Greenie stood deliberately back from the reunion of father and son. For once, she was content to be a witness. She had been awake for nearly four days straight, making roasts and cookies, pâtés, English puddings (Yorkshire and plum), half a dozen bûches de Noël. Ray might instruct his staff to surround the mansion with a thousand flickering farolitos, but he was a sucker for all the Dickensian trappings.

She followed Alan and George down the escalator to Baggage Claim. The airport was close to vacant; they had a bank of plastic seats to themselves. As Alan talked to George of gifts and food and snow and sleds, Greenie watched the blades of the carousel turn in a gleaming oval, awaiting the onslaught of trunks, duffels, skis, and alpine backpacks. Just like her: waiting to see what sensations would hit as she reentered her old life, or what remained of that life.

She was glad that she had already run the gauntlet of Christmas entertaining on someone else's behalf. She had become a placid, willing vessel of Ray's private nostalgia and public benevolence, an all-consuming project that had left her mind both spent and purged. Just as fortunately, she'd had precious little time in recent weeks to think about, let alone see, Charlie. Perhaps, she thought (or wished), I won't even miss him. After all, she reasoned, they were just friends. While you, she thought as she watched Alan lean toward their son (looking so pleased, his love so hungry and sated all at once), you are my *husband,* you are my husband of *ten years.* This meant, she also reasoned, that Alan would always be to some degree transparent: not invisible but impossible to see, the way you can't see great portions of your own body except in photographs or elaborately positioned mirrors. Wasn't a husband, after a while, just another part of you, a part you were destined never to see without unflattering distortions?

She watched Alan touch his son on the nose and then, having captured his attention, reach into the shopping bag. "And now . . ." He pulled out a large present and gave it to George. Repeating the motion, he held out another to Greenie.

George said, "Dad, this is rapted in the newspaper!"

"Well, okay, so maybe I forgot to buy real wrapping paper. Some details I've had to fudge. But look, I managed real ribbon."

"Yes," acknowledged George. He shook his present, sniffed it, and examined its underside. "Can I open it now?"

"That's the idea, guy."

After Alan helped loosen the ribbon, George tore off the paper in one dramatic gesture. "What is it!" he exclaimed, staring at a plain cardboard box. He shook it from side to side till the bottom fell out, leaving the lid in his hands. Holding the lid above his head, as if he mustn't let go of it, he looked down. "It's a . . . it's a . . ." Finally he dropped the lid, sat on the floor, and rummaged in the box.

"Oh my goodness, a cowboy suit," said Greenie, her first words since getting off the plane.

George looked from the box to his father. His expression was neutral, almost pensive.

"Let's see!" said Greenie.

Carefully, George held up a black suede vest. Tassels sprouted from shiny round grommets along the bottom.

Greenie reached over and felt the material. "This is the real thing."

She picked up the shirt from below; it, too, was black, with white piping and pearl snaps. Across the chest, a graceful linear drawing in reds and blues, galloped a crowd of horses. "George, look at this."

George dropped the vest and turned his attention to the shirt.

"A herd of mustangs!" said Greenie.

"Maybe," said George. "Or maybe Chingo Teak ponies. They're wild ones, too." He looked at his father. "You know, Dad, cowboys don't really wear their clothes like this."

"Yes, they do," said Greenie, "when they're dressed up. I see them at Ray's house all the time. You should see how fancy some of their outfits are."

In the same box, under a pair of black jeans, cocooned in tissue paper printed with horseshoes, sat a small gray Stetson hat—identical to one that Ray wore—and beneath it the requisite boots.

"Oh Alan." Greenie was both touched and worried, because like so many extravagant gifts that parents dream will answer their children's most fervent longings, this one seemed to be falling flat—not entirely, as George continued to examine the shirt with fascination, turning it around to verify that (yes) the horses galloped full circle around the wearer, but his reaction seemed to be one of ingenuous caution or even skepticism.

"Open yours," Alan said to Greenie.

"Later. Look, here come the suitcases."

"No, now," he said. "Really."

"Here," Greenie said to George, "you're so good at tearing off the paper, why don't you help me?"

Inside Greenie's box was another pair of cowboy boots. Hers were red, with cutouts shaped like soaring swallows, cameos of blue against ivory leather. The swallows made her think of Ray's ranch, where swallows built nests in the rafters, yet also of Maine, where sometimes you'd see them careening and flitting, like stunt pilots, over the water. The boots, so beautiful, embarrassed her. Inexplicably, she felt herself recoil at the perfection of Alan's present. Was she too exhausted for gratitude?

"What do you think? Honestly. Will you wear them?" said Alan. "Because I can return them. I don't want to see them gathering dust."

Behind him, Greenie caught sight of the one suitcase she had packed for both herself and George, toppling through the chute. "How did you know my size, Alan? Men never know their women's shoe size."

He frowned briefly. "The shoes you left in our closet. I'd like to say I know all your physical dimensions by heart, but that would be a lie."

And we never lie to each other, do we? thought Greenie. "Alan, I'm overwhelmed," she said. "I'm going to put them on right now."

As they walked from the terminal to the parking garage, people who passed her would look down and smile. "Look! Bluebirds of happiness!" said an older man to a little girl at his side. "Merry Christmas," he said to Greenie.

"Same to you," she answered.

"Do mine have bluebirds?" asked George, whose cowboy outfit, repacked, was now under Alan's arm.

Alan said, "Yours have lasso designs stitched right into the leather."

George was silent for a moment. He clasped Alan's hand, the one that also carried the suitcase. "I don't like lassos," he said softly. "They're mean."

Greenie could see that he had struggled not to make this complaint, but honest declarations held powerful sway for children. She said, "Did you know that lassos can be used to rescue animals? If a calf or a foal gets caught in a river and can't swim, a cowboy can lasso it and pull it back to shore."

"Oh," said George. "I didn't know that."

As Alan unlocked the car he'd borrowed from a friend, he said, "Before I forget, Walter told me that if you don't call him by tomorrow morning, he'll never forgive you."

Walter. For days now—some of the busiest days of her life—Greenie had forgotten that Alan would not be the only person to see on this trip. She'd known there would be Tina and Sherwin; that was business. Tina wanted to buy Greenie out, and Greenie had agreed. (Walter had told her that he knew a lawyer who'd do the deal without fleecing them.) But there were also the friends to whom she'd sent brief, hasty e-mails, assuring them that she couldn't wait to get together when she came back for Christmas. Now, all she wanted to do was climb beneath a pile of blankets and sleep. "Are we invited to parties?" she said. "I think I'm a little partied out."

"The Christmas parties you missed," he said dryly. "But New Year's, yes, same as always." He named an old friend of his from the institute, one with a pair of twins the same age as George. They had an annual

New Year's Day buffet: borscht, ham, and black-eyed peas. Greenie and Alan had been to eight or ten of these parties, each one nearly identical to the last. Just as dependably, all the children went home with indelible beet stains on their brand-new holiday outfits and came down with whatever virus one of the other children had passed around with the carrot sticks and hummus.

To be back in New York was thrilling and enervating, familiar and strange. Nothing had changed, yet suddenly there were too many people, there was too little sky, and the damp air was a visceral affront. The weather wasn't much different from the weather she'd left behind here nine months before, as if in her absence the climate hadn't bothered to change. Only Greenie had changed.

GEORGE WAS NOW THOROUGHLY obsessed with horses. He neglected his miniature railroad and had abandoned his dinosaurs to concentrate on a collection of lifelike model horses he'd started when Diego gave him two duplicates: a bay gelding, head down to graze, and a trotting Appaloosa mare with a billowing mane of pearl-colored plastic. In six months, Greenie had added four more to the collection, Ray two, and Mary Bliss the one that Greenie liked best: a roan pony with a bridle and western saddle. The leather was tooled with looping vines, the fastenings a good imitation of antique silver. But George had promptly removed the saddle and bridle; riding was not the point of his horseplay.

"Wild, wild, you are wild, the Connemara king of wild!" he proclaimed in a joyful, breathless murmur as he galloped the pony along a bookcase, past the long-forgotten Sneetches and an all too pedantically human Harold; past Mr. and Mrs. Mallard in distant, irrelevant Boston; past Frog and Toad, whose genteel voices had not been heard for months.

On one visit to the library after school—Consuelo took him twice a week—George had apparently asked the librarian for "bigger, betterer" books on horses; so now, nearly every time, Consuelo would read aloud to him from a large dusty reference book called *The Golden Equine Encyclopedia.*

When Greenie returned from work, George would tell her something new he had learned. "The Hackney has a very short tail and it steppens very high," he might say, demonstrating with raised forearms. Or "Did you know there are horses who don't live here, in the United States? The Suffolk punch lives in England. The Tendon Sea Walking Horse lives by the Tendon Sea. The grass is blue by the Tendon Sea." Greenie was surprised how many kinds of horses she had never heard of. She knew a little, but nowhere near as much as George, so she did not tell him that the Tendon Sea Walking Horse came from and was named for Tennessee or that Kentucky was the bluegrass state or that fancy show horses like the Lippizan stallions were trained on a lunge line, not a lunch line.

His favorite storybook was called *Bronco Busters*. In it, three crude, swaggering migrant cowboys failed to break the spirit of a young black horse. Every night, a small boy would visit the horse in its corral. Gradually, through music, food, and quiet musings about their future together, he won the animal's trust. At the end, after the insolent cowboys drove off in their sinister pickup, the boy freed the horse, climbed up on his back, and rode him away toward the mountains.

George had made two friends in his kindergarten class—a boy named Sven and a girl named Hope—but when they came over, they had very little interest in the horses. Sven liked the dinosaurs, though mostly he wanted to browse again and again through the Pokémon trading cards he brought along, displayed in a binder of plastic sleeves (which gave Sven, in Greenie's eyes, the unsavory air of a traveling salesman). Hope liked putting on the plastic masks that Greenie had bought for George after he'd shown so much interest in the Hopi mask at the Governor's Mansion. But his friendship with the enigmatic Diego was still the one he treasured most. Greenie's schedule did not permit her to do much of the driving to and from Diego's house; about once every two weeks, Consuelo drove George out to Tesuque at three (when Diego got home from school) and brought him home by six. This was easier for Diego's mother, who had other children to look after and, according to Consuelo, no car of her own. George would return from these visits energetic and open, dispensing tales about the hand-fed squirrel on the roof, the goats that liked to stand in the sun on top of their shed, and, above all, the horses that grazed the fields of the neighboring ranch. He had learned to identify all of them by coloring and most of them by name. ("Carumba! What do you think about *that* name, Mom?" he would say proudly. Or "My favoritest one today is Fengali. Fengali has the longest tail of everyone. It's black.")

Greenie would have found George's fixation funnier than she did if she had not felt equally yet shamefully enthralled by something other than horses. Greenie's obsession was Charlie, and it was not a matter of pretend. In October, before the parade of holidays began, Greenie had met Charlie in town two or three times for lunch, but he had not dropped by her house again and never asked to see her at night. Nor did he mention her mother again. He spoke much more often now of his visions and ideals, what he readily called his "crusades," than he did of the past. With relief and regret, Greenie wondered if Charlie was backing away. When she began to wonder if his motives might be noble or cowardly, *Stop!* she warned herself. It simply did not, could not matter.

NO CHRISTMAS DAY HAD EVER FELT SO EPICALLY LONG. To catch their flight, she'd had to get herself and George ready to leave Santa Fe by four in the morning. Tall George had picked them up in the fading dark and driven them to Albuquerque, but while Small went back to sleep, Greenie had stayed awake and talked with grown-up George. She had never spent time alone with her son's name-mate and occasional playmate, though she had learned secondhand that he grew up in Harlem, was a Yankees fan, and liked to Rollerblade.

"How'd you end up working for Ray?" she asked.

Predictably, he laughed. "Long story short? I was stuck on this girl who says, Hey, let's hitch to L.A.! Like we're in some Robert Redford movie." He laughed. "Like who's gonna pick up a couple of black teenagers, man. Clueless, man. But somehow we end up here. We get a ride for two whole days in the back of a pickup with this Indian dude. We make it here and I figure, hey, don't push our luck. I get a job delivering groceries, which gets me driving a truck, which gets me driving an airport cab, which gets me driving a limo at night for extra money, which gets me, well sort of, to this place."

" 'Well sort of'?" said Greenie. "Sounds like a logical progression to me."

"Yeah, well, on the surface like." Tall shook his head. "But see, Ray puts the eye on someone and, wham, before you know it, you in his *collection.*" He caught Greenie's eye in the rearview mirror. "Know what I'm sayin'?"

"Yes, I suppose I do."

"Guvna sees, Guvna wants. Guvna, man, he *conquers*. Not in a bad way, I'm not saying that. But it goes, like, deeper than you'd think. Big Daddy stuff. He hired *me,* see, because he saw me hangin' out on my blades with a crowd near the Plaza. What he saw, why me, who knows? He needs a driver, so I get tapped by some dude who works for a law firm near where I hang out. He knows my name, he knows it all. A weird thing. Weird but good. Stroke. Of. Luck." With each of those three words he tapped the steering wheel with his right hand. She noticed that he wore a wide silver band on his pinkie.

"So you know how he found me then," she said.

"Something about your singing's what I heard."

"My singing!" Greenie laughed loudly, and Small George stirred against her. She stroked his hair.

"Yeah, and some ballbustin' cake."

"The cake, yes. But what did you hear about singing?"

"Mary B. says you start the day with goofy singing. Well, she *can* spin a tale, that girl."

Greenie leaned forward. "George, is it just me, or is it obvious to everyone that Mary Bliss is mad for Ray?"

"That girl," he said again. "She be in for a serious bruising. Not like he's led her on. She ought to *know.*"

The car slowed, curving away from the highway, toward the airport. At the curb, Tall took their suitcase from the trunk. For the first time, Greenie looked at his face and saw that he was younger than she would have guessed, twenty-five at most. What sort of a life would he be leading now if Ray had not pulled him off the street? Or would he have been in school, on his way to becoming a teacher or a lawyer? What did it mean that Ray seemed to choose people rather than let them come to him, plucked them like fruit, ripe or not, from a vine? When Greenie reached into her purse, Tall George looked wounded. "I ain't no Red Cap," he said, but he gave her a forgiving smile. He turned to his small, sleepy friend and held out his hands. "What do I need, my man Small?"

Greenie saw her son smile and shake off his crankiness, then go through the ritual of slapping hands and gyrating bodies.

"Bon voyage," said Tall. "Know what that means?"

Small shook his head.

"Means come back soon, amigo." He winked at Greenie.

Small George giggled. "Okay, amigo."

Hours later—though days later was how it felt—after a slow crawl through the Holland Tunnel; after the joyful reunions of George with Treehorn and then with his seemingly immortal goldfish; after the opening of presents; after the eating of stuffed Cornish game hens and vegetable salads that Alan had insisted on buying from a gourmet market and that she had found blessedly delicious; after second helpings of a pear-almond tart sent by Tina in a Ms. Duquette pastry box that brought tears to Greenie's eyes; after George had inspected every decoration on the tree and every nook of his old home and then, in a moment when neither of his parents were looking, fallen asleep on the floor under the coffee table, nestled against his dog; after Alan had tenderly changed him into pajamas and tucked him, utterly unwaking, into his bed, which now looked so tiny; after phone calls from Alan's mother and Walter and Consuelo had been left for the machine to answer—after all this, Greenie and Alan collapsed side by side, alone together for the first time in four months, on the couch they had bought together just before their marriage.

At first, they looked not at each other but at the enveloping mayhem— crumpled paper, empty boxes, a ransacked half-empty suitcase, a table covered with leftover food and wine, candles melted to puddles of wax—and laughed. Delicately, lips pulled back from her teeth, Treehorn was nibbling at the wild rice strewn on the rug under George's place. She looked up, regarding them with alarm and then curiosity.

Staring at the table, Alan groaned. "Flowers. I knew there was something I forgot." When he started to get up, Greenie said, "Don't touch a bit of it. Don't you dare. We'll deal with it all tomorrow."

For a moment, they turned their nervous attention to the tree. By mistake, Alan had replaced some burned-out bulbs with blinkers. They kept up a syncopated rhythm, casting onto the ceiling a mute display of fireworks.

She knew she ought to thank him for working so hard on everything— the tree, the meal, the presents—but Greenie wanted Alan to speak first. And yet, as she looked around the room at the things she'd expected to see and the things she'd forgotten about, she heard herself say, "Where's my chair?"

"Your chair?"

"My big pink chair. The one I rescued from execution by garbage truck."

"I moved it. To make room for the tree. It's in the bedroom."

"I didn't see it."

"I covered it," said Alan. "Okay, I covered it about two minutes after you left. I can't stand the color. As you know."

Greenie nodded. "But not permanently."

Alan rolled his eyes. "No, Greenie, not permanently. With an old bedspread of mine."

"That denim thing?" said Greenie. "Blue. What is it with men and blue? Why is blue so boring, so safe?"

"Maybe because it's a color that isn't intrusive. Because the sky is blue."

"Yes. And always there." *The important thing about the sky,* she remembered from Margaret Wise Brown, *is that it is always there.* But Alan, who hadn't read to George much at all in the past year, wouldn't know the allusion. One of the unexpected difficulties of their separation was that when Greenie made passing remarks about her everyday life, often she would have to explain them to Alan. Because he *wasn't* always there.

They still hadn't touched. Were they shy? Were they intimidated? Or were they, deep down in the compressed molten core of their selves, still angry, even justifiably angry? *Let go,* thought Greenie.

She turned to Alan, pulling her knees up and resting them against his thigh. "Would you tell me about your visit to Joya? You never really explained that. Did she have a breakdown of some kind? I worry about her, you know."

"Joya's okay," Alan said firmly.

"Well, she *would* be okay, that's the kind of person she is. But last time I talked to her, she was so . . . fed up. She was so depleted about this baby thing. She said she wished she could have that part of her brain cut out, whatever part holds that bourgeois cuckoo clock—that's what she called it! Funny even when she's furious. She wishes she could love her life as it is, with her—Alan!"

Alan had let out a great, full-throated sigh. He said, "I don't think Joya is what we should be talking about, do you?"

Treehorn jumped up on the couch, on the other side of Alan, and laid her long jaw on his opposite thigh. She gazed at Greenie as if to remind her (the renegade wife) that Alan was the one who deserved an ally.

"Greenie, there's something I have to tell you right now that's terrible, that's confusing, or it is to me, that's . . ."

"That's what? What is it?"

Alan stared at the tree. "I'm so afraid you'll leave me when I tell you."

Don't you feel I've left you already? Didn't you say that months ago? Greenie thought. But she waited, listening, feeling the excess food, the second slice of pie, sitting too high in her chest. "Just tell me. You're a worrier, Alan. Things are rarely as bad as you think they'll be." She put her hand on his leg. Treehorn shoved her nose against Greenie's hand.

"Okay," said Alan fiercely. "That time I went to my high school reunion, way before George, when we were fighting all the time—at the last minute you refused to go, do you remember that?—I ran into a girl I'd known, Joya's best friend, and I—"

"You slept with her."

Alan started to speak, but Greenie interrupted again; she had no patience for a confession of something so stale. *Now* was the problem: right this very *minute*. "That was how many years ago? That was ages ago. God, why are you telling me now? Alan, I don't need to know this." She turned to look at him. "Or is this because you're seeing Jerry again? I hope you're seeing Jerry again. If Jerry thought you ought to come clean with me—"

"Greenie, I'm not seeing Jerry. There's more than just this."

"You mean other women? Other reunions?" Greenie could no longer look at her husband's face, which seemed to grow darker, more miserable, by the minute. Everywhere else she looked, clutter abounded: a toppled pile of picture books (Alan had given them both so many books!), a tousled knot of ribbon and tissue paper, a sweater, a card, a plaid scarf, a box of chocolates . . . "God, Alan, are you having an affair? Some would say I deserve that, don't I?" She laughed.

"Greenie!" he shouted. She jerked away from him, stunned. Treehorn dropped to the floor, looking up at Alan in fear. He reached a hand down to pet her. "Shh, it's okay, girl." To Greenie, he said, "Listen to me, please! Stop thinking so damn fast, galloping ahead of me like you always do."

"I'm sorry," she murmured.

"I am not having an affair. There is no one—lamentably, maybe—no one but you. There was *one* woman, *one* night, it was stupid, it was petty. I'll be mortified to the end of time. But it's more complicated. There are complications."

"Complications?" She thought of cancer and AIDS. *The wife died from complications of infidelity.*

"I might be the father—accidentally, Greenie—the father of another child."

Greenie remembered telling Alan that she was pregnant. She'd said it the way so many adoring wives do: *I have some incredible news for you. You're going to be a father.* Perversely, she felt for an instant as if she were hearing good news, as if somehow he might be telling her that now *he* was pregnant, that this other child was their next child. Just as perversely, she smiled. "But Alan," she said, and then she drew in her breath, as if to take back the affection with which she had spoken his name.

Alan began to cry. Greenie stared at him. At first he just kept repeating how sorry he was, and then a torrent of words came out of her normally nontorrential husband, her husband who spoke in carefully chosen, intelligent phrases, even when expressing profound emotions. He was saying, over and over in a litany of careless repetition, that he had no idea what to say, he had been a terrible coward not to tell her before, he had not seen this woman in all those years till he went to San Francisco, he had only wanted to know for sure, he needed just to *know,* he had no intention of leaving Greenie and George, he loved George— "and you, *you,*" he added too hastily—more than anything on earth. He wanted them together more than ever, he hoped she could forgive him, maybe not now, maybe not for a while; he would sleep in his office or go to a hotel that very night if she needed to be alone, he would—

"Did you meet the child?" she asked sharply. She wanted him to stop talking, to stop blubbering. He stopped. He wiped his face. She had never seen his face like this: so strangely, unkindly softened; streaked with red, his eyes swollen. "No," he said. "But I tried to. Just to see him."

"What would you have done?"

"I don't know. It was just a . . . need. I wanted an answer from . . . the mother. I wanted to know. That's all."

"What do you mean, 'That's all'? Like, if you'd seen the child, met the child . . ." Greenie gasped. "Is it a boy? Another boy?"

Alan nodded. "He's a little older than George."

More than once, George had asked Greenie if he could have a big brother. She had told him that maybe one day he could have a little brother, but never a big brother. "You would always be the oldest," she said. "You would always be the first. If Daddy and I ever have other babies, and we might or we might not, you will always be our very first baby. Very first babies are very special. Forever and always, they came before all the rest. No one can ever change that."

Now she said, "George has an older brother."

"Honestly, Greenie, I don't know. That's not how I think of it. That's not the part that matters."

"No?" She didn't mean it sarcastically, though she could tell Alan heard it that way. She focused on the facts, and the conversation took on the sound of an interview. She found out that the woman was married to a wealthy doctor, so at least child support might not be an issue (though Greenie kept this thought to herself). She found out that Joya, out of sheer anger, had claimed she told Greenie about the child, that this explained Alan's message of love on the answering machine; he had been desperate, not drunk. She found out that the boy was named Jacob. Jacob's ladder. Jacob's pillow. Her mind—tired beyond the bounds of sanity—looped about with the new names Greenie must fold into her consciousness of family.

"Alan," she said suddenly. "I have to sleep now."

He stopped talking. He looked at her with such abject grief that she had to close her eyes. She felt him move closer, to sit against her, his right arm around her shoulders. It was their first true physical contact since the airport, nearly twelve hours before. It rippled through her body like a chill. "This is just too much for someone as tired as I am right now," she said. "I'm too tired to be angry. I'm too tired to be hurt. I'm too tired to . . . think."

He said, "I understand completely," and he asked if she wanted him not to sleep in their bed. She told him of course not—of course they should sleep together. Whatever they figured out from the next day forward, they would figure it out together, she assured him. As she lay down in the clean sheets he had stretched across their mattress, she felt bruised but calm. She also knew, with an unavoidable ruthlessness, that she was now the one in control. This was both ominous and soothing.

She said one more thing before she fell asleep. "Alan, I know it's still a week away, but can we skip the New Year's party?"

"Absolutely." He, too, sounded calm. They knew they would have a superficial reprieve for the day to follow; George, refueled by the thrill of new possessions, would not sleep late, never mind the change in time zone. In just a few hours, he would burst through the bedroom door and leap on their bodies, begging for pancakes, begging for someone to play his new games, solve his new puzzles, sit down and listen to him read all those brand-new books.

TWO MORNINGS AFTER CHRISTMAS, Greenie met Tina at Walter's Place, where a lawyer helped them complete and sign the transfer of Greenie's old pastry business. Walter had opened the restaurant just for them, but his chef was there as well, and Walter instructed him to cook a large, indulgent breakfast, the kind that Ray loved to eat when he was out on the ranch. Greenie thought of Ray with unexpected longing. She missed him, the way you might miss a tall strong tree that anchored the view from your living room window.

Trying to concentrate on the papers laid before her in fans and paper-clipped sheafs, Greenie felt as if she gave not a hoot about the future of the business she'd infused almost literally with her own sweat, the kitchen she had fashioned precisely to her habits and tastes, the green boxes with their delicate veils of blossoms. She felt the urge to push all the papers toward Tina and say, "Take it all, under any conditions, take it all out of my sight—and here, take all the years that go along with it. Pack it all up and take it away."

As if in a dream, here was this kind, patient, handsome man, a friend of Walter's named Gordie, explaining each and every clause yet one more time. Now and then, Tina looked intently at Greenie, as if to check for a change of heart. Greenie's weariness and lack of appetite must have appeared like reluctance. After the papers were signed, Tina embraced Greenie and asked if she'd come to the kitchen later that week for a celebratory lunch.

Greenie could still remember the expression on Tina's face when she'd entered the kitchen the first day she came to apprentice: a look of covetous awe, which had stirred in Greenie a corresponding possessiveness. "I've made this place to suit no one but me," she had said, "so I hope you like it, too." How easily she seemed to be giving it up—for a comforting amount of money, with a modest share of profits and the right to take back her name in the future, all this was true—yet she felt a sense of foreboding. She had been so certain, back then, of what "suited" her. What in the world would suit her now?

After Walter had closed the door behind Tina and Gordie, he spun around dramatically and said, "Before we break out the champagne— even though I should be scolding you for sealing the deal on your expatriate status out there in the wagon-train boonies—I have a confession to make. That was him."

Greenie smiled; Walter's theatrics were irresistible. "Who was who?"

"Gordie. It's *him*. The guy I've been *telling* you about, the one I've been *seeing*. The one whose name I wouldn't tell you because I wasn't really sure what was what. So, what did you think?"

"Oh my," she said. "Well, cute. That's for sure. Nice. Smart. And he must be crazy about you, because even I know that lawyers charge a hell of a lot more than two hundred dollars just to shake your hand." She kissed Walter on the cheek. "So when's the date?"

"For heaven's sake, we're not hetero college sweethearts looking to register at Bergdorf, lay in the layette and all that."

"And I'm not lining up to be your bridesmaid, Walter. But am I the last to know?" Greenie sat down again. Hugo, who had long since cleared the table, was back in the kitchen; preparations for lunch sounded like a percussive free-for-all. If she'd had more energy, she might have offered to help, just to spy on Hugo for inspiration. Ray would have loved Eggs Hugo, a layering of brown bread, rare beef, roast peppers, and hollandaise sauce.

"No, no, it's still kind of secret," said Walter. "But we've been seeing each other a lot. We spent Christmas Day at my place, just us. Scott's back in California for the week—a break I definitely needed from playing surrogate dad to the grunge poet laureate of Bank Street. So I fumigated the place and decorated up the wazoo, half Martha, half Bauhaus, and it was . . ." Walter sat down across from her. "Romantic. Simple as that."

Greenie was pleased to see Walter blushing. She put a hand on one of his. "Walter, that's fantastic. What's to keep secret?"

Walter reminded her about the lawyer's ex-partner, who lived in the neighborhood and was still getting over the breakup. "Thirteen *years* they were together. In my world that's a monument, that's *Rushmore*. So I'd be cruel to trumpet this thing from the rooftops. Though boy would I ever love to do just that! A whole brass *band*. The Boston *Pops*."

"He treats you well? He knows how lucky he is?"

"Sometimes I think we are so compatible that we don't even need to speak of the future. At this point." Abruptly, Walter sat up and stared straight at Greenie. "Oh my stars. The future! You! You and the home-town Romeo!"

"Oh Walter. No. That is the furthest thing from my mind."

"What do you mean, no? No what? No, don't go there? No, he's a psycho? No, mind my own beeswax?"

"No future. Not that kind. It's just a dormant crush. I don't know what I was saying when I told you I'd fallen in love. It's just . . ." If she'd been petty, Greenie could have told Walter about Alan's shocking news, but she feared that Walter might gloat, remind her that he'd always suspected there was something undeserving, some fundamental fault in the man. Not unlike George, Walter often saw the world in primary colors.

"It was just a passing thing," she said, understanding now just how big a lie this was. "I'm not sure I told you, because I've been so knocked out the past two months—all those turkeys and stuffings and cookies and pies—but Alan's getting his act together. It's taken him more time than I would have liked, but he's definitely moving out with us soon."

"Well," said Walter. "if I were him—though, lordy, am I ever *not*—I'd get my Freudian derriere on that plane and pronto!"

"Yes, me too," said Greenie, and she left it at that.

Now that Alan had told her his messy story—worse, confided in her that he'd had his fears about the other child for over a year—he had left her almost no choice but to forgive him. In one way she felt terrible for him, filled with pity; thank God a woman couldn't find herself in such a plight. But who wouldn't feel the urge to boot the man out, to let him twist in the wind, hoist himself on his own petard, stew in his bitter juices? All the angry euphemisms lined up in Greenie's brain like cars before the Lincoln Tunnel at rush hour. Yes, she thought, Alan had better get his ass in gear, bite the bullet, fish or cut bait. Go west, young man, and pronto! Except that he wasn't so young, and neither was she. *Life is short*, Ray liked to say, *but here's worse news: what remains of it gets shorter all the time. It does.*

SHE RETURNED TO ZINC SKIES, a garden glazed with snow, a kitchen (her own) colonized by spiders, and her first e-mail from Charlie: *happy new year. i missed you. too much. see you thursday with wb's but call sooner.* She e-mailed back, *I missed you too. New York was bleak. Come to the kitchen on Thursday. Bring me another gift?*

On Thursday, the sandwiches Greenie made were pork tenderloin with chipotle mustard, the soup a purée of beets and pears with Beaujolais wine and dill. For dessert, she made lemon wafers, rosewater marshmallows, and Amazon cake powdered with cocoa. Ray said, eyeing her preparations that morning, "Fancy-schmancy. That soup looks like something we'd serve to folks from the White House."

Greenie said simply, "Thank you."

Four hours later, she heard the Water Boys enter the dining room—their voices, as usual, more raucous than those of any other group. Not long after, she heard their soup spoons clattering too often and too emphatically. As courses were served and plates were cleared, she stayed away from the kitchen door.

When Maria went out to refill coffee cups, Greenie retreated to her office. She stood by the window, looking at the mountains, waiting. Almost immediately, she heard Charlie's footsteps, and then his hand came down on the sill beside her. When he pulled it away, there was the skipping stone from Circe.

"I wish I could have you back," he said. "I never quite had you, I know that, but all the same, I wish I could have you back. I guess that's obvious by now. I feel like I had you first, or I could have. I feel like it's just not fair."

She turned around. "Don't talk about it in terms of having. Or fairness. You sound like George." She was appalled to find herself scolding him; perhaps it was her last, feeble attempt at resistance.

"I'm sorry." He looked sad, but irritated as well. He crossed his arms.

"Don't be," she said, and quickly, because she knew just how long it took for Maria to refill the Water Boys' coffee cups, Greenie uncrossed his arms and put them around her back. She kissed him forcefully, without a hint of regret, because she wanted him to make no mistake about her intentions, and she stepped away. Gently, she laid a hand against his mouth and pointed toward the kitchen, showing him out. "Later," she said.

What she saw on his face, before he left, was shock more than anything else, but that night he was in her bed till four in the morning.

She assumed that she had forgotten his body, but she hadn't. His hips were wider, the veins in his legs and hands more pronounced, and there were various scars he might or might not have had since childhood, but the hair, nearly everywhere, was still a rosy blond, his nipples perfectly oval, his fingernails bluish along the crescent cuticles. How strange the recognition felt. The one thing she knew she had never forgotten was the squareness of his joints. As the two of them had bungled through their first embrace, beside a stone wall in the Maine woods, he had cried out quietly when one knee struck a rock hidden by a layer of twigs and leaves. Greenie had helped him hold the knee until the pain subsided. Briefly, they had laughed. She'd noticed then that his knees—and his elbows, too, when she had reached to cup them in her hands—seemed blunt and hard as stones themselves. This one memory she'd kept all along.

NOW SHE WOULD ARRIVE AT THE MANSION having slept very little, if at all, with swollen eyes and lips, with aching limbs and heart. She thought about Alan more than she had in their first months apart. As angry as she felt, her guilt was stronger. It did not really matter that she had found out about this Marion and her child—the child!—because only a self-righteous fool would equate Greenie's infidelity with that one. No, this was *not* revenge.

It took Ray just a week to guess. It was a Friday, and there was a bluster of snow in the pink morning air as she arrived. To her astonishment, Ray was already on his stool, reading his newspapers. According to his official schedule, circulated by Mary Bliss, the governor would have a short day in the capital, then head out to the ranch to check on the calves born that week. But an earlier morning for Ray had never before meant an earlier raid on the kitchen.

He'd helped himself to the remains of a vegetable terrine and a beef stroganoff.

"Ray, what are you doing here so early?"

"Too cold to run, and I am sick to death of the treadmill. I'll ride off extra this weekend. Somehow ridin' in the cold don't freeze your butt so bad."

"That's because your butt is up against another living creature who *is* freezing its butt off," said Greenie.

"Girl, don't talk horses to me. Your son knows a hell of a lot more about horses than you do. Bet you did not know that in Mexico they call a Palomino an Isabella. Or that George Washington's warhorse was an Arab named Magnolia. I sure as hell did not. Hey, Magnolia! Takes a mighty secure man to ride a horse into battle with a name like that; well, to ride a horse into battle at all. You watch out or I'll send Small to the ranch to study up. Like Rumpelstiltskin. You would never see that boy again, no you would not."

Greenie had brought together ingredients for cherry bread. It was a variation on Irish soda bread, baked in a cast-iron skillet with dried cherries and pepitas instead of raisins and caraway seeds. At lunch, she would serve it with a spinach gorgonzola salad (the dressing sweet, to appease Ray) and a veal roast studded, porcupine fashion, with long, thin slivers of garlic, ginger, and chili pepper. She'd heard everything Ray said, but her body was a fugue of memory: fingertips, kneecaps, soles of feet, palms of hands, eyebrows, the hairs at the very top of her spine, every part of her playing its own hectic tune.

When Ray had been quiet for several seconds, Greenie turned around. He was chewing his food, but he was also staring at her, squinting, unsmiling. "Nor would you see that boy—or so much of him—if Alan were to find out what kind of cookin' you appear to be doing outside my kitchen."

"Ray," she said, a quiet warning. Just because there was no fooling Ray did not mean she owed him explanations. "I don't want to talk about this."

He laughed rudely. "Boy oh howdy you don't. I'd bet the ranch you don't."

"Fine. You need to tell me you disapprove? Now you have." She crossed the room to the sink. She ran water briefly into a large bowl. She put two towels in to soak, then squeezed them out and laid them across the bowls of dough. "So, would you fire me?"

"Oh please, let's not get dramatic here, Greenie. I'm thinking about your son. I'm thinking about that husband of yours, who just needs the well-placed steel toe of a Lucchese boot to get his ass in gear. I'm not sure you tried that hard when he was out here last summer. Mystified me just a little, it did."

"How would you know? Did you bug my bed? Does my daw-see-ay now include my pillow talk? My bathroom talk with George, my views on cavities and bath toys and drinking milk? And what would you know about marriage and monogamy and what it's like to be the number one parent?"

"Who says I know nothing about monogamy?" said Ray.

Greenie carried his dishes to the sink. "Sorry. That was low."

"You do not know me that well," said Ray. "You think I'm a western chauvinist gas-guzzling stripper-craving horny old phony cowpoke blowhard. You do."

Greenie couldn't help laughing.

"You do not take me seriously because you'd never vote for me if I didn't keep you employed. You 'like' me, you find me funny and generous and charming, right? You might even concede I have a decent if misused brain in my head. But a high-paid cavalier dilettante, that's me."

Greenie looked directly at Ray for the first time since he had alluded to Charlie. She did not believe he was seriously angry, but he had never spoken so aggressively to her.

"Well today," he said, "here's what I think of you. I think you are a never-tested righteous-thinking petunia-garden liberal with a conscience like a Barcalounger. You got talent and smarts, you got kindness, you're a good mom, but that ain't everything. It just ain't."

She could not have spoken if Ray had poked her in the chest with one of his antique cavalry sabers.

"Oenslager, he's not a bad man, I'm not saying that," Ray said. "I suppose that's part of the lure. That he's not your typical bad-boy rebellion. And no, before you get all feminist-righteous on me, I do not intend to say a word to him. I know my church from my state."

"So tell me what you do intend," said Greenie, speaking softly to steady her voice.

"I'm just putting you on notice," he said. "Notice, I mean to say, that you need to think mighty hard about what you are doing with your wonderful life. Excuse the cheap Gary Cooper reference."

"Jimmy Stewart."

"Right. Jimmy Stewart."

They stared each other down from across the kitchen.

"Notice taken," she said.

"Fair," he said. "My conscience goes forward clean as a plate licked by a hungry coonhound. Yours is your business. It is." He stood, slapped his stack of newspapers, then gathered them up. "You know—and I am not sayin' this describes you, but there are a mighty lot of folk around these days who just don't think they have to make choices. Your Water Boy's got a point when he gets to ranting about resorts and fountains and lawns and the got-to-have-it-all greed in these parts. But it's easy to be smug when you come from where the *all* is taken for granted. You should give that a good thought or two. My advice, welcome or not."

Ray squinted at Greenie again, as if she were fading before his eyes, and then he startled her by dropping his newspapers back on the counter, crossing the room, and clamping his large callused hands on the sides of her head. He kissed her so fast, hard, on one cheek, that by the time she gasped, he had already pulled away.

"That's not harassment, by the way, Ms. Duquette. That's a half apology. Half. Are we straight?"

Greenie said, "Hardly straight, but I get your point."

"I got to tell you, Greenie, I had my eye on your paramour for Mary Bliss. She needs a good guy bad. You already got one." He held up his hands. "Okay, end of tirade. Lunch looks stupendous. And would you fax McNally the recipe for that dude-ranch meat loaf you made last night? His version tastes like it's held together with mink oil."

Left alone, Greenie stared out a window, waiting for something to pass through her empty view: anything to distract from her shame. When nothing, not even a cloud, would oblige, she turned and put the pans of bread in the oven. As she closed the door, the phone rang.

Darling was the first word out of Charlie's mouth, a word of such old-fashioned tenderness that it made Greenie ache with happiness. Her mother had called her *darling*—but what a different, far less intimate endearment it had been, for her mother had called everyone darling, from her husband to the girls who passed hors d'oeuvres at her parties. "Darling," when Charlie said it, felt like a whirlpool of rapture. Whenever Greenie answered the phone, he would say just that word, and Greenie would say "You," which was her way of expressing that he was now the world to her, that he was the one for whom she was always waiting, that he was the high cliff on which she was happy to stand and from which she had come to realize she might, at any moment, jump. Jump with open eyes and outspread arms. *Anything,* she might have been saying, *everything, anything, all.*

Greenie and Alan had married each other in a secular ceremony, their words egalitarian, rational, and modern, but privately, she'd always had a soft spot for the antique Episcopal vows, most of all that ravishing phrase *with all that I am and all that I have.* In that moment your beloved was gravity itself, pulling you in, holding the wide world together, everything held on the surface of a spinning sphere. "Burn the bridges, damn the torpedoes, just take me; take everything!" you were saying. "If it isn't yours, it couldn't possibly matter."

FOURTEEN

ENTROPY, ATROPHY, FECUNDITY—what was that word for nature run organically amok? Whatever the social equivalent, this was the insidious force that threatened Walter's life, or his peace of mind, as the snow shrank away and the buds on the trees began their suggestive swelling.

First and foremost, there was Gordie's reticence, which Walter could no longer see as a sign of sensitivity. It was more like a sign of stagnation. Back in January—high fireplace season—Walter had decided that he felt flush enough to close the restaurant for one night in order to throw a dinner party for his friends . . . and for Gordie's.

"Sounds terrific, but what's the occasion?" Gordie asked.

"You don't have to have an occasion to throw a party," said Walter. "But if you want one, well, why not let the occasion be . . . us?"

"That's a very sweet idea, Walter."

Walter waited. He wasn't hearing, *Yes, absolutely! Why not on Valentine's Day?* "I think I sense a looming *but,*" he said.

"Well, no, but—"

"There it is! The *but*! 'Now here comes the zeppelin.' That's what Granna used to say whenever we started to make excuses."

Gordie laughed. "My mom wasn't so original. We got the old saw about saving our buts for the billygoat. We'd drive her nuts with bleating."

Gordie loved Walter's stories about his grandmother. Walter, in turn, enjoyed stories about Gordie's big, bursting-at-the-seams Catholic family. He had already nurtured fantasies about flying with Gordie out to Montana, where most of his siblings still lived. They sounded like a civilized, educated, miraculously unjaded clan, so it didn't seem unrealistic that Walter might one day be a welcome guest at Unsworth family weddings, christenings, perhaps even Christmas parties. Walter might take up skiing again.

"So? What do you think?" He hated to press, but he had no choice.

"Well," said Gordie slowly, "the only thing is that my friends, for so long, were . . . well, they became Stephen's friends as well."

"Of course they did," said Walter.

"So it still feels awkward to . . ."

Walter realized that Gordie, once again, was hoping he would finish the thought, lending it legitimacy. "To . . . ?"

"To invite them to a big, formal affair where I'm not with Stephen and I'm not, well, I'm not alone."

"I note your choice of the word *affair*," Walter said tartly. "And so, does this mean your friends, after all this time, think you *are* alone? Think, perhaps, that you're suffering in solitude, as you seem to feel you deserve? Gordie, my love, life goes on! Has no one ever slung that cliché in your face? Because you need to hear it loud and clear!"

Gordie laughed nervously. "Walter, you have a very concise way of hitting the painful nail right on its head."

"Gordie, how old are we now? Old enough to have seen a lot of sewage ooze under the bridge, are we not? If anyone knows about seizing the moment, it's people like us. For Stephen, that meant having a kid—and you know what? Good for him, I say. So what does it mean for you and me? Not waffling around the bush, I bet you'd agree with me, right?"

They'd been having a midnight dinner at Gordie's apartment, as they did two or three times a week; facing each other across the table wasn't the best situation for talk like this, Walter knew, because they became accidentally adversarial. "I don't know about you," he went on, "but I need a very soft place to rest my overworked anatomy." He picked up the wine bottle and took it to the living room.

Gordie followed with their glasses. "You're completely right, Walter, and maybe it's time you called my sorry bluff." He sat down not on the couch beside Walter but on the armchair across the coffee table, only replicating their positions over dinner.

"Okay then, buster, I'm calling it now."

Gordie did not smile. He refilled their glasses. "Walter, I have to confess something. Lately I've been feeling like I might . . ."

Walter held his breath.

". . . I might be falling into a kind of depression. I mean, I'm working as well as ever, business is good—practically too good—and I have a great time with you, but it's like I, like I didn't end it with Stephen the way I should have; like I did it so fast I left a big piece of my soul in that life, and I can't figure out how to go back and retrieve it."

Walter worked to conceal his relief. This was no fun, but it was progress. As gently as he could, he said, "You're not telling me you want to go back to Stephen, are you?"

"No, I'm not. Definitely not. But I'm just not up for replacing him. Yet. And I feel like that's what you're hoping."

That was exactly what Walter had been hoping, but what fool would say so? "I haven't exactly suggested we merge closets, have I?"

"No, you haven't. But I have a feeling that if Scott weren't a part of the picture—and listen, Walter, I am so impressed with what you've done for that boy—well, if he weren't in the picture, I have a feeling you would. Suggest we move in together."

Walter felt a great sinking. He was tired of calculations. "And you also have a feeling that if I did, you would say no. Without much ambivalence."

Abruptly, Gordie stood up, and for one blessed second it looked as if he would come around the table and sit beside Walter, embrace him, tell him he was mistaken there; but instead he covered his face with his long, smooth, lovely, lawyerly hands and let out a muffled scream.

So, thought Walter, almost calmly, he is going to break my heart again. He is going to do it because, once again, I've set myself up to *let* him do it.

"Walter, I'm sorry, so much of this is timing."

But Gordie had not gone on to tell Walter this was it, it was over, the usual mortifying severance. No. He'd said that he needed not to feel rushed, he wanted a little "break," and Walter—oh how desperate could he *be*?—Walter had meekly agreed. For a month, it was decided, they would settle back into their separate lives. And then (oh really, as *if*) they would "see."

Matters with Scott were, in a way, equally dicey. Walter tried to remind himself of all the extenuating circumstances—Scott's age, his trophy-hausfrau mother, his post-adolescent oblivion—but the bottom line was that after a month or two of good behavior, Scott had rapidly settled into predictable teenage slapdashery. Now that Walter was home a good deal more often, the worst of Scott's traits became even more conspicuous.

One night, Walter came in after midnight to an apartment that, except for the slot of radiance under Scott's door, was dark. This was fine—or would have been if Walter had not twisted his ankle on a foreign object in what should have been a clear path to the light switch. When he yelped, the laughter in Scott's room stopped for an instant, then resumed at a lower pitch. After turning on the light, Walter identified the offending object as a backpack plunked in the middle of the floor. Morticia's, no doubt. He left it there. Pick it up, he mused, and Cousin It might leap from the tie-dyed patch pocket.

There were CDs on the couch, beer bottles and Chinese take-out containers on the coffee table. With delicate revulsion, Walter lifted a greasy chopstick from the rug. In the kitchen, he found an empty sink, but candy bar wrappers and a bottle of hot sauce had been left on the counter. Two of Granna's samplers hung askew, as if there'd been a commotion nearby. As he assessed the disarray, Walter heard scratching on the inside of Scott's door. Without showing a face or saying a word, someone opened the door just enough for the dog to squeeze his way out. The door closed, and T.B. sauntered into the kitchen. Oddly, he wasn't wearing his collar.

"Hello, boy. How's life in the den of hormones?" Walter, whose ankle had recovered, kneeled down to hug The Bruce. "So what's up, you pawn your collar for a box of Omaha steaks?" He stood and frowned toward Scott's door. He threw the candy wrappers in the garbage and put away the hot sauce.

In the morning, the beer bottles and take-out containers were still in the living room, though the backpack had vanished. T.B. emerged from Scott's room once again, this time wearing his collar. Scott emerged wearing a begonia-pink T-shirt declaring, I'D RATHER BE HERE NOW.

"Than where? Or, for that matter, than when?" said Walter, looking up from the paper.

"Excuse me?" said Scott. "Like, top o' the morning to you, too, dude."

"Your shirt, your slogan du jour. Last I looked, your preference was to be in Manitoba. But I see you've changed your mind. Just what does *this* mean? Is it some kind of Zen message? No matter where you are, things are always hunky-dory? Something like that?"

Walter wasn't sure whether Scott's smile betrayed approval *(Exacti-mento, dude!)* or mockery *(You hopelessly left-brained fool!).*

"Yeah, in a way." Scott shrugged oafishly and poured himself a cup of coffee. "You're like, so totally literal, Uncle Walt."

"Knowing how to follow directions is something that comes in handy, young man. Understanding and processing all the messages around you."

"Hey, I know my 'Walk' from my 'Don't Walk.' I know a third rail when I see one. The life-or-death stuff, no sweat." Scott addressed his confident views to the interior of the refrigerator, his back to Walter, playing air guitar as he compared the merits of a half-empty container of strawberry-kiwi yogurt with those of a tinfoil tray of old french fries.

"Scott, let's not refrigerate the entire West Village."

"Word!" Scott declared, then deftly grabbed both offerings and spun full circle on one foot, slapping the door shut with the opposite knee. "T-t-toong, t-t-toong, t-t-toong toong *toong*," he chanted softly, a per-fect cymbal, as he bopped to the table and sat down. He pushed the fries toward Walter. "Want some?"

"Ugh, no," said Walter. "But thanks, I suppose."

Scott proceeded to eat the cold fries, dipping them into the yogurt.

"That cannot be good."

Scott pointed to the slogan on his chest. "Be happy with what you have and in the present moment, that's the message. This"—he gestured at the food before him—"represents the here and now."

"And what," said Walter, "does that represent?" He gestured toward the coffee table, the white boxes of petrified rice and jellified lo mein noodles.

"Oh. Yeah. Sorry. I thought you'd be out for the night. On Tuesdays, you usually . . . Hey. Sorry."

"Okay, Scott, but even if I hadn't come home, did we have the talk about vermin? I really don't want mice in the here and now."

His mouth working away, Scott nodded. "Gotcha," he said, allowing half of a masticated fry to escape. T.B. was there to retrieve it.

"So," said Walter, determined not to be the big bad uncle, "are you having fun with . . . Sonya?"

"Yeah. She's cool." Scott stopped chewing and smiled slyly at Walter.

"You know, she knows you, like, can't stand her. She says it's okay. Older men are threatened by her looks. They don't like her till they get to know her."

Walter snorted. "Threatened by her looks?"

"Guys associate her look with death. It's like an unconscious, archetypal thing. The dark-haired, light-skinned lady. It gives 'em the creeps, but it's totally irrational. They're, like, kowtowing to the purely symbolic."

"Ooh, that sounds dangerous," said Walter.

"I know it sounds bogus, and I sort of agree? But I also get what she means. The succubus, the siren. She plays with it, kind of like a controlled experiment of the self. It's even got me doing a little mythological research. I might write a song about it. But, hey, is it true you can't stand her?"

"Look, I'm going to have to plead the Fifth on this one. And you'd better plead your way into the shower. Hugo's expecting you in fifteen minutes."

Scott stuffed the last fistful of fries in his mouth and bolted for his room, leaving Walter, once again, to pick up all the food containers. Was this a battle worth fighting? Walter calmed and amused himself by composing a letter to Dear Abby. He could sign it *Parent in loco*. "Word!" said Walter to no one, since even T.B. had deserted him for the younger, cuter model.

WALTER INVITED THIRTY-NINE GUESTS for the first Friday in March. At first, he could not decide whether to seat them all together—in one great quadrangle, Knights of Columbus style—or spread them around the room in clusters of four and eight. He decided on the latter, in part because he'd also decided that if Gordie wasn't a party to the party, why not let Scott invite a few pals? But just to be safe, he'd let the punksters entertain themselves. There were limits, thought Walter, to the power of assimilation.

Hugo planned a five-course meal: smoked duck, oyster stew, roast beef with mashed yams, a salad of apples with beets and blue cheese, then chocolate banana cream pie. Rich, rich, and richer still. Ben made pitchers of martinis and set aside thirty-five bottles of a tried-and-true

Napa cabernet, pure purple velvet, and an Oregonian pinot gris, grassy and effervescent.

Of course, it *would* have to snow.

All morning, the sky had been a sturdy, ominous gray. Toward noon the first flakes fell, their descent a sly, flirtatious meandering. But Walter knew the ruse. He walked out the front door and shook his fist. "Gods!" he shouted at the sky. "Do you never, never have mercy?"

"Mercy from heaven? Why, what a daft notion," Walter heard in reply.

Bonny Prince Charlie, just down the sidewalk in front of his shop, was also regarding the sky. "You're not worried about tonight."

"Oh people are sissies," said Walter. "Or, I should say, a lot of my dear friends are sissies. They don't like to ruin their shoes. Or they're certain they'll be stranded, the subways and taxis all paralyzed in apocalyptic drifts of snow."

"I'll be there. You'll have me, at the very least."

Walter, in a moment of neighborly beatitude, had invited Bonny. He had also invited Greenie's husband and the puppy woman, who appeared to be friendly with both of those men. Walter had caught sight of her more than once through the window of the bookshop, and he had chatted with her twice when she was walking Greenie's husband's dog (for whom T.B. had the futile hots).

By six, the tables were set, the stew was ready, and Walter had managed to run home, shower, and change. On the way back to the restaurant, in the chilly, windy dark, he marveled at an hour's transformation. The cars along Bank Street had been engulfed by two tenderly undulating dunes, sparkling like quartz, spilling over to fill the sidewalks. Falling as fiercely as ever, the snow made a faint hissing sound as it replenished the drifts. Overhead, the larger boughs creaked like antique doors.

Quite thoughtfully, McLeod had shoveled the sidewalk from his shop to Walter's Place, but the rest of the way was impassable. Walter and T.B. walked straight down the middle of the street. Though it had yet to be plowed, tires had pressed the snow into a stippled, corrugated track, still a clean and brilliant white. Ahead of them, the wind would knock loose great chunks of snow from the branches above, spilling them onto the road with explosive glee.

Four of Walter's least rugged friends had called before three, from

Hoboken, to say that they feared the PATH train would close. Now Ben told him that seven more had canceled. Walter put away place settings, rearranged name cards, and pushed the empty tables against a wall. He lit candles and stoked the fires that Ben had laid.

Alan Glazier was the first to arrive, bearing a bottle of wine. (Walter refrained from joking about the infamous coals.) Right behind him, thank heaven, came several of Walter's old acting buddies. Two still acted, one a relentlessly successful villain leapfrogging from one soap to the next; the others had taken their talent to advertising and public relations. Out of a much larger original clique, they were the only ones left standing, not just alive but healthy. He hugged them one by one and called Ben over with his tall glass pitcher. "Mulled cider ought to have been the cocktail tonight," joked Walter. "Eskimo pies for dessert. Maybe we should all go out later and have an igloo-building contest."

There was a commotion of stamping at the door. Walter let the men hang their own coats. When he stopped to listen to the music, he realized that Ben had put on an Ella Fitzgerald Christmas CD. "Very, very funny!" he called across the room. "Get out the mistletoe, why don't you!" He laid an extra mat before the door, and when he stood up, right there, holding a large potted plant wrapped in green tissue, stood Bonny.

"A man of his word," said Walter. "What's this?" As he pulled off the tissue paper, he thanked McLeod for shoveling the walk. "Is this heather? I'm sorry to laugh, but *heather*?"

"I like to live up to the cultural stereotypes," said McLeod. "White heather's for luck, my mum always told us."

"Thank you," said Walter. "Luck is something you can never have too much of. Kind of like mashed potatoes."

"Luck is like a good dog," replied McLeod, thickening his accent so that *good* would have rhymed with *shrewd*. "Na take it for granted when it's by your side. Then long and loyal may it bide. . . . Again, my mum. I think she invented that one."

"Well, amen. Bet I'd like your mum." Walter carried McLeod's plant to the longest table and centered it there, replacing a glass globe filled with white tulips. As he went to dispose of the tissue paper, he realized that snow had dampened the paper and its color had bled onto his hands and linen shirt. They were splotched with forest green.

He closed his eyes and willed himself to enjoy the evening thoroughly, come what may. When he opened them, he saw the heather. It was lovely. He looked around: everything, everyone looked lovely.

For the next half hour, Walter hugged and kissed, hung the women's coats, passed a tray of cheese puffs and cherry tomatoes stuffed with crab. He had no time for a drink, and he forgot about his ruined shirt and the dozen friends he'd lost to the storm. The sadness he'd felt about Gordie's absence seemed to have fallen away, as if by special dispensation. Just after Hugo gave him a nod from the kitchen door, he went to the window and peered out. The street, empty of people and traffic, was dazzling. The snow continued to fall, and where it clung to the branches of the wide sycamores, the slender gingko and pear trees, it etched a vivid urban forest. "Oh my stars," Walter whispered. His breath clouded the window, then vanished. He felt the urge to breathe again and draw on the pane a transient design or, boyishly, his own initials. He turned around and called out, "Dinner, my friends, is about to be served!" Such glorious words. There was a smattering of applause, and people jostled one another at the tables, eagerly seeking their place cards.

Impulsively, Walter instructed Ben to help him push the tables together into one large clump and told everyone to sit wherever they pleased.

ONE DAY IN HIGH SCHOOL, when the snow had fallen so mercilessly that afternoon classes were canceled, Walter had come home to find Granna talking to her husband. She was sitting at the kitchen table with a cup of tea and the framed picture that Walter had never seen anywhere other than on her bedroom dresser. Granna kept the ornate silver frame so rigorously polished that you could catch fragments of your reflection in its minutest leaf or blossom.

She stood and greeted Walter with pleasure, taking his wet coat and draping it over a radiator. "Off with your coat, and I vill make hot chocolate." She started toward the stove but then turned to pick up her husband's picture. She kissed it quickly, smiled at Walter, and set the photo on a bookshelf against the wall, safe from spills and careless reachings.

"I talk to your grandfather about many things," said Granna as she stirred the pan of milk. "It may be I say more to him since he is dead than when he was alive."

"Was he a big talker?" Walter was the one who felt embarrassed.

"Oh no. More a big reader. But he liked to read out loud. He read me a little bit of everysing. A little bit newspaper, a little bit history, a little bit Bible. English and German both. I miss all the little bits." She concentrated on stirring the milk as it heated, then filling a cup. The spoon sounded so musical, so soothing and civilized, against her shapely porcelain cups.

When she set the cup on its saucer in front of Walter, she said, "He needed a listener for his reading, I think. I was a listening wife. It's a good thing, a listening wife. Listening husband, that is good too." She tapped Walter's hand with one finger and gave him an encouraging smile.

He thanked her for the chocolate, wishing he knew the right thing to say. Years later, he was ashamed that he'd never offered to read to Granna himself. What an insensitive lout he had been! A little bit Shakespeare. A little bit *National Geographic*. A little bit Sherlock Holmes. Or perhaps that wasn't what she'd have liked; maybe the reading-aloud was a part of the marital intimacy she'd had with her husband. Maybe it had been like an ongoing courtship.

But these were thoughts Walter had much later, after Granna died. That day in the kitchen, all he thought of was loneliness: spending a life without finding one person he could talk to in solitary kinship again and again, face-to-face or, if the worst should happen, at least through a picture frame. How will I ever find that one person if I can never marry? he thought. What if no one ever needed Walter—needed him to read *or* to listen?

THE CONVERSATION AT THE PARTY was dense and eccentric, the talk of friends who no longer need the ordinary everyday topics. The rich food led them to talk about the diets of vultures, parrots, and Aztec kings; parrots and kings led them to argue about the future of zoos and the future of elections. In smaller groups, they rhapsodized about Shakespeare's sonnets, laughed at Arnold Schwarzenegger's political ambitions, marveled at how C. S. Lewis had found God, and listened to the soap-opera villain recount in detail how the entire crew of the *Endeavor* managed to survive shipwreck in conditions that made the weather that night look like July in Ibiza.

And then, long after Walter had forgotten they should already be there, the door blew open and in sauntered Scott, Morticia, and another teenage couple. A gust of wind entered with them. In the arresting chill, as the dinner guests turned away from their meal, Walter realized that his friends might see the newcomers as crashers, as a band of *Clockwork Orange* hoodlums. He stood and said, "For those of you who haven't met him already, allow me to introduce my nephew, Scott, and his . . . entourage." The word *henchpeople* had come to mind.

"Welcome!" someone called out. "Get the hell in here and close that door!"

"Do any of the lot of you wear watches?" whispered Walter as he pressed the sodden group toward the coatroom.

"Uncle Walt, we had to check out Central Park in this totally awesome blizzard. It is so unreal up there!"

"Get your overclothes off before you flood the place with all that unreality," said Walter, though his main intention was to move them out of sight for a moment or two. "Boots, young fellow," he said to the male companion. "Those boots will go no farther than this. If your socks are wet, I've probably got a spare pair in my office."

"Thanks, Grandma," said Scott with a sly smile. "Hey, cool shirt. Is that like some kind of batik, or did your pen explode?"

Walter looked down; he'd forgotten about the tissue paper disaster. "It's yours after tonight. But don't try that bait-and-switch on me." As the other three peeled off their parkas and droopy sweaters, Walter whispered to Scott, "This is really beyond rude, I have to tell you."

"Sorry, man, but don't you ever get like a kid when it snows?"

Walter sighed. "Well, you have a point. Just go into the kitchen and ask Hugo for plates. Serve yourselves. Your table's back there." He pointed. "Hello there, Sonya. And you would be . . . ?"

The two tagalongs, Tyrone and Lisa, had firm enough handshakes, but one of them—or probably all four—smelled of marijuana. *Later,* Walter scolded himself. And really, what did he expect? The tykes from *Mary Poppins*?

By the time Walter sat down again, Alan Glazier was telling the others about his son, George, how he had suddenly become quite shy in his kindergarten. He was far ahead of his peers in his ability to read, but perhaps this had only served to isolate him socially.

"Well, what are you doing so far away from him, if I may ask? Don't you suppose that has something to do with it?" asked one of Walter's actor friends.

Alan laughed nervously. "I'll be moving out there soon."

"Yes, but what kind of consolation is 'soon' to a five-year-old?"

"I'm sure a five-year-old is far more complicated than either you or I can imagine," Walter suggested. "We, after all, are not parents. As I am discovering in the most explicit fashion." He looked ruefully toward the back table, where the teenagers were happily emptying a bottle of wine. "Crimonitely!" he exclaimed, to the open amusement of his friends. He excused himself and made a beeline for Scott.

"I can be closed for underage drinking, my dear nephew. I believe you know this," he said. "This is not precisely my living room." He picked up the bottle as they clutched their glasses possessively.

"Hey, it's called Walter's Place, right? So, why not? And by the way, I'm twenty-two," said Sonya. T.B. lounged in her lap. She was scratching his jowls, and he was drooling in ecstasy.

Ignoring Morticia, Walter took Scott to the kitchen, where Hugo was carefully dissecting the pies. "Look, Scott. I thought that including you and your friends in my party would be something you could appreciate—by which I mean have a good time while minding your manners. I'm not even going to ask who's stoned here, because I presume you all are—"

"You won't call Dad," said Scott, sounding plaintive.

"Of course not! Or not, I should say, if you start minding your p's and q's. This . . . this Sonya, I fear—"

"Uncle Walt, you introduced us."

Walter wanted to scream. "I don't know why I should expect to be treated like the cool dude you once believed I was, but the alternative is that you treat me like a big, fat, square-as-baloney parent, okay? Meaning . . . oh for crying out loud, Scott, *meaning* that if you don't behave, I can ship you back to your real parents. Message loud and clear?"

"Deafening." Scott had gone from fearful back to cocky. He leaned close to Walter and said, "Baloney's round, man."

"That's all she wrote, my friend." Walter turned away decisively and took a tray from Hugo. The chocolate and banana custards had been marbled in such a way that the wedges of pie resembled plump triangular bees. His chef gave him a wry smile. Hugo's family story had always been murky to Walter, though he knew it involved a couple of grown children and a jilted wife or two.

Walter thrust the tray at Scott. "Practice your serving technique, Junior."

Not long after their access to booze was cut off, the teenagers left. Walter's last glimpse of them was of Scott and Morticia framed in the doorway, merged in a flagrant, convoluted total-body kiss.

The party lasted till one o'clock. The two dozen guests left as a group, perhaps hoping somehow to pool their warmth against the winter night. Walter hugged them all gratefully before sending them out the door. The snow had stopped, but the wind persisted, and they wrapped their collars up around their cheeks, pulled knit hats down over eyebrows, wincing and bracing themselves. Already, Walter's memory of specific conversations was fragmentary but bright: the stained-glass-window effect of all the best parties.

Walter had just collapsed on the velvet couch, assuming that he and Ben were now alone, when the door to the men's room opened.

"I'm not sure I've ever been the last guest left standing." McLeod blushed faintly.

"It's a compliment," said Walter. "I thank you."

"Please, don't get up." McLeod looked around. "One doesn't appreciate the small touches when a restaurant's filled—as yours so often is." He examined an antique rectangular platter that hung on the wall; it had been glazed with the image of several spotted rabbits running through grass. The detail was lovely, though Walter couldn't help thinking that these helpless, adorable creatures, in the artist's eye, were about to be pounced upon by a vicious pack of hounds.

"You should publish a cookbook," said McLeod as he pulled on his coat. He looked reluctant to leave, but Walter did not invite him to linger. Walter wanted to have a brandy with Ben and recollect the evening in the solitude he had to accept as his fate yet again.

"A cookbook? What, you mean by Hugo?" Walter laughed. "I'm sorry. I don't mean he isn't outrageously talented, but we're more of the upscale-diner mind-set. None of this Mad Mario showmanship—orange clogs and Bermuda shorts fit for Babar, sweetbreads garnished with squash blossoms stuffed with cheese from the milk of Angora goats who live in the Pyrenees. Litchi sorbet veined with coconut milk and honey from Crete." Walter shivered. "Spare me."

"I know what you mean," said McLeod, "but lately I've noticed that's the sort of recipe book we're selling—what you call the diner mind-set. People want to cook closer to home. If they want Escoffier, they go out. I had a customer the other day who said she wanted a book with recipes for deviled eggs and Welsh rabbit. I hadn't a clue what she meant."

"Ah, right up our alley," said Walter. "But I'm no idiot. If I coaxed Hugo into a book, I'd lose him to some Idaho ski lodge where they charge twenty bucks for s'mores."

"S'mores?" McLeod wrapped a long dark scarf around his throat.

"Oh my dear, how long have you lived in this country? You are a babe in the culinary woods till you've had s'mores."

"Do you serve them?"

Walter laughed again. "You know, that's not a bad idea. Seems I'm obliged now to make them for *you,* my friend. But not in the dead of winter."

"Springtime then."

"You supply the campfire, we will oblige," said Walter.

McLeod nodded and smiled, but still he did not leave. "May I ask you, Walter, what in the world is 'crimonitely'? An obscure sort of mineral or antique motorcar?"

At first Walter thought he was serious, and then they fell to laughing almost at the same instant.

"I haven't laughed so much in ages as I did this evening," said McLeod. "Thank you."

"Me neither," said Walter.

"Thank you for inviting Emily too. She needs a wider world."

Walter yawned. He was curious about the puppy woman but had not a pebble of energy left. "You are welcome," he said, and struggled to his feet, apologizing that he had to boot his last guest out into the snowdrifts.

After closing the door behind McLeod, Walter looked around, realizing that he'd forgotten about T.B. The dog was nowhere to be seen. Ben, who came out from the kitchen, saw his panic and said, "Cousin Brucie left with the potheads."

Walter groaned and returned to the couch. "Without his coat." He asked Ben to bring him the brandy he'd been craving, and the two of them sat down together and joked about s'mores. The party had been a success. People had gone home happy and sated: with food, with lively silly talk, with the kind of companionship that, however brief, replenished the inner streams as they yearned toward the sea. "Heavens to Betsy," said Walter to Ben, who was putting another log on the nearest fire. "I think I just caught myself thinking in Roy Orbison. I *am* getting old."

FIFTEEN

"VIETNAM IS THE NEXT FRONTIER. I'm sort of ashamed to say so, but the thought of going over there all by myself is just terrifying."

"Nothing terrifies you, Joy. Nothing I've ever seen."

"Oh, put me in a roomful of angry teamsters and I am a fish in water," she said. "Correction. I'm a *hammerhead* in water. But this is . . . this would be like parachuting into the Arctic Circle wearing a bikini."

"You'll do fine," said Alan. "You do everything fine."

"Yeah? How about find a nice guy and settle down? Even a not-so-nice guy and settle down."

"Maybe settling down isn't really for you, Joy."

Alan recognized the silence of exasperation. His heart quickened; he wanted so desperately to have Joya completely back on his side, the sister whose provocative loyalty he must learn to stop taking for granted.

"Alan, you've seen how I live. I *am* settled down. I'm settled down *alone*."

"I'm sorry."

"Oh, for God's sake stop walking on tacks. You're reminding me too much of Mom." She paused. "Oh God. How is Mom?"

"She likes her physical therapist, but she's as pessimistic as ever. She acts like my going out west will be the end of her life. She's started talking about where she wants her ashes spread, how cremation will spare us unnecessary expense, how dying sooner than later will save us money."

Joya sighed. "That's our mom. She probably *will* die sooner when she finds out she's going to have an Asian grandchild. If I go through with this. She still lives in about 1963. In her world, the Beatles are still a bunch of scruffy boys in a Liverpool garage."

"You'll go through with it," said Alan. "And she'll be thrilled."

"Enough Mom talk," said Joya. "Listen, speaking of moms, I have to go. Feely-mealy group of single mothers who want to adopt. My lawyer recommended it, so I go and grit my teeth. I'm glad you called."

Alan had spoken to Joya only three times since his misbegotten trip to San Francisco, and neither of them had ever mentioned her false drunken assertion that she had betrayed him to Greenie. During their initial truce, back in January, she had listened quietly, never interrupting, as he told her about his confession. The only thing she said, after he finished his tale, was "Christmas Day? Wow, Alan, they say the holidays make people do irrational things, but you take the cake."

Whatever sins he had committed, however much penance he had yet to fulfill, both women had forgiven him. He would not lose sight, he told himself, of just how lucky he was.

"Joya," he said before she hung up, "what if I could go with you—to Vietnam, or wherever it is you have to go? We could be terrified together."

AS IF TO PROVE THAT HONESTY was the best policy, that telling a difficult truth could be like opening all the windows of your house on the first day of spring (as he used to tell patients before it became too painful to hear himself say), Alan felt a new resolve. He had given his patients nearly two months' notice and was guiding them through discussions of how they felt about his move. He had given each of them an appropriate referral for continuing therapy after he left.

The one patient Alan really did not want to leave behind—and it puzzled him—was Stephen. Stephen was healthy and rich and found his work exciting. Stephen had countless friends, two active still-married parents who loved him "anyway" (as he put it), two godchildren, and a dozen fellow board members on two separate not-for-profit arts organizations who revered his opinion. Stephen had fine looks, a semblance of youth, a resilient ego, and a decent sense of humor when he wasn't pissed off at the world.

But people, as Alan had once reflected to Greenie, were not at all like recipes. You could have all the right ingredients, in all the right amounts, and still there were no guarantees. Or perhaps they *were* like recipes, he pondered now, and the key to success was in finding the ingredients you had to remove, the components that turned all the others bitter, excessively salty, difficult to swallow; even too jarringly sweet. He had seen Greenie clarify butter, wash rice, devein shrimp, and meticulously snip the talons from artichoke leaves.

April first, he told Greenie—by which time his mother should be soundly on her feet again. He would be there, lock stock and barrel, or dog and baggage, on the first of April. Their earthly possessions—yes, even her big, obscenely pink chair—would follow. When he had made his declaration, early in February, she had uttered a small noise that clearly expressed surprise but sounded almost like a cry of pain, the reaction to very *bad* news.

She had exclaimed, "Oh, just a couple of months!"

Alan was amused. " 'Just'? Are you scolding me or teasing me? I know I've taken my time, but this is the way I had to do it. You know me."

"Yes," she said. "I do."

"So I thought I'd tell George, if he's there."

"Not yet," she said. "I mean, I don't think you should tell him yet. You know how he is with too much anticipation. Two months is an eternity for him."

"If you ask me, he's extremely patient for his age." As if in contradiction, George piped up in the background, demanding a story. It was later than Alan had thought. "Let me talk to him for just a minute," he said.

"I'm in my pajamas." George sounded out of breath. "Daddy, is Treehorn there?"

"Treehorn's sleeping. Do you want me to wake her up?"

George hesitated. "No. She needs her sleep for running."

"Just like you," said Alan. "So tell me what story you're reading with Mom tonight."

"The one about the pet wave."

"Pet what?"

"Wave, Daddy. It's the boy who gets a wave at the beach and takes it home to keep, but it gets mad and turns into monsters and the cat gets really scared even though it likes the fish and then the dad has to take it back in a quilt. Like a big icicle. Then the boy is going to get a cloud for a pet. And that's the end. Actually, you don't get to see him bring the cloud home."

"A pet wave. Sounds like trouble."

"It *is* trouble, Dad. That's the moral in the story."

"I haven't seen that book. Is it from the library?"

"No. It's from Charlie."

"Oh," said Alan. "Is Charlie a friend of yours from school?"

"No, Charlie is Mommy's friend, only he's my friend, too." In a rush, he said, "I have to go now, my feet are cold, good night."

"Charlie's that guy from my hometown I told you about." Greenie was back. "The water lawyer."

"A book about a pet wave from a water lawyer?"

"Ha ha," said Greenie.

"It sounds like a very weird book," said Alan, "but at least it's a departure from horses."

"You know," said Greenie, "there's nothing wrong with George's thing about horses. You should see his classmates. They're obsessed with these weird Japanese trading cards or these put-together space warriors that all have futuristic weapons. I think it may be the age of obsession, that's all."

"It's fine. I didn't mean we had to worry. George seems great." He heard George clamoring for his mother once again, for his story. "Go," he said. "Call me later."

But she didn't, and he wasn't surprised. Though his confession had, perversely, given him a certain relief, Alan was—not so perversely—afraid to bring up the subject of Marion's child. He had faith that Marion would be in touch with him soon. Her upright husband had basically promised she would. (Whom could you trust if not a guy who cured cancer?) And she lived in Berkeley, the land of spiritual and sexual freedom, the land of counter-bourgeois truth-telling, did she not?

He had decided that he would give her six months before he tried to speak with her again. He had told Greenie as much, and she had replied that this was absurd—if, in fact, he was the father. (Yes, she insisted, genes did make you a father; to hell with some New Age logic protesting otherwise.) But Greenie also understood that aggression would probably backfire. They had discussed all this in the first conversation they had on the phone after Christmas. The conversation had been almost alarmingly calm, even cool. Alan had reasoned that what made it easier than their late-night agonizings together in New York was a matter of proximity: how much less complicated not having to see (and react to) each other's facial expressions, not having to worry about whether or when they should touch each other.

STEPHEN WORE THE SMILE of someone with a happy secret. He took off his pale green jacket, doubled it with care, and laid it over an arm of the couch. He adjusted the pillows and lay down. "Guatemala!" he said, in a tone of surprise, just as his head came to rest. "So I have just found out that even single guys can adopt babies from Guatemala. Isn't that fabulous news?"

"That's great," said Alan.

"And my friend Roberto's been telling me all about the home-study. It's really more paperwork than anything else, he says. You don't have to be Erma Bombeck or even Mel Gibson to pass. He said I'd do fine; I can just be myself."

"Mel Gibson?"

"You know: the arch-conservative dad with big bucks, religion, and a certifiably female Stepford spouse."

"Well, one out of four's not bad."

Stephen laughed. Since he had started doing research on how to go about adopting a baby, he came to Alan's office filled with energy and excitement, even joy. That joy was like a great iridescent bubble, Alan knew, gorgeous but delicate. Either it would deflate gradually, to a more realistic size, as Stephen did all the necessary work, or he would find that his passion for a child was only masking his heartbreak—in which case the bubble might burst.

Alan felt uneasy. He had believed, in his gut, that Gordie would return to the relationship. He had no idea whether Stephen could have convinced Gordie to become a parent, but he had seen the two men as more than simply used to each other. They had seemed right for each other, *good* for each other, perhaps as much "in love" as two people together that long could be. Or was Alan projecting assumptions and wishes about his own marriage onto these men?

Just the week before, Stephen had declared that he knew he was finally getting past Gordie. "Not *over*—that takes much longer," he said. "But something remarkable happened yesterday. I saw him, on the other side of Sheridan Square, walking along with this big Swedish-looking guy. Not the restaurant guy, but cut from the very same mold. How well we always knew our weaknesses! Only mine were less pernicious, I like to think."

"Merely walking along with someone doesn't—"

"Oh please. I know what Gordie looks like when he's . . . I know the look he's got when—" Stephen stopped short. "You know, I've been dreading that kind of coincidence for months. Seeing him with someone else. I was sure I'd drop dead if that happened, dissolve in a puddle like the witch from Oz.

"The amazing thing was that I could see him with that big hunk and think, mostly, Poor Gordie. I wasn't pissed off and sad and jealous; I just felt like he must be going through this . . . I don't know, he must really be *flailing about.* I was more . . . embarrassed for him. I thought, Oh this is so foolish, Gordie, you're smarter than *this,* there's no *there* there, honey! I could even hear myself sort of talking him down, the way we always used to whenever we . . ."

Stephen let out a brief sob of laughter. "You know where I was headed? I was taking Skye to that movie about Iris Murdoch, and we were in such a rush that not till I was watching the movie did I really realize that I had *seen* him, seen him with another man, just like that. So I'm processing it, thank God in the dark, and of course, what movie is this? Not some action thriller, not some skin flick, someplace I can lose myself, but a sensitive, weepy, romantic *film* where this devoted crusty old guy takes care of his dear lifelong partner, and there are flashbacks to how they met and how madly they fell in love and all the compromises they made and . . ."

Alan heard another sob. He waited for Stephen to collect himself.

"Well!" A deep breath. "I always assumed we'd end up like that, old and devoted, with lots of friends but in the end relying on *ourselves.* For a long time, you know, before we were sure we'd made it through, that we were going to escape with our health as so many people did not; well, for a long time I also envisioned exactly that—one of us nursing the other right to the bitter end."

Both Stephen and Alan were still for a few minutes, one thinking, one waiting. Stephen's arms lay folded on his chest, which rose and fell slowly as he breathed. "But you know what?" he said, almost inaudibly at first. "When I got out on the street with Skye, I felt like I did the last time I was tested. Free. Purged of something." He craned his neck to make eye contact with Alan. "Really."

Stephen had then declared that he did not want to talk about Gordie anymore—not for a long time.

So now, for the third meeting in a row, they spoke about the practicalities of adoption. If Alan had not been Stephen's therapist, he would have put Stephen in touch with Joya. Only a few nights before, Alan had had a dream in which he entered his office to see, hanging over the couch, an enormous, intricately rendered map of the world. *I never knew my geography,* he thought as he approached it, excited to find this surprise on his wall. Right away, he saw that several countries were covered with a texture that looked from a distance like a cartographer's marking for mountainous terrain but that proved, up close, to comprise hundreds of upturned cherubic faces, all rendered photographically. They were the faces of orphan babies scanning the sky. He knew this without question just as he woke up, to his alarm clock. Well, he thought as he rose from his bed, wasn't it obvious what they were looking for? Planes full of American adults who were wealthy and loving yet driven by a specific loneliness and the longing to cure that loneliness: cure it with the faces and bodies and arms of those very babies.

ALAN HAD AGREED TO HELP SAGA, every few weeks, distribute leaflets for her animal-welfare group—notices from owners who'd lost their pets or, conversely, pleas on behalf of pets who needed owners. Alan told Saga he'd be happy to place the notices on neighborhood bulletin boards and bus shelters while walking Treehorn, so long as he did not have to traffic with the surly Stan, who (talk about the rigors of adoption!) had peered rudely around Alan's apartment, grilled him mercilessly, and made him sign about two dozen forms before allowing him to take the puppy home.

Why were so many people who devoted themselves so passionately to animals so odd, even misanthropic? Saga herself—whose own saga he had never been able to elicit, at least not by indirect means—often seemed vaguely autistic. He had watched her at Walter's dinner party (where she appeared to be the "date" of Fenno McLeod, though everyone knew McLeod was gay), and though she had joined in the conversation often enough, sometimes her face had looked blank or intent, as if she were not a native English speaker. She had slipped away before dessert, claiming that she had to catch "the last train out."

Her largely incurious attitude toward other people was something Alan now realized he might have seen in that boy Diego—another animal lover—and he hoped that George, through his devoted association, would not take on the same demeanor. The boy had appeared at times to be disconnected from the flow of human interaction around him, even from his friendship with George.

Alan was mulling this over, heading into the newly fashionable Meatpacking District with Treehorn, trying not to entangle the leash with a roll of masking tape as he posted neon-yellow flyers about an abandoned litter of Airedales *(We are cute and healthy but homeless!)*, when he saw Jerry, his old therapist and mentor, step out of a boutique on Gansevoort Street. They saw and recognized each other at the very same moment.

"Yo!" said Jerry. In the year and a half since Alan had last seen him, he had rejuvenated his hair color and grown a trim mustache. He carried a shiny silver bag frothing with pink tissue paper. "Man, look at you."

Alan wondered what Jerry was seeing. "Well, yes, and you. You're thriving, that's obvious."

"In most ways; in the important ways, I guess." Jerry leaned down and extended the back of his hand to Treehorn. "Wow, a dog! Hi there, lucky dog of Alan." Treehorn licked the hand. "How's Greenie? How's your son—George? How are those heavenly *pastries*? Is she giving Martha a run for her money?"

"We're all just fine," said Alan. "Fine."

"Are you still down here in the same place?"

"More or less."

Jerry tilted an eyebrow. "What's the less part?"

"I just mean that we're ready for somewhere else. We're working on it."

Jerry nodded. "My rent's about to shoot through the roof. I'm actually down here myself doing the rounds with a broker. Condos are sprouting up like mad"—he gestured at a tower rising above the warehouses, conspicuous and scornful—"and this is the only way to keep Daphne from dragging me off to Pelham. The bad news I have to give her is the price per square foot. The good news . . ." He swung the elegant shopping bag aloft; it caught a flash of setting sun. And then he asked, as Alan had known he would, "How *are* you, Alan? I left you a message last fall—you get it?"

Alan saw Jerry trying to read, discreetly, one of the flyers with the photo of the Airedale pups. Feeling bad about his earlier evasiveness, he said, "I'm sorry. I wish I could say I was too busy to call back, but the truth is, I don't have as many patients as I'd like. I'm hoping it's a temporary lull."

"Maybe," said Jerry. "But too many people are turning to pills." He sighed. "Could you see yourself teaching? Doing something institutional?"

Sure. Like committing myself. "I suppose I ought to consider that."

"I'm in on a few public health projects," said Jerry. "We're in one of those cycles when the city actually attends to its conscience, when the powers that be include social workers. How's that for political paradox?"

Alan laughed politely.

"Call me if you're interested. Right now there's room at the top."

"I appreciate the offer," said Alan. Treehorn pulled on the leash, eager to walk along the last remaining block where bisected cows, not handbags and cashmere sweaters, were still the prime commodity on display.

Jerry swung his silver bag again, as if to draw attention to his prosperity. (What possessed Alan to project such pettiness onto a man who'd never been anything but good to him?) "Let's get together," he said, and Alan could see that he meant it. Before Alan could reply, however, Jerry had spotted the rare vacant taxi and waved it down over Alan's shoulder. "You know where to find me!"

Alan dumped the last few flyers in a garbage can and aimed for the river, into the sharp wind of early March yet also toward a bright rosy sky, the shine and scent of the water, sensations to which he and Treehorn looked forward nearly every afternoon.

It was close to ten o'clock when Greenie called. Realizing that he had only a month left in which to pack, Alan had just sealed his first box of books, psychotherapy texts that he had not opened in ten years yet could not discard because they had become talismans of his profession. He was about to tell her this news *(You see, I'm serious, I'm really finally doing it!)* when she said, urgently, "Alan, you're going to despise me for what I have to tell you, and I won't blame you at all if you do."

For twelve minutes, she did not allow him to interrupt her. He became aware of the time as minutes because he was sitting on the couch, directly across from a ship's clock that Greenie's father had given Alan for his thirtieth birthday. The minute hand moved not smoothly, imperceptibly, but in discrete, isolated clicks. As he tried to concentrate on Greenie's self-deprecating yet fiercely calm confession, stray thoughts worked their minor sabotage. The ship's clock posed a thorny question: Would Greenie have dared to leave him if her parents were still alive? The cardboard box at his feet, one that formerly held bottles of gin, seemed to sigh with relief: Oh now I won't *have* to pack. And when Treehorn, seeing Alan immobile, wormed her way onto the couch beside him, he felt a wave of consolation: At least I'll still have *you*.

As Greenie spoke precisely yet defensively about this guy from her past, this guy she now knew she had probably "always loved," this guy she needed to "know about, one way or the other, or I'd never be able to live with myself," Alan realized that—as she had told him months ago—this probably *was* someone he'd met; more accurately, even absurdly, whose congratulations he had accepted as he stood in the formal reception line that Greenie's mother had treated like a ritual of life-or-death importance.

"Can I say something now?" he said at the end of her soliloquy.

"Yes. But please don't try and convince me to change my mind."

Perhaps Alan was an idiot not to have expected exactly this; some might say he'd been asking for it. Yet he was also convinced that he and Greenie had been joined far too long to be divided by a single conversation, no matter what Greenie believed. "You know that I still love you," he said. "You know that I am packing up, intending to join you in less than a month. You know how long we've been together, no matter how many years ago you knew this other guy."

"I know all that," she said. "I'm sorry."

Alan thought carefully. He knew better than to ask how long she'd been sleeping with the man. "Let me come out next week, for a few days."

"No, Alan, not now. Not right now. Please."

You can't stop me, he wanted to say. "You're implying later would be better? How much later?"

"I can't keep you away, I know that," she said, as if reading his mind. "And I can't ask you favors anymore, but then, I don't owe you any either."

Alan knew what she meant, but he would not mention Marion. If that's what this was about, there was nothing he could do.

Her voiced softened when she said, "Alan, is it too late for you to keep the apartment?"

Why answer this coldhearted question? Or why not lie outright just to stab her in the heart? "No," he said coldly. "They were planning to renovate."

"I never thought I would do anything like this to anyone," she said, her voice so subdued that Alan could hardly hear her. "Least of all to you."

Cheating and lying and wounding, he might have said, *are hardly childhood aspirations.* How did they manage to sneak up on you the way they did, the motives of real live bumbling grown-ups that justified such acts?

He must make you very happy. Also unsaid.

"Alan? Alan, are you still there?"

"I don't feel as if I am, Greenie. I don't know what to say except that I won't let you end our marriage like this. I just won't."

"You have to let me go."

"I don't have to do anything." He wanted to tell her that, if he chose to, he could arrive on her doorstep anyway, with all their belongings. Did he suddenly love her more, want her more, because this Charlie wanted her too?

"Alan, when was the last time we were together without fighting?"

"Come on, Greenie, what married couple doesn't fight? Fighting is never the real issue."

"That's not true," she said.

He sighed. "You're right. But only about that." He felt his resolve begin to falter. "We have to stop talking for now. But we have to keep talking."

She agreed, or she pretended to. She said she would call back in a few days, when she wasn't working and George was asleep or at school. A week went by in which Alan cocooned himself in routine. Every time he spoke with George, the boy was with Consuelo. Alan questioned his own judgment—his desire to feel that George, like him, was filled with sorrow—but he sensed a new distance or apathy in George. He seldom asked about Treehorn, and when Alan asked him what friends he'd played with or what he had done that day, he offered not a single detail. In the midst of weary silences, Consuelo could be heard urging George on in a poorly disguised whisper. ("Tell your daddy about the donkey that came to your school, the way you rode him!")

Then Alan came home one night to a message from Greenie that sounded fearful and obligatory: how bad she felt; how she was "check-ing in"; how she hoped he was talking with friends. . . . He erased it and did not call back. He drank half a bottle of Scotch and worked himself into a silent rage—not at Greenie but at Ray McCrae. It was a good thing he had no way to reach the man. He would have made a lout of himself.

Some might have thought it strange, or repressed, that Alan did not feel immediately angry at Greenie. He simply canceled the mover he had reserved. He shoved the one box he had packed into a corner. Whenever he left the apartment, he took circuitous routes to avoid his own street. He did not want to run into Walter or Fenno McLeod or anyone else who might inquire about Greenie. It struck him, in a rush of bitter shame, that Walter might *know.*

He called Jerry. He said nothing about Greenie but listened as Jerry described his good works for the city. He began to think about Marion again; he had to make her look at him as something other than a threat.

Something would give, he thought. Something had to give. There was a physics to emotion as well as to matter. This was the one thing Alan knew.

SIXTEEN

"I THINK THIS PLACE IS RUN BY THE MOB," he whispered across the table, an obvious bid for her trust. "But the soufflés are out of this world."

Saga watched Michael unfold his napkin and smooth it across his lap. She did the same. "It's very pretty," she said. "I haven't been to many restaurants other than Uncle Marsden's favorites."

Michael made a face of friendly disbelief. "You don't really still call my dad 'uncle,' do you?"

"Of course I do. You still call him Dad."

"Touché." He beckoned to a waiter. The waiters wore tuxedos and carried their noses high, like hounds sniffing the wind. "Glass of wine?"

Saga shook her head.

"She'll have a Pellegrino," Michael told the waiter with confidence. "And what reds do you have by the glass?" After describing a number of wines to Michael, the waiter told them about food specials—and warned them to order their soufflés now or it would be too late. Fancy restaurants were exhausting, thought Saga. She did not enjoy having to focus on the waiter, on his lofty nose, to pretend they were having a real conversation, so instead she looked around at the breathtaking cavern of a room in which they were seated. The ceiling was surely over two stories high; hanging from it were fans that wobbled as they turned, making her even more nervous than she already was. Thank goodness there was no fan over their table, nothing that threatened to fall on her head.

"You've got to have a soufflé," said Michael. "The special sounds great, but they're all stupendous. You can't go wrong." He pointed at her menu.

Saga looked down, for an instant unable to decode the choices before her.

"Does madame like citrus flavors?" said the waiter, pretending to be helpful (now, she decided, he looked like an angry bull terrier). "The Grand Marnier is quite superb. It's made with a touch of tangerine."

"Yes, that one sounds fine," said Saga; anything to make him go. The combined scrutiny of Michael and the waiter was too much to bear.

She followed Michael's suggestions for an appetizer and a main course, even though she was nowhere near that hungry.

"Dad says you're getting into the city a lot these days. I'm glad to hear that," said Michael. "He says you're working for the ASPCA."

"No," said Saga. "It's a smaller group. We don't have that kind of money or so many people." She didn't want to say the name, for fear of Michael's reaction. "True Protectors" had come to sound silly even to Saga.

"From what I hear, they should be paying you."

"No, it's strictly volunteer. Not even the guy who runs it gets paid. He does it in addition to a full-time job." She felt a surge of admiration for Stan.

"Ah." Michael buttered a roll. Saga wished he would get it over with; she knew exactly why he had asked her out for this expensive lunch. "Would you give me a tour of the headquarters sometime?" he said. "If it's anywhere downtown, I could meet you there at lunch one day. Maybe my firm could make a donation. They'd match anything from me if it's a five-oh-one C three."

A brief explosion of laughter escaped from Saga. She was glad she had no food in her mouth. "Well, it's in Brooklyn, and it's kind of private. It's in someone's house. It sort of *is* his house."

Michael frowned. "Is it regulated by any kind of agency?"

"Stan does a great job. You don't need any agency to figure that out. You just need to know animals." She hoped she didn't sound annoyed. She couldn't afford to irritate Michael, not any more than she knew she already did.

He nodded, chewing. The waiter came with their twin servings of snails in little pools of butter. The round dish, with its circle of round compartments, reminded Saga of a watercolor tray, though in this case there was no color (unless you counted the flurry of parsley).

"How's Denise?" she said. "How's she feeling?"

"Denise is so great, I am in awe," said Michael. "Four months to go and she is already just enormous. I don't know how Mother Nature does it!"

His phone rang just then, and to her amazement he took it out of his pocket and turned it off. "A fine meal shouldn't be spoiled by interruptions," he said. "Eat up! They're really wonderful in a completely old-fashioned way." Saga watched him press a piece of bread into one of the butter pools. She picked up the tiny fork and forced herself to eat two snails. She thought of Uncle Marsden and his contribution to the advancement of salad.

Enough, she decided. She took a deep breath. "Michael, did you ask me out so we could talk about the house?" She hated the high, uncertain sound of her own voice, but Michael's face loosened with gratitude.

"Yes, I did, Saga. Did Dad say something? He said he wouldn't— not because I didn't want him to, but because he . . . well, we've had disagreements."

"Okay," said Saga. "He didn't need to say anything. I've heard you talking. About the house closer to town." No expression, she thought. Let me say these things with no expression.

"Saga, Dad's getting older."

"So are we all, Michael. Please, just let's tell the truth about all this."

Michael glanced out the window. Saga looked, too. Between two buildings across the street, she had noticed a view of the Hudson River when she sat down. She was startled to see that now, all of a sudden, the river had been replaced with another building—a building that moved from right to left. She gasped.

"What is it?" said Michael.

"The—" She saw the tail end of the cruise ship, then the river view restored. "Oh."

Michael laughed nervously. "You okay?"

"I just remembered something, that's all."

The waiter took away their snail plates. "You didn't like that," said Michael. "I'm sorry."

"I'm not relaxed here, Michael. You want to take away my home."

He did not smile or look away. "I want you to see this house, with me and Dad, next weekend. It's really cute."

"Cute," said Saga. No expression. No expression!

"Okay," said Michael, drawing out the word. "You think I mean tiny. You think I'm talking real-estate lingo. I'm not. Saga, that house is just too big for the two of you. Have you noticed that mice and bats have moved into the back attic, under the eaves? I think the local wildlife believes the place is abandoned!"

Saga was aware of the creatures who shared the top floor with her, though she had never seen them. She was fairly certain that in fact a family of squirrels, not mice, had moved in. At night, she heard their cavortings through the upstairs walls and found them comforting. Uncle Marsden, with his poor hearing, was probably none the wiser.

"You can hire an exterminator if you think they're wrecking stuff," she said, though the thought that he might do this made her sad. She knew she had to make—what was the word?

Accommodations. (A long, long train, all its cars the same dark blue.)

Now two businessmen in glossy suits took the table beside them. One placed a briefcase on the cushioned bench right next to her thigh. Saga smelled an intense cologne. The scent was exotic but slightly sickening.

"I guess you and Denise want the house for yourselves. That's it, right?"

"You make us sound so greedy."

"You're having these babies, which is great, and you need more space. But why do you have to take your dad's house?"

"Because it's my house, too, Saga. And Pansy's and Frida's, but they . . ." Michael closed his eyes briefly. "Saga, do you think Dad's emeritus salary pays the taxes on that place in this day and age? The heating bill? I'm afraid not."

Saga was glad to see the waiter this time. He set before her a plate with a piece of pearl-colored fish, a cluster of tiny potatoes, and something oily and green, all in a ring of rosy-colored sauce. It did smell good, but she wondered how she would eat it. She stared for a moment at her oddly shaped fork and remembered, painfully, the way it had felt just after the accident to confront any array of tools, things she saw as familiar but was not certain she knew how to use. She picked up the fork. She'd had no idea Michael was helping pay for the house—if it was even true. Well, it probably was.

"Listen, Saga, you're my cousin, my flesh and blood! The last thing in the world I'd ever want to do is throw you out, but I think you and Dad have settled into a . . . I think you need each other in ways . . . I don't want to pass judgment here, because I'm grateful he's had your company the past few years. I think he'd have gone downhill much more severely after Mom died if—"

"He hasn't gone downhill at all, if you ask me."

Michael raised his hands in defense. "You're right. He's amazing for his age. I've heard he still gives a great lecture, too, and that he stays up with the new science, even though he pretends to be a curmudgeon."

"Let's not change the subject," said Saga.

"I'm not. Let me tell you one of my biggest fears: that Dad will fall down those treacherously crooked stairs to the basement or electrocute himself rewiring a lamp or . . . well, the house itself is a bit of a peril, let's forget about Dad's state of mind. Or body. Though you cannot ignore the physical reality. Because once you get older, no matter how sharp you are, all it takes is one misstep and next thing you're in the hospital with a busted hip or ribs, then in the nursing home. People fall apart fast at that age if they have an accident. They just don't have the resilience . . ." Michael wasn't dense. He saw Saga's cold, hard stare and knew he had begun to offend her.

He raised his knife and fork, glancing down briefly at his steak; this discussion had not spoiled *his* appetite. Abruptly, he set them back down and looked almost piercingly at Saga. "Please try not to see me as the bad guy. How can I make you believe that I'm also concerned about *you*? Dad is old, Saga, but you're *young*. You shouldn't be swallowed up by the demands of that huge house and a man who takes so much for granted."

Saga stared out the window for a moment, then back at Michael. "Tell me about the house."

Michael frowned. He looked down at his plate and ate a bit of meat. He sighed loudly. "Okay then. So Saturday we are going to look at it. We've got first refusal. Even if we don't want it, it's not likely to go on the open market. It's a real gem." He continued to eat. Saga could see that her coldness had unsettled him. She felt both ashamed and triumphant.

"This is my idea," he said. "Denise wants to have the babies here, in the city, with the doctor she knows, start this new life in the place we know best. We figure we'd be looking to move out in October, November at the latest."

No expression. Saga felt the tears rise. *No expression!* "You've just gone and decided without us," she said.

Michael finished chewing his mouthful of food. He looked sad but impatient. "Dad knows all this. He's the one who's refused to tell you about it. I have no guilt there."

"So he's agreed to this other house."

"Contingent on seeing it," said Michael.

Contingent: mustard, ridged like bark, rough to the touch.

"What if he doesn't like it?" said Saga.

"I'm pretty sure he will. I'm pretty sure *you* will. It's got a beautiful modern kitchen with everything built in."

How awful that sounded. She thought of the cabinets with their wavy old glass, reflecting back and forth across Uncle Marsden's beautifully *un*modern kitchen. "And will you be paying the taxes there, too?"

One of the men at the neighboring table looked right at her. Her tone now had plenty of expression.

"Oh Saga," said Michael, "I was so afraid it would get hostile like this."

"I'm not hostile. I'm just . . ."

Michael waited.

"I'm just sad. That's all. Just incredibly sad." And murderously angry.

Michael reached across the table and grasped her left hand with his right. "I am trying to be honest with you. Which is more than some members of my family have been. If Dad . . . if he really saw and respected who you are, he'd make you get out more, meet other people. When you were with David, you had a very full life, and you can have it again. You weren't married, but it was obvious that once you . . ." Was Michael clenching his teeth? He glanced at the ceiling, then said, "Ask Dad to tell you more about your life before the accident."

"It's my life now that matters," said Saga. But how could she talk back to Michael now that she knew he had been supporting her? It made him almost noble; never mind all his snooty, unkind remarks in the past. She *was* a charity case. His charity case.

"I hate it that I've made you cry," Michael whispered. "Please."

Please what? she wanted to say. Please disappear? Please act like what's good for me is terrific for you? Please don't be so attached to a home that's never really been yours in the first place? Please get a brain transplant and go to law school, maybe in California? But answers like those were not fair to *this* Michael.

If someone out on the sidewalk had peered through the grand window beside their table, that person probably would have thought that she and Michael were a couple in the middle of a breakup. They'd have wondered, What is that dashing, well-dressed man doing with that rough-around-the-edges woman who isn't dressed up enough for that restaurant? Saga thought of David (for this she *could* blame Michael), who by now quite probably had a wife. In Zimbabwe or even in Connecticut, maybe the next town over. And that did it: now she could not stop crying, though she cried as silently as she could.

"Oh dear God," said Michael. "I am sorry, Saga."

The waiter seemed to appear from nowhere. "Finished, sir?"

Michael looked at Saga, a question. She nodded to her lap.

"Yes, yes," he said.

"The soufflés will be ready in ten minutes. May I bring coffee or tea?" Saga heard the waiter but did not look up.

"Maybe we'll just have the check," said Michael.

"No!" said Saga, but still she kept her face down. "I do want my soufflé."

Michael sighed. "Good. Then coffee for me. Double espresso."

Again, she felt his hand on hers. "My life is good now. I want yours to be the same. I don't know what else to say."

Saga pulled her hand away, though she knew it was childish. She wiped her eyes and looked up at her healthy, successful cousin who couldn't be content with what he had; no, he had to take what she had. Or that was how it felt. "Well, you *could* say that you and Denise will take the cute house."

Michael smiled at her, a Saint Bernard smile, mournful and guilty.

"Never mind," she said. "Let's have our soufflés, okay?"

"You're going to love this place," said Michael. "I promise you."

"Be careful what you promise, isn't that what they say?" said Saga. Or was it be careful what you *wish*? And then it came, the small steaming delicacy that looked like little more than a droopy brown hat. She inhaled the steam; it smelled woefully similar to the cologne of the man at the very next table. She ate it anyway: every bite and slowly. It was food the texture of love, sweet and airy, warm and moist; the taste didn't matter so much. She and Michael did not speak again until they stood on the street and he embraced her.

"If it makes you feel any better," he said, "Frida and Pansy are pretty pissed at me too these days. They think Dad's favoring me because I'm giving him the grandchildren he never knew he wanted so much."

Saga tried to smile, to share his simple joke. "I guess you must be very sure about what *you* want," she said.

"It's becoming a father. I feel like I have so much catching up to do."

"Oh, well," said Saga, "I could tell you a thing or two about that. The catching-up part."

Michael gave her a searching look. They said good-bye; they would meet again on the weekend, to see the cute house, the consolation prize. That would make sense, wouldn't it? Just about all of Saga's life was a consolation prize.

SHE WALKED UPTOWN. She had an envelope of notices to post, this time about meetings. As much as he did not like having too many people in his life, Stan needed more volunteers. "We've been discovered," he said. "Which is the good news and the bad. It means we're about to become a dumping ground for half the abandoned creatures of Brooklyn and Queens. Yesterday I got a call from a Dalmatian rescue league on Staten Island. Katy bar the friggin' door."

The notice read:

Join the **TRUE PROTECTORS!** Make a real difference in the lives of the city's **SMALLEST, MOST HELPLESS CITIZENS!** Be a part of the **REVOLUTION** against malice, abandonment, so-called "mercy killing," and overpopulation!! You will **SAVE LIVES.** Come see what a **MEANINGFUL MISSION** we are on, and meet your **FELLOW CRU-SADERS.** The beer and coffee are on us. Drop by and check us out, **YOU WILL NOT BE SORRY!**

At the bottom, it gave Stan's e-mail address and information about how to get to the falafel place. Saga had suggested to Stan that he hold the meeting in Manhattan, where more people were likely to show up, but he had barked, "I want people who are serious! Committed! No fuckin' dilettantes need apply. Subway scares 'em off, then screw 'em."

In his typically grumpy way, he'd muttered something about how it was finally time to "get real," make it an organization with some kind of official recognition. "By recognition, I mean cold hard cash," he said. "I mean, like these taxi fares are busting my balls." They were in a cab, taking the Airedale puppies to the vet. "But to get the cash, I need the status. I need to knock the socks off those executioners in Midtown who call themselves animal lovers. Yeah, like Hitler loved kids. Did you know he gave medals to women who had lots of kids? The right kind! Not the scruffy kind!" Stan laughed his creepy laugh, all the while petting the puppies, soothing them with his pale bony hands.

Saga tried to imagine Stan raising money. This was difficult.

Perhaps people could grow into what they needed to be. Sometimes they didn't even know what they wanted to be until it stared them in the face. For example, it was true what Michael had said: after years of claiming he couldn't care less, Uncle Marsden was in love with the idea of being a grandfather. "Now I'll be a bona fide patriarch," he'd said to Saga after Denise and Michael admired the cradle. "What do you say to that, my dear?"

Patriarch. Brown, she thought: a temple of a word, a shiny red brown, like the surface of a chestnut. "You're a natural," she had assured him.

After that, he began to dig deep into the storage rooms on the third floor, searching for further mementos of childhood: not just Michael's but Pansy's, Frida's, and his own; even Aunt Liz's girlhood. He'd sanded and repainted a wooden rocking giraffe just before Christmas, tied a large bow around its neck to make it a gift for Denise. But when Pansy showed up first on Christmas Eve, she saw it and cried out, "That's mine! Where did you find that?"

"Well, if you have a child one day, I'm sure Michael will be happy to hand it on to you," Uncle Marsden told her.

"Dad! Dad, it's mine, to save for my children first, not Michael's!"

Uncle Marsden had been unable to convince her that she should give it up, even temporarily, and the grudging rift between them had made Christmas tense. In the three months since then, Uncle Marsden had given Saga the job of finding out which unearthed treasures belonged to which cousin.

Two weeks ago he had declared, "Time to clean all this stuff out of the attic, once and for all! And I will not be a party to any materialistic feuds. If those girls are planning on families of their own, I'm all for it— but they'd better get cracking. Time waits for no man, and Mother Nature waits for no woman!"

Now it was clear that he was preparing not just for the arrival of his grandchildren but for his own departure—and Saga's—from the house. Perhaps she should have felt angry at him rather than at Michael, but she couldn't.

Most of her cousins' belongings were in boxes they'd already labeled, but Saga did have to bring down all the old books and lay them in piles on the living room floor so that Pansy and Frida could divide them up properly. This was comforting work, because it was so much like working with Fenno.

Just this past weekend, Frida had come down from Boston and filled her car with boxes. Afterward, she'd had lunch with Saga on the porch. They'd carried out mugs of chicken noodle soup and pulled quilts across their knees. It had been humid, almost warm for March; fog hovered over roads and lawns.

"How are you, Saga? I mean, really?" asked Frida.

"Pretty good, I guess," Saga had answered.

"Do you feel like things are still improving, like you're . . ."

"Getting better?"

Frida laughed nervously. It took a lot to make Frida nervous. "I hate to phrase it as if you're sick. Obviously, you're not sick."

If she needed to answer that, Saga didn't know how. So often she *had* felt sick, sick the way that maybe people with vertigo felt sick, like a sickness of not knowing your place, the place you were supposed to occupy in space. "The worst things don't seem to bother me much anymore," she told Frida. "I don't get the headaches, I haven't had seizures, writing's no problem, or using . . . everyday things. Mostly."

She wondered if Uncle Marsden had told Frida about her checkup the week before. Saga hadn't been to the neurologist in six months, and he was pleased, saying that she had made unexpected progress. Though Saga could have said no, she always allowed Uncle Marsden to sit with her while she took the peculiar series of tests measuring eyesight, hearing, coordination, and memory skills. He was the one to fill out her medical history. Letting him take over made her feel more like a child, but when she looked at the forms—the fine print, the numbered questions and rows of boxes to check—she felt queasy. Uncle Marsden's certainty was a relief. "I know it all by heart, my dear," he'd say as he ticked off the boxes. "Easy as pie."

Frida nodded at Saga's good news. "I'm glad to hear it. And Dad says you get away a lot." She said this with a smile revealing that her dad had expressed his displeasure.

"I go to the city on the train."

"You've made friends there?"

Saga hesitated, but why should she keep friendships a secret? "I've met a Scottish man who runs a bookstore and another man who's a therapist."

"A psychotherapist? He's a friend?" Frida sipped her soup. "If this is too nosy, just say, but are you seeing anyone? I mean, a therapist?"

"No. That stopped a little while after the PT stopped." Saga braced herself for more advice. Why did people always think she wanted their advice? But Frida just stared into the fog and drank her soup in rhythmic little sips.

"Well," she said at last, "I've been seeing someone for more than a year. I fought against it, but now I'm glad. I was lonelier and angrier than I wanted to know."

"Angry?" Saga meant it more as an expression of surprise than a question. But Frida seemed happy to answer.

"Mostly at Dad, because he seems so oblivious to me." She turned to Saga and smiled. "And for a while I was angry at him because of you. As if you'd taken our place—as if you were the one and only daughter now. His Cordelia."

Saga's confusion over the name must have looked like fear, because Frida leaned over and touched Saga's knee. "Don't worry. I'm past that. Pansy can't stop being angry about it, but she's angry about everything these days. You might not know this, but that nice guy she brought with her for Thanksgiving and Christmas broke up with her last month."

"Oh," said Saga. "That's sad."

Frida nodded. "Sometimes I'm just as glad I never get asked out these days. I seem to have reached the end of my shelf life. Maybe I've been too passive, assuming my brains and my sense of humor would hook some passing suitor." She peered into her mug. She spooned up noodles from the bottom and ate them with a satisfied look.

Saga said, "You haven't given up, I hope."

Frida shrugged. "I have a crush on my therapist, and sometimes that seems like enough. But Pansy's still out there fighting the good fight. She's paid to join some fancy matchmaking service. I think she has a date this week."

Saga nodded. She didn't want to talk about Pansy's love life. Pansy was prettier than Frida by far, but if Saga had been a man, she'd have gone for Frida over Pansy any day.

"What about you, Saga?"

"Me?" The quilt slipped from Saga's knees.

"Any guys in the city? How about the guy with the bookstore?"

"Oh no," she said. "Not like that." She couldn't help thinking of Fenno, how she'd missed understanding that he was gay.

"Wouldn't you like to go out with somebody other than Dad?"

Saga laughed. "Maybe there's a fancy matchmaking service for half-wits."

"You're not a half-wit."

"I'm not a full-wit, that's for sure."

Frida looked as if she were measuring Saga with her eyes. Saga looked away. The fog was clearing. She could see Commodore Perry's front porch. The commodore was sleeping in his giant basket.

"Saga, do you think you hold on to the half-wit thing? Have you made it a habit, a pair of comfy old shoes? I saw you in the kitchen just now, making our lunch. You didn't consult your labels once."

Saga continued to watch the fog lift—or drift, really, as if retreating. Fog didn't really lift; it backed away. Out of nowhere came an image of Japanese girls bowing as they tiptoed backward. *So sorry, so sorry, so sorry.*

"Saga, did I offend you?"

She looked at Frida. "Michael didn't put you up to this talk, did he?"

Now Frida was the offended one. "Saga, everything around here isn't about Michael, though it may seem like that right now, now that he's flaunting his reproductive vigor, like some kind of sports car. *Vroom, vroom,* twins!"

Saga laughed. "He's taking me out for lunch, you know."

Frida was quiet for a minute, then spoke cautiously. "Michael is a good man, and I admire him, even though I don't like to think about what he does for a living. Pansy would kill me if she knew I'd told you this, but he cosigned the mortgage for her condo, and he's even tried to fix her up with a couple of guys from his firm."

This was when Uncle Marsden came around the corner of the house and sprang up the stairs, carrying a pair of shovels. "Girls!" he exclaimed, smiling. He held out the shovels, one in each hand. "Girls, I am putting you to work!" He had a replanting project. Though it was barely spring, he'd become a sort of garden dervish that week. He seemed bent on moving shrubs around, front to back, shade to sun, from one corner of the porch to another.

That heart-to-heart with Frida was the first time Saga could recall, since her coming to live there, when one of her cousins had really wanted to talk to her and also to listen. It meant something. It was an omen, not necessarily good—because now she could not remain outside the circle.

That was when she'd known that no matter how much Frida cared about her, or even Uncle Marsden, there would be trouble ahead.

Well, she thought after her lunch with Michael, after putting up her last notice, here it is. The question was, could she face it?

Saga checked her watch. It was four o'clock. She was on Horatio Street, not far from the bookshop. It would be open for another three hours, but Saga did not feel like seeing Fenno, whose kindness would encourage her to confess all the rage and panic she felt. Lately, she was surprised at how much she found herself telling Fenno in the pockets of time when they were alone together.

Not that he hadn't told her a lot about his own life. The evening she had gone up to his apartment for dinner, he had shown her photographs of his family in Europe—they looked like a happy clan: happily married, happily overrun by children, happily overworked in their privileged jobs—and Saga had seen, or guessed, one of the things that made her want so badly to be with Fenno. Inside himself, just like her, he was basically alone. People surrounded him, and people loved him, but he had accepted in their midst the role of the Lonely One.

This was something she could only guess. Fenno had spoken with great affection about his Scottish home and his relatives, and then he'd asked about Saga's family. So she had told him about Uncle Marsden and her cousins—she could speak about them lovingly, too, if she was fair—and she'd told him about her accident, how her dad died of cancer right before it, her mother of a stroke just a couple years after. It turned out that Fenno's parents and hers had died of almost exactly the same causes, though his mother was the one who went first, with the cancer. They had a lot to empathize about, a lot more in common than Saga might have hoped.

It was while he cooked the curried shrimp, at the stove, that he told her he was gay. "Not that I've ever been a success at making a good match," he'd said while his back was to her, while the shrimp sizzled in the pan with the garlic. He'd pretended to find this funny.

"But you fall in love," Saga heard herself say, "don't you?"

He had turned around for a minute, looking surprised. (Why did she have to be so blunt?) He didn't tell her it wasn't her business, though. He cooked for a minute or so without answering, and then he said softly, "Of course I do."

She had not gone so far as to ask if he was in love with anyone right then.

Fenno was more her friend now than he had been before her embarrassing, gushing confession in the store that day. But still, she wanted to think in private about all the things Michael had told her. If she were to stop by the bookshop now, Fenno would see that she was unhappy, and he would ask why, and she would tell.

When she found a phone booth on Hudson, she called Stan.

"Come out and help me bathe some kittens," he said without any small talk. "All hell is breaking loose."

With his griping and his bossing around, Stan would leave her no time for self-pity. The animals, he might say—homeless, discarded, starved, bitten, diseased—now *they* had problems.

Saga could still taste the garlic from lunch as she walked from the subway. She hoped Stan wouldn't smell her breath and make some nasty comment. But when she turned onto his block, she knew there'd be little time for idle comments. Sonya's van was in the driveway, and the house was like a big jukebox, broadcasting the sound of ten dogs barking.

"Jesus, Story Girl, get yourself in here. I've got a howler on my hands."

Once Stan let her in, Saga could discern the sound of one dog howling its heart out, that baying-at-the-moon persistence, which had worked up every other dog and even a couple of the cats. Stan explained that Sonya was going to take the loudmouth to her place for the night, after she dropped off another dog she had to take back to its owner; in the meantime she had begun helping him with a flea bath. Saga could hear, through all the ruckus, the pitiful bleating of kittens.

The bathroom on the first floor was given over to caring for the animals. The shelves in the medicine chest and the back of the toilet were crowded with flea and tick shampoos, gauze pads, tubes of ointment, vials of eyedrops, and pills from the charitable vet. Hanging on a rack, along with towels, were leashes, harnesses, collars, and a muzzle. A tattered poster of the cartoon dog Snowy faced the toilet.

"Hey," said Sonya when Saga looked into the bathroom. "Don't slip on the floor. These guys are ninjas." She'd taken off her shirt. Saga tried not to stare at Sonya's black spiderweb bra and the snake tattoos coiling around her arms.

"Hi," said Saga. "Can I help?"

Stan pushed past her and reached out to Sonya, who handed him a kitten bundled in a washcloth. He didn't seem to notice or care that Sonya was shirtless. Stan held the kitten up to his face and spoke to it sweetly, stroking its wet little head. He sat on the toilet and gave it a gentle rubdown. "Get me that plastic laundry basket by the back door," he told Saga.

The howler had taken a break, but now he was at it again.

"Christ!" Stan exclaimed. "It's a good thing my neighbors are too psychotic to get the cops' attention!"

Saga finally asked, "Do you want me to take over for Sonya?"

"We've got a system going here," said Sonya. She gave a second kitten to Stan. The first was nestled in a towel lining the laundry basket.

Sonya turned to Saga. "Listen. Do me a favor. There's this dog in the van out there, I think he probably needs a walk. He's a cream puff. Can you do that for me? Take him around the block, and by the time you get back, I can take the werewolf too. You got a crate for that monster?" she said to Stan.

"He's not a monster," said Stan. "He's just being expressive. Probably has a lot of legitimate gripes."

The "cream puff" sat in the passenger seat, his nose to the crack Sonya had left above the window. When Saga opened the door and the light went on inside the van, she laughed. "I know you," she said. "You're . . ." She couldn't quite remember his name, but she knew this dog from that restaurant near Fenno's store.

He licked her hand. "Hello, you," she said. He wore a wide leather collar with metal studs; Saga twisted it around, to read his tags. Sure enough, next to his rabies tag was a big silver heart engraved *The Bruce,* with the name of his owner (Walter, yes, the one who gave the party the night of the storm) and a phone number. "Good to see you, The Bruce!" she said. Though he showed no interest in escaping, she held him by the collar with one hand and reached past him to take his leash off the seat.

As she fumbled with the fastener on the leash, Saga realized that something was stuck to the fingers of her left hand. Green chewing gum. "Disgusting!" She stopped to fish for a tissue in her pocket. She came up with an unfamiliar fine blue handkerchief. She stared at both the gum and the handkerchief in confusion. She remembered now that Michael had given her the handkerchief at lunch. But the gum, where had that come from?

She looked down at The Bruce, who stood on the sidewalk, waiting patiently. More of the gum stuck out from beneath his collar. With the unpleasant wad of gum, once she managed to pull it free, came a folded slip of paper, about the size of a fortune from a Chinese restaurant cookie. It, too, must have been stuck on the underside of the collar.

Saga unfolded the slip of paper. In thin, spidery letters, it read, *Miss Sea Urchin pines for your la la la luscious tongue. Lick her till she's a razzmatazz rose, a big wet shiny rose. Tonight. Alice in Wonderland, under the mushroom-roomba. Xxxxx you know exactly WHERE.*

Quickly, Saga refolded the paper. Unsure what to do with it, she let it fall to the floor of the van. She walked The Bruce around the block, stopping whenever he wanted to stop, trying not to think about the message under his collar. Had it been written by Sonya? Was it for . . . for *Walter?*

Sonya was waiting by the van. Crated in the back, a surprisingly small dog, quite nondescript and harmless-looking, whined and scratched at the bars.

"Hey, thanks a mil," Sonya said. She unsnapped the leash and helped The Bruce up to the front seat.

"You're welcome," said Saga.

"Want a ride into the city?"

"No. I've got something I need to ask Stan," she said, a lie. She felt herself blushing. Sonya drove off with a wave.

"Hey, Story Girl, come in and have a beer," said Stan when he opened the door. He walked to the kitchen. "You could hear a pin drop now."

"I just need my knapsack," she said. Everything that day seemed off balance, thought Saga. What made Stan so suddenly cheerful?

He saw her suspicion and laughed. "Hey, business, all business."

She blushed and accepted a Coke. It turned out that Stan meant business about the business. He'd found out about an intensive seminar, less than a week long, for people who wanted to establish a not-for-profit group. The only problem was that the seminar was held in Washington, D.C. He could easily take the vacation time, but who would look after the animals?

"And then I figured, you and Sonya could do it together," he said, looking pleased with himself.

"Me?" said Saga.

"With Sonya, yeah, sure. She'd be the brains, you'd be the brawn, right?"

Saga said nothing.

He reached across the table and shook her arm gently. "Story Girl, I am *kidding*. You could stay here, you know the routines. And Sonya's got wheels. Hey, how 'bout I even change the sheets?" The first seminar with an opening was six months away, so they'd have plenty of time to plan.

SHE THREW HER JACKET over the fence and climbed after. She worried for a moment when her hem caught on the iron spears at the top, but she managed to disentangle the skirt without tearing it, without losing her balance either. When she landed on the other side, she looked up quickly at the windows in the buildings across the street to make sure no one was watching.

The night wasn't as chilly as it might have been, but she was sorry she did not have pants and a heavier jacket—or her sleeping roll. She hadn't been drawn to this place, to sleep here, since the fall. What had changed? It had to be the bookstore; this was the first thing that came to mind. Despite Michael's bad news—which she had expected, so it wasn't really news, not the part of it that mattered—she knew there was plenty for which she could be thankful. (Though, really, when your skull had survived collision with a tree, that would always be the case, wouldn't it? In some ways, that was annoying, the way you knew you should always feel grateful, even when you had good reason not to.) Saga helped Fenno two or three times a week now, for which he paid her fifteen dollars an hour. She had told Uncle Marsden about the shop, that it was a place she liked, where she helped out a little, but she hadn't told him about the money. She hadn't wanted him to have more cause to agree with Michael, to feel that Saga might need him less somehow.

Because she didn't need him less. At the same time, she found now that she was finally furious with Uncle Marsden. How could he not have warned her, at least, about what Michael intended to tell her at that lunch? ("Save your appetite! I bet he'll take you somewhere swanky," Uncle Marsden had told her at breakfast. And he had known exactly why!) Was he such a coward that he had to hide behind his son? All those times she'd seen him stand up to Michael's cranky bursts of temper, had he been little more than a rooster showing off his tail? When things really mattered, did he scuttle away to the henhouse?

Saga had never stayed in the open on a winter night—her risky behavior had limits—but a certain amount of cold she could take, in exchange for perfect solitude, a place where no one could find her. Especially when she couldn't bear to go home. She buttoned the top button and the cuffs of her blouse (the doctor had just observed how much better she was at this very task). She put on the sweater she kept in her knapsack and, over that, her jacket. She turned up the collar.

She wriggled back till she'd wedged herself between the two great flowerpots that held the trees. She looked up at the sky. It was the usual chocolate brown of city sky: no stars, alas no moon, just the occasional winking plane. She was thirty-four years old; what would become of the rest of her life? If she moved with Uncle Marsden to the Cute House, it wouldn't be the same, not at all, as simply staying on at the big house. That was the real problem. She would be telling the world that she was helpless, which wasn't true. She wasn't helpless. She was directionless, that's what she was. She lived the way dogs did, trusting in food, the next day, the next sleep, taking small expeditions, short-term missions. In truth, dogs were smart, resourceful, and strong if they had to go their own way. They were dependent because it's what they knew and it was easier, not because it was necessary. She closed her eyes.

SEVENTEEN

Dear Marion,

Forgive me if I have to say this protracted silence has become absurd. I understand and respect your need to consider so many things, and I know that my own behavior, when we saw each other last, must have seemed belligerent, confused, even paternalis

Just as belligerent, confused, and paternalistic as this letter itself. How about hostile? Did he neglect to mention hostile?

Dear Marion,

I was determined to let you decide when we should be in touch again, but several months have passed now, and events in my life have recently been so tumultuous that I feel a renewed urgency to open up the lines between us. If that seems selfish, and I know it must, then please

Oh God. He felt as if he were writing to a patient who had quit in a huff, walked out the door in a peremptory snub (not that Alan would ever have written to a patient who did that, and not that any patient ever had; not quite).

Dear Marion,

I hope you won't consider this letter an intrusion on whatever process you are going through. I can't help worrying that you fear I would enlist a lawyer or make threats of some kind. Believe me, I would never do such a thing. I know that I've behaved badly enough already. Whatever decisions you are

thinking of making about Jacob, all I wish is that we, you and I,
could at least discuss them, or perhaps exchange e-mails if that

Why should she care what he wished? What if, after all, Jacob were
not "his" child? But somehow her silence, as time went on, only proved
to him that the opposite was true.

He still had two blank sheets of paper, but at this rate they, too,
would shortly lie crumpled at his feet. He'd grabbed the slim sheaf in his
printer, a last-minute notion as he raced around the apartment packing
clothes, rinsing dishes, trying to figure out what to do with Treehorn.
Fenno had answered the phone at the bookstore but told Alan he was
about to leave the country for a week, to attend a family christening. To
Alan's uneasy surprise, Fenno gave him a phone number for Saga, in
Connecticut. There had been an awkward confusion over her name;
Fenno apparently knew her as Emily. What else, Alan had wondered,
did Fenno know about her that Alan did not? (Why did he feel a
spark of *jealousy* over a woman who, by objective standards, seemed
vaguely pathetic?) After speaking to a man who sounded older and
rather imperious—Saga's father? surely not a husband—Alan had been
relieved to hear her voice. She would pick up his keys from Fenno's
assistant at the store. Treehorn would be fine.

Other than the bond he had forged with his dearly predictable dog,
every close relationship in Alan's life seemed tattered or bruised. So
then, why not smash this one to smithereens? Perhaps Marion would
change her name and move to Las Vegas, consigning Alan to the oblivion he probably deserved. Didn't bad omens, daunting ordeals, and personal catastrophes come in threes?

He raised the plastic window shade, which he had closed soon after
takeoff. Already they were over the desert. Ah, talk about omens! When
he turned back, he saw the flight attendant making her way up the aisle.
She acknowledged Alan's wave with a Styrofoam smile.

"May I get you something, sir?"

"Do you by any chance have paper?"

"I think I saw a spare copy of *USA Today*. Will that do?"

"No, just paper. Blank paper."

Her smile looked like a patch sewn on her face.

He said, "To write on."

"I'm sorry, we don't have that," she said. "Could you write on a napkin? Or . . ." She reached into the seat pocket next to him and, pleased with her resourcefulness, presented him with the paper bag designed for airsick passengers. "Would this do in a pinch?"

Alan shook his head. On impulse, he asked if he could still order a drink.

"Why sure," she said. "That I can get you. What'll it be?"

"Vodka," he said. He never drank on planes. He never, out of habit, did anything he was doing at this moment in his life.

The previous morning, barely two weeks after letting him know she was in love with somebody else, Greenie had called with more bad news. Whether it was worse news remained to be seen. George and his friend Diego, wearing primitive animal masks, had opened Diego's window after his parents fell asleep, climbed down over the roof where he fed his tame squirrel, slipped under the rail fences that bordered the corrals of the ranch where Diego's father worked, crept into the barn, and unlatched the doors to the stalls of three horses, urging them out of the barn, then out a back gate into the wider world, where they were lost, confused, and possibly panicked, running not toward the mountains, where the boys intended them to run, but toward the road—perhaps because civilization, however dangerous it might be, was far more familiar to them than wilderness of any kind.

Only then, on hearing this news, did Alan's fury at his wife begin to blossom, spreading through him steadily, quietly, outward in all directions, like the red stain from a glass of wine spilled on a white tablecloth.

Alan gazed again at the parched, unpopulated land beneath him; would that he could will his mind to be so blank, his emotions so neutral in color, his temper so flat. When the attendant returned, he gave her a handful of singles; she gave him the tiny bottle, a tiny napkin, and a plastic cup filled with ice. Alan could actually smell the ice, how old it was. It smelled like a closet. He twisted the tiny bottlecap and poured out the crystalline liquid. His nose stung and his eyes watered slightly as he raised the cup to his mouth. Through the gap behind the tray, he fished in the seat pocket and pulled out the airline magazine.

"The Tetons!" he cried out softly when he found the table of contents. "Oh do let's read about the Tetons." Among the smallest of blessings he could count, both seats beside him were empty. He was free to mutter (or laugh maniacally, or growl, or weep) without visible censure.

THE UNEXPECTED WARMTH STRUCK HIM FIRST, then the sight of Greenie. After pulling up to the curb and leaning across the passenger seat to catch his attention, she opened her door to come around and greet him.

"Don't get out." He threw his bag on the backseat. "Where's George?"

Greenie stared at Alan. She sat there without driving, though he had closed his door and fastened his belt.

"He's back at the house. He's with—"

"Your beloved Chuck?"

"Consuelo," she said quietly.

"Your fabulous, attentive nanny?"

"It's not her fault, Alan. It's completely my fault. I've been—"

"Let's go. Let's just get there." He would not look at her. He had seen in one glance that Greenie's face was drawn and swollen from crying.

As she drove them through the airport catacombs, leaning forward to see every sign, she said nothing. She'd switched off the radio when he got in.

He looked out at the mountains flanking the city. Snow covered the peaks, though the air around the car was hot. Alan opened his window.

"Sorry. The weather is a fluke," said Greenie.

"Sorry for the *weather*?" *Sorry.* How many times had she said that inadequate word in the course of their recent conversations? Eat your heart out, Erich Segal.

They had been driving for ten minutes when Greenie said, "Alan, we can't make this whole trip in silence. You have every right to be very, very angry at me, not to want to say a word to me ever again, but we have to figure things out, and we can't look like this to George, especially not now."

"Look like what? His parents who are about to split up? Or did he figure that out a long time ago, before we did? Maybe we're the childish ones here. Maybe we're the delinquents, the guilty ones, the ones who've let the animals loose. Whatever sins you want to claim, let me be the first to claim stupidity."

Greenie cried silently. He could tell without looking at her, just from the way she was breathing. "Stop crying," he said, willing his voice to sound gentle. "Please stop crying." He opened the glove compartment and found a paper napkin. When he handed it to Greenie, she apologized again.

He said, "Tell me again what happened. I want to get the story straight."

"Okay." She blew her nose. She was driving fast, possibly too fast, but Alan made no comment.

"George was overnight at Diego's. Consuelo drove him there because I had a dinner party at the mansion. Consuelo told me—yesterday, after everything happened—that he was very excited before he went. He told her they were going to play a special game and he needed . . . black clothes." More tears.

Alan wanted to put a hand on her shoulder, to stop her more than to console her, but he didn't.

"So—I told you—the police phoned at two in the morning. They had a call from someone driving on Bishop's Lodge Road who had to swerve to avoid a horse. And then there was . . . By the time they got out there, one horse had been hit." Her voice broke. "So now they'd had other calls, and they went to the nearest ranch; they found the open stalls. It took an hour for someone to mention how the boys were hanging around that evening, so they went straight—"

"The horse," said Alan. "Tell me about the horse, the one that was hit. Before we cope with everything else, I want to know what we're dealing with, the liability."

"What is your problem!" shouted Greenie. " 'Everything else' just happens to be your *son*! Don't you care how George is? What matters more to you, George or some *horse,* some goddamn potential lawsuit?"

"I might ask you, Greenie, what matters more to *you,* George or some goddamn . . . what should I call him, childhood sweetheart? This guy you've been running around with, ignoring what anybody else could see was an intense if not *bizarre* situation with this other child!"

"At least I haven't thrown any illegitimate children into the fray!"

"Good for you. And please be sure that if—*if* that's what I've done, I've done it with great delight. I said to myself, Let's see, what's missing from my life? I know! What I need is another child, with a different mother, one who will vanish, have that baby in secret, and never speak to me again. That's what I need!"

Greenie turned to glance at him for a moment, and she actually tried to smile when he met her eyes. "I guess this is what they call clearing the air," she said. "So, do we hate each other now? Is that where we are?"

Alan wished they were anywhere but in a speeding car. He wanted to grab her, with longing as much as rage, to shake her. He understood what it meant to want to *shake sense* into someone. "I can't speak for you, Greenie, but it would take a great deal for me to hate you. Or a great deal more than this, which I can't begin to imagine." He stared at her. She kept her eyes on the road.

"The horse," she said slowly, "is going to be all right. The leg is badly bruised but not broken. I've offered, through the police, to pay the vet bill. I haven't spoken yet with anyone from the ranch. Mary Bliss said it's not a good idea, not yet. Ray's vet, the one who takes care of his horses, is going to double-check the X-rays, free of charge."

"What about Diego's parents? Are they taking no responsibility here? Their son was the instigator, that has to be obvious even to them."

"Diego's father will be lucky to keep his job, Alan. The mother feels terrible, I know she does, but her English isn't so terrific, and I think the father won't let her tell anyone how sorry she is about all this."

Alan was aware of the cruel, even racist remarks ready to leap from his mouth. As if to mock him, four dark-skinned men crowded in a pickup truck, jostling one another, their radio blaring, passed Alan and Greenie on the right. Through Alan's open window, the music hit him, briefly, like a shock wave.

Greenie said quietly, "Isn't George the most important thing right now?"

"Of course he is. When I see George, I want to have a fix on every-thing that's going on *around* him so that I pay attention just to him."

"I think George is terrified."

"Greenie, he should be."

"Alan, *he's five.*"

"Yes. And for that, in some ways, we are lucky. And I intend to be as reassuring to him as I can. But he needs to know how serious this is. It doesn't matter if the horses were *unscathed,* if they returned happily to their own stalls, tucked themselves in, and turned off the lights. We need to figure out how a kid so smart could do something so reckless. He's not so young he could really believe those horses wouldn't be in danger, set free near those roads. Unless . . ."

"Unless what?"

"Unless he's been . . . well, for lack of a better word, brainwashed."

"Alan, I'm sure it was a matter of being coerced. Of being convinced by this older boy—"

"He wasn't coerced. I saw him with that boy. George was fully, joyfully involved in their games. Did you ever look at their games, listen to what they were doing? Were they practicing this escapade the whole time they were playing with those model horses? This is how teenagers end up on drugs; their parents pay no attention to the details of how they're living their lives."

"Alan, that's not fair."

Alan said nothing. He did not want to think about justice.

"I don't believe Diego is a bad child or even a bad influence," Greenie said. "He got carried away with his imagination. There are much worse crimes than that. But George will never see Diego again, I promise."

"Of course he won't, Greenie. Because as soon as we deal with the police and the people who own the ranch, I'm taking George back to New York. Honestly, I don't even give a damn about Diego or his parents."

There was no traffic to hold them up and no exit looming, but the car began to slow. Greenie pulled into the breakdown lane. She put the car in park and stared at Alan. "Please, don't do this."

"Do what?"

"Take him. Oh Alan."

Alan closed his eyes and tightened his jaw. How could he be in this tawdry place? How? He'd heard couples exchange deadly threats from opposite ends of the couch in his office, vile threats involving homes, pets, friends, and yes, not infrequently, their own children. Sometimes, after they had left, he'd felt shamefully smug and lucky, knowing that he and Greenie, whatever their troubles, would never be forced into such extreme places.

When he did not respond to Greenie's plea, she began to sob loudly. "You can't *do that*. You know he belongs here, he needs to be here with me. I'm his mother! He has another two months of school! To change his life all over again would be disastrous, I know it would. He would be sure it was a punishment!"

"Would it be a punishment," Alan said quietly, "to return, with his father, to a neighborhood he's always known, with his old friends, the places he still remembers as his 'real' home? You heard him at Christmas. And send him back to school here? He will be certain that everyone knows what happened, what he did—and you know what? They will."

"Please, Alan—"

"Look, Greenie, there's no reason for me to move out here now. Would I be correct in saying that? Though the irony is that, as of today, I am seeing precisely two patients. I would have seen one of them for the last time this very afternoon!" He pointed at Greenie. "You—you can always come back to New York, even if we're not together. You could start another venture and—"

She gripped the steering wheel, as though Alan were threatening to take the car. "Why did this have to happen?"

Which thing? Alan nearly asked. Greenie teased out the one crumpled napkin she had been using to soak up all her tears. She blew her nose, stuffed the napkin in the breast pocket of her shirt, and put the car in gear. Alan noticed that she wore clothes he had never seen, that her yellow shirt fastened with snaps, even the cuffs, which were rolled up to her elbows. She had lost weight since Christmas (the sweet wasting of passion, he thought bitterly), yet she looked more, not less, substantial. In her leanness, she looked more serious, experienced—more burnished by the sun, as if she'd become a mountain climber when Alan wasn't looking. By contrast, he felt as pale and shapeless as a city snowbank. There had always been great differences between them, differences they liked to acknowledge with pride and pleasure, but the contrasts he saw now seemed like those of people destined always to clash.

THE TV WAS ON. George watched, laughing at cartoon buffoonery. Consuelo was on the phone, speaking rapidly in Spanish.

As soon as they walked through the door, Consuelo said good-bye and hung up. George remained riveted to the television a few moments longer. Only when he heard Alan's voice did he look away from the screen.

Consuelo was embracing Alan, and try as he might, he couldn't freeze her out. Greenie was right; Consuelo was faultless. She was a kind, grandmotherly pillow of a woman who saw her job as cuddling, nurturing, and taking this little boy from place to place—not disciplining him, spying on him, or second-guessing his motives. "George's Daddy, we are so glad to see you!" she said.

"I'm glad to be here," he said. What else was there to say? It occurred to him, as she pulled away and smiled at him, that of course she had no idea Greenie was dumping him. She might not even have met this Charlie fellow.

George had not moved from the couch. "Hi, Dad," he said. "Daddy, did you bring Treehorn?"

Alan sat next to George and put an arm around his shoulders. "No, guy."

"You could have putten her in a suitcase."

"You have to make special arrangements. I didn't have time. A friend of mine will take good care of her while I'm gone, and then . . ." He faltered. Greenie was staring at him with desperation. She had seated herself on the opposite side of their son. Consuelo busied herself in the kitchen.

Over George's head, Alan gave Greenie a pointed look. The look was meant to convey that they mustn't crowd George and that it was Alan's turn to speak with him, but she did not, or did not want to, understand. She pressed her cheek against George's hair. "Have you had dinner, sweetie?"

Without looking away from his cartoon, he shook his head. Alan took the remote and turned off the TV. George looked up at him in wordless protest.

"Show me what's new in your room while your mother makes dinner," said Alan. The look he gave Greenie this time fell just shy of a threat.

In George's room, Alan was shocked to see the row of horses on top of the bookcase below the window. Shouldn't they have been swept away by now? Hidden—vaporized?

"I see your collection is larger than when I was here before."

"Yes," said George. He rushed forward and picked up a black horse. It was rearing up, as if in defense. "This one's newest. He's an Arab."

Alan took the horse. To hold it, now, felt like holding a toy revolver. He pretended to examine the horse, then put it back in its place. He sat on the bed. "I'm so happy to see you, George. I've missed you so much. But you know why I've come right now, don't you?"

George nodded. He looked his father straight in the eye, his expression shaded with defiance, not shame.

"I love you, George, but I'm upset about what happened with Diego. Can we talk about that?"

George held a plastic Appaloosa. Casually, as if he were alone, he made it gallop along the mattress toward Alan's thigh. "You can talk," he said furtively.

Alan lifted George to sit on the mattress beside him. He turned sideways to face his son. "You let those horses go. You scared them into running away."

George said, with a confidence that impressed Alan, "We let go the ones they were breaking. They were making them wear the saddles. They were making them be ridden when they didn't want to be ridden. We knew they didn't. We saw them. Diego can read what they feel in their faces."

"You thought they were unhappy."

George nodded with passion.

"Did you know that horses are a lot like dogs, George? What I mean is that they aren't wild animals. They are meant to live with people. They wouldn't know what to do without people to take care of them. And they learn certain things so that people can be closer to them. They learn to be ridden just the way a dog learns to walk on a leash. Sometimes it's hard to learn, but they do."

"Daddy, there are *wild* horses."

"Yes, but not on that ranch, guy." Gently, Alan took the toy Appaloosa from George. "You know that what you did was wrong and that you put the horses in danger, don't you?"

George nodded.

"Didn't Diego know the horses might run into the road? They might even have panicked and hurt you by mistake. Horses are very strong animals."

George shook his head. "They would never hurt us, actually. We are friends. Diego said they would go to the mountains, to their rightly home. He said our masks would send them in the right direction and then they would find their way, like cats who know how to get home from far away when they get left behind. Like *The Incredible Journey*."

"Their home is that barn. And George, those horses belong to the people who own the barn."

"Diego's dad owns the barn."

Alan could see how George might believe this, how perhaps even Diego might think that his father, spending all day in the barns, caring for the horses, must have a say in their fate. "Diego's dad has a job in the barn," Alan explained. "That's different. He's responsible for the horses, but they are not his."

"Is that why the police came? They thought we stole the horses?"

"No, George. But one of the horses was hurt. It's going to be all right, but it was hit by a car. It was scared, and its leg was bruised."

George reached for the Appaloosa. Alan let him take it. Was it too painful for George to accept the harm he'd inflicted, at least indirectly, or was there something sinister in his refusal to apologize? Alan felt a flash of anger.

"George." Greenie stood in the door. "I made pig-in-a-poke. With the tiny tomatoes you like."

George smiled at his mother. Alan raised a hand. "In a minute," he said. If he had to be the bad cop, he would. There would be so much time to make up for it now. "George, did Diego ever ask you to do . . . did you ever make plans like this together before?"

"Daddy, we love the horses. We wanted the horses to get free from the ranchers and the cowboys. Actually, we wanted them to be happy. So they could play games. We only let the baby horses go. Diego says they're only one year old. That's too young for riding, I know it."

Alan nodded. "We'll talk about it later. Let's go find your dinner, and some for me too. I'm very hungry." *I could eat a horse,* he thought, as George dropped the Appaloosa on the bed and rushed from the room.

AFTER GEORGE HAD FALLEN ASLEEP, the phone rang. Greenie listened solemnly, talking very little, for the first few minutes. Alan began to wonder if it was Charlie, if the man had enough nerve to call when he must know Alan was right there. He was restraining himself from snatching the receiver when Greenie said good-bye. "Thank you, Officer," she added.

She told Alan that the policeman who had answered the call about the horses had good news and bad. The good news was that the ranch owners, who had been fond of Diego as well as his father, were willing to forgive the whole incident if the veterinarian's bill was covered. Somehow, the indirect connection with the governor seemed also to have impressed and possibly mollified them, the policeman confided in Greenie. But the woman whose car had sideswiped the horse, she was out for blood. Her car had sustained only minor damage, and she hadn't suffered so much as a broken nail, but she claimed that she had been so traumatized she doubted she would be able to drive again without extensive therapy. She might be looking into suing someone, the officer suggested to Greenie. He knew the type all too well.

"This is exactly the sort of thing I was afraid of," said Alan.

"I'll deal with it," she said. "I'll talk to her, and I'll deal with it. This is a very small town. Maybe I have a connection to her somehow."

"Guess you have a lot of connections now, don't you?" Alan spoke quietly, wearily, and when Greenie did not reply, he said, "I'm just too tired to stay awake any longer."

He went into the bedroom. To his surprise, Greenie followed him. She had already insisted he sleep in her bed. No doubt this was for George's benefit.

Hastily, as if he were suddenly modest, he stripped to his T-shirt and shorts and went to bed first. Greenie undressed with her back to him, her every movement exuding resignation and sorrow.

Alan did not bother with a book, nor did she. She stood beside the bed and pulled the chain to start the ceiling fan, then switched off the lamp. As she turned back the covers to join him, Alan noticed the print on the sheets, a scattering of tiny blue flowers that she would never have chosen when they were living together; the moonlight invading the room made the flowers stand out brightly.

Alan and Greenie lay awake a long time, careful not to touch. How bitterly he thought of the shared wakefulness they had savored when they fell in love. One night she had said, into the silence of their patiently waiting for sleep in the dark, "Do you think our parents forgot to teach us how to go to sleep? Do you think it's a life skill they skipped by accident, the way my parents never told me the facts of life because they knew my school taught sex education? Maybe they thought we got sleep education too." This had delighted Alan. "Interesting theory," he'd said, "but don't you hate those people who snore the minute their heads touch the pillow?" Greenie had agreed. "And I pity them. They miss out on so much fretting. All that extra time to think about unpaid bills and invisible tumors. Birthday cards you forgot to send."

Now, as he longed to be one of those despicably somnolent citizens, he waited for her to start pleading her case, the case to keep George, but she didn't. Above them, the fan made a shushing sound, like futile consolation.

ALAN PRETENDED TO SLEEP when he heard Greenie rise before dawn. She did not linger in the house but dressed, without showering, and left for work. Alan got up as soon as he heard her drive away. He went into the kitchen. Oddly, there was no coffee. In New York, Greenie had relied on coffee, every day without exception, to get herself out the door. He had to search the refrigerator thoroughly before he found a bag of beans, shoved to the back behind a dozen jars of mustard, chutney, and jam. The coffeemaker seemed equally forgotten, exiled to a cupboard below the counter.

He ate an orange from a bowl of fruit. He watched the back garden lighten from incandescent blue to milky gray. As he began to hunt for a newspaper or a decent magazine, anything for distraction, George came into the kitchen. "Daddy, where's Consuelo?"

Alan extended his arms, inviting George onto his lap, but George chose a chair of his own. "She's taking a day off, guy. You're with me."

"You'll take me to school?"

Greenie had agreed to keep him out of school for the time being—but soon, she said, he should go back as if nothing had happened. His parents would solve whatever legal and logistical problems his folly might have engendered.

"No school today," Alan said.

"Why?" asked George.

Alan wished he could pretend that everyone had this day off. "Well, for one thing, I'm here and I've missed you very much."

George smiled at his father. Alan wondered, again, if there was any kind of manipulation here, if he and Greenie had been underestimating their son's awareness of nearly everything. George was not a horse or a dog, to be treated like a deaf and dutiful bystander. Even if he couldn't eavesdrop, he could probably read between the emotional lines.

"Okay," said George. "So let's have breakfast and go see what Mommy's cooking today. Actually, the cereal is there." He pointed to a cupboard.

Alan fetched the cereal, the milk. "Breakfast was my idea, too, but after that let's . . ." He was going to say *drive somewhere,* but then he realized that he did not have a car. George waited for him to finish his sentence.

"Let me call your mother and see about her plans." Other than leaving him for another man.

Greenie answered on the second ring. She told him her car was still there, at the house. She told him where to find the keys and the road maps. "Do anything you like," she said. "Just, please, can you be back by six? I think I can make it home by then. I could come back for a couple hours after lunch, if you want, but I thought you might rather—"

"Yes," said Alan, "you thought correctly there."

"Alan, are you all right?"

"Of course not!" He spoke cheerfully, for George's ears. "We'll see you later."

So she had been picked up that morning. By Charlie? Alan would rather that she had driven her car and left him in the house all day, two days, three days, any amount of time that would allow him to deceive himself into thinking that she was with no one other than Ray and the rest of his staff.

HE TOOK THE NEAREST WAY OUT OF THE CITY. The signs told him they were heading for a place called Galisteo, though the only destination he had in mind was New York.

He did not have the conviction to forbid George from bringing two of his horses; really, what was the point? For the first fifteen minutes of their drive, Alan listened to George, in the backseat, fabricating a whispered dialogue.

You are going over the blue hill?

I am going to the cave.

I'll go too.

But the cave is scary.

I'm not scared of the cave. I like the cave.

My brother is waiting for us at the cave. He has the secret message. He has the magic stones from the volcano. It's the cave of treasures.

They passed small, opaquely windowed churches that looked as if they might crumble apart and clatter to the ground at any minute. They passed the occasional donkey, the occasional vaudeville cactus.

So insistently that the words felt as urgent to expel as his own breath, Alan wanted to tell George that he would be returning to New York with his father, to their old home, in just a few days.

He wanted to ask George about Charlie.

He wanted to tell George that Diego might have been a fun friend, but he had not been a good friend, because good friends did not get you in trouble or put you in danger. He wanted to ask George—no, not George, and not Jerry, but someone impartial—whether he deserved to be left by Greenie, whether his crimes were unpardonable, or whether she was probably telling the truth when she said that Charlie had nothing to do with Marion, nothing at all. How had their childhood longings caught up with both of them, pulled them up short from behind, whipped them around and yanked them apart?

"George, do you like enchiladas and burritos?" he said.

"Yes! The cheese kind," said George. "With the not-spicy salsa. With the chips, but not the purple ones. I don't like the purple ones. I like guacamole, but not if it has chunks or the red stuff in it."

"All right then. I read about a restaurant that's on an old farm. Maybe we could go there for lunch. I'm getting hungry. Are you?"

"Yes!" said George. "I think we went to that farm with Charlie."

Alan was glad, for a change, that child-safety regulations required George to ride behind him. "Have you been to lots of places with Charlie?"

"Not *lots*, Daddy. Look, I see a llama! They have llama farms out here! Do you *believe* it?"

"It's very different from New York, that's for sure," said Alan.

"Mrs. Rodrigo says llamas are from South America. A different America."

Let the evening come quickly, thought Alan. Let everything be decided so that I can talk to my son about how his life is going to change. Again.

"But you know what?" said Alan. "You know where your Nana lives, in New Jersey? There's even a llama farm near there! We could go see it next time we visit her. She misses you, too."

"I'd like to see Nana. I miss Nana. She gave me the Legos at Christmas when we went there. And the book of giants."

"You'll see her soon," said Alan, feeling in this assurance a nugget of pure relief. He had told his mother as little as possible over the past year; she did not know about Marion, and she certainly did not know about any of this new mess. He had told Joya, mainly so she'd know how to reach him.

At the restaurant, they were waited on by an older woman who was so friendly that Alan wondered if she had mistaken them for customers she'd met before. She lavished tactile affection on George and winked at

Alan. Over a body like a compact mountain range, she wore a Mexican apron striped yellow, pink, and green. Out of her silvery bun protruded an artificial rose. She introduced herself by pointing to the rose and announcing, "I am Rosalita." She bent toward George and said, "Smaller people have permission to call me Rosa."

When Alan turned down her offer of beer or tequila, she poured lemonade into two green glasses.

"There are actually bubbles inside the glass of the glass!" George exclaimed. "And why are there limes if it's lemonade?"

Rosalita put her pitcher down on the table and touched George's nose. "Observant boy." She said to Alan, "Watch out for this one. He will slip secrets from under your feet like a magician slips a cloth from under dishes."

That's just what I'm afraid of, thought Alan.

He was grateful for the starchy food, rice and beans and delicious puffy rolls that Rosalita called sopaipillas. (Had Greenie learned how to make these for His Royal Fucking Highness in the mansion?) He ate half a roast chicken with a rust-colored pumpkinseed sauce. Except for one large happy family, they were the only customers. Rosalita kept an eye on them from beside the kitchen door, where she sat in a lawn chair and spoke on a cell phone, laughing often.

"Where are you driving to?" she asked as she cleared their plates.

"Not really to anywhere," said Alan. "Just around. Seeing things. My son loves the animals on the ranches."

"Well then," she said to George, "we have chickens and goats out back. There are baby goats you can pet, if you don't mind having your sleeves nibbled. We sell goat cheese that is very, very good."

"I know about the nibbling. Actually, I've petted goats before."

"Ah. Also, we have a very big white rooster. When he crows, he scares away the coyotes, he is so loud. A bear could not sleep through his crowing."

George said that he would like to see the rooster. "Can you pet the rooster, too, or does he peck?"

This bland conversation soothed Alan, and as Rosalita told George a tale about how the rooster had routed a pack of dogs that menaced the goats, he took in her physical particulars—smooth reddish skin, thick solid arms and neck, enormous breasts beneath the voluptuously colored apron—and it struck him full force that he might, not long in the future, accept into his life a woman other than, probably quite different from Greenie. For so long, Greenie had been the only woman he looked at so closely, the woman he considered his human home.

Rosalita seemed to be appraising him as well. "If you will not have tequila, you will have chocolate."

She returned to the table with two shallow bowls of chocolate pudding. Onto George's, she spooned whipped cream; onto Alan's, she poured a small amount of dark liqueur. "Stir," she ordered, twirling a finger in the air.

Before they went out back to meet the celebrated rooster, Alan told her that he hadn't had such a delicious meal in ages. "You needed that, a good meal," she said. She pointed at her own chest. "I see such things."

Though he knew it might spoil before they returned to Greenie's, Alan bought a cake of goat cheese, wrapped in one large shiny green leaf.

THE HORSE PROVED RESILIENT, its leg completely salvageable. Thank heaven it wasn't a racehorse, Greenie observed, to Alan's irritation. The owners of the ranch had installed a video security system and planned to put more elaborate fastenings on the stalls in the barn.

Within two days, the threat of a lawsuit vaporized. Alan was never sure what happened, but he imagined that Ray was involved. Ray could probably vaporize anything—even Alan himself, if Greenie had asked. But this was conjecture, since she was the one who handled the phone calls, all conversations about the horses, the accident, the awkwardness with Diego's family.

Except in his role as a father, Alan's presence seemed immaterial to the crisis at hand. Finally, there were no more reasons to prolong the torture of his stay. On his third unhappy evening in Greenie's place—whose native charms were now nothing more than a reminder that she had become an alien being—he called her in the governor's kitchen and asked when she would return.

"I told you: probably nine, maybe sooner."

"Sooner would be better," he said.

"Is George upset I can't put him to bed tonight?"

"No."

Dishes. Laughter. Unintelligible conversation. The roar of a blender.

"We need to sit down and talk as soon as George is asleep. Not too late. I'm leaving day after tomorrow. I need tomorrow to talk with George."

Over the blender, someone called Greenie's name. The blender stopped. She called back, "The soup bowls are to the left, above the butter plates! For the salad, I want those blue glass plates. Yes. Those." Where wasn't she in charge?

She was back at eight-thirty. George was still awake, though his lights were out. She went into his room to kiss him good night. Alan waited at the kitchen table.

When she came in, she sat down across from him. She forced a smile, but it was unmistakably wary. "So, should I have a lawyer present?"

"This won't be easy," said Alan, "so let's not be sarcastic."

"You're right. I'm sorry."

"Listen, Greenie, if I thought I had any kind of moral footing, I'd try to get you back. It's you I'd take on the plane day after tomorrow. You as well as George." Did he actually utter the words *moral footing*? Christ.

Greenie whispered, "Please don't take George. I know it seems like the right thing to do, but it's not."

"I know it's not the right thing for you, Greenie. I'm not doing this to punish you. That's the first thing you have to know."

"And what's the second? The third? Listen to you, Alan. Who needs a lawyer with you here? You're cold enough for a whole boardroom of lawyers!"

"I'm not cold. I'm holding myself together," he said. "That's the truth, Greenie. You've always been good at that, holding yourself together. You are Iron Woman. I'm not saying it won't be hard—"

"What about George's school? You can't just take him out like that."

"I can enroll him at P.S. 41. You know that, Greenie. He can miss a couple weeks of kindergarten."

"His friends . . ."

"You mean, Diego?" Alan stared sadly and pointedly at Greenie. "Do you see how, in a way, this will be easier for George? I'm not saying I'll act as if this never happened. I'll keep a very close eye on him—"

"Like you're sure I didn't."

On the plane from New York, Alan had wondered if he would take any pleasure in this moment, if he would feel as if he were finally the one in control. But now he saw that his hands, on the table before him, were shaking. He stood, walked around the table, and knelt next to Greenie. He would have sat if there had been a chair beside her, but there wasn't.

"Don't put George in the position of choosing. Because that's the alternative." Alan tried to put his arm around Greenie, but she kept her back firmly against her chair. Her head hung down so that he could not see her face. It was obscured by her beautiful hair.

Greenie turned to him with a gasp. He recoiled, sure that she intended to hit him, but she threw her arms around him and held him tight. He was pinned to her sideways, his shoulder uncomfortably wedged between her breasts, but he made no attempt to move. He said nothing as she cried.

When she let him go, she said, "Just promise me you won't go to court. Promise me that."

"I promise." To Alan's surprise, Joya had already pushed him to find a good lawyer. She was someone who lived and breathed the air of the legal troposphere, but he had assumed she would not be so quick to abandon her sympathy with Greenie.

They sat quietly at the table for a few minutes. Alan listened for sounds of the outside world but heard none: no crickets, no wild animals, no cars, not even water in the ditch out front, now apathetically dry and sprouting weeds.

ALAN'S READING LIGHT WAS ON, and when he sat back, its beam shot past him directly onto George, who slept beneath a thin blue blanket on the two seats between Alan and the window. He felt a profound, protective relief in this island of light. The pilot had announced that he would have to take a circuitous route to the north, to skirt a thunderstorm building over the center of the country, but Alan did not mind the delay.

This time he wrote to Marion about what he remembered from their common childhood. The more he wrote, the more memories he felt erupting in his mind. Like fireworks, they filled a vast dark space with color and excitement—while illuminating face after face with a supernatural clarity. What he needed to show Marion, or simply to remind her, was that they had known each other for years, even if those years were now long in the past. They were not two strangers who'd fallen idly, drunkenly in bed. He was the boy who had—prehistorically, perhaps, but it was history all the same—fallen in love with her. She was the best friend of the big sister, the girl who'd had the grace to humor him just enough, to never quite break his heart. He mentioned Jacob only in passing, their meeting in Berkeley not at all. *I'm going to confess to a fantasy,* he wrote at the end. *I like to imagine that we could go on knowing each other, or know each other all over again, even if we hardly ever meet. What do you think?*

Alan folded the letter in thirds and tucked it into a safe pocket of his shoulder bag. He sat back and laid his right hand on George's hip; ink stained his thumb and middle finger. Outside, he watched the unmistakable brilliance of Chicago rise above the wing of the plane, its shimmering sprawl clipped into a crescent embracing the lake. From here on, he would try to sleep. He might even, for the first time in days, sleep well.

III

Every
Corner
on
Bank Street

EIGHTEEN

QUITE UNLIKE HERSELF, Greenie became superstitious. If Mike Chu passed the side window an even number of times, Charlie would stay; odd, he would leave her. If she found fewer than three blue eggs among the first dozen she opened from the organic farm that delivered on Mondays (the pullet eggs she used for omelettes and fritattas, charmingly varied in size and color), Alan would try to take George away for good. If Ray showed up for breakfast even seconds before the hour, some unknown terrible thing was sure to befall her and soon; just seconds after the hour and she would be safe. Not long ago, she would have been surprised by this change in her nature, baffled and dismayed, but nothing much surprised her anymore.

When she was alone with Ray, she felt sheepish—though after his initial sermon on her infidelity, he'd never reaffirmed his disapproval. Never again did he try to convince her that Charlie was a mistake. He went so far as to ask if she needed a good New York lawyer to win back George. "No," she told him. "George is where he belongs for now." Ray nodded and said nothing further.

She no longer had the guts to partake in the political sparring matches Ray seemed to relish. Sometimes she professed to agree with him when she didn't. She rarely played Broadway songs before he arrived; she did not want him to catch her in the middle of "I Feel Pretty" or "Shall We Dance?" Even alone, she did not feel she deserved to bask in the orchestral ardor of Rodgers and Hammerstein, the sprightly wit of Cole Porter. It seemed improper to mime such happiness, such coy satisfaction. Now she worked in silence; even Billie Holiday was much too superficial.

When she was not with Charlie, she was miserable—not just because he was elsewhere but because the tides of conscience and motherhood rushed to fill the void. You could not lay waste to a heart without suffering your punishment.

When she was with Charlie, Greenie was incurably happy. They spent every night together. Even when he went to Albuquerque, he would drive back, no matter how late, and wake her in his bed. Greenie's place was larger and prettier, but they did not stay there. By virtue of his absence, George was much too present. She had shipped most of his books and toys and clothes to New York, keeping a few for his next visit. She was to see him in New York in September; she wanted to go earlier, but Alan was still too wounded.

So now it was Greenie who called George every day, often morning as well as evening. Almost as soon as he arrived in New York, he seemed to find his place, the rhythm of his old life made new. After one week, he told her that Treehorn had slept beside his bed. He was over the moon. "And Dad bought a bigger bowl for Sunny. Sunny might get bigger, like the bowl, my dad said."

"Really?" said Greenie, fighting her selfish sorrow at George's pride when he said "my" dad.

"Some fish do that, you know. If where they live gets bigger, they get bigger too. We'll see, says Dad. The new bowl is called an acclarion. I want to measure Sunny, but he won't stay still for my ruler. Dad got me a ruler with a Spiderman that leaps when you twist it! I've learned about inches in my school! We measured our bedrooms, you know. Mine's is six feet in one way and eight feet in the other. We drew pictures of the rooms. I drew Treehorn on my bed, even though Dad says she shouldn't sleep up there."

Greenie noticed that he now said "you know" where he once said "actually."

"Do you have friends in your new school yet?"

"Mommy, Ford! Do you remember Ford from my old school? Ford's in my class!"

Yes, Greenie remembered Ford: Ford the Evangelist. God-Is-Everything Ford. "That's amazing," she said. "I am so glad." Ford, Alan told her later, was just one of several kids in the class whom George had known in nursery school. He was doing fine, Alan reassured Greenie, though she could tell from his guarded tone that he knew this good news might also make her feel useless, forlorn, even guilty that taking George with her in the first place had set him on the wrong track.

She tried not to tell George too often that she missed him. Once every few days, she allowed herself to voice that blaring truth. In her house, she kept the door to his bedroom closed so that she would not be tempted to wander in, lie on his bed, hold one of his dinosaurs, and weep. The toy horses, all but the two he'd insisted he take on the plane, she had thrown in the garbage. She told George that their legs would probably break in the mail, that it would be better to give them to another child in Santa Fe who might enjoy them. She believed this was the only outright lie she had told him. But lies and truth overlapped so relentlessly now; that's how it was when you left a marriage, no matter how high the ground you took. How calmly could you look at broken vows, at certainty unraveled? Shortly before their wedding, Alan had taken her to the Cloisters to see the Unicorn Tapestries; later, she came to envision her marriage as a shining blue tapestry hung on a wall, proudly, for all to see. Now it lay on the floor in heaps of tangled thread: bright flashes of memory among the knotty strands of gray and faded browns.

Not that she was in mourning. She loved the foursquare Boy Scout spotlessness of Charlie's life—of his apartment, his mission, his very soul. He did not seem to be one of those men who had never married because he feared other people's disorder. The orderly life he led, inside and out, was one he did not feel compelled to force on others. Greenie's sneakers and sweaters, tossed off in exhaustion when she let herself in, stayed where they were without comment; dustings of flour she might leave on his counter after making a piecrust sometimes lingered until she wiped them away the next morning. (Alan had loved her breakfast pastries best; Charlie craved her pies. He liked them true-blue American, folded roundabout in a blanket of pastry so that when you cut through it, out rushed the captive soft flesh of peaches, apricots, rhubarb, berries. His favorite was a pie she made with Anjou pears and blackberries, the bottom lined with frangipane. If she made a pie, any pie, he would eat a large piece at every meal, three meals a day, until it was gone. "Oh, encore," he would say when he'd swallowed the final crumbs. And she would make another.)

Charlie was pleased that he could live contentedly in so small a space—Greenie knew this without hearing him say so—and he seemed to be happier still that they could share it, if only at night and on snatches of weekend, in a way that kept them so physically close. "I would never want to share a house with you," he said. "You could get too far away from me."

Small spaces are easy to share, of course, when two people are newly in love, when every coming together ends, or begins, with sex; when nakedness is a state both savored and taken for granted. It was a marvel to Greenie that Charlie did not seem skittish after Alan left with George. Secretly, she'd feared he would have to flee or at least retreat for a time. She was wrong: it became immediately clear that he wanted to rejoice.

For the first week, he held back because of her sadness at losing George—but then, one evening, Charlie met her at his place with a bottle of expensive champagne and take-out dinner from a four-star restaurant where only Ray could get a table without a month's notice. Ray was at the ranch, in the culinary care of McNally, so Greenie had spent the day taking inventory in the governor's pantry, clearing out stale nuts, rancid condiments, cereals and snacks that had lost their appeal. After that, the weekend was hers.

She stood idly at Charlie's table examining his collection of rocks, creating an imaginary atlas of his life from the places inscribed on their undersides. He must have opened the door with deliberate stealth, then set down his packages silently, for the first thing she heard was a whoop, close behind her, and then she felt herself upended, slung over a shoulder, thrown down on the bed. He stood above her, beaming. "You are mine, you are mine, you are *mine*," he said. "Tell me it's true—no, tell me nothing, Charlie, nothing for now." He sat beside her and began, slowly, to open her blouse.

"Nothing," she whispered. "For now."

After they made love, Charlie got to his feet and began to jump on the bed. He wheeled his arms upward and back, like a child gaining maximum height on a trampoline. His blond hair stood on end when he descended, and though he was fit, his body betrayed its age, every bit of spare flesh jostling haplessly up and down.

"Charlie, you are crazy," she said. And then something occurred to her. "Did you win? Did you win the appeal? Is that what we're celebrating?"

He stopped abruptly and looked down on her. She'd stayed on her back, moving to the very edge of the mattress. He said, "I am celebrating you."

With George, she had lived her life in close concentric circles. Despite her determination to take him on small-boy adventures, they had hardly ever left the city. Now Charlie took her everywhere. He drove her to dams, so she could feel their fearsome, insidious power, a dark hum along her skin, tunneling down to her bones. He drove her to a mesa—a place where she felt consumed by sky—and told her about a plan to drill for oil that would, without question, endanger the water stored up over millions of years beneath their feet. He took her to a desolate place where people stood in line at a pump to retrieve their water in metal drums and haul it home in their trucks and rattletrap cars. "This water is theirs—it comes from a river that should flow where they live— but now, thanks to government shenanigans, it doesn't, so they have to drive for miles to get it," Charlie told her. He wanted Greenie to know all the things and places he knew; she had to know them not by hearing stories or by looking at pictures—that wouldn't bring her close enough— but by seeing them herself. He could not wait to take her to his favorite places in Oregon, Canada, Mexico.

Yet still she felt a nervous kind of unreality, an off-balance footing, to her altered life, to being loved with such inebriated fervor.

Being in love again summoned forth being in love before: with Alan. She remembered their day at the Cloisters, a memory she had not examined in years. Two weeks had remained before their wedding, and Greenie had let herself fall prey to petty material panic. As she called the florist in Massachusetts for a third time to make *triple* sure they understood that the peonies on the tables had to be white, *pure* white, she was faintly ashamed—because she knew all too well just how appallingly a woman could behave as her wedding loomed. She had seen brides throw last-minute fits about almond paste that tasted too "almondy," about piped roses that looked too "crude," about white icing that did not "precisely" match the shade of a wedding gown. Confronted by such women, she had kept her cool by telling herself that they would never behave so badly under ordinary circumstances, that they would feel embarrassed later. She'd seen a yoga instructor scream herself blue over how much she hated even the suggestion of pink; she had listened to an investment banker whine about Greenie's "unreasonable" policy of charging more for a five-tiered cake that would serve two hundred guests than she would for a three-tiered cake to serve the very same number.

Alan had walked into the kitchen for a glass of water as she was saying to the florist, "None of those peonies with the red on the petals—Festiva maxima, my mother says they're called. . . . No, not those, *not* those! Your e-mail mentioned freesia, but we asked for stephanotis." She'd seen Alan set his glass by the sink and fold his arms, smiling at her with deep amusement. After she'd hung up, he said, "Which of us will the media be covering at this event? Will my crooked tie be mocked in the Style section of the *Times*? Heavens, what if my shoes don't match my belt?"

"Alan, my mother is involved here."

"Yes, and she's taken charge, as only she can do, but this is a day I intend to . . . well, that I will try my damnedest to enjoy. Will you?"

"Of course, but—"

Very gently, Alan had clamped his hand over her mouth, and then he had replaced his hand, for a tantalizing instant, with his mouth. He said, "Tomorrow is your day off. You will not use it to phone seamstresses or chauffeurs or chair rental agencies or klezmer bands. I am taking you to see something sublime."

"What's a klezmer?" she asked.

The shuttle from the Metropolitan Museum had been packed with their fellow cultural aspirants, all tolerant of the torn vinyl upholstery and moldy aroma of a school bus put out to pasture. They had clung to the seats in front of them as the bus wound jarringly up the approach to the monastery; along with the other tourists, they murmured appreciation for its sequestered medieval beauty.

"Eat first, then look," said Alan, who had packed the perfect picnic according to a man: French bread, Swiss cheese, Greek olives, a tub of hummus, sliced sausage, Granny Smith apples, and a bottle of viscous red wine. There were paper cups and napkins, even a corkscrew, but not the utensils with which to slice the cheese or spread the hummus. (Greenie had brought along molasses cookies.)

In the end, she gave in happily to tearing the loaf and using the foil cutter on the corkscrew for slicing cheese, dragging bread through hummus, spitting olive pits into a napkin. "Your teeth are purple," said Greenie after she sat back to look at their fairy-tale surroundings.

"Do you still want to marry me?" said Alan.

"I like purple teeth. Purple is my favorite color," said Greenie.

"I'm serious," said Alan. "I want to make sure you're not just caught up in the wedding. That happens, you know. All that fussing distracts from the importance of being sure right down to the wire."

Greenie had been touched. It wasn't like him to sound so earnest. "Alan, I will be sure beyond the wire. Way beyond the wire."

"Thank you."

"And you?"

"I am never sure about anything," he said, "and I am sure about this."

"Does that make you worry?"

Alan nodded. "Good question. It has made me worry, but I'm past that now. I just want all the flowers and the music and the hemlines and your parents' expressions and the weather and the dancing and the bubbles in the champagne and the—"

Greenie laughed. "Stop!"

"—to be perfect," he said. "I want all of it to be perfect not because I give a damn but because I want you to see it all as background. I want you looking at me, so you can't say later that if only your shoes hadn't been so tight or the clouds so heavy or your snooty Bostonian cousins so late . . ."

"You didn't mention the cake," she said.

"How could the cake not be perfect?" said Alan. "Amazing cake is the one thing I know I can count on. For the rest of my life if I get to spend it with you, right?"

When he led her into the cool stone hall where the tapestries hung, Greenie felt the sleepy thrill of the wine as it seeped into her capillaries and made her skin feel effervescent, the perfect degree of tipsy.

She was surprised that Alan had taken her to see something so violent—though the violence in the tapestries, the hunting down and slaying of the unicorn, was so formal and stylized that it nearly resembled a dance. "I don't want to look, but I can't stop looking," she said as they stood before the tapestry that showed the wounded unicorn, pierced by spears and bleeding, being paraded toward a castle. "The colors are exquisite," she said, almost reluctantly. "But these hunters look like zombies! It's cruel, really. Don't you think?"

He led her to the tapestry, the famous one, of the unicorn held captive: fenced and chained but unharmed. "I suppose this is the happy ending," she said. "As happy as it gets for a unicorn."

"Some scholars," said Alan, "believe the tapestries are a narrative of how the bride captures her groom."

Greenie gave him a skeptical look.

"Really," he said, grinning.

"Is that why you brought me here?"

Alan laughed. "No. I just read that now, on the wall over there."

They spent the rest of the afternoon in the galleries and gardens, holding hands like teenagers on a date.

"Why didn't you bring me here before?" she asked as they waited for the bus in the parking lot.

"I was saving it for a special occasion."

"Are you saving other incredible things? I don't like the idea that you're holding them back. What if something happened and I never got to see them?"

Alan shook his head and laughed. "Greenie, you don't need to seize it all now. You've got plenty of time."

"You don't know that for a fact," she had teased him back then.

"I'll take my chances," he'd said.

And now, here was Charlie, almost tragically the inverse of Alan, cramming as much of what he knew and loved into her life as fast as he possibly could. You would have thought there was a deadline, that they were on a lovers' scavenger hunt, competing for the prize of perpetual joy. Greenie knew that if they had been in New York, a place where she had saved up her own collection of significant things, he would have expected her to reciprocate. But other than her work—which exerted fewer demands than ever on Greenie, now that it was summer, now that Ray spent as much time on the ranch as he possibly could—she had no deadlines whatsoever; she had, now that George was gone, all the time in the world to waste or spend wisely as she pleased. What to do with all that time, however, was simple, almost humiliatingly simple: lose herself in love. Who would choose to do anything else?

AND THEN THERE WAS RAY. So much had shifted between Greenie and Ray in the past few months that she did not know precisely which changes had come from her and which from him. Their morning companionship, because the provocation and teasing had diminished, became almost peaceful. They were together the same amount of time, but they said less. Without George, Greenie worked any and all hours demanded of her, no longer having to negotiate Consuelo's needs as well. This made her work suddenly much easier than it had ever been—and now that she had lived and worked here through a round of seasons, she knew the traditions of the house both public and private, the foods and native customs each holiday called for, the hierarchy of Ray's taste for the many kinds of food she knew how to make. She had been the closet hostess not just of a Santa Fe Christmas Eve (for which she'd filled the mansion with green chili garlands and a promenade of ghostly farolitos), a Mexican Catholic Easter (candies arranged to portray the Virgin of Guadalupe), a Fourth of July (ice cream in colors to match the splendor of fireworks over the valley), and a birthday celebration for Ray (Angus piñatas, persimmon-glazed suckling pig, and coconut cake for thirty friends), but of banquets to celebrate the piñon harvest, the Day of the Dead, and Zozobra.

Ray, too, was in love. This was no secret to most of those around him, though gossip about his ostensibly clandestine courtship passed, within his house, only by way of lingering glances and satisfied smirks. Yet one day Greenie knew, just knew, that he had made up his mind. She knew, too, that six months of tabloid runoff from his out-in-the-open affair with the Hollywood actress had led him to treat his attraction to Claudia like a covert operation, even if it was perfectly proper. Claudia had come to the mansion only twice, for Ray's birthday and for Christmas Eve. Ray saw her mainly when he was out on the ranch. McNally knew her, and her tastes, far better than Greenie did.

One morning in late July, as Ray polished off a bowl of cold asparagus soup (having stirred in half a cup more of heavy cream), Greenie could no longer stand it—the chitchat to cover their placid détente or, for that matter, the suspense.

"Are you going to marry her?" she asked.

Ray frowned. "Her? What her would that be?"

"Ray."

"Well, yes, I am," he said. "On the twentieth of October, that's what I've been thinking."

As usual, he had trumped her. Keeping her cool, she asked, "So how many people know this?"

"You'd be the first."

"After Claudia."

"What did I say? I said you were the first."

They regarded each other with competitive amusement, like two old friends forgiving each other a foolish rift in their affection.

"Don't hug me," he said, seeing her intention. "I'm coming down with a cold. Besides, understand that business is not irrelevant here."

"You love her. I've seen you with her."

"Love flows through many different contours, just the same as a river," he said. "It does."

"The poetry gives you away," said Greenie.

Ray shook his head. "The only poetry I know is the poetry of popularity polls. Oh sing to me of reelection! A liberated woman—a damn smart independent tall bossy woman—will take me far. I am no fool."

"If it's all so calculated, why tell me your intentions?"

"You asked, my girl. And you will be cooking for the guests, so you'd best get cracking."

Panic washed over Greenie. Later, she realized that it wasn't the fear of masterminding a wedding but the fear that if she were there, if she were still doing her job on the day of his wedding, three more months would have passed in which she would not be living with her son or even near him. But her response to Ray's second intentional bombshell was simply a nod.

"Which you will do incognito until I make this fully public. You will."

"Do you mean incommunicado?" she said.

"Make it a song and, yes, that's it." He stood and picked up the hat he had laid on the counter. "You don't sing anymore. I've noticed that."

"I don't sing for you," said Greenie.

"Did you ever?" He laughed briefly, as if to have the final word without speaking.

"Congratulations," said Greenie.

SHE DECIDED TO TAKE ON A NEW CUISINE, to delve into North African foods, introduce spices that she knew Ray would like, that would marry with the local produce she used for dinners to impress visitors from other parts of the country. She made a harissa with chilis from Mike Chu's garden and a rich harira with Ray's beef, stewed with tomatoes, lemons, and heirloom beans from a farm near Chimayo. That weekend she would learn to make warqa, the Moroccan pastry used for bastilla, and jelabi, a fried dough meant to be served with fish. The traditional filling for bastilla was pigeon, but come shooting season, Greenie could use whatever game birds Ray and his cronies brought back from the hunt.

She sat in the cool silence of Ray's vast kitchen, where she could lay out several books on the counter at once, to read and compare. The books, which were new, had to be weighted open with cutting boards and meat mallets. The antiseptic smell of their pages made her feel as if she were in a laboratory, back in a classroom at cooking school.

Except for maids changing linens and dusting tables, Greenie knew she might be the only occupant in the house that day. She had just called New York; Alan had handed the phone almost directly to George, who told her he was going to Ford's for the afternoon. "Ford has a *Star Wars* game, you know," he said. "It goes with the new movie. Daddy says we can see the first *Star Wars*, maybe, but the new one he says is too old for me. Except that the new one happens *before* the first one, you know."

What had become of the horses? How quickly his young, supple mind had moved on to other interests. As she listened to him prattle on, Greenie was disturbed to feel a haze of resentment settle over her affection. Did she have to carry the burden of their separation—and its cause—all by herself? And *Star Wars*? Wasn't even the original movie too old for George?

As she read about what made warqa distinct from phyllo, Mary Bliss entered the kitchen. "Oh, I am sorry," she said.

"No reason to be sorry," said Greenie. "But how come you're not riding, or having a manicure? How often do you get this kind of time off?"

"These days, more than you'd reckon. Am I botherin' you?"

"I could use bothering." She took a pitcher of iced tea from the refrigerator.

Mary Bliss drank two sips of tea, pretending interest in a diagram of how to cut and fold the warqa, before she burst into tears.

To ask Mary Bliss what was wrong would be dishonest, but she did.

"He is fucking engaged," she said through her tears.

Greenie looked at her with concern but said nothing.

"You must think me a certifiable loon," said Mary Bliss.

"No, not at all." Greenie pulled a paper towel from the dispenser by the sinks and handed it to Mary Bliss.

"I can't believe I am *crying*. Lord! All because there's going to be a fucking first lady in this house."

"He's not going to fire you, or even demote you," said Greenie. "He's going to need you more than ever now." This was true but also dishonest.

Mary Bliss looked around. "Do you keep anything here like sherry?"

"Honey, I have it all," said Greenie. "Bourbon?" she guessed.

"Oh lord no."

Greenie opened the liquor cabinet.

"That bottle of Bordeaux, if you please," said Mary Bliss. "And give me the fuckin' corkscrew. I am so sorry I can't clean up my mouth today."

"We all have those days. Recently, I've had a few of my own." Greenie took the bottle from its rack and opened it herself. It was the last of a case, an exceptional vintage sent by a Frenchman who patronized the Santa Fe Opera. She took a heavy blue Mexican goblet off a high shelf.

Next to Mary Bliss, thought Greenie as she filled the goblet, am I lucky? Am I unlucky? Isn't she more deserving of love?

Then something occurred to her. "How do you know he's engaged?"

"He sent me an e-mail this morning. An e-mail, if you please. He's announcing it from the ranch this evening. Six o'clock news. I plan to have passed out by then. Let the fucking phones ring themselves silly."

At which the kitchen phone rang.

"I am not here. I am not on this cruel planet today," said Mary Bliss.

"Darling," Greenie heard when she picked up the phone.

"Hi," she said. "Can I call you back?"

"Can I come pick you up?"

"I'll meet you back at the apartment. In an hour."

"I love you," he said.

"Same here," she said lightly. "But I have a visitor."

Mary Bliss shook her head. "I'll go, I'll go."

"Stay," said Greenie to Mary Bliss.

She closed her cookbooks. She listened to the story of how Ray had plucked Mary Bliss from a gaggle of secretaries over at the Capitol. This was early in his campaign for governor, and she had stayed up so many late nights with him that people began to joke about the matching pairs of circles beneath their eyes come morning. "And I began to think, Oh if *only.*"

Then the movie star had made her entrance. Mary Bliss never minded the actress, mostly because she knew it couldn't possibly last. All the time he played out his fantasies with "Miss Box Office, Emphasis on Box" was time in which Mary Bliss could reveal to Ray her own genuine charm and compatibility. The longer the actress stayed, in some ways the better.

"Bidin' my time, is what I was," said Mary Bliss. "My precious, idiotic time. I even thought I saw him turnin' toward me these past few months, noticing me in a new way. But it was *reflected* love, that's all it was!"

Greenie tried to reassure her that she still had all the time in the world to find a good man and have a family. She could even stay in her fine job and still get over the man. "You'll get a chance to see what he's like married, and I doubt it will be anything close to ideal."

Mary Bliss began to cry again. Greenie tried to embrace her, but she was too miserable for consolation.

"I only wish I'd gone and told him!"

But he knew, Greenie wanted to say—exactly the wrong thing to say. Nor could she tell Mary Bliss that Ray had claimed the marriage to Claudia would be a power marriage—Greenie didn't believe him anyway—because it would reveal that Ray had confided in Greenie before telling Mary Bliss. *Take my husband, a mostly good man I've betrayed and wounded.* She thought of saying that, too. Because there was nothing, really, to say to Mary Bliss. Ray had led her on by never leading her on. Ray, like most politicians, led the world on simply by throwing his grand flirtatious self in every direction.

Mary Bliss had drunk most of the wine. Now she stood up, carried the bottle to the sink, and poured the rest of it down the drain. "Goodbye to my vintage years," she said. "Adios. A Dios. To God. Fuck God." She left the bottle lying on its side in the sink. "I'm going home to watch Cartoon Network. Hope I catch *Road Runner,* that's my favorite." She smiled sadly at Greenie. "*Meep meep!*"

"I'm driving you," said Greenie. "No, you've got no choice in the matter." She took Mary Bliss to her office and helped gather up her things. She held her by one arm as they left the house, afraid that the sudden change of temperature, the harsh light, would make her faint. It was so hot that the sky was nearly white, as if the sun had burned away the blue.

Or no, Greenie thought as she drove, the blue was now inside of her. She felt (unreasonably, but never mind) as if she were the one who'd broken Mary Bliss's heart.

After getting Mary Bliss inside her apartment and turning on the central air, Greenie drove to Charlie's. She told him she needed a nap before going out on yet another adventure. He lay down beside her, and once they slept, they did not wake till after dark.

MAKING LOVE SO OFTEN, with someone new, reawakened Greenie to the history of her body. They never mentioned that long ago, just once, they had been naked together before. Greenie did not want to reignite Charlie's resentment of her mother, and she did not want to find herself wishing that if only they had known then what they knew now, perhaps . . . But to have her body so fondly interrogated—because that's what Charlie's attentions felt like sometimes: a series of urgent, adoring questions—did take her back, time and again, to George's birth.

Objectively, the birth itself had been average; but for Greenie, George's emergence had felt like an athletic event. *This is what a football huddle feels like,* she could recall thinking in the midst of nauseating pain; close about her, exuding the smells of toothpaste, cologne, laundry detergent, raw onions, and disinfectant (temporarily obscuring her own smells of sweat, blood, and far less savory excretions), were Alan, the labor nurse, a female intern, and the essential, necessarily heroic Dr. Gilmorrison. ("Call me Dr. G," he'd once suggested, and that day, perilously short of breath, she had discovered why.) They pressed around her coiled, grunting, pushing body—as if afraid it might suddenly fly away, like a lost balloon—and cheered her on, just as if she *were* a football player.

Afterward, her body was shockingly flaccid: not just her belly but suddenly her arms and thighs and neck—as if they, too, had been taut with the pregnancy and then, once George was born, rendered idle and spent. Purpose seemed to return to her body, all of it, only when she had mastered nursing. This was as painful as her friends had warned her it would be, but George was a good student and latched on almost too well from the start.

When she fed him during the day, her body felt as if it had been made to ensconce a nursing baby the way a saddle was molded to carry a rider—the crevice between her thighs a perfect seat for George's bottom, her waist calibrated to support his flexed knees and, later on, his arm as he rhythmically kneaded her back. The remarkable, unexpected thing was not that the baby yearned for the breast but that the breast seemed to literally yearn toward the baby. At night, she'd take him from Alan, or from his cradle, without turning on a light, and she would guide him carefully toward her right breast, the one George liked best. He would appear to search for only a second or two, and then his mouth became a tiny heat-seeking missile. Gasping, she would feel the magnetic draw on every duct, like dozens of reins pulled tight from behind her rib cage. George drank intensely and fell asleep still joined to her breast. She'd insert the tip of her pinkie at the edge of his mouth, and when his head rolled away, milk would spill across his cheek like sugar glaze poured across a rose-colored cake. Her left breast, ignored, would often ache until morning.

She could not indulge memories of that time without including Alan. After the birth, after a lesson at nursing, after George had conked out, she could not decide which urge was stronger: the urge to sleep or to eat. The first won out, but not, Alan would tell her later, before she had muttered to him exactly what she dreamed of eating. By the time she awoke, night had surrendered to a sunny morning. Her room was filled with a brilliant snow-infused light and a startling amount of activity. A nurse was teaching Alan to swaddle George; an orderly was replacing her pitcher of water; the mother behind the adjacent curtain was babbling to her own brand-new child. Pain had invaded Greenie like an army while she slept, pitching camp in the most unexpected places: her wrists, her throat, her thighs.

"My baby," she said, reaching toward Alan. "Drugs," she said to the nurse.

Alan carried George, uncertain but beaming. Greenie had laughed. "You look like you're carrying a porcupine," she said as she took the baby—whose face seemed to twitch and agitate at the sound of her voice. His mouth opened in a plea, the mouth of a baby songbird.

"I brought you something," said Alan. Then she noticed, on two paper plates on the ugly beige chair where Alan had spent the night, an enormous sandwich and a miniature cake. "Roast beef and coleslaw, that's what you asked for. And devil's food."

For one greedy instant, she forgot her baby. "I'm not supposed to come first anymore, am I?" she said as she wrestled with the task of feeding George, but she found it hard to take her eyes off the sandwich. When she ate it—all of it—and half of the cake, each bite tasted like the answer to a separate prayer.

Late that night, as Alan snored on the foldout chair and George lay cocooned in his Plexiglas box, she took out the greasy carton with the last of her cake and ate it as she marveled at her husband and son. This, she thought, was the true meaning of romance.

Now, by contrast, she could not stop picturing George as he had appeared when she arrived at Diego's house in the middle of the night, after the police had called. She had made the drive in stunned bewilderment, certain only of the need to get to her son and fold him as close to her as possible. But in the moment just after she found him, sitting on a lawn chair while grown-ups milled about him, agitated, ignoring him, he had looked to Greenie shockingly separate from her, too much his own self.

When he saw her, he did not stand. He did not look upset; he looked confused.

"Honey? Honey, what happened?" she said. "Are you all right?" She knelt before him and tried to pull him out of the chair and into her embrace. In his lap was a wooden mask, a crude likeness of a bird with a long hooked beak. He kept his hands firmly on the mask. As she hugged him, she noticed the animal smell in his hair, just like the inside of Ray's horse barn.

"I'm okay," he said. "Diego is okay, too. He's inside the house. They told me to wait for you here. Mommy, I'm cold. My sweater's inside."

Greenie took off her jacket and wrapped it around his shoulders. "What happened?" she asked again, but at this point a police officer approached her. He held a pad and began to reel off a list of questions.

"Wait," she said. "Can I talk to my son alone?"

Not now, she had been told; someone would talk to her son along with her, to find out just what had happened. But did they want something to drink?

By the time Greenie was alone with George again, not for another two hours, he had fallen asleep in her lap in the back of a police cruiser. Only after she had carried him to her own car and laid him in the backseat did Greenie realize that he was still holding the bird mask. As if it were a soiled object, she carried it quickly to Diego's house and set it down on the doorstep. All the lights inside were out, and as she returned to her car, the cruiser drove away. She was the last to leave, the last one awake. She looked into the backseat at her sleeping son. She felt the same old instinctive, marrow-deep love, but for the first time she also felt dismay: disappointment, shame, and the fear that she had forgotten to teach her child something essential and might not be given another chance.

WHEN RAY RETURNED FROM THE RANCH ON SUNDAY, Greenie found herself thrown full tilt into work, as if Christmas had vaulted forward to the middle of August. Phones could be heard ringing throughout the mansion all day on Monday, along with the patient voices of Mary Bliss and her assistant repeating again and again, "Would you please hold?"

Ray told Greenie that Claudia would be coming to dinner the following night and that she couldn't wait to begin discussions about the wedding meal.

"Ray, I think this is beyond me," said Greenie. "I'm not a caterer."

"You've got McNally to ride shotgun," he said. "Between the two of you, we'll have a fandango of a party, I know it. I do."

"How many people?"

"Claudia wants it small. Maybe two hundred."

"Two hundred is small?"

"Hey, that's not even half my best friends."

Greenie uttered what she hoped was a suicidal-sounding laugh. "Two hundred, five hundred. All the same to me."

Ray had been eating lunch alone in the dining room, scrolling through e-mail on a laptop. He looked up. "I'd go with five hundred. Claudia claims that would be in poor taste, since she was married before. What do I know?"

"Does that mean no white dress, no veil?"

"Turquoise, she says. I leave the fussy stuff to her. I'll show up—'specially if you're cooking. I always show up for your meals, don't I?"

Again, he met her eyes. "We need the people in charge to be people we trust. You'd have to resign your job to say no."

"Sink or swim."

"Swim! Swim! Butterfly, breaststroke!" said Ray, his arms undulating to either side of the computer screen. "You'll get all the help you need. Use your city-girl know-how. Hey, why not import that other city girl, the one you sold your business to? Now let me eat your food in peace."

Greenie phoned McNally. He told her that Claudia wanted barbecue. "Ribs, jicama slaw, a buttload of peppers, and a gigantic, special, totally unique cake. Quote unquote," McNally said dryly. "Glad to say *that*— the 'totally unique' part—would be your department."

"*That* I can handle. Can I leave the rest to you?"

"Not on your life."

CHARLIE WAS THRILLED. "Can I be your date? Can you poison just the cake that goes to the state engineer, the reclamation guy, and the director of the BLM? Can I watch them die slowly right there, under the big top?"

"You know, we did get this lecture back in school. 'How to Poison Absolutely Anybody Absolutely Anywhere Without Getting Caught.' But I had the flu that day. Sorry. Anyway, I don't get a date. I'm the hired help. Christ, I'm the *boss* of the hired help. And on your own, I regret to say, you would probably not make the governor's top-two-hundred list."

"Nor his top-one-thousand list."

"He does like you, Charlie." She thought of Mary Bliss, wiping her forehead with a dish towel. She thought, too, of how Alan had made a similarly tiresome joke about poisoning Ray the very first time she had cooked for him.

Greenie and Charlie stood in her kitchen, which was stifling, though she had opened the door to the garden and turned on the fan. Charlie frowned on air-conditioning except in the very worst heat. They had come to pick up her mail. She hadn't been home in three days; she didn't really live there anymore but held on to the place with the hope that somehow George would return for good. George could never have lived with them in Charlie's place; even Charlie agreed.

She tossed catalogs on the floor and separated bills from not-bills. Near the bottom of the pile was an envelope from Alan.

Charlie had picked up the catalogs and was telling her that she should write to the companies and get herself removed from their lists, that this was a terrible waste. He stopped when he saw her sitting at the table, motionless.

"What is it?"

"I don't know," she said. "I don't want to know."

"You think it's legal?"

"I don't know." She placed the envelope in the center of the table, by itself.

Charlie set the catalogs on the counter and put his hands on her shoulders.

Still she did not move. "I suppose he's asking for a divorce."

"Is that what you're afraid of?"

"No, not that."

"Would you divorce him, or let him divorce you?" Charlie went to the opposite side of the table and sat down to face her.

"It has to happen, I guess. It's just . . . so much more agony."

Charlie leaned toward her. "Would you take the divorce," he said, "and then marry me? We could have George live with us here, at least for the school year. I know we could make that happen. I promise you it wouldn't be ugly."

Greenie felt as if she had touched an electric fence. "Oh Charlie."

She tore open the envelope. Inside it, without a note, was another sealed envelope, addressed to her in New York, from one of her cousins in Boston. Except for Christmas cards, she hadn't been in touch with any of her cousins since shortly after her parents' funeral. The letter was typed on the cousin's law-firm letterhead; bitterly, she laughed at the irony.

"Oh," said Greenie after she finished reading. "Oh my."

"What?"

"My cousins are wondering if they can buy me out of my share in the house on the island."

"Is that good news?"

Greenie folded the letter and replaced it in the envelope. "I haven't thought about that house for a long time. I mean, not as part of my future." She blushed, but Charlie did not appear to share her memory. She sighed. "It seems so far away. Well, it *is* so far away."

She realized that she had all but ignored his marriage proposal, shoving it aside for a real-estate proposal. She opened her mouth to turn back the conversation, but Charlie was paging through a clothing catalog. He looked worn out.

IF THE TEMPERATURE GOES ABOVE NINETY-FIVE TODAY, I will marry Charlie. If the phone rings before ten, I will get to have George again. If the butter in the skillet melts before Maria returns from setting the table, Charlie and I will have a baby of our own.

Claudia was easy to work with because she knew exactly what she wanted. She'd been through a wedding before and remembered all the mistakes she had made ("other than saying 'I do' to that S.O.B.").

"A completely grown-up wedding," she told Greenie. "Except that reporters will be present." One photographer from each of the New Mexico and Colorado dailies would be allowed to take pictures between the ceremony and the reception. The entire affair would take place on the grounds of the mansion.

McNally's presence in the city kitchen was nearly comic. Against the polished beige surfaces, he looked like an outtake from a colorized western: his face too harshly red, his clothes clumsy in bulk and shape. They sat on stools at the center island, listening to Claudia go through her lists; Greenie could feel the vibration as McNally swung his short legs back and forth, leaking nervous energy. Every so often, he'd catch himself reaching up to pick his teeth, force his hand back into his lap. Looking meek and claustrophobic, he deferred to Claudia as "ma'am," waiting a full beat before answering any of her questions or making comments. Greenie realized that any necessary amendments to Claudia's plans would have to come from her.

Claudia had changed her mind about the ribs. She had decided on filet mignon, the beef to come from the affianced ranches, to be grilled out in the open. She went to the window and pointed to a place where she believed the grills could be placed so that the cooking smoke would be blocked from the reception area behind the mansion. Greenie had no idea what direction the wind, if any, was likely to come from. She looked pointedly at McNally—surely he had an indigenous sense for such matters—but he was gazing at Claudia (or her back) with undisguised sorrow.

Like Mary Bliss, McNally was not happy to see his boss getting married. Greenie should have figured this out the minute he arrived in her kitchen; never mind that, like Greenie, he had seen it coming. Ironically, now that their earlier prediction had proven true, they were powerless to predict anything further. When it came to Ray's wedding, McNally would follow Greenie's orders, but he would take no initiative. He was too fearful of losing his job.

Greenie joined Claudia at the window. She liked this woman, but at the moment she felt piercingly alone, as if her life were an open prairie, bright with sun but far too wide and empty. She felt as if someone had handed her an edict informing her, with cosmic authority, that she was entirely, absolutely, unforgivably in charge. Of weddings, of hearts, of fates, if only a few. A small-time monarch, that's what she felt like as she stood in the smallest of kingdoms, a kitchen, peering at the world beyond its walls. *Be very, very careful what you wish for,* said the edict.

AUGUST PASSED IN A SCORCHING BLUR, a rippled vision like a desert mirage. Ray was out of town for two weeks, and Greenie would gladly have gone to New York, borne its mean urban heat to be with George, but Alan said he'd rather wait, as they had agreed, till George was well settled in first grade. Alan would stay with them in the city for a few days, so George could be with his parents together, and then Alan would go to San Francisco. His sister was planning to adopt a baby, had he told her that?

They exchanged their news, concisely and politely, by e-mail. Though Greenie phoned New York twice a day, Alan now gave the phone straight to George. Or George himself would answer. "It's me!" he'd shout against the mouthpiece, sounding more exasperated than eager. George was going to "camp" at his old nursery school. The little campers played in the classrooms and up on the roof, where an awning sheltered a wading pool, a fleet of tricycles, and a flower garden planted in bathtubs. Dutifully, Alan had described the particulars in June, going through the motions of including Greenie in the decision of how George would spend his summer.

They went on field trips, George told her. They had been to the Union

Square farmers' market and the nearby museum with the toy soldiers, but they had also been to Coney Island and to the merry-go-round in Central Park. When Greenie commented on how far from his school these places were, he informed her cheerfully, "We have special T-shirts with the camp name, for if we get lost on the subway." Greenie tried not to envision such a mishap.

For the first time in months, Charlie ventured farther away than Albuquerque. He went to California, to meet with lawyers who worked for the Sierra Club. He would be gone for several days. Greenie spent her free time wandering the sunstruck town. Shoulder to shoulder with summer tourists, she browsed through galleries filled with colorful blankets and baskets. She sat quietly one afternoon in the Santuario de Guadalupe, inhaling the scents of resin and incense, trying to understand the story told in the church's cameo paintings. Had a cloakful of roses become a radiant image of the Virgin, was that it? Greenie felt tears begin to gather. This happened so easily now, at both ends of the emotional spectrum.

She did not drive anywhere except to the mansion, and there was little reason at all to do that. Mary Bliss, who had gone home to Nashville to look for another job, urged Greenie to take a week off and leave the city.

On the day before Charlie's return, she stood gazing at a red couch in the window of a stylish furniture store on Marcy, wondering how you could recognize a certain kind of beauty as Italian, when she noticed, in the window's reflection, that a woman had stopped across the street and was staring in her direction. When Greenie turned around, the woman started to hurry away.

"Wait!" Greenie called after Diego's mother.

Theresa allowed her to catch up. Her expression was aggressively neutral.

"I don't know what to say," said Greenie. "I've been meaning to call you, but I haven't, I'm sorry. I guess you know George went back to New York."

Theresa nodded.

"He misses Diego, you know. He adores Diego." She had nearly said "adored" or "still adores," as if the affection had to be a thing of the past.

Theresa nodded again. She was a broad woman, but she was pretty, with a youthful, coppery Mayan face and lovely dark eyes. The expression in those lovely eyes, aimed steadily at Greenie, might have been contemptuous or simply aloof. Greenie tried not to look away.

"I didn't handle that evening well at all," she said.

"It doesn't matter," Theresa said quietly. "It's in the past. Diego is not allowed near the horses now, and we do not talk about it. He is gone away for the summer. He works for my sister at her house in Albuquerque. He comes back when it is time for school."

"Is he . . . is everything okay with his father?"

Theresa shook her head, not to say that things weren't okay but to brush off the question. "I have more children than Diego. Diego is a part of the family, and if he is doing his chores and his schoolwork, this is all we ask now. I did not think the friendship a good one. That was the trouble." She spoke fiercely, inflicting the wound she had intended.

"George is a good boy. He did love Diego," Greenie said.

"He was too curious, this was the trouble. A nice boy, but too many questions. Too many questions lead to trouble. When you are a mother longer, you will understand this."

In the silence of her own embarrassment, Greenie thought of Diego's placid nature. Was this the intangibly peculiar thing about Diego, that he rarely asked questions? Had he been taught not to ask questions? She felt herself scowling at Diego's mother. *It could have ended far worse,* she was tempted to say. *Be grateful we got off as well as we did.* But the conversation was finished.

"Take care," said Greenie as Theresa started on her way. She could not be sure, because the woman's back was turned, but she thought Theresa might have laughed.

Greenie turned the corner and leaned against a shaded wall. Its rough, cool surface calmed her. From there, she walked into the nearest shop. A woman beamed at her from behind a luminous jewelry case: the familiar confectionary array of turquoise in its many hues; corals in orange, scarlet, even purple; lapis lazuli, malachite, obsidian.

"Shopping for a gift?" said the woman. "Everything for men is half off today."

Greenie saw a row of silver bracelets, some sleek and slim, others broad and braided; men's bracelets. "Yes," she said when the woman asked if Greenie would like a closer look.

She left the store with a box that contained, on a wafer of cotton, a clipped oval of silver, narrow but inlaid with a long straight channel of old green turquoise. Charlie's proposal had hung over both of them, like a pine bough weighted with snow, for nearly a month. Why hadn't she accepted? What was she waiting for—everything to turn out just right, everyone to love her, the charming, gregarious, talented Greenie Duquette, all over again as if she had never done anything wrong? That was the root of her superstition: the fear that whatever pain she inflicted must earn her pain, and much more of it, in return. But the world, as Small George already knew, was never just.

NINETEEN

SCOTT AND SONYA NO LONGER WENT OUT on the town every night. Now they had taken to hunkering down in the apartment, a hipster version of the old married couple, eating takeout at midnight while listening to incomprehensibly jarring music on Scott's CD player and then, until two or three in the morning, composing songs of their own. Walter, in turn, had taken to wearing earplugs when he went to bed, though he hated blocking such a vital alert system before entering the defenseless land of nod. For more than a week now, they had been working on a song called "Purple Tarmac Blues," which pondered (abrasively) the many colors and textures of asphalt and the likeness of love to tar itself, how it would ultimately trap you like the poor creatures fatally mired at La Brea. *Behold the dinosaurs of passion, the fuh-fuh-fuh-fuh-futile fuh-fuh-fuh-fuh-FOSSILS of love!* was one line Walter kept hearing loud and clear, even with his door closed and the air conditioner turned up full blast, because it seemed to be the song's wailing climax. Their hour-long efforts to find a rhyme for *violet* (apparently the color of upper-class suburban macadam—which they rhymed with *Mill Valley madam* and, if Walter's ears could be trusted, *smokin' señoras lemme at 'em*) finally drove Walter out in search of a club, the sort of outing that had lost its luster ever since the fizzling, yet again, of his relationship with Gordie. Walter understood now that when Gordie had proposed a "separation," he'd known there would never be a reunion. Yes indeedy, if love was tar, then Walter had been royally tarred and feathered. Still, however cowardly Gordie might be, at least he was discreet.

Now Walter walked the streets of the Village—blessedly balmy, as they had been for most of August—and reassessed his determination to be just as magnanimous and tolerant to Scott as Granna had been to him. Writing songs, however bad (though who was Walter to judge modern music?), was an art. Scott might not be talented, but he was not dealing drugs. Walter delighted in continuing to flummox his brother by keeping the boy out of trouble; what were a few lost hours of sleep next to proving that you were superior to the older brother who had left you in the lurch when you needed him the most?

Werner, Tipi, and the suddenly buxom fifteen-year-old Candace had come east for a visit over the Fourth of July. They took a suite at the Plaza, on a high floor with a view of more than one fireworks display. Almost shamefully, Walter was impressed, for he had always made it a policy to escape New York on this particular holiday; how loathsome, he'd always maintained, that real estate should render the celebration of populist power such an elitist occasion. (Candy Kinderman, cell phone addict, seemed *un*impressed, disappearing into the master suite to talk to her friends back home.)

Walter had arranged to take time off so that he could squire everyone to the Ellis Island Museum, the Guggenheim, and a classical guitar concert at the Winter Garden. For meals, he'd planned on oysters at Blue Ribbon, sushi at Tomoe, and classic Italian at Da Umberto. (Scott suggested an evening at the Knitting Factory, which Walter answered with an are-you-out-of-your-*mind* smirk.) How silly not to have guessed that Werner had made plans of his own: a Mets game, drinks at a revolving bar, dinner at Windows on the World (which Walter skipped; what overpriced déclassé fodder), a chartered boat from South Street Seaport (okay, *this* was fun), shopping at Barneys and at the weary, sclerotic galleries remaining in SoHo. Werner had also finagled five insanely expensive tickets to *The Producers* (how wickedly Walter wished that they could have gone to *Naked Boys Singing* or *Hedwig and the Angry Inch*).

For the week of his parents' visit, Scott seemed to have the surprisingly canny instinct to minimize the presence of Sonya. Thanks to a suspiciously coincidental meeting, she did show up once, just in time to join them for the private cruise. Candace spent most of the cruise yakking on her phone, and Werner and Tipi were too busy playing with their new digital camera, taking pictures of the skyline from the water, to pay much attention to their son's punksterette pal. Walter realized that, to Scott's parents, this year away from the life they wanted him to lead was just an insignificant hiatus, like a stop on the highway to grab a burger, use the rest room, and fill up on gas.

Walter had counted on making a visit to his apartment as inconvenient as possible—though he needn't have bothered—and instructed Scott on compliance with the plan. "If your dad sees how we are living, the close quarters, he is sure to call the vice squad." Scott uttered a predictable "Copa, dude." Walter's real reason for hiding the apartment, however, was pride. If Werner saw how modestly he lived, it would reinforce the elder brother's superior standing.

The only gap in Werner's choreography was the final night of the visit. "You surprise us with a favorite restaurant of *yours*. Except, of course"—chuckle, chuckle—"for your place, which we know and love."

So, on that blessedly final night, as they sat in Union Square Café, Werner poured out a bottle of champagne (overruling the waiter's efforts to do so) and raised his glass. "To Stanford," he said, directing a leonine smile at his son.

Tipi smiled more timidly, while Candace gulped down her glass, concentrating on the luxury of booze condoned by her parents. She was wearing a pink cashmere sweater, which Walter thought much too tight for her age, and had painted her nails the very same color.

"Yeah, long may it wave," toasted Scott. "Yale and Harvard too. Masters of the universe, unite! You got nothing to lose but your scalps!" He laughed carelessly.

Werner ignored the jest. "Rourke tells me admissions has a spot for you in September."

Oh this will be more delicious than the meal, thought Walter.

"Whoa, Dad. That's like dropping the boom."

"That's telling the facts, son. You've had a great year with your uncle." He nodded reverently at Walter. "For which your mom and I are endlessly grateful. You needed to get a fresh perspective, and I'm sure it will serve you well."

"Yeah, but like, I'm practically off the waiting list for this amazing workshop and really finding my voice. I'd never, like, even considered the blues as a plausible art form till now."

Werner's confident smile bore just the hint of a threat. "You'll be singing more than the blues without a solid education."

Across the room, Walter watched the host seat Julianne Moore and her scruffy-adorable boy-man, along with that tall blond actress who'd clearly been born with a harelip (Laura Linney? Diane something?). He whispered in his niece's ear and pointed. She looked both tipsy and awestruck.

"Dad, I can always get a college education. I can't always seize the moment of inspiration. I feel like it's totally now or never with my music."

Walter watched *never* flash across his brother's face.

Tipi blinked, doelike, at Scott. "Honey, they have plenty of music at Stanford. It's not the army."

"Even the army has music," said Candace. "Do you know how much the government spends on military bands? Like more than they do on public education." As she spoke, her eyes scanned the room for other celebrities.

"Nobody said anything about the army, for God's sake," said Werner. "Let's not exaggerate here. Your mother is right. I'm sure they have bands and orchestras and things like that. Some colleges even have their own . . . cabarets. Radio stations. You could be a deejay on weekends."

"Perhaps you could have a minor in music," said Tipi. Werner flashed her a let-me-handle-this scowl.

Scott was stacking his silverware, looking down and slowly shaking his head. Suddenly, he pinned his gaze on Walter, a piercing plea across the table.

Walter cleared his throat. "Werner, Scott is learning the ropes in a sophisticated, potentially quite lucrative business. Where's the harm in another six months or so? It's not like he's lounging around strumming the banjo and smoking weed. He's not a Beatnik. You never know—he could grow up and be the next Danny Meyer." He realized Werner had no idea who Danny Meyer was. "Or Colonel Sanders."

"Very funny," said Werner. He turned to Scott. "What aspects of the business have you learned thus far?"

Scott shrugged. "Like, lots of running-the-kitchen stuff, and like . . ."

Walter broke in. "He's been helping me go over the books. He's been learning about the division of labor in a professional kitchen, soup to nuts." He smiled. "Or should I say stew to sorbet. Garde-manger. Booking reservations. Compliance with health regulations."

"Like washing your hands after going to the bathroom?" said Candace, who'd poured herself the last of the champagne. "Duh."

Werner was not distracted. "A very narrow range of skills."

"Keeping the books is practical," said Tipi.

Werner ignored her. "Of little use if he wakes up one day and wants to be a doctor. Which happens far more often than you'd guess. My dermatologist majored in *philosophy,* but at least he had that B.A. when he needed it.

"You are now nearly twenty years old," he said to Scott, attempting to sound more conversational than autocratic. "When I was twenty, my parents were dead and I had no cushion to fall back on. I was on my own. You are a lucky young man."

You had Granna, thought Walter. *You were headed for Haight-Ashbury, all expenses paid.* He clamped his lips together.

Yearningly, Candace followed Julianne Moore's elegant trajectory toward the ladies' room. Walter had also spotted Dame Edna, but none of his white-bread relations would have known—or wanted to know— who *she* was.

"So you're, like, going to disown me or something if I don't go to Stanford like *right away*? Wow, Dad. Wow."

Surprisingly, Werner seemed to have no ready answer.

Walter raised his hands, the benevolent traffic cop. "Werner, listen to me. Chill a teensy bit, will you? Twenty these days is young—and I admit, I'm jealous too! But I am willing to take responsibility here. Let's say I raise the bar for Scott, make him take on more challenging work. Maybe he could take a class in business accounting. You know, I've been thinking of starting a second restaurant. He could be very helpful there." Had he been thinking of this? Why in the world was he so keen to hang on to Scott? How nice it would be to have the apartment—even The Bruce—all to himself once again.

Tipi looked at her husband and then at Scott. "Sweetheart," she said, "do you really love this work? Is there a possible career for you in this? I mean, one that will support you in the manner to which you are accustomed? The music just isn't likely to do that."

Werner snorted faintly, but he had lost the spotlight.

Scott shrugged. Walter glared daggers in his direction, forcing him to straighten up and declare, "Mom, I'm not a liar. The restaurant is cool, it's a cool place, cool work. But it lets me be on for my music, too. It's like a ripe combination. The right job at the right time. Dad, I am not going to morph into some kind of deadbeat, okay?"

Werner shook his head with dismay, but Walter could see that Scott, for now, had won. "So much for the Taittinger," said Werner, and flagged the waiter to order a more modest, less celebratory wine.

Instinctively, Walter watched to see how quickly the waiter would respond—and looking in that direction, he saw Stephen enter the dining room. Not with Gordie, saints be praised, but with a middle-aged woman. Still, Walter did not want to make eye contact with him. Yet why in tarnation should Walter feel guilty? Alas, the host led Stephen right past their table. He saw Walter and looked away. Walter wondered if Stephen knew that he, too, had been dumped by Gordie—forgotten more than cast aside. Yet how could Walter even *think* of such a comparison? He had never lived with a lover at all, never mind a lover who became, over more than a decade, a mate. When his attention returned to the table, Werner and his family were discussing Julianne Moore. Candace had just said how amazing she was in *Boogie Nights;* from a twitch on Candace's face, Walter could see that she realized, too late, she ought not to have mentioned this movie.

Tipi looked at Werner. "I think we missed that one. Is it out on DVD?"

Scott covered his mouth, trying to hide his laughter. When Walter met his eyes, they lost control in unison.

Tipi smiled. "May I ask what's so hilarious?"

"Oh," said Walter, "that movie is kind of like a remake of *The Sound of Music*. But it's not well done. You can give it a pass."

"Yeah," said Scott, "like Julianne Moore, Julie Andrews—same diff."

"Can Julianne Moore really sing?" asked Tipi.

Walter and Scott were now laughing so hard that tears ran down their cheeks. Candace, blushing scornfully, excused herself.

Stephen, seated two tables away, stared right at them all with such menace that Walter became instantly sober. "But seriously," he said, his voice low, "you have got to see her in *The End of the Affair*. Her accent could have used some extra coaching, but does she ever have gorgeous *breasts*. Werner, would you pass that sinfully exquisite bread?"

THAT NIGHT, ONLY A MONTH BEFORE, had been a high point in Walter's connection to his nephew. It did not take Dr. Freud to interpret Walter's longing for that connection as much more than family feeling. Walter knew he was grasping at youthful straws (now that he was grecianizing his hair), pathetically hoping that Scott's loose-limbed ways and callow sense of immortality might rub off on him just a little, lending him that peerless sheen.

Now, as he walked brazenly along the Hudson River at two-thirty in the morning, something else occurred to him. All Walter really wanted (well, not all, but quite a lot of all) was to be genuinely, uniquely needed. He had believed, falsely, that the risks Gordie took to be with him in the beginning were sure proof of such a need. The greater the risk, the greater the need; wasn't that logical? And though Scott had never conveyed anything but a sense of independence, Walter had believed that his nephew's gratitude would grow into a yearning that paralleled his own. But now, if there was anyone Scott needed, or believed he needed, it was probably Sonya.

"Of all people," Walter said aloud, "I've been robbed by Spiderwoman." He laughed quietly. He wished he had brought The Bruce along, not for protection but to look up at him when his own lame jokes broke the surface of his lonely, opinionated psyche. Well, T.B. needed him. That was nothing to sneeze at.

The towers that defined the city's skyline remained bright even at this ungodly hour, like punch cards coded with fluorescent light. Were all those illuminated offices empty, or were bankers and traders still up there, alongside the janitors tending to trash cans filled with the documentation of yesterday's monetary tides? Walter sighed as he turned back east on Christopher Street. He had a much nicer life than any of *those* people, no matter his measly troubles.

When he entered the apartment, it was, as he had hoped, silent. It smelled of pizza, and half of Sonya's grisly garb festooned the couch—but at long last it was silent. He went to the kitchen for a glass of water. On the way, he realized that his right shoe was sticking to the floor.

Green chewing gum: Sonya's trademark substitute for conversation with grown-ups. Walter threw it in the sink, where it landed on a long tomato-stained knife laid across a stack of plates. The pizza box protruded from a garbage bag that ought to have been trussed up, taken downstairs, and replaced. Walter resolved to have a paternalistic word with Scott. Again. Sonya's gum would give him a more than justifiable entrée. *It's her or me!* flashed through his mind. As if.

When he filled his glass, he noticed a small slip of paper adhering to the bottom of the water pitcher. He peeled it off. It had been folded several times, and the ink was waterlogged and blurry, but the message still stood out, as legible as it was blunt: BIG   HARD   PRIMED TO FUCK YOUR DAYGLO BRAINS OUT   MAKE YOU EXPLODE LIKE A TANK UNDER SIEGE.

Walter gasped and dropped the note. He knew this language well—no Tipi Kinderman, *he*—but in his own kitchen, right under Granna's demure samplers, written out boldly, no qualms whatsoever . . . Was that Scott's handwriting? Sonya's? It was unnaturally tiny and cramped, though the intentions expressed were anything but.

Walter crumpled the message and pushed it deep into the garbage, past the pizza box. When he pulled out his arm, there was grease on his sleeve.

DURING THE LAST WEEK OF AUGUST, Walter accepted an invitation to Fire Island. Scott would play host at the restaurant, with Ben looking over his shoulder. "I warn you, Ben will let me know if you are so much as a nanosecond late," said Walter. "And if you get in over your head, you can always call me. I don't think we'll have a full house, even on Saturday, so reservations shouldn't be a problem, and Hugo's a genius at guessing how much of everything we need. Really, the place should run itself."

T.B.'s eczema had flared up again, as it always did after prolonged exposure to heat. That was another good excuse to get out of town. They'd be staying in a huge glass house shared by two wealthy couples, and the parties promised to be dense with beefcake. In one fell swoop, Walter would renew his sorry tan and his moribund libido. And heaven only knew, maybe he'd *meet* someone.

On the morning he packed, the phone rang. For the first time in nearly a month, he heard Greenie's voice.

"Dear stranger!" he exclaimed. "You very nearly missed me! I'm off to the land of no cars and way too much sex."

"I can't say I'm envious," she said. "I'm too tired for way too much sex."

"How are you?" he said, sitting down on his bed. "How's that glistening man from your past?"

The pause that followed was so long, Walter expected the worst.

"Walter, I think we're going to get married." Her voice was soft, almost resigned, and it took him a moment to understand.

"Bless my jaded soul," he said. "But could we sound a little less blue?"

"I feel . . . I'm like an outlaw these days. I've lost touch with so many people—entirely my fault, I know they wouldn't judge me, but suddenly it's like I'm this pioneer woman off in the desert, severed from everyone I knew before."

Walter knew all about the child and his misbegotten prank. Greenie had called Walter during that mess, and twice in the past month he'd spotted the boy on Bank Street. He rode on his father's shoulders, grasping at branches, laughing as if his little life were perfect. Alan looked happy too, though more quietly so. Once, seeing Walter, he'd lifted a hand from George's sandaled foot to wave. Walter waved back, but they had not spoken.

"So when will I meet him, this Galahad?"

"You'll have to come out here," said Greenie. "You can have my house, throw parties, do whatever you like. Basically, I live at Charlie's."

"A house to myself in Santa Fe? Honey, count me in."

"But I'll see you soon anyway. I'll be back there in a month."

"I can't wait to see you, sweetie," he said. "But if you don't have much time for me, I'll understand. And business promises to soar, so I may not have a *life*. Is the good governor jumping on this all-eggs-no-toast bandwagon?"

"Walter, he's practically driving. But it's not a diet, it's just his innate sense of immortality."

"Talk about comebacks," said Walter. "First John Travolta, then Tony Bennett, now What's-His-Face Atkins. Bacon is the new bok choy! Hugo's made enough omelettes this summer to sink the *Titanic* all over again." Walter sighed. "But you know, I liked it better when I was the countercuisine. I've got these customers who talk to me now like I'm their nutritional guru. All these neo-carnivores raving about *ketosis*—frankly, I wouldn't know ketosis from halitosis."

Greenie laughed. She sounded more like her old self. If Walter was good for one thing, it was amusing people out of a funk. No small talent, though he would rather have charmed them into commitment. Greenie's life right now wasn't one to be envied—but still. This was the *second* man whose heart she'd won over completely.

Walter told her he had to fly but that he'd call her when he returned. He packed all his most flattering pale-colored clothes, including a vintage dinner jacket à la William Holden that he hadn't worn in three years, along with a toilet kit monopolized by an optimistically thick accordion of condoms and a large plastic bottle of T.B.'s eczema cream. He taped the cap to the bottle, to be sure it wouldn't burst inside his suitcase. Odd miniature disasters seemed to lurk in wait for Walter these days, so he took whatever precautions he could.

THE WEEK ON FIRE ISLAND was pleasant but predictable. Predictability was a great relief at times, but on this occasion it felt vaguely sad to Walter. There was plenty of fine beach weather, and he saw everyone he expected to see, whether by design or happenstance. Along the boardwalks, he had that funny sensation of spotting one familiar face after another—only to pass them and realize, from the mirroring of his own baffled geniality, that he recognized them from the restaurant. These encounters were satisfying—especially when someone nodded or greeted him in such a way as to express approval—yet each time a twinge of loneliness passed through Walter, the transient fear that he knew everybody a little bit and nobody all that well.

He regaled his friends and new acquaintances with tales of what it was like to be the surrogate parent of a rock 'n' roll teenage boy, while The Bruce made time with a new crowd of pooches, mostly upscale purebreds. T.B. had more success on the romantic front, stealing the soul of their host's Rhodesian ridgeback—while Walter had more success in the zipless department. What was it about the ocean that made you think of nothing but sex, sex, sex? Did salt draw lusty fantasies from your reptilian brain the way it drew moisture from flesh?

Walter had hoped to meet someone he'd see again, in the city, through the fall and winter, when lying against another person, night after night, the whole night through, mattered most of all. Once again, wishing for love had kept it at bay. No matter: by the end of the week, thanks to sex and sun (and sleeping late), Walter could look in the mirror and see, no small consolation, that he glowed.

Ben had called Walter just once that week, to double-check on their credit with a vendor. When Walter asked how Scott was holding up, Ben had said, "Needs a haircut, but no complaints." Thus believing that everything was "copa," Walter could not have anticipated the state of his own apartment when he walked through the door that Labor Day afternoon.

Granted: Walter did not often see the place in full sun. Right away, the veneer of dust dismayed him. But dust was insignificant next to the clutter of clothing, musical instruments, dirty dishes, empty beer and soda cans, and used *ashtrays*—that is, dishes used as ashtrays. Scott did not smoke; not even Sonya smoked—or did they? Walter dropped his bags and examined the ramekin-ashtray on the coffee table: nothing illegal, at least.

Some kind of speaker (amplifier?!) stood under the dining table. Black cords meandered and coiled beneath the furniture to join to it a guitar and an odd-looking flute. Two other guitars leaned against the couch, over which drooped a couple of T-shirts and a denim jacket encrusted in rhinestones.

"Holy smokes," he exclaimed. He laughed aloud at his prissiness. The amusement was brief. Here he was in the middle of a frigging opium den (well, not quite) and he was talking like Anita Bryant. "Jesus Christ!" he said for good measure. Which, automatically, redirected his eyes toward the kitchen wall. Corner to corner, the glass that covered the sampler with the little dog was cracked.

Dishes filled the sink and covered half the counter. (*There vuz a party?* Like, was George W. Bush the goddamn court-appointed president?) Out of curiosity, Walter opened the dishwasher. In the bottom lingered a pool of brackish water. "That explains *something,*" he muttered. But then he saw the two wineglasses, stems snapped, balanced atop half a dozen liquor bottles in the recycling bin.

Walter walked in the front door of Walter's Place just behind a family of tourists looking for an early dinner (for whom he held the door). Scott greeted them—and then saw his uncle, along with his uncle's expression.

"Show them a table," Walter said through his clenched smile. T.B. made a beeline for the front hearth and stretched his plump body on the cool brick floor.

While Scott escorted the family to one of the rustic booths and handed them menus, Walter went to the bar and greeted Ben. Ben welcomed him back as if he'd been absent for two hours. Walter glanced over a copy of the evening's menu. *Heirloom tomatoes grilled with blue cheese. Hudson Valley corn on the cob with maple butter.* The catch of the day was stuffed bluefish. *Some* things did not fall apart. Walter took a deep breath as Scott came slowly back toward the bar, stopping at empty tables to straighten place settings.

"Scott!" Walter pointed back toward the kitchen.

As they passed through, toward the office, Walter waved at Hugo and said, "I owe you my firstborn. You are responsible for my sanity. What remains of it, that is!"

The minute Walter closed the door behind them, Scott said, "Okay, man, I know you're pissed. I'm really, really sorry about the mess. I thought you'd be taking like the last bus back."

"Well, at least you didn't blame it on a poltergeist. Just when, may I ask, have you found the time to turn my nice neat apartment into a lowlife nightclub? Oh—at *night.* Silly me. Have I been served an eviction notice yet?"

"Look. Really. I'm totally sorry," said Scott. Walter could not tell if he looked genuinely contrite or simply terrified. "Like, we did have a couple friends over to jam, but we kept it pretty low. I promise! We're totally in this momentum you wouldn't believe, and I guess I lost track of time and I figured I'd clean up when I got back tonight, and really, man, you wouldn't have noticed a thing."

Walter wondered whether it would have made a difference only to *suspect* that the place had been trashed in his absence. Should he maintain something like the army's don't-ask-don't-tell protocol on queers? Out of sight, out of mind? "And these 'friends,' they, like, smoked up a storm?"

Scott looked sheepish. "You never said no cigarettes, Uncle Walt."

"Right. And I never said no pottery kilns, no prostitution, no . . . let's see, off-track betting? Use your common sense, Scott! Do I smoke? No. And what's with the dishwasher?"

"Sorry. Like I had no idea who to call. For repairs." Scott was looking at his shoes by now—a pair of orange high-top sneakers. Had Walter's dress code for Scott's week as boy maître d' even specified shoe restrictions? Probably not. Maybe orange high-tops were fine. Don't get hysterical, Walter warned himself.

He sighed. "I'll take care of that. Appliances break. But *listen.*" He told Scott that he would take over for the evening while Scott went back to the apartment and cleaned both the kitchen and the living room, top to bottom. "I'm going to ask for a moratorium on the music this entire week. Doesn't Sonya have a place of her own where you can practice? Never mind. Just give it a break. I am going to have to gauge how angry the neighbors are. And frankly, I wouldn't mind a break from Sonya herself."

If Scott was annoyed, he didn't dare show it. "Was your vacation cool?" he asked Walter, as if he wasn't sure he should ask.

"Just dandy," said Walter. "Now vamoose. And take T.B. He needs a long walk. That, too, if you please."

Scott saluted.

"Don't test my sense of humor," Walter said. "And—not so fast—get a haircut. Tomorrow morning. I will have your great-grandmother's sampler reframed, but you will reimburse me."

After Scott left, Walter checked his reflection in the mirror and was comforted to see that the island glow had not yet faded. It was back-to-school time now, auspicious season for all things new—but to hope too far along that avenue would lead him to yet another dead end. *Vork, it must be your daily anchor.*

Out at the bar, theatrical deadbeat Dagger was on his first drink, warming to the subject of Gwyneth Paltrow as the perfect example of nepotism unbridled.

PEACE AND CALM RULED FOR NEARLY A WEEK. Never before had the last days of summer made the city feel like a place of such privilege. By day the air was almost dry, the sky ever blue. Nights felt clean, even chilly; often there were stars to be seen. A few leaves were fooled into turning at their tips, flashing like gold sequins in the perpetually soothing breeze that blew from the harbor.

As ordered, Scott went to the barber. "Your ears are quite handsome, you know" was Walter's only response. The boy still wore his orange high-tops to work; Walter decided to ignore the issue of footwear. At closing time several nights running, Sonya showed up and lurked by the door. On Friday, Walter softened and told Ben to give her a glass of champagne. He tried not to be annoyed when he caught sight of her rolling her eyes at Scott in what he assumed was a mockery of his gesture. Whatever did Scott see in that arachnid creature? Was it simply that she was older, was that the allure? Walter tried to amuse himself by imagining Tipi taking Sonya for lunch at her country club.

On those nights, Scott went off with Sonya—Walter never asked where—and, as in the old, pre-Scott days, Walter and T.B. walked home by one circuitous route or another. Walter fell asleep alone in his own bed, but with the windows open to the velvety air, no earplugs, no need for Granna's firm hand to keep his cool. Even the car horns sounded softer.

And then came Sunday. First, a child threw a plate of waffles on the floor, splashing maple syrup onto a pair of expensive purple suede pumps at the adjacent table; Walter soothed the wearer's conspicuous indignation by picking up her tab. Another customer complained loudly that the Scottish salmon on his bagel had gone bad (it most certainly had not). Thereafter, no one ordered salmon in any form. By one, Walter was tempted to have a drink. He ate a piece of chocolate cake instead. This made him think of Greenie; but for his big mouth, she would still be there, nearly next door. What had he been thinking?

With Walter's permission, Scott left early, in the lull between brunch and dinner, to go to his "guitar workshop." Minutes later, Ben asked to have a word with Walter in his office. A case of wine had gone missing, and though he couldn't be sure, he had to suspect that it had been pinched by Sonya (which had to mean Sonya in cahoots with Scott).

"She's a bad influence, that's my firm conviction," said Walter. "But theft?"

Ben shrugged. "Just a suspicion. Needed voicing."

"Have you ever seen Scott behind the bar?"

Another shrug. "Wouldn't think twice if I had."

"Ben, this is my nephew."

Ben gave Walter a bland, impenetrable smile. "Just a suspicion."

"Ben! Articulate, please! I love the way you never talk my ear off, but I need a little more to go on here. And please don't do that what-the-heck thing with your shoulders again!"

"If I had evidence, I'd show you," said Ben. "I don't want to have a suspicion, not raise it now, then have you come to me later asking why. Whole story."

Walter groaned. "Whole story. Great."

Ben rose to go. "I'll keep an eye out."

"You do that."

Walter laid his head on his desk. What should he do, install nanny cams at home and at work? How long ago had he last checked the shelf in his closet where he kept Granna's silver flatware? When, in fact, was the last time he'd had occasion to use it? Whatever happened to entertaining at home?

The Bruce nudged his thigh.

"Here you go." Walter took one of T.B.'s well-masticated phone receivers out of a lower drawer. Immediately, The Bruce curled up at Walter's feet and began his ritual of licking and gnawing at the plastic.

"That does look like a good way to relieve stress," said Walter as he stroked his dog's neck, massaging the warm folds of skin around the collar. As he did so, he felt a small nub of something foreign at the edge of the leather. Probing with two fingers, he withdrew a tab of chewing gum and a minute rectangle of paper.

After flinging the gum into the trash, he held up the paper. It had been folded many times, down to the size of a thin matchbox, to be hidden inside T.B.'s collar, fastened there with the gum. (Another probing brought forth a second rubbery wad.)

"What in tarnation," said Walter as he unfolded the paper. He thought of desperate pleas enclosed in bottles, flung out to sea. Were old people at T.B.'s nursing home being held prisoner against their will? (*Anywhere* in the Bronx would be prison to Walter.) Was this a cry for rescue?

Apparently not.

"Christ Almighty," he said when he read the note.

Slick and all aquiver, Miss Urchin waits like a rainflower, You Boy Cock Red Lava God. Slave to your mountainous rumbling. She says pluck my petals NOW she says DRINK MY NECTAR till I am a prune, a dry hag, a she-shark in your molten ocean!

An extremely tiny pink photograph adhered to the paper. Walter held it close to his desk lamp. A vagina, an actual, wide-open, devil-may-care *vagina*. Walter groaned and dropped the note in the trash, then fished it out again. He stuffed it in his pocket. He bent over and pulled T.B.'s collar around his neck, feeling under its entire circumference. T.B. dropped his phone and looked up at Walter, concerned. Walter was hyperventilating.

"It's okay, boy," he said, though his tone was not consistent with the statement. How he would get through the evening without an aneurysm or a shriekfest, Walter had no idea, but get through it he would. And then, once Scott showed up at his apartment, well let the chips fall where they fucking might.

"YOU HAVE BEEN USING MY DOG AS A, what, a porn conduit?"

Scott looked dumbstruck. It was six in the morning, and he had just walked in. Walter had slept very little the night before, finally surrendering to his rage by taking a very long, very hot shower, dressing for the gym, and eating a large bowl of Grape Nuts. The heavy chewing was almost cathartic.

Scott leaned his guitar case against the wall. Nervously, he laughed.

"*This* is not funny. Or *I* don't find it funny." Walter held out the four sex-slave messages, all resembling eviscerated origami, that he had found by scouring the sea of clothing in Scott's room. (He had almost hoped to find drugs; why not shoot the moon?)

Scott was clearly holding a private debate. Finally he said, "Those are totally private, Uncle Walt. Like you thought I was a virgin or something?"

"Please don't insult me." Walter threw the messages onto the coffee table. "Do you really have no idea how . . . repellent and perverse this is?"

"The dog can't read." Arms crossed, Scott had struck a sullen pose. If there had been a moment to choose repentance over defiance, it had passed.

"Listen, nephew of mine. I have put up with a lot here. Maybe I didn't know what I was getting myself into, sharing my place with a Mick Jagger wannabe—" Walter heard Scott's faint snort of derision. "All *right.*"

Scott waited for a moment. "All right what?"

"I am just about fed up. I mean, I am fed up! How dare you laugh at me. I am suddenly feeling mighty sympathetic with your father!"

"Hey, man, I'm sorry we offended you, okay?"

The *we* put Walter over the edge. "That is *it,*" he growled. "You are out of here, young man. I will keep you on at the restaurant—though we will be having a good talk about that, too—but I want you to find your own place. Move in with Morticia Addams if you please, but forget about using poor T.B. as your envoy of lust. I simply cannot believe your lack of respect. Shame on you."

T.B. cowered at the sound of his name in such an angry speech. He slipped down from the couch, retreating to Walter's bedroom.

Scott stared at Walter, and then he sighed. "Suit yourself, man. We were just having the bit of harmless fun. You are one hypersensitive dude, you know that? I mean, I appreciate everything you've done for me, really, man, but you need to like, I don't know, get laid more often yourself."

Walter's heart was beating with the cadence of a polka. He spoke not a word, went to the coatrack, and took down T.B.'s leash. "Come, boy," he said quietly, aware of the ironies in his command. He would drop T.B. off at the restaurant and go to the gym from there. He picked up his workout bag, refusing to meet Scott's eyes. Scott did not move from his post near the door.

"Are you actually going to, like, leave?"

To get out the door, Walter was forced to speak once more to his nephew, if only to say a courteous, cold *Excuse me.* "Take today and tomorrow off. You can leave your stuff in your room until you find another place to stay."

The boy looked utterly deflated, though it might have been nothing more than an aftereffect of all-night sex with the repugnant Miss Urchin. On his way out, Walter read what he hoped would be the last idiotic T-shirt he'd ever have to face so early in the morning. On magenta cotton spandex, it read THE SWEDISH WOMEN'S VOLLEYBALL TEAM SLEPT HERE.

Charming as ever, Walter was tempted to say as he opened the door, but Granna warned him to hold his tongue. He had said more than enough for one miserable Monday morning.

At the gym, he increased his weights. At his office, he tackled several money matters he had been postponing. In the kitchen, he offered Hugo a modest but unexpected raise. *For effry dark deed, trade a light one.* After last call at the bar, he took T.B. for a marathon walk down to Battery Park City. At the marina, T.B. made no protest when Walter sat on a bench to listen awhile as the yachts conversed at their moorings. As they walked back north, the warm tranquil lappings of the river against the piers and the wooden rim of the city itself soothed Walter as much as anything could. When he arrived back in his apartment at two A.M., he found a note from Scott saying that Sonya would be taking him to Newark first thing in the morning, to catch a flight to San Francisco. He was heading home to "chill" for a couple of weeks before returning to New York. He'd get the rest of his stuff then. *If you decide to fire me, that's totally fair, but this whole thing just makes it clearer what my future is really about. I think you kind of get it, too, Uncle Walt, and I forgive you for blowing off the steam. I'm sorry I said that lowly thing about you not getting laid. I hope we'll stay friends. High five to the B-man. I'll call from Camp Werner if I survive the deprogramming stuff.*

Walter was sad but not surprised. In fact, he suspected that Scott would *not* survive the "deprogramming stuff" to return to New York. Still, Walter would have rooted for Scott. Really, had mash notes under a dog's collar been reason enough to evict the boy? In the end, Walter knew nothing about what it was to be a parent, let alone a grandparent who had to do it all over again because her own child had failed at the job.

He called Sonya's number but (thankfully) got her machine. Channeling Granna, he wished Scott a safe trip and told Sonya she could pick up T.B. at the restaurant after taking Scott to the airport. Walter would rise early and work like a madman.

He slept heavily and got up at six. From the window near his bed, a forgiving, reinvigorating breeze swept through the room. Walter dressed and gave T.B. a hasty brushing. On the way to the restaurant, they stopped to share a bagel under the sumptuous greenery by the playground. "Let's get fat, my friend, what the hey," Walter said to The Bruce as they relished their respective halves of schmear.

The wide-plank floors of the restaurant had been newly waxed the day before; they gleamed softly when Walter turned on the lights. He opened every window, to admit the extraordinary morning, and turned on Hugo's radio, opting for jazz.

Almost to Walter's surprise, Sonya showed up. He turned his dog over to her without a word. He did not even meet her eyes. She was persona non exista to him, but he would not give her the satisfaction of mentioning Scott or of breaking his promise to the old folks in Spuyten Duyvil just because he wished she would fall through a hole in the ground.

When the first plane hit the north tower of the World Trade Center, Hugo was writing lunch specials on the blackboard. Oddly, Ben was in as well; like Walter, he had awakened early, filled with energy and a sense of purpose. He had decided to recheck his wine inventory. So there they were, all three men, in the kitchen together, Ben having just confessed to Walter that he might have made a mistake about the missing case of pinot grigio. He realized now that a large bridal shower, which took up half the restaurant on Saturday night, had asked him to set aside an entire case, so they wouldn't have to order by the bottle. Man, but those girls had whooped it up. They'd tipped him like a king.

TWENTY

IT COULDN'T BE SNOWING; how in the world could it be snowing? Saga stood at the kitchen window and stared into the small sad yard behind Stan's house. The ground was white, and the air appeared to be filled with the coiling currents of very large snowflakes. The window was filthy, its lower panes covered with paw prints and the smearings of eager noses, so Saga could not see all that clearly. Stan no longer let the dogs out back, because he worried that someone would report him to the Board of Health.

She had been staying at Stan's, basically *being* Stan, since Friday evening. Stan was in Washington, at the nonprofit seminar. He called several times a day, and though she could tell he was a little anxious leaving her in charge, he was never sarcastic. Every time, just before saying good-bye, he thanked her.

And really, his thank-yous mattered. Being Stan was no picnic. It was harder work than Saga had thought it would be, even with Sonya's help. Sonya stopped by every evening to help take the dogs on one long walk. Stan had "pared down" to six dogs for his absence, including a three-legged collie and a spaniely mongrel that cowered and peed every time something spooked him. There were also seven cats, one with a litter of kittens; a guinea pig with an eye infection; and a chameleon someone was supposed to have picked up on Saturday but hadn't. Saga felt slightly ashamed that the chameleon gave her the creeps, but at night, after she turned off the downstairs lights, the lamp in its tank continued to glow. Its snakelike tongue would lash out, presto—always disturbing because the lizard's facial expression never changed.

Scott, Sonya's boyfriend, thought the chameleon was "genius cool." He'd even wanted to take it out and hold it, but Saga told him she didn't know if he should. (Now she wished she had let him do it, just so she could have cleaned the smelly tank.) They had come by together the evening before, and it was nice to have the extra help. While Sonya held and medicated the squirming guinea pig, Scott told Saga that he was moving in with Sonya but heading out to California for a little vacation first. "Do the family thing," he said, the way you might say "Do my taxes" or "Do my hair," as if it were shorthand for a task that everyone had to do at some point, more or less the same way as everyone else.

Saga wondered what it would mean, to her, to "do the family thing." Right now, it meant acting like a deaf-mute in the presence of her warring cousins, just so she could keep her tentative place in the constellation. Being Stan was tough, yes (and the longer she stayed here, the more she admired him), but being Saga at Uncle Marsden's house was, at this delicate moment, tougher still.

On the Fourth of July, after everyone had watched the fireworks from the porch, after a hugely pregnant Denise had gone to bed, Michael had announced that he'd closed on the Cute House. This was no surprise to Saga, who had gone to see it, as promised, with Michael, Uncle Marsden, and a real-estate broker. Aside from her uncle's complaints that the ocean was out of earshot and the garden little more than a "vulgar profusion of forsythia," there was nothing not to like. And, in a sneaky way, Michael had won her over at the fancy lunch with the snails and soufflés.

But that night on the porch, Frida and Pansy were not won over. They told Michael that they had decided they did not want to be bought out, that if Michael wanted to live in the big house, he'd have to rent it. This led to a stormy, teary argument, to Uncle Marsden trying to duck out for a walk, to Pansy screaming at him that he'd always loved Michael best, to Michael calling Pansy an ingrate, to . . . well, Saga had simply sat there, unable to move, as if watching a real war unfold.

It became an all-out cold war—Uncle Marsden and Michael versus Frida and Pansy—until, one month later, the twins were born. Both girls: Elizabeth, after Aunt Liz, and a flourishy name that Saga had a hard time remembering (Leonora? Isadora? Ramona?), after Denise's mother. They came out from the city for their first visit in the middle of August. You'd have thought he was expecting royalty, the way Uncle Marsden behaved. Saga had never seen him clean anything other than the leaves of ailing plants, but there he was, down on his knees scrubbing behind the toilets, standing on a ladder sweeping cobwebs out of hidden corners they'd occupied for months or maybe years. He shook rugs over the porch rail, bleached countertops, and filled the house with flowers from his garden. Meanwhile, he moved the houseplants he knew to be poisonous into his salon of mosses, locking the door as if they might escape.

"Those babies aren't even close to crawling," said Saga.

"I know, I know," he said, "but supposing the wicked old wind blew a geranium leaf into a cradle? Mother Nature is cruel!"

Saga decided to take his hysterical preparations as just that: crazy and amusing. After all, he'd asked nothing extra of Saga. But Pansy and Frida, who arrived a few hours before the royal family, did not find their father's behavior funny at all. Frida had called a truce, and she'd made Pansy come along. Pansy spoke to Denise but not to Michael and hardly at all to her father. Uncle Marsden didn't seem to care. He only had eyes for those babies. He couldn't get enough of holding them—one then the other, the other then the one, as if they were old enough to guess at a preference—and Saga could see from the looks on both Pansy's and Frida's faces that they were feeling literally replaced, traded in for these two tiny, perhaps more promising girls.

Michael seemed gentler. He could not get enough of holding his daughters either. He still spoke on his phone pretty often, but he kept the conversations short. During many of these conversations, as he paced the far wall of a room talking numbers and money trends, his eyes, warm and adoring, stayed fixed on those babies.

When Saga mentioned his softened manner to Frida, as they washed dishes together after that first dinner, Frida laughed harshly. "I think what you're seeing is the effect of losing sleep. But don't be fooled. He hasn't changed his plans." Saga said nothing; she'd been careful not to take sides, and thank goodness no one had asked her to do so. Well, what power did she have?

Later that night, thinking that the others had all gone to bed, Saga had walked out to the front porch, wanting only to sit by herself and gaze at the sky. But there was Uncle Marsden, on the swing beside Denise. They rocked together; Denise, humming faintly, held one of the babies on her lap. The adults looked at Saga and motioned silence, fingers raised to their lips in unison.

It was an odd picture: this young pretty mother in her short white gown, its thin summer fabric almost see-through across her swollen breasts, both she and her baby watched closely by this much, much older man. He leaned toward them with an accidental kind of . . . not lust, thought Saga . . . lechery? No. But it was clear that Uncle Marsden was thrilled at the intimacy. *Memory,* thought Saga with all the longing and pain contained in that single word. He was in thrall to his memories, that must be it, of sitting on this porch with his own wife and his own babies so long ago. He was in love again, in love with the way he'd been shuttled back in time, in love with the people who'd sent him to that happy place.

Saga waved her understanding, went back indoors and up to her room.

SHE SCRAPED HER HAND AS SHE UNFASTENED the three locks on Stan's back door. But finally she yanked it open and stepped out, careful to close it right behind her. She found herself in a silent storm not of snow but of paper: torn, shredded, singed, at times nearly *powdered* paper. It brushed her face and hands as it continued to drift to the ground, settling with a festive leisure.

How could paper fall from the sky? Saga looked straight up. The sky was perfectly blue. She looked at her feet. At first she was fearful of touching the paper. Silly, she told herself.

She reached for a sheet that looked almost whole. It was part of a menu from a Chinese restaurant. Some of the names of the dishes were red, others green. *Two delight chickens. Gold phenix prawns. Double happiness. House ginger chicken with dry-greened beans.* The red ones were starred: spicy, that's right, she remembered. Uncle Marsden didn't like Chinese food, but she'd had takeout at the bookshop—and with Stan. Was the menu from Stan's kitchen? He'd shown her where he kept the menus, but she had forgotten. She looked at the window, as if the kitchen might have an answer. The spaniel and the German shepherd had jumped up and were watching her, panting with excitement, licking the glass. Most dogs loved snow; could they see this wasn't snow? Of course, they could *smell* that it wasn't snow.

The next several papers she picked up—all whole, barely creased— were covered with numbers. Rows and columns, with dashes and spaces: numbers that, without being able to read them, she knew stood for sums of money. They looked like the pages of numbers in the newspaper business section.

She waded farther out, up to her ankles. She kicked at the paper. She thought of confetti, of weddings.

Numbers lay everywhere about her, layer upon layer, shred upon shred. This could have been a joke of a nightmare for Saga: a blizzard of the very thing she had lost touch with most permanently, designed to drive her mad. But of course it wasn't a nightmare. It had to be some kind of comic mishap. She bent over and pushed away layers of numbers with her hands, searching for more words. Another menu; anything. She came up with a page from a magazine: movie reviews on one side, on the other an advertisement for a hand cream that promised to kill germs while making your skin soft.

Now the paper had stopped falling. There it lay, in shallow drifts about her. It did not melt or disappear or flutter about. She looked up. High overhead, she saw what might have been more paper, floating by in the sun—or perhaps the wheeling shapes were birds, pale pigeons or seagulls.

Squatting down, she found memos to people she had never heard of, a piece of the directions on how to use a copy machine, a photograph of a group of people posed in front of a boat. They wore matching pink T-shirts with white palm trees. There were pinholes where the photo had been tacked to a board or a wall.

One of the watching dogs had begun to bark.

Saga knew suddenly that something terrible had happened. For one thing, there were signs of burning on some of the papers. Was the building next door on fire? How would she take all the animals to safety? Alarmed, she looked up the brick wall to her left: no smoke, no sign of panic. Could someone have tossed all this paper off the roof of the building?

She let herself into Stan's house, pushing the dogs gently back, and refastened each lock. She went to the living room and pulled aside a curtain. There was paper in the street as well, drifting along the ground.

Saga returned to the kitchen and poured herself a glass of water. The problem with things that did not make sense was that they might seem worrisome or absurd only to Saga. The senselessness might come from inside herself. She could never be quite sure. She focused on the notion of paper falling from the sky and whether there was a plausible, ordinary cause she had forgotten. As usual, exerting her mind, trying to use it like a muscle, got her nowhere.

She found her notebook and called Sonya's cell phone. She got the recording and hung up. What would she say? Next, she tried Uncle Marsden. She got his answering machine and left the message that she was just checking in (though Uncle Marsden seemed far less concerned with her whereabouts these days). "Hope you're getting lots done in the garden," she added, knowing that's where he'd be on a day this fine. Unless something *hugely* terrible had happened. She thought about calling Fenno but did not want to make a fool of herself. She could call Stan in Washington on his cell, but if she told him his yard was full of somebody's trash, what could he do? It would probably ruin his day.

She had fed all the animals early that morning and taken the dogs, two at a time, for walks around the block. She had changed the litter boxes. She had changed the chameleon's water, shuddering when the long tongue snapped out and nearly touched her hand. "Buster," she had scolded the lizard, "I hope you can see that I am not a fly." She'd been sitting at the kitchen table looking at a big photography book about dogs when the flurries outside the window had caught her attention.

Now, looking around at the animals, most of them busy in their own quiet forms of letting time pass till the next outing or meal—grooming, sleeping, sniffing, pacing—Saga was gripped by a sense of panicked isolation. She must leave the house and go somewhere, even if she failed to solve the mystery of the falling paper. She had to know that this weird thing was happening to someone other than *her*. Rushing, as if fearful of an impending threat, she filled all the water bowls, put out cat chow and teething bones. She took food and water to the closed room upstairs, where the kittens were clustered against their mother in a large cardboard box.

She grabbed up her book, her knapsack, and the keys to the house. Out on the street, she saw a confusion of people walking here and there, looking dazed or angry. Some cried. People stood on nearly every roof, all facing the same way. Where they faced, often pointing, a billow of smoke rose from behind the shabby row of stores on the avenue. The height of the smoke was shocking; something hugely terrible *had* happened. Was it happening still? Birds fluttered everywhere—or once again, it could have been paper, literal reams of paper.

Reams. A golden word, smooth and slippery. Or was that because it made her think of *beams*? Not rafters but rays of sun.

People filled the streets in a way that was physically aimless yet emotionally urgent. As Saga walked away from Stan's, at first aimless herself, she heard an audible ebb and flow of *Oh my God oh my God oh my God.*

Something enormous was on fire, but from Stan's neighborhood, from the ground, you couldn't see what.

"What's happened?" she asked a young man who stood in a patch of sun, as if he'd found a spot of safety and did not intend to give it up.

"The second one just collapsed." He looked plaintively at Saga. The tears in his eyes were so startling that she couldn't bring herself to ask, *The second what?*

She walked in the direction of the smoke, curiosity stronger than fear. The fire had to be in Manhattan, she could guess that much, and there was water between that place and this.

People everywhere spoke rapidly on cell phones and stared at the sky—not just at the smoke but all around at the sky. She couldn't be sure, but when she did the same, she thought something might be *missing* from the sky.

Fenno. Saga would call Fenno, because it was a local call. But at the first pay phone she came to, she found a long line of people; and at the next one, and the one after that. The buildings were low in this neighborhood, but still she could not see the source of the great, widening geyser of smoke. It must be coming from a very tall building. On she walked, the sun peculiarly pleasant, straight toward the unseen disaster.

She walked until she came to a modest, homely park by the river, where all of a sudden she could see that the smoke—and she gasped at how broad and thick it was, how furious and dense, a vertical roiling *river* of smoke—came right out of Wall Street. The park was filled with people exclaiming, weeping, pointing, shouting into phones. *Oh my God oh my God oh my God* from every direction, like the sound in a movie theater.

Saga stood beside a woman in sweat clothes who had a dog on a leash. The woman watched silently; the dog sniffed Saga's legs. Saga bent to pet the dog—a wiry beige creature, part basenji perhaps—and then the woman spoke to her. "I knew something like this had to happen one day," she said, nearly whispering. "We were all just too damn pleased with ourselves."

Saga said, "I'm sorry, but can you please tell me what happened? From the start? I don't know what happened."

The woman's eyebrows rose. "Oh, I wish you could stay that way," she said. "Not knowing."

"Tell me," said Saga.

"Two planes flew into the towers there, the trade towers, and just like that, in an hour, they're gone. They *fell right down.*"

"Why? The planes, I mean," said Saga.

"Oh terrorists." The woman made it sound like an Irish name, *O'Terrorists.* "Goddamn fucking towelhead terrorists. Arabs. You really have to ask?"

The woman's rage sent Saga spiraling back down into her uncertain self. She waited till the woman was staring again at the smoke before slipping away, out of the park. She stopped on a crumbling sidewalk beside a huge brick building whose windows were boarded over. Saga had no idea where she was. She had never been to this spot before—or if she had, it hadn't stayed with her.

She felt as if she might start crying, but not because of the tragedy. She was lost. She needed to call someone. She would find another phone and wait in line, no matter how long it took. Maybe Sonya could come pick her up, if Saga found her way to one of the bridges along the river. She could see the Manhattan Bridge and the Brooklyn Bridge not too far away. And now she saw, despite the smoke, just how empty the sky looked there, behind the bridges. "Oh my God," she said.

The first pay phone she found was broken. After that, she walked several blocks without seeing another. This was an old warehouse neighborhood, not one of the places rich people had claimed for gigantic apartments but a real urban ghost town. Grass grew between some of the slabs on the sidewalks. Except for the effect of the brilliant sunshine, she might have been afraid.

The air had begun to smell oppressive and rubbery—like a fire in a stove, not in a fireplace—but you couldn't see the smoke from these canyonlike streets. Where would she go?

Fenno, she thought for the third time that day, with even greater longing. Having left Stan's neighborhood, she had no idea where she might find a subway stop. She would simply have to walk. She knew she could cross the Brooklyn Bridge; people talked about the walkway down the middle. She had always wanted to walk a dog across it, but she was never in the right place to do it. From there, she could figure out the right direction, or she could ask her way to Bank Street.

Staying as close to the river as possible, she aimed for the bridge. Already you could see that it was filled with people walking—all walking away from Manhattan. But she would go against the tide. That never bothered Saga.

WALKING ACROSS THE BRIDGE TOOK FOREVER, and it was terrifying. No one questioned her going the wrong way (along with a few other brave souls), the way toward the fire. Some people spoke to one another, but most of them looked stunned, alone in their minds and not happily so. There was no rushing, no panic. No one seemed to fear a fire at their heels. Several people looked as if they'd been dipped in chalk. Or was it the papery snow? Some of the women, the ones all dressed up, the ones with mascara and lipstick, looked clownish—slovenly, smudged, their faces streaked. Some walked in bare feet.

"Where are you going? You're out of your mind," said one woman shouldering past her. The woman's tone was exhausted, not angry.

O'Terrorists, o'terrorists, Saga kept thinking. Once upon a time, when she lived with David, she read the paper nearly every day. They had talked about Israel and Bosnia and unions and civil rights and Romanian orphans. Now she avoided the paper, along with radio and TV. Too much busy noise. Sometimes a swatch of current events from another time dropped into her consciousness like a comet—that's how she knew now that once she'd known about Bosnia and Romanian orphans. *Herzegovina:* there, a sudden shaft from nowhere. The word a deep blue lavender, the color of Uncle Marsden's favorite hyacinths.

So she had to wonder: were terrorists in the headlines these days? Had they made threats that only she, Saga, did not know about? Had conversations spun around her that she had forgotten—or, in her narrow life, simply never heard? She remembered a terrible news story from long ago, a man in a wheelchair on a cruise ship executed, tossed overboard.

She stopped near the center of the bridge. Were these terrorists still at large, right here? She checked people's faces again. They did not look like they worried that they would be chased, even though many were crying.

Planes, she kept hearing. War planes? Terrorists in war planes?

Her thoughts, however worrisome, unspooled in a way that calmed her. She made her way into Chinatown. Since the accident, she had been to Chinatown only a few times (always with Stan), but despite its disorienting smells and crowded sidewalks, she had liked it better than ever. She loved seeing language everywhere that *no one* could read—or no one she knew. Ordinary people could have a taste of what she had felt when, for a time, so many known things became *un*known.

And it was the closest she'd come in a long time to anything like the exotic travel she'd planned to make her living. She loved all the red everywhere. She loved the pagodas. Pagodas on phone booths, pagodas on banks, pagodas on public schools. Restaurants were not stylish—restaurants here were the opposite of pretty—but they had tanks of bizarre, fascinating fish or murals in curious colors.

Streets going toward the fire were thick with policemen; some were blocked off. Saga tried to fix in her mind a map of the city, imagining how she would get where she needed to go. She paid attention to shadows, which kept her heading vaguely north until she could go west again. Yet she felt a separate conviction, as if, like a dog, she could now find her way by intuition alone, no matter how roundabout the route she must take. Maybe the company of all those dogs at Stan's, for days on end, had immersed her just enough in their dogness.

She stopped again. How would she get *back* to Stan's? She would have to reach Sonya. Already, she began to sense that the city was closing down, sealing up at the edges like a wound. From the crowds on foot, filling sidewalks, spilling onto streets, it was clear there were no buses, no taxis, perhaps no subways. She walked on. Now half the people were walking her way, too, which made her progress easier, faster. Now she had company, fellow travelers.

Everyone moved as if in predetermined paths, though Saga understood that the steady, docile movement, the peeling off of smaller groups onto each side street they passed, was more a sign of shock than true direction. Yet she found herself remembering the poster in the bathroom at the bookshop: the migration of birds. She remembered how, the first time she'd seen it, she had imagined all those dependable pathways embracing the world, flocks of birds binding it together like ribbon. *The whole world over,* she remembered thinking; *birds fly the whole world over but always, no matter what, find their way back home.*

A song came to her. "Marching to Pretoria." Where was Pretoria? Was it a real place? But she wasted no effort on yet another riddle. She turned a corner and saw the arch in Washington Square. She knew her way from there.

SHE WOULD TELL NO ONE THIS, but she had begun to picture herself in the Cute House with Uncle Marsden, how they would live their lives. He could take over the dining room for his collection of mosses. They could have a dining table in the kitchen or on the sun porch. He would have the largest bedroom, but one of the others had a prettier view, to a neighboring yard with a great elm tree, a rare survivor. From its branches hung a long, old-fashioned swing. On the expedition to see the house, Saga had lingered alone in the room to watch a little girl swinging on the swing. Maybe Saga would get to know that girl. She wondered if the girl had any pets.

There was a chimney smack in the middle of the house. Upstairs, the floors all slanted downhill from that chimney, as if the entire floor were a tutu flaring from the waist of a stout ballerina. When Saga realized that the house had a personality, she knew it would become, if she were patient, a fine place to live. Maybe she could get a bird. She'd have to find out if Uncle Marsden was allergic to birds. She could borrow a parakeet from Stan's menagerie.

SHE WALKED INTO THE BOOKSTORE like a child returning home after a long, long trip. Yet the minute she looked around, she knew that relief was a feeling no one shared. Fenno looked calm enough, but next to him, crying in loud, disturbing sobs, was the man who ran the restaurant—Walter, the one with the bulldog. She looked around but did not see The Bruce. Two other men stood together by the garden door. They were listening to a radio, which stood on the glass case containing binoculars and telescopes for people who liked to spy on birds. Felicity sat on her perch by the window. She bobbed up and down, side to side, like a boxer; she watched the sobbing man as if he might be her opponent across the ring.

There was no one else in the store; who would be shopping for books on a day like this?

Fenno nodded at Saga and waved her in. "Oh lass, I'm glad to see you safe and sound."

Walter glanced at her, then quickly away. "Oh God, oh God, I am so ashamed," he said. He was facing a bookcase, clutching an upper shelf with both hands, as if he might otherwise slip to the floor. Fenno continued to stand beside him.

"You're not the least bit sure, you mustn't panic," Fenno said gently. "There are scores upon scores of airplanes which we know have landed safely—or never left the ground to begin with."

"I know it, I know it, I just *know it*," cried Walter. "He told me Newark, he was planning to leave from *Newark*."

"I'm sure he's fine," said Fenno. "Stranded somewhere, unable to phone, but he'll show up. The Bruce will show up, too. He may be overly coddled by his Bronx grannies, but he'll be fine as well."

Walter cried more loudly. "Oh God, for once in my wretched life it's not the dog I care about!"

Saga saw Fenno touch Walter's back, lightly, nervously, then pull his hand away. "I wish I could make you sit down and take a drink," he said. "I can fetch something good and strong from my flat."

"I would pass out," said Walter, shaking his head. "Oblivion is a blessing I do not deserve." His large strong back moved in spasms beneath his shirt.

The two men by the radio moved toward Walter. "He's right," said the one with black curly hair (she'd seen him at the restaurant, at the lovely party). "Sit down, Walter." He reached up and grasped one of Walter's wrists, pulling him away from the bookcase.

The second man who'd been listening to the radio was round and bald, dressed all in white—a cook's uniform. He put an arm around Walter's back and helped the curly-haired man coax Walter toward the armchair beside Fenno's desk.

Saga realized she was staring. She went over to Felicity, who calmed down once Walter was seated. She squawked at Saga, who held out her arm. Felicity jumped on and sidestepped up to her shoulder. Saga leaned her cheek into the bird's warm, fragrant scarlet feathers. *The realm of you,* thought Saga. She glanced at Fenno—would she always be a little in love with him?—and saw him, beside Walter's chair, looking unusually helpless. Embarrassed, she looked away.

As she stood by the garden door, letting Felicity prod and tease at her hair, Saga began to listen to the radio. A plane had flown into the Pentagon. In New York, hundreds of firefighters might be dead. The president, on his private plane, was being hustled from hither to yon, from yon to hither, and there were people calling him a coward. Then there were people who claimed this was no time for talk like that. Someone with a thick accent was talking about Saudi Arabia. Someone else was talking about an attack on a ship, a bomb. An attack on an embassy in Africa. Was this the start of a world war?

"Is there a war?" she blurted out.

Walter had stopped crying, but he kept his face behind his hands. Fenno was suddenly nowhere in sight.

"Likely as not," said the curly-haired man.

"Oh sweet heaven no," said Walter. "Oh no."

"I think you jump to conclusions," said the man in white to the curly-haired man. "But how terrible this is, we cannot yet know." He was foreign; *I sink,* he said. *Ziss iss.*

Now the mayor spoke. He told everyone to stay home, to keep listening, to be alert. The air force was guarding the city. Home was the safest place to be.

Startled, Saga turned toward the radio. Felicity nipped her ear.

Was Uncle Marsden at home now? Had he taken Aunt Liz's radio out of the closet? Was he listening? How would he *know* to listen?

Fenno came in the front door carrying three bottles. "Emily, do you know where I keep those cups downstairs, the ones we use at the readings?"

As Saga passed Fenno, Felicity leaped to his shoulder.

When she came back up from the basement, the bottles were standing on the counter by the register. Scotch, club soda, fizzy lemonade. Fenno introduced her to Ben and Hugo. Behind them, she could just hear Walter whispering, "I've lost him. *I've lost him.*" Saga wanted to ask Fenno why Walter was so upset, who it was he thought he'd lost, but she didn't want Walter to overhear her and grow even more hysterical.

She asked Fenno if she could use the phone to call her uncle.

Once again, she was greeted by the machine. "Uncle Marsden," she said, "I'm still in the city, but I'm not at Stan's. I'm at the bookstore. I'm okay. I guess you might be out somewhere, at someone's house with a TV? I'll call you later. But I'm fine, I just thought you'd want to know." She did not hang up. Was there something else she should say? Should she give him the phone number there, at the shop? But the machine, allowing no silence, clicked off.

She tried Sonya's cell phone. She got a busy signal.

Ben handed a glass to Walter, who looked up at Saga. "I'm so sorry," he said. He turned to Hugo. "I'm so mortified. I'm so . . . I can't believe I let him go like that. I lost it over—what? Vulgar love notes?"

Hugo began, "Walter, what are the chances—"

"Stop talking to me about statistics and probability!" shouted Walter. "I haven't heard a word from him! He would have called! He may have driven me crazy, but he doesn't hate me! And I certainly do not hate him!"

"Called where?" said Hugo. "Not here, he would not."

Walter pulled a phone from his pocket and shook it. "Here!" Again, he began sobbing. Saga noticed Fenno watching Walter from across the room. Fenno had tears in his eyes.

"We already know most lines they are not working," Hugo said in his awkward English. "Most regular phones I have tried to call, here in the city they are busy."

Saga wondered if she should leave, to let this poor man grieve among his friends, but where would she go? The radio had announced that no trains were running; she might be stuck in the city for days. She thought of the animals at Stan's. She should never have left them alone.

"Walter," said Ben. His voice was calm yet sharp. He held something out in his hand, a very small box.

"*Drugs?*" Walter shouted. "Ben, who do you think you are talking to here?"

"It's just Valium. You're not yourself," said Ben.

Walter took a tiny pill from the box and held it in his palm, just staring at it.

Ben poured a glass of soda. "Take it, will you?" Walter did as he was told.

Fenno went out to the garden. Saga saw him search the sky; the small area visible through the treetops was blue as a baby blanket, smooth as a china plate. Saga joined him. He said in a low voice, "Walter's nephew left to catch an early flight to San Francisco. They had a row. He thinks it has to be one of the planes that was hijacked. One was bound for San Francisco, but I can't believe . . ." Fenno sighed. "He's . . . well, just imagine. There's not a bloody thing I can say."

"I'm glad he's with you," said Saga. "You're someone good to be with when things get crazy."

Without smiling, he looked grateful. "You, too, Emily." Before going back inside, he touched her lightly on one cheek.

Over the next hour, Walter sat listlessly as Ben, Hugo, and Fenno talked with one another about the attack, what it might mean in the city (would everyone flee, now and then for good?), how the hothead president was sure to want instant revenge. Walter nodded off in the armchair. Using Fenno's phone, Saga tried again and again to reach Sonya. Between these attempts, she stood by the front window, watching people pass.

Finally, Hugo and Ben told Fenno they had to go, to check on the restaurant and close down the kitchen, but they would be back to look after Walter. They waved politely, forlornly, to Saga.

At last Sonya answered her phone, shouting, "I am stuck in the mother of all traffic jams!" But the traffic jam (Saga secretly rejoiced) was in Brooklyn. Sonya agreed to head for Stan's; she might stay there if she couldn't make it back to Manhattan. Stan had called her, too.

"Is he mad at me for leaving?" Saga asked her.

"He didn't know you weren't there. Phone's been busy all day. You can call out, but you can't call in. Like jail. Stan just wanted to know you were okay. So you are, right?"

"Yes," said Saga, though something else began to nag at her, a sense that she had forgotten something crucial, something beyond the animals, beyond the problem of how she'd get home.

"Good. Gotta go," said Sonya.

Fenno went out on the sidewalk to speak with friends who had waved at him through the window. They embraced him before they went on their way. He came back into the shop looking worried and sad.

So this was tragedy true and large. Saga had known tragedy personal and small, but this . . . "Where is Oneeka?" she asked.

"She's at home, a long ways uptown. She couldn't make it in," said Fenno, "and I'm glad. She would've been stranded here, away from Topaz."

He excused himself and went to the basement, returning with a blanket. He knelt beside Walter's chair and tucked the blanket around his legs and chest. Carefully, he removed the cell phone from Walter's loosening grasp. Fenno then went to the front door and locked it. "Emily, I'm going to go upstairs and try to call the airline from there; I don't think it'll do much good, but I'll try. Would you mind hanging about in case he wakes? Answer the shop phone if it rings—and this one as well?" He handed Walter's phone to Saga.

Walter slept on, sometimes breathing in shallow gasps. Saga placed his phone on Fenno's desk. She opened a book displayed on a table nearby. It was filled with pictures of beautiful gardens.

Uncle Marsden. Saga realized that two hours had passed since she'd left her second message on their answering machine. She closed the book. She went to the counter, to the store phone, and punched in the number again. So loudly that Saga had to hold the receiver away from her ear, Pansy said, "Hello?" Her voice was urgent, as if she'd been terribly startled, yet Saga's first feeling was relief: Uncle Marsden had company.

"I'm glad you're there," said Saga, speaking softly, to keep from waking Walter. "It's so awful, isn't it? Did you get my message? I'm okay. I might spend the night at the bookstore here."

Pansy uttered a short, ugly cry. "Saga, we are waiting to hear from Michael! Have you given a single, solitary thought to *Michael*?"

Saga held the receiver farther from her ear; Pansy's voice was so shrill.

Michael? Saga gasped. This was it, the thing she'd forgotten. Michael's office was in one of those towers.

"Of course not!" said Pansy before Saga could speak. "Of course not!"

"Pansy?" Saga said. "Can I please talk to Uncle Marsden?"

"We need the phone free right now, Saga. We're just praying like hell that Michael is all right, that he made it out of there."

"Can I give you the number where I am?" said Saga.

"No! We don't need your number! You are *fine*!"

Saga heard Uncle Marsden's voice in the background but couldn't tell what he was saying.

"Saga, you have to call later. I have to go," Pansy said. "Dad isn't talking to anyone now. He is very upset." She hung up, just like that.

Saga held the phone for a moment. Was Saga simply "anyone"?

In the garden, the sun had just passed beneath the roofline. Birds went about their business in the big tree above her. Saga felt the instinctive jab of fear, but really, she could no longer pretend that trees were a menace.

Michael used to talk about his amazing view of the harbor. Why on earth hadn't she thought of him, realized the danger he was in? Because she'd never doubted that Michael would always be fine, that Michael's life simply *had* to follow its sunlit path, with never a detour, never a pitfall.

How unfair of her to think that only she could fall prey to catastrophe. How meanly selfish. How almost convenient her forgetting began to seem, how lazy. Had her flawed memory become an excuse for remaining outside the pain of other people? Had she become *irresponsibly* forgetful?

When she went back inside, Fenno was sitting at his desk, talking quietly with Walter. Walter's chef had returned, no longer wearing his uniform.

"I have to call my brother," Walter said. He sounded close to calm now. He looked up at Saga. One of his cheeks was ruddy and scored where it had been pressed against the chair. "Are you all right?" he asked her. "Do you need a place to stay?"

"I'm fine. *I* am," she said. "How are you?"

Walter simply shook his head, but his eyes were dry. Fenno went to him and leaned over, lifting the larger man to his feet from the chair. "Come then. You'll be a mite unsteady on your feet."

When Walter stood, he threw his arms around Fenno, holding him tight. Saga thought at first that he had lost his balance, but then she realized they were hugging each other out of commiseration and comfort, their eyes closed. "I never knew you were such a friend," she heard Walter say.

"Here I am," said Fenno.

Walter made a muffled sound, a groan. "Not that I deserve your friendship, or anyone else's, right now."

Fenno, his head resting on Walter's shoulder, smiled. His eyes were still closed, so Saga could take in that smile and just what it meant. What right had she to be jealous?

When the two men released each other, the chef held out an arm to Walter. "Come back with me. I have made us a little meal, steak and beans. You can call from your desk. We will take you home later. Come." He turned to Saga. "Do you want to come with us? We must not forget to eat. Eating, we will keep our wits about us."

She thanked him but said that she had to go.

"I'll be right here," said Fenno. "If anyone needs me, I'll be here or upstairs in the flat. I should ring my family." Saga felt disappointed, as if it were Fenno's job to worry about *her*. Of course it wasn't; that was nobody's job but hers.

Fenno kept a hand on Walter's back as Hugo led his boss to the door. Saga followed them out. On the sidewalk, she saw Walter straighten up from his old-man stance. "Come over," he said to Fenno. "Please?"

Saga slipped away quickly, before they could notice her departure. Walking west, she had to shade her eyes to see. The sun faced precisely down the center of the street. Her shadow, when she looked backward, was long and elegant; what she could see of the world was undisturbed, lit up golden as a flower. A few people passed, and though the trees and fences and buildings hadn't changed, the people had, Saga right along with them. Exactly how, that part remained to be seen.

Saga looked all around for the moon; had it risen yet? The night before, getting up after midnight to check on the animals, she had seen it through Stan's bedroom window: low, newly risen. A half moon, a wedge of honeydew, white as the papery snow that would fly from the towers.

Oh Michael. She thought of their lunch together, which had begun so bitterly for her yet ended on a far less certain note. Was the cousin she'd thought the most self-involved in fact the most concerned about the family as a whole—a family she had not made the effort to properly join?

When she crossed Hudson Street, she saw the smoke, high and thick as ever, to the south. How impossibly long the day had been; how deeply her legs ached. But she would rather walk, anywhere—where did not matter—than be in any particular place. She could not bear the company of those men in the store, all so much kinder than she was: kind to their families, kind to one another, kind to people they hardly knew. At kindness—kindness to other human beings—had she faltered? Was she turning into just another version of Stan?

She found a pay phone without a line of people waiting to use it. She fished in her knapsack for the change purse filled with quarters. Before Saga could even ask whether there had been news, Pansy flew into a rage. It was panic, Saga knew, and probably guilt, but this made little difference. "Stop calling every minute like this!" yelled Pansy. "Stop acting like Dad's your father, like Michael's *your* brother, like our house is your house! Stop making Dad pretend he needs you and get a life of your own for a change!"

"I have my own life, Pansy. There and here, I do," said Saga. Did she? She was shaking, and she longed to hang up, but that's what Pansy surely wanted. "Can I please just talk to Uncle Marsden for one minute? One minute, Pansy?"

Pansy ignored the request. "You don't have a life. You're just jealous of other people's lives. You think Denise doesn't see the way you look at her with those babies? It gives her the creeps. Everybody knows how you—"

Saga heard Frida shout, "Jesus, Pansy!" Frida took over the phone. "Saga, I'm sorry." She covered the mouthpiece and said something to Pansy, then, to Saga, "Everybody's insane here."

Saga asked, yet again, if she could talk to Uncle Marsden.

"No one can," said Frida. "He's shut himself up with his mosses and says he won't come out till we hear something, one way or the other. I'm trying to make him eat a little dinner." She paused. "Meals! How trite, I suppose."

Saga asked if there was anything she could do, there in the city. Frida seemed to think for a long while. "If you're near a hospital," she said slowly, "you could see if he's there. But not really. I can't think of anything, really. I wish I could. I wish I could think of anything constructive right now." After a pause, Frida asked if Saga had a place to stay. Saga told her that she did.

The sound of a radio rose in the background. Pansy must have raised the volume, to make her sister hang up. "Frida," said Saga, "I know you need the phone to stay free, but can I ask you a weird, selfish question?"

"Why not?" Frida might have meant to be sarcastic, but sadness made her sound earnest. "The truth is, Michael would call Denise before he'd call us."

"Frida, was there something people didn't tell me about the accident? Mine, I mean."

A chaos of shouting came over the radio. Frida sighed loudly. "This is so not the time, Saga. Just try to get back here as soon as you can."

Saga noticed that she did not say *get home*. "I will," she said. "But please just tell me. Michael was the one who told me to ask."

"Well then," said Frida. "Well then, on a day like today, what choice do I have?" She shouted at Pansy to close the goddamn kitchen door.

TWENTY-ONE

"WHO'S THAT MAN?"

"He's someone they think may have ordered those men to fly the planes into the towers."

"Who thinks it?"

"The president. The people who run the United States." *The spies,* he did not say. *The idiotic spies who bungled it all so badly, who could have foreseen this and stopped it if they hadn't believed us so high and fucking mighty.*

"Will they catch him?"

"Well, he's very good at hiding," said Alan.

"When they find where he's hiding and they catch him, will they turn him into a good guy?"

"Oh George, if they could do that, that would be something."

"Something great, you mean."

"Yes."

"But people are dead because of him? Aren't people dead?" George's tone was so straightforward, so ingenuous that Alan could only nod and place a hand on his head.

Ten minutes ago, the news artists had placed a picture of Osama bin Laden's face—a face that Alan now realized would look bizarre and striking even to a child raised in a city of freely eccentric people—in the upper left corner of the television screen. It resembled a postcard tucked in the frame of a mirror—for across the rest of the screen burned the World Trade Center, or the rubble that remained, pathetically diminished yet inconceivably, appallingly massive. What a ghastly mirror it was.

"Don't stand so close," Alan said gently. "Sit here, beside me. Please."

"Have you seed my toy planes, Daddy?"

"Seen," said Alan. "No, sweetie, I have not seen them in ages. But let's go out now. Treehorn needs a walk." He turned off the TV.

George frowned. "How will we know if they catch him?"

Alan hesitated. "We don't need to worry. He's not in New York. He's very far away from here, in fact."

"But he ordered the men to crash the planes *here*."

"Yes. That might be true," said Alan. "But it's over. The damage is done." Though of course it wasn't. The many, many kinds of damage yet to be inflicted were utterly unpredictable. The damage had only begun.

George looked skeptical. "Daddy, who knows where Osaddam is hiding?"

How strange, and in a way how canny, that George, absorbing the news for those few hours, had already conflated the names of the two villains about whom there was voluble speculation.

"Everyone's trying very hard to find out," said Alan. "Now where did we put the leash? Is it in your room?"

Greenie would not be happy that Alan had left the television on all afternoon. In retrospect, Alan wasn't happy about it, either. He had not realized how events would unfold (who could have?), in what directions they might take George's imagination. But George had seen the towers on fire, right there against his very own sky, when Alan brought him home from school, so what was there to hide? In Tulsa or Boston, you might shelter a five-year-old from news like this—though even in distant places they would soon hear all about it. Still, as father and son left the apartment with their dog, Alan knew that he must take them due west, avoid even a glimpse of the hospital. There would be hundreds of ambulances—dozens, at least—filling every lane of the avenue, carrying people burned and crushed.

Alan had yet to speak with Greenie. At noon, when it occurred to him that he had not heard from anyone outside the city, he called his mother and found her mad with worry. ("All morning long, I've dialed and dialed and dialed!") After reassuring her that he and George were safe (no, there was no human way they could get to New Jersey), he called the kitchen at the Governor's Mansion. It rang a long time before someone answered: Maria, who'd cooked for Alan and George and Greenie the night they ate dinner with Ray.

"She is not here, she is gone," said Maria.

"She's at home?"

"No, no, she is gone to you. Half an hour."

"To me? What do you mean?"

"She tries to call you, but she did not get through. She is driven by George."

You had to wonder if the terrorists had messed not just with buildings and planes and people's lives but with the minds of everyone everywhere. Well, in fact they had. If no one could think straight today, would that be so strange?

"Ray's driver?"

"Yes. Tall George. He will drive her to New York."

"Here? All the way here?"

"That's it, *sí*, yes. All the way to you," said Maria.

Alan asked if there was any way to reach her, to reach Tall George; she did not know. He started to ask if he could speak with Ray or Mary Bliss, but really, who was he, now, to get through to either of them? "Never mind, Maria. Thank you. If she calls there, would you tell her we're all right? We're fine?"

ALAN HAD BEEN IN HIS OFFICE WITH STEPHEN, looking over the brochures and documents Stephen had brought along. Alan had told Stephen that his sister was adopting, too, through a different country with different rules. He confessed that beyond what he'd learned about this process from Stephen and Joya, he knew nothing. "That's completely okay," Stephen had told him. "You're like my second set of eyes, my second set of shoulders. Sometimes it feels like I'm lifting a Dumpster to do this thing." Alan was touched.

That morning Stephen told him about a dream in which he had discovered that in order to adopt a child he had to move to a medieval building in Brooklyn that looked a lot like a monastery. In the dream, this seemed fine—the monastery had views of New York Harbor and the Statue of Liberty—until Stephen found out that Gordie would also be living there.

"I guess the Statue of Liberty would have to represent my freedom from my anger at Gordie. What do you think?" said Stephen. "And it's right beside Ellis Island, so that seems like a good omen for the adoption, maybe."

"But you have to live in a monastery?" asked Alan. He smiled. "Stephen, have you been seeing anyone?"

"*Seeing* anyone? Other than nosy matrons and paper pushers? Dream on."

They had talked about Stephen's hunch that he would be adopting a daughter, how his fantasy was tied up with his goddaughter, Skye. They had talked about Stephen's vision of caring for a baby. Alan felt almost fatherly toward him now; he wanted to make Stephen feel welcome to the world of impending parenthood, to understand that it both did and did not merit any sort of fanfare. Once Stephen had the child he yearned for, too many people would give him grief or shut him out, and Alan wanted to inoculate him, however modestly, with approval and a sense of inclusion.

After the session had ended, Alan left his building with Stephen, knowing that they would part ways on the sidewalk. As soon as they stepped outside, Stephen said, "Good grief, will you listen to that?" He was referring to the sirens, which wailed insistently from every direction.

A few blocks to the east, where Bank Street met Greenwich Avenue, Alan saw a throng of milling people. It was just before nine, and though people would still be heading to work, there were never crowds of commuters, not the hordes you'd see farther uptown. A man walked swiftly toward them, a brooding look on his face.

"Has something happened?" Alan asked him.

"A jetliner's flown right into the World Trade Center. Right *into* it. Like six floors of it. A terrible, terrible accident," said the man. "Terrible." He looked as if he wanted to discuss it with someone, but neither Alan nor Stephen knew what to say. The stranger continued on his way.

Alan had meant to go west, to a stationery store on Hudson, but now he walked with Stephen, toward the crowd. When they emerged onto the avenue, they looked south. They heard a muffled roar, like the muttering of gathered birds—but it was human, the sound of far-reaching, inarticulate amazement. They saw a second plume of smoke breach the horizon of rooftops.

Along with the crowd of which they were now a part, they made wordless noises of incomprehension.

Across the avenue, on the stretch of sidewalk in front of the hospital, a line began to form. Out of the hospital, from the emergency room, from around both corners, emerged figures in green and white: doctors and nurses, all fully suited in scrubs the color of Caribbean water, their heads covered, nunlike, with crisp white bonnets. At their throats they wore cloth masks, ready for the worst. They stood in rows spanning the entire block. As they stepped from the shadowed margin of the building and into the sun, their white pants and headcoverings gleamed. Shading their eyes, they stared in the direction of the smoke.

Alan saw cops pushing barricades against the curbs, the way they did for big parades. Almost abruptly, there was no traffic; the avenue was utterly empty. It was empty because it was expected to fill, at any moment, with ambulances.

Alan turned to Stephen, whose astonished presence he had forgotten for several minutes. "I'm going to my son's school," he said. "I have to go." As if they'd been headed somewhere together.

Stephen looked shaken. "Yes. Go there now."

"You should go home, I think," said Alan.

"Yes," said Stephen, but after Alan had crossed the avenue, he looked back and saw Stephen, fixed to the spot, looking south.

Alan had dropped George off by eight, for breakfast in the school cafeteria. He did this on Tuesdays and Thursdays, in order to meet with Stephen. Alan saw four patients now, restricting their appointments to the margins of his days.

He joined a crowd of distressed parents in the cafeteria, just in time to see the principal climb up on a chair. She waved her arms, trying to silence the uproar. She was a small rotund woman—Madam Cog she was called by the parents who found her policies too cold, too unionized—and though she seemed for once *admirably* cool, she looked like a hen on a precarious roost. Most of the parents swarming about her were mothers, several of them the same mothers who spoke so warmly, so unctuously to Alan on other mornings, looking him over as a prospect for their lonely friends: the ultimate prize, a single dad. Here and now, these women had no time or courtesy for Alan, elbowing around him, blind to anyone but the authority figure who held their children hostage.

"Parents! Parents! Parents, listen to me!" the principal called out over their heads. Finally, there was a begrudging semblance of quiet. "Parents, school is the safest place for your children," she intoned, her voice as ceremoniously condescending as ever. "I advise you to leave them here until further notice, to maintain as much normalcy as possible. But if you must take them home—if you feel you must—then proceed to my office and follow the usual procedures. Please. That much I must require."

She had more to say, but her words were lost in the sound of feet running toward her office. Alan ran with them and took his place in a long, long line. If the city were to be bombed right then, he wanted to be under the same roof as George. Let me be with him now, *now,* he thought as he waited for his turn at the attendance ledger, where children could be signed out like library books or prescription drugs.

What would you do, he had thought, if at that moment you'd had two children, or more, all in different places? How could you decide where to go first? What parent, honestly, would *go home* and wait out the day?

Yet now, as Alan detached his reluctant son from the television screen, he understood what Madam Cog had meant. In the classroom where he had picked up George, the teacher had been conducting first-grade business as usual. The children had been sitting on a brown rug, at "meeting time," discussing the seasonal changes of autumn, what those changes meant about the earth and its relationship to the sun. The teacher had smiled as, one by one, parents took their bewildered children's hands and led them out toward the bedlam beyond the classroom walls. "Take care!" the teacher had called after each departure, her voice light as a billowing scarf.

When they left their building, Alan paused at the top of the stoop, holding Treehorn back, and looked in every direction, even up at the sky. At a glance, their neighborhood looked as it always did in the long, lovely shadows of late afternoon; but today people stood in tight, animated groups on every corner of Bank Street, to east and west alike. Alan led George and Treehorn through these knots of people, hearing excerpts of their outrage and grief. *But we are the safe ones, the spared ones,* he wanted to say—till he realized that this might be only fleetingly true. When they reached the playground, George stopped. A surprising number of children were swinging, climbing, digging in the sun-warmed sand. One of George's playmates came to the fence.

"Can we go in?" George asked his father.

Alan shook his head. "You know Treehorn can't go into the play-ground."

The friend's mother, who had followed her son to the fence, looked intently at Alan; they both understood that though they wanted desperately to share the horror they felt, to find out what details the other one knew, there was little they could say in front of the children.

"Everyone in your family all right?" asked Alan.

"Yes," she said. "Yours, too, I hope."

"Yes," he said. At least Greenie, he thought in a flash, was not a chef at Windows on the World. He wondered if, in what she had always described as a very small cosmos, she knew anyone who worked there. Who had worked there.

"Can we come back later?" asked George. "Please?"

"Let's give Treehorn a good walk, and then we'll see," said Alan. But he wanted to get home quickly. He hoped Greenie was trying to call. At some point, the telephone lines had to clear. "Come on, George. I'm sorry."

At first, George wouldn't move. He whined in protest. Alan held out his free hand until George surrendered and took it. They walked toward the river, where the sky had begun to turn from blue to a buttery yellow. The open water seemed to amplify the sirens as they rose and fell, some prolonged and moaning, others staccato, ululating, pleading. At times their collective noise became nearly symphonic.

WITHIN A WEEK OF RETURNING from New Mexico with George, Alan had accepted his mother's offer of her aging Toyota, and he had phoned Jerry again. "I think I need to work with crazier people than I do," he said. "Is that a terrible thing to say?" Jerry had laughed. "Not in the slightest. Let's get you up and running with the wolves."

Alan did these two things to keep himself from curling up in a corner and mourning the death of his marriage. Not that George, with his emotional resilience and energy, would have let his father curl up for so much as a catnap. Alan enrolled him in a simple summer camp, run by his old nursery school teachers (this was to make *Alan* feel secure), but every weekend they got in the car and left the city. They went to New Jersey, where George's grandmother was happy to see so much of him, where the boy could run and dig and splash on the beach; to friends' country houses; to trails that wound along cliffs in the Catskills. One weekend they stayed in a lighthouse on the Hudson River. They bought food to cook in the decrepit kitchen, inviting the keeper (a former dot-com boy wonder in a Deadhead T-shirt) to join them. Warily, George ate lobster for the first time.

Perhaps Alan had made the mistake, for too long, of expecting Greenie to broaden his horizons. Now he would do it for himself, and for George. In time, he suspected, he would have to give George back to Greenie, but for now he would make the most of having him close. He took George to the *Intrepid,* to the Cloisters, to a Yankees game where they sat near the very top and—Alan having forgotten the sunscreen—felt their noses turn pleasantly pink. A fine layer of gratification began to form, like a dusting of snow, in Alan's psyche. Yet George alone could not have brought his father this much peace.

Marion had called the day she received Alan's letter—also less than a week after he had returned. She began with an apology. She had been much too cruel; she had held against him the petty sin of silence. How was he to have guessed that she had become pregnant (to her own surprise, she insisted), that she hadn't really meant to make their good-bye in that parking lot so final? She'd been trying to be tougher than she was—tougher and less attached to her past. "I was furious when my parents told me they were selling that house. Never mind that I'd grown up to see it as tacky, as so *New Jersey.*" She laughed. "I mean, it's the only place I grew up, right? I went to that reunion knowing it was the last time I'd be there. My house."

She had called late at night. Alan had sat on his bed and listened to her talk. Just her voice, all the tension and resentment of their last meeting fallen away, gave him enormous pleasure. He enjoyed the sound of her voice so much that he felt no urgency to speak.

"Little brother, are you still there?" she said after a long pause. "Were you listening to everything I said?"

"I've always been here. It's you who went underground," he said, but affectionately.

"Will you forgive me?"

"Of course. But please don't call me little brother."

"I'm sorry." Another long silence, and then she told him, "Now here comes the hard part." This was the part where she acknowledged that Jacob was his son as well as hers ("Yes, *yours,* no more mincing words") but that she could not imagine complicating what the boy knew about his universe already. He knew that Lewis wasn't his "original" father, but he'd stopped asking who that father might be.

"For now," said Alan. "He's stopped asking for now. And he hasn't stopped thinking about it."

Marion sighed. "You're not the only head-science guy around here." She told him that she hoped Alan, maybe Greenie and George as well, could find their way back to California soon, that they could all get together. "Have a picnic in Golden Gate Park? Would that be insane?" She wished that something could bring her east, but her parents were happily settled in Del Ray Beach and didn't miss New Jersey one bit. "And no more reunions for me," she added. "None of any kind whatsoever."

She mailed him five pictures of Jacob, two including herself, none including Lewis. Alan gazed at them, trying to feel a recognition. He didn't—but it didn't matter. He kept the pictures in his dresser, under his T-shirts.

They spoke every few weeks all summer long. They traded stories about George and Jacob, the common phases the two parents had gone through, the great differences in the two boys' temperaments and tastes. Without planning it that way, they took turns calling. Once when Alan called, Lewis answered. "Why hello there," he said, as if Alan's voice were a delightful surprise. Only in August, because Marion had mentioned Greenie a third or fourth time—clearly wanting him to open up and talk about his wife, his marriage—did Alan tell her that they were separated. "Irrevocably, I think." At the risk of sounding callow, he told her quickly, almost dismissively. Marion told him how sorry she was. He told her that he was sorry, too. Why hadn't Alan told her before? At that, he laughed honestly. He said, "I'm not the only head-science guy around here."

Jerry—in Alan's book, king of all head-science guys—worked now not in a doorman building on Madison Avenue but in a defunct school building on Flatbush Avenue. He had become a tribal leader, dispatching guerrillas to fight for the city's walking wounded. By September, Alan was working four hours a week in the defunct school's defunct gymnasium, running group therapy sessions for couples with drinking problems. There was no air-conditioning, and sometimes the portable fans were turned up so high that the participants had to shout their confessions and grievances. Alan went home to George hoarse and exhausted but mentally vibrant and drained of self-pity. He had also enrolled in two forensic social work courses. That afternoon, he would have been attending the third class of each course, back to back, if the terrorists had not interfered.

ALAN WONDERED WHAT GEORGE, years from now, would remember of this day. Even in the weeks to come, would it change the way he saw his world? His *little* world, Alan thought, but that was not right. Wasn't the world, to any child, much larger than it was to the adults around him?

Alan had said to Greenie that he would speak to George in greater depth about the incident with Diego and the horses, once they had settled back in New York. But his efforts to keep that promise were feeble at best. The first time Alan tried to edge his way toward asking what had happened, George cut him off brusquely. "Nobody talks about that now," he said, looking his father straight in the eye with a confidence that was nearly chilling. For an instant, Alan could easily see the younger boy as the one who had cooked up the foolish scheme.

Once George left New Mexico, he seldom spoke of anything he'd left behind—not counting his mother. He was vocal in his compassion toward animals. He scolded a friend at the playground who chased pigeons; he asked Alan why rats had to be poisoned. Whenever he saw a horse—on trips outside the city or in Washington Square, where mounted police patrolled in pairs—he stopped to be impressed, but there was no more talk of palominos, Appaloosas, or Tennessee walking horses. He mentioned Consuelo once every few days at first—he might tell Alan the way she made his favorite sandwich or what books she liked to read with him—but even these references had ceased by the end of summer.

Was George a cold child at some level? Did he have no lasting remorse? Or was he simply resilient, strong because—like his mother—he was happy by nature? For all that Alan had learned about human motivations and pathological patterns, he could not fathom the innermost George. No matter how well you knew your own child, wouldn't your love always distort your perception?

Joya grilled Alan constantly about being a parent. She was reading every book under the sun, despite his warning that once the baby arrived, she would throw them all away. She expected to hear by Christmastime that a baby was waiting for her across the Pacific Ocean. The agency would send a picture of the baby by e-mail. Alan had agreed to go with her, and now he realized that perhaps this would help him find a natural way to meet Jacob as well. He would fly George to New Mexico, then travel to Vietnam with Joya. If they could return to San Francisco in good time, he might be able to spend a week there before returning home. Joya told him she had enough frequent-flyer miles for a round trip to Pluto, so she'd send him wherever he needed to go. "Those miles were supposed to be my honeymoon in Thailand and Japan," she said, "but I guess I'm skipping that phase. At least I knew I'd be going to Asia. I just didn't know why."

Joya was so busy redesigning her life that she no longer had the time to scrutinize Alan's. Or that was how Alan chose to interpret the way she steered clear of discussing his estrangement from Greenie. At first he missed Joya's bossy advice, her editorials on what he'd done wrong and how he should fix it; was he now a lost cause? But once he realized the selfishness of this anxiety, Alan was content to devote all their communications to his sister's plans.

That evening, when he and George returned to the apartment from walking Treehorn, Joya's message—concerned but chastising—was the first of two on the answering machine. The second was from Marion. Alan wanted to speak with both women, but he would wait until George was asleep. And then it dawned on him: the lines from the outside world had cleared.

As soon as Treehorn had settled down, George began eyeing the blank television screen, though he did not ask Alan to turn it on. Yes, it was clear he did understand that the world was very large. "Is Mommy okay?" he asked suddenly.

"Yes," said Alan, surprised at his own less-than-honest conviction. "Let's read," he added quickly. "Why don't you read to me?"

George chose *Bartholomew and the Oobleck*. Halfway through, Alan wondered just how coincidental this choice had been. Watching Bartholomew Cubbins run frantically about the Kingdom of Didd, trying to thwart the green goo, he couldn't help thinking of Rudy Giuliani.

Greenie called when the royal trumpeter's trumpet filled with oobleck.

She cried when he answered.

"We're fine, we're both fine," he said twice.

"Where have you been, where have you *been*? Why haven't you left the city? Why haven't you answered your cell phone?"

"I haven't used it in months," said Alan. "I'm sorry. Where are you? You know, I tried to call *you*."

"Can I speak to George?"

"It's your mother." Alan handed the phone to George.

"Mommy, hi, we're reading. We are in the middle of the story." He listened to his mother. Alan heard the flow of her voice, rapid, expressive.

"Treehorn is okay, too. We went for a walk and we saw a lot of police cars." After another minute, he turned to Alan. "Daddy, is my school canceled?"

"I don't know about school, George." Since taking George out of his classroom, Alan hadn't given school a thought. How could life of any normal sort resume—yet what would take its place? He asked for the phone.

"Listen, Alan, I want you to take George to Maine, up to the island— for a week or something, just till the city seems safe again, and then we can talk—"

"Greenie, where are you? You're skipping so far ahead here. Listen, we are fine, we really are—"

"How do you know you're fine? Think of all the people in those towers who were certain they were fine when they got up this morning, Alan!"

"Greenie." Slowly, insistently, Alan drew from her that she was calling him from a rest stop in Oklahoma, that there were no rental cars to be had in New Mexico—or anywhere else—once all the planes had been grounded, that Ray had forbidden her to drive cross-country alone and had, so generously, loaned her his driver, to get her at least partway back to New York. Nothing, however, would have kept her from George. She spoke breathlessly, almost angrily, in a headlong rush of words.

Alan suddenly understood that she was on her way *there,* to the very room in which he sat, and that once she reached George, she might refuse to leave again without him.

"Alan," she continued, "I need you to call one of my cousins in Boston and go to Maine. There are keys to the house in my dresser, but you need to let them know you're going. Please. I cannot sleep—I will die of worry—if you don't do this."

"I have a life to live here, Greenie," said Alan. *With George,* he was tempted to say. She had her life with Charlie.

"Alan, no one there is going to be leading a regular life for days, probably weeks. Maybe never again!"

"First I was supposed to move to New Mexico, Greenie. Now I'm supposed to move to an island in Maine? Where next? Marrakesh? Beijing?" Alan glanced at George, who was watching him, newly worried.

"No, Alan—just, please, for now . . . I'll get there in a few days. I want George—I want you both out of the city. They're saying the air from the burning towers could be poisonous to breathe. Please. Until they know more."

"I'm paying close attention to the news right here, and I haven't heard a thing about poisonous air," he said. But he wrote down the numbers of her cousins. She told him that the marina would still be open; he could get a launch to take them over. There should be a boat at the island. No one closed up the houses before October. She asked him to find his cell phone and keep it with him. She would call him twice a day until she could get there.

"And what will you do once you get here?" he asked. "You're planning to quit your job?"

"No," she said. "No, I'll go back. I just—"

Just what? Just want to have your motherly cake and eat it too? he thought, before recognizing how hilariously apt that would sound. "It's okay, Greenie," he said. "We'll talk tomorrow morning. We'll be fine, we really will."

After he hung up, Alan realized that he could not remember the last difficult conversation in which he had been the one to reassure her.

In bed, in the dark, he listened a long time to the never-ending sirens. It had become the sound of extreme mourning, but you had to see it as hopeful, too. *Let each siren be a rescue,* he thought, as close to prayer as he'd ever come, *someone pulled from the wreckage and restored to a family.* He imagined an aerial view of the city, the city as river upon river of throbbing red lights. Ironically, the only people up there to see it would be fighter pilots, tucked tight in their armored cockpits. When Alan listened hard enough, sometimes he heard them, too.

~~⌒~~

EVERYONE WANTED TO GIVE BLOOD. Or clean socks. Or blankets. Or musical entertainment. Or, as a last resort, money. In an epidemic of survivor's guilt, people were haplessly desperate to give. On Seventh Avenue, donors whose blood was not needed, and who knew it, lined up anyway along the walls of the hospital. Cooks at the James Beard House, across the street, piled tables with pastries and fruit to feed these superfluous donors.

Alan saw the first newly flaunted flag on Thursday—safety-pinned to the backpack of a roller-skating teenage boy with shredded jeans and fuchsia hair. Graffiti became patriotic, public spaces religious. Bus shelters were shrines, papered with pleas that reminded Alan, inescapably, uncomfortably, of the missing-pet notices he posted for Saga. On Friday, when the rain came down in torrents, when George's school resumed, the candles guttered and collapsed, the ink on the notices ran, the photographs of the lost people buckled and blurred.

The air had begun to smell not just foul but ominous. Alan believed the smell was one of burning circuitry and building components, but others believed it was flesh. Jerry said it smelled much worse in Brooklyn. *Even the wind is a capitalist, mindful of real-estate values. What a world,* he e-mailed Alan. Alan had not been to Brooklyn since Monday; he had been looking after George, talking to clients on the phone. When he returned, said Jerry, there would be more work than ever. City officials wanted to subsidize therapy for people traumatized by the attacks.

Alan dropped George off at school, where the halls echoed with absence, and told the teacher he'd be back to pick up his son before noon. He went home, packed their bags, and took Treehorn for a walk. After stopping at the bank for cash, he found himself on the northwest corner of Bank and Hudson, fighting the wind to keep his umbrella intact as Treehorn strained against the leash, pulling him off balance. He shouted the dog's name twice, wondering what could be so urgent, when he heard "There's a good girl. That's my girl."

Saga came toward them from under a café awning, clasping a paper coffee cup. It was obvious that she had not wanted them to see her. She was wet, and her clothes looked filthy. If he had been wrong to think she was homeless the day they met, he had doubts all over again.

To hide her face from Alan, she bent low, petting and murmuring to Treehorn.

"I like the coffee here," she said to Alan, meekly, when she stood. She motioned toward the café.

"Saga, you look terrible!" Alan exclaimed. "I'm sorry, but it's the truth! Are you staying in the city—at Stan's? You don't look like you're staying anywhere." He held the umbrella over her head, but the gesture was pointless.

"He's back now," she said. "He got a ride."

Alan ignored the non sequitur. "Why aren't you home, in Connecticut? Did you get stuck here? You should have come to me!"

She shook her head. "I think my cousin's dead. Well, he must be. I don't think they're going to forgive me. Even if it isn't my fault."

"Oh Saga, stop talking in riddles, please! Where *are* you staying?"

"Around the corner."

"Let me walk you back there," said Alan. "You need dry clothes, you need . . . Who are you staying with?"

She shook her head again. "It's just somewhere I stay." No longer avoiding his eyes, she looked miserable yet defiant.

"Come home with me now," said Alan. "Please."

Saga let him take her arm, which he managed to do by giving up on the umbrella, which he closed and forced into a pocket of his raincoat. Almost immediately, it soaked through the lining and then his pants.

He could hear her teeth chattering as they walked along. Just before they reached Alan's building, she said, "I can't believe he's dead, but I know he must be."

"Let's talk when we get inside," he said.

"We've been here before, haven't we?" she said as they climbed the stairs.

Alan stopped to look at her, alarmed. "Many times, Saga. You've been to my place a few times now." Was she in shock?

She laughed weakly. "No, no. I'm not that bad. I mean, you've rescued me in the rain before, only then we had the puppies. Including you, little girl," she said to Treehorn.

"Yes," said Alan, relieved. "That's when we met."

"Oh I know that," said Saga.

⁓

THERE WAS INDEED A PECULIAR déjà vu to that morning: Saga freshly showered, hair in a towel, wearing clothes abandoned by Greenie, sitting at Alan's table with a cup of tea, a view of rain pummeling the neighbors' bushes and tiny plots of flowers. Yet this time, perhaps because Alan was focused on other things (locking windows, suspending the paper delivery, changing Sunny's water), she could not stop talking.

Saga had not returned to Connecticut because, in the trauma of Tuesday, she'd had a series of phone conversations with her family—mostly with a spiteful-sounding cousin named Pansy (her name a real-life red herring if ever there was one). "After everything she accused me of, it's like suddenly I had nothing to lose," Saga told Alan as they left the apartment to pick up George and get the car. "I wasn't so afraid of them anymore."

As a therapist, you were both privileged and condemned to hear the stories of every conceivable family arrangement under the sun. Saga's was not so terribly eccentric—a group of highly functional siblings with a rational parent—yet Alan marveled at the strange symbiosis of the relationship Saga described with this uncle of hers (the older, imperious voice on the phone).

For all that he had once impatiently wondered about her, suddenly Alan knew more than he might wish to know. He worried that she had begun to see him as a savior, a role he felt unsuited to play for anyone, even someone he liked as much as he did Saga. But as Jerry used to say years before, during Alan's training, "Don't worry so damn far into the future. The future does its own thing without a lot of help from you."

Alan was glad he'd provided so many toys and other distractions for George, who sat in the backseat amid books, trucks, stuffed animals, and half a dozen tapes. Poor Treehorn had squeezed herself down on the floor. Alan had decided, in part because the aura and the odors of the city had begun to dig into his soul, that he would comply with Greenie's wishes and meet her in Maine. He had no intention of staying there for more than a few days, but perhaps George needed a break from the air of disaster as well. In the sandbox, Alan had seen some of George's playmates reenacting the attack itself. And now, after the strangely serendipitous meeting with Saga, he was glad that he could insist, so logically, on making sure she got home.

Leaving the city was even more difficult than on the average Friday. They inched along the West Side Highway, north toward the George Washington Bridge, for half an hour. George, oblivious to the delay, listened to *The Lion King* on Alan's Walkman. "Oh I just can't wait to be king!" he sang along, off-key. In the past few days, whenever George caught his father with a brooding expression on his face, he would say, "Hakuna matata, Dad." It made Alan smile every time.

Saga had been quiet for a while, and Alan thought she might be falling asleep. For the first time in hours, he became preoccupied again with his fears about what might happen when Greenie finally arrived. So he was completely unprepared when Saga, there in the traffic jam—and thank God for once that George's ears were blocked by Disney—confided yet something else.

"I found out I was pregnant," she said without emotion.

Alan had contemplated changing to a lane that appeared less sluggish. He stayed where he was. He had to look at Saga. "Saga, you're pregnant?"

"No. Was. I was pregnant before the accident, when it happened. Frida told me."

"And you forgot? Is that it? Oh Saga."

"I forgot, but then no one told me. Uncle Marsden and my mother made everybody promise not to tell me. Maybe my mother would have told me, but then she died." Saga delivered this news as if it had very little to do with her.

Alan had a hard time containing his anger. He was about to ask how the hell anyone could keep this from her—what about her doctors, for God's sake!—when he realized that the answer was obvious. You didn't even have to have met this uncle to guess that he'd needed Saga to remain, or return to being, a little girl.

"You know," Saga said quietly, "maybe that's why David left me. Maybe not just because he thought I'd be a cripple. Okay, like that wouldn't be enough!"

"Don't try to make this funny," said Alan. "It isn't funny at all."

She told him then that for a long time she'd felt as if the people around her were withholding something from her, a particular thing about her life before. She'd thought it might be that she and her boyfriend were going to break up anyway. Her voice became barely audible. "But maybe the opposite was true. Maybe we were going to get married."

"Saga, this is so hurtful," said Alan. "It's outrageous. No one had the right to keep any of your life a secret from you."

"I guess they wanted to keep me from being too upset."

Alan could not see her face; she was looking out the window. She might have been crying, trying to find a moment of privacy. He let her be. In the backseat, George was doing his best to sound like the evil Scar, singing along with Jeremy Irons.

One thing was certain: Alan did not relish the thought of meeting Saga's relatives, which he was likely to do in about an hour—or four, if the roads did not open up. They sounded like a bunch of narcissistic jerks, but there was no way Alan would have dropped Saga off at her doorstep and driven away—not after what she had just told him.

The cars in front of them picked up speed after the toll bridge to the Bronx. What little conversation he and Saga shared after that was idle talk about the countryside and responses to jokes that George was now reading to them from a book called the *Jokelopedia*. ("Why *did* Mrs. Crow have such a huge phone bill?") In less than two hours, they pulled up in front of Saga's uncle's house. It was a huge shingle house, stark and gray as the weather. "I'm coming in with you," said Alan. "That's a den of lions in there."

"I'm no antelope. They can't devour me."

"Well, there's devouring and there's mauling."

Saga looked mournfully at Alan. "They're my family."

"They are, and they aren't," said Alan. "Right now, Saga, they are Michael's family." What Alan knew, but did not say, was that when she walked in the door, they would grieve that the one returning was *not* Michael.

In the backseat, George had fallen asleep. Right up against him, Treehorn slept as well, having somehow made a place for herself among the toys.

There were four cars in the driveway but no sign of life beyond a pair of seagulls swooping over the massive chimney. Alan did not see the ocean, but he could smell it.

Saga went in the back door; Alan followed. They emerged in a kitchen nearly the size of his apartment. The sink overflowed with dishes.

On a blackboard he read: *pasta   garlic   aa batteries   TP
babywipes   TOMATOES   call dentist*

Boxed in pink chalk: *Public Hearing Thurs.!!*

"Hello!" called Saga.

They passed through a wood-paneled dining room into one of the largest living rooms Alan had ever seen—impressive yet shabby, its furnishings so well used that they had been all but used up. He heard footsteps on a staircase from the second floor. He looked at Saga, who waited quietly, hands folded before her in the attitude of a schoolgirl.

"There you are, my dear," said the man who was obviously Saga's uncle, perfectly casual, as if she were ten minutes late for tea. He was tall, with an Einstein head of hair, and his shirt was open one button too low; perhaps he had just put it on. "We did wonder, but I said you were fine."

Saga moved toward him quickly as he reached the foot of the stairs. "I am so sorry about Michael," she said. She hugged her uncle; he returned her embrace almost absentmindedly.

"We're still waiting, you know. He told Denise he was getting out. His last words to her were 'Don't you worry.' No one outsmarts Michael. Let's not forget about that. Let's not. He will turn up yet." Alan was apparently invisible to him.

"Where is everybody?" asked Saga.

The uncle walked past her and sat on a couch. "Pansy and Denise are shopping, with the little girls. Michael and Denise have a new car, the biggest you've ever laid eyes on." He raised his eyebrows, as if he might smile, but his expression returned to one of docile fatigue.

Saga remained standing. "Can I get you something, Uncle Marsden? Something to drink?"

"No, my dear, but thank you." Alan had never seen someone look so dignified yet so extremely sad.

Hearing lighter footsteps on the stairs, Alan looked up at a slender woman with long, straight graying blond hair. She wore a brown batik dress and an earthy type of sandals he hadn't seen since college. She stopped midway down. "Saga? Saga, where on earth have you been?"

"She's been *fine,*" said the uncle. He did not bother to turn around and look at the woman on the stairs.

Saga said, "I'm sorry, Frida."

"We've had way too much to worry about, never mind worrying

what became of you when you didn't call back. I've been on the phone for days. I seem to be the only one around here who can hold anything together. It's just . . ." She sighed, as if she'd used up every word she possessed.

The two women looked at each other for a long, uncertain moment. This was the cousin who had told Saga the secret of her pregnancy; couldn't she guess what effect it would have had on Saga? Alan could sense a sympathy between them, but Frida looked angry. Well, she had a right, a small right, to be angry at Saga. People shouldn't disappear for days without calling (or disappear for good, Alan thought sadly).

"Do you think there's a chance Michael's coming back?" asked Saga.

Frida glanced at her father, who seemed transfixed by a stuffed elephant wedged against the arm of the couch. Frida shook her head. Saga started to cry.

"Stop all this crying!" said the uncle abruptly. "All this weeping is driving me mad! Girls weeping their heads off day and night!" Now he was addressing Alan. He didn't seem to wonder who Alan was; he was simply a fellow male, one who must have suffered the weeping of girls. Alan nodded once, just to acknowledge that he'd been spoken to.

"Everything's changing," the cousin said to Saga, and the change she referred to did not sound good.

"I know," Saga said. "I guessed that. I'm not an idiot."

"No one's ever said you were, Saga." She turned to Alan. "Who are you? Are you the book guy or the dog guy?" She did not sound as if she really cared or even wanted to know, and in that moment Alan made a decision. To hell with his fears about playing the savior. Looking at Saga, he did not think it would be hard to convince her to leave this place, at least for now. Before taking her aside, however, he went out the front door, quickly and without excuses, down the steps and to the car. For a few horrified moments, he'd forgotten all about George. To his relief, George still slept, but Treehorn was awake. Through the opening at the top of Treehorn's window, Alan whispered, "I'll take you out in just a minute, girl. Hang on there."

TWENTY-TWO

MCNALLY CLEANS THE GRILL, scowling as he shoves the wire brush back and forth, so vigorously that it looks like a penance. He does not notice that someone dances just behind him, bumping and grinding within inches of making contact. The someone is Walter, his widespread arms threatening to enfold McNally's torso. Greenie told McNally that he did not have to do this ghastly chore, but the massive grill is one he made himself and trucked in from the ranch. It won't be done right, he insists, if it's left to anyone else.

Walter's responsibilities have ended, and he is filled with the expendable joy of a hard job impeccably done. He is at his most abandoned and gleeful, moving his mouth to "Some People." Ethel Merman is the one doing the singing, her voice blaring from Greenie's boom box, which Walter has brought outside to entertain them now that the party is over.

When Greenie cannot contain her laughter (still a startling sound after a month of so many miseries), McNally turns around. "Just what is so hilarious?"

"Walter wants to ask you for this dance," she says.

McNally levels a withering gaze at Walter. Feigning innocence, Walter stands three feet away, arms at his sides.

"Let me tell you something," says McNally, shaking his sooty brush at Walter. "I am too worn out for jokes. This has got to be about the longest day of my sorry life—we won't mention a couple in lockup back in the army."

"We won't ask for what crimes," says Walter.

"You don't ask about mine, I certainly—certainly—will not ask about yours," McNally says.

The guests have left, but the lawn still swarms with people. Mike Chu checks his flower beds for flotsam. (Greenie sees him pull a sequined purse out of the chamisa. He shakes his head.) The musicians lay their instruments in their cases and fold up their stands. Employees of one rental company fold tables and chairs; those from another stack plates and box up glasses. Volunteers for a food charity gather leftovers for a shelter, while the cops, now relaxed, chat in twos and threes along the service driveway, stopping only to inspect the trucks that come and go. They are not accustomed to being so suspicious, but they are learning.

The blue tent will not be taken down until the following day. It luffs like a sail in the breeze, its shadow wavering over the grass. Against this azure backdrop, two television reporters address their cameramen.

One of the reporters stands so close to Greenie that she can hear his words, even in competition with Ethel Merman. "Yes, Anita, that's right. Governor Raymond Fleetwing McCrae was married today, on his own lawn, under skies as blue as his bride's eyes, in a ceremony whose friendly, informal tone was a welcome balm in the face of all the unspeakable horrors of this past month and the great sorrow that so many Americans continue to endure," says the buff, slightly sunburnt reporter. Greenie notices that his tie is red (as well as his nose), making the tableau, with his white shirt and the blue tent, an obsequious tribute to the fierce resurgence of the flag. "Indeed, Anita," he continues earnestly, "the governor's act of unity and hope for the future only serves to strengthen the new unity we feel now, all of us together, in the midst of our mourning and healing."

Greenie turns up Ethel Merman and begins, with great care, to wrap and pack the top tier of the cake. McNally will take it back to the ranch, where it will be frozen for Ray and Claudia's first-anniversary celebration.

The size of a pillbox hat, it was the crown to a widening skirt of seven tiers, an impressive yet fragile creation held together with a complex system of hidden pillars and platforms. ("My word, it's like a parking garage!" said Walter as he followed Greenie's orders to help construct it.) This final tier, by itself, is a small coconut cake—still Ray's favorite sweet—encased in the same white chocolate fondant that Greenie laid over the entire creation. One of the only vetoes that Ray imposed on Claudia's wedding scheme was her vision of a spun-sugar bride and groom, in western attire, on top of the cake.

"Claudia, there is a fine line between whimsical and tacky, and there you have it. You do," he said in the only planning session with Greenie that he attended. To Greenie's relief, the lone embellishment on the smooth white surface of the cake was a garland of flowers fashioned from the icing. Ray suggested yucca, the New Mexico state flower, and it took Greenie a great deal of practice to make the blossoms look like something other than wilted larkspur.

"I want a cake like no other—and I mean that," Claudia said to Greenie, almost sternly. "I want a cake that, when you cut it, there's some kind of big flamboyant surprise. Maybe fancier inside than out. Just like true grown-up love, what do you think?" Standing there in Ray's kitchen, Paul Bunyan fists on her denim hips, she looked anything but the romantic bride.

Greenie remembered the three-flavored cake she had wanted for her own wedding—yet surrendered in the face of her mother's notions of good taste, what Olivia Duquette called "the class of understatement." Understatement, now, looks laughably overvalued. Better say what you think much too strongly than risk not being heard.

"But no chocolate," said Claudia. "I happen to be one of three people in the world who don't care a hoot for chocolate."

They agreed on four flavors of cake—vanilla, maple, orange, and coconut—to alternate, almost randomly, in twenty-one slim layers throughout the seven tiers beneath the one to be saved, the crown of coconut. A syrup infused with ginger would be brushed on the sponge beneath the icing. Greenie spent four days in early September testing recipes, tasting the flavors together, manipulating and reweighing ingredients to strengthen the cake itself. She made measurements and ordered pans. She had an hour-long phone conversation with the master pastry chef who had taught her how to make cakes to feed a small army. At times, with all the intricate planning, the entire wedding did feel like a military maneuver.

In the kitchen, Greenie's first passion has always been cake. Most inexperienced cooks believe, mistakenly, that a fine cake is less challenging to produce than a fine soufflé or mousse. Greenie knows, however, that a good cake is like a good marriage: from the outside, it looks ordinary, sometimes unremarkable, yet cut into it, taste it, and you know that it is nothing of the sort. It is the sublime result of long and patient experience, a confection whose success relies on a profound understanding of compatibilities and tastes; on a respect for measurement, balance, chemistry, and heat; on a history of countless errors overcome. In Greenie's favorite antique cookbook, an eloquent curmudgeon named Louis P. De Gouy devoted eight closely typeset pages to "Common Causes and Remedies in Cake Baking Failures." How she wishes sometimes that Master Chef De Gouy had written such a treatise on love, even just motherly love.

Yet she felt almost completely happy as she immersed herself in the perfection of Ray's wedding cake. At the end of each long day, for nearly two weeks, she would return to Charlie's place with a sample of her work in progress; after dinner, he would savor cake while Greenie sipped from a glass of cold wine, their bare feet pressed together under the table. The sleepy days of August were over, the pace of life at the mansion was accelerating slowly, and the weather was exquisite. Soon, very soon, she would see George.

How quickly everything in the world has changed in the weeks since then: lives, dreams, assumptions, excuses, plans, priorities; everything except for the date of Ray's wedding. In late September, when Greenie returned from seeing Alan and George in Maine, Ray told her that to postpone it would look defeatist. That was when she realized she could not pull it off if she was the only one in charge. Late one night, with only three weeks to go, she called Walter.

"Walter, I need you," she said.

Before she could tell him why and how, perhaps before he was even fully awake, he said in a muddled voice, "Honey, I am there." Greenie will never forget this. She is tempted sometimes to ask him what he imagined, in that instant, she might need him for.

Now Walter continues to dance about, a ne'er-do-well bystander next to everyone else's last-minute labors. But at the height of the party, he was a commander-in-chief (with all the extra security on hand, the wedding was like a military maneuver after all). Greenie was astonished—and, in the face of McNally's initial resentment, also proud—to discover that Walter spoke a little Spanish, flirting equally with the girls in the kitchen and the fetching young bartenders weaving their way among the guests.

He kept her distracted from so many worries, both immediate and distant, and Greenie knew that Walter did so consciously. "*Real* cowboys?" he whispered when four men arrived in Stetson hats, silver bolos, and sharp-toed boots. "What do they call that, Full Fargo?" As

Ray and Claudia made their heavily cheered and confetti'd departure, Walter turned to Greenie and said, "I'm sorry, but with her decked out in that tasseled frock, they just *beg* comparison to Roy and Dale—thank heaven they're sexier. She has the right little smidgen of butch, and he has this complementary dash of Robert Mitchum."

Among the comings and goings at the back gate, two of the cowhands from Ray's ranch lean against the hood of their pickup, smoking. When McNally spots them, he yells, "Make yourselves useful!" He holds out a hose and directs them to rinse off the grill.

"Will you stay for a beer?" says Greenie. "The cake will keep in the fridge till you go."

"One sip and I will keel over dead. Have to get back tonight."

"Who's to cook for?" asks Greenie.

"These boys, they couldn't make a burger to save their sorry asses." He nods at the hands, who are struggling to rinse the underside of the grill, and shakes his head. "Hard to believe they're capable of roping a steer, ain't it?"

"You are not leaving without giving me your number," says Walter. He hands McNally a pen and a turquoise cocktail napkin. "He's coming out after Thanksgiving," Walter tells Greenie. "He's in major trouble if he doesn't."

"Like what, you'd send me a dead rat?"

"I would send you subscriptions to several magazines *no one* would want to see arrive at the governor's ranch, least of all you."

"Hard to refuse, in that case." McNally writes on the napkin and hands it over. Awkwardly, he shakes Walter's hand. "Did a fine job, Walt."

"Yes, I did," says Walter, "and I enjoyed every minute. Thank you."

McNally turns to Greenie. She makes it easy for him by hugging him lightly, kissing him on a cheek. "The cooler!" she says, and heads for the kitchen.

ALL HER SENSELESS SUPERSTITIONS ought to have prepared her. Ray came down for breakfast an hour early. Greenie was so absorbed in rolling out pastry that at first she saw nothing unusual in his arrival. When he said her name and then just stared at her, she told him he looked like he'd seen a ghost. "Something's going on in New York," he said. He told her about the planes; he also told her he knew her family would be safe.

"You know? How do you *know*?"

"My sixth sense." He tapped his forehead, the gesture he always made when bragging about his intuition, and Greenie was suddenly enraged.

"This is no joking matter!" she shouted.

"Call right now," he said. He put an arm around her shoulders and squeezed hard. "You need anything, you go talk to Mary Bliss. She expects it. I have no time to stop, but I wanted to tell you myself. I'll be downtown all day, I'm guessing. All day and all night." Greenie heard phones ringing throughout the house, every phone except the one in her office.

"You'll be A-okay, you will," said Ray. "And drop all that." He gestured at the pastry. Before leaving, he waved, as if they were parting at a train station.

The apartment phone was busy. She punched the one, speed-dial to Alan, over and over, until she was driven nearly mad. It shouldn't *be* busy; their phone in New York had call-waiting. She rifled through her desk to find Alan's cell phone number, which she had rarely ever called. No answer, no voice mail. She opened her e-mail and typed, *Are you all right? What's happening? I can't get through on the phone. Answer now, PLEASE.* Next, she wrote to Charlie, who had left for Albuquerque at five that morning. She told him that she was going out of her mind trying to reach home. She told him to call her as soon as he could. *TAKE CARE OF YOURSELF,* she typed, as if the pressure of her fingers on the keyboard could strengthen her words.

She turned on the radio; after ten minutes of nearly unbearable listening—how could any of this be true?—she went to see Mary Bliss.

"I can't get through to my family," she said.

"I know, honey. None of us can get through to anyone there."

"Ray? Not Ray?"

"Ray's gone downtown. I'm keepin' this ship afloat, such as it is."

"I have to get home to my son," said Greenie.

Mary Bliss nodded. "If you can wait fifteen minutes, George'll take you."

"To the airport?"

"Oh no, honey. There won't be planes for some time. Rental cars're all gone, too. I've managed to hijack a *schoolbus* for a group of CEOs we've got stranded out at Los Alamos. Honey, the world's gone catty-wumpus."

"Then where would he take me?"

"We'll see, but I would say all the way there, if need be."

Greenie pointed out that she had a car of her own; she could drive herself. Mary Bliss said that Ray had expected she'd try that foolish stunt. Paternalistic as ever, he would not permit her to go by herself. She could return whenever planes got back in the sky. They couldn't keep planes on the ground forever. "You know Ray. He runs the show," said Mary Bliss, her tone quietly ironic, as if Ray would decide when the planes should come and go. After Mary Bliss had returned from Nashville and given notice, Ray had offered her a raise she couldn't refuse. According to Tall, Ray had even offered to buy her a horse.

In the half hour before Tall picked her up, Greenie thought of nothing but her own George, wishing for nothing at all but his safety. *His and only his, no matter what it costs:* the prayer of all mothers, even those without a god.

Tall showed up not in the sedan he used to transport the governor but in a compact car that looked and smelled new. "A spare," he joked quietly. He had the radio on, and for most of that day, until they stopped for the night in Oklahoma City, the two of them said very little. Many times, Greenie used Tall George's phone to try New York. When they stopped at a drive-through for burgers, he took the phone away and told her he'd let her call again in another two hours. "They be smart, they're fine and outta there. Me, I'd be at a friend's. Safety in numbers, you know?"

For the first time since leaving Santa Fe, she thought of Charlie. "Oh God!" she cried out. She also remembered, the trite alongside the momentous, the pastry she'd rolled out that morning, the eggs she had left in a bowl to warm for custard.

"What, they got no friends?" said Tall.

Greenie shook her head. "I forgot something. I'll cope with it later."

"Need to stop at a drugstore; like that?"

"It's nothing." She would call Charlie, to explain her departure, the first minute she could be alone. All that mattered now was to drive, drive, drive. Her body was so charged with adrenaline that if she could have reached George just as fast by running all the way on her own two feet, she'd have done that instead.

Greenie was aware that she and Tall made an odd couple when they entered each new diner and motel: dark with light, hip with sedate, grace with guilt. Mile after mile, they listened to news on the car radio, changing stations only when the static overcame the voices, as if their lives depended on it. At the start of each day, they read newspapers; at the end, they went to separate rooms and slept.

Greenie spoke to Charlie each night of her journey, from Oklahoma City, Saint Louis, Pittsburgh, and, on Friday night, from the apartment on Bank Street, where she stayed alone before driving to Maine. She had expected, even wanted, Alan and George to be gone already, but still she was disappointed.

Charlie had returned to Santa Fe from Albuquerque as soon as he heard the news. By the time he got there, Greenie had left. When she spoke to him late that Tuesday afternoon, she had not yet spoken with Alan or George, and she was frantic. Charlie tried to calm her down.

"Do you want me to try them, too, from here?" he asked.

"No!" she said. "Why could you reach them if I couldn't? And what would you say to Alan? God, no."

"Something like this suspends everything else. He'd know you wanted to know they were safe. I could speak with George."

"I don't want to hurt Alan more than I have." Charlie said nothing to that. "It's you I love," she said. In some form, she said so every time they spoke along her journey. Yet the farther away she traveled, the more desperate it felt to tell him how much she missed him, as if there were only so much distance their attachment could take, as if there were a literal breaking point to the emotional line connecting them.

It was hard to talk about anything other than the drama unfolding in the world at large, events they could do nothing about. Charlie was right: something like this suspended everything else. Even the two of them were suspended.

When she called him from New York, she said, "Well, I'm here. And they're not. It's strange. It's strange how calm everyone seems. There's this ghastly hole in the sky, yet all these people are walking around with strollers and briefcases and bags of groceries. People are renting videos and ordering Chinese food. It's all normal, but *they* are gone."

"Charlie, you asked them to leave." He sounded weary.

"I know that. I'm glad I did." She asked him about his day.

"I think we might win."

"Don't sound so happy, Charlie." She tried to laugh.

"Well, you're not here. And it's just one step. There are always more challenges, more appeals. It's chess. We take one piece, but they take another."

"I don't know how you have the patience."

"I have some," he said, "but it's not endless."

She told him again that she loved him.

"I know that," he said. "But I wonder if you'll come back."

"I've said I would, Charlie! How could I not come back?"

"To me, I mean."

"I know what you mean!" Why was this conversation suddenly like conversations she'd had with Alan when she had been in Santa Fe and he, Alan, had been where she was now? She saw herself in a passage of dueling mirrors.

"Ssshhh," said Charlie. "I didn't mean to upset you. You just need to get to George. It's the right thing to do, I completely agree."

"But maybe I was being hysterical, making them go to Maine."

"It made sense," said Charlie. "You feared for their safety. I would have done the same thing. I'm not even sure I like the idea of *you* in New York. Are you staying the night there?"

She told him that she would set the alarm for four in the morning. She needed a shower and sleep. She might not be able to call him for a few days. Would he mind?

"Whatever you need," he said, "I'm fine with it. I have work to do. Lots of it. So don't worry about me. You wouldn't see much of me anyway if you were here. I'll be off pretty early tomorrow."

Greenie climbed into her old bed, between sheets that smelled of the husband she had already left.

WHEN SHE REACHED THE BOATYARD, it was raining. She parked the car—which she had rented in Pittsburgh, almost physically forcing Tall to turn around—and ran to the office above the dock. Inside was a boy she'd never seen before; at one time, she'd have known the faces, if not the names, of everyone working here, but she had not been to Circe in three years. The boy would take her to the island; he mentioned that he'd taken her husband's "party" the day before. "They looked to be pretty well stocked," he said, trying to sound like the adult he almost was. "Like they were planning to stay through Christmas! You need the wheelbarrow, too?"

"No," she said, indicating her small bag. The clothes she'd packed, days ago in haste and shock, would not be warm enough for the island in this weather. She'd have to hope there were clothes she could borrow in the cabin.

The motor launch wore a smart blue awning, with see-through plastic flaps along the sides. Greenie chose to stand in the open air at the stern, in part to distance herself from the boy—she had no energy for small talk, least of all island small talk—but mostly so she could turn her face to the elements. She needed a little ruthlessness.

Motoring slowly along (the boy must be new), they took the strait between Mare's Rock and Collared Cove. The boy sped up slightly as they passed String of Pearls. Someone had built onto the guesthouse the only way you could—vertically—so that now it resembled a watchtower. A sailboat nearly as large as the island itself was moored off its tiny dock.

A gust of wind sent rain down the neck of Greenie's jacket. She gasped at the sharp cold as it funneled between her breasts.

Rain—rain everywhere, agitating the trees on the islands, pelting and coarsening the wide gray waters of the bay—took her back to Charlie. Water: Charlie. Charlie: Water. How could she survive if rain and open water—so abundant in her part of the world, though so scarce in his—made her think of Charlie? Tumbling streams, melting snow, dripping eaves. NO LIFE WITHOUT WATER, read a sticker on the fender of Charlie's bike.

Her island (her mother's island) grew in detail, its idiosyncratic rocks and trees, none changed; the mouse-colored houses still huddled together like three shy girls at the edge of a dance floor. There should have been fog, but despite the domineering, monotonous gray of everything in sight, even the farthest horizons were crisp.

The important thing about rain, remembered Greenie, was its wetness. The greenness of grass, the whiteness of snow, the fact that shoes must contain your feet: according to Margaret Wise Brown, the important things were always the obvious things. George had never loved *Good Night, Moon*; he preferred *The Important Book*. Greenie found the pictures hauntingly frumpy, but the litany of what made each thing "important" gave a sweet illusion of comfort.

What was the important thing about a mother? Was it that she loves you no matter what? Was it that, like the sky, she is always there? (Could you count on anything as much as you could count on the sky?)

No. The important thing about a mother is that she shows you love—not just gives you love but shows it: shows how it's done. She shows you love like a museum exhibit, laid out in good light and calm surroundings. She shows it to you, thought Greenie, like a tray of pastries, every one so perfect that you are at a loss to choose. But that's fine, because any one you choose will be exactly what you need. You cannot lose. Nothing is stale or runny, too sweet or too yeasty. That's how it should be. Should be.

Greenie's face was dripping with rain, her hair nearly soaked to the scalp. She felt water beneath the waistband of her jeans and inside her sneakers. As the boy turned the boat's shoulder toward the dock beneath Circe, she was reminded of the way she'd seen Ray's cowboys rein their horses away from the edge of a herd: close but never too close. And as the boy lowered the throttle and cut the motor, allowing the boat to drift the last several feet on its own momentum, it occurred to Greenie that she could not remember anyone other than her father at the helm when she came to this place for the first time each year. He'd always docked the boat like a predatory bird coming in for a sideways landing, compensating for wind shear yet showing not an ounce of timidity. Always, this approach had enhanced her excitement about the time ahead. Yet now that this boy from the marina had brought the boat to a standstill with such perfect aim and timing, she saw that her father's way had been little more than stylish, like a pointless curlicued flourish at the end of a signature.

When we leave, she thought, I will sell my share in the house. To be reminded of Charlie and her father all at once was simply too much.

She looked up. There, right away, almost too soon after all her yearning, was George: in the rain, leaping from rock to rock, with Treehorn just behind him. Treehorn's short legs did not serve her well on this terrain. She'd scramble down a wet slope only to find herself stranded in a crevice, then crouch and leap, stiff and cautious, to the next rise—then do it all over again.

"Mommy!" George cried joyfully. Alan appeared just behind him, calling Treehorn, trying to show her the path whose twists and turns George had refused to follow.

The boy from the marina helped Greenie out of the boat, and she tipped him. George arrived on the dock at the same moment, making a song of her name. Alan waited behind George, at the foot of the notched gangway, perhaps for some kind of signal, but she didn't have one to give him. After holding and rocking George until he wriggled free, Greenie leaned down to greet Treehorn. She still did not know what to say to Alan, other than the simplest thing, an echo to his careful "Hello." He picked up her bag. "We're so relieved to see you," he said. "Saga's good at building fires, I've discovered. A good thing, or we'd have frozen solid last night. I was the world's worst Boy Scout."

I remember, she might have said, because that had always been one of his self-effacing refrains.

"Icicles!" said George, tugging at Greenie's sodden jacket as they crossed the gray rock that led to the lawn. "We'd've been turned into icy icicles. That's what would have happened, you know."

There had been precious little time—or precious little space in her mind—to picture what it would be like returning to Circe for the first time in so long. It was certainly not like those Hollywood movies where the heroine steps through shafts of dusty sun, sweeps aside draperies of cobweb, unveils the furnishings to find them (while eerie music plays) exactly as she had left them. Greenie could not run her fingers over cushions last plumped by her mother, did not find in the sink a ghostly wineglass bearing still the impression of Olivia's lipstick, a spoon still encrusted with oyster bisque.

Greenie's cousins had—quite reasonably and with no disrespect to her mother—freely changed things around. New curtains, in a faux-Hawaiian print, hung from the window by the stove. The picnic table at which they'd eaten all their meals had been replaced with a bona fide dining table and ladderback chairs, probably from L.L. Bean. A shag rug, blue polka dots on white in the shape of a boomerang, now occupied the floorspace in front of the woodstove. As Greenie took in this comic touch—was it hideous or hip?—Alan said, "My first thought was, where's the matching lava lamp?"

Greenie looked him in the eye for the first time, and she couldn't help smiling. "I'm trying to imagine what my mother would say."

Alan returned her smile. In the old days, he would have ventured to guess Olivia's remark, and he would have nailed it precisely, making Greenie laugh.

She took a towel from a rack by the sink and dried her hair.

"Hello. Hello." Through the back door, shaking out an umbrella, came the friend Alan had mentioned, the one he'd told Greenie he was bringing along to the island. He had described her as a woman whose life was in serious crisis. (*And what am I?* Greenie had thought self-ishly.) George had come on the phone and described her as Treehorn's godmother, leading him to ask, "Do I have a godmother, Mommy? Why don't I? Does God have a mother?" According to Alan, Ford was no longer proselytizing, but George's world had grown wider all on its own, demanding further questions alluding to the supernatural. Greenie had her work cut out there.

Alan had warned Greenie that, physically, Saga was a "lopsided" woman, that she'd had an accident years ago. She did not look so pecu-liar to Greenie. She had a crooked smile, and she walked with a subtle lope, but these quirks seemed nothing more than colorful to Greenie. Saga's age was hard to guess; was she twenty-eight or forty? With her intense blue eyes, she was taking a cat's measure of Greenie. (How much had Alan told *her*?)

Greenie laid aside the towel and shook Saga's hand. In a cowardly way, she was glad to have someone else there, a chaperone to protect her, for at least a few hours, from facing Alan alone.

"I have a present for you," Greenie told George. From her pocket, she pulled a small parcel of newspaper, now damp.

George did not seem to care about the wrapping or the ink that came off on his fingers. "Mommy, it's a knife! Thank you!"

"Yes, I know it is, and you must be careful with it. There's a note, George. It's not from me." She sat on the couch—the same old beat-up blue corduroy couch—to warm herself by the woodstove. She invited George into her lap.

After picking up the note, which he had dropped, George sat beside her instead. He allowed her to put an arm around his back. On a piece of hotel stationery from a Pittsburgh Days Inn, it read, *From me to you, Small Man. Keep the faith. Come visit. 5 up, 5 down, 5 twist around! Tall.*

It was a modest Swiss Army knife, with a single blade and a few extra gadgets, but to Small it was a magnificently grown-up object, one that promised transformation. This was obvious in the reverence with which

George squeezed and stroked it. Before Greenie and Tall had parted, he had taken the knife off his key chain.

"I miss Tall," said George as Greenie showed him how to pull out the nail scissors and the elfin tweezers.

"You'll see him again. Don't worry." She removed her arm from around his shoulders. Her jeans were soaking the cushion. She excused herself to change.

She went into the downstairs room where her parents had slept. She stopped in the doorway. The double bed was gone; two bunk beds stood against opposite walls. The same painted bureau was there, but in its drawers she found not her parents' extra sweaters, the tar-spattered khakis her father had worn when he worked on his boats. Instead, she found board games, a scruffy electric blanket, a set of souvenir lobster-claw pot holders still wrapped in plastic, two flashlights, and a faded Red Sox baseball cap. Next door, the smaller room where Greenie had slept was furnished with a crib, a changing table, and a rocking chair.

"You probably want to sleep upstairs." Alan was standing behind her. "Unless you want to sleep in here with Saga and George." A tangle of George's clothing spilled from a bag in the corner. A small suitcase lay open beside it.

"My things are in the big room up there," he said. "Borrow anything." That's how it was now: she needed permission to wear Alan's sweaters. Was another woman wearing his sweaters and shirts? This hadn't occurred to Greenie before. She looked down, so Alan wouldn't see her face, and passed him to go upstairs.

The four-poster bed—the one her mother had found at a yard sale off Route 1 and painted white out on the rock above the dock—now occupied the big bedroom on the second floor. This arrangement did make more sense; grown-ups should take the best view. Here was the familiar loose-jointed bookcase, but its collection of paperbacks—the plump, ruffled copies of *Hawaii, Future Shock,* and *Tora! Tora! Tora!*—had vanished. A dozen newer books leaned along one shelf—novels by authors that her scholarly father would not have heard of: young, stylish New York City authors. The other shelves were empty.

The top dresser drawers were empty too, but when she opened the bottom drawer, *here* were her parents' sweaters, her father's work pants. She let out a sob. She lifted an Irish cable-knit sweater and held it open.

It was pure white and smelled of rich dark cedar. Greenie cradled it to her face.

George called up to her. They were hungry; wasn't she hungry too?

"Yes I am!" she called back. "I'll be down to cook in a minute!"

She changed into a T-shirt of Alan's, her mother's sweater, and a pair of anonymous sweatpants drooping from a closet hook. Beneath her father's trousers, she found a pair of blue fleece socks.

As she left the room, something Greenie had not seen in ages caught her eye: on a bedside table, the small leather book in which Alan had once, every morning, written his dreams.

Downstairs, a meal was already on the table, bowls of fragrant brown soup and a loaf of bread. (Was it lunch or dinner? She'd lost track of time, not just hours but days, perhaps entire eras.) "Oh my," she said. "Thank you."

"We're very good at shopping, aren't we?" Saga said to George.

"I know how to use a can opener. Saga showed me," he told his mother.

"In the right place at the right time, a can opener might just save your life," said Greenie. It was something Charlie had said when she teased him for using canned foods in the meals that he had insisted on preparing for her. She could count those meals on one hand.

George was alarmed. "What do you mean, save my life?"

"That's a joke," said Alan. He did not look at Greenie.

After dessert—made by Sara Lee—Greenie put George to bed while Saga and Alan washed the dishes. When she pulled out *Owl at Home*— which she had found behind her sofa in Santa Fe and carried with her across twelve states—his eyes widened. "Mrs. Rodrigo's book! Did you take that from her?"

"No, that's our copy. Do you remember that I bought it for you?"

He shook his head.

What else had he forgotten? Greenie asked if he wanted to read it to her.

"You read it," he said. "I missed you reading."

He leaned against her for all five tales, which related the neurotically foolish mishaps of a character who was a literalist yet also a romantic. In Greenie's favorite, Owl made himself a pot of tear-water tea by thinking up, laboriously, as many sad things as he could: chairs with broken legs, forgotten songs, clocks that had stopped, mornings that no one witnessed because everybody was sleeping. More than sad, they were invisible, neglected, or simply lost to memory.

When she finished reading, George asked, "Can I sleep with my knife?"

"I don't think so, honey."

"Please? Please?"

Greenie saw the knife on the dresser. She brought it back to the bed, along with a T-shirt of George's. "Listen, George. I'll wrap it in this shirt and tuck it under your pillow, but you must promise me not to take it out, all right? Just like when you leave your tooth for the Tooth Fairy."

"I promise," he said.

For the first time that day, she indulged in simply gazing at her son. Though she had braced herself, he hadn't changed so much. The great difference was that he felt more separate from her than ever before. His promises would grow increasingly complex, along with what he understood about the world. His secrets would deepen too, and one day his mother would no longer be the one who knew him best.

On the third day of their marathon drive, Greenie and Tall George had talked about Small. Before then, she had worried that to ask anything about her son would be to violate a private friendship, but Tall didn't see it that way. He told her several amusing stories about Small, and Greenie was pleased to hear in this man's voice an echo of her own pride in her son's curiosity and oddball logic. Tall became serious, however, when she asked what he knew about the incident involving Diego. Tall had never seen the boys together, he had to admit, but from what he had gathered, he believed that Small George had been desperate for something to change. When Greenie asked urgently, "For what to change? What?" Tall had given her a long, almost insolent look and then shrugged. "Your guess be as good a mine," he'd said. "Come to think of it, better." If he'd meant her to feel shame, he had succeeded.

"Can I give you a really big hug?" she asked her son now. He laughed and told her yes. She lay beside him on the bed for several minutes until he said, "Mom, you can go now."

Before she left the room, he said, "Mommy, I like this place. Have we ever beened here before?"

"Yes, we have," she answered from the doorway, "but I'm pretty sure you couldn't remember. It was such a long time ago."

"We'll come again, won't we?"

"Yes," she said.

When she returned to the main room, Saga and Alan were sitting at the table by the woodstove. On the table was a game of Scrabble. It was the original edition she remembered from her childhood, in the dour cardboard box that Greenie had always thought precisely the color of a scab. It came from an era when fun did not have to look garish or even shiny. Here were the baby pink and blue Chiclet squares, the dowdy beige letters like scraps from a carpentry project, the racks like dollhouse church pews.

Greenie's parents had been clever at Scrabble. On the island, they had played every night after Greenie went to bed. She had heard their murmurs of surprise, frustration, triumph, disgruntlement; they concentrated so hard on the game that they rarely exchanged words other than those on the board. For long stretches of time, if the ocean was still, Greenie could hear the tiny clatterings of the wooden letters in their racks. Once in a while there would be a challenge—generally from her mother—and out would come the dictionary. (She'd never known of a word from her father that did not pass the test.) Olivia and George had kept score year by year for their entire married life. Every New Year's Day began with a tallying of the score; the winning spouse would choose where they'd go on their next big vacation. Greenie's father (who generally won, though never by a landslide) was the one who had chosen Scotland.

As Alan turned the letters facedown in the lid of the box, he told Greenie and Saga about the work he would be doing with Jerry, at the clinic for people traumatized by Tuesday's attacks. Though he might have seemed relaxed to anyone else, Greenie knew he was nervous, because against his very nature, he was working to fill every silence. From across the table, she looked at him now the way she had just looked at George. He was thin and uncharacteristically tanned, as if he had spent the summer sailing or hiking. Alongside his ears, his hair was almost entirely gray. He looked more beautiful to Greenie than he had in years—unattainably beautiful, as if she had found his picture in a magazine.

Saga went first, laying down the word S O F A, descending from the star at the center of the board. Alan, almost immediately, put down S E L K I E.

"Well," said Greenie. "Well, I forgot how good you are at this." Now she remembered that they had played two or three times with her parents. Her mother had been tense—amusingly, at the time—when Alan beat everyone the first time they played.

"What's that?" asked Saga, her question one of genuine curiosity.

"A selkie is a creature from Irish folklore, part seal, part woman."

"How could you think that up so fast?" asked Greenie.

"George had a book from the library. *The Selkie Girl.* A fisherman falls in love with a selkie and forces her to marry him by hiding her pelt."

"Something terrible must become of him," said Greenie.

"No, not really, but he does have to let her go in the end. It's your turn."

Greenie had a decent assortment of letters—enough vowels, no wallflower consonants—but she could not concentrate. She laid down three letters. "Onto."

"That's all you want to do? That's five points."

"Yes, Alan," she said. "I need to warm up."

He wrote down her score. She recognized his neat handwriting, his straight columns. In his precise way of doing things, he wasn't unlike Charlie; yet they were so different, Charlie so much more expansive, someone who looked ever outward. She wished that she and Charlie had been together long enough that some of the things she admired and loved about him had become cause for irritation—that his ardent resourcefulness had come to seem like rigidity, his sense of adventure like restlessness; that his playfulness could look immature, his lack of sentimentality cold instead of wise. But they had not been together that long. To recall even one of those qualities made her feel as if her heart would crack in two.

Saga placed A R M Y at the tail end of S O F A. "Double word score," she said, as openly pleased as a child might have been. (This was a woman in crisis? Greenie inspected her critically for a moment, but what could you really know from the surface? Alan had taught her how well people hide things, often for the sake of their own survival.)

"Eighteen," said Alan. "Excellent." He began to fiddle with his letters.

"Can I ask you a nosy question?" Greenie said to Saga. "Can I ask you about your name?"

Saga laughed, self-consciously. "It's really Emily."

"Mine's really Charlotte," said Greenie. Alan looked up at her, briefly, then back at his letters.

Saga told Greenie that when she was five years old, she'd run away from home. "I sat with my stuffed dog behind a bush at a bank down the block. I wanted them to be good and sorry. You know, like kids always do when they feel wronged. So nobody came, and nobody came. It felt like I was there for hours. A lady I thought I knew from my school saw me there and asked me what I was doing. But she was nice. So I told her. She said she'd take me for a treat. We walked down the street, and we stopped to look in a toy store window, and she bought me an ice cream cone and we sat at a table while I ate it. I thought for sure my mom would show up then, or maybe pass me in her car and be shocked to see me with somebody else. Then she'd be sorry. But no. So then I went with this lady while she bought herself a pair of sunglasses in another store— I tried a bunch on myself—and then she walked me home. She didn't take me in, she just waved to me while I walked to the door."

Starting at the left edge of the board, Alan spelled B A I R N, the final N forming N O where it linked up with Greenie's O N T O. The B occupied a red square. "Seven times three, plus three," he said quietly.

"Bairn?" Greenie laughed. "What is this, Celtic Scrabble?"

"I don't know what's come over me," he said. He looked at Saga. "What happened then?"

"Oh." She shrugged. "My mom was inside the house. She never noticed I was gone. She thought I was in the yard. When I told her where I'd been, she told me I had a big imagination. When my dad came home, she told him I had quite the saga to tell him. 'You *are* a saga!' he said, something like that. I thought I'd get in trouble. I *wanted* to be in trouble—but no one believed me."

"You never told me that story," said Alan.

"It's true," she said, "something I remember clear as anything."

They traded smiles, the expression of people who understand each other in the midst of much confusion.

Greenie felt Alan nudge her foot with his. "You again," he said. "Don't rush." He got up and went to the stove, took the kettle to fill it.

Greenie hadn't looked at her rack since picking up three new letters. She saw R H M I E L A. The E was a substitute. Many years before, when a real E had gone missing, Greenie's father had penned the letter on one of the two blank tiles. "Ha! Just like life," he had joked. "Occasions for free choice diminish as you age. Though your mother will probably tell me I'm wrong about that."

Jostling the letters, she found H A R E, H A I R, H A I L: was H A I L E R
a word? She could make A L I E N with an open N. "Alieno?" she said.
Saga laughed. Greenie happened upon M A R I E L, but that was a
name. M A R E. M A L E. She focused on the L in S E L K I E. M A L L. *My
mind is refusing to do this,* she thought, moving the letters arbitrarily:
M A R H L E I, M H A R L I E. She stared.

M   H A R L I E

Mournfully, pointlessly, she searched the board. No C. Of course not.
No place for such things. No proper names allowed. What about
improper names?

Alan returned from the kitchen with three mugs and a mason jar
filled with a variety of tea bags.

"Can you remill something?" Greenie placed R E M I L above the
open L.

"I think so. Flour, if it's not fine enough the first time around," said
Alan. "You of all people would know about that."

Saga nodded. Over B A I R N, she made O A R. "Believe it or not, I
need consonants."

They chose tea bags. Alan put the bags in the mugs and lined them up
on the table. He leaned down to pet Treehorn, who slept close to the
stove. He returned to the table. "You're both going to hate me." With
an R, he turned O A R into R O A R and then, using both hands, built a
bridge all the way to R E M I L L, crossing a double word score, to make
the word R E Q U I E M. He wrote, but did not say aloud, 40.

"Is this what they call a rout?" said Greenie.

"It's early yet," said Alan, pointing to the unchosen letters.

Greenie smirked at him. "I don't think we have to be telepathic to
predict this outcome."

Saga continued to stare at Alan's latest word, as if she might challenge its legitimacy. "Copper," she said. "Greenish."

"Requiem?" said Alan, who seemed to understand.

She nodded.

"I'm not sure I'd have come up with that word at any other time,"
he said.

They grew quiet, reflecting. Each of them took another turn, no one
scoring remarkably, and then they agreed that it was very late. They
poured the letters straight from the board back into the box and put the
game away. Though the wind complained incessantly through the trees,

the rain had stopped. The next day was to be a nice one, according to their crank-up radio—which they consulted only for weather and, now and then, a hasty sampling of news. Next day, they decided, they would explore the other side of the island.

Saga whistled gently to Treehorn, who jumped up to follow her into the nearby bedroom, which George had requested the three of them share. Awkwardly, Alan and Greenie said good night to her as she closed the door.

Greenie whispered to Alan, "Someday he'll be sharing that room with a girl his own age, and they won't be in separate bunks. We'll pretend we don't care. We'll be very modern about it."

Alan stared at her. She had hoped he would hear the implications. She wanted to tell him that aside from anything else, they were parents. They were the parents of George Glazier, a boy nearly six years old, inquisitive, loving, optimistic, and—whether or not he'd outgrow it—a little secretive. They were parents, and for the time being that's all they were.

"Are you staying with me?" he said. He added quickly, "Upstairs?"

She told him she was, if he didn't mind. They brushed their teeth together at the kitchen sink, using the last of the water in the kettle. It was still warm and a little salty. Greenie went up first, while Alan went to the outhouse.

She turned on the battery-powered lamp. The wet clothes she had shed lay in a heap beside the window. She hung them on hooks; next day, if the forecast was correct, she would lay them on rocks to dry in the sun. Quickly, she climbed into her parents' old bed. Alan had made it up with two splayed sleeping bags, their puffy linings patterned with fishermen and leaping trout.

She'd made a last call to Charlie that morning, from a phone booth in a town just south of New Hampshire. She had stopped the car when she knew that he would be awake but still at home. He'd greeted her with wary surprise. Where was she? Was everything all right?

"I'm in Massachusetts," she'd said.

"Our home state." He spoke warmly but without enthusiasm.

"I didn't really sleep last night."

"I'm not surprised."

From the phone booth, Greenie had watched two women herd several small children across the street. A crossing guard held up traffic.

"Are you still there? Are you sure you're all right?"

Greenie told him then that she was not all right. She told him that she loved him, that she couldn't believe she was going to tell him what she had to tell him. She did not insult him by saying she had no choice (she did) or by repeating over and over how much she loved him (oh God, she did, repeating it endlessly inside her head). She did tell him that by spending the previous night in New York, among Alan's and George's things, she had been confronted by just how much she would lose—and how much she would risk never knowing.

"That doesn't surprise me," he said, and then he was silent a long time. Greenie let him think—or compose himself. At last he said slowly, "You know, when you e-mailed me before you left, you told me you were going home. Home. That's the word you used."

Greenie sobbed. "I'm so sorry. I didn't mean it that way."

"Yes, you did." His tone was almost forgiving. "I always thought this would happen, if you want to know the truth. I don't mean that vindictively."

Greenie was about to protest—what kind of an I-told-you-so was this?—when she realized how stupid and selfish it would be; like Owl when he tried to be upstairs and downstairs at the very same time. "Can I see you when I come back? Because I'll be back. I don't know for how long, but I will."

Charlie had sighed, then sighed again. "Oh Charlie, I don't know," he said. "But if we don't see each other soon, we'll see each other later. If life doesn't throw us together again, we'll figure out something. Something different." Halfheartedly, he laughed. "Yeah. Different. Because you know what's so obvious now, Charlie? That you're not Charlie. Not the long-lost soul mate I thought I'd found."

While she struggled not to tell him he was wrong, he said, "That's not the slightest bit your fault, Greenie."

"Can I write to you?" she asked. "Please?"

Firmly, he said, "No. Not now."

After hanging up, she'd stood in the phone booth and cried into her hands until the crossing guard caught sight of her and motioned concern. Greenie had run to her car and driven on through the rain to the marina.

When she was in high school, a couple whom Greenie's parents knew had split apart, the husband leaving the wife for another woman. A few months later, he returned. When Greenie had remarked that the wife must be happy to have him back, Olivia had raised her eyebrows and said, "Yes and no." A marriage that survived an affair, she said, was like a fine china cup whose handle had snapped off. You could glue it back on, but you would always see the place where it had broken, and you would never be completely confident that, as you held it in your hand, it would not break again in that very same spot.

Now, in her parents' bed, waiting for Alan, Greenie felt herself fill with rage, not just at her mother but at herself, for taking at face value so many judgments Olivia had made. What, then, would Greenie and Alan's marriage look like if it "survived"? A porcelain sugar bowl, *both* handles snapped off and glued back on? Was something broken and then salvaged automatically devalued? What if it became more precious *because* you saw how fragile it was?

Like Greenie, Alan had dressed for bed in two layers of clothing. When he joined her—without hesitation, because the air was so frigid— she asked him about Saga. Whispering, he told Greenie about Saga's accident and about her family. He said, "She's someone who went through a terrible, sudden loss of self and doesn't realize how much she's recovered. And now this."

"Are you taking her as a patient?"

"No," he said. "Or I wouldn't be telling you this. But I'm going to help her. She has other friends too, in the city. She's not helpless."

Wind trespassed loudly on the silence. Windows rattled in their frames.

"You remember that old cliché, ordinary unhappiness?" said Alan. Greenie said she did. "Well, Saga needs to understand that she's nearly achieved ordinary forgetfulness. Not quite, probably never, but almost. It's like she's come to idealize memory itself. She thinks the rest of us walk around remembering everything we ever did or saw or said."

Because they were whispering so softly, and because the room was so cold, they pressed against each other, side to side. "It's amazing what people get through—or get over," Greenie said, and then there was nothing more to say. They had no further ways of reasonably delaying their arrival at each other.

Alan asked if he could look at Greenie's hands.

"My hands?" She pulled them out from under the sleeping bag. Alan took them and held them toward the light from the lamp, turning them.

"Ouch," she said when he twisted one of her wrists too far.

"That's new." He pointed to a thin welt across the back of her right hand.

"Thanksgiving pies," she said. "Twelve. Six flavors."

"Impressive. And this?" A patch of scar tissue on the center knuckle of a pinkie.

"I've had that since school. It shows up when I get a lot of sun."

A chef's hands were like a map, a history of culinary mishaps, scattered with scars from slashes, punctures, burns, run-ins with cheese graters, meat cleavers, grills on open fires. Greenie bore no scars from cuts—she had always been good with knives—but she had a collection of tiny burn marks, some white, others pink; a plum-colored lozenge on her inner left wrist. After Alan finished his examination, he turned off the lamp.

"You're still wearing your ring," he said.

She couldn't answer. Even in the panic of departure, she had remembered to bring it with her. She had put it on when she left New York for Maine. If Alan had looked closely at her finger, uniformly brown beneath the ring, he would have known that she had not worn it all summer.

He sighed: such a familiar, freighted sound. "Greenie, I don't know what we're doing here, really, but George and I have to return to the city in a few days. At the latest. You can stay—but we're going back. My life is there, and it's very busy now. George's school is back in session."

Her throat felt as if it had shut completely; how was it that she could still breathe?

"So that's up to you," he said. "Well, obviously." He waited. He sighed again. "There's a lot I have to tell you, a lot I've decided."

She managed to say, "Same here."

"I guess I need to know how much time there is to tell it in."

"A great deal of time, I think."

"A 'great deal'? You 'think'? Greenie, if you came all this way, dragged me all the way here just to separate one more time—"

"What I meant was, I *hope.*" She said, carefully so that she would not have to repeat herself, daring to elevate her voice from a whisper, "You'd let me stay, wouldn't you? I mean, go back with you and George?"

Through a window, bright light entered the room. Greenie knew the sound of a cabin cruiser, loud and guttural. This was its headlight, which passed away before the puttering of the motor.

"Are you coming back to George or to me?" he asked.

"The truth," she said, "is that to me, right now, you are inseparable. I want you both. I can't think of you apart right now. Or myself apart from you." She laid a hand on his chest, so that he knew she meant *him*.

THE MORNING OF THE WEDDING, Greenie arrived at the mansion before six. McNally was to arrive at seven, Walter at eight.

"Well, *this* half is calm. It is."

Greenie jumped at the sound of Ray's voice. She had not expected to see him that morning.

"Didn't mean to scare the pants off you, girl."

"Oh Ray, look at *you*."

"Well, no, look at that. Hot dog, Ms. Duquette. Hot dog, and jump up singin'!" He gazed with awe at his wedding cake. She had just finished piping the flowers onto its upper tiers. Ray leaned in and held up a finger as if to run it through the icing.

Greenie slapped his hand. "Don't you dare."

"My mama always let me steal a taste of birthday icing before my party," he said. "She'd let me lick the beaters too."

"I am not your mama," said Greenie. "Sorry."

"Be sorry for much more than that," said Ray.

Greenie stared at him, just to stop the teasing. "Can I say, in all seriousness, that I will miss you?"

"In all seriousness," said Ray, "I will miss you too." He clicked together the long shiny toes of his black cowboy boots, as if in fact he could not bear to have anything be purely serious. "Others will as well."

"I know."

"McNally won't say it, but he wants you on speed-dial."

"The feeling's mutual." She glanced at her cake: It was her Mona Lisa. Fully assembled on the cart, it stood as tall as Ray. The air conditioner was turned high, to keep the cake cool until Walter arrived. He would help her move it into one of the large refrigerators and then, before the guests arrived, out to the tent.

"Can I ask you something?" Greenie said.

"Ask away."

"Did you give Charlie his win?"

"Greenie, judges decide these things, not me. If I could've given the man and his doggone fish a break, just to avoid a buttload of red tape and spleen, believe you me, I would have."

"But didn't you appoint that judge?"

Ray pointed a finger at Greenie. "I don't mess with judicial matters. I make my opinions known—I broadcast 'em far and wide, I do!—but judges make up their own minds."

She nodded.

"Oenslager's in Sacramento now. The man is in high demand wherever the people are thirsty."

"Or wasteful," said Greenie.

"This is not a morning on which to argue. Bad luck," said Ray. As he had done once before, he surprised her by kissing her, quickly, on the mouth. "That's for good luck."

"You already have it, Ray."

"I meant for you," he said. Then he left, looking glossier and more handsome than he had ever looked, even in his tabloid days. During the festivities, under the tent, he passed close by her once, squeezing her shoulder and winking, but Greenie did not see Ray again that day outside the context of a crowd. After he'd gone, she wondered if she would ever see him again.

ONCE MCNALLY AND THE RANCH HANDS have driven away, Walter and Greenie start cleaning the kitchen. Greenie has sent Maria and the others home. They worked hard enough, and she must finish packing up the belongings she will take with her when she leaves for good.

She pulls from a shelf certain rare spices and sugars that her successor is unlikely to use. Insulating the jars with softbound books and sheafs of cooking notes, she packs them in a carton that came to this kitchen holding boxes of Italian pasta. She examines the fanciful designs on a container of sugar imported from Turkey, a favorite finish for the surface of cookies: bearclaws, butter wafers. The large, faceted granules glitter like bluish rhinestones; children always choose those cookies first. She wonders if she will be able to get this sugar anymore, if borders will tighten so austerely that she will lose some of her most precious, treasured ingredients: the best dried lavender and mascarpone, pomegranate molasses. But in the scheme of things, does it matter?

She comes upon her collection of vinegars, which she uses to brighten the character of certain cakes, to hold the line between sweet and cloying. She takes down a spicy vinegar she bought at a nearby farm; inside the bottle, purple peppers, like sleeping bats, hang from the surface of the liquid. Greenie used it in a dark chocolate ice cream and a molasses pie. She will have to leave it behind.

Walter scrubs the counters—no mean task, for McNally's barbecue sauce has dried in spatters and spills, nearly everywhere, like a sugary version of superglue. Walter works away at the mess with a wiry pad, still singing. He's carried the boom box back inside, and from Greenie's neglected Broadway tapes he's chosen *Camelot.* At the moment, Robert Goulet is doing his best to convince the world he's Lancelot, not a lounge singer from Vegas.

Exaggerating the stuffy diction, Walter croons loudly, about cleaving dragons and resisting the ways of the flesh. He has Greenie in stitches by the time he cries out, "*C'est moi, C'EST MOI!* The *angels* have chose, to fight their battles below—" He stops short, finally succumbing to laughter himself.

"Egad." Walter lets Robert Goulet finish alone. "You know, I think neurologists have it all wrong, the sectors of the brain." Facing Greenie, he cups his hands over his forehead. "This part here—and it's pretty large—is taken up with schlocky song lyrics, the ones you desperately wish you could lose, like Captain and Tenille, disco Bee Gees. Todd *Rundgren,* for Pete's sake." He groans. "Now this part?" He spreads a hand across the left side of his head. "This is where you've got—stored archivally—the worst family arguments you ever had to witness or be a part of. And this other side"—his right hand mirrors his left—"is a grand little warehouse of all the most embarrassing sexual encounters you've ever had to endure. In Panavision and Technicolor."

Greenie is almost always grateful for Walter's zany, tempering humor, but today he is antic with pleasure. "Walter," she says, "if ever I saw a man in love, *c'est vous.*"

"Is that what ails me?" He leans down to work at the knobs on the stove, which are badly encrusted, though it's obvious that his main intention is to hide his blushing face.

Greenie knows—and Walter knows she knows—that he and Fenno have become nearly inseparable over the past month. Even when they are working, Walter says, they go back and forth between the bookshop and the restaurant (Fenno for meals, Walter during the lulls between). She knows—because he's told her, marveled at it more than once—how the two men came together in the midst of Walter's panic over his nephew, how Walter now realizes that Fenno had been looking his way for months, perhaps longer. ("My neighbor! Right there under my snooty, vainglorious nose!") Walter jokes that it took a hit of Valium, mixed with mortification and grief, to slow him down enough to return the looking. "He's one of those guys," said Walter, "who's practically incapable of making the first move—not just in love; in anything! Normally, that would drive me berserk. My guess is that somebody up there is telling me to chill."

Hanging about with a bookish man (whose restaurant nickname, courtesy of Ben, evolved from Bonny to Britannica) has led Walter back to Shakespeare. He's even begun to memorize a few soliloquies. "Please keep reminding me it's just for *fun*," he's told Greenie. "If you ever catch me planning a cabaret, it's your job to shoot me."

Walter takes a break from the stove. Claiming he's had enough of knights in shining armor, he picks through the tapes stacked loosely on an open shelf, takes out *Camelot* and clicks in another.

"So what did he do with himself today?" asks Greenie.

"He told me his plan was just to 'faff about the town.' Don't you love that? After today, you and I certainly deserve a bit of faffing about!"

Heartily, she agrees. Over the past month, Greenie and Walter have spoken to each other so often, borne so much upheaval and change, for better and worse, that they have become the most effortlessly intimate friends.

"Maybe I shouldn't ask this," she says, "but whatever happened to that nice lawyer, Gordie?"

"Nice? Well." Walter groans as the overture to *My Fair Lady* begins. "I'm trying to get to the no-hard-feelings stage—which should be easy now, right? But get this: Gordie is a friend of Fenno's. They don't see a lot of each other, thank heaven, but ages ago they had a friend in common, a very close friend, who died of AIDS. Which means that it's a *sentimental* connection, the kind that lasteth forever." He presses his hands together in mock prayer. "Lessons in humility abound. . . . Though apparently, I am not alone. According to my trainer, Gordie's been trying to go back to his old relationship. Where he should have stayed put in the first place! But his ex is onto something entirely new. A *baby*. So Gordie's in purgatory. That is, until he gets distracted again." Walter laughs derisively.

Politely, Greenie laughs too. She didn't mean to open a wound.

They work in tandem now, comfortably silent. Walter hums along when Julie Andrews sings "Wouldn't It Be Loverly?"

Both Walter and Greenie knew people who died on September 11. From the cooking world, Greenie knew three corporate chefs trapped in the towers; Walter knew a flight attendant on one of the planes, though he learned of the man's death only a week ago. But they share the good fortune of having lost no one they love dearly—or not to death, thinks Greenie.

She has heard Walter tell the tale of how he was certain for many hours that his nephew had taken the flight that crashed in Pennsylvania: how Scott—"typical lame-brain testosterone slave!"—overslept that morning at his girlfriend's apartment and so did not bother to go to the airport as planned; how, once it got through his blithe young skull that the whole world was watching, he called his mother in California but not his uncle right there in New York. Greenie pointed out that Walter had evicted Scott; why should he have called? "Because family is family!" Walter snapped. "Honestly now, did he think I wished he'd go down in flames?" Only when Walter found the courage to call his brother did he find out that Scott was alive, stuck in Brooklyn with the girlfriend on whom Walter still liked to blame Scott's every bit of thoughtless behavior. The Bruce was stranded right along with them. ("Did she call to reassure me? I rest my case.")

Almost as soon as they'd heard about the first plane, Walter, Hugo, and Ben had gone down the street to the bookshop in search of a television; Fenno had no TV, but they wound up lingering there, for the company. "That's where I heard about the flight from Newark—and went ballistic," Walter confessed. Greenie doesn't have the details straight on all the comings and goings on Bank Street that day, but she does know how Fenno showed up at the restaurant much later, just to check on Walter, and found him collapsed in hysteria, exhausted with abject humiliation and grateful relief after speaking with Werner, the older brother who, once again, knew more and had known it first. "As if pride had a place in *anything* that day!" Walter said when he told his tale to Greenie. Only when Fenno urged him to lock up the restaurant did Walter realize that Ben and Hugo should go home—and that they would not go until he did.

Once they had said good-bye to the other men, Fenno convinced Walter, firmly and gently, that he shouldn't be alone. They went up to Fenno's apartment, where they ate scrambled eggs and fried tomatoes, drank Scotch, and watched a romantic old black-and-white movie called *I Know Where I'm Going*.

"The eggs were overcooked, I loathe Scotch, and the movie was like this bizarre dream sequence with everybody trilling away in brogue on some craggy quaint island," Walter said, "but I couldn't begin to imagine going home, especially without T.B." He told Greenie that he and Fenno had spent virtually the entire evening in silence ("Can you imagine *me* silent for more than about three seconds?"), talking now and then only about the most insignificant things—food, Fenno's parrot, the pictures of his family that stood about on shelves—until partway through the movie.

"I think I might have dozed off," said Walter, "and when I came to, it was in the middle of this weird dramatic scene where a wedding dress flies off a boat in a storm and gets sucked down into a whirlpool—don't ask!—and Fenno's looking at me, smiling, and he doesn't look away. I said something nervous and stupid about what a terrible, terrible day it was, how I couldn't remember a worse day in my whole life, and do you know what he said?

"He stopped smiling, and he said he agreed with me, it was an unimaginably terrible day, but . . . 'But as I sit here beside you, 'tis a day I wouldn't trade for any other, not a one.' That's exactly what he said, in that beautiful Old World voice of his. And I couldn't say a thing more, and we watched the rest of the movie, and then we went to bed." Walter did not bother to fight back tears when he told this bit to Greenie, but then, embarrassed, he laughed and said, "You should see this movie, though. It's totally wacky and totally old-fashioned but wonderful. Wonderful." Walter is so happy these days that "wonderful" is a judgment he passes on all manner of things several times an hour.

Greenie has never heard of this movie, but *I Know Where I'm Going* could have been the title of her bygone life. She is aware that she remains a deeply fortunate woman, but her inner certainty, the logic of that former self, is gone. Fate, or responsibility—or maybe Ford's ubiquitous God—has caught up with Greenie at last.

George is fine, almost irritatingly fine. He is matter-of-fact when he talks about that day—"the day those men crashed the towers with their planes"—and asks questions about it as if he is a child researching a school report on a war that took place long before he was born, but Greenie knows she will never look at her son's future the same way again. For the first time, she imagines him as a soldier going to war. She can even fear that he might *choose* to fight. She still feels the urge toward a second child, but how do you bear the anxiety of sending *two* children out into a world with so many new (or newly discovered) perils? Of course, hasn't it been this way for most mothers in most places at most times? Such silent debate exhausts her.

Greenie closes and tapes up a second box. Walter sprays disinfectant on the counters, the drawer pulls, the faucets. "How is Saga?" she asks him. Saga is staying in Walter's apartment, taking care of The Bruce.

"One thing's for sure," he says. "She's got to stay in New York. The uncle's going into some kind of home, one of those morbid assistance condos, and the huge, incredible house where they lived together has become this female family fortress—sisters, widows, babies; something out of Ingmar Bergman. Except that Saga's been shut out. She doesn't seem all that sad, but Fenno says not to be fooled. He's keeping an eye on her." Walter looks up and smiles at Greenie. "He's good at that."

Greenie carries the boxes into her office, where she has already packed up her books and files. Glancing around, she sees, on the windowsill, nearly hidden by a curtain, the flat stone from Circe, the one Charlie placed there the day he came in from lunch and surrendered to her. She clasps it tightly in one hand, then puts it in her pocket.

Back in the kitchen, she takes the spray bottle away from Walter. "Enough. It's too lovely to stay in here."

They silence Rex Harrison and go back through the empty dining room; two hours ago, it was filled with uninhibited dancing. The French doors stand ajar, admitting a pine-scented breeze and the bright prospect of Ray's plush, well-watered lawn. Remarkably, nearly everything's been cleared away: tables and chairs, television cameras, flower arrangements. Beneath the tent, all that remains is a grand piano. Greenie and Walter carry the piano bench into the sun. They sit, facing the mountains.

Walter is still talking about Saga. "She's going to work for Fenno part-time, and he's going to help her put out a newsletter for that militant animal group, which is going legit. Scott's vixen works for them, too—though let me tell you, T.B.'s days in her clutches are over. Like, man, so totally over. As she would say if she could ever stop snapping her gum."

"Walter."

"I know. I promised not to get bitchy. I promised to even be *civil* to her."

"Once Scott comes back, you'll have to be."

"Unless they break up! Don't you know any nice little pâtisserie mademoiselles?"

"Don't let her bother you, Walter," says Greenie. "She's nothing more than a restless middle-class girl dolled up as a punkster princess."

"In case she hasn't heard," says Walter, "Halloween lasts for just one day a year." He stands up to stretch. "I think I have a name, by the way. It came to me last night, walking around under this gorgeous sky. Blue Yonder. No 'wild' because I think we're both past wild by now."

"Do you think references to the sky are a good idea these days?" Greenie remembers that Wild Blue was the name of the fancier restaurant at the top of the towers—but she will not mention that now. She looks up; the actual sky above them is fading, passing through the soft linen colors of late afternoon.

"Oh, listen," says Walter. "The blooming sky will be there when the planet has been burnt to a raisin thanks to no more ozone layer. And maybe *blue* is a word for the times. How about Greenie's Blue Yonder? How do you like *that*?"

"A clever way to keep me from backing out."

"You won't. You're mine now. I know it in my aging bones."

Greenie would tell him not to joke about possessing her, but she doesn't want to talk about possession. For now, she wants to be owned by no one, not even her son. She says, "That's sweet of you, Walter. Let's figure it out when we get back."

Walter reminds her that they need to get cracking. He wants to open the new restaurant well before Thanksgiving. He wants a name, so that word of mouth can spread even before they finish the storefront. He longs to commission a sign, to dream up a look for the menu.

She tells him it will be a success, no matter what they name it. "You decide," she says. "I trust your instincts far more than my own right now."

Walter strokes her back. "Your instincts are just fine," he says.

They look straight ahead at the view, as if they're attending a concert. In its own way, the landscape does rival a symphony. Three mountain ranges—the Sandias, the Sangre de Cristos, and the Jemez—enclose a valley, cities and villages built along a river. Steadfast against the tentatively colored sky, they give the illusion of witnessing and sheltering the lives of those who see them every day. Greenie feels the stone in her pocket and holds it fast, like a secret. If Charlie were here, he might remind her that the mountains are indifferent. Well, of course they are— but they are stirring, even comforting, all the same. It is Alan, though, to whom she will replay this vision, along with everything else: the wedding, the cake, the drunken dancing, the pompous toasts; the way Walter, with his wry, playful authority, made it run so smoothly. Suddenly, she cannot wait to tell him.

"Walter, do you know what I've never asked you?" She looks directly at him. "What exactly did you say to Ray?"

"I said, 'Congratulations. May you have a hootenanny of a married life together and a caboodle of little Roys and Dales.' "

"I mean in New York, way back when he ate at your restaurant."

"Do you really want to know?"

"Yes."

"I told him you were a monstrously talented cook. I told him you sang like an angel. I told him you were looking for a change to shake up your life. He said, 'Sings like an angel?' He thought that was funny. I told him about your show-tune mornings, how I liked to walk by your kitchen and eavesdrop."

"You did not."

"Eavesdrop? Oh yes I did. And will again. I won't even have to sneak. Because there you'll be, working beside me every day."

"Walter, you did not tell him that."

"Does it matter?"

"*Walter.*"

"Do you know what my beloved nephew has tried in vain to teach me?" Walter says. "Live in the here and now. So here and now, I have to ask, is there more of that amazing cake? I'm hungry again already."

Greenie's consent is a murmur. As she stands, someone calls out their names from the house. Walter rises quickly, turns around, and waves energetically. "Hello, you!" he exclaims. He remains beside Greenie, but she can feel his emotions, his tenderness and excitement, radiating as tangibly as heat.

Fenno waves back as he steps from the French doors and crosses the grass. "Hello to both of you!" he calls in return. "How did it go, your grand event?"

ACKNOWLEDGMENTS

A grant from the National Endowment for the Arts, a fellowship at the Radcliffe Institute for Advanced Study, and membership in the Writers Room of New York City enabled me to complete this book more quickly and under more privileged circumstances than I would have been able to afford on my own; my deepest thanks go out to these generous institutions.

I thank Barbara Burg and Pamela Matz of Harvard's Widener Library for their terrierlike detective skills; Ann and Charlie Harriman for the twin inspiration of their island retreat and their epic rivalry at cribbage; Bette Brown Slayton for calving tales; Larry Olson of Wiley & Sons for culinary texts; Dr. Andrew Wilner for early counsel on the effects of head trauma; Lucy White for the porcupine lamp; Archie Ferguson for the rare combination of a brilliant eye and an open ear; Shelley Henderson for life-changing conversations; and my sons, Alec and Oliver, for enriching my work far more than they interrupt it. For help with crucial details, especially in the final stages, I thank Millicent Bennett, Joanne Brownstein, Matthew Iribarne, Margot Livesey, Maria Massey, Ann Marie Romanczyk, Katherine Vaz, and Joan Wickersham.

The political New Mexico that I portray in this novel—its governor, the workings of his household, and his professional challenges—is pure invention, though for helping me ground the virtual in the actual, I am indebted to Lorraine Rotunno, director of the Governor's Mansion in Santa Fe, docent Florence Lloyd, and First Lady Barbara Richardson, who graciously welcomed me into the real-life mansion. My dear friends Lisa Wederquist and Larry Keller also supplied much local color. For background on the 2000 Cerro Grande fire, "The Shape of Things to Come," by Keith Easthouse, was most helpful, while Marc Reisner's astonishing book *Cadillac Desert* opened my eyes to the western water crisis. On both fire and water, articles in the *New York Times* and the *New Mexican* provided more timely details.

Ten years of reading to and with my sons have reawakened me to the stimulating language and vision of children's books, some of which I have folded into this story. Over my entire life, few authors have given me as much delight as the peerless Dr. Seuss, whose books need no special mention. I would, however, like to cite, in admiration, a few less celebrated books to which I refer: *The Important Book,* by Margaret Wise Brown; *The Selkie Girl,* a legend retold by Susan Cooper; *Mordant's Wish,* by Valerie Coursen; *My Life With the Wave,* by Catherine Cowan (inspired by Octavio Paz); *The Shrinking of Treehorn,* by Florence Parry Heide; *Album of Horses,* by Marguerite Henry; *Bronco Busters,* by Alison Cragin Herzig; *Roar and More,* by Karla Kuskin; *Wee Gillis,* by Munro Leaf; *Owl at Home,* by Arnold Lobel; and *Me and My Amazing Body,* by Joan Sweeney.

My good fortune as a writer over the past few years I owe to much more than my own abilities. I owe it to the enthusiasm of my readers, many of whom have come to readings, written me perceptive and moving letters— even stopped me on the street—and to the loyalty, wisdom, and kindness of my agent, Gail Hochman; my publisher, Janice Goldklang; and Deb Garrison, my incomparably talented and generous editor. Thank you all.

PERMISSIONS ACKNOWLEDGMENTS

Grateful acknowledgment is made to the following for permission to reprint previously published material:

CROWN PUBLISHERS: Excerpt from *Me and My Amazing Body* by Joan Sweeney. Copyright © 1999 by Joan Sweeney. Illustrations copyright © 1999 by Annette Cable. Reprinted by permission of Crown Publishers, an imprint of Random House Children's Books, a division of Random House.

HARVARD UNIVERSITY PRESS: "I have no life but this" (poem 1398) by Emily Dickinson, from *The Poems of Emily Dickinson* edited by Thomas H. Johnson (Cambridge, Mass.: The Belknap Press of Harvard University Press). Copyright © 1951, 1955, 1979, 1983 by the President and Fellows of Harvard College. Reprinted by permission of the publishers and Trustees of Amherst College.

RANDOM HOUSE CHILDREN'S BOOKS AND DR. SEUSS ENTERPRISES, L.P.: Excerpt from *The Cat in the Hat Comes Back* by Dr. Seuss. TM and copyright © by Dr. Seuss Enterprises, L.P., 1958, renewed, 1986. All rights reserved. Reprinted by permission of Random House Children's Books, a division of Random House, Inc., and Dr. Seuss Enterprises, L.P.

SCOTT TREIMEL: Excerpt from *Roar and More* by Karla Kuskin. Copyright © 1956, 1990 by Karla Kuskin. Reprinted by permission of Scott Treimel.

VIKING PENGUIN: Excerpt from *Wee Gillis* by Munro Leaf, illustrated by Robert Lawson. Copyright © 1938 by Munro Leaf and Robert Lawson, renewed copyright © 1966 by Munro Leaf and John W. Boyd, Executor of the Estate of Robert Lawson. All rights reserved. Reprinted by permission of Viking Penguin, A Division of Penguin Young Readers Group, A Member of Penguin Group (USA) Inc., 345 Hudson Street, New York, N.Y. 10014.

A NOTE ABOUT THE TYPE

The text of this book was set in Sabon, a typeface designed by Jan Tschichold (1902–1974), the well-known German typographer. Based loosely on the original designs by Claude Garamond (c. 1480–1561), Sabon is unique in that it was explicitly designed for hotmetal composition on both the Monotype and Linotype machines as well as for filmsetting. Designed in 1966 in Frankfurt, Sabon was named for the famous Lyons punch cutter Jacques Sabon, who is thought to have brought some of Garamond's matrices to Frankfurt.

Composed by Creative Graphics, Allentown, Pennsylvania
Printed and bound by Berryville Graphics, Berryville, Virginia
Designed by M. Kristen Bearse